THE
TWELVE
CHILDREN
OF
PARIS

Also by Tim Willocks

Bad City Blues
Green River Rising
Bloodstained Kings
The Religion

TIM WILLOCKS

THE
TWELVE
CHILDREN
OF
PARIS

JONATHAN CAPE
LONDON

Published by Jonathan Cape 2013

2 4 6 8 10 9 7 5 3 1

Copyright © Tim Willocks 2013

Tim Willocks has asserted his right under the Copyright, Designs
and Patents Act 1988 to be identified as the author of this work

First published in Great Britain in 2013 by
Jonathan Cape
Random House, 20 Vauxhall Bridge Road,
London SW1V 2SA

Map by Darren Bennett; adapted from 'Map of Paris, 1572', by Braun and
Hogenberg, reproduced by permission of the National Library of Israel.

www.vintage-books.co.uk

Addresses for companies within The Random House Group Limited can be found at:
www.randomhouse.co.uk/offices.htm

The Random House Group Limited Reg. No. 954009

A CIP catalogue record for this book is available from the British Library

ISBN 9780224097451 (cased edition)
ISBN 9780224097468 (trade paperback edition)

The Random House Group Limited supports the Forest Stewardship
Council® (FSC®), the leading international forest-certification organisation.
Our books carrying the FSC label are printed on FSC®-certified paper. FSC is the
only forest-certification scheme supported by the leading environmental
organisations, including Greenpeace. Our paper procurement policy
can be found at www.randomhouse.co.uk/environment

Typeset in Adobe Caslon by Palimpsest Book Production Limited,
Falkirk, Stirlingshire

Printed and bound by CPI Group (UK) Ltd, Croydon CR0 4YY

To my friend
DAVID COX
who walked every step of the way

CONTENTS

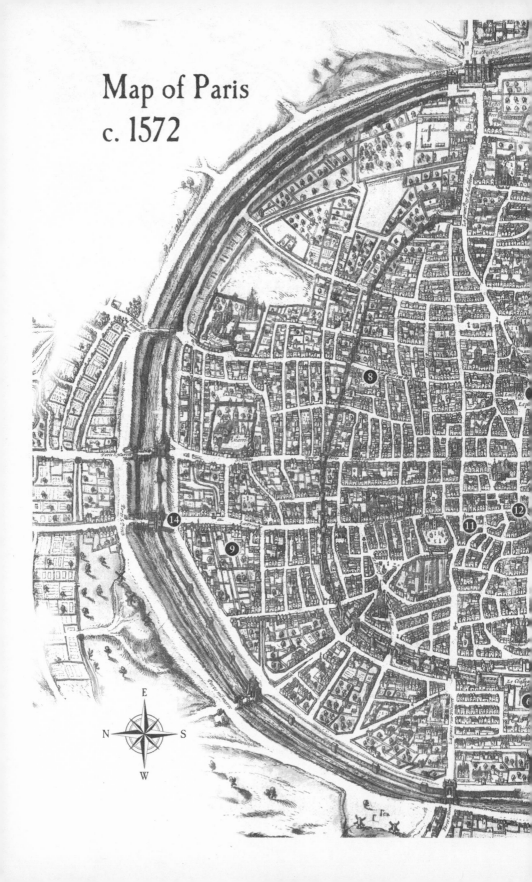

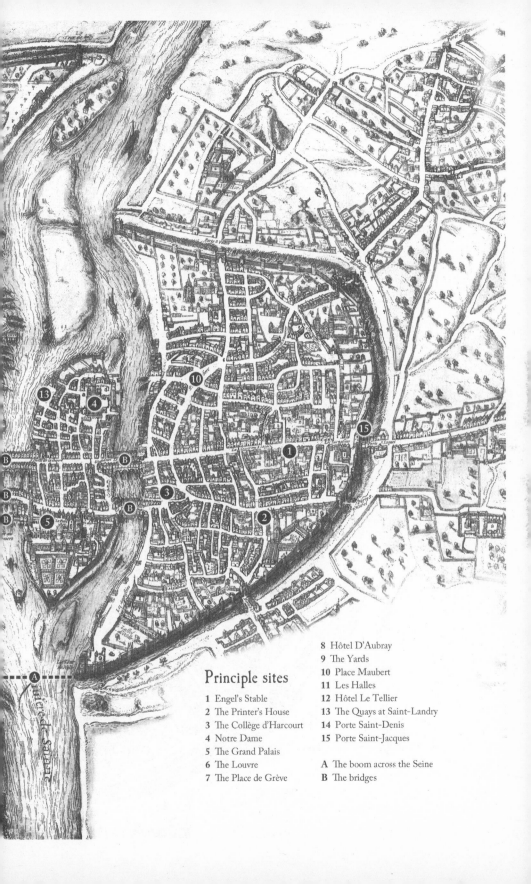

Principle sites

1 Engel's Stable
2 The Printer's House
3 The Collège d'Harcourt
4 Notre Dame
5 The Grand Palais
6 The Louvre
7 The Place de Grève

8 Hôtel D'Aubray
9 The Yards
10 Place Maubert
11 Les Halles
12 Hôtel Le Tellier
13 The Quays at Saint-Landry
14 Porte Saint-Denis
15 Porte Saint-Jacques

A The boom across the Seine
B The bridges

PART ONE

THIS FEARFUL
SLUMBER

CHAPTER ONE

The Printer's Daughters

Now he rode through a country gutted by war and bleeding in its aftermath, where the wageless soldiers of delinquent kings yet plied their trade, where kindness was folly and cruelty strength, where none dared claim his brother as his keeper.

He passed gallows trees where red-legged crows roosted black as their carrion, where knots of children in rags and tags returned his gaze in silence. He passed the roofless hulks of burned churches where shards of stained glass glimmered like abandoned treasure on the chancel floor. He passed settlements tenanted by gnawed bones, where the yellow eyes of wolves gleamed from the darkness. A blazing hayrick lit some yonder hill. In the moonlight the ashes of vineyards were white as tombstones.

He had covered more miles in fewer days than even he had thought possible. Yet here at last he was and there it stood. The walls quavered in the distance, warped by the August heat, and above them glowered a swag of ochre haze, as if the walls were not walls at all but, rather, the lip of some vast shaft sunk into the nether realms of the earth.

Such was his first impression of the Most Catholic City in Christendom.

The sight brought him little comfort. The forebodings that had driven him were undiminished. He had slept by the road and taken to the saddle in the cool before the dawn, yet every morning his destiny had risen before him. He felt it lying in wait, behind those Plutonian walls. In the city of Paris.

Mattias Tannhauser pressed on to the Saint-Jacques Gate.

The walls were thirty feet tall and studded with watchtowers as high again. The gatehouse like the walls was stained by time and the shitting of birds. As he crossed the drawbridge his eyes watered from the fumes of the putrid garbage filling the ditch. Through the blur, as if in a dream, two families tottered out between the enormous timber doors.

They were dressed in black and he took them for Huguenots. Or Calvinists, Lutherans, Protestants, or even Reformers. To the question of what to call them he had never found an answer that served all needs. Their new conception of how to live with God had hardly learned how to walk, yet their factions were already hard at each other's throats. To Tannhauser, who had killed for God in the name of more than one creed, this came as no surprise at all.

The Huguenots, women and children too, staggered beneath a diversity of bags and bundles. Tannhauser wondered how much more they had left behind. The two men, who had the look of brothers, exchanged a glance of relief. A slender boy craned his neck and stared at Tannhauser. Tannhauser mustered a smile. The boy hid his face in his mother's skirts and revealed a strawberry birthmark on his neck below the angle of his jaw. The mother saw him note it, and covered the mark with her hand.

Tannhauser pulled his mount aside to ease the pilgrims' progress. The elder of the brothers, astonished by this courtesy, looked up. When he saw the Maltese Cross on Tannhauser's black linen shirt, he dropped his face and hurried by. As his brood followed, the little boy looked back into Tannhauser's eyes. His features lit up with a grin, and it was the gladdest sight Tannhauser had seen in many a day. The boy tripped and his mother caught his arm and dragged him across the bridge towards hazards unknown.

Tannhauser watched them go. They put him in mind of a flock of ducks. They were poorly equipped for the road, whose dangers were considerable, but at least, or so it seemed, they had escaped from Paris.

'Good luck.'

Tannhauser received no reply.

He pushed on beneath the first of two portcullises and into the gatehouse, where a customs officer was too busy counting coins to afford him more than a sour glance. Here more emigrants were being fleeced and they, too, were clad in black. He entered the city and stopped in the shade of the wall. The humidity was suffocating. He mopped his brow. The journey north from the Garonne had consumed eight days and a dozen mounts, and had almost wasted him, too. He felt as if he didn't have a mile left in him. But this was his first time in the capital and he roused himself to take some measure of its spirit.

The Grand Rue Saint-Jacques ran ahead, downhill towards the Seine. For most of its length it was no more than five yards wide. Every square foot teemed with human beings and their animals. The clamour of voices, the bellowing, the bleating, the barking, and the snarling of flies, would have made a field of war seem tranquil; and those among the damned whose eternal task it was to scour Satan's piss pot with their tongues knew not a fouler smell. All this he might have expected, but beneath the workaday turmoil he sensed a more malignant tension, as if too much fear and too much fury had been swallowed by too many for too long. Parisians were a truculent lot, prone to disobedience and public disorder of every kind, but even they could not sustain a mood so febrile as a matter of course. In a different circumstance, this might not have caused him much unease, but he had not travelled the length of France to pull on trouble's braids.

He had come to find Carla, his wife, and take her home.

Carla's foolhardiness in visiting Paris had caused him an agony of worry and exasperation, emotions compounded by the fact that she was, by now, exceeding late in pregnancy. It would be their second child, and God willing the first to survive. Yet her behaviour had not much surprised him. Carla's mind, once resolved on any matter, evinced an iron fixity of purpose, and practical hurdles of any kind aroused her scorn. This was one of the qualities he loved in her, and a wall he had cracked his skull against more than once. If one added to this the fact, as he had it on good advice, that pregnancy was a temporary state of insanity, then her journey to Paris, along roads unimproved since the fall of Rome, might even seem unremarkable.

And few women can resist an invitation to a wedding, especially one between two royal houses and celebrated far and wide as the union of the age.

A pair of child prostitutes tottered towards him through the muck, their faces caked with white lead, their cheeks and lips daubed with vermilion. The little girls were perfect twins, which no doubt added to their asking price. The radiance that had once lit their eyes had been snuffed and would never shine again. As if trained in the same school of depravity, they mimed lewd smiles for his delectation.

His stomach turned and he searched the press for their pimp. A brutish adolescent caught his gaze and realised he was staring down the bore of a thrashing or worse. The pimp let out a shrill whistle. The wretched girls turned on the spot and scurried back to his side, and they vanished into the crowd to be raped elsewhere.

Tannhauser urged his horse into the throng.

His knowledge of the city and its geography was primitive, gleaned from the letters of Orlandu, his stepson, who was here to study mathematics and astronomy at the Collège d'Harcourt. This southern half of the city, on the Left Bank, was called the University. The island in the Seine was the City. The Right Bank beyond the river was known as the Ville. Beyond that he knew only that it was the biggest city on earth, a vast overpopulated warren of uncharted streets and nameless alleys, of palaces, taverns, churches and brothels, of markets, abattoirs and workshops, of multitudinous hovels too desperate to contemplate.

He had travelled using the relay network of post-horses re-established after the wars. The final stable in the chain lay on a side street west of the Rue Saint-Jacques. He found it easily enough – the Écurie D'Engel – but not without repelling further entreaties from the off-scourings of humanity. Paris was home to more beggars, whores and thieves than existed in the whole of the rest of France. Hired assassins were so numerous that, like the goldsmiths and the glovers, they boasted their own guild. Criminal gangs flourished in league with various of the *commissaires* and *sergents*. And at the other end of the hierarchy, the Crown and the great aristocrats, when not plotting against each other or fomenting mindless wars, devoted those energies surplus to their debaucheries to robbing their subjects with ever more ingenious taxes, these latter being, in Tannhauser's view, the most heinous of their many crimes.

After the street and its open sewer the smell of the stable afforded his nostrils and eyeballs some relief. He heard the sound of someone being flogged, and it wasn't a horse for the victim was too quiet. The grunts of pleasure accompanying the lashes came from the flogger's throat. Tannhauser dismounted in the yard and followed the sounds to a stall, where a muscular fellow, stripped to the waist, worked up a sweat by whipping a boy with the sharp end of a bridle. Tannhauser glimpsed bloody rags, an ungainly body curled and writhing in silence on a mass of straw.

It didn't sit right with him.

He caught the bridle by its bit as the hostler cocked his arm, and looped the strap around the hostler's neck and heaved. As the hostler choked on his own fist, Tannhauser stomped on his Achilles tendon and rammed a knee into his spine. He rode him down with his full weight and the hostler's face bounced from the flagstones. A piss runnel carved into the floor ran past the stalls, replenished by the frightened mare. Tannhauser crammed the hostler's nose and mouth into the stream and let him inhale. He wondered if this were Engel himself. The hostler squirmed and wheezed in the piss until his strength fled. Tannhauser let go of the bridle and stood up.

The flogged boy was on his feet. He was a big lad but otherwise nature had been no kinder than life. A harelip exposed his gums as far as the left nostril. His age was hard to guess, perhaps ten or so. To his credit, there were no tears on his cheeks. His lower jaw was misshapen and Tannhauser wondered if he might not be an idiot.

'The mare needs a rub.'

The boy bobbed his head and disappeared.

Tannhauser booted the hostler in the chest until he crawled out of his way, then unloaded his gear and stripped the saddle. As the boy arrived with a currying glove, Engel stumbled past, dragging one leg and clutching his ribs, and reeled towards the street. The boy watched him go. Tannhauser wondered if he'd done him any favours. Future beatings would likely be more vicious than before. He contemplated the weight of his belongings and the prospect of hauling them through crowded streets and crippling heat.

'How well do you know the city, boy?'

The boy garbled something unintelligible. He uttered a strange, halting laugh. He hunched his shoulders and made odd gestures with his spade-like hands. All Tannhauser gleaned was a sense of enthusiasm.

'What's your name?'

He had a stab at interpreting the strangled, nasal reply.

'Grégoire?'

Again the laughter. Furious nodding. Tannhauser laughed, too.

'Well, Grégoire, I'm going to make you my lackey. And I hope my guide.'

Grégoire fell to his knees with his hands clasped and chanted what might have been a blessing. The boy would make a singular Virgil, not least because Tannhauser could hardly understand him. He raised him to his feet and looked in his eyes. They were bright with intelligence.

'See to the horse, Grégoire, and we'll find you some decent clothes.'

Grégoire, reattired in Engel's white cambric shirt, bore up well under the burden of two enormous saddle wallets, a canvas sleeping roll, a goatskin of water and a pair of holstered horse pistols, from which Tannhauser had blown the priming so that the boy wouldn't blow off a foot. Tannhauser carried his wheel-lock rifle cradled in his arm. His hand-and-a-half sword was slung by his side. As they approached the Grand Rue Saint-Jacques, Engel reappeared.

His nose and lips looked like a mass of rotten pears, and one eye was swollen shut. He was in the company of two *sergents à verge* armed with short bows. Tannhauser wondered how much Engel had paid to recruit them. The *sergents* weighed up the large, well-armed figure striding towards them and concluded that their fee had been inadequate.

'Thanks be to God,' said Tannhauser. 'You've arrested him.'

The *sergents* stopped.

'I found that man buggering my horse.'

Engel's jaw dropped. Blood drooled from the new gaps in his teeth.

'In fairness, it was a mare, but I trust that the penalty is no less severe.'

Engel took a breath to protest and Tannhauser stepped up and fed the butt of the rifle into his brow. Engel toppled as if his feet were nailed to the ground, his fall only broken when the back of his skull cratered a mound of filth. Tannhauser smiled at the *sergents*, who had retreated and grabbed at their sword hilts.

'My lackey here can testify to his crime. Can't you, Grégoire?'

Grégoire garbled something incomprehensible.

'Now, do you officers need anything else?'

'Carrying that gun contravenes the law.'

'Your laws don't apply to the Knights of Saint John.'

The *sergents* looked at each other.

'As the last thief I met discovered, this gun enforces statutes of its own.'

To compensate himself, and with the pleasure of a connoisseur in life's injustices, one of the *sergents* smirked at the luckless hostler.

'Don't worry, sire. We'll make sure this sodomite gets everything he deserves.'

They left the *sergents* to rifle Engel's pockets and walked to the Grand Rue where Tannhauser stopped. Somewhere in this vast midden was Carla, and in her belly was their child. As to her exact location, he had no clue. His hopes of finding her hinged on the assumption that her son, Orlandu, would be rather better informed.

'Grégoire, I want to find the Collège d'Harcourt, on Rue de la Harpe.'

Grégoire emitted one of his cackles and set off through the crowd.

Tannhauser followed. They gave a wide berth to a pair of lunatics

9

chained together and shovelling sewage into a cart. They saw a priest and a slattern rutting in an alley, their skirts pulled up round their waists. From Saint-Jacques they turned west into a seething maze, where the buildings were piled so high their roofs almost touched above the thoroughfare. At length they entered a quarter full of students and a corresponding ubiquity of whores. Tannhauser caught fragments of several different tongues. If any among this elite were wrestling with metaphysics, he did not hear them, though he did see one pair wrestling in the filth, to the amusement of drunken friends who spoke in English.

The stern ambience of the Collège d'Harcourt restored some of Tannhauser's hopes for the groves of academe. The entrance hall was deserted but for an ancient porter on a high stool in a recess behind a counter. The old man looked as if he hadn't left the stool in years. He wore a short horsehair periwig a size or more too small and which partly concealed the disease consuming his scalp. Grey lice scouted the wig's edge above his ears. His eyeballs bulged proud of his cheekbones and flitted back and forth beneath closed, blue-veined lids. Tannhauser rapped on the counter.

The porter awoke without moving, like a lizard. His eyes were a shocking blue, as if the ancient carcass were inhabited by the spirit of some other being. They took in Tannhauser's clothes, the white cross on his chest, the cradled rifle. They took in Grégoire, festooned with luggage and dripping sweat. They returned to Tannhauser. They saw everything that he was: a foreign, lowborn killer, upon whom Fate had smiled. The porter despised him. The porter did not speak.

'I'm looking for Orlandu Ludovici.'

'The college term is long over, sire.' This seemed to gratify the porter. 'Few of the students remain in these lodgings at this time of year.'

'But do you know Orlandu Ludovici? And is he among those few?'

'The Maltese has not lodged here since, oh, Michaelmas last.'

'Do you know why he moved out?'

'I am not privy to Master Ludovici's thoughts, still less his motives.'

'Do you know where I can find him, or where he lodges now?'

'I'm afraid not, sire.' This ignorance, too, appeared to please him.

Tannhauser had been warned that any interaction with Parisian officialdom, no matter how petty, would require considerable tenacity.

'But he remains a member of the college.'

'As far as I know, sire.'

'When did you last see him?'

'I don't recall, sire.'

'A week? A month?'

'I don't recall.'

'You recall his moving out a year ago but not when you last saw him.'

'At my age, sire, memory becomes unreliable.'

Tannhauser had last written to Orlandu four months ago, before the voyage that had detained him in Velez de la Gomera and parts far beyond. He pointed to the rack of lettered pigeonholes that hung at the rear of the porter's domain. Filed in the box marked 'L', he saw papers. He propped his rifle against the counter.

'Has he any messages or letters?'

'No, sire.'

'I'd be grateful if you'd make sure.'

'I am already sure, sire.'

Tannhauser swung open the hinged flap and strode to the pigeonholes.

'No one is allowed behind the counter, sire.'

Tannhauser shuffled the papers from box 'L' through his fingers. There was nothing for Orlandu. The box marked 'O' was empty. He turned.

There was a smile in the old man's eyes. His lips didn't move yet conveyed the depth of his scorn. Tannhauser had the disconcerting sense that the porter had been expecting him, that his visit had been foretold; that the porter knew who he was.

'You know who I am.'

'A gentleman of very great eminence, I am sure, sire.'

'Orlandu must have friends, tutors.'

'No doubt, sire. But it's not my job to be expert in such matters.'

'Is there anyone else here I can question?'

'On a Saturday, sire?'

'Then, so far as the college is concerned, Orlandu has vanished.'

'There are ten thousand students in Paris, sire, from all over Europe. Who knows what such young men get up to? Especially in times such as these?'

'Orlandu is my stepson. He is dear to me.'

The porter's indifference had been hardened by an endless horde of whining youths, each of whom believed himself the most notable person in the world. Perhaps a whiff of royal intimacy would loosen his tongue.

'Orlandu may be with his mother, Lady Carla, Countess of La Penautier. She was the Queen's guest at the royal wedding. Do you know where I might find her?'

'If you don't know where your wife is, sire, how should I?'

Tannhauser ignored the pain in his skull and deployed a final stratagem.

'If you have any information at all that would help me find Orlandu, or Lady Carla, I can show my gratitude with gold. A contribution to the college, perhaps.'

The porter arched a hairless brow as victory was delivered into his hands.

'A bribe? You do me a grave injustice, sire.'

Tannhauser had offered said bribe with all due delicacy. Any insult offered lay in the porter's reply and the old scab knew it. Tannhauser dropped the papers and put an index finger against the old man's chest. He sensed the mean, sinewy carcass under the greasy coat. He pushed the porter backwards from the stool. The porter's limbs jerked outward as he crashed to the floor. The groan that arose therefrom was the first sincere sound to have escaped his lips. Tannhauser ignored him. He rummaged beneath the counter and found paper and ink. Amid a bundle of used quills he found one whose tip looked functional. He wrote in Italian, in a crude hand.

Dearest Orlandu, I am in Paris. I do not yet have lodgings. Leave a message here, at the college. Tell me where I can find you and your mother.

He paused. He had little faith that Orlandu would find the message in the near future, or that, even if he did, the porter would not tamper with any reply. He had noted a tavern on the opposite corner of the street.

He added: *Leave a copy at the Red Ox. I must find Carla at once.*

He searched his mind for the date. Tomorrow was the feast of Saint Bartholomew the Apostle. He signed his name and dated the message *p.m. Saturday 23rd August 1572*. He flapped the paper to dry the ink. He looked at Grégoire, who observed the proceedings with wide eyes, an open mouth and a runny nose.

'The taverns,' said Tannhauser. 'We will search the student taverns.'

Tannhauser folded the paper twice and wrote 'LUDOVICI' and 'MATTIAS' on the back. The letters that identified the pigeonholes were painted on wooden tags nailed above the slots. He prised the 'L' tag free and used it to pin the message to the box where its title could be read from beyond the counter. He returned to the porter and kicked him in the ribs.

'Get up.'

Despite his apparent decrepitude, the porter scrambled to his feet with an agility a younger man might have envied. Indeed, denuded of the wig, and with his face taut with rage, the porter might have passed for fifty rather than seventy. His scalp was a mass of scabby, peeling lesions. Tannhauser stepped back in case they were catching. He retrieved his rifle and nodded at the pigeonholes.

'Make sure my message reaches Master Ludovici.'

Out in the street, the sun was hotter, the crowds denser, the stench more odious than before. Tannhauser scraped his fingernails through his beard. Sweat crawled down his flanks. His eyes felt gritty. He wanted a bath, if such existed in Paris. He wanted his horse back, so he might ride above the slime congealing on his boots. Grégoire pointed at a long row of clamourous, over-crowded pigsties.

'The student taverns.'

The first three alehouses roared with drink and argumentation but proved barren in respect of his search. In each he had the landlord bellow Orlandu's name above the din, but no one responded. When this tactic failed in the fourth, the Red Ox, Tannhauser took a table near the door. He ordered wine, a cold goose pie and two roasted pullets. The conversation of the surrounding clientele had an undertow of dread. Some urgent news had broken, it seemed. Tannhauser tried to catch the gist but he was tired, and his ear was poorly attuned to the local accents.

He heard mention of the Queen, Catherine de Medici; and of her son, King Charles; and of his brother, Henri, Duc d'Anjou; and of the Duc de Guise, the Catholic champion of Paris. More often than he liked, he heard the name of Gaspard Coligny, the Huguenot demagogue and Grand Admiral of France. The man had starved Paris in '67; his German mercenaries had despoiled much of the country; and now, so rumour had it, he hungered for conflict with Spain in the Netherlands. The same cast of imbeciles and villains had thrice plunged France into the horrors of civil war.

Tannhauser had abandoned all involvement and even interest in political matters, for there was nothing he could do to alter their course. The high and the mighty remained spellbound by their own self-importance; their basest emotions turned history's wheels. The rulers of France were no more corrupt and incompetent than those who governed anywhere else, but because he had come to love the country, their crimes caused him a deeper despair. He brightened as the drink and the pie arrived.

The serving girl was unsure as to whether Grégoire was to be included in the meal. When Tannhauser indicated that he was, the boy was more surprised than she. Grégoire appeared not to have eaten so well since the milk from his mother's breast, if he had ever known that pleasure. Tannhauser had changed the boy's destiny on a whim. As a child his own life had changed on the impulse of a stranger. He might have picked someone better made, who might have lent him more prestige; but his heart rebelled against the notion. He had chosen this boy, and he would do right by him.

Grégoire exploded in a fit of violent coughing. When he turned beetroot-red, on the way to turning blue, Tannhauser rose and pounded the flat of his hand between his shoulders. Fragments of pie scattered the table and the boy heaved for breath. He snorted hard and more detritus flew from his nostrils.

'Take small bites and chew twelve times. Can you count to twelve?'

'I can count to fifty.'

'Then you're better informed than most but twelve will do.'

As Grégoire followed these orders, he caught sight of something behind Tannhauser, and his face once again turned red and he lowered his eyes to his plate in shame. Tannhauser turned.

At the next table a pair of students sniggered while twisting their lips into grotesque shapes and mimicking an idiot's speech. Two girls in their early teens sat with them, though neither seemed impressed by their companions' antics. Tannhauser wiped his mouth on the back of his hand and stared at the students, who must have been the worse for wine for this entertained them, too.

'If you find misfortune amusing, I can give you plenty to laugh about.'

This too provoked a titter, more likely due to nerves than insolence, but a man was entitled to enjoy a pie without scum making mock of his lackey. By the time he was on his feet, he had one youth by the throat. The other lurched from the bench but Tannhauser seized a handful of his hair. He let them get a closer look at his face and they wilted in his hands. He dragged them to the door and into the street.

He hauled them towards the open sewer, where mounds of filth lay in stagnant pools awaiting the shovels of the lunatics. He slammed their skulls together and left them sprawled in the ordure. He returned to the tavern. Standing in the doorway was the taller of the two girls. Her fists were clenched by her sides. He noted that both her hands were stained with ink. She stuck her chin out at him.

'Why did you do that?'

Her eyes were dark and fierce, her hair as blue as a raven and cut short, almost like a boy's. She was skinny and he guessed her age at around thirteen. She wasn't exactly pretty but she lacked for nothing in spirit, which in his book was the better end of the bargain. She wore no face paint but her fury lent high colour to her cheeks.

Tannhauser dipped his head in courtesy.

'A lesson in manners will stand them in good stead.'

'Manners?'

She seemed to imply that his own were less than impeccable.

'You forget I invited them to apologise.'

'They were cruel to your boy, yes. But you attacked them before they had a chance to reply.'

'You'll forgive me if our recollections differ.'

She glared at him, unwilling to relinquish her ground. Tannhauser looked over his shoulder. The youths had clambered as far as their hands and knees, and were assessing the damage to their clothing, which was catastrophic. They saw him watching them and must have seen the girl, too. They stood up and fled.

'You see? No harm done that a soak in the river won't repair.'

He turned back to the girl. She was not mollified.

'Though if I may say so,' he continued, 'abandoning you to the company of a brute is a black mark against their gallantry.'

'I am not in your company.'

'Then accept my invitation to share our table, and make it so. Mattias Tannhauser, Count of La Penautier, Magistral Knight of the Order of Saint John.'

She did not reply but no longer clenched her fists.

'I'm hardly an hour in this city, and for the first time, too. So far I've found the natives less than cordial.'

She folded her arms beneath her breasts. 'I do not wonder.'

Tannhauser inclined his head in acceptance of this rebuke.

'In any event, I apologise for any distress I may have caused you.'

Her lips were compressed, as if now she were as vexed with herself as she was with him. She looked away and stood aside. Tannhauser bowed again and went indoors.

The roasted chickens had arrived on a large platter. Tannhauser dismembered them and told Grégoire to fill his plate. The boy turned aside to expel a green pea from one nostril, then set to. As Tannhauser ate, he brooded on what to do next.

He was here, indirectly, because of the wedding of the King's sister, Marguerite Valois, to her cousin Henri Bourbon, Prince of Navarre, which had taken place the previous Monday. Marguerite was a Catholic, the daughter of Catherine de Medici. Catherine was Italian, a species generally loathed by the French, and credited, even by her devotees, with diabolic powers. She had ruled the country since her husband's death in '59. Because Charles IX, now twenty-two, remained little more than a monstrous child, Catherine, despite her son's fantasies, continued to do so.

In the eyes of many, Catherine's policy of toleration towards the Huguenots had caused three civil wars. The marriage of Marguerite to the Protestant Henri, neither of them twenty years old, represented Catherine's latest effort to secure the fragile peace between provincial warlords. The union was at best unpopular, not least with the newly-weds. Much of the Huguenot nobility, and most Catholic Parisians, considered it an abomination.

Such Tannhauser had gleaned on his journey north.

During the week now ending, which had followed the royal wedding, numerous grand balls, tilts, masques and feasts had been held in celebration. According to the letter that Tannhauser had discovered on returning home from the sea, Carla had been invited 'by the Queen' to perform at the climactic gala on Friday the 22nd – last night – in the Louvre palace.

Carla's mastery of the viola da gamba was no news to Tannhauser; she had bewitched him with her music before he had ever set eyes on her. That her fame had spread quite so far had surprised him. She had assured him that she would be safe, for an armed escort had been sent to bring her to Paris. She was also under the protection of the one man Tannhauser suspected he might not best in combat, the Serb and former janissary Altan Savas. The letter had contained no details as to where Carla would be quartered in the city, because at that time she had not known herself. She had made plain her intention of contacting Orlandu on her arrival. Now that his hopes of finding Orlandu were thwarted, he was left with only one avenue to explore.

'The Louvre,' he said to Grégoire.

Grégoire nodded and smiled.

The sight of his gums made Tannhauser want to turn away. He didn't.

As for the Louvre, Tannhauser did not relish the prospect. Once inside, numberless practitioners of virtuoso obstructiveness would stand between him and whoever it was might know of Carla's whereabouts.

The royal household, the *Maison du Roi*, was a vast and parasitic entourage. Thousands of functionaries, in scores of different departments, competed to squander the nation's wealth in a frenzy of extravagance and corruption. The largest department was the *Bouche du Roi*: the King's mouth. By all accounts the King could not put his shirt on, the 'Chamber' being the second largest department, without a dozen men in attendance, most of them nobles on enormous public pensions; and His Majesty's every royal stool – the expulsion of which required the nobles to assemble at the royal commode – was the subject of scrupulous study, though what fragrant auguries might be writ there, Tannhauser could not guess. He doubted that Catherine de Medici, prior to the ball, had been aware of Carla's existence. But someone in that palace had put Carla's name on a list, and had organised her travel and accommodations.

He fended a wave of despondency and drank wine.

He remembered that Carla had mentioned some fellow in the *Menus-Plaisirs du Roi*, the department of the King's 'lesser pleasures'. This, surprisingly enough, did not include those specialists who attended him at stool, but it did include those responsible for his lavish entertainments. What was his name? Carla's letter was in his saddlebags.

Tannhauser started as the two girls appeared at his table. The second was the meeker in manner, her hair summer-blonde. He clambered to his feet and bowed.

'We accept your invitation,' said the girl who had confronted him.

'I am delighted,' replied Tannhauser, while wondering why on earth he had extended it. He saw that Grégoire remained seated, wolfing food. 'Grégoire, a gentleman stands and bows when a lady approaches.'

Grégoire leapt from his bench and bowed with such zeal that he banged his forehead on the table. The girls laughed. Grégoire directed a deformed grin at Tannhauser, as if to suggest that their mirth should not provoke him to violence. The view of his gums was as revolting as before. Tannhauser joined in the smiles.

'This is my elder sister, Flore Malan. I'm Pascale Malan.'

'I'm charmed. Eat and be merry.'

The girls crowded onto his bench and fell upon the food with even greater gusto than Grégoire. Tannhauser's appetite waned. His eye fell on his heaped luggage and another problem loomed. The palace guard would hardly let him stroll into the Louvre loaded down with guns.

'So you're another of these Catholic fanatics,' said Pascale.

She tossed her chin at the white eight-pointed cross blazed on his chest.

'My days as a fanatic are long behind me.'

Pascale stared at him.

'In any case, the Huguenots enjoy bloodshed as much as anyone else. Their atrocities may be less widespread, but that's a problem of manpower, not morality. And both parties hate the Moslems and the Jews, so all is right with the world.'

She broke into a smile. She had a distinct gap between her front teeth. The gap gave her a certain gawkiness, which magnified her charm.

'Martin Luther hated the Jews for all the same reasons the Catholics do,' she said, 'but he also invented some new reasons, which considering the centuries the Church had before Luther came along, was quite an achievement, don't you think?'

If she was poking fun at him, Tannhauser was enjoying it.

'Luther was so brilliant he worked out that you could hate the Jews for exactly the same reasons he hated the Catholics,' she continued. 'He argued, for instance, that Catholics and Jews both believe that salvation comes from obeying the laws of God, not from faith alone. So Lutherans get the best of both worlds. They can combine a hatred of Jews with a hatred of Catholics without sacrificing theological consistency.'

'You are forcing me to a complete reassessment of the man's genius.'

'However, you will find that Calvin's attitude to the Jews is very different from Luther's. For one, he includes them among God's Elect, and provides arguments to demonstrate that the whole offspring of Abraham, uniquely among the nations, will enjoy eternal life.'

'Have the Jews heard these glad tidings?'

'And unlike Luther, and Rome, Calvin doesn't blame the Jews for the death of Christ. He blames everybody. You see, Calvin says you can't say that the Jews are exceptionally wicked, because all men are just as wicked as each other, and not just relatively speaking, but entirely so. Though, by the same token, neither are the Jews less sinful, or depraved, than anyone else.'

She smiled as if daring him to feel mocked.

'You've led me out of my depth,' he confessed. 'My life has seen very little theological consistency.'

'No one is more consistent than Calvin. All you need know is that all men, without exception, are evil and corrupt to a radical, irredeemable and absolute degree – believers and non-believers, the saved and the damned, the good and the bad alike.'

'I do indeed know that, though it's a conclusion I'd reached by myself.'

'Nevertheless, some will be welcomed into Heaven, even though they are every bit as wicked as those who will go to Hell.'

'Then there's a chance for me after all.'

'So you're not as holy as your shirt proclaims.'

'My shirt fools men, not God.'

'But you do believe in Him?'

'I believe in a God beyond any name or doctrine we can hang around His neck.'

Pascale turned to her sister. 'He sounds just like Father.'

Flore nodded in agreement. She gave Tannhauser a wary look. She was a year or so older than Pascale, but not nearly as saucy. Pascale turned back to Tannhauser.

'My father's a freethinker, too.'

'I'd beware of painting either of us with that brush, unless you'd see us hanged.'

'He says men in times to come will stand in wonder at the miseries we have made for ourselves.'

'They'll be too busy wondering at miseries of their own manufacture.'

'He says that this royal wedding – and this peace – are a sham. He says that war only slumbers and little it will take to reawaken it.'

'Your father should teach his daughter to be wary of strangers.'

'So I must live in fear of speaking my mind?'

'We all must live in fear of speaking our minds.'

'Even you?'

'I have nothing to say that's worth dying for.'

She studied him, as if seeking to read some darkness in his soul.

'That's a pity.'

'I would once have thought so, too.'

Tannhauser poured more wine. He drank.

'What's your father's work?'

'I'm his apprentice.' Pascale brandished her ink-stained hands. 'Guess.'

'A printer,' said Grégoire.

'A publisher,' corrected Flore. 'Mainly texts for the Collège de France.'

'A daring profession for a freethinker.' He noted that Flore's hands were clean. 'And your mother?'

'She's dead,' said Flore. She did not elaborate.

'You don't look much like a chevalier. Or a count, for that matter, but I'll bet you've been for a soldier.'

'I'm a merchant. I trade with the East, Spain, North Africa. My ventures in the English trade ended in total loss when your co-religionists started a third war, and the Sea Beggars commandeered the ship and all my goods.'

'So that's why you don't like us.'

'I like you both a great deal.'

'What do you trade in?'

'Saffron. Pepper. Opium. Glass. Whatever comes my way.'

'Is that what brought you to Paris?'

'No. I've come to find my wife and take her home.'

'Does she have a lover here?'

Tannhauser had never considered the possibility, not on account of Carla's virtue, though her loyalty was not in question, but because the thought that she might prefer some other man over himself was inconceivable. Even so, had a man suggested such a thing, Tannhauser would have struck him dead. Flore sprang to Carla's defence.

'Shame on you, Pascale. He loves her as a chevalier loves, it's clear. As an eagle loves the wind. A woman so loved would never be unfaithful.'

'Carla was invited to the royal wedding. She's expecting our child.'

This information begged so many questions that Pascale was struck silent.

'Tell me, how would I find the lodgings of a given student?'

'Is he a good student?' asked Flore.

'He'd better be.'

'Then you might ask his Master at the college. Your student might even be lodging with him. It's not uncommon, if he's keen enough.'

'Excellent advice, thank you. And where can I rent a room, where my gear would be safe from thieves for a few hours? I've important matters to settle at the Louvre, and as you see I'm overburdened.'

At mention of the Louvre, Pascale's eyes widened further. Flore spoke again.

'Every room in the city is packed with visitors here to celebrate the wedding. Thousands came, along with thousands more hoping to profit from the rest. As to an inn that's safe from thieves, even at the best of times . . .'

Tannhauser frowned. He cursed the wedding.

'We can keep your gear safe for you,' said Pascale.

'Pascale,' said Flore.

'Of course we can. You trust us, don't you?'

Strangely enough, he did.

'I hope I may insist on paying you for that good deed.'

'You may,' said Pascale.

'Where would you store the gear?'

'At our home. No one would ever find it and it's not far.'

'There's nothing of great value. Except for a spare shirt. And a pound of Persian opium. And the guns. The guns are the problem.'

'The guns?' said Flore.

'I doubt I can wander about the Louvre carrying a rifle and a pair of pistols. So with your father's permission, I'd count your offer a very great boon.'

Outside the Red Ox stood four buckets of water in a row, watched over by an urchin boy. It seemed that in Paris buckets were worth stealing, too. Pascale gave him a double handful of leftovers from the chickens, which the boy thought more than fair payment. Pascale and Flore each hefted two buckets and set off.

They turned the corner and came upon a brawl in the street. Four young men were kicking and punching a fifth, who knelt clenched and bloody by a wall. A jeering crowd egged the assailants on. Tannhauser plotted a course that would take them clear of the melee. He herded the girls and their buckets across the road.

'Please!' The beaten youth screamed, all dignity stripped. 'Please!'

His entreaties were only an incitement to greater violence. It was a fact strange to contemplate that a man who begged for mercy made the job of his tormentors all the easier. Tannhäuser felt disgust, for the victim as well as the brutes.

'Can't you stop them?' said Pascale.

The brawlers concerned him not at all. The crowd did.

'He's no friend of mine.'

He looked in the direction of Pascale's backward glance. A double crack rang out as a boot smashed the victim's head into the wall. He slithered to the cobbles where the stomping continued unabated, the aggressors grabbing one another's arms for balance, like revellers in some monstrous dance.

Pascale shouted. 'Leave him alone, you bastards.'

Heads turned and obscenities flew back.

Tannhäuser ushered the sisters onwards, their buckets sloshing water over his feet. He sensed Grégoire at his heels. They cleared the hurly-burly and reached a cross street and turned right. He was relieved. Both sisters were white-faced, Pascale more with anger than with fright. They set down their buckets to catch their breaths.

'Where is the Huguenot neighbourhood?' asked Tannhäuser.

'Protestants are spread all over the city,' said Flore, 'but there are more here, in the sixteenth, than in most others.'

'If they don't keep their heads down,' said Pascale, 'they get them kicked in.'

He looked at her. Her opinion of him had fallen, he could see, though why this should matter to him as much as it did, he could not fathom.

'I salute your courage,' said Tannhäuser, 'and even your compassion, but the world is as it is, not as you might like it to be. Helping that fellow would not change the world, it wouldn't even change the street. It would only change our own circumstance, for the worse.'

'I will not call you a coward, for that I do not believe, but if the world can't be changed by small acts of virtue, it can't be changed at all.'

'No doubt, Pascale. Again I salute your ideals. But a mob can't be predicted. It might have shown me its throat, but, had it turned, there is no beast so fierce. And then I might have been forced to kill them all.'

Pascale stared at him. It took her a moment to realise he was serious; another to believe him capable of the deed. She blinked, unwilling to abandon her outrage.

He said, 'From such small acts of virtue are wars born.'

'Huguenots are killed every day in Paris. They're beaten and robbed and insulted. No one is ever punished. No one even dares to speak out against it.'

Tannhauser's sympathy for the Huguenots was not great. They regarded themselves as God's chosen and wallowed in victimhood, yet their appetite for bigotry and violence was as healthy as any he had seen during a long career in such trades. They had imported whole armies of Dutch and German mercenaries, and at the war's end had left them to ravage the countryside unpaid. Thousands were out there still, inflicting wounds that wouldn't be healed for generations. In sanctimoniousness, a habit he despised more than malice for it brought greater evils, the Protestant leadership could not be matched. In all other forms of moral degeneracy, they were fully the equals of their Catholic foes.

'You're a Huguenot.'

'I don't know,' said Pascale, with a stiff smile. 'You'll have to ask my father.'

'I would be glad to. Where's his house?'

Pascale pointed to a shop across the street. The building was three storeys high and no more than fifteen feet wide. Exposed timbers poked through crumbling plaster. A sign splattered with thrown filth read: **Daniel Malan . . . Printer to the Excellencies of the Collège de France**. The windows were shuttered from without. Beneath them he noted the remnants of broken glass.

Pascale said, 'My father is out at one of his meetings.'

'Are you sure my gear is welcome?'

Flore said, 'Of course. And please forgive Pascale her sharp tongue. You were worried for our safety and you were right.'

Flore grabbed her buckets and crossed the street. She opened the front door with a key on a cord around her neck. She turned on the threshold.

'Your belongings will be here whenever you want them.'

'Are you sure your father is out? I'd value his blessing on this arrangement.'

'You protected his daughters from an unpredictable mob and avoided a war,' said Pascale. 'Why wouldn't he bless it?'

Tannhauser smiled. He opened the pan cover and blew out the priming. He handed the rifle to Pascale. Its weight caught her off guard. She stacked it inside the door. Grégoire gave the holstered pistols to Flore. Tannhauser rummaged in his saddle wallets and at length found Carla's letter, wrapped in oilcloth. He pushed it into his boot top. He gave the wallets to Pascale. She stowed them inside. He glanced up and down the street.

'Promise me you'll lock the doors and stay inside, until either your father returns or I do. No rubbing elbows with students in taverns.'

'They were actors,' said Pascale. 'On their way to an audition.'

'Actors? I did you a better turn than I knew. Let me hear your promise.'

'You have my word.'

'Let me hear the lock turned and the bolts thrown.'

Tannhauser gave Pascale an *écu d'or*. She was astounded.

He bowed goodbye. Pascale showed him her gap-toothed smile.

'You be careful, too,' she said. 'There are a lot of angry Huguenots at the Louvre. And unlike that wretched boy you left in the street, they carry swords.'

'Why should they be any more ill-tempered than usual?'

She looked at him as if he were stupid, a diagnosis she at once confirmed.

'Because Admiral Coligny has been shot.'

'Shot or killed?'

'Shot, by a Catholic marksman. But by all accounts he will survive.'

'When did this happen?'

'Yesterday morning. The city talks of nothing else.'

'Has the would-be assassin been caught?'

'Not as far as I've heard.'

'I appreciate the intelligence. Now mark your promise.'

Pascale closed the door. He listened for the scrape of key and bolt. He pulled the letter from his boot and unwrapped it. The most wondrous handwriting he'd ever seen. The sight of it made his heart clench. With each word he heard Carla's voice and love stabbed him. With each stab, he felt afraid. He found the functionary's name that had eluded his memory.

Christian Picart. Steward of the *Menus-Plaisirs du Roi.*

Tannhauser folded the letter and stowed it away.

Admiral Coligny, the Huguenot demagogue, shot but not dead.

A fourth war in the offing; if not in progress.

The Louvre doubtless a swamp of frantic intrigues.

Carla was over eight months pregnant.

And he didn't know where to find her.

'Come, Grégoire. The day is far from done.'

CHAPTER TWO

A Very Great Philosopher Indeed

Tannhauser returned to the Collège d'Harcourt. It was deserted. They left and crossed the Pont Saint-Michel to the City, past shops selling gimcracks and tawdry apparel, and Tannhauser decided to buy Carla some token of affection. Carla was not an acquisitive woman; her habits and tastes were more austere than his own, yet for this very reason he was puzzled that his gifts always brought her such delight.

'Grégoire, where would I find fashionable goods, fit for a lady?'

Grégoire garbled. The boy had a tendency to speak through his nose, interspersed with the growls and grunts he seemed to require to get any words out.

'Speak slowly so you shan't appear an idiot. I can't keep asking you to repeat yourself, so I shall do this –' he wagged a hand at his ear '– to tell you I don't understand.'

'I'm sorry, master. No one listens to me except the horses.'

'In this respect, at least, I'm a horse's equal. What did you say?'

Grégoire pointed to the façade. 'The Grand Hall in the *Palais de Justice*.'

In the Grand Hall hundreds of stalls sold velvets, silks and linens; decks of cards for playing tarot; jewellery, feathers, buttons, hats, elegant clothes. As Tannhauser wandered the market the burden of selecting a gift for Carla descended upon his spirits. The silks on display were superb. When first they'd met Carla had captured his eye, and more, by wearing Neapolitan silk. Red and diaphanous. The memory of her nipples haunted him yet. Such fabrics appealed to his own appetites but were hardly apt for a woman advanced in pregnancy. Or were they? Might the thought not flatter her? It was the sentiment that counted; but which sentiment? He caught sight of a baby's christening robe in white silk. He scrutinised the seams and invisible threadwork. Carla would adore it.

'How much for this baby's smock?'

'Sire, this is not a "smock" but, rather, a christening gown, and one that – for a garment in which to receive the most sacred of the Sacraments – would be fit to clothe a princess or a prince.'

The merchant launched into a paean to the gown's Italian weave, its artful lace fillings and the cloth-of-silver embellishments to its collar.

'They ship these from Venice by the bale, so spare me the performance.'

The draper named his price. Tannhauser laughed at him.

'Make me a fair bargain and you'll go home with some silver in your pocket. It will likely be the last you'll earn in a good while.'

'Why should that be, sire?'

'Why? The Huguenot rebellion. You haven't heard?'

'Is it true? The Huguenots intend to cut the King's throat and pillage the city?'

'I am at this moment on my way to the Louvre. If I were you I'd load this stock on a mule and head south. These fanatics despise finery and bright colours, as you well know. The only use they'll have for these silks is stringing up our priests, and perhaps us, too.'

The draper surveyed his merchandise in agony.

'I wasn't going to open my stall today but we were ordered to do so by the Bureau de Ville. "To maintain a semblance of normality." I ask you. Why can't they maintain such a semblance? The country is run by maniacs and thieves.'

'Does that pass for news in Paris?'

'To the Louvre, you say.'

'I've already said too much. But keep it to yourself or we'll see a panic.'

The draper glanced at his fellows who crammed the hall. He nodded.

'Now,' said Tannhauser. 'Do you want to sell the smock or not?'

The bargain was so favourable that Tannhauser headed down

the hall and purchased breeches, nether socks and shoes for Grégoire. As the bewildered boy was trying on the latter for size, Tannhauser spotted a man of thirty years or so, and dressed in bottle-green velvet, watching him from behind a display of shirts. There was something of the weasel about him; he seemed malformed without actually being so. The weasel turned and disappeared. His face was vaguely familiar but Tannhauser could not place him. He had seen more faces in the last hour than he had seen in the past year. The episode itched him. Before he could dwell, a throaty voice roared above the din.

'Ho! By the hairy chin of the Prophet, can that be Mattias Tannhauser?'

At an alcove in one of the galleries stood a Spaniard, a year or two over forty, who wore a fine but understated livery. It was badged with crossed maces and crossed keys on a red and gold field. Tannhauser knew him to be an Estrameño. As if that wasn't enough, nature had built him to inspire fear in all but the bravest; a decade of killing for the Tercio of Naples, and exterminating Waldensians for the Inquisition, had done the rest. He was armed with sword and pistol, and at least two concealed daggers that Tannhauser marked. Under the livery he wore a breastplate.

Tannhauser walked over.

'Guzman. Why don't they have you in the prison down below?'

Guzman laughed. They shook hands. Both spoke in Italian.

'I've come up in the world. So, it seems, have you. Shopping in the Grand Hall?'

'Something for Carla, my wife.'

'Blessings and congratulations. I trust it is a happy match.'

'I'll be happy when I find her. I have just arrived. Carla's some-where in the city but I don't know where.'

'Many a wife's been lost and found in Paris. Perhaps I can help. I'm not without a measure of influence, thanks to my master. You've heard of Albert Gondi, the Comte de Retz?'

Retz was a Florentine soldier who had entered the service of Henri II at the time of Henri's marriage to Catherine de Medici, some twenty-five years before. He had remained, and survived, and risen, in the inmost circle of the royal council ever since. Tannhauser nodded.

'I'm Retz's bodyguard. That's to say, he has guards by the regiment when he wants them, but I'm his shadow. It's mine to take the bullet or the blade.'

'How did you come into his service?'

'I saved him from three assassins on the street, in Tours, October of '69, just after Moncontour. I didn't know who he was but I knew God's luck when I saw it. Wasn't much of a contest. But can you guess why Retz gave me the job?'

'I would have kept one alive.'

'The times I've set that riddle and never got the answer. They use a water torture here that makes the victim beg for the thumbscrews, and beg that fellow did, and so did those he named, and those that they named, until I wondered if they'd run out of rope.'

'As long as there are necks, there'll be rope.'

'Retz has been the King's personal counsellor since the King was a boy, and there's no one closer to Queen Catherine, though if he ever swived her, as some whisper, it was before my time. Retz has worked for peace. He calculates there's more money in it. But if war it must be, he's the man.'

'How badly is Coligny hurt?'

'He turned to spit in the gutter at the moment the shots were fired, or he'd be dead.'

'Shots?'

'A double load. One ball smashed his right hand, the other his left arm. Paré amputated some fingers, but Coligny will live. The marksman was a member of the Guise faction. Retz and I haven't slept since. Meetings here, soundings there, parleys galore. What was that knot Alexander cut?'

'The Gordian knot.'

'That's the task fallen to Retz.'

'Does he have the sword to do it?'

'The King is his sword, if Retz can unsheathe him. But tell me more about this wife.'

'She was invited to this cursed wedding.'

'Cursed indeed.'

'Am I right to worry for her safety?'

Guzman shrugged, as if not to overalarm him.

'If any lady of sufficient note to be invited to the wedding had been murdered, I'd have heard of it. At the same time, the sooner she's with you, the better. Who is she, if I may ask?'

'A contessa of old Sicilian blood. Her fief is on the Garonne. She was invited to play music at Queen Catherine's ball last night.'

'There was no music. The Queen's Ball was cancelled, because of the shooting.'

Tannhauser absorbed this irony without comment.

'A steward at the Louvre knows where Carla is lodging. Christian Picart.'

'The court's attendants number over ten thousand, with this wedding even more. But stick with me.' Guzman nodded at a door in the alcove. 'When this cabal with the magistrates is over, that's where we go. The inner circle is summoned to cut the knot.'

A handsome man, around fifty, emerged in a pale grey doublet. A man playing dice with history and who expected to win, whatever the throw. He sized up Tannhauser.

'One of your old comrades, Guzman?'

'Your Grace, may I present Mattias Tannhauser, *Cavaliere di Malta*, and even within that brotherhood a man amongst men. We faced the heathen Turk together on the Bastion of Castile.'

Retz bowed, 'Albert Gondi, Comte de Retz.'

'An honour, your Excellency. Mattias Tannhauser, Comte de La Penautier.'

'The honour is mine. The best of us are humbled by the epic of Malta. In the Queen's own words, *the greatest siege of them all.*' His Italian, like his voice, was refined. 'But you must excuse me for I'm expected at the palace.'

'I've some business of my own to conduct there,' said Tannhauser.

'Ride with me. With your permission, I would take your counsel along the way.'

Tannhauser took a breath through his nostrils.

It would take a very great philosopher indeed to explain the wars that had drenched the country in woe and set kin and lifelong neighbours at each other's throats. Tannhauser was content to wait for that sage to emerge, though he did not expect his arrival much before Armageddon. Nor did he expect such wisdom as might be revealed to in any way mitigate the madness and hatred certain to be swilling about the globe when that day dawned. Differences in scriptural exegesis so fine that few bishops understood them were the ostensible cause for the violence between Catholics and Protestants, but to Tannhauser such grand causes were no more than the usual devices by which the elites persuaded the gullible to die and degrade themselves, in enormous number, on their behalf, and to their advantage. Diverse political feuds and rivalries, the ambitions of provincial warlords, and the general economic disaster engineered from on high, were the stronger poisons in the brew. The wagon of War was always filled to the raves with sordid motives; and always sheeted in a gaudy banner. The faithful might fight for God, but the winnings would be reckoned in power, land and gold, and divided among the few.

Such as Retz.

Tannhauser said, 'I've no particular grudge against the Huguenots.'

'Good,' said Retz. 'Neither do I.'

The windows of Retz's carriage were curtained with muslin. Bags of lavender and perfumed cushions meant that Tannhauser could breathe without clenching his teeth. He had rarely ridden in a carriage and thought them both uncomfortable and effeminate, but in Paris this was a civilised way to travel. The coachman cracked his whip and bellowed at the riff-raff in the thoroughfare. Guzman rode on a lookout platform bolted to the rear. Grégoire ran behind the carriage. Tannhauser waited to hear what price the ride would cost him.

'The journey is short, so I'll be brief,' said Retz. 'There are some two hundred Huguenot nobles in the city, the higher echelons of their movement, along with their retainers. They are lodged in the old apartments of the Louvre and in various of the nearby *Hôtels Particuliers.*'

He said this with the certainty of a man who possessed a list.

'The attempt on Admiral Coligny's life has left these noblemen shouting for justice. Some have threatened the person of Queen Catherine. Our young King is of a sensitive temperament and he holds the Admiral in very great affection and esteem. His Majesty is enraged that parties unknown should shoot his honoured guest while His Majesty was playing tennis. He smashed his racket in frustration. He wept with grief and shame at Coligny's bedside. He has forbidden the people of Paris to take up arms. He has cleared all Catholics from the streets around the Hôtel Béthizy, so that the Admiral might be surrounded by his own men. He has sworn to avenge this crime or lose his soul. This morning a judicial inquiry, staffed at the King's insistence with Huguenot sympathisers, concluded – but did not prove – that Henri, Duke of Guise, was behind the plot.'

He paused and studied Tannhauser.

An assassin acting in Coligny's interest had murdered Guise's father almost a decade before. Like the King, who loathed him, Guise was twenty-two. Some believed he coveted the throne on the basis of a bloodline to Saint Louis. Catholic militants, and the people of Paris, adored him.

'If Guise wanted revenge for his father,' said Tannhauser, 'he has greater patience than I.'

'Unrequited revenge is a potent elixir. Sip it every day and life has a meaning, a purpose.'

'The true identity of the plotters is immaterial. The Huguenots will convince themselves that the scheme was hatched long ago – by the Queen, the King, the Guises, the Pope, and anyone else whose name they want to blacken.'

'Would you suspect Catherine of the plot?'

'It runs against the grain of her policy.'

The satisfaction with which Retz received this made Tannhauser wonder if he, and most others, had not been gulled precisely as the Queen intended.

'Suppose we yield to the King's sensitivities,' said Retz. 'What next?'

'That depends on Coligny.'

'Coligny will carry himself like Christ Resurrected and garner more power. That's why he's stayed in the city, instead of leaving, as his comrades have urged. Which brings us to the heart of the problem. Coligny has been pressing the King to go to war with Spain, in the Low Countries. He believes it will unite French Catholics and Protestants under a single banner.'

'That is hard to credit in a man of sound mind.'

'He claims such a war was the price agreed for his consent to the marriage.'

'The wedding required Coligny's consent? And he's allowed to say so?'

Retz did not respond to this critique of the Crown's diplomacy.

'A month ago a Huguenot army crossed into Flanders. Alva crushed them at Mons. A letter from the King was found on Genlis, the leader of the disaster, promising His Majesty's support for the Dutch rebels.'

Tannhauser grunted and left it at that.

'The Crown is massively in debt and dependent on Italian bankers,' continued Retz. 'Another conflict with Spain would be a catastrophe, yet His Majesty wavers, at least when Coligny has his ear.'

'Why is an habitual warmonger like Coligny allowed anywhere near the King's ear?'

'The King is only twenty-two years old.'

'By that age Alexander was sizing up the walls of Persepolis.'

'You are right, up to a point.' Retz paused. 'On the night that His Majesty first slept with a woman, I was present throughout the occasion, to help make sure that all went well. And all did go well, for to make things go well for His Majesty is my calling. So you see, beyond that point, you are wrong, for, whatever his abilities, the King is the king.'

Tannhauser gritted his teeth.

'Tannhauser, I am surrounded by sycophants and liars. Your bluntness is gold, unaccustomed to it though I am. Now. Two days ago Coligny made an explicit threat: that the King must choose between a foreign war or a civil war.'

'Does threatening a king no longer pass for treason?'

'His Majesty loves Coligny, almost as the father he hardly knew.'

'Coligny loves only war. Without war he's just another provincial grandee. He is nothing. Hence he has nothing to lose and I'd take him at his word: the next war has already begun.'

'A Huguenot army of four thousand men is bivouacked a day's march from Paris. They have no intention of attacking and have no need to do so. Coligny claims they are loyal subjects, but they are not commanded by the King, and therefore their very presence is a challenge to royal authority. They are also a source of terror to the common populace.'

'Why do you tell me all this?'

'I would like to know what you would do in this circumstance.'

'If I were you?'

'If you were the King.'

Tannhauser felt a pressure in his skull. The months he had spent in the wilderness, at sea and in the desert, had cleansed him of such concerns. He had melted into the power of being alive in the world as God had made it. He had forgotten the world that humans had fashioned in its stead.

'Please, speak freely,' said Retz.

'Coligny is a strongman. He knows, as does any beggar, that the King is – or is seen to be – weak. It galls strong men to take their orders from a weakling. Or worse, a weakling's mother.'

'Then you don't approve of the Edict of Toleration.'

'One tolerates an attack of the piles, not warlords like Gaspard Coligny.'

Tannhauser had so far escaped the former affliction but was familiar enough with the latter. He wished he were back in the Land of God, with the travellers of Timbuctoo.

'Are the Huguenots not entitled to freedom of conscience?'

'Coligny's captains don't sit in the taverns debating the Real Presence of Christ in the Mass. They talk of women and horses, not the nature of the Divine. They've no more a clue what they fight for than the Catholics. This is a war between believers who don't understand what they believe in. It's a question of power, not religion. Does power reside in the state, as embodied by the King? Or is power to be dispersed among the warlords and their mercenaries? But you don't need me to tell you that.'

The carriage rattled to a halt and creaked as Guzman climbed down. A rap on the door.

'The Louvre, your Excellency.'

Retz looked at Tannhauser. 'How would you answer that question?'

'The King doesn't need my advice.'

'To the contrary. A man of the world, untainted by the intrigues of the court? A cooler mind. A man who has no cards to play in this game.'

Tannhauser grimaced.

'The Huguenot elites defy the King, in his own palace. They speak treason. They demand wars. They threaten his kingdom. They threaten his mother.'

Tannhauser paused. Retz worked his charms well. He did not much like it.

'I'd kill them all,' said Tannhauser.

'The entire Protestant aristocracy?'

'Just their grandees.'

'A radical solution. Can you elaborate?'

'I doubt I'm the first to suggest the stratagem.'

'The particulars are of interest.'

'Decapitate the high command and the next war will be a lesser war. If the game is resolved with a modicum of political skill – a treacherous conspiracy decisively crushed, taxes will be cut, apples of solid silver will fall from the trees, etcetera and so forth – there may be no war at all.'

'You advocate the killing of, let us say forty nobles – and their guards and retainers – who are guests in the King's palace and under his protection.' Retz's voice suggested the stratagem was indeed familiar. 'Men from many of the oldest families in France.'

'You want me to multiply the arguments in favour of this scheme.'

'Do you have reason not to supply them?' asked Retz.

'The oldest families in France are no more than its oldest criminals.'

'His Majesty counts some of them among his dearest friends.'

'A king who cannot kill his dearest friends for the good of his people is no king at all,' said Tannhauser. 'Suleiman strangled his own sons to preserve the peace. He strangled the wrong ones, but that's another matter.'

'I can't use an argument that compares His Majesty unfavourably to a Turk.'

Tannhauser wanted to get out of the carriage. He didn't.

'His Majesty must demonstrate raw power. At so late an hour as this, the only currency that buys such power is blood. Coligny's alone is no longer enough, for his is now the blood of a martyr. But if such blood were diluted with that of his fellow conspirators while quelling a plot to seize the throne – which, in effect, is what Coligny is attempting to do – then the martyr would become the traitor that in truth he is. Be scrupulous to avoid any wider repression of the Protestant religion and the rest of the Huguenot nobility will come to heel. It worked for the English. The more dear friends he kills, the better. And he should seize the Protestant strongholds, in particular La Rochelle, preferably by riding up to the gates in person and demanding the keys. If he had the mettle to do that, I doubt they'd have the mettle to shoot him.'

Tannhauser did not expect this last advice to be taken seriously. It was not.

'Dilute the blood of the martyr.' Retz relished the phrase. 'The King will say it is wrong.'

'Has the King seen the state of his kingdom?'

Retz did not answer.

'I've just ridden the length of this country from the dock at Marseilles. It should be the Garden of Eden. It's a wasteland. It's a disgrace to its keepers. But I'm not finished.'

Retz nodded at him to go on.

'A strong king would go beyond a cull of the Protestant elite. He'd arrest Guise and a dozen more Catholic schemers and have their heads, too. He would cleanse his palace of the libertines and live like a man. With the fear and respect thus earned he could banish civil war. If at that point his subjects wanted to worship idols carved from mud, he could let them do so, for no one would dare break his peace.'

'You would spill a lot of blood.'

'Hundreds of thousands have died in these wars for the vanity of men like Coligny. The King wept no tears of grief and shame for them. He played tennis.'

Tannhauser sat back on the scented cushions. The carriage was too small for him. He felt that if he took the deep breath he needed, the walls would be rent apart.

'I see it,' said Retz. 'Yes. I see it all.'

Tannhauser reflected on his advice. Some might consider it monstrous. Carla, for one. Perhaps it was. He couldn't think of anything he had said that wasn't true. It wasn't his problem.

'You have armed me with some powerful propositions,' said Retz. 'Now, what can I do for you?'

'For me?'

'No one gets as close to the throne as you now sit without asking for something. Preferment, a pension, a pardon, a grant of monopoly, a contract of supply. The very life of the court consists in a perpetual seeking of advancement and advantage by all who manage to gain access.'

At another time Tannhauser might have squeezed Retz, but he felt tainted. He had spoken the truth, but he knew he had been used. He did not want to be paid for it.

'I appreciate your offer, but it sits ill with me to stand in any man's debt. I want to be reunited with my wife, nothing more.'

'I'm disappointed.' Retz smiled. 'Your answer makes me wish you were indeed in my debt. Instead, I am in yours. I salute you, sir.'

'In looking for my wife I need to locate a palace functionary called Christian Picart. If a word from you would make that task easier, I'd be grateful.'

'A simple courtesy is no reward, but yes, of course.'

They climbed from the carriage.

Across open ground to the east stood the Louvre: part fortress, part palace, fashioned by diverse kings in diverse times, and currently a composite of different architectural eras. To the west, the city walls loomed. A gateway pierced the wall just short of the river and this was where the carriage had stopped. Through this gate Tannhauser saw lavish gardens and the wing and pavilion, both incomplete, of another half-built structure of elaborate dimension and design. Building materials littered the area in massive stacks but workers were nowhere to be seen.

A section of Swiss Guard met the carriage. Their halberds and harness shone in the long yellow light. They avoided eye contact, as professionals will. Also present were three courtiers. Their self-esteem seemed injured by the sight of Tannhauser emerging from the carriage. He watched them wonder who he was and what entitled him to such fellowship with Retz. Most of all they wondered what threat he might pose. Retz chose the youngest, who happened to be the most corpulent.

'Arnauld, escort the Comte de La Penautier into the palace. He will tell you what he needs, make sure he gets it.'

Arnauld grovelled to hide his chagrin at being expelled from distinguished company into that of a ruffian. He glanced at Tannhauser with unconcealed distaste.

'They feed them well at the palace, then,' said Tannhauser.

Retz laughed as if a laugh were what he needed.

In response to Retz, the courtiers tittered, the bloated youth included.

'I regret our meeting was so short,' said Retz. 'God bless you and happy days.'

They exchanged bows. Retz headed towards the gardens with his entourage. Guzman winked in passing and Tannhauser nodded. He turned as Grégoire ran up. He was drenched in sweat. The cloth wrapper tied with ribbon that contained the christening robe was crumpled under one armpit. He appeared to have developed a limp.

'Are the new shoes nipping you? If so, take them off.'

Grégoire, though in pain, was horrified. 'The shoes are a marvel, sire.'

Arnauld's horror was the greater. 'That creature is coming with us?'

'Grégoire, this kind young gentleman has volunteered to take us into the Louvre.'

'Tannhauser!' Retz had paused at the gate. 'One last question.'

Tannhauser looked at him and waited.

'Would you kill your dearest friends for the good of the people?'

'My dearest friends are the only people I have. For their good, I'd kill anything that breathes.'

CHAPTER THREE

Swine

Arnauld de Torcy led them through a sequence of corridors, salons and halls whose extravagance left Grégoire agape and filled Tannhauser with contempt. He was not immune to architectural beauty, but of late he'd seen too much scorched earth; and the Italians did it better.

Statuary inspired by the Romans abounded, along with ornamented masonry, delicate friezes, and allegories in relief that portrayed the fantasy of Valois genius. Each gallery and ceiling sang the praises of its patrons and recast historic acts of violence and greed as grand myths. All was newly built and on a scale so lavish that Tannhauser did not wonder that Italian cash, at excruciating interest, was paying the bills. He foresaw years of fresh taxes with every step he took. Household officials scuttled back and forth to assuage the whims of the lordly, who were as numerous as they were repellent. As Arnauld strutted towards each new room, footmen bowed and opened twin gilt doors.

'Note that most courtiers merit the opening of only one door,' explained Arnauld.

'Did you hear that, Grégoire? For such as we, you must open both doors.'

'Very amusing. But here, in the jewel box of civilisation, such distinctions are not inconsequential, nor are they empty ceremony. Each detail helps to define one's rank in the court hierarchy. If such details are neglected or ignored, then how can we tell who – or indeed what – a given individual truly is?'

In the salons of the pavilion, as on the streets, an undertow of disquiet was general, but this did not prevent a determined display of the decadence for which the court was famed. Women of outstanding beauty and high station, perhaps in an attempt to raise morale, displayed their tits for the languid gentlemen who sprawled about the furniture, several of whom wore silver cages hung about their necks in which they carried miniature dogs. While a handsome young footman served a reviving cordial, one of the gentlemen stroked the former's crotch bulge with a tongue-moistened forefinger, to a chorus of titters and squeals. The footman bore this ordeal with admirable stoicism and of the cordial he did not spill a drop. The smell of urine lingered everywhere.

'To a provincial this must seem a paradise,' said Arnauld, 'but what you are seeing is an intense struggle to conquer the pyramid of precedence. The ambitious are constantly developing elaborate manoeuvres, either to establish superiority or to undermine rivals, which latter are in endless supply. It may look gay but there is little real enjoyment, rather a perpetual commerce in suspicion, jealousy and spite. I doubt you would do very well here, but that you may take as a compliment.'

As they passed from one wing to another, Tannhauser saw a woman topped with a mass of golden curls hoist up the skirts of her blue silk dress, the pearls on which alone must have cost the price of a modest farm. She squatted over a mound of human faeces piled beneath a staircase.

'What am I seeing now?' he asked. 'An elaborate manoeuvre to establish her superiority? Or her intense struggle to conquer the pyramid of precedence?'

'That is why the court has to move every month from one palace to another,' tutted Arnauld. 'The stench becomes intolerable and the building has to be aired for fear of the plague.'

'And what do the midget dogs in cages signify?'

'One expects the centre of power to attract the dishonest, the greedy, the venal, the vain and even the wicked,' admitted Arnauld. 'It would be a shabby little court that did not. The elite must be allowed their privileges or what is the point? What is so dispiriting is that nine out of ten courtiers are also stupid, ignorant, talentless and scared. In every respect, except perhaps physical beauty, they are mediocrities. Yet they prosper.'

Swiss and French Guard were stationed so that every room and corridor was watched. Ranks of Swiss steel walled off certain stairways and entrances all together. The apartments of the royal family stood above. They left the *Pavillon du Roi* through a grandiose portico.

A huge courtyard opened out before them, perhaps a hundred paces square. It was walled in by buildings old, new, demolished and half-complete. The north and east wings were ancient, and unlike the new to the south and west, which were created to satisfy the vices of degenerates, the old Louvre was built to be a fortress. Its three conical towers rose above the courtyard's angles at all but the south-west corner. The courtyard swarmed with armed Huguenots.

Most of them were young and milled in truculent cliques. Some affected a silence suggesting righteous anger straining at the end of its tether. Others held vehement debates. Some, probably drunk, yelled insults and threats at the windows of the royal apartments. A handful wore armour. The white cross on Tannhauser's chest marked him out as someone worthy of their scorn. Some had already noticed him and were pointing him out to their fellows.

Tannhauser said, 'Where are the Swiss Guard?'

'His Majesty has posted them indoors, for fear of further inflaming high passions.'

'Where do we go next?'

'The office of the *Plaisirs du Roi*, where we'll find Picart, is in the North Wing.' Arnauld stared across the courtyard as if wishing for an underground tunnel. 'Unless this fury passes we will witness some terrible madness. Don't these fanatics understand? The King is the best friend they've got.'

'Perhaps not for much longer.'

Tannhauser studied the armed cliques. He wondered if he could reach the other side without shedding blood and decided he didn't much care. He set out across the courtyard with Grégoire behind him. He realised that Arnauld had not budged from the portico. He turned and looked at him. Arnauld pointed to a narrow gateway at the centre of the North Wing.

'Today the duty captain of the military household is Dominic Le Tellier, of the Scots Guard.'

'Vicious, dour and intemperate, and given to drink?'

'I doubt the Guard have a real Scotsman left. I was in the Guard for a year. It's a prestige posting, the senior company of the King's Life Guard. We swear to protect His Majesty wherever he goes – that is, to banquets, on hunting trips, to take the waters, and so on. The Life Guard only take to the field of battle when the King himself does so in person.'

'Not exactly veterans then.'

'That does not stop us having a high opinion of ourselves. I'm sure Captain Le Tellier will gladly take you to find Monsieur Picart.'

'Retz said anything I need. You will take me yourself, gladly or not.'

'We could adopt a different route,' offered Arnauld.

'You should've thought of that sooner. I'll walk where I choose.'

'You're as much a fanatic as they are.'

'If we turn tail now, they'll know why. We can't do it, can we, Grégoire?'

Grégoire hoisted the waist of his new red pants. In hindsight, they ended too far short of his knees, but the boy seemed not to mind. Under his arm the package for Carla was a sodden mass.

'No, sire,' he said.

'Then let this creature be your guide.'

'I could drag you across the yard,' said Tannhauser.

Arnauld stepped from the portico as if into a pool of vomit.

'Walk beside me, on my left,' said Tannhauser. 'Imagine you're still a Scots Guard. Head high. Eyes on the gatehouse yonder. If it comes to swordplay, grab Grégoire and run.'

They started across the courtyard, Arnauld almost trotting to match Tannhauser's stride. Though it galled him to do so, Tannhauser navigated the cliques in a series of straight lines designed to avoid a petty confrontation. If any of them moved to block his way, he'd take the man's measure. They skirted several bands without encountering anything worse than stares. When they reached the halfway mark, at the centre of the square, the catcalls began.

'Who's that fat swine?'

'His arse is bigger than the Queen's.'

'I bet it's seen a lot more cock.'

Laughter. To distract Arnauld, Tannhauser struck up a conversation.

'I've been getting about the city on foot but I'm hoping to find a horse.'

'Shit, shit, shit,' said Arnauld.

'Can I get a mount here at the palace?'

'Not without an authorisation.'

'You seem lordly enough to provide one.'

'I'd rather provide a warrant for your arrest.'

Twenty feet ahead, a Huguenot detached himself from the bunch. He stepped into Tannhauser's line of march and crossed his arms over his barrel chest. He was sturdy enough to try such a manoeuvre and angry enough to want to. He had sufficient lumps and scars on his face to prove himself a brawler but men who indulged such ploys as this drew half their courage from their fellows. Tannhauser checked the group to see if the brawler was a decoy deployed to set him up for someone more dangerous. He saw no candidates.

Arnauld quailed. 'What shall we do?'

'Give me some room but don't stop walking.'

Arnauld put his hand on his sword hilt and loosened it in its scabbard.

'Take your hand from your sword and do as I say.'

As they approached the burly Huguenot, Tannhauser did him the favour of altering course so that a confrontation was not inevitable. But the brawler was not to be denied. As he stepped once more into their path, he pointed a finger at Arnauld's face but spoke to Tannhauser.

'What does his arsehole taste like?'

Tannhauser grabbed the extended finger and cranked it backwards. The brawler howled with pain. Tannhauser stepped past him and the brawler, his strength rendered useless, was forced to bend backwards from the waist to avoid the dislocation of his knuckle.

With the back of his right leg Tannhauser swept him behind the knee. As the hulk crashed into the flagstones Tannhauser felt the finger snap at the second joint and let go. Tannhauser had barely altered pace. He didn't stop walking nor did he look back. He didn't need to. The fallen brute – and not them – now formed the focus of the courtyard's attention. Arnauld craned his head back over his shoulder.

'Eyes front,' said Tannhauser. 'It'll take him a minute to get to his feet, another to get over his shame. By then we'll be inside. By the time the buffoon gets angry, he'll be a problem for the Guard, not for us.'

They reached the gateway without further incident. On the steps a pair of guards stood grinning from behind their halberds. They nodded to Tannhauser but avoided looking at Arnauld, who was further incensed.

'This kind of insolence is the cross I bear for being so close to Anjou.'

Henri, Duc d'Anjou – a man who by all accounts preferred wearing women's jewellery to wearing a sword – was the King's younger brother and no friend to the Huguenots. He made amends for his decadence with periodic bouts of self-flagellation.

'Ignore it,' said Tannhauser. 'You did well.'

'Really?'

'You didn't lose your head and you were ready to fight.'

Arnauld gained a couple of inches in height and strode on into the lobby. He looked back and forth then set off down a corridor. The windows of the old palace were hardly more than slits in the stone. Lamps and candles struggled to fend off the gloom.

'You're one of Anjou's *mignons*?' asked Tannhauser.

'I am his friend and counsellor. He's in great need of both.'

'Counsellors seem to outnumber footmen round here.'

'The palace is a stew of rivalries and plots.'

'Perhaps that's why.'

'And by the way, my lord Anjou's taste in clothes does not

necessarily make him a sodomite, nor does his tolerance of masculine love among some of his favourites. I myself saw him take a maid-servant from behind while she was scrubbing the floor, though, I admit, he was intent on proving himself to his mother, who was also witness.'

'Buggery's not a practice to which I've given much thought. Must I?'

Arnauld smirked. 'Tell me, why did you insist on crossing the courtyard?'

'Aren't you glad we did?'

'I do believe I am.'

'There's your answer.'

They entered a large room stacked with the detritus of diverse theatrical productions.

'Wait here,' said Arnauld. 'Christian Picart, yes?'

Tannhauser nodded. While Arnauld went to question the man in charge, Tannhauser studied the room. Artificial mountains, painted silver and topped with thrones, lined one wall. Here were sheaves of scenery designed to recreate the flames of Hell. The masks of demons and imps filled several shelves. Animal costumes and angels' wings hung from racks. A strange sequence of noises drew him deeper into the clutter.

Hidden from view was a large cube covered by a sheet of black velvet. From beneath the cover came rustlings followed by silence, then whispers and croonings, then more silence. Tannhauser lifted the velvet and was greeted by a gale of shrieks so violent he took two steps backward and dragged the cover off with him.

The cage was made of hardwood slats. Its interior teemed with scores of monkeys, each no bigger than a squirrel. Their coats were short and yellowish. Their mouths and eyes were rimmed with black fur, which gave them the look of skulls. Their tiny and perfect fingers clung to the slats, which showed the marks of their teeth. Their ribs heaved rapidly beneath their skins. When they pulled back their lips, their gums were grey. Their eyeballs were shrunken from the rims of their sockets. Some lay on the cage floor, too lethargic to move. Grégoire stared at the creatures with a sigh of pity.

'What are they?'

'They're called monkeys.'

Grégoire made a fair attempt at pronouncing the word.

'They live in trees. These are from the New World, across the ocean.'

'They're scared and hungry. And there's no water in there.'

'Well spotted. Lend me a hand.'

Tannhauser threw the velvet cover aside. With a deafening exacerbation in the violence of the shrieks, he and Grégoire manhandled the cage from its obscure location and left it at the door. Arnauld reappeared and studied the monkeys with distaste.

'What are you doing?'

'The poor creatures are dying of thirst. Here they can let their keepers know it.'

They left the monkeys to raise the roof and Arnauld led them back down the corridor.

'Why do you want to find Picart?' asked Arnauld.

'He can tell me where to find my wife.'

'His nickname is "Petit Christian" because he was born with a deformity of the genitals. He has no testicles and his penis is barely visible, or so I am reliably told. In his younger days this made him sexually desirable to those of more outlandish tastes, whom this place draws as a manure bin flies. Christian submitted to these humiliations in the belief it would advance his ambitions as a playwright. If he had trace of talent as a writer, perhaps it would have.'

'He's a writer?'

'He wrote a single play, crudely borrowed from Gringoire but lacking his wit, and outstanding only for its pretentiousness and vacuity. In some circles these qualities are highly valued but the bloom quickly faded from his buttocks and with it his career. He now pens spiteful pamphlets aimed at dramatists more gifted than he and erotic doggerel for a private clientele. He is most valued for the sexual freak shows that he stages to titillate his former abusers at the court. He can draw on a whole stable of grotesques, midgets, freaks and children, or so I am reliably told.

49

In his official role, however, he is an administrator of court entertainments.'

'Not a man of great importance, then.'

'Who is of lesser importance than a failed playwright?'

Tannhauser said, 'I've never seen a play.'

'After spending half an hour in your company I will never watch one again.'

Arnauld investigated three further offices. Christian had been busy enough that morning but had not been seen at all that afternoon. No one knew where to find him.

'I've done my best,' said Arnauld. 'I'll order Dominic Le Tellier to send his guards to find the wretch. Then, with your permission, I'll attend to my other obligations, which are many.'

Tannhauser nodded.

They returned to the vestibule and stopped. Two men stood in the shaft of light thrown from the gateway, engaged in urgent conversation. Tannhauser could only see the face of the taller, an officer dressed in an expensive buff jerkin and matching hose. His handsome features were set off by a figure-of-eight ruff. He glanced over the other's head and his eyes stopped too suddenly on Tannhauser. Once again Tannhauser had the sensation of being recognised by someone he was certain he had never met.

'At last, there's Dominic Le Tellier,' said Arnauld.

Dominic nodded in their direction and the second man looked over his shoulder. It was the weasel in bottle-green velvet from the Grand Hall. Alarm flitted through his eyes. As in the market, he turned away.

'And that's Petit Christian,' said Arnauld. 'Do you want me to introduce you?'

Tannhauser studied him. There was nothing in Arnauld's eyes to suggest duplicity.

'No. If all goes well, our paths won't cross again. But I won't forget your generosity.'

'Then hear my counsel. Imagine a nest that is home to a family of vicious and overfed rats, all of whose members harbour secret hatreds for each other. Imagine further that the nest is festooned with webs spun from the purest lies, and that on those webs scuttle venomous spiders almost as big as the rats. Finally, imagine that this nest is located in a pit filled with vipers and poisonous toads.'

'You have there the material for a painting that would cheer the King of Spain.'

'I would not joke, because such a nest in such a web in such a pit is where we stand right now. Loyalties turn on a rumour. A sacred oath may be broken on a whim, an old friendship betrayed for a promise that will never be kept. Even an honest man, and they are few, may go to bed sworn to one faction and wake up supporting another because his master has changed allegiance while he slept. In short: leave as soon as you can.'

'I plan to quit the city with the sunrise, if not before.'

'Good.' Arnauld bowed. 'May God go with you.'

'Be careful crossing the courtyard.'

Arnauld smiled. He turned and headed for the gateway.

Tannhauser indicated Christian Picart.

'Grégoire, look at the man talking with the captain. He holds his arms like a monkey.'

Grégoire nodded.

'Have you ever seen him before?'

Grégoire nodded again.

'Where?'

'Across the street from the Red Ox. By the college gate.'

'Was it before or after we ate?'

'Just after. When the girls took us to their shop.'

'Well done. Go and stand by the gateway and watch for young Arnauld crossing the courtyard. If he chances on trouble, come and tell me.'

Tannhauser walked over to Dominic.

'I'll be having a word with this fellow Petit Christian.'

Dominic swallowed the discourtesy without comment.

'As you wish.' He left.

Christian turned with a false smile, as if seeing Tannhauser for the first time.

'Christian Picart, at your service, my lord.'

'Mattias Tannhauser, Comte de La Penautier. I understand you can tell me where my wife, Lady Carla, is lodging.'

'Lady Carla is the guest of Symonne D'Aubray.'

'I'd appreciate directions.'

'I can take you there myself, sire, if you can wait a short while.'

'Who is Symonne D'Aubray?'

'The widow of Roger D'Aubray,' said Christian.

'Both widow and husband are unknown to me.'

'Roger was a merchant and a much admired rector among the Protestants of Paris.'

Christian paused, as if waiting for Tannhauser's reaction to the fact that his wife was lodged with a prominent Huguenot. Given the state of the city, the news was hardly welcome.

Tannhauser said, 'Go on.'

'Roger was murdered last year in the Gastines riots, during the Third War. Symonne has continued his business. She imports gold braid from the Dutch, with considerable success.'

'I am delighted for her. Why does she play hostess to my wife?'

Christian flapped his hands.

'They both are wonderful musicians, as are also the four D'Aubray children. Since the underlying theme of the royal wedding was religious conciliation, a joint performance at the Queen's Ball – a musical allegory so to speak – was considered an excellent idea.'

'By whom?'

'Why, by all involved, including, we must assume, since she accepted the invitation, your good Lady Carla. Due to the recent unfortunate events, the ball, and so the allegory, were cancelled.'

'Who conceived this allegory?'

'I'm afraid I don't know,' said Christian. 'As you will appreciate, over a thousand guests were invited. I was instructed to make the arrangements for Lady Carla, just as I was for many others who had roles in the celebrations.'

'It was your decision to lodge her with Madame D'Aubray?'

'No, no, sire,' said Christian. 'I'm far too humble a servant.'

'Then who was responsible?'

'I am given lists of names and instructions. Long lists. The means are complex and many by which a name appears on such a list. A friend, a favour, a bribe, a debt. I cannot account for the habits of the court.'

Petit Christian was lying, or, rather, he was concealing what he knew under a mass of factual generalities. Tannhauser was certain that the playwriting pimp had followed him. If he quizzed him on the matter, he would only invite more mendacity. He would not get satisfactory answers short of inflicting fear and pain, which methods were not practicable here.

'Tell me where to find the Lady Carla.'

'You don't want me to act as your guide? I could do so within the hour.'

'Are you trying to delay me?'

'Why of course not, sire.'

'I have a guide. Directions will do.'

Christian's eyes flickered about, as if hoping assistance might arrive.

'For Paris, they are simple enough. Follow the river east to the Place de Grève, which will make itself obvious by the presence of the Hôtel de Ville and the gallows. Turn due north and you will by turns find the Rue du Temple. You will pass an old chapel and a priory on your right. A little further and you'll see the remains of the old city walls, beyond which lies the Temple itself. Just south of the old walls, on the west side of the street, you will find three fine houses in the new bourgeois style, not more than ten years old. You won't mistake them for they're dressed with an abundance of glass. The middle house is taller than the others and has a double façade. Carved in the lintel above the door are three honeybees. That is the Hôtel D'Aubray.'

'It had better be.'

'I hope the proximity of the Temple reassures you.'

'Why would I be in need of reassurance?'

'I meant only to be courteous, sire. Can I be of any further service?'

Tannhauser said, 'You can tell me where to locate the Collège d'Harcourt.'

It was hardly the subtlest of snares but Petit Christian did not expect it. In the Louvre dissembling was so habitual some didn't know when the canniest move was to be honest.

'There are scores of colleges, sire. I'm afraid I know little about them beyond that most can be found on the Left Bank.'

'I'm told it's near a tavern called the Red Ox.'

'Taverns outnumber the colleges ten to one, sire.'

Tannhauser didn't speak.

Christian shuffled, as if unsure who had outwitted whom. He knew that Tannhauser already knew the location of both buildings, for he had seen him there. Yet he dared not say so. A profession of complete ignorance must have seemed the safest course, and he stuck to it.

Christian said, 'Shall I make enquiries for you, sire?'

'I'll be making my own.'

Christian's lies confirmed he had followed Tannhauser up to the moment he met Retz. The porter must have sent a messenger while Tannhauser was eating. What had Orlandu been doing to justify this espionage? The answer would have to wait. He was eager to see Carla and the details of her location he believed.

'One last matter, but an urgent one. Your monkeys are dying of thirst.'

'My monkeys, sire?'

'See that they're watered and fed. See to it now.'

Christian bowed as he retreated to a safe distance. He turned and scuttled away.

Tannhauser heard footsteps and the rattle of weapons and tack.

'There he is, the swine.'

Tannhauser turned.

Four Huguenot nobles stood in a menacing formation. The eldest was the brawler from the yard; the youngest was a stripling. They were flanked by two Scots Guard. Dominic Le Tellier stood at the fore but off to one side. His features bore no trace of charity. One of the Huguenots held Grégoire by the scruff. A red welt from a slap marked the boy's cheek. Tannhauser took a breath to gentle the sudden urge to violence in his chest.

'So you're men enough to best a helpless boy. Let him go.'

Dominic spoke up. 'These noble gentlemen –'

'These noble gentlemen will let the boy go.'

The Huguenot shoved Grégoire forward.

Tannhauser tilted Grégoire's chin to examine the welt.

'Are you all right, lad?'

Grégoire nodded.

'Stand behind me.'

Tannhauser looked at Dominic.

'Which of these great warriors struck him? Or did the Scots Guard need practice?'

'I chastised him as he deserved,' said Dominic. 'He cheeked me.'

'Can you quote him?'

'Enough of this,' said the brawler. 'Let's get to the business.'

'Wait your turn or draw your sword,' said Tannhauser.

The sword remained untouched. Tannhauser looked back to Dominic.

'Grégoire is my lackey. I'll do the chastising.'

Dominic dipped his head. 'I was unaware, sire. I beg your pardon.'

Tannhauser said, 'Let's to the business.'

'These noble gentlemen claim you have impeached their honour.'

'All four of them? I didn't know I'd had the chance.'

'They are brothers,' said Dominic. 'A slur upon one is a slur upon all.'

Weighty texts expounded the formalities of the Code of the Duello, designed, like the laws of chivalry, and the supposed conventions of war, to preserve the illusions of those too civilised to celebrate pure savagery. Under the Code an insult might be offered by word or deed, and since the latitude extended to either category was wide, duelling was rife. Tannhauser had never taken part in a formal duel; he preferred to set to without the mummery. But unlike the violence indulged by the lower orders, the duel enjoyed the protection of the law, and this he was more than happy to accept.

Dominic indicated the brawler. 'This is Benedykt of –'

'Let him save his name for his tombstone,' said Tannhauser.

This discourtesy further inflamed the brothers. Dominic began again.

'Sieur Benedykt claims that you did injure him in an unjust, cunning and dishonourable manner. It is his right, therefore, without further debate or questioning, to challenge you to the combat – unless you decline the same by making satisfaction for the offence.'

The thought of Carla's disapproval pierced Tannhauser's conscience. If a formal apology, however insincere, would see him on his way, he owed it to her to make it.

He swallowed. 'How might I give this gentleman satisfaction?'

He managed to make the word 'gentleman' sound like 'turd'. All present noted it.

Benedykt stepped forward. 'Submit the first finger of your right hand to be severed.'

Tannhauser felt a burden lift from his shoulders. 'And if I refuse?'

'A refusal would impute me liar,' said Benedykt, 'and in such a state life is unsupportable, till death terminates either my existence or yours.'

A second brother stepped forward.

'However,' said this one, 'since the said dishonourable injury renders my brother unfit for combat, I, Octavien, as his second, claim the right to fight in his stead.'

Octavien was taller and leaner than Benedykt, younger by several years and a sight more handsome. He sported one of the long quadrate rapiers fashionable among those who had never seen a battlefield. The way he wore it said he fancied himself a swordsman. He weighed up Tannhauser's shorter, broader, cut-and-thrust sword with confidence.

Tannhauser looked at Dominic. 'Do you call this lawful?'

Dominic shrugged. 'Seconds often enter the fight.'

Octavien said, 'Consider my brother's offer. In the Duello I have slain five men.'

Tannhauser laughed at him. He turned to Benedykt.

'Let me see this crippling injury.'

Benedykt brandished his index finger in front of Tannhauser's face. It was swollen like a bobbin and mottled black beneath the skin. Tannhauser grabbed it and wrenched it sideways. The pop echoed from the walls, as did Benedykt's agony. Tannhauser felt sundry tissues and sinews snap their moorings. Benedykt fell to his knees, jaws clenched. Tannhauser looked at Octavien.

'Walk away or I will kill you. Think of the stripling.'

Tannhauser nodded at the blond-haired youngster, who was terrified.

Octavien looked at the boy. His resolve wavered.

Benedykt's malice exceeded his pain. 'Octavien! Kill him.'

Tannhauser drove a knee into his chin and splayed him on the floor.

Octavien had turned a shade paler. He put his hand on his rapier.

'Will you be known as a coward?' asked Dominic Le Tellier. 'Or does your challenge stand?'

Tannhauser stared at him.

The captain retreated to stand behind his guards.

Octavien said, 'The challenge stands.'

Tannhauser said, 'Then the choice of time, place and weapons is mine.'

No one took exception to this ordinance of the Code.

'Now is the time. In the courtyard. With those.'

Tannhauser pointed above the gateway. Mounted on the wall was a pair of ball-and-chain maces, their iron-bound handles crossed. A murmur. Octavien turned paler still.

'I've no skill with such a weapon,' he said.

Neither had Tannhauser. He smiled.

'Then I will instruct you.'

In the courtyard the crowd formed a square in which the duellists would contest their lives. Tannhauser gave his belted sword and dagger to Grégoire.

'Grégoire, you're my second.'

He pointed out Octavien, who was in conference with his kin.

'I'm going to kill that man, do you understand?'

Grégoire passed his tongue over his sundered lip and licked mucus from his gums.

'If anyone else enters this square, you must bring me my sword. Run as fast as you can. Grip it tight by the scabbard and hold the hilt towards me. Show me, now.'

Grégoire kicked his shoes off. Blistered and bleeding toes poked from holes in his new socks. He took a breath and gripped the sword by the scabbard. He proffered the hilt.

'Like this?'

'Perfect. You will make a fine second.'

'Are you going to die, sire?'

'Not today.'

He took up the mace. The chain clanked as he examined the links to make sure they were sound. The tarnished iron sphere, the size of a large apple, was welded about its surface with blunt pyramidal spikes, designed to destroy plate armour. Tannhauser had never used one in combat. He had chosen the mace because the choice itself had defeated Octavien already. He could see the brothers clustered around him, bemoaning the injustice of it all and further undermining his spirit. Benedykt was sobbing, and this time not from pain.

The sun had dropped below the roof of the West Wing, whose new tiles and chimneys were chased in a virulent red. Tannhauser hefted the mace with his left hand and swung it and the swivel spun. He turned his back to the sunset and started forward. Silence fell on the crowd. Tannhauser went down on one knee and crossed himself and rose to his feet. He sensed that many eyes were on him. He took in the Huguenot spectators with a slow turn of his head.

'Does Octavien intend to fight in the dark?

Octavien parted from his brothers, their hands slapping his back, their last words of advice lost in the gloaming. As he approached he took an underhand swing with his mace and shifted to correct his balance as its weight arced behind him. He would aim for the legs, the best of his options. He circled to Tannhauser's right and tried some footwork and again he almost stumbled.

Tannhauser advanced head-on, his mace held limp before his chest, the haft in his left hand. In this fight he was the bigger dog and he stared Octavien full in the eyes. Had he been the underdog, and times enough it had been so, he would have stared at the mouth, for the eyes of the stronger are a dark abyss inviting one to fall. Octavien tried to match his gaze. Tannhauser bore down. Three yards. Octavien still circled, still whirled his mace, the mace still the master of the man, the man puzzled more and more by the fact that Tannhauser did not wield his weapon.

Tannhauser stopped. 'Yield,' he said.

Octavien's lips compressed and signalled his move. He struck out for Tannhauser's thigh, as expected, but he lost control of the tension in the chain, thrusting the haft too eagerly, too far in advance of the arc, and the chain clanked and the swing was slow. Tannhauser pulled his left foot back, avoiding the blow by inches, and grabbed the ball of his mace in the palm of his right hand. The momentum of Octavien's swing wrapped his right arm across his chest.

Tannhauser shifted his weight and lunged, the iron ball cocked to the crook of his neck, like an artilleryman in a wager to heave a cannon shot. With the whole of his bodyweight behind it, he shoved the ball of the mace through Octavien's face. The force of the impact shivered up his arm.

He braced his shoulder and followed through.

The sound of the iron on flesh and bone broke the silence. Blood spattered Tannhauser's chest. Octavien uttered a dull cry and hurtled to the ground. Tannhauser stood over him and looked down. The iron ball had caved in the left side of his face from the upper jaw unto the brow. His eye appeared to have vanished upward, into his skull. The blunt spikes had ploughed runnels through the muscle and skin of his cheek. Bloody teeth gaped through the rents.

'The surgeons have healed worse,' said Tannhauser. 'Yield.'

Octavien shook his head. Tannhauser looked around the square of dour men. None spoke. The brothers were in shock. Tannhauser took the haft in his right hand and raised the mace.

'I ask him a third time to yield.'

Octavien shook his head.

Tannhauser estimated the strength required to punch a hole through the vault of Octavien's skull. His muscles decided they didn't want to do it. There was no morality in the decision, just an arm that had had its fill. He had had his fill, too. He turned away, towards Grégoire.

Grégoire exploded into a sprint.

Tannhauser looked back. Benedykt was lumbering across the square, a sword in his left hand, his face crazed. He let out a roar. At the sound of the roar, the other two brothers followed him. Tannhauser turned to the slap of bare feet as Grégoire extended the sword.

'Brave boy. Get back.'

Tannhauser spun with his sword to meet Benedykt's charge. The brute was beyond reason, his rapier extended to run him through. Tannhauser let him come. As the thrust was launched he side-stepped right and parried, his heavier blade swatting the rapier aside across Benedykt's body. Benedykt's impetus carried him past a pace too far. Tannhauser followed him round, the rotation of his body at one with the rotation of the chain, and lashed the mace through the inner side of Benedykt's lower left leg. He felt the shinbone shatter like porcelain, and to that very bone was Benedykt's weight committed as he stalled his rush. Benedykt fell screaming, on his face.

Tannhauser glanced athwart his shoulder as the third brother ran at his back. Sword and dagger, right and left. He had not the fury of Benedykt, nor the skill of Octavien. Or perhaps he knew that his actions were those of a scoundrel. He hesitated. Tannhauser stepped and spun to his left, covering and parrying, and swung the mace from maximum vantage, all his might in the blow. The ball hummed through its arc and flailed the scoundrel through the ear. His skull collapsed and an eyeball burst from its hole amid bloody fragments. Groans and whistles of approval rose from the crowd and the carcass dropped. Tannhauser turned to the fourth and last of the brothers.

The stripling, for he was fourteen at most, stood with a sword in hand, agape at the speed with which his family had ceased to exist. He was fair of face. He stared at Tannhauser without any notion of what to do. Tannhauser turned to Benedykt, who sat panting like some foundered beast in a swill of gore.

'Die in the blood of your kin, for it's you that spilt it.'

Tannhauser maced him with the motion one might use to split a log and this time his arm was willing. The ball lodged so deep in the vault of Benedykt's skull that it looked as if it had grown out from within it. Blood cascaded over his shoulders in remarkable quantity. Tannhauser let go of the haft and Benedykt dragged it with him as he toppled.

Octavien was choking on the spillings of his shattered sinuses. Tannhauser stabbed him in the heart. He turned and looked at the stripling. He had no intention of harming him, but he gave the lad the respect apt to the field. He had little else to offer.

'No dishonour falls on you. Shall we two make peace?'

The stripling did not answer. He was yet too bewildered for sorrow.

'Tell me your name,' said Tannhauser.

'Justus.' His voice caught. 'They, my brothers, called me Juste. I am the last.'

'Sheath your sword, Juste. Go to your Huguenot companions.'

Juste clenched his lips to stifle his emotion. His sword clattered to the stones.

'Pick it up. Show them some pride. And go.'

Juste's shoulders trembled. He picked up the fallen sword and sheathed it. He turned and stumbled away. Tannhauser spat gall. He watched Dominic Le Tellier approach with his two Scots Guard. Dominic stopped before him.

'By the laws of the Duello the bodies are yours to do with as you please.'

'Feed them to the dogs,' said Tannhauser.

'As you wish.'

The Huguenots forming the square began to break up. Dominic nodded to his guards. Instead of tending to the corpses, they moved to take up positions surrounding Tannhauser, halberds at the ready. To their surprise and unease, Tannhauser moved backwards, at the same time circling so that one was obliged to line up behind the other. Neither of the guards looked like a master, or even a killer. From this angle he could take the first at the knees and be onto the second. He smiled.

'Hold fast,' ordered Dominic.

The guards stopped in their cramped formation.

Tannhauser continued circling, counting on the guards to hold their ground, which they did. As he stopped within range of Dominic, the latter realised his error but could hardly retreat.

'Explain this treachery or there'll be more than the dogs can stomach.'

'You are under arrest,' said Dominic.

'I've broken no law.'

'It is a measure for your own protection.'

'From whom?'

'These men will take you to your quarters, which I assure you are most civilised.'

Tannhauser flicked his sword and stippled the buff of Dominic's chest with Octavien's blood. Dominic flinched. The guards tensed. Again Dominic swallowed the insult. His master had a minion with unusual self-control. It suited Tannhauser to be seen as a man with none.

'I'll not surrender my weapons to anyone lesser in rank than Alberte Gondi.'

This gave Dominic pause. 'A gentleman can be trusted with his sword, even in confinement,' he said. 'You may take your lackey, too. You have my word there need be no more bloodshed.'

'Tell me who you serve.'

'I can't.'

Tannhauser raised the sword point to Dominic's throat.

Dominic said, 'It's enough you know I'd choose your mercy over his.'

Some intrigue was mounted. By whom? Why? He could kill these three with less trouble than the first. He doubted anyone watching would try to prevent him leaving the courtyard. Then he would be on the run, in a strange city on a hot night, where his only friends were a stable boy and two half-grown girls. Could he call on Arnauld or Retz? Both were waist-deep in their own complots, and their fealty to a man who had killed three palace guards could not be counted on. If he ran, he would have to make a fugitive of Carla, too, or she would be questioned. What that might mean was best not imagined.

He saw Petit Christian watching from the gateway.

If he killed Dominic, the deformed playwright would raise the alarm. They knew Carla's location better than Tannhauser did. He didn't see how he could reach Carla much ahead of a pursuit, if at all. He struggled with his instincts. He had surrendered once before. But he had to do what he reckoned best for Carla. If they had him where they wanted him, at least for the moment, Carla would be safe. Or as safe as she currently was. He thought of Altan Savas and felt some comfort.

'Where am I to be confined?'

'Gentlemen prisoners are kept in the East Wing.'

The cell was a suite comprised of a parlour, a study and a bedroom. Numerous men of noble estate had given their kings reason to confine them. Some had gone from here to the block; others had been released or restored to high office. Coligny himself had once been sentenced to death before regaining favour. There was no reason to embitter a foe who might one day become an ally by shoving him in a dungeon with the rabble.

Dusk had fallen and candles lit the gloom. Tannhauser found a pitcher of water in a basin. He quenched his thirst. He washed the blood from his hands. Sooner or later whoever had concocted this riddle would make himself known. Until then there was no point dwelling on it. His worry for Carla was extreme but she'd survived this long without him; at least he hoped so. In the study he found a desk equipped with pen, paper, sealing wax and ink. He doubted Guzman could read but if Fortune would place the letter in his hand, he could have someone read it for him. Tannhauser wrote the message in both Italian and French.

Guzman, I am imprisoned on the second floor of the East Wing. Get me out, at once. I will be in your debt. Your brother from the Bastion of Castile – Mattias Tannhauser.

He sealed the letter with wax. On the front he printed: *Albert Gondi, Comte de Retz.* Few would dare break the seal, and if Retz was the reader, so much the better.

Carla's image returned to his mind. He shouldn't have made the voyage to North Africa at such a time. But was the world to grind to a halt on account of a baby? What had Petit Christian told him of Carla's location? He couldn't remember. He turned to ask Grégoire; but the boy had not been present at that conversation. Gallows. A church. Symonne, widow of some Huguenot rabble-raiser.

'Grégoire, where are the gallows?'

'The Place de Grève, sire.'

The Place de Grève. North on the Rue du Temple. It came back to him. A fine house with a double façade. Three honeybees above the door. On the west side of the street. Symonne D'Aubray. He noted it on paper. He put down the pen.

'Grégoire, I've a labour worthy of Hercules to set you.'

'Hercules?'

'A hero of mighty strength and courage.'

'I'm not very strong,' said Grégoire.

'It's the courage that counts. Are you game?'

'Yes.'

The boy had put his shoes back on. Tannhauser tucked his shirt in and tidied up his slops. He wiped his face and hands and smoothed his hair with a wet neckerchief. The lad would not pass as a page to the Duc d'Anjou, but neither did he look like a beggar just in from the street.

'Do you remember Guzman, the Spaniard?'

Grégoire nodded.

'Find him and give him this letter. Bring Guzman back here to set me free.'

Tannhauser held out the letter.

Grégoire took it as if it were a fragment of the True Cross.

'You must walk these halls as if you walked them every day. Hold the letter out before you – just so. Perfect. If anyone stops you, show him the name on the front. Retz is a man of great importance and with luck they won't interfere. If you are asked any questions, recite an *Ave*.'

'An *Ave Maria*?'

'Exactly. Shout it as loud as you can and with passion. No one will understand a word you say. Do you remember the first grand building we entered?'

'Where the men wore dogs around their necks?'

'That's the place that Retz is most likely to be – upstairs in conference with the King – and that's where you'll find Guzman, if you find him at all.'

'I will find him.'

'If you don't, do not think you have failed me.'

'I will not fail you.'

Tannhauser summoned the guard by means of a chain by the heavy door that rang a bell.

'My page has an urgent message for the Comte de Retz.'

The guard frowned at Grégoire, who held out the letter like a talisman.

'I was with Retz this afternoon,' said Tannhauser. 'His mood is testy. Tell me your name.'

'I'll see your page through the gates at once, sire.'

Tannhauser tossed the guard a silver franc. He motioned to Grégoire.

'Good luck, lad.'

Grégoire bowed. The door closed. The key turned.

The bedroom was dark. By the candlelight from the parlour Tannhauser glimpsed a bed. His exhaustion was so deep he was almost glad to be in gaol. He stripped his weapons, his boots and his shirt, and did what good sense demanded. He lay on the bed, and thought not of his troubles, and fell into a sound sleep.

CHAPTER FOUR

The Lady from the South

C arla awoke for the third time that night with a desire to use the pot, and she sighed. The moonlight was so bright it might have been dawn. Her back ached, as usual, as did her ribs and much else, but the pain that sometimes extended down her leg had remitted. She put her hand on her belly, wherein her babe was sleeping. She was reluctant to wake him again. Once roused, his energies would thwart her own rest.

She was sure she carried a son. His kicks and punches – his impatience to enter the world – seemed altogether too masculine. She thought of Mattias, as she thought of him a hundred times a day, and she smiled. Boy or girl, the baby had inherited his spirit. She could feel the two of them, father and child, connected to each other through her. The feeling made her happy when she was sad. It helped make Mattias's absence tolerable. It helped keep him alive in her heart until the day she would fall in love with him, all over again.

She cast aside the sheet, which was limp with humidity, and swung her legs over the edge of the bed. She pushed herself upright. She prided herself on being a woman of vigour, but the weight of the child had lately seemed enormous, as did the bulge swelling over her thighs. The transformation of her body continued to amaze her. She pulled her nightgown above the bulge and tucked it beneath her breasts, which were also enlarged. By her reckoning she was thirty-eight weeks along. She braced her arms and lowered herself into a squat beside the bed. Squatting was one of few postures she found comfortable. She drew the pot beneath her and relieved herself. The volume was small. In another hour, she'd probably have to relieve herself again. Some women, she had been assured, adored pregnancy, but despite its wonders, Carla was not one of them.

She pushed the pot back under the bed. She remained on her haunches, wide awake now, as her belly grew hard with a contraction. She had grown familiar with such throngs in recent days, since the babe had shifted down into her pelvis and the shape of her belly had changed. Two days before she had found a show of pink mucus on her nightgown. She hadn't planned to give birth in Paris, but now it looked likely to be so. She was not alarmed; rather she felt a heady excitement, and relief that the ordeal would soon be over. She wanted to hold him in her arms.

She was well cared for here. Symonne could not have been kinder. The midwife who had delivered Symonne's four children was ready to attend her at a moment's notice. A fine surgeon, Monsieur Guillemeau, a protégé of Ambroise Paré, had paid a visit the day before and was prepared to intervene in the event of complications. But as he had pointed out, she was strong, the baby was both strong and well positioned, and she had given birth before without extraordinary difficulties.

Her invitation to perform with Symonne at the Queen's Ball, which she had thought a delightful idea, had coincided with one of the bursts of energy and elation that had been scattered throughout her pregnancy. Strange as it seemed now, she hadn't considered refusing. She had expected Mattias to return in time to join her, for the invitation had included him. When he did not return, and when her official escort had arrived – six mounted men at arms under the command of Dominic Le Tellier – courtesy had obliged her to leave without him.

The journey had been staged so as not to overtax her, her accommodations had been generous and the weather fine. She had a passion for riding and being in the saddle had proved more agreeable than standing, sitting or lying. She had enjoyed the trip and felt that her babe, too, had appreciated his first taste of adventure. She had now been in Paris for ten days.

The throng passed and had been mild enough, yet she noticed for the first time that her womb did not completely relax. Soon, then. She was glad. She rose and peeled off her damp nightgown and threw it on the bed. The contraction had woken her babe. Not only could she feel him, she could see him move, the shape of her bump shifting. A foot perhaps, or a shoulder. She laughed. And then she felt alone, for she wished she could have shared the sight with Mattias.

It was hard not to think of Mattias. Whenever she did, she worried for him, but since leaving for Paris she had no longer felt angry with him for not coming home. Such anger had in part provoked her to come here, for she knew his worry would be greater by far than hers. She was ashamed of such pettiness. She had married him well knowing his trade and his venturesome spirit. He had tried for over three years to play the country gentleman, to manage tenants and livestock and orchards and vines, all of which skills he had at first enjoyed learning from her, but all of which turned on a dial so slow she had watched it begin to drive him mad. He was ingrained with the rhythms of commerce and war, not of nature. In the end the spectacle had been so like that of a bear on a chain that, while dreading the long periods they would be parted, she had urged him to follow his ambitions. Even so, his recent absence had hurt her, then angered her, and now scared her. With an effort, she put him from her mind.

She walked to the rear window.

Carla had left both casements open for the air, hoping that the muslin summer drapes would fend off the gnats. Her room was on the third floor. The moon was a day short of full. It hung in the west amid a mass of stars and cast a silvery green light across the dense black blot of the Ville. She wondered if it was true that the full moon made men mad. Staring at it, she felt a tinge of delirium. With sundown, the city as a whole descended into darkness, but here and there in the vast concentration of humanity, pinpoints of yellow glowed.

When she had first arrived, and being used to the countryside, she had sensed the presence of so many as a physical force, even when alone in this room. It was as if their countless and individual psyches formed a single entity, as drops of water a sea. The sense was both exciting and sinister. Would her barque be swamped and wrecked or borne along on the swell? After ten days she felt the presence less strongly. She had been neither wrecked nor borne along, she had been absorbed into the waves.

Paris repelled and fascinated her in near equal measure, fascination emerging triumphant. Within four days she had lost all sense of smell, despite that she had drenched her clothes in perfume. Its people, high and low, lived their lives with a rabid ferocity, as if few expected to see another day. Its vitality thrilled her. Its casual cruelties filled her with dismay. The thought undammed her other source of worry, for Orlandu, her son. He was out there, somewhere in the night, but she knew not where.

Seeing him had filled her with a greater joy than she had known in many months. Far more than the wedding, which had given her both an escort and an excuse, the prospect of throwing her arms around him had been her prime motive in coming to Paris. For a week they had been together for several hours a day. He had spent most nights here at the Hôtel D'Aubray, though, not to be outdone in matters of manfulness, he had insisted on pitching camp in the garden at the rear with Altan Savas.

She had been shocked, almost disappointed, to find how completely Orlandu had become a man. He had been gone almost a year but fending for himself in the capital had worked deeper changes than time. Orlandu had not lost the exuberance that made him shine and which she so loved, yet its light was shadowed, as a candle by stained glass, by some brooding awareness she had not seen before. Survival in Paris might explain the change, though he had been wary of telling her much about his life outside the realm of college and his studies. Perhaps that was normal. She had told her own parents nothing of her inner life. What had disturbed her most was how much like his father, Ludovico, he had become, not merely in his broadening build and obsidian eyes, but in the darkening intensity of his mind.

She had not seen Orlandu since Friday afternoon, yesterday, when he had arrived in some agitation to tell her that Admiral Coligny had been shot and the Queen's Ball cancelled. She had invited him to keep her company, a prize she preferred to the ball, but he had intimated urgent obligations and promised to return as soon as he could.

Carla put her hands on her hips and arched her back. The baby kicked. Carla smiled, with the quick change of mood that she was now used to. The travails of her elder son would have to wait. She didn't want to wake anyone else – the children next door or Symonne on the floor below – but she needed exercise. She missed her daily riding, a practice less easily accomplished here. The Hôtel D'Aubray was one large room deep, in the new, spacious style of Monsieur Cerceau, and a second window on the far side of the bedroom overlooked the Rue du Temple. She walked across the room and leaned on the front window sill to ease her loins. Through the gauzy drape a movement across the street caught her eye. She pulled the muslin aside.

A young girl sat cross-legged with her back to the wall of the building opposite. She did not move – her small white face was still – and yet, at the same time, her body appeared to be writhing in a slow convulsion, and her torso appeared to be cast in abnormal dimensions, too large for her head. Carla wondered if this were not some trick of the night, or yet another strange symptom of pregnancy. She looked again. Something detached itself from the girl and scurried away.

Carla turned away with revulsion.

The girl was covered with rats.

Carla's skin crawled. She put both hands on her belly. The baby seemed unperturbed. She felt compelled to look again. It was true. The writhing was caused by a living coat of rats. To her relief, Carla saw that the girl was not under attack. Rather, she appeared to be quite at peace with the creatures. More than that, her chin was raised in a kind of ecstatic swoon. Her hands slid among the creatures, stroking their rank brown coats as if caressing the hair not of a pet but of a lover. Carla stepped back from the window. She swallowed a surge of bile. She needed a glass of water.

Before she could dwell on the girl further, two men emerged from the alley to the side of the building where the girl sat. Carla retreated further and watched.

One man was so huge in the shoulders and head that his gait rolled from side to side as if to stop him losing his balance. He conjured in her mind the Titans of Greek lore, the children of Gaia who had once ruled earth until thrown down by the gods. He wore a yellow shirt and his face was in shadow. The second man was as thin as a reed and wore his hair in a tarred pigtail. Knives hung from their belts.

The manner in which men planned acts of war was particular; it expressed a passion that no other task could rival, not even seduction. It penetrated their muscle and bone. Only surgeons at the slab could compare. Carla had seen men at it hundreds of times – knights, sappers, surgeons – too, during the fabled Siege of Malta.

Neither seemed bothered by the sight of the rat girl.

The girl scrambled to her feet and caused a brief and spectacular flood of vermin, which vanished into nowhere with the speed of an interrupted dream, and left just as strange an aura behind them. The titan spoke to the rat girl and pointed to something in the sky above the Hôtel D'Aubray.

Carla's stomach dropped inside her.

The object of their campaign was the building in which she stood.

The rat girl looked up – at a point so directly above Carla that she almost looked up herself. The girl shook her head with vehemence and said no. The pigtailed man stooped to yell in her face then slapped her with such violence that she fell to the ground. Carla flinched. She flinched again as the titan grabbed the man by his pigtail and rammed his face into the wall. Had he not held him upright, pigtail, too, would have fallen. The titan muttered in his ear and let him go.

The rat girl got up and listened to the titan's instructions, and this time she nodded. She took a small knife from a belt around her waist and handed it over. Pigtail took her by a stick-thin arm and they walked south down the street.

The titan looked over at the Hôtel D'Aubray. Carla could not make out his features, only the huge clean-shaven rim of his lower jaw. He raised his face. For a moment she had the impression he was looking straight at her. She took a third step backwards. The titan turned and rolled away down the alley.

The street was once more empty but for moonlight, yet the titan had left in his wake that uncanniest of all guests: not mere fear, but the premonition of disaster.

Carla paced the room, naked. She called on her reserves of calm. She asked herself if what she had seen was just another bizarre incident in the life of the turbulent city. But the titan had not merely looked at the Hôtel D'Aubray; he had studied it. She hurried to the rear window and looked down.

She had been accompanied from La Penautier by Altan Savas. He was a Serb by birth, a galley slave whom Mattias had bought from the Knights in Malta four years before. Like Mattias, he had once been a janissary of the Grande Turke and he enjoyed her husband's absolute confidence, an honour bestowed on so few she could not name another who was still alive. Despite the three-week journey from the south, Carla felt she hardly knew Altan Savas. He lived in a world unto himself. He prayed to Allah, though he let few know it. She rarely heard him speak French, though he and Mattias would talk for hours in Turkish. Altan, at his own request, had been bivouacked on a palliasse in the garden. If she had understood his explanation, a mixture of word and mime, it had been, 'If the lion sleeps indoors, he cannot smell his prey.'

As she looked down she saw that the palliasse was empty.

Carla put on a gown of pale gold linen tailored to accommodate her state. Her heart was beating so fast she could hardly think. To slow it, and in one of those irresistible whims that characterised this pregnancy more than her others, she took the time to braid her hair. The chore soothed her and the braid made her feel stronger; she didn't know why. And since, on a similar whim, she had not cut her hair since learning she was expecting, it fell almost down to her waist in long waves.

She went to the door and stepped out into the upper hallway. Windows lit the stairwell from the front and the rear. A ladder led up to the cramped attic bedroom of the housekeeper and her husband, poorer in-laws of Symonne, Denise and Didier. Across the hallway was the children's room. Carla opened the door and peeked inside. The four D'Aubray children – Martin, Lucien,

Charité and Antoinette – were asleep in two beds. Martin and Lucien had vacated their room to make way for Carla.

Carla closed the door. Another contraction began. She leaned on the wall and breathed. The contraction was the strongest yet. She questioned the alarm bubbling in her stomach. It was the dead of night, when all things seem strange. She had seen some peculiar characters in the street. In Paris such figures were legion. Should she wake Symonne on the floor below and frighten her? Where was Altan Savas? The contraction passed but left her feeling faint.

She returned to her room and closed the door. She drank some water. She went once more to the front window. The Rue du Temple was empty. She made up her mind to go down to the garden. As she turned she heard a sound – a dulled clattering – as if from behind the gable wall. Carla started for the door. A muffled squeal, of fear marbled with fury, stopped her. Cinder fragments tumbled into the fireplace followed by a billow of soot. A moment later a pair of arms appeared, and coils of hair, then a head. A small, scrawny body slithered from the chimney, naked from waist to feet.

Carla stared at the rat girl.

The girl crawled into the hearth and coughed on her hands and knees. Her rough woollen smock had slipped up past her hips, which bore fresh grazes. She was filthy, though perhaps not much more so than was usual for her. The descent had grazed her elbows, too. Her long, corkscrew hair was so matted with grease that the soot had hardly gained purchase. The ringlets looked dark red but it was hard to be sure. She recovered with remarkable speed, as would a wild animal, and hawked black spittle onto the rug.

She looked up and saw Carla.

Wild grey eyes glittered in a soot-smeared face.

Inspired by the girl's example, Carla recovered quickly.

'Are you hurt?'

The rat girl didn't answer. She scrambled to her feet. She was all skin and bone, poorly nourished, but rather older than Carla had imagined, perhaps nine or ten. Perhaps street life had aged her beyond her years. She coughed again. Carla went to the table and poured a glass of water. She stepped forward and offered it to the girl. With quick glances the girl took in Carla, the room, the glass.

'If you try to stop me, I'll kill your baby.'

'I won't try to stop you.'

The girl grabbed the glass and drained it. She gave it back to Carla.

'You came down the chimney head-first?'

'Gobbo pushed me down head-first, so I couldn't climb back out.'

The rat girl went to the window. She seemed scared, but not of Carla.

'I'm in the wrong room.'

The chimney stack on this side of the house served the fireplaces in Carla's bedroom, the parlour below, and the business office on the ground floor. None had seen use during the summer. The second stack, on the southern gable, served the children's room, Symonne's bedchamber and the kitchen stove. Carla wondered how much so small a thief had expected to steal. Then she realised.

'You were sent down the chimney to open the front door for your friends.'

'The back door.'

'Is Gobbo the big man?'

'No. That's Grymonde, the Infant of Cockaigne.'

She recited this bogus title with a fierce solemnity, as if she expected Carla to tremble. When she didn't, the girl bared her teeth and clawed her fingers and growled. Without meaning to, Carla laughed. There was something elvish about the girl, elvish in spirit, and Carla couldn't help but be charmed by it. The spite in the girl's threats reflected the world she lived in.

'Don't laugh at me. You won't laugh when Grymonde comes.'

'I didn't mean to be unkind. If you look in my mirror I think you'd laugh too.'

'You have a mirror?'

'You can use it if you tell me your name. My name is Carla.'

'Estelle.'

'I love that name. It's one of the prettiest of all names.'

'Grymonde calls me La Rossa. Because he loves my hair.'

'I'm sure it's beautiful when it's clean. Why don't you stay with me, Estelle? I can help you wash your hair and find you some clean clothes. Then we can eat breakfast if you're hungry.'

Estelle considered this, with a mixture of innocence and guile. Fear won out over hunger. She shook her head. 'I have to go. Don't try to stop me.'

There was a hard knock on the door. An accented voice said, 'Madame?'

'Come in, Altan.'

Estelle glanced about in panic. Her eyes fell back on the fireplace.

'No. Don't be afraid,' said Carla. 'I won't let you come to any harm.'

The door swung open. Altan Savas took in Estelle as he bowed to Carla. His sword was sheathed but he held a dagger tight along his forearm. Estelle bolted for the fireplace. Altan sheathed the dagger as he strode across the room.

'Your pardon, madame.'

'Don't hurt her.'

Estelle was scrambling back up the chimney when Altan seized her by the waist and dragged her down. She struggled. Altan slapped her face. Estelle's eyes rolled up.

'Altan, no.'

Altan held the girl's wrists behind her back in one hand. He wore a thick black moustache in the style of the janissaries, which he smoothed with finger and thumb.

'I find a man.' He searched for words and failed. He indicated the roof then raised two wriggling fingers through the air to illustrate someone climbing up, then climbing down. Then Altan flipped his hand down flat, palm upwards.

'Gobbo fell?'

With the same two fingers Altan mimed the draw and release of a bowstring.

'He fell, yes.'

Altan jerked Estelle's arms. He gave her a look that said he would kill her if he deemed it necessary. Estelle understood such looks. She stopped struggling.

'Is he alive?' asked Carla.

'He talks. Now he is dead. More men come.'

'How many more?'

Altan hesitated.

'Tell me.'

Altan spread the fingers of his free hand. His palm was smeared with dried blood. On his thumb he wore an ivory ring. Five. Carla felt queasy as he closed and opened the hand again. Altan spread his fingers a third time.

'Fifteen?' Carla wondered how he knew, but didn't ask. 'Is it true?'

Altan shrugged. 'I demand many times.' He mimed cutting with a knife. 'I say: More? Less? He say, fifteen. Always.'

Carla looked at Estelle. The girl had followed what had passed. She dropped her gaze. Carla took this for confirmation. She turned back to Altan.

'Where is Madame D'Aubray?'

Altan put the back of his hand to his cheek and tilted his head.

'We must give them what they want,' said Carla. 'We will collect all our valuables and leave them in the street outside.'

Estelle said, 'You're the lady from the south.'

Carla felt her scalp prickle. 'What do you mean?'

'Grymonde wants you. The lady from the south.'

Carla realised her hands were cradling her child. He was still.

'Why does he want me?'

'Grymonde will kill you all. Then he will take everything. The tables, the chairs, the clothes, the food, the candles, and all the gold.'

Again, Estelle seemed to be quoting as if from a speech.

'Why does Grymonde want me? How does he know about me?'

'I don't know. Don't you?'

'I've never heard of him. Who is he?'

'Grymonde is the king of thieves, the king of us all. All the Ville is afraid of Grymonde. The police. The assassins. The pigs of the palace. He's my dragon.'

Carla was seized by another contraction of her womb. She closed her eyes. She used the pain to focus her thoughts. Estelle was infatuated with this criminal, this Grymonde, and no doubt exaggerated his power; yet no doubt he had power enough. She put her hands on her belly and felt her child through the tightened muscles. He gave her strength. The throng passed. She reassured herself that this was not labour. Her waters were intact. It was normal. She looked at Altan.

'Can we run?'

Estelle answered for him.

'The rich think these houses belong to them – but not tonight they don't. And the streets of Paris belong always to us. We can take them whenever we want.'

This, too, sounded like a quotation from a harangue.

Estelle added, 'Where will you run to?'

'Then we must hold on here until the *sergents* come to help us.'

'The *sergents* won't come. They're cowards. And Grymonde has promised them a fifth, but be sure, he'll give them only a tenth.'

Carla thought of the four children sleeping next door. She had played music with them every day since her arrival. She had grown to love them. Their mother, Symonne, was more remote, still trapped in loss, but she had given over her home to Carla and Carla was fond of her. Despite Estelle's conviction, Carla did not believe that this Grymonde meant to kill her. There was no sense to the idea. There was no logic, let alone passion, to drive such a murder, nor any profit. If even a shadow of what Estelle said was true, then a man, a leader, like Grymonde must be a man of reason, or at least of greed. Carla was worth a decent ransom. She would face him and tell him so.

She had faced dangerous men before.

She had married the most dangerous man she had ever met.

'You say Grymonde wants me. So he doesn't want to hurt my friends, the other people here.'

'Of course he does, they're heretics. Tonight all the heretics will die and they'll go to Hell, every single one, even the children.'

'What do you mean?'

'This is a Huguenot house. All the Huguenots of Paris must be killed, by the order of the King.'

Carla was aware of the hatred in which the city was steeped, but this was inconceivable. Not a week ago she had watched the King give his sister in marriage to Henri of Navarre. The King and his mother wanted peace and conciliation. Besides, there weren't enough soldiers in Paris to accomplish so vast and heinous a task.

'Grymonde told you this?'

'A spy from the palace told Grymonde. You can't save your friends.'

Carla did not know what to believe.

'The time goes,' said Altan Savas. 'The bad men come.'

Carla mastered the tide of fear that rose within her. She felt Altan watching her. She could not fight as he could, but she could ease his burden. She could take command. She knew what Mattias would expect from her. She wondered if she would ever see him again. And there lay her first task: to exclude all those many thoughts that would make her weaker. She indicated Estelle to Altan.

'Let the girl go. Put her outside the door.'

Altan pursed his lips beneath his moustache. 'Please. I kill her.'

'There is nothing she can tell Grymonde that he doesn't already know.'

'She sees us. The house. Kill her. Or keep her.'

'I don't want another child in the house, especially in a fight.'

'She is no child. She is the enemy.'

'I will not give you permission to murder a child. No, Altan. No.'

'A battle comes.'

'Then you make your preparations. And I will make mine.'

'We go, now,' he said.

He pointed at Carla, then at himself. His fingers mimicked walking away.

'You, me.' He pointed at her belly. 'The boy of Mattias.'

'You mean abandon the others? Symonne, the children?'

He made a spacious horizontal circle with his free hand, then slashing gestures.

'Outside, you, alone, I can defend, in the street, yes. With the bow, the sword. They are not soldiers. Thieves. But the others? The women, the children? Too many. Many, many. Too many. In here?' He shrugged and grimaced. 'Perhaps.'

'I will not abandon those children.'

Carla said it without thinking because it was the thing that everything she believed in, everything she believed about herself, expected her to say, provoked her to say. Yet at once she regretted it. Having said it, she couldn't retract it.

Altan started towards the door, dragging Estelle with him, then stopped, his ear cocked. He went to the window at the back of the house and listened. He looked at Carla. Carla now heard the sound too: the toll of a bell, rolling across the city from the south-west. The sound filled her heart with an inexplicable dread.

Estelle said, 'You see? You're all going to die.'

CHAPTER FIVE

The Rat Girl

A s the mad Turk Altan dragged Estelle downstairs, she took in every detail to report to Grymonde. She knew that the thieves could not be kept outside for long.

The house was built with too many windows and none of them were barred or even shuttered. The rich put sheets on their windows, as if they were too grand to need protection. At the second-floor landing the stairway doubled back on itself and bent down towards the front door hallway. To the left at the ground level was a room full of desks and big books. To the right was the kitchen. Each had a shorter, higher window to stop people peering in from the street. Through the kitchen door she saw a quiver of arrows and a strange foreign bow laid out on a table.

Moonlight filled the hallway from the windows in the stairwell on each floor. Towards the rear of the house, black blood was pooled and smeared on the hallway floor. She guessed it was Gobbo's.

Altan grabbed her hair and lifted her from the ground.

Estelle squirmed and kicked at his thighs. She knew he wanted to kill her but she remembered madame's order and she knew Altan would obey. She also knew Altan was right: he should kill her. Estelle liked madame, the lady from the south. Carla? She was sorry Grymonde would kill her.

Estelle screamed as Altan threw her down and rubbed her face in the gore. It was still warm, thick and greasy. She clamped her lips tight but the blood went up her nostrils and she was forced to breathe. The blood clung to the inside of her throat and she coughed and opened her mouth and breathed in more. She couldn't scream any more.

She was going to die in Gobbo's blood.

Altan hauled her upright. Coughs racked her. She retched blood. She was blinded but Altan held her wrists and she couldn't wipe her eyes. He shook her by the hair. She tried to spit at him. He slapped her face again, hard, but not as hard as Gobbo had hit her in the street. He pulled open the back door of the house.

'Look,' said Altan.

He twisted her around to face the outside of the door. A cord was strung from a wrought iron knocker twice the size of her fist. The knocker was fashioned in the shape of a bee. The end of the cord was looped around Gobbo's neck. Gobbo was dead and he was naked. His broken legs were canted at strange angles. Both were covered in stripes of blood that ran from the black hole tufted by his pubic hair. His eyeballs bulged at the moon. He'd been stabbed in the chest. Shoved into Gobbo's mouth were his severed cock and balls.

Estelle lived with Gobbo. He and his brother, Joco, slept in the same bed as her mother, Typhaine, though Estelle didn't think she let them swive her, at least not unless she was drunk, which wasn't very often any more. Estelle had never liked either of them. She only liked Grymonde. She loved Grymonde. Grymonde was her dragon.

She looked at Gobbo's bleeding corpse and felt no pity. She wondered if Altan had cut his cock and balls off before he died. She hoped so.

Altan shoved her into the courtyard. He pointed at Gobbo.

In his strange voice he said, 'Tell your master: come and see! Come and see!'

Estelle stumbled across the yard towards the alleys beyond. She saw movement there. That was where most of them were hiding – Altan must know it – waiting for her to open the door. Instead they would be looking at Gobbo and getting afraid. Afraid of the mad Turk who had hung him on the door and cut his balls off.

Grymonde would not be afraid. He didn't know how to be.

Altan was as vicious as a cornered rat, and as clever. But he did not know that no matter how much the others were afraid of him, and his bloody door, they would always be more afraid of Grymonde. Estelle was afraid, too. She had failed her dragon.

She scrubbed Gobbo's blood from her face with the skirt of her smock. She thought of her rats. Her rats would lick her clean. She promised herself she would bring her rats to feast on Altan's corpse.

CHAPTER SIX

The Gentle of Spirit

T annhauser awoke to some obscure sound and swung to his feet with his dagger. A spasm knifed his back and he blasphemed. He grabbed his sword. The atmosphere was stifling. After the darkness of his dreams the glow from the open door was sufficient to see by.

He walked into the parlour where the candles had burned down to their nubs. He saw a platter of bread and meat and a jug of wine on the table. Someone had been in and out while he slept. The lock in the front door scraped and he realised he had been woken by the jangle of keys. The door opened to reveal the night guard. Behind him stood Grégoire and Arnauld de Torcy. Something had changed in Arnauld since that afternoon. His youth had vanished.

'The madness has begun.'

'What madness?'

'With luck, you can make use of it. Hurry.'

Tannhauser cut a wedge of mutton. He ate as he returned to the bedroom. He pulled on his boots and his black linen shirt, the white cross spattered with blood. He buckled on his belt and sheathed his weapons. As he turned back to the door he saw for the first time that there was a second bed, or, rather, a low pallet, in the room. It lay in an alcove, against the far wall. Under a damp sheet lay a body. The body lay with his face to the wall and shivered in the gloom, as if some ague were shaking his bones. Tannhauser hoped it wasn't catching. He returned to the parlour and rifled a pint of wine down his throat and cut another slice of meat. He joined his saviours in the corridor.

'The frock for the baby,' said Grégoire. 'I left it in there.'

Tannhauser swallowed the mutton. 'Go and get it.'

Grégoire dashed inside the cell.

'What time is it?'

'Almost four,' said Arnauld. 'The screams of the King have been terrible to hear.'

'Why? Did he lose a game of tennis?'

Arnauld was not amused.

'This is a darker night than you can imagine. Your creature was arrested trying to climb into a second-floor window of the *Pavillon du Roi*, from the building works of the new South Wing.'

'He's a resourceful lad.'

'He was lucky not to be killed before I was called.'

'You've earned my eternal friendship, a treasure few can claim. Why was I arrested?'

'I have no idea.'

Arnauld glanced back into the cell for some sign of Grégoire.

Tannhauser went back inside. The robe was precious only in sentiment. He saw Grégoire going into the bedroom with the water jug in his hands. Crumpled under his arm was the cloth package.

'Grégoire, what are you doing?'

'The other prisoner asked for water in his sleep.'

'Let the other prisoner be damned.'

A parched groan drifted from the bedroom.

Tannhauser grabbed a candle, snatched the jug from Grégoire and plunged into the room. He hoped he was wrong. He set the light down by the pallet. He rolled the prisoner onto his back.

'Orlandu.'

Somewhere beyond the windowless walls a bell began to toll.

Orlandu's cheeks were sunken beneath a clammy brow. Tannhauser thumbed his eyes open. They were socketed too deep in his skull. His pupils were shrunken to dots. He showed no sign of awareness. Tannhauser slid an arm beneath his shoulders. Through the saturated shirt, he could feel Orlandu's body burning. Opium and fever. He raised him up and Orlandu groaned. Tannhauser put the jug to his lips and poured. Orlandu swallowed.

Tannhauser set the jug down and lowered Orlandu back to the pallet. He stripped away the wet sheet, which released a whiff of putrefaction. Orlandu was fully dressed. The left sleeve of his shirt had been cut away and his arm was bandaged from elbow to armpit. Tannhauser ran his fingertips over the bandage. It was stained brown and boggy to the touch. The bandage was wrapped too tight; the arm had swollen grossly. At either edge of the dressing the exposed skin was fiery and tense with the spreading corruption. Tannhauser felt Orlandu's neck and found lumps beneath the jaw. A mortifying wound; perhaps even gangrene. If the poisonous humours spread to the blood, they could kill the strongest man within hours. Arnauld arrived.

'The tocsin has sounded. We must go.'

'Fetch the guard.'

Tannhauser looked down on Orlandu. The putrefaction had to be drained, the rotten flesh trimmed. The arm might even require amputation. Arnauld returned with the guard.

'Tell me your name.'

The guard shuffled. 'Jean, sire.'

'Tell me, Jean, when did Captain Le Tellier bring this prisoner here?'

'Yesterday evening, sire.' He frowned in thought. 'That is, Friday evening, not Saturday.'

Thirty hours since. And it was Le Tellier.

'And the prisoner was already wounded.'

'He was as you see him, sire. That is, his wound had been dressed, though he has taken much more poorly since last night. That is, early Saturday morning.'

'Did you call help?'

'Oh yes, sire. A physician attended him and left that potion.'

Jean pointed to the floor beneath the bed. A small bottle lay there, its glass stopper uncorked. The bottle was empty, its essence fled. Tannhauser picked it up and licked the rim. Tincture of opium. He threw the bottle at Jean. It bounced from his face and shattered.

'A physician? The lad needs a surgeon.'

Jean cringed at this injustice. Tannhauser leaned over him.

'If he dies, you will answer to Anjou, who holds him most dear.'

The name dwarfed any authority Dominic Le Tellier might wield.

'What should I do, sire?'

'Can you spare two men to carry him?'

'All the guards are called to arms. I'm holding the night watch alone.'

'Help me get him over my shoulder.'

The bell continued to toll.

As they stalked the ill-lit corridors of the East Wing Tannhauser was grateful for the opium. Without it Orlandu would have found the journey unendurable; in the event, he hardly stirred.

'Tell me where to find Ambroise Paré.'

'The King's surgeon?' said Arnauld.

'He treated Coligny. He must be nearby.'

'At the King's request Paré is lodging with Coligny, at the Hôtel Béthizy.'

'How far is that?'

'From the gate, ten minutes on foot, but it's not possible –'

'My son is dying.'

'The streets will be impassable. The killing is about to begin.'

Tannhauser felt his bowels shift. Arnauld stopped and opened a door.

'Coligny is to be murdered – along with his brethren. See.'

Arnauld led them into a room that looked out from the east face of the building and opened a window. Beyond the *hôtels* on the far side of the square stood the church whose bell was ringing. To the north of the church, a mixed column of troops, bearing torches, wound through the streets, roughly parallel to the river. At their head were two score horsemen, followed by squads of arquebusiers, their match cords pinpoints of red. At the rear came the hedged blades of the halberdiers.

Tannhauser guessed their number at around two hundred.

'Who commands them?'

'Guise.'

'Tell me everything.'

'After many hours, His Majesty was persuaded – much against his conscience – to order the execution of the Huguenot leadership. That was the scream I heard from outside the room: *God's death, then kill them all! Kill them all, so that not a single one may blame me!*'

'And the nobles here in the Louvre?'

'Their throats are being cut as we speak.'

'Ambroise Paré is a Huguenot,' said Tannhauser.

'Paré's genius will be spared, at the King's explicit command.'

'So he's not so distraught as to waste his finest surgeon.'

'Catherine's suggestion. Navarre and Condé will also be spared, for they are princes of the royal blood. But no one else. I begged Anjou for the life of my friend, Brichanteau. Anjou said that everyone had a friend they would like to spare. Even La Rochefoucauld, who has been intimate with the King since childhood, must die along with the rest. Anjou said: *A king who cannot kill his dearest friends for the good of his people is no king at all.*'

Tannhauser grimaced.

A volley of gunfire reached them. He squinted. Knots of fighting had broken out in the streets. Men stumbled from the houses, half-dressed, the moonlight winking on their swords. The Huguenots were turning out to defend their leader. Muzzle flashes lit up the darkness.

'The bells of other churches are ringing,' said Tannhauser. 'Why?'

'I don't know.'

'Are they calling out the militias?'

'The militia have orders to maintain peace and tranquillity throughout the city.'

'Nothing more?'

'The militia is to stand by, ready to prevent anarchy and disorder, nothing more. The assassinations are in the hands of Guise and the Swiss Guard. His Majesty has been assured that this business will be accomplished neatly, before the sun is up.'

Tannhauser headed back to the corridor. He looked either way and found it empty.

Gunfire echoed through the palace.

Arnauld and Grégoire joined him. They descended a broad staircase through the tang of powder smoke. Screams of fear and pain echoed around the walls below. They were halfway down when a man started scrambling up the steps. He was barefoot and wore a nightshirt that was slashed and wet with blood. He stopped as he saw them. Two Swiss Guard emerged from the gloom.

'Alas, I have done nothing, good sirs,' said the fugitive. 'Grant me refuge, I beg you.'

Tannhauser anchored his balance with a hand on the banister rail and kicked the refugee in the chest. The wounded man flung out his arms and rolled down the stairs. He landed on his back at the feet of the guards, and their halberds ploughed his gut and chest until his cries had long ceased and his blood and entrails lapped over their boots.

Tannhauser stopped three steps above them. They saw the body over his shoulder. Troops were schooled to a certain tone of command, one Tannhauser had employed the world over.

'The upper floors are clear.' Tannhauser nodded at the disembowelled corpse. 'Haul this traitor to the courtyard. Don't let any more of them get away from you.'

The guards grabbed the dead man's ankles and dragged him away. The nightshirt rode up round his armpits and the wounds that punctured his nakedness oozed ropes of blood.

Arnauld made a sound of disgust. 'The man asked for mercy.'

Tannhauser continued to the foot of the stairs.

'Be thankful you weren't skewered, too.'

'They would not dare,' said Arnauld.

'They reeked of grog. One noble looks much like another, and for men like these the chance to make a noble scream is a treat indeed.'

Arnauld pointed at the Maltese Cross on Tannhauser's doublet.

'No one will take you for a Huguenot.'

'Someone takes me for worse.'

Yellow light exploded through the arrow slits in the wall. Another volley. Tannhauser hefted Orlandu on his shoulder and followed the trail of blood left by the guards. It wound across a hall where he counted five more bodies sprawled in puddles on the polished marble floor. One was a woman and two were the size of children. He stopped at the gate to the inner courtyard.

He looked out upon a torch-lit slaughter.

The West Wing, it seemed, was where the bulk of the Huguenot nobles had been housed. Here and there a window would light up with the blast of an arquebus. From the main gateway of the wing a sorry string of Huguenot nobles were chivvied between ranks of palace guards towards the centre of the courtyard. And not just nobles but their pages, grooms and valets, and a handful of wives and children, too. Many were in a state of undress, some already bleeding. None were armed. A handful of the boldest tried to get at the throats of the guards beyond the blades of the halberds. They were lanced like boar and their co-religionists stumbled over the corpses towards their doom.

Crossbowmen and arquebusiers were assembled on the south side of the square. They fired at will into the mass of Huguenots herded out before them. The east side of the courtyard bristled with steel. Those unfortunates crazed enough to flee were speared and hacked by guardsmen competing for their quota. The maimed and the dying slithered about in a foul bog of gore and final excretions. Last words were uttered, and some kissed each other goodbye, and some knelt down on the bloodslaked stones and prayed. Outrage and terror and laughter wheeled about the night. The King was cursed and God was entreated but neither intervened in the butchery.

On a balcony of the *Pavillon du Roi*, Tannhauser saw a group of figures standing at a balustrade. As still as the statues around them, they watched the unfolding catastrophe. King Charles and his brother, Anjou. Catherine de Medici, their mother. Albert Gondi, Comte de Retz. Other high and mighty statesmen. At least they had the stomach to bear witness to their deeds; unlike most of their ilk, who preferred a brief summary on paper.

Tannhauser turned at the sound of a sob. It was Grégoire. For all the ill treatment and danger he had borne, the lad had made no complaint, let alone shed a tear. Now his cheeks were wet and mucus streamed from his deformed and gaping nostrils and over his gums.

He was a child, and gentle of spirit. The mindless horror of the bloodbath had stormed his soul. Tannhauser pulled him away from the gate into the hall.

'Wipe your face, lad. Tears won't help us here, nor pity, either for them or ourselves.'

Grégoire scrubbed his cheeks and nose on the sleeves of his cambric shirt.

'And Jesus wept,' said Arnauld.

'They came to provoke a war. They have one.'

'This is not war. This is a massacre.'

'Massacre is war's oldest tool. And when every other tool devised by man lies blunted in the ashes, when every wheel has been broken and every book burned, and we're back to grubbing in the mud, massacre's edge will be as sharp as ever and just as often honed.'

Arnauld shrank from his eyes. 'That is a counsel of despair.'

'I forgot. We're in the jewel box of civilisation.'

Arnauld turned away and said no more.

Tannhauser felt Grégoire tug on his sleeve. The boy had regained his composure and was pointing at Orlandu's head. Tannhauser realised he wasn't feeling much movement against his back. He spotted a bench against a wall and hurried over. He lowered Orlandu and laid him flat on the wood. Arnauld brought a torch from its fitment on the wall. Orlandu's lips and face had turned purple. As they watched, his chest rose and fell and his colour grew paler.

'His weight must have cramped his lungs. How far to the street?'

'If we're not waylaid, a minute or two,' said Arnauld.

'The gate will be well guarded?'

'By Anjou's Swiss, who know me well.'

'Can you get me that horse?'

'That would cost more time than it will take you to walk.'

Orlandu looked as well as he was going to.

Tannhauser rolled his shoulder and hauled him aloft. He followed Arnauld.

They headed east, away from the courtyard, then north through a maze of corridors. They passed another corpse. And another. Then more. Arnauld jumped as they passed a piece of statuary in an alcove. His hand flew to his sword.

'In the King's name, show yourself!'

Tannhauser backed away, his hand on his dagger.

A slender figure emerged from hiding, pale in the torchlight. When he saw Tannhauser, his terror increased. If a flicker of hope remained in his breast, it died with the sight. It was the blond and sole survivor of his clan, Juste. He was clothed in Huguenot black and bore no arms.

'His name is Juste and he's harmless,' said Tannhauser. 'Let's go.'

'If we leave him here he'll be hunted down and murdered,' said Arnauld.

Tannhauser continued down the corridor. A moment later the light of Arnauld's torch caught up from behind. He had brought Juste by the arm. They took another turn and Tannhauser saw a well-lit guardhouse thirty paces hence. He glanced at Arnauld.

'You'll not keep that boy alive in this bloodbath,' said Arnauld.

'No, I won't, because he's going with you. You will keep him alive.'

'I will take that as a jest.'

Arnauld stopped. Tannhauser stopped and turned. Arnauld's eyes were aflame.

'The lad won't want to go with me. I killed three of his mother's sons.'

'I might say all the more reason to take his part, but now I know you too well. Perhaps I am worse, for this is my world, not yours, and I have helped make it what it is. But Tannhauser, for the love of God, we – you and I – will do something decent on this most shameful of nights.'

Tannhauser looked at Juste. The boy was trembling.

'I don't love God,' said Tannhauser. 'And I am doing something decent. I'm caring for my family.'

'I have cared for your family, too.'

To this, Tannhauser could find no reply. Arnauld's eyes bored into him.

'You promised me eternal friendship, and suggested that it might prove "a treasure". I claim my treasure. I call upon your friendship. Take this boy with you and protect him. As I believe you would protect me.'

Tannhauser looked at Juste, who stared at the ground with no part to play in his own destiny. All Tannhauser could see was another burden. Juste might even seek revenge; but Arnauld would not believe that; and neither did he. The youth's heart was not made for such a road. Juste, too, was gentle in spirit.

'Juste,' said Tannhauser.

Juste looked up at his chest and no further.

'You will do exactly as I say, and as soon as I say it.'

'Yes, sire.'

'If in doubt, follow Grégoire.'

Juste looked at the grotesque child. 'Yes, sire.'

'I'll tolerate no snivelling nor any of your Calvinist gibberish. If it's martyrdom you crave – as some of your kind do – then stay here.'

'I would not have you think me a coward, sire, yet I do want to live.'

'Then let's go test our mettle, before Arnauld asks me to change the water into wine.'

None were amused, so Tannhauser laughed alone.

Arnauld led them onwards. They approached three guards at the gate. Tannhauser touched the hilt of his dagger with his elbow. Orlandu would slow him up, but, by the same token, they would not expect to die at the hand of a man carrying a body on his shoulder.

'Juste, take Grégoire by the hand and don't let go.'

Tannhauser took the lead. Arnaud gave him a look and slipped in front of him.

'Open the gates, in the name of Anjou,' ordered Arnauld.

Two guards and the sergeant of the watch eyed the group with the suspicion it deserved.

'May I humbly ask for what purpose, my lord of Torcy?'

'Lombarts, isn't it?'

'Yes, my lord.'

'As you can see, Lombarts, the favourite page – the most

cherished favourite – of His Highness, Anjou, has been wounded helping to suppress the rebellion.'

Tannhauser gleaned from Lombarts' reaction that Orlandu was taken for a sodomite.

'This learned doctor and Chevalier of Malta must deliver the unfortunate page to Ambroise Paré, the King's surgeon, at the Hôtel Béthizy, before His Highness's beloved page expires.'

'My lord?' said Lombarts.

'Before he dies,' snapped Arnauld. 'If he dies we will all have to answer for it, and blame will fall most heavily on the man who blocked the way. Every passing minute threatens his life.'

Tannhauser gave Lombarts a stare.

'While you're at it,' continued Arnauld, 'assign one of your men to carry the invalid.'

He pointed at the burlier of the guards, a corporal.

'That man will do.' As Tannhauser blessed him for this unexpected stroke, Arnauld looked at him and said, 'They feed them well at the palace, as you see.'

Before Lombarts could quibble, Tannhauser strode to the corporal and hefted Orlandu from his shoulder. The corporal grunted as the body landed in his arms. Lombarts glanced at the youngsters holding hands.

'The idiot and his guardian are going too,' added Arnauld.

Grégoire started babbling an *Ave*. Lombarts decided his duty was more than done. He unhooked his keys from his belt and unlocked the gate that led from the Louvre.

Tannhauser motioned to Grégoire and Juste and they walked out. The big corporal followed them, carrying Orlandu. Arnauld held out his hand. Tannhauser took it and squeezed and looked in his eyes, and something passed between them that had not existed bare hours before.

'Thank you, Arnauld.'

'The bargain is square. I pray you find your wife safe. Godspeed.'

Tannhauser looked out into the absolute darkness beyond the lamps.

'In Hell I'd rather fly the Devil's colours.'

PART TWO

ACTS OF BLACK NIGHT, ABOMINABLE DEEDS

CHAPTER SEVEN

In the Vein

The heat was a damp weight on Tannhauser's chest. Sweat plagued his brows and trickled down his flanks. Such was the coolest hour of the coming day. He took a deep breath. It coated his tonsils with an oily sediment exuded by a dozen different species of manure. He walked to the edge of the light thrown by the gatehouse lamps.

The moon had gone down behind the palace. The Plough pointed him north. To the east, Jupiter was bright. He turned towards the cramped *quartier* whose nearest buildings encroached on the far edge of the palace yard. Paris could be crossed on foot in less than an hour, yet some claimed that if its streets and alleyways were straightened and placed end to end they would stretch to Jerusalem. Pandemonium seemed the likelier destination. In all of man's creation there stood no labyrinth more lunatic or unmapped. Carla was out there, somewhere.

He didn't know what he would do without her, or what he would become, and he was afraid. As Petrus Grubenius had told him, all things, whether dumb stones or almighty God Himself, are of necessity founded in their *telos*, their purpose in existing, and his fear reminded him that Carla was his purpose. With age his understanding of the world had turned darker. Carla, with her love and her music and her hope, had saved him from the encroachments of despair. Such goodness as was within him he nurtured as a tribute to her, and to his love for her, and to her inexplicable love for him. Without Carla he would expend himself in destruction, for then such would his *telos* become.

She was well protected, or so he told himself. He feared for the child in her belly. The news of its existence had been welcome but a shock. Would the child be strong enough to live or would it die within hours of its first breath? Thus had died its brother not two years since, christened Ignatius Bors by his own hand, no priest being near. Carla took grief quietly. Her silence was terrible to witness; it had taken all his will to endure it. But such thoughts would only sap his strength. He pushed Carla from his mind.

He was on the run, on alien turf, amid a multitude of villains who called it home. He had to walk these streets as if he owned them. He had reasons enough to hate this reeking bitch of a city, but a wolf was wise to love his hunting grounds, and he resolved to love Paris. She had little kindness for her subjects, that much was plain, and he decided he would follow her example. With luck she would whisper some of her secrets in his ear.

Ox-drawn wagons lumbered across the square. Scullions ran out to unload them, nervous and subdued, as if they'd just found out there'd be fewer mouths for breakfast. Piles of materiel spoke further of a city half-ruined and buried in debt yet determined to outbuild Rome. To the south, by the edge of the Seine, pigs and street curs rummaged among a long pile of garbage stacked by a jetty, presumably awaiting transport. In the warren of streets to the east gunfire was general. He heard collapsing windows, splintering wood, bellowed orders, death cries. Behind the rooftops, the rose window on a church façade reflected the last of the moonlight. From the tower to the church's rear the bell tolled on.

Tannhauser turned. The two boys huddled shoulder to shoulder. Grégoire plucked at his crotch with a finger and thumb. Tannhauser ordered them both to take a piss. The advice seemed sound so he joined them. He took a torch from a bundle soaking head-down in a pail and lit it at the gatehouse lamp. He turned to the big Swiss who carried Orlandu.

'Corporal, tell me your name.'

'Stefano, my lord.'

'Where do you hail from, Stefano?'

'Sion, my lord.'

'The Valais? I knew it the moment I set eyes on you.'

Tannhauser accompanied this bald lie with a clap on the back. Despite his load, Stefano's chest swelled with pride.

'Now, Stefano, deliver this boy to the King's surgeon and there'll be some gold in it. If we run into any of your comrades, let them know right sharp that we're on Anjou's business, you hear? If anyone tries to stand in our way, friend or foe, I will kill them.'

Tannhauser gave him time to look into his eyes and appraise his new commander.

Stefano clicked his heels and bowed his head.

'Yes, my lord.'

Tannhauser shook excess oil from the torch. Flames billowed up and a shower of drops flared and died as they tumbled at his feet. He handed the torch to Juste.

'Juste, you will go with Stefano and light his way.'

Juste cringed from the torch. His head sank between hunched shoulders. Grégoire reached for the torch but Tannhauser motioned him back. He offered it again to Juste.

'Tilt the flame away and you won't get burned.'

Juste shook his head. Panic had him. He clasped his hands to his face.

'No. I don't want to go. I won't. I can't.'

Tannhauser slapped him across the head. The blow was mild enough but Juste staggered sideways and Grégoire sprang to hold him upright. Juste's lip trembled. His eyes swam. He covered his face with an arm and tried to stifle his sobs. Tannhauser remembered those feelings. Terror, confusion, humiliation. He took Juste's wrist and pulled the arm away. Juste kept his eyes cast down, the lashes beaded with tears. Lit by the torch he could have stood for a painting on the ceiling of a basilica, but here beauty begged to be defaced. Tannhauser lifted Juste's chin so that the boy was forced to look at him.

'Your comrades are betrayed and butchered. The King is a fiend. You are lost in a universe of lies. And no god will help you, neither yours nor any other.'

Juste stared at him, his eyes swimming as they darted back and forth.

'Are you listening, Juste? Answer me. Say yes.'

'Yes.'

'Good. Listen more. Your nostrils are choked with blood and shit, your bowels are churning, your brain feels as if it boils inside your skull.'

'Yes.'

'You are alone.'

'Yes. Yes.'

'Your brothers are dead and gone to the dogs.'

Juste let go a sob. Tannhauser swallowed and pressed on.

'I killed them. I killed your mother's sons. And in my power you stand.'

'Yes.'

'It is night and the night has no end.'

'Yes.'

'And in all this dark and bloody world you have no friend.'

'Yes.'

'Or so you believe.'

Juste's yearning was painful to behold. Tannhauser remembered that, too.

'Yet in that particular at least, you are wrong. Because I am your friend.'

Juste's tears ran down his face. His breath shuddered in his chest. Grégoire, who still had hold of him, patted him between the shoulders as if comforting a poorly horse.

'I am your friend,' repeated Tannhauser. 'And you could do worse. Furthermore, since Stefano is my friend, as is, also, brave Grégoire, they are your friends, too. And so, far from being without a friend you are surrounded by them. Do you agree?'

'Yes.'

'Will you light the way, through this black night, for your friends?'

'Yes.'

'Good lad. Wipe your face.'

He pushed the stave of the torch into his hand. Juste closed his fingers around it and held on. Tannhauser took Juste's other hand and anchored that around the stave, too.

'The torch will blind me to the dark, and the dark is where I must be master, so I will go on ahead. You won't see me but I will be close.'

He drew his dagger in his right hand.

Grégoire said, 'It's the cage.'

He ran towards the garbage. Tannhauser took another oily breath and blew it out. He gestured to Stefano to wait and set off after Grégoire. Juste trotted behind him.

'Grégoire.'

The cage lay on its side by the jetty. Grégoire stood staring at the monkeys. They were dead. The tiny bodies were heaped upon the slats in limp tangles of limbs, heads and tails.

'They came all that way across the ocean. And all they needed was water.'

'We have to go.' Tannhauser squeezed the boy's shoulder.

'Look – there – they tried to chew through the bars. To get free.'

'We tried to help them.'

'We didn't try very hard.'

'No, we didn't.'

Tannhauser noticed a dog and a pig contesting a heap of naked corpses in the trash. The bodies looked stiff enough to have died hours before. He pulled both boys away, before Juste could spot them.

Tannhauser crossed the square with his entourage. Stefano directed him along the river, due east, past wharves and a broad stairway down to the beach. At the next turn he headed north towards the street along which, if he had his bearings right, he had seen the Duke of Guise lead his assassins. A halberdier stood guard. He glanced at the cross on Tannhauser's chest, and at Stefano bringing up the rear, and did nothing to delay them.

Tannhauser forged ahead, crossing over, keeping close to the buildings on the far side of the street. His eyesight adjusted. With the torch ten paces behind him anyone coming towards him would see only its flames.

The *quartier* was a patchwork of inns, boarding houses and artisanal businesses devoted to the special trades required by the palace. He caught the scents of candle wax and turpentine. Behind the lightless windows and locked doors he sensed huddled families praying for day. Some doors were smeared with crude white crosses. Their locks had proved no barrier, for they had been smashed from their hinges, and those who had hidden behind them had been slaughtered within and without. Barefooted bodies sprawled in the filth, their nightshirts badged with wet black stains.

A wedge of buildings cut a fork in the road before him, the wider arm curving east, the narrower north. He headed east. More doors, more corpses cooling in coagulating pools. Alleys opened right and left, then an archway, now another street to his right. He followed the curve, the alleys and gated yards multiplying, until he saw a larger crossroads and, in the distance beyond, torches by the dozen, bunched and milling in the blackness. Shouts of triumph; of bloodlust not yet requited. The sweep's momentum had spent itself in a mob of horses and men.

He glanced back. Stefano lumbered into view, festooned with boys. As Tannhauser turned to the crossroads, he saw a man sneak from the last of the alleys on the far side of the street.

The man was wigless and though not much over thirty as bald as a monk. He was stark naked but for a single shoe. Tannhauser loped across the street, the tolling bell masking his footsteps. He saw no confederates. A leather purse hung round the wigless one's neck and judging by the way it swung its contents were heavy. He carried a long dagger in his left hand, like one who had little idea how to use it. As he limped towards Stefano and the boys, Tannhauser fell on him from behind.

He approached on the oblique and trapped the fellow's knife hand by the wrist. At the same time he stabbed him behind the collarbones, again over the shoulder. As the hilt thumped home he churned the blade and felt the vital tissues rend and burst. Whatever life was, it fled in an instant yet its passage was palpable. The corpse dropped to its knees without a spasm or a sound. As it fell

Tannhauser steadied it upright with the hilt and grabbed the draw-string of the purse and looped it forward and untangled it from the ears and chin. He pulled his dagger free, alert for spray but blood's force had spent itself inside the chest. He let the bald skull flop backwards into the gutter. He chased the gore from his blade with a flick and sheathed it.

The soft leather purse was impregnated with perfume and Tannhauser took a deep sniff. He knew the heft of gold pieces without needing to look. It had a strap to permit firm attachment to a belt. He stooped for the dead man's dagger – Milanese, he guessed, a third the length of a sword, and well suited to tight spaces. The pristine steel, the lapis lazuli pommel and the small side ring suggested it had been commissioned as a parade piece, but its lethality had not been compromised. With its sheath it would be worth as much as the gold in the sack, but the sheath was nowhere to be seen.

He stowed the dagger in the back of his belt, the hilt towards his right elbow. He stripped the dead hands of two rings. He put them in the pouch. For the first time he looked at his victim's face, but its features were lost in the gloom. He stretched and grimaced.

Torchlight approached and with it the steady tread of Stefano. When he saw Tannhauser, he shook the sweat from his eyes. Orlandu was still breathing in his arms. Juste tilted the torch and he and Grégoire stared at the dead man, who lay nude and leaking blood, his body folded backwards at the knees as if slaughtered while committing some act of perversion. They watched Tannhauser buckle the purse at his side.

'You robbed him?' said Juste.

'No fort is so strong that it can't be taken with gold, and we must take Paris.'

'I don't believe Cicero intended to justify murder.'

'The man was dead before we met him, which is why he was armed and desperate. You were in his path. And Cicero justified the plundering of half the world.' He looked at Stefano. 'Have we far to go to find the surgeon?'

Stefano pointed with his chin. 'A little way beyond the commotion.'

Tannhauser started towards the crossroads a hundred paces distant, but heard the sound of running behind them. He turned.

Two young nobles, or so he supposed them to be from their gaudy costume, emerged from the same alley as had the naked man. Each wore a white linen cross pinned to his cap. They carried rapiers over their shoulders, neither one blooded. They were panting and frightened but recovered some bravado on escaping the slit. They noticed the corpse and the shorter fell to searching it with mounting indignation. They noticed Tannhauser.

Tannhauser walked on.

'Ho! Sirrah! We were after this heretic!'

Tannhauser kept going and considered it an act of mercy. The two hurried to overtake him. Juste grabbed Grégoire's hand, and the torch he held, released from its double grip, swayed towards Orlandu's head. Tannhauser took the torch from him and held it high and to his left. He stopped, for the rash pair barred his way, their swords still shouldered as if this were the current fashion.

'That was our heretic,' said the shorter.

Tannhauser saw no witnesses in range. He looked at Juste.

'What might Cicero say to this?'

'What a marvellous question,' said the taller of the youths.

Juste said, '*O praeclarum custodem ovium lupum.*'

'My Latin is poor,' said Tannhauser.

The taller young noble smiled, eager to be helpful.

'He said: *how splendid a protector of sheep is the wolf.* But Cicero was almost certainly employing irony. After all, he did coin the word. Don't you agree, George?'

'That was our heretic. We flushed him out.'

Tannhauser stepped within the limit of their rapiers, where they were useless and he could get to grips. Each youth flinched but had sufficient pride and stupidity to hold his ground. Their faces were those of creatures who expected the world to conform to their every whim, because the world had never done otherwise.

'Get out of my way.'

George held Tannhauser's eyes, oblivious to what he was looking at.

'The heretic stole Nicole's dagger.'

He pointed to an empty sheath on Nicole's sword belt. Nicole obligingly turned to display it. The sheath was enamelled and chased with silver wire and lapis lazuli.

'We want the dagger back,' said George.

'The dagger is spoil.'

'So now you have stolen it.'

'Courtesy would have won its return. That opportunity has passed.'

'And you've stolen the heretic's gold, too.'

'George, detain me no longer. I am in the killing vein.'

Nicole stepped to one side, but out of obedience, not martial guile.

'The dagger is of no great importance, chevalier,' said Nicole. 'It was a gift to my late father, and he had so many, why, I can't even remember from whom. And the gold isn't ours anyway, nor, in any case, do we need it. So we shan't detain you any longer at all.'

George's instincts remained wanting. He pointed a finger at Juste.

'Who is this boy so black in dress and so white with fear?'

'Be off, egg. Or be cracked.'

George tilted the sword from his shoulder.

'I'll not be seen off by a thief.'

Tannhauser doubted he intended much more than to strike a petulant posture, in order to get his way, a method he had probably refined in dealings with his mother. But such were the hazards of going about armed, and seeking the excitement of killing, in the middle of a massacre. He stuffed the head of the torch into George's mouth and stepped to his left, drawing the contended dagger from the back of his belt.

George's shrieks were muffled by flames. His nostrils sucked up tendrils of fire. Burning naphtha ran down his chin and set light to his doublet. He dropped his sword and grabbed the torch and

Tannhauser let him take it. He stabbed the little turd in the side of the neck, the outer edge angled downward so that he might exert more weight when it came to the pull. The dagger was so sharp, his thrust drove it through to the quillions. George squirmed and gargled. His right hand gashed itself bloody on the blade transfixing his gullet, his left waving the torch at arm's length. Tannhauser knocked his cap off and seized him by the hair to hold him still. He looked at Nicole. He leaned into the pull and divided George's windpipe and severed his throat entire. A tide of gore drenched George's chest and spurted up past his ears, and with it spilled his life and all his dreams of manhood. The torch hit the ground, and so did George.

Nicole gaped, as if frozen by a vision of a nightmare world, where he and his titles meant nothing and were worth even less. He moved not a muscle. He uttered a thin cry.

'Nicole, drop your sword and give your belt to this lad. Quickly now.'

Nicole unbuckled his belt and handed it Grégoire. He twisted his lips in an attempt to further prove his acquiescence. Tannhauser stepped over and stabbed him and burst his heart. He chased blood from the blade's grooves. It was at once pristine.

'Grégoire, give me the sheath for this dagger. Leave the sword here.'

Juste said, 'You didn't give them a chance.'

'A better chance than they'd have given you. Or your brethren.'

Tannhauser plucked the white linen crosses from the dead men's caps. He retrieved the torch. He gave the crosses to Grégoire and Juste.

'Wear these on your chest, they will mark you servants of the Pope. And ask Grégoire to teach you the *Ave*. His Latin is excellent.'

Neither dead youth had carried a purse on their homicidal jaunt, the only intelligent, if unwelcome, decision they had made. Tannhauser took the ornate sheath from Grégoire and slid in the dagger and stowed it in his belt. He spoke to Stefano in Italian.

'You are my accomplice in this.'

'In what, sire? Two brave loyalists slain in pursuit of a dangerous rebel?'

'Stefano? You've doubled your share of the gold.'

Tannhauser and his band reached the crossroads, where the powder smoke smelled as strong as brimstone and drifted in swags on the hot and windless air. Corpses were everywhere strewn in great numbers. They watched as a dozen dazed prisoners were herded at spear point to stand before a rank of arquebusiers, twice their number. The latter blew on their matches and checked their pans. At a series of commands, they aimed and fired, and the luckless Huguenots were smitten down in a vortex of lead and smoke, some so close to the muzzles that their clothing sprang briefly ablaze. Not all died in the salvo and these lay calling out to God until the Swiss moved among them like gardeners hoeing weeds, and finished them off with their glaives.

Warnings were shouted to those below as corpses were pitched from windows and roofs. Elsewhere, by the light of torches, more guards dragged the dead into leaking, saturated piles, some of them recruiting horses and ropes to the job. Boots, hooves and bodies alike slithered through the puddled blood and churned it up with the street filth into a nocuous batter that was splattered far and wide. A lone gunshot flared beyond the rooftops. There would be a few last hares to flush and run down, and a wagon of sawdust could be put to good use, but on the whole a dirty job appeared well done.

Bells still rang all over the city.

Tannhauser called to a guard who seemed underemployed.

'You, soldier, run to the church and silence that bell. Corporal?'

He glanced at Stefano. Stefano barked.

'Do as his Excellency says. Jump to it.'

As they got closer to the Hôtel Béthizy, it was clear that some of the Huguenots had put up a stiff fight while going under, probably in an attempt to reach Admiral Coligny. Among the dead were men with crosses on their caps or white armbands on their sleeves. Wounded Catholics lay on cloaks or blankets, tended by friends.

George and Nicole would raise no eyebrows on the Rue Béthizy. Tannhauser pressed on. In that numbed bewilderment that tends to follow a slaughter, no one was inclined to bother them.

The horsemen up the street started forward at the amble. Those in their path made haste for either side of the street. Tannhauser herded the boys out of the thoroughfare. The riders were richly dressed and superbly mounted on some of the finest gaited palfreys in the country. Even by the light of flames the muscles of the horses shimmered like silk, their hooves stepping high through the muck. Tannhauser wanted one. At the head of the column was a man scarcely older than George, but the contrast in character was great. He shouted, as if to reinforce a point.

'Remember! It is the King's command!'

Tannhauser realised this was Henri, Duke of Guise, champion of Catholic Paris, and commander of these nocturnal revels. Guise had fought at Saint-Denis, Jarnac and Moncontour, and had even travelled to Hungary to campaign against the Turks. Perhaps for that latter reason in particular, when he saw the Maltese Cross on Tannhauser's chest he slowed his horse and saluted. Tannhauser didn't bother to return it. Their eyes met in the torchlight and Guise, giddy on blood and glory, smiled as he rode on by. A number of his followers saluted, too.

At the crossroads, Guise turned south towards the river. As the last of his horsemen rode from sight, the bell of the nearby church stopped tolling. Though others more distant continued, it felt as if silence had fallen.

Stefano said, 'There is the Hôtel Béthizy.'

The narrow-fronted building and its courtyard were less imposing than Tannhauser had hoped. The second-storey windows gaped open. A variety of armed men milled around the yard. Lying in the gutter beneath the windows was the bloodstained body of an old man in his nightshirt. A gentleman took it upon himself to kick the corpse in the face. A second followed suit. Tannhauser realised who the old man was. A third bravo, not to be outdone, took out his cock and started to piss on the remains of Gaspard de Coligny.

Coligny had come to provoke a war and he had died a fool. Yet he had also been a famous soldier and the spectacle did not sit well with Tannhauser.

He strode over, grabbing a half-pike from a stack against the wall, and struck the pisser in the base of the skull with the iron-shod butt. The pisser dropped at the feet of his companions, whose laughter abruptly ceased, and lay there insensible, pissing on himself. Tannhauser looked at the others and they looked away. He returned the pike.

He grasped each boy by a thin shoulder. He mustered a smile.

'You two lads have proved yourselves my hardy, stout and resolute mates.'

Grégoire's mouth fell open. Juste dropped his gaze.

'But though we have reached one goal, others beckon. Juste, Master Paré may not feel inclined to help us, so you, as his co-religionist, will help me win him over. Grégoire, there are stables hereabouts whose rich and eminent clients will never return to claim their mounts, and I am tired of treading in shit. Go and find me the finest horse in the neighbourhood.'

CHAPTER EIGHT

Dogs on Fire

S ymonne D'Aubray's reaction to the news that her house might come under attack was to sit on her bed in her nightgown and stare into the gloom like someone who had lost her wits. Childbearing had left her plump, yet it sat well with her sweet, rosy features. When Carla suggested she get dressed and that they rouse the children, Symonne appeared not to hear a word. She was younger than Carla, twenty-nine years old, and a woman of intelligence and enterprise, but even the most steadfast mind could be undone by fear. Perhaps the poor woman was revisiting memories of her husband, Roger, murdered by a mob during a previous persecution less than a year ago, during the Gastines riots. Carla did not press her. She laid out Symonne's clothes on the bed.

'I'll wake the children. Then I'll help you put up your hair.'

As Carla reached the door, Symonne said, 'If we are not prepared to suffer under the cross, we betray our faith in the promise of salvation. These afflictions are imposed by God to test that faith.'

Carla heard the echo of Symonne's husband in the brave words. In Symonne's voice, she heard only desperation and defeat. There seemed no point in theological debate. Carla left without speaking.

Her heart pounded and her stomach churned. She thought of Mattias and his strength and wished he were here. She laboured up the stairs, candlestick in hand, already tired, the weight of her child enormous. She woke the housekeeper, Denise and her husband Didier, sleeping in the roof space. She roused the D'Aubray children in their beds. They sat up blinking. Antoinette, at six years old the youngest, asked for water.

'It's still dark,' said Martin, at twelve the eldest.

Carla forced a smile. 'Martin, you're the man of the house. I want you to make sure you all get fully dressed as quickly as you can.'

'Why?' asked Charité.

'Do as Martin tells you and come down to the parlour,' said Carla. 'Your mother and I will explain everything there.'

'Should we wash?' said Martin.

'No,' said Carla. 'Just get dressed. Quickly now. Wear stout shoes.'

Carla went back to her own room and closed the door. She leaned her back against it and caught her breath. The despair she had sensed in Symonne crept into her heart. Despair was more poisonous than fear. She put her hands on her belly and felt her child.

Her body encompassed his; her waters washed around him. Mattias had suggested, though he had taken pains to point out that it was only a speculation based in alchemical possibility, that every-thing that went through her went through the babe and in some sense found a home in his growing being, for, after all, the babe was a part of her and was being made from her deepest fibre. With this in mind, she had taken pains throughout her pregnancy to share with the babe her most inspired and elevated feelings. Her love for Mattias, her joy in horses and Nature, her exhilaration while riding in the wind, even, while asleep, her most marvellous dreams. In part she had taken this journey to impart to him a love of adventure. She would not nurture him now, at this crucial juncture, the verge of his birth, with fear and despair.

The Siege of Malta had taught her that hope, and faith in God, could conquer desperation even at its darkest, and that when hope and faith were exhausted there remained yet a final refuge in defi-ance. She thought again of Mattias. She should have been more patient. She shouldn't have left on such a whim. She heard him laugh, as if to say he would have expected no less, and she saw his face, and she thought that her heart might burst.

She heard a sound from the street and went to the window. Twelve armed men marched south in the direction of the Place de Grève. Though incapable of keeping in step and not in uniform, one carried a drum and another a flag. Each wore a white band around his arm and a white cross pinned to his hat.

Carla leaned out over the window sill.

'Messieurs! Good sirs, your attention, please.'

'That's a Huguenot house,' said one.

'Remember Roger D'Aubray?' said a second.

'Aye and he was a right bastard.'

Their leader looked up without stopping. 'Stay indoors.'

'We are threatened with burglary and murder by a gang of criminals –'

'The Huguenots are in revolt. We militia are called out to stop them.'

'They've tried to kill the King!'

'God save His Majesty!' A rough cheer was joined.

'I am no Huguenot.' The words almost stuck in Carla's throat. 'I am a Catholic noblewoman in grave danger. There are children here.'

'Stay home and lock your doors. It's the safest place.'

'We are not safe.'

Her baby kicked. Anger flared inside her. The candle flame trembled.

'On your honour. Will not any of you brave men stay to defend me?'

The militia marched on without another word. As their torches disappeared into the darkness, Carla sensed figures moving in the shadows on the far side of the street. She heard a dog bark. Another replied and then another. She was sure she heard a voice curse. Then she wasn't sure. She closed the window. She fingered the small gold crucifix at her throat.

The house could not be defended against determined invaders. The new style was far from the miniature forts of the old. The windows were too many; it was designed to let light in, not to keep burglars out. On the streets three women, four children and a manservant would be devoured. Estelle said that they were coming for Carla, the woman from the south. Was her presence a danger to the family? Should she escape the house alone with Altan Savas, as he had suggested? The Temple wasn't far, a quarter-hour even at her pace. Could she leave Symonne and her children to their fate? The siege had also imbued her with the ethic of loyalty. But she realised that if deserting them might save her baby, she would. She would let them all die.

She thanked God that Orlandu was not here. She wished Mattias was.

She felt a moment of absolute helplessness. She had a sudden urge to surrender, to give herself over to these unknown enemies, to abandon resistance. The idea produced a sense of relief. She remembered she had once seen a sheep surprised by one of her dogs. The sheep stood quite still while the dog tore at its throat. It made no attempt to run or to shy away from the teeth. When the dog paused to choke up a mouthful of wool, the sheep stood quivering on the spot, waiting for the dog to resume its attack. The spectacle of a terror so profound had disturbed her. She had felt no pity for the sheep; only disgust. The sheep had deserved to die. Symonne downstairs was in the same state as that sheep. The dog had gone on to kill a dozen more in a frenzy, and Carla hadn't been able to stop him.

Carla had to move.

She went back to the children's room and found them half-dressed and squabbling. Again she ordered them below. Antoinette, who was still in her nightgown, started crying. Charité took her hand.

'To the parlour, now.' Carla stamped her foot. 'You can cry down there.'

In the parlour their instruments were still laid out from recent rehearsals. Carla had no plan but the instruments offered a means of keeping the children occupied, and a disciplined routine with which they were familiar.

'Everybody sit down and tune up.'

'But it's still dark,' whined Lucien. 'And I'm hungry.'

'Martin, I leave you in charge. If you're not ready when I return, there will be trouble.'

The other room on this floor was the master bedroom. Carla

looked in on Symonne. She hadn't moved, her clothes still spread on the bed beside her. Carla left her alone and found Denise and Didier had come down. She could not imagine either of them would be anything other than a handicap in the coming fight. She wished she had left them asleep. Martin issued half-hearted orders. Gut strings pinged.

'Denise, make the children some breakfast,' said Carla. 'Didier, let us see if we can help Altan Savas. Madame is unwell. Do exactly as I say.'

They followed her down the main stair to the hallway, bewildered and made even more afraid by the mention of Altan's name. She explained nothing. She did not know what to explain. Noises came from the rear hall, clatters, blows and grunts, but not of combat. She found Altan Savas rigging a variety of wedges and timber props, improvised from planks that he appeared to have ripped from the floor, in such a way as to buttress the lock and hinges of the back door against the hole the planks left behind. Altan Savas did not seem much impressed, though Carla was. He glanced at Didier as if the man was a woman or worse. He beckoned her back towards the entrance hall that enclosed the front door and the foot of the staircase. He pointed to her candle and motioned about with his hands.

'Candles, here. Here. Many, many. Light.'

'Didier,' said Carla. 'Tell Denise to forget our food. Both of you place as many lamps and candles as you can find here in the hallway and light them. Quickly, now.'

Altan stabbed a finger at the front door.

'The bad men come. Here. Yes.'

'Yes, I know, we can't stop them getting in,' said Carla. She did not plan to but she found herself asking him, 'Tell me, can we go? Can we get away, just you and I?' She made a walking gesture with her fingers, and pointed to his chest and to hers.

Altan nodded. 'Yes. You want?'

Carla didn't answer. She heard the pluck of strings above, the sleepy voices.

She shook her head.

Altan pointed to the back door. 'They want to come there. To be not seen.' He threw back the bolt on the front door so that only the lock held it. 'But we make they come here.' He again gestured about then nodded up the stairs and made the motion of drawing and firing an arrow downwards. 'When many dead, they go.'

Carla understood. Encourage the invaders to come through the front door on Rue du Temple, where there was at least a chance of others witnessing the assault and summoning help. Then use the front hallway as a killing ground, defending the stairs from the first-floor landing outside the parlour and the master bedroom. If enough of them were killed, if the price was bloody enough – and she was certain Altan Savas would drive a hard bargain – the others would give up.

She felt hope rise in her chest.

'Yes, yes. Good. Mattias would be happy.'

Didier brought in a pair of candelabra and Denise began lighting the wall lamps. From above came the sound of reluctant bows sawing at strings.

'Should I join them?' She pointed upstairs.

Altan nodded. 'One candle. Not more.'

Carla took her seat with her viola da gamba propped almost against her belly. The position required her to bend and stretch awkwardly to finger and bow, but she had adapted. She knew that when she played the instrument vibrated against her womb. The music filled her child's entire universe. She had been playing to him all his life and she knew he loved it. Music had nurtured him as surely as had her blood.

She had played for her dead child, Bors, too, throughout his life inside her. Even now it consoled her to know that his existence had been filled with the purest beauty. And if it was so, as Mattias, following Petrus Grubenius, insisted, that in the womb there is, and can be, no such thing as Time, but only Before Time, then Bors had heard her play through that same eternity which ruled before the dawn of creation. As Mattias said, Bors had not only always listened to her music, he had listened to her music for forever.

She took her bow and looked at the children. Their eyes were wide in the semi-dark, not even sure whether or not they should be afraid.

'We did not play for the Queen so we will play for your mother.'

'Maman has heard us before,' said Antoinette.

'True. But not as she will hear us now, for we will play like never before.'

Carla counted off and they began the *chanson spirituelle* that she had composed for the occasion of the royal wedding. It was a rondeau for four voices, one human, sung by Martin, and three instrumental. Antoinette had a recorder part, often improvised but rarely, thanks to Carla's glances, catastrophic.

Previously Carla had been much concerned in their practice with achieving a respectable performance. This morning she played for herself and her baby. She closed her eyes. If her baby was not going to emerge into Time at all, if all he would ever know was forever, then she would try her best to fill it with magic and not with her terror. She let the music, the wood, the gut strings, her skin and muscle and bone, carry her deep into his world, into the world Before Time.

If they died, together, then together they would continue into the world Beyond Time. She thought of Mattias whose spirit, she believed, was near as large as eternity – for as he might say, *What right soul is not?* – and could encompass all things and all loss. She grieved for the pain that would gore him. Yet Mattias would endure until he joined them, as she knew he would, for any Paradise inclined to reject him she would scorn. The baby joined them, here and now. They all three played together. Somehow she knew that the baby sensed his father and felt his presence through her.

When Martin's voice stuck in his throat, Carla did not waver.

When Antoinette dropped her recorder, she did not care.

When Lucien and Charité stopped playing, Carla played on.

When the battering of metal on wood began, and Symonne started screaming and the children joined in, Carla closed her ears to their din.

She played on.

When glass began to shatter all over the house, Carla did not open her eyes nor did she miss a note. She played on and her baby listened and he loved her and she loved him. Let Death, too, join them in their song if he would. They would die amid love and music.

She did not stop playing until Altan Savas wrenched the gambo violl from her hands. She didn't open her eyes until he pulled her to her feet and out of the parlour.

The big window which lit the hallway from over the main front door gaped glassless but for saw-toothed fragments in the rabbets. Stones and lead balls lay among the gleaming debris and the over-turned candles on the tiles of the hallway floor. At the foot of the stairs the front door shuddered in its frame with blows from the street. They alternated between the upper hinge and the lower. Two hammers. The door was heavy but no door is stronger than its hinges and the hinges rattled and twisted on creaking screws. Throughout the house more windows burst with such exuberance that one might think them freed from bondage, their original purpose fulfilled. Above the clamour of despair from the parlour, Carla heard strange animal yowls and human curses.

Altan's hand was immensely strong. His grip hurt her arm.

He shouted in her ear. 'We go, now.'

He released her and Carla followed him down the stairs without questioning the change of plan. Altan wore his Turkish horn bow on one shoulder. He drew the short, heavy-bladed *Messer* sword that he favoured. He drew a dagger. Carla felt a hand grab hold of hers. It was Antoinette's. Carla held onto it and pulled her along.

Halfway down the staircase their limbs were quaked by a hideous squeal that seemed torn from the outraged spirit of all living things. A spiral of flame erupted outside the jagged frame above them, and, as if the hole were a portal to some darker and more vicious Hell than any of those the prophets had foretold, a dog on fire soared through the broken window towards them.

Antoinette screamed. For the first time, Carla screamed too.

She dragged the girl behind her, stumbling back up the steps as Altan hacked the piteous animal, alight from neck to tail, in mid-air. The sword cut the dog half through its mid-section and hurled it to the tiles in a smoking frenzy, its jaws panting and agape, its eyes whited with terror, its muscles squirming beneath the flames. Its paws scrabbled and skated in the tinkling shards and with a howl it took off down the corridor.

Carla retreated further as a second burning dog came through the window.

She could smell the pine pitch in which it was smeared. The stench of burning fur and flesh turned her stomach. She felt Antoinette's fingers clinging to her skirts, heard the girl's racking sobs. As the second dog writhed to its feet, the first returned down the hall in its blind sprint of agony and panic, the fire fluttering, the yowls pitiful to hear. The two blazing animals collided and exchanged snarls, and seemed about to fall to fighting, then exploded together up the stairs. Altan Savas kicked them aside, tongues of fuel flaring from his boots, and spread his arms wide about Carla and Antoinette.

As the dogs on fire spread their fever to the crowded parlour, Altan guided Carla down to shelter in one front corner of the hall. Carla heaved for breath in the sulphurous air.

Yet more dogs appeared.

These dogs were not ablaze but were almost as panicked and surely more enraged. They were tossed through the ground-floor windows at the front and rear – six dogs? Eight? – street curs of indeterminate breed, small in size but large in energy. They hurtled about and up and down in a deranged tintamarre, barking in terror and confusion. From the parlour above Carla heard the voices competing in terror – in pleas, in prayer – dog goading human and human goading dog into a lunacy of fear absolute.

Nor was Altan Savas immune. His head twitched from side to side, eyes glazed as if waiting for ranks of demons to emerge from the walls.

Carla hit him hard across the cheek. Her hand stopped dead, as when one slaps the hindquarters of a horse, but Altan blinked and his senses returned.

'Thank you, madame.'

He stood to one side of the door, watching the hinges come loose. From the darkness upstairs came a renewed burst of distress. With a suddenness that made Carla jump, the door flew inwards and crashed to the floor. A man lunged in right behind it, off balance, carried by the momentum of his last hammer stroke.

'*Allaaahu akabar.*'

Altan Savas chopped him through the nape of the neck and would have severed his head but that he pulled the stroke in order to dash on through the blood spray to swarm the second of the hammer men. In the space of a heartbeat Altan stabbed him four times, dagger and sword, in the gut, chest, throat, then stepped back as he glanced across the street. Three bodies lay on the baked dirt, pierced by arrows, one still mewling, clutching his leaking belly. Carla realised Altan must have shot them from the windows above while she was playing. Something whistled by and cracked and careened around the hallway but Carla heard no gunshot.

Altan pegged his sword in the doorjamb and belted his dagger and unslung his bow and produced and nocked an arrow with movements no less swift and precise than those of Carla's fingers on the frets. Across the street she glimpsed a figure make an overarm throw with a sling. She retreated, face to the wall, and again came the whistle and the crack of the stone. Altan Savas swung into the gap, the horn bow flexing, the arrow coming up to the aim. He loosed from the ivory thumb ring and she couldn't help but peer around the door.

The slinger was on his knees, his hands cupped before his chest from which blood spouted like wine from a skin. The arrow quavered in the timbers of the building ten feet behind him. He fell forward onto his face and didn't move.

Altan had already knocked and drawn again, aiming at some target she could not see. But at the last moment he swivelled back inside and Carla flinched and ducked back into the shadows as the broad head tip of the drawn arrow swung in her direction. Altan swooped the arrow tip up above her head and levelled it again.

Or tried to.

Later she wondered if the swoop had cost his life. And so much more.

Glass crunched behind her. She was deafened by the roar of a gun.

Flame and powder smoke blasted Altan Savas in the face.

He was thrown over backwards. The arrow vanished behind her. An enormous figure charged past her and fell astraddle Altan's body, a knife rising and falling as if to kill some fabled creature known to be immortal. But Carla knew from the way he had fallen that Altan had died the instant he was shot. The ringing in her ears faded. The enormous shoulders stopped stabbing. He stood up and looked down at his victim.

'Hellfire. Even so, he nearly killed me.'

Despite the shock in his voice, it was the deepest Carla had ever heard.

He didn't turn.

She realised it was his head and shoulders that gave the impression of a giant. He was over average height but not as tall as Mattias, and, apart from his feet, which were huge, his lower half was of reasonable proportion. His shoulders and head were those of a man who might otherwise have been twice the size. He looked out of the front door, his back still towards her, and she caught sight of the immense lower jawbone. A thick gold ring pierced his ear, as if in some defiant act of vanity; or to dare someone to take it. A pair of crazed dogs slithered through the weltered gore and careened between his legs, snapping at each other in their desperation to escape the deranged women and wailing children, the barking and the broken glass and the stench of burning hair.

The killer waved a two-barrelled wheel-lock pistol across the street, smoke curling from one muzzle. He bellowed into the night.

'The Turk is dead. We're in. Bring up the carts.' He glanced at Altan's corpse and murmured, 'If there's enough left to pull them.' He bellowed again: 'I want to be gone by first light.'

He shoved his bloody knife into the back of his belt and looked down again at Altan. He shook his head as if counting his luck. He belted his pistol and stooped and took the ivory ring from

Altan's thumb. He looked at it curiously, then tried to slip it over his own. It didn't fit. He slid it over his little finger and seemed pleased with the trophy. He turned and looked at Carla.

His features were not deformed in design, yet his nose, his lips, the heavy ridges of his cheekbones and brows were so huge, so overgrown, that the effect was grotesque. His eyes were deep-set and dark. Strangest of all, he gave off something of the air of a monstrous boy. Perhaps it was the disproportion of his head; perhaps something inside him. The Infant of Cockaigne.

'Six. Six of my young lions your Turk has killed.'

Carla remembered a principle that Mattias had pressed upon her, and how hard it had been to accept it. To appear weak invites the fate of the weak, and that fate is to be crushed without pity by the strong. She closed her senses to the blood gluing her shoes to the tiles, to the foul smoke, to the chaos, animal and human, echoing around her. She took a deep breath.

'Monsieur Grymonde, I regret he didn't kill you all.'

Grymonde's mouth opened. He put his fists on his hips. He didn't reply.

'I am Carla, whom you call the lady from the south.'

Grymonde sought some adequate response. He failed and scowled at Altan.

'And who was he?'

'Altan Savas was my protector, and my husband's brother-in-arms, and in both respects to be reckoned a man among men.'

'Where is he, this brave husband?'

Her last coin was her courage. She wagered it.

'Harm me further and he'll give you cause to curse the day you were born.'

Grymonde twiddled the ivory ring on his finger.

'I already have such causes. Why not another?'

'That ring is not made for any gaudy purpose. It enables the drawing of the bowstring, though few can boast the strength to draw that one.'

Grymonde stooped and levered the horn bow from Altan's grip. He hefted it and grunted. By the way he handled it, Carla knew he was no archer, and he was canny enough not to accept her challenge. He slung the bow across his shoulder and grinned.

'The lady from the south has sauce, I'll give her that.'

Carla's baby shifted inside her. Her womb cramped.

'Your arm, monsieur, if you will.'

She stepped from the shadows and Grymonde saw her figure for the first time. The deep-set eyes swam with sudden emotion, as sudden to him as it was to her.

'The Devil take my eyes, you're quick with child.'

Though she didn't need to, Carla took hold of Grymonde's arm and leaned on it. His hand looked big enough to hold a gallon of pears. He gave off a smell so strange that she was lost for a comparison. His skin was filmed with a greasy exudation and was coarse without being pocked. She did not break his gaze. At this moment there was only one ally worth having, and that was Grymonde. If by small increments she could appoint him her defender, her defender he would become. The more her defender he became, the harder he would find it to retreat from that role.

'Help me outside. I want to take some air.'

She took a step towards the threshold. Grymonde supported her weight and stepped with her. She felt Antoinette clutching her skirt. They were outside.

As if chewing on an unforeseen dilemma, Grymonde said, 'You're pregnant.'

'Yes, I am.'

'Our intention was to kill the lot of you.'

'Clearly you don't want to kill me, or my unborn babe.'

Grymonde pursed massive lips. She did not blink.

'So why would you? Are you not master here? The king of thieves?'

'Do you mock me or appeal to my vanity?'

'I speak for what I see in your heart.'

'I am not ruled by my heart.'

'If I may be so bold –'

Grymonde laughed.

'– I don't believe that's true.'

He stared at her, and she wondered if she had gone too far.

To mask his abashment he turned to rally his decimated crew.

'Gather round, gather round my bold and faithful blackguards. It's time to reap the harvest we have sown. And no appetite here's so gaudy it won't be gorged.'

A rabble of youths congregated from every direction, some from behind the Hôtel D'Aubray. There were more than the nine that six dead should have left, but some were too young to be counted men, even in this crew. Their clothes were improvised from multi-coloured rags and hides. Most walked barefoot in the filth as if to go otherwise would be unnatural to their breed. Their faces were scarred, ingrained, with the violence of utmost poverty. Some were scorched and stank of naphtha and burned hair. All wore strips of white cloth tied around one arm. They dragged with them half a dozen two-wheeled carts of the type one saw at markets.

They were in a state of high excitement, sweating with uncontainable energies, sniggering to mask their shock at their slaughtered mates. They were alive in the midst of death and wielding fire in the night, come to spill blood and spread fear, to seek plunder, to scratch some proof of their wretched existence on the cheeks of the world, to hold their betters at the tips of their knives, their every waking dream come true.

Yet their jubilation was muted as they awaited Grymonde's permission to explode.

Carla had lived among armies. She had a sense of the diverse and powerful forces required to bind men together and to hold them to a common purpose. That force was Grymonde. His army was a crowd of tatterdemalions, hardly better knit than a common mob. Carla saw only one among them who appeared much over twenty years old. He seemed disinclined to smile. He had an ugly V-shaped scar branded into his forehead to mark him a thief. All except he held Grymonde in awe.

'Send for a chair,' said Carla. 'If you'd be so kind.'

'What?' said Grymonde.

'A chair, I feel faint. And a cup of wine. You'll find both in the kitchen.'

'Joco! A chair and a cup of wine from the kitchen.'

Joco, the one branded a thief, gestured to two lesser minions.

'Papin. Bigot.'

As they two ran into the house they had to wade through the pack of dogs which had gathered in the hallway to lap up the blood. The dogs snapped at their bare ankles and the other tatterdemalions laughed.

Joco sneered at Carla. She felt his hatred. He saw what she was doing and it galled him. The more Grymonde took her part, the less would he feel able to retreat from that choice in front of his gang, especially if challenged. If she was to gamble on such a throw, she had to gamble all. She arched one brow of scorn at Joco to provoke him further. Joco bared his teeth at her. He threw his hand out towards Grymonde.

'Are we here to slaughter these pigs or to wait on them like slaves?'

'The pigs are ready for slaughter because I killed the boar.'

'If it's the baby that troubles you,' said Joco, 'I can cut it out of her stomach before we rape her. It's been done before.'

Sniggers and exaggerated groans. Grymonde's eyes silenced them.

'Poor Joco is sad because poor Gobbo, his brother, is dead –' began Grymonde.

'Have you seen what they done to him?'

'Gobbo is dead because he did not do as he was told. If Joco does not do as he is told, he will be dead, too. So will you all. Is this but a game we play here?'

Grymonde looked about him, enormous palms outspread and quite the performer. His audience was spellbound. None dared answer. At the climax of his turn he rested his gaze on Carla and she realised that the question was for her. She sensed his bizarre glamour. It might in another circumstance have repelled her, but she needed it. She needed to embrace his charm, for men love few things more than to believe they have it. And it would help her charm him. She dared. She smiled.

'Perhaps so.'

'Perhaps so, says the lady. Why not? What brave man – or lady – does not love a game? None more than me. But if game it be, let all be warned – and let these dead comrades testify – it is a dangerous one.'

'What right game is not?' said Carla.

Grymonde clapped his hands in delight. The sound was like a gunshot.

'The Lady Carla shames you all. Papin, give the chair to Joco.'

Papin had just braved the dog pack with a chair, Bigot was close behind carrying a pewter cup. Papin proffered the chair in his hands to Joco. Joco ignored him.

A smouldering dog, the one Altan Savas had hacked, its body gaping open behind the shoulder, hobbled over the threshold on three legs. It leaned against Joco's calf, as if in the blind hope of procuring comfort. Joco kicked it in the chest. The dog skittered and whimpered and fell panting on its side. The boys laughed.

'I'll shove that chair up her, one leg at a time,' said Joco, 'but I'll not wait on her.'

Papin looked to Grymonde.

'Papin. Bigot, you, too.'

Grymonde waved them over. He took the chair in one enormous fist and with an elaborate twirl set it down for Carla. With a bow he indicated that she sit, which she did. She laid one hand on her stomach. With the other she smoothed her braid and pulled it down across her breast. With another bow, Grymonde offered the cup of wine.

She took it.

'Thank you, monsieur.'

'You have your chair, your wine. May we proceed?'

Carla pointed at the burned and bleeding dog.

'That poor creature did you a service. You owe it more than cruelty.'

Grymonde pulled back his vast shoulders. He frowned.

'Did you hear that, Joco? We are in debt to a dying dog.'

Joco twitched. The door was open but he knew not how to walk through it.

'I am in debt to no dog though much is owed me. Gobbo's share, too.'

Grymonde stooped to pick up a sledgehammer. His palm enclosed close to a quarter of the shaft. He altered his grip for the balance.

'A double share? On what grounds? Did you and Gobbo write wills before going to war? Like the soldiers of David?'

'David who?' asked Joco.

'Carla, the noble lady from the south, is right. This dog served us well. Just as the foxes served Samson against the Philistines.'

The hammer swished down as if it weighed no more than a fly-whisk and crushed the dog's spine just behind the skull. He looked at Joco.

'Do you know who Samson was?'

Joco grimaced with effort. 'Didn't Jesus raise him from the dead?'

'No, no,' said Papin. 'That was Lazarus. Samson kicked the Jews out of the temple, then pulled the roof down with his bare hands.'

'And the Philistines crucified him right next to Jesus. Didn't they?' said Bigot.

A babble of competing theories arose. Grymonde looked at Carla.

'Now you see why these poor children need a father.'

He put his free hand on the head of the hammer and rammed the butt into Joco's gut. Joco folded over, too winded to make a sound. The babbling stopped.

'Now I will show you all why you must obey him.'

Grymonde swung the hammer into Joco's ribs where they met the backbone.

Carla didn't flinch at the crack and the woeful groan. Others did.

'Now we will watch Joco eat the dog.'

Grymonde seized Joco by the back of the skull with one hand and dragged him on his hands and knees and crammed his face into the carcass of the dead dog.

'Eat the dog, Joco, before the maggots get here. Bite. Chew. Swallow.'

Joco struggled and Grymonde stubbed the hammer into the small of his back, pinning him, forcing his mouth open and into the scorched mass of pink and blackened flesh, the burned hide sloughing off in sheets and reefing up around his nostrils until he had to open his mouth to gasp for air.

'Chew, you turd. Swallow that tasty morsel. Eat I say.'

Joco gnawed a charred mouthful and swallowed.

Carla saw Estelle, the rat girl, watching Grymonde. Clotted in soot and blood, she looked like a rag doll recovered from the ruins of a sacked town. She was the only female in this bestial company and Carla wondered why she was included. Earlier, the girl's awe of Grymonde had been evident. Now, in her eyes, Carla saw that she adored him. Her love made the scene that she witnessed all the more perverse. Estelle turned her head and looked at her. Her eyes changed.

They burned with hatred.

Carla realised the girl was jealous. She saw her as a rival for Grymonde.

Carla felt her baby move inside her. She felt his curiosity, the lust for adventure she had helped instil in him. She put her hand on his backbone, to calm him, to send him to sleep, to let him know that this was not the time to be curious, that he should wait inside her for adventures less hazardous than these. A contraction clenched her womb and tightened its grip. It tightened for longer than any she had known before it. She felt vast natural forces rise within her, yet seemingly from far beyond her – from the earth, from Time – forces capable of any extreme without regard for her wishes or feelings, without respect for the bounds of her body or the peril around her.

She braced her hands on her knees and, though she closed her eyes, she kept her head erect, and she stifled the urge to groan. She didn't want to distract the pack from Joco's humiliation. She breathed in and out with all her concentration. The contraction eased but did not completely relax.

She realised that there would be no more complete relaxations until the baby was born; if she stayed alive that long. The journey had begun; rather, the last stage of the long journey she and the babe had taken. The journey that would end with the beginning of another. Or so she must believe. She felt herself spinning on the wheel of life and death, her perceptions both exquisite and numbed. She had to open her body, her very soul. She had to surrender to her child's will. She had to match him in courage; or neither would survive. If he wished to be born into a world of demons, then in a world of demons she would suckle him.

Were those real bells that rang with such abandon? Or did she dream them?

She opened her eyes.

Joco was half-choked and wholly broken. Grymonde let go of his head but replaced it with a foot on the back of his neck and straightened up. Carla felt an impulse to shout: *Finish him. Kill him.* Almost as if he had heard her, Grymonde turned and gave her a questioning look. He had murder in his eyes and she wondered if indeed she had not spoken the words out loud. He turned away.

Grymonde wagged the hammer at his band of young scurvies, who seemed only to admire him the more for having turned on one of their number with such savagery.

'He who has a mind to beat a dog will always find a stick.'

He raised his foot and Joco crawled away on hands and knees, vomiting. He squirmed to his feet and stumbled away down the alley by the side of the house.

'Do you want us to bring him back, chief?'

'He is dead to me.'

Grymonde pointed the hammer at Estelle.

'La Rossa, you brought Gobbo and Joco into our band. They failed us. As you failed us.' He gestured at the slain. 'You failed to open the door.'

Estelle stared at him in disbelief. She looked around at the feral young men and found no supporters, only grins and jeers. She looked at Carla.

Carla felt a terrible sympathy for the girl, despite her enmity; but so overwhelmed were her senses by the gruesome theatre about her, and the violent change inside her body, it was all she could do to stay upright on the chair.

'But I was brave,' said Estelle. Her voice was clearer than the bells. 'Altan almost killed me. If I hadn't told you about him, he might have killed you.'

Carla thought she saw pity in Grymonde's eyes. No one else did.

Estelle raised a pale, thin arm and pointed at Carla.

'Carla will tell you I was brave.'

'It's true,' said Carla. 'Estelle could not have been braver.'

She caught a glimpse of Grymonde's face and realised she had only sealed Estelle's banishment. Having shown the gang he would take no dissent from them, he had to show them he would take none from Carla either.

'Sometimes bravery is not enough.'

Estelle held her hand out. 'I want my knife back.'

'See her off, lads, back to her rats.'

Three of the louts made to grab her. Estelle slithered through their hands, avoided their kicks. One of them pursued and grabbed the neck of her smock as she pulled away. It tore down the back. She spun and grabbed at his crotch with a hiss and he let go to defend himself and Estelle fled naked down the street. As she disappeared, Carla thought she heard her sob. Though it was not true, for Estelle was no friend, she felt as if she had lost her only ally in that street of the violent and the crazed.

'Now listen,' said Grymonde. 'The bourgeois militia is called out and there's no telling what those stupid bastards will do. They're no friends to beggars like us and they won't be bribed like the police. We must be finished and on our way by first light. You've got your orders and they're good ones. The back door is still barred so go and open it, we've carts out there, too. Don't neglect the cellar – it's full of stock, the prize pickings – and don't forget to bring the ladder either. And drive out those dogs.'

'Look, there's another woman, up there,' cried Bigot.

Carla told herself not to do so but had already lifted her head. Symonne peered down from the shattered window of the parlour. Their eyes met.

'Can we spoil her before we kill her?' asked Papin.

Carla looked away.

'She's rich and she's tasty, with fine fat teats and a crack in her arse that could strangle a live eel,' said Grymonde. 'I dare say she'll spill a river of tears to soften your tender young hearts, but be not tender. Your mothers and sisters scrubbed her floors and emptied her pisspot, and she never even cared to learn their names, for when do her kind ever? Show her what her fine floors look like when you're down on your knees. And the inside of her pisspot, too.'

Carla heard a sob at her shoulder. She turned to pull Antoinette close.

'Antoinette, kneel here beside me and put your head in my lap. Feel the baby. Hum a lullaby for him, but very softly.'

'Can we kill all the other Huguenots, chief?'

'The King himself decreed it. The one in the Louvre.'

'Chief? Are the Huguenots as bad as the Philistines?'

'They are worse than Philistines. Of them Samson killed ten thousand with the jawbone of an ass – heaps upon heaps, we are told – and he is reckoned a hero for the deed. So unsheathe thy knives with gladness, and go and do likewise for Charles.'

The tatterdemalions cheered and charged into the Hôtel D'Aubray.

Carla closed her eyes and put her hands over Antoinette's ears and braced herself. Violent screams, from the killers no less than their victims, echoed in gusts from the shattered house. She heard the terror and pain of Martin. Of Charité. Lucien died last. The cries of the women intermingled, and continued, in a single unbroken scream. The strange odour filled her head and Carla opened her eyes.

Grymonde crouched in front of her, his face a hand's breadth

from hers, his granitic features lost in the darkness but for the gleam
of his eyes and mouthful of widely spaced teeth.

'Is the wine good, my lady?'

'I have not tasted it.'

Inside the house, one woman stopped screaming. The other –
Carla knew it was Symonne – didn't stop. Antoinette knew, too.
Her body shook as she hummed.

Grymonde put a hand on Antoinette's head. He stroked her
hair. Carla resisted an urge to strike his hand away. The girl's lullaby
turned to whimpers.

'You'd have me believe this Huguenot is your daughter.'

'No. I would have you make your boys believe it.'

'You set Joco against me.'

'He wanted to kill me. And you were willing. Thank you.'

'Should I have killed him?'

'Yes.'

Grymonde scraped an enormous thumb down his cheek.

Symonne's screams subsided into breathless grunts, muffled by
obscene outbursts, laughter, and the squabbling of her defilers.

Grymonde's enormous head tilted in thought, then righted
itself.

'You may keep your "daughter". But tell me no more lies.'

'I have told you no lies, nor will I.'

'Then pull no more strings for I am no puppet. Ask me for
nothing more.'

'You know I must ask for more. I believe you will help me.'

'Why? Have I lacked for villainy?'

Carla remembered an aphorism that Mattias sometimes quoted,
which he had learned from Sabato Svi.

'The Jews say, *In the place where there are no men, be a man.*'

'You quote the Jews at me?'

'Samson was a Jew, and so was Christ, though I will place no
reliance on your fealty to Him. You have proved yourself a villain.
I dare you to prove yourself a man.'

For a moment Grymonde was still. His eyes shone into hers
from beneath his bone-cragged brow. His black curls shone. He

was the Infant of Paris, of its streets, its logic, its cruelty, much as
an owl is of the forest. He glanced beneath the chair. He ducked
his head. He reached out his hand and withdrew it.

'The bag of your waters has burst.'

Grymonde rubbed his thumb against his fingers and examined
them.

'The waters are clean. A good beginning.'

For a man to make such observations startled her. She did not
dwell on it.

The throes of her labour had begun.

'Will you take me to the Temple of the Hospitallers?'

'Those monks know nothing of women. I wouldn't let them
calve a cow.'

'Then please, just leave us to find our way. For my child's sake.'

'For your child's sake, and yours, I will take you to Cockaigne.'

'Where is this land of plenty?'

'You've heard tell of the Yards?'

The Yards were dens of criminals and beggars, so notorious for
bloodshed and worse that they remained inviolate to all but their
own. Carla nodded.

'Cockaigne is my yard.'

Carla felt the baby move inside her as her womb seized them
both with a tremendous convulsion. It came in a rising wave, rolling
downwards, its strength more astounding than the pain. Antoinette
recoiled and retreated behind the chair. Carla took a deep breath
and made no sound.

Grymonde took her hand in his and squeezed, with a gentleness
that should have been beyond him. She squeezed back with all her
might. She clasped her other hand around his knuckles. The throng
lasted for what seemed a long time. It waned, but not entirely. Her
abdomen remained more tightly knotted than ever.

She pulled her hands from Grymonde's, confused by the
unwanted intimacy of the moment just past. Confused because she
had appreciated his grip. In his face she saw no lust, only an amused
concern, as if his confidence in her were as firm as that he placed
in himself. Though her mind rebelled, on instinct she knew she

should trust him; not because she had no choice, but because the choice was a good one.

'My child and I place our faith in you, and in your protection.'

From the Hôtel D'Aubray came a fresh cycle of appalled screams.

'Here, this will give you strength.'

Grymonde offered her the cup of wine. She took a sip.

'I don't know how far I can walk like this.'

'Walk?'

He laughed and showed the great gaps between his teeth.

'What manner of man do you think I am?'

CHAPTER NINE

Clementine

'I told Cosseins that I refuse to treat your wounded,' said Ambroise Paré. 'As he knows, I am obliged to take orders from no one but the King.'

Tannhauser laid Orlandu on the bed. The carpet was bogged with blood but the sheets were clean. He pointed to one of the lamps.

'Juste, the light.'

Juste held the lamp over the bed. Orlandu had remained under the opium throughout all that had happened. His chest still rose and fell.

'He's alive and he's young,' said Tannhauser. 'Plenty have survived worse.'

'Did you not hear me, sir?'

Tannhauser turned towards Paré. The great man stood at the rear of the room near an open door leading to a staircase, as if the fantasy of escape gave him some comfort. He was bearded, of distinguished good looks, and in his early sixties. Tonight he looked much older. While his posture mimed defiance, his eyes were sickened and fearful.

'Forgive my manners, Master Paré, and allow me to put the blame on these dire events. I am Mattias Tannhauser and I stand before you with the highest respect. In truth, with awe. As you see, I am a Knight of the Hospital of Malta, and among that noble crew your fame as a surgeon has no equal. During the siege, the application of your methods saved many a life and I often heard your name invoked. I invoked it myself, to my friend Jurien de Lyon.'

'You knew Jurien?'

'Knew him and saw him die. He was still working at the slab when the Turks cut his hands off and beheaded him.'

Paré's pride, at first flattered, was now stung.

Tannhauser said, 'In bloody times, it's no easy thing to go on. Yet we must.'

Paré walked over to the bed, pulling a pair of spectacles from inside his sleeve.

'I have spent my life in bloody times, in bloody tents, on bloody fields. Nor am I new to treachery as policy. But on this scale? Guise has gone too far. The King will have his head. His Majesty sat by this very bed and wept over the Admiral's wounds. Wept with pity and rage, and swore to see justice done. Now they say all this is done by the King's command.'

'I'm not privy to the King's councils, but I'm certain it is only by the King's command that you are still alive.'

While Paré absorbed the implications of this, he donned his glasses and his hands examined Orlandu as if they had a life of their own. Pulses, fingertips, the nodes in his neck, the texture of his skin, the condition of his tongue. He bent forward to sniff his breath.

'Bring the lamp closer,' he said to Juste.

He peeled back Orlandu's eyelids.

Tannhauser clapped Juste on the back. 'It's thanks to me this young lion is still here. You and he may be the only living Huguenots in this *quartier*. Is that not so, Juste?'

'Yes, sire. I should have been murdered in the palace with the rest.'

Paré looked up. 'They're killing our brethren in the Louvre, too?'

'Sire, I believe they are killed already.'

'They were herded into the courtyard for the sport of the archers,' said Tannhauser. 'The royal family watched from the Queen's terrace, as if it were a masque.'

Paré closed his eyes. Tannhauser feared he might faint.

'They consorted with snakes,' said Tannhauser. 'They got bitten.'

Paré looked at him. Perhaps the surgeon read in his face the brute and knowing callousness that this world demanded of its survivors. If so, it was a skill that Paré had mastered long ago, albeit against his every deepest instinct. He nodded.

'You are right. We must go on. When was this man last given opium?'

'More than ten hours ago.'

'And still so insensible?' Paré opened a case of instruments. 'He must be a strong lad to survive the dose he was given.'

'Orlandu has an unusual pedigree, reckless on one side, fanatical on the other, and stubborn on both. He is my son, though not by blood.'

'Chevalier, you can better assist me from the far side of the bed. Juste, you stay as you are. The lamp will get hot, so use that towel.'

With tweezers and scissors, Paré began to cut open and tease apart the foul dressing congealed around Orlandu's upper arm, and which was now twisted and compacted by the rigours of his journey. Tannhauser circled the bed.

'This bandage has baked the wound like a suet pudding,' said Paré. 'Nature alone would have served him a lot better. There's a bullet in his arm along with a gill of pus.'

'I thought to lance it myself but had no dressing. The Hospitallers, after your writings, use egg yolk, Venice turpentine and oil of roses.'

'That concoction I devised for fresh wounds. When infection is established, as here, Ægyptiacum attenuated with wine and *eau-de-vie* is more effective.'

'Of course, of course.' Tannhauser dug into his memory. 'Verdigris and honey?'

'There are surgeons in Paris who know less about their art than you do, or than you seem to, and yet, if I may say so, I would not have made you for a surgeon on first sight.'

'I'm a soldier and a killer of men, for preference with blades, for they're more certain, to which end I've made a primitive study of Anatomy. It also helps to know a thing or two about how to treat wounds as well as to inflict them. To that end I also have dabbled in the sciences of Alchemy and Natural Magick.'

The smell of putrefaction arose as Tannhauser pulled away the sodden bandages. The linen clung to the skin and the skin started to tear like the peel of an overripe apricot.

'Stop. If he's not to lose the arm, we will have to soak the bandages off. With a decoction of black wine mixed with oxycrate, and warmed over the lamp flame.'

'Excellent,' concurred Tannhauser. 'Marvellous.'

'He may lose the arm in any event.'

'Or his life. Can you say how old the wound is?'

'A day and a half, perhaps more.'

Paré opened a portable chest crammed with drawers, pill boxes, powders, bottles and vials, and prepared his decoction in a glass retort.

'Juste, put the lamp back on the table and hold this retort over the flame. Your hand is steadier than mine. Slowly swill the decoction so that it heats evenly. When you see the vapour start to rise from the surface, pour it into this dish.'

Juste took the glass receptacle and did as asked. His concentration was such that for the first time since Tannhauser had met him, the cares seem to melt from his face.

'You would make a fine assistant,' said Paré.

'Thank you, sire.'

'My last assistant was soon to take his Batchelor's degree. He was stabbed in the back, there on the stairs to the garret, not an hour ago. Teligny and the others got as far as the roof before they were shot down.'

'I am sorry, sire,' said Juste. 'A surgeon's assistant, more than most men, should be spared so cruel an end. I will pray for him.'

'What part of Poland do you hail from?' asked Paré. 'The Lesser? Or the North?'

'The Lesser. Near Krakow.'

Tannhauser, who had been enjoying an unearned pride in Juste's intelligence and bearing, was taken aback. He felt somewhat oafish. Paré noticed.

'His accent is subtle. Yours I can't place, though it is less so.'

'That at least does not surprise me.'

Tannhauser had spent the last seven years refining his command of French, a language he had previously found abominable but had come to love. That Carla was his primary instructor was not immaterial. He now thought in French. The course of his life could be plotted in the languages Fate had forced him to think in: German, Turkish, a confection of Italian dialects.

Tannhauser said, 'You travelled a long way for a wedding, lad.'

'We did not come for the wedding. Our good king, Sigismundus Augustus, is dead. Henri of Anjou has designs on his crown.' Juste swung the retort from the lamp and emptied it in the dish. 'The Lutheran electors sent my brothers to meet Anjou, to find out what kind of man he is. But we were never able to get past your friend Torcy. Benedykt was furious.'

'Anjou doesn't want to live in Poland,' said Paré. 'He considers them pig farmers.'

'In Poland Catholics and Protestants do not fight endless wars. Our people are not starving. Our fields are not burned. We have not spent all our gold to pay Germans to destroy our country. And we have invented the means to dispose of our shit instead of letting it rot in heaps as it does inside the Louvre.'

Tannhauser, knowing him better, was more surprised by this than Paré.

'I meant no disrespect to your great and famous nation,' said Paré. 'All you say is true. I pray God we had a statesman of Sigismund's genius on the French throne, but we do not. I meant, as a point of fact, that it is Catherine who has designs on the Polish crown on her son's behalf. She will persuade the Polish electors to choose him. And Anjou will obey his mother whether he likes Poland or not.'

'Whereupon they'll empty the Polish treasury of all but the mice droppings,' said Tannhauser. 'But Anjou is a degenerate. Why would the Poles want a king who dresses like a woman?'

'That's the question my brothers would have taken back to Krakow.'

Paré took the dish of warm wine and oxycrate and handed it to Tannhauser.

'Enough politics. Soak the dressing. I will cut the poison from your son.'

Paré's speed and decisiveness were marvellous. He opened the wound and trimmed the dead flesh until it bled, removed shreds of cloth, and through a second incision extracted a small iron ball, which he gave to Tannhauser.

'A pistol bullet,' said Tannhauser.

'No powder burns, no wadding or patch in the wound. Shot from behind at some distance, at least twenty feet.'

'A shot meant to kill, then.'

'Most shots are,' agreed Paré. 'Unless he was an exceptional marksman.'

'A marksman would know that the chances were greater of missing him or hitting him in the back. Yet they didn't finish him.'

'He also took a blow to the back of the head,' said Paré. 'We must assume to stun him. Who are "they"?'

Tannhauser said, 'I don't know.'

Paré completed the debridement and applied the concoction of Ægyptiacum. Orlandu tried to pull his arm away. The pain must have been exquisite yet at no point did he wake. The entire bottle of tincture must have gone down his throat.

'I have dressed him,' said Paré. 'It's up to God to heal him.'

Tannhauser grabbed a pair of gold coins from the lavender-scented purse, the clink of one against the other hard to resist. As he withdrew them, their weight told him they were Spanish double pistoles, double doubloons each worth twenty livres. Before he could drop one back, and the clink having revealed that he held two, thus making palming one appear devious, Paré had already extended his hand and raised an expectant brow. Tannhauser gave him the golden ounce. Paré's smile must have been his first in at least two days.

The surgeon advised that it would be unwise to move Orlandu, at least before the youth awoke, if wake he ever did. For the moment Tannhauser did not have a safe place to move him to. Later in the day he could hire a wagon and take him to the Hôtel D'Aubray, or perhaps the Temple. Until then, Orlandu would have to convalescence at the centre of the carnage. It was a better spot than most. That there was no one left here to kill was general knowledge. Paré wouldn't be taking to the streets until he received orders from the Louvre, and a guard to boot, and the King had much else on his mind.

'With your consent I'll post my man Stefano up here to ensure your safety. I can warrant he took no part in the massacre, should that ease your mind. Though no doubt he would have done so if ordered to.'

'If you trust him with your son, I can hardly complain.'

'Juste will stay here, too. As you have seen, he is an excellent companion.'

'Absolutely not,' said Paré.

'I want to come with you, sire,' said Juste. 'You made a promise. You killed my three brothers and you promised to protect me.'

Tannhauser became aware of Paré's scrutiny. He felt the prestige he had taken such pains to establish wither beneath the surgeon's gaze.

'The brothers forced me into a duel. It had nothing to do with religion.'

'No,' said Juste. 'You'd kill anyone.'

'If I'd known you were Poles I might have been less harsh.'

'Why? Because you despise us?'

'Because men of the north ought to be allies.'

'Then we should be allies, and I should come with you.'

'Your wishes are immaterial.'

Paré said, 'I hope mine are not. I have faith in my authority to protect my patient, while I'm here, but I can't protect Juste.'

Tannhauser was about to point out that Stefano would do the protecting.

'I've seen enough murder. I'm sorry.'

Tannhauser bowed. Paré was right. And were Juste to be exposed as a Lutheran, his presence could endanger Orlandu, too. He would take him.

'Master Paré, I am in your debt.'

'I thank you for protecting Coligny.'

'Monsieur?'

'I saw you from the window. You stopped them desecrating his body.'

'An old soldier shouldn't be treated that way. It means the world has no future worth knowing.'

'The only future worth knowing is reunion with God.'

Tannhauser saw that the light outside had changed, from indigo to pale violet.

'I'll settle for reunion with my wife. There's one last favour I will beg of you, though it's an urgent one. Can you recommend a midwife?'

'You wife is expecting a child that imminently?'

'I can't be that exact, but imminently enough.'

'Then bring her to see me, the sooner the better.'

'You'll deliver our babe?'

'Childbirth is the matter of my next book. I have skills no midwife can match.'

'You've lifted a tombstone from my chest.'

'Coligny's wife is in the same advanced condition. He was planning to leave Paris to be with her for the birth. Instead . . .'

Tannhauser didn't like this coincidence. It smacked of ill omen. He put his superstitions aside and acquired Paré's address, on the Left Bank. He took his leave.

He went downstairs, past Cosseins' guards. Gelid lumps of blood slithered under his feet. Ambroise Paré had agreed to deliver Carla's baby. On reflection, he could think of no more valuable prize to have won. The man had written a book on the art. A book. Had anyone else in the world? Had anyone else even thought to do so? That sufficient knowledge on childbirth to fill a book existed at all was astounding enough. And Paré knew it all. It was as if the hidden motive driving Carla's rash journey had at last been revealed. Having replaced a dire superstition with a more auspicious variant, he felt better.

Tannhauser resolved to be cheerful.

In the courtyard outside he found Stefano waiting in the dawn. The long light fell straight down the length of Rue Béthizy and the great swill of clotted gore that stiffened in the gutters and grouted the stones turned from black to russet as he watched. He motioned Stefano over and told him what he required. Stefano tightened his lips and without voicing his reluctance, bowed his assent.

'Hold out your hand.'

Stefano did not need to be told twice. His demeanour changed to one of reverence as Tannhauser dropped a double pistole in his palm.

'Have you ever held one of those before?'

'Sire, I don't even know what it is. But its weight is sweet.'

'Half an ounce of Spanish gold at twenty-two karats. If it were any more pure it would melt in your fist. To you, it's four hundred sols.'

A good month's wages. Stefano didn't speak.

'If when next we meet, Orlandu has suffered no new harms and you are still by his side, you'll get two more. If events force him to be moved, go with him. Whatever happens, do not leave him. You're canny enough to stretch Lombarts' orders as needed. Use Arnauld de Torcy as your warrant. If you and Orlandu do move, or if there's anything else I should know, leave word for Mattias Tannhauser back at the gatehouse.'

'Sire.'

As Stefano stepped back to salute, Tannhauser noticed that Coligny's corpse had been tied by its feet with a rope. At the other end gaped a neck stump. Coligny's head was nowhere to be seen. Tannhauser looked at the Swiss.

'Guise's followers,' said Stefano. 'The head is to be packed in salt and sent to Rome. A solemn promise made to the Pope, they said.'

'I'm sure it will bring the pontiff great cheer.'

'They said that, too.'

Juste said, 'You fed my brothers to the dogs.'

'Stefano, you may go.' Tannhauser turned to Juste. 'What?'

'You despise the dishonouring of Coligny yet you fed my brothers to the dogs.'

'Different principles at stake,' blustered Tannhauser. 'Different traditions.'

'Is it because we are Poles?'

'Of course not. I fancied you for Normans. You were fierce enough.'

'Does the world have a future worth knowing when men feed each other to dogs?'

'I know that too sharp a wit in the young portends an early grave, a fate you've avoided only narrowly at least twice.'

'My brothers have no grave. Why should I deserve one?'

'Dogs or maggots, your brothers came from Poland to die. Their names were writ in that book before they crossed the Oder.'

'Perhaps your name, too.'

'That page won't be turned in Paris.'

'You sound like Bendyckt.'

Tannhauser reflected that he had sounded like a lot of people recently. The printer. The circle around Retz advising the cull. Now, a belligerent Pole. That was the problem with living among people. One's pettiness and the base unoriginality of one's thoughts were exposed. He decided it was no apt time for the sympathy he felt for the boy.

'You are a burden to me, but I will shoulder it. I've taken you behind my shield but you're not my prisoner. If my company offends you, you're free to seek your own way. But if we are to be in league, we must agree to stop these bickers. If not, Death will claim you like a bad debt. And with that, perhaps Grégoire too, for his character at least is not in question, much less his loyalty to a friend. Do you agree?'

'I agree. I beg your pardon.'

'You have it, free and full. And I beg yours, though I don't expect it.'

Grégoire emerged around a corner leading an enormous grey mare.

The only horse of comparable stature Tannhauser had ever seen had been harnessed to a wagon hauling thirty hundredweight of cannonballs. She was, to be sure, an extraordinary animal, seventeen hands at least, with a Roman nose, a deep chest, tremendous hind-quarters and extravagant white feathering over her hooves, which were the size of meat platters in circumference. Her hide showed numerous signs of ill use in a city too puny to appreciate her essence: the scabs, burns and gouges left by accidents; the vindictive slashes inflicted by humans offended by her passing; the marks the large of spirit bore in a world that wished them smaller.

All this called to Tannhauser. Yet, vanity being the humiliating affliction that it is, and having coveted the lustrous horseflesh of Guise's crew, the scarred and lumbering mare fell short of his image of a mount on which to flaunt around Paris.

Somehow, Grégoire had managed to get a saddle on the beast.

'Grégoire, that's a carthorse. I can hardly see over her back.'

Grégoire babbled and Tannhauser wagged a finger at his ear.

Grégoire began again.

'This is the best horse for you, sire. Look at her – calm, strong, fearless. All the others, the fine horses, were affrighted by the shooting, the smoke, the smell of blood. She was eating hay. The others are country horses, but she knows Paris. Nothing will scare her. Also, she will not run away when you leave her outside the tavern. Also, you will ride much higher above the shit. Also, Paris is crammed between every wall and every other wall with people, but Clementine will drive the rabble from your path.'

'Clementine?'

Tannhauser had hoped at least for a suitably intrepid name.

'You don't like Clementine?'

'I like it,' said Juste.

They looked at Tannhauser as if awaiting the verdict of Solomon.

'It's the very name I would have chosen myself.'

He stood before the great creature and looked at her and let her size him up. Wisely, having no good reason at all to trust the likes of him, she grunted and reserved judgement. He murmured some endearments in Turkish and was rewarded with a whicker that made his chest vibrate. He took this for permission and swung into the saddle.

'Grégoire, as a judge of horses you have no peer.'

The moment his arse hit the leather he knew the lad had picked a legendary steed. His thighs, his backbone, his heart, were connected to a massive force of life whose spirit was undaunted. The strength of his own spirit redoubled. Yet bells still tolled all over town and he had kept too many appointments he hadn't made.

'Grab a stirrup strap, lads, and hold on tight. Take me to the gallows.'

CHAPTER TEN

Out of the Strong

At first, the streets were quiet. Any Sunday would have muted the turmoil of dawn; rumours of slaughter and rebellion must have prompted thousands more to stay indoors. Through a gap between the houses lining the Seine, Tannhauser saw a solitary boatman punt across the river. Seagulls patrolled the strand.

They began to pass armed citizens wearing white armbands, with white crosses pinned to their caps. Some carried flags so colourful they would have embarrassed an Austrian duke. No archers or cross-bowmen; not the regular city guard. They roamed the wharves with the malign self-importance of those whose bigotries were backed by the state. The cross on Tannhauser's chest was saluted with waves of their banners and spears.

By the time Clementine reached the Pont Notre-Dame the militia were stretching a chain across the road between iron hooks moored to the houses lining either side of the bridge. Tannhauser pressed on, though so many armed men now filled the thorough-fare he had to slow the carthorse to a walk lest she plough them down.

Grégoire had slung his shoes around his neck by the laces. He held onto them with both hands to avoid being kicked in the mouth. He let go and patted Clementine's enormous shoulder.

'A good choice, master?'

'She must have been sired by Pegasus.'

The boy's gums gaped in a warped grin. Tannhauser masked his disgust.

The Place de Grève opened before them. It was congested with bands of militia flying their colours. A pair of drummers practised a tattoo but no one marched. A preacher harangued the troops with apocalyptic fantasies. Cooks fired up their braziers. Enterprising drabs tried their luck. A miscellany of dogs scouted the doings with a nose for scraps.

Tannhauser saw the gallows, the pale mare foaled by an acorn that had taken so many on their short last ride. The timbers were stained and saturated with the final evacuations of the doomed. Even at this distance, the stench of the distillate was piercing.

Beyond the gallows stood the half-built town hall, the Hôtel de Ville, where those who believed themselves the city's best devised new catastrophes for its people. The façade was inscribed with the motto: '*One king, one law, one faith*'. Archers, crossbowmen and halberdiers were drawn up outside and passed a wineskin from hand to hand. Artillery crews manoeuvred eight bronze cannon. The church bells tolled.

Grégoire guided them north to the Rue du Temple. Like all but two or three of the largest streets its surface was unpaved. Here, too, an iron chain had been stretched across the street. A sentinel leaned on the shaft of a glaive whose tip stood an arm's length taller than he. He held up one hand to stop them.

Tannhauser stared at him.

'You'd best use that hand to lower the chain or I'll cut it off,' he said.

A diversity of expressions battled on the sentinel's face, none suggesting the judgement he was in need of. Juste stepped forward to save the fellow pain.

'If it please you, good sir, let me lower the chain for my master or he will slay you, and that would make seven the men he has slaughtered in less than half a day.'

Juste's plea was so heartfelt that the sentinel tripped on the shaft of his spear in his haste to unhook the chain. Clementine clopped forward with a snort.

'Tell me, sirrah,' said Tannhauser, 'what exactly are your orders?'

'Hervé the plasterer at your service, sire! Our orders are to prevent the Huguenot rebels from escaping. Or from attacking. It is not certain which they intend, though it is certain that they intend evil.'

As far as Tannhauser's eye could see, the Rue du Temple was deserted.

'Has a rebel force been spotted?'

'I wouldn't know, sire, but I do know – everyone knows – that these devils have been sneaking in for years from all over the country. Normans. Southerners. Foreigners, too, of course, starving for blood and pillage. This here *quartier* – Sainte-Avoye – crawls with heretics. They've faggots and powder stashed in their own homes ready to burn the city down – that's fanatics for you – just like in '65, when they torched the windmills. Can't trust your own neighbours. I had to sell a good coat to buy this spear, but you can't put a price on safety –'

Tannhauser urged Clementine into a trot.

'If we don't protect our city who will? The magistrates? The Knights of Malta? And gramercy for your generous contribution to the cause!'

The street remained empty, the hoof beats loud in the early morning shadow. The shuttered fronts of the houses, some three storeys, some as many as six, showed no signs of occupation, not even kitchen smoke from their chimneys. They could not all be inhabited by terrified Huguenots, but it wasn't much safer for peaceable Catholics. Only the reckless, the militant and the criminal would venture out this morning. The city was caged by swords. In some form or other every living soul he had met had been afraid. Now that he was so close to Carla, he realised how afraid he was himself.

The boys at his stirrups ran at full pelt now, each of their steps, should it falter, threatening to pitch them under Clementine's irons.

'Let go the straps, lads. You'll find me up ahead.'

He left them behind and almost at once Clementine cleared her nostrils with distaste. Tannhauser smelt it, too. Burned flesh and hair. Blood. Death.

Up ahead he saw the old city walls of Philippe Auguste to either side of the road. Petit Christian had mentioned the wall. Three honeybees above the door. On the west side he saw a splendid house, designed with an abundance of glass. In its faith in light he saw the hopes of a new era, of a new way of thinking, of living, of being. The windows were shattered, the door agape. A body was suspended from an upper sill and clots the colour of aubergines were splashed in fantastic patterns on the paving stones below. He didn't need to see the honeybees.

He reined in Clementine and walked her slowly past the charnel house in which he had hoped to find his wife, and in which he knew he would find her corpse.

He saw drag marks in the puddled blood in the street. The half-burned carcass of a maimed dog lay in the gutter. A dead man, naked, lay inside the doorless threshold.

The body at the second-storey window was a woman, nude and suspended by one ankle from a golden cord tied to the mullion. Her free leg was bent and twisted behind the other. Her throat had been cut by someone with insufficient practice, or will, for the gashes were many and most of them shallow, and some had carved her jaw as she struggled. One breast had been cut off and an attempt made on the other but abandoned. Trickling gore had caked her head entire and was congealed in her dangling hair like melted wax. Dark drips still fell, but so drained was her corpse that her skin was the hue of lard. She looked to be of middle years, perhaps forty. She had been dead less than an hour. As far as he could tell in such a condition, Symonne D'Aubray – if this was she – had not been the most handsome of women, in either face or build. The observation was unkind but he could not help making it.

Carla was fair.

The contrast would not have been lost on those who had done this.

Most windows on all three floors had been broken, which at six panes per casement was a lot of glass; yet little had fallen into the street. Only slings, or an unlikely band of arquebusiers, could have reached so high and done such damage. No sound came from within. He scanned the houses either side of the street, but the

Black Death might have swept them clean for all the signs of life they showed.

He rode through a side alley to the courtyard and garden at the back of the house. Here, too, all the windows had been smashed inwards. The only reason to break so much glass – and to do so had required many hands – would be to create chaos, to distract the defenders while one or more intruders forced an entrance. And there: one window in the first storey was not smashed; but gaped wide open. The main back door was also open but showed little damage, the lock none at all. It had been opened from inside.

The lower half of the door was streaked with crusted blood. A gelatinous pool, now trampled, had hardened on the outer steps below. The bloodstains puzzled him.

He dismounted and left Clementine to crop grass and white cabbage. The trampled dirt of the vegetable patch was carved with the tracks of several two-wheeled carts. There were no hoof prints. A palliasse lay on the ground: Altan's, he guessed.

He drew his dagger and approached the back door.

On the flagstones that bordered the house he noticed a raw lump. He crouched and poked the lump with his dagger. It was a man's severed cock and scrotum. One ball was missing, though its owner must have been past caring. He noted the heavy knocker on the door, and again the congealed puddles, the vertical stains. Someone had been hung from the knocker and left to bleed.

He stepped inside and stopped and listened. He heard nothing. Several planks had been pulled from the floor just within. They were not to be seen. To his left a door led down into a cellar; to his right was a large kitchen suite that spanned the depth of the house. Glass on the floors. Pantry, cupboards and shelves ransacked and emptied. There wasn't so much as a wooden spoon to be seen. A little flour had been spilled but not scattered. Burglars who considered flour and spoons worth stealing.

He thought about that. It was easier than thinking about Carla. He walked down the hallway where numerous feet, many of them shoeless, had trampled through a mass of blood. The blood clung to the soles of his boots. Like that spilled by the back door, it was black and the consistency of warm tar. In the front hallway lay a great deal more blood, this as thick as cold gravy, also well trodden but more recently spilled by perhaps an hour. Glass. Glass. Bare feet hard enough to brave it. His own feet trod on a lead musket ball. He picked it up and found it distorted by impact but without any trace of burned powder. Slings. He had faced them in the grain riots in Adrianople; cheap, but in expert hands or massed attack, deadly enough.

He examined at closer quarters the body he had seen from the street.

It was Altan Savas. He was set in a great pool of jellied gore like an edible figurine on a confectioner's fancy. Rats, as if thus tempted, squatted on his thighs and chest and nibbled at his wounds. Tannhauser kicked them away. He sheathed his dagger.

He had expected to find Altan dead since the moment he had seen Symonne D'Aubray bleeding from the window. Altan had not been a man to abandon a breach, nor anything else to which he had committed himself. When Tannhauser had bought him from the Sea Knights, in Malta, there had been other janissary slaves in the dungeons of Saint Anthony. Instinct had prompted the choice, that and his broader faith in Serbian mettle. He recalled the words that had sealed their understanding, when Altan, after brief reflection, had said, *If, as the price of freedom, you expect me to forswear the Prophet, blessed be his name, you'd best leave me chained to an oar.*

Red Dawn Rising was his Turkish name. In a bloody dawn he had died.

Their friendship had been the more profound for being without much warmth. Altan had only ever smiled at him after a fight, when they were cleaning the blood from their weapons. During the recent wars, when the countryside had been scourged by rabid bands of mercenaries and deserters, there had been more than a few occasions for such smiles. Looking at his corpse, Tannhauser felt pain.

He studied Altan's injuries.

Altan had been shot in the left eye at close range, with a pistol. His face was blackened and peeled by the powder burns. His skull was otherwise intact. A number of knife wounds were well grouped to pierce the heart. He had been stripped of his clothes and weapons. Large patches of skin had been incised and peeled from his thighs. His killers had taken his janissary tattoos for trophies. They had not taken his privates; but even among killers, to cut off a man's pizzle took the coldest blood.

Tannhauser guessed that Altan had captured a forward scout, mutilated him and strung him from the back door to deter and unnerve further intruders. Several candle stubs burned on the hallway floor. There had been light to fight by. A killing floor and choke point. Altan had been ready for those who had come through the broken door and, judging by the quantity of blood, he had killed several. Attacking from the street, Tannhauser himself would not expect to get the better of Altan, and never to get close enough to shove a pistol in his face. His killer must have come from behind. A single shot at close range had taken him unawares, probably intended for the back of his head.

Tannhauser looked up the staircase.

The stink of burned hair. Glass and blood and silence.

Altan Savas had died to protect Carla, but in dying he had failed. Murderers, rapists and thieves came to murder, rape and steal. From what he has seen so far, these villains set few bounds upon their appetites.

Carla would be up there. Nude, dead, probably mutilated, perhaps eviscerated of her babe. Raped. Trophies taken. He had often seen women used thus, in every corner of the world. Just such a woman – his mother – formed the floor of his memory, for he had no memories at all that predated the last time he had seen her. In that image she was splayed naked and defiled on the flanks of a dead horse. He thought of Amparo, whom he had loved, and then he tried not to think of her, for his last image of her, too, was of an atrocity he had failed to prevent.

Now Carla was a victim of the curse the stars must have laid upon him in the moment of his birth. It was the price cosmic justice had demanded in advance for the crimes he had been destined to commit. Carla was gone. He had no fears for her soul. What would be the fate of the soul of her child unborn? He did not know.

He was alive and they were not.

And now he was free.

No longer would he have to endure the toil of love, to carry its vast weight, to live with the fear that accompanied it. He would no longer have to miss her, only mourn her. The relief that flooded through him revolted him, but he could not deny it. He would love no more. He would lose no more. He had lost too many. He felt no pity for himself. He neither needed it nor deserved it, nor would it profit him, for whom did it ever? Neither would he suffer. By an act of will he would keep suffering at bay, for its purposeless ubiquity had come to disgust him. Carla was dead and he was free and he would feel free. Free to join hands with the Devil and dance his pavane. Free to cast aside tenderness, hope and joy, and all other trappings of weakness. Free to wander the desert places of the world and of his own inner realms. Free to become what Fate, time and again, had invited him to be: a beast at last unburdened from the pain of being a man.

The staircase was still there.

So was whatever he would find at the top.

He didn't move.

'Master?'

Tannhauser was leaning forward, hands on his knees, and breathing hard. He had not noticed. He looked up and out into the street and saw Grégoire and Juste. They were concerned. For him. He laughed an ugly laugh. The candle stumps guttered.

'Master?' Their fears for his sanity were plain.

'Clementine is at the back. Give her water. Juste, come here.'

Juste stopped at the edge of the maroon pudding setting on the floor.

Tannhauser waved his thumb. 'Use the back door.'

Juste disappeared at a run.

Did he need to send the boy upstairs?

Could he not go himself?

He could; but in matters of squeamishness he was decades beyond the need to test himself. He had enough pictures of dead women graved into the marrow of his mind. If he saw Carla dead he feared it would unhinge his reason. He was in the killing vein. They had murdered his wife. His unborn child. At that thought – and with the thought a sudden cascade of sounds and visions: her voice at daybreak, her face in the throes of passion, the laughter she reserved for his follies – his every muscle clenched in a paroxysm. He thirsted for absolute destruction, for absolute waste, absolute chaos, absolute violence and annihilation. He would cleanse himself of the clinging filth of his humanity.

'I will wade through rivers of blood.'

'I brought you some water, sire.'

Tannhauser turned. He nodded and took the cup. He drank.

He should go upstairs alone. He decided he would not.

'Juste, I need your help. I want you to go upstairs and look all about, and I want you to tell me everything you see. Everything. It will be ugly. Can you do that?'

Juste studied him. 'Yes, sire.'

'There'll be corpses but you've seen your share. To you they are strangers.'

'You don't want to see your wife dead.'

'Not just dead.'

'I understand. I saw dogs eating my brothers.'

They looked at each other.

'Thank you,' said Tannhauser.

Juste skipped up the stairs through the tinkle of glass. He stopped.

'A man lies on the landing, stabbed many times. He is old, older than you. A servant or gardener, I should say. He has rough hands.'

'Good lad. Go on.'

Tannhauser waited. His conscience nagged him to follow. His gut swilled with dread. His mind, aware of the precipice on which it stood, advised patience.

'I am in the parlour. Dead boys, two dead boys, stabbed many times. A girl, stabbed, stabbed, stabbed. My God. All dead.'

For a moment Juste didn't speak.

'At the window is a woman. Her ankle is tied to a golden rope. And the rope to the window post. She is quite old, I think, but not very old, it's hard to tell. She has been cut, everywhere, and her –'

'I saw her. Madame D'Aubray, I presume. Anyone else?'

'No. Three dead children, the servant, the hanging woman. It is very empty. No carpets, no paintings, no furniture. Not a stick left.'

'Good. Go to the next room.'

'It's a bedchamber.'

Tannhauser waited. He drove down his nausea by seeking some thread of logic in these events. The thieves had come for plunder, to kill some wealthy Huguenots. Why not? He had killed and robbed one himself hardly an hour since. But why this house? Their determination in pursuit of such profit as this house offered did not ring true. Burglars wanted easy pickings, not a battle; a defenceless house, not one adorned with the castrated corpse of one of their fellows.

He looked again at Altan's body. His killer had breached the upper rear window during the storm of breaking glass. A daring man. A dangerous man. A man whose design – a clever one – had hinged on his own courage.

The attack must have been synchronised with the assault on the Hôtel Béthizy – signalled by the tocsin – which would not have been possible without forewarning. From some confederate in the militia or the palace guard? The militia had not been thus coordinated; they were late and even now confused. How much forewarning? To prepare an attack on this scale, even with a disciplined crew to call on – to be ready to haul away furniture, clothes and flour, in the dead of Saturday night – would require at least, what? Four hours?

No one could have taken Altan Savas the way they did without foreknowledge, not only of his presence but of his ability. Had they been mere burglars, even had they come by the score, Tannhauser would have found Altan building a wall with their bodies. To design and execute so elaborate a siege, the killers must have had detailed intelligence of the building. It could not possibly have been improvised.

More than hours. Perhaps days.

Tannhauser had worked beyond the law, in Messina, Venice, Istanbul. He could put himself in the shoes of the Parisian criminal brotherhoods. By now every criminal in the city was rubbing the drink from his eyes and staring at the chance of a lifetime. The best would have got wind of the attack on the Huguenots before the police or the militia. Perhaps even before the palace guard. Their people were the lowly – and thus the invisible – who enabled the Louvre to function, who disposed of the royal stool, whose women were raped by the Duc d'Anjou to demonstrate his manliness to his mother. Even so, this crew had sacked the Hôtel D'Aubray, against stiff opposition, and vanished before day had broken. And while there had been booty in this house, hundreds of others offered richer plunder at lower risk.

This house had been targeted.

This was not a random crime exploiting chaos.

This was not bad luck.

Neither were the delays that had prevented him from getting here sooner.

The appointments he had kept but hadn't made.

Carla had not been murdered; she had been assassinated.

The only alternative was that Madame D'Aubray and her children were the targets, and Carla an unfortunate bystander. But that did not explain why he and Orlandu had spent the night in a cell. Or why Orlandu had been shot in the back.

The assassins had been instructed by someone with advanced knowledge of the plan to kill Coligny and his supporters, a decision that, according to Arnauld, had not been made until late the previous evening. That decision was merely the final assent of a weak king. The plot itself could have been concocted long before; there were sufficient liars and schemers for the job. In either event, this plot against Carla had depended on intelligence from the inner councils of the Louvre.

He looked up to find Juste coming down. He was pale and scared.

'The chamber has been plundered too – even the mattress is gone –'

'You found a dead woman in the chamber.'

'Yes, sire.'

'Tell me everything.'

'Everything?'

'Is she old? Young?'

'She is not so young, but not old. A normal age for a woman. Thirty years?'

Carla was thirty-five. 'What colour is her hair?'

Juste frowned and looked upwards to think. He shook his head in apology.

'I don't know. There was a pot on her head.'

'A pot?'

'A chamber pot.'

Tannhauser's jaws clenched. Juste retreated one step upwards.

'I took it off, but there was blood, too, a lot. Should I look again?'

'Is she pregnant?'

Juste hesitated. His eyes darted this way and that.

'Is she carrying a baby inside her? Is her belly swollen?'

'Yes, I think so.'

'You think?'

'Yes, she is pregnant, perhaps.' Juste's pallor turned red. 'That is, I don't know for sure. I can't. She is stabbed, cut –' He made vague gestures about his torso.

'Did you see the baby? Did they cut it out of her? Speak, lad.'

'No, I don't know. I don't know! I am sorry.'

Tannhauser took a breath. 'I'm not angry with you. Please. Go on.'

'She is – kneeling, her face down. There are – things – stuck in her.'

'Things?'

'A chair. The leg of a chair, but the chair is still complete – '

Juste covered his mouth, perhaps to stop his words; perhaps his nausea.

Tannhauser turned away. He couldn't let the boy see his face. He was in the wrong. He should go and look for himself. Yet he felt less able to do so than before. He reached out to pat Juste. Juste cringed away.

'Juste, I shouldn't have asked you to see that. Forgive me.'

'I am glad to protect you. It wasn't so bad as seeing my brothers.'

'No. That must have been worse.'

He wondered if there were not some small satisfaction in the youngster's heart. If there were, he could hardly blame him. Perhaps that was his own malice speaking.

'Go and wait with Grégoire and Clementine.'

'I didn't go up to the floor above.'

'Were there any other bodies in the chamber?'

'No. Just – the woman. What are you going to do?

'Go and wait outside.'

When Juste was out of sight Tannhauser gave in and vomited into the blood caked around his feet. He felt better. He headed up the staircase.

The dead footman, the parlour of dead children, Symonne D'Aubray strung by the ankle from two yards of gold braid, all as Juste had described. The severed genitals lying by the back door had belonged to no one here. The victims had been cut and stabbed numerous times, their hands and arms slashed, killed with enthusiasm but without skill, without knowledge of the lethal organs and vessels. The man who had killed Altan would have known better. His crew were not seasoned cutthroats, but even among criminals, killers were few.

Tannhauser climbed a narrower stair and found two bedrooms, both stripped. In the second room he smelled Carla. Her natural scent. The perfumes she favoured. He quelled a surge of grief. He was not entitled to it.

Fresh soot lay piled in the hearth and was smeared on the floor. Now that he looked back, it was smeared in small tracks out of the door. An old trick. They had sent a little boy down the chimney to open the door. Obviously, he had failed. He was certain Carla would not have permitted the killing of a child.

He saw a chamber pot, half-full. Grief swelled from his chest and up through the bones of his face, a black tide of sorrow and shame, love indistinguishable from penetrating pain. He leaned out of the broken window to the rear and breathed deep. He had scolded Juste for less. Much less. He had slapped him. He choked on some inchoate sound expelled by his deepest vitals.

'Master?' Juste's voice rose from the garden below. He was afraid.

The sound had been louder than Tannhauser realised. He mastered himself.

'Don't fear,' he called in reply.

He had hoped to find a corpse whose head he might have paraded around the fouler taverns of the Ville; but they had taken their dead away with them. No small chore and surely not to honour their fallen. They – he, the dangerous one – did not want to be identified.

Tannhauser left the room and went down the narrow steps. At the top of the main staircase he hesitated. The bedchamber door was just behind him. He should at least cover her up. But with what? Anguish. Nausea. Rage. He did not know how to do the right thing any more. The very notion of right seemed a lie. He could not bear to see Carla butchered and pierced by the leg of a chair. He did not want to smell her blood, or whatever else they had deposited inside her and on her. He had walked through sacked towns the world over. He had seen such things, the same things, the ugliest things, too many times before. He had heard the laughter, the excitement, the glee, of those who thought they were inventing such atrocities, when in truth they were as old as human time.

He could bear it. He took a step towards the chamber and stopped.

The part of his mind that remained always cold stopped him; the part that knew no feeling and mistrusted the parts that did. He would need his judgement. He would need some bridle on his sanity. The coldness, cold as it was and well as it knew him, had no idea what the violation might provoke.

He could not risk seeing Carla as he would find her in that room.

He did not want to remember her that way.

He did not want such an image to join the others.

He could not blind what little was left of his humanity.
Tears rose in his throat and he was ashamed and amazed.
He swallowed them.
He would find a priest to consecrate her remains.
Then he would see her.
He continued down the stairs and out of the death house into the street.

The Rue du Temple was still quiet. Right by the front door, so incongruous that it had escaped his attention, stood a heavy wooden chair. On the pavement by the chair was a pewter cup near filled with wine. He imagined the master criminal enjoying his triumph. Tannhauser sat on the chair. He picked up the cup and sniffed the wine and took a sip. He swilled out his mouth and spat. Then swallowed a mouthful. It was good. From a pocket sewn into his sword belt he pulled a Jerusalem whetstone and put it in the wine to soak.

Grégoire and Juste returned with a sheet of mouldy hemp.
'We found this in the cellar,' said Juste. 'If it please you –'
'With your permission–'
'We'll cover your wife with it. And take away the chair.'
'And say a prayer for her.'
'I would like that,' said Tannhauser. 'Thank you.'
'You should say a prayer for her, too,' said Juste.
'Carla needed many things from me and did not get them.'
He furrowed his brow at a trembling mass concealed in Grégoire's shirt.
'Are we truly your hardy, stout and resolute mates?' asked Juste.
'What have you got there?' said Tannhauser.
'We found this is in the cellar, too, master.'
Grégoire produced a small, ugly but muscular mongrel by the scruff of its neck. It panted rapidly, eyes bright with shock, its mouth a toothy rictus. Its body was scorched in a patchwork of singed hair and raw skin.
'Can we keep him?' asked Juste.

Tannhauser said, 'He will slow us down.'

'Master, he can run faster than us, or even Clementine, I'm sure.'

'He can guard us when we sleep,' said Juste.

'He's very brave.'

'I don't approve,' said Tannhauser. 'He stinks.'

'We'll wash him,' said Grégoire.

'You won't smell him from high on Clementine's back,' said Juste.

'So you're in this together.'

Tannhauser fished the whetstone from the wine and drew the dagger he had stolen. He sighted down the edges and decided to lower the angle. The boys stepped back.

'What are you going to do?' asked Juste.

'I'm going to cut new edges on this blade.'

The morning light revealed an inscription on the dagger's ricasso. On one side: *Fiat justitia*. On the other: *et pereat mundus*. He showed it to Juste.

'Can you read this for me?'

'*Let justice be done – though the world perish.*'

Tannhauser drew the blade across the whetstone. The feel of grit on steel soothed him. As the material world around him dissolved, these materials at least he could believe in. The hard honed by the hardest and greased by wine.

Grégoire tried to put the dog back in his shirt but its wriggling betrayed him.

'Does that poor cur have a name?'

'We didn't want to name him too soon, in case you decided to kill him,' said Juste.

'Because if you gave him a name his death would make you more sad?'

They both nodded.

'You protect your feelings at his expense. A dog without a name may be easier to lose, but he's also easier to kill.'

The boys looked at each other in alarm. They looked at the blade.

'Did not the naming of Clementine transform her from a cart-horse into a myth?'

They both opened their mouths at once but he stopped them.

'I never killed a dog in all my life. Carla doted on them. I'm simply giving you a lesson. I'm hurt that you think me capable of such a deed.'

'We are very sorry, master.'

He wondered if his dead and unborn child had been a daughter or a son. Though he had not said so to Carla, he had hoped for a daughter. A daughter needed no instruction in the arts of war or in how to handle the pain of being a man.

'Master, why did they burn the dogs?' asked Juste.

'*Out of the eater, something to eat. Out of the strong, something sweet.*'

'The riddle of Samson,' cried Juste. 'He set fire to the tails of three hundred foxes and burned the crops of the Philistines. And in revenge the Philistines burned Samson's wife —' Juste stopped. 'I'm sorry.'

'And he smote them hip and thigh with a great slaughter,' said Tannhauser.

For a moment he was lost in thought, yet his thoughts were empty.

The boys shuffled as if still uncertain of their dog's fate.

'Cover Carla with her shroud. Go on. And give that cur some water.'

'Juste?' said Grégoire. 'I named Clementine, so you should name the dog.'

They headed for the alley, at once deep in discussion.

Tannhauser watched them out of sight.

The street was still in shade but getting hotter. He sleeved sweat from his brow. He felt choked again, though provoked by which sentiment he could not say, for too many competed for the honour. He drew the blade of the lapis lazuli dagger across the whetstone. He raised the burr and polished the edge with the slurry of wine, grit and metal. He blunted the tip sufficient to render it less inclined to lodge too deep in bone. He sheathed it on his right hip. From his left hip he drew his own dagger.

There was a void inside him that could only be filled with blood. Not knowledge, nor mourning, nor God, nor love; for this yearning for blood was his truth and the measure of his failure as a man. It had taken him a lifetime to learn nothing. Again he must be Death's bondsman. He would solve the riddles. He would descend to the floor of the pit. Yet he knew there was not blood enough in Paris to fill the void, nor in the perishing of the world. Even so, he would spill it. Sooner or later the blood would be his and then, perhaps, he could rest.

He drained the cup of wine.

He sat by the dead dog in the gutter and sharpened his weapons.

He realised that the bells had stopped tolling.

PART THREE

FALSE SHADOWS FOR TRUE SUBSTANCES

CHAPTER ELEVEN

Cockaigne

I n a two-wheeled cart, on a mattress stained with blood, Carla and her unborn child travelled west into the thick of the Ville.

Towards the Yards.

And the kingdom of Cockaigne.

The narrow street was deserted but for the plunder train, five carts in all with Carla's in the van. Grymonde led from the front. The dogs capered among them, their recent indignities forgotten in hope of reward. Papin and Bigot, the brawniest of the scurvies, hauled on the shafts of Carla's cart and grimaced through the trickles of sweat that muddied the dirt on their faces. They had orders not to speak to her and neither glanced in her direction. Antoinette lay curled at Carla's ankles and clung to her skirts, entirely mute. Carla was grateful for her silence; she had nothing to give the girl beyond a chance to survive. Everything else she had, all that she was, she needed for her baby.

Carla would not have felt much more exposed if she had been nude. Her thighs were wet and slimy. Her waters had left dark stains on the pale gold linen of her gown. The ache in her back was severe and she pushed her hands into her loins without finding relief. Grymonde had filled the front of the cart with her baggage, along with cases of musical instruments and Altan's bow and quiver. The mattress was doubled over in the wagon bed, along with a heap of pillows, but despite this gesture she could not get comfortable.

She did not expect to.

At a broader cross street Grymonde raised his hand and the train stopped. He disappeared for what seemed like a long time. His gang maintained a hush that at first surprised her, yet their terror of Grymonde was tangible.

In the quiet she noticed that the whole city seemed still.

She had got used to the ceaseless din that accompanied daylight and its absence was striking. Yet she could sense the hidden multitudes. It was as if the whole city, like the gang, was holding its breath. She was reminded of the first day of the Siege of Malta, when, in the hour before the first battle commenced, a similar eerie quiet had prevailed.

Grymonde came back, scrubbing his palms on his thighs. He waved the caravan forward. As the cart lurched into motion, a fresh contraction tightened on Carla's innards.

She scrambled onto her knees and turned to face the backboard. She clung onto its timbers with both hands. She lowered her head between her arms and sucked for breath. She held her groans inside. The spasm was so inexorable she was certain even her death could not have stopped it. She wondered how long the ordeal would last this time and if it would kill her. Such thoughts would undermine her endurance. Nature squeezed her in its fist. Life strained her sinews to the snapping point. Around her whirled the vortex of cruelty. She had to stop thinking. Thinking was the doorway to panic. To defeat.

She could not allow defeat.

She delivered herself to instinct and a strange exhilaration rose in her chest. The wild horse was running and she sat astride its back. To ride a wild horse, you had to open your heart to its spirit and let it merge with your own. If you fought it, you would be thrown.

The throes faded and left her belly tauter than before. She felt her baby move inside his fast-shrinking chamber, but barely. A rustle of sensation, his last message from within her as all he had ever known rushed away from him, as his world turned upside down and prepared to cast him out into this one. He rode a wilder horse than she did. How brave he was. She was filled with a love so intense she feared it would burst the buckles of her heart. Her love reached out to Mattias and she felt his spirit touch her in reply. For a moment he was in her, as surely as was their child.

He was with her, she knew it.

He was near.

She let out a single sob.

The sob emptied her mind. For a moment she floated in silence. Then she heard the creak of axle and wheels, the grunts and oaths of the hauliers. She felt the heat of the rising sun and the weight of her belly. She relaxed her hold on the wooden board and sat back on her heels. She raised her head and looked into the face of Grymonde.

In daylight his eyes were the loveliest shade of brown she had ever seen. Tawny as an owl's, and they seemed to see as much. They did not belong in that grim and disproportioned visage at all, but were the eyes of a younger man and an older soul, as if his features had been moulded around them by a spiteful sculptor. They looked into hers without blinking. His immense brow was furrowed.

'Don't be afraid,' he said.

'I am not afraid.'

'No. I see that now.'

Grymonde walked along behind the cart, his chest almost touching the backboard, whose width was only narrowly greater than his shoulders. He smiled.

'You'll be in my company for a while. At least until the babe is born and you're feeling fit. So tell me, how should I call you? My lady? Madame? Your Grace? My manners are rough, but I don't want you thinking I have none.'

'You may call me Carla.'

Her answer surprised them both. She didn't question it.

'A good choice. And a strong name. It does you justice.'

'How does one address a king of thieves?'

He laughed and the backboard trembled.

'Grymonde will do. As for king, my army is as you see it, a fistful of ants crawling through a wilderness of tigers.'

'I'd rather liken them to scorpions.'

The cart jarred to a halt and tilted over as one wheel rolled into a pothole. Carla grabbed the sideboards. With no more than a shrug, Grymonde lifted the cart and shoved it on its way with such force that Papin and Bigot struggled not to fall underneath it.

'Scorpions, I like that better,' said Grymonde. 'The scorpion is the symbol of death and these lads live with death. They sleep with him, they eat with him, they have carried him on their backs from the day they were born.'

'So have we all.'

'Indeed. Yet most hear him whisper in their ear but rarely, while for us he hardly ever holds his tongue. If any of these knaves were to dwell on it, none would wager a spoonful of honey on seeing three more summers, and they'd be right. But they do not so dwell. They live for this day, when the honey tastes good, and thus they know more of freedom than the highest in the land. If that be a kingdom, I'll wear its crown.'

Carla saw he needed her to be impressed. She was. More, she was moved.

Yet she said, 'A kingdom of raped women and murdered children?'

His immense brow darkened. He blinked to hide the flames in his eyes. He looked away. Beyond her sight, she sensed the tightening of his fists.

'You don't know,' he said. 'You can't know.'

'I have known horror in the round,' said Carla.

Grymonde looked at her and doubted it. Then doubted his doubt.

'Horror, perhaps. But humiliation? Shame? Disgust at the sound of your own heartbeat?'

'Yes, yes and three times yes.' Her own anger flared. 'I've known them all.'

Grymonde's lips curled and she saw the immense pain and violence within him.

'You were not born to be a whipped dog.'

'Perhaps not. Yet I have been one. If you want my pity, it's yours, take it. But I will not bear your scorn. You know nothing of me. Nothing beyond that which you have seen. My shame is my own. So, too, is my pride, so let your scorpions do their worst. I am ready to face our Maker, and so is my child. Are you?'

Carla put her arms around her belly. Her first born, Orlandu, had been taken from between her thighs, his cord cut, and his yelling, struggling figure stolen from her before she'd even seen his face. She had been sixteen years old. She had not found the courage to even try to find him for twelve years more. Mattias had found him for her, in a sea of blood and tears, and at the cost of the only close friend of her life, Amparo.

She looked full into Grymonde's eyes. She didn't speak.

The rage in his shoulders eased.

'We will say no more on this.'

She doubted it, for his pain was too keen. Somehow, she understood.

'Take me to a surgeon. My word is good, and I swear on my child's life that I will see you richly rewarded when I can do so.'

'Among whipped dogs we have a saying. When the surgeon is called to a woman giving birth, only one will leave the room alive.'

'You would also earn the gratitude of my husband, a man whose loyalty is beyond price.'

'Where is this loyal husband?'

She didn't react to this sting, though it struck deep.

'A midwife, then.'

'If you wish I will leave you here, in the street, with your mattress, your pillows, your fiddle and your Huguenot daughter, and even with a share of our gold to pay your way, a bigger share than any of these poor scoundrels will see. Say it and it will be done. I will set you free.'

She knew he meant it. Reason screamed that she accept his offer.

But the wild horse was running.

'I am already free.'

Carla and Grymonde studied each other.

At length Grymonde raised his hands above the backboard. He held them out.

'Give me your hands. That you might trust me.'

Carla leaned back on her heels. She sensed nothing seductive in his gesture. Despite his intense maleness, she sensed no element of desire in him, not merely for her but for anything. She had lived among men, fighting men, in the closest proximity; she knew that emanation – that look – no matter how well masked by piety or courtesy, or even by impending oblivion. She had watched the faces of men who had never known a woman as they took their last breath, watching her; and even then she had sensed the ghost of their yearning, not for her but for that knowledge. She had known, too, men who loved only men. But Grymonde was like a rose that had no scent. He bewildered her. He terrified her. Yet the trust he asked for sat inside her, waiting to be affirmed, as heavy as her womb. She wondered if her child knew something she did not.

She kept her left hand on her belly, to connect her son to her heart, and offered Grymonde her right. He took it in both of his. They were strong yet soft, padded with flesh. She thought of Mattias's hands, which were strong but as calloused as hooves.

'I am a king of rapists and murderers and liars and thieves, yes. Of the wicked, but not of the worst. Such is our world and as such we both know it.'

'As above so below.'

'As above so below. But there's a difference. Down here, if the wind is blowing right, you get told the truth. So here is the truth. If not for your child the flies would be crawling on your eyes with the others, for I was paid a fine price to see it done. Instead, I take you to a woman who's delivered more sturdy babes than all the surgeons of Paris.'

'May I know her name?'

'Her name is Alice. She is my mother.'

The cart pulled out and turned into a much wider cross street, which Carla believed was Saint-Martin. It ran south towards the bridge and she was surprised to see not a soul. Grymonde held up a hand to halt the carts coming behind them and strode forward past Carla. She heard him mutter instructions to Bigot and Papin, who lowered the shafts and followed him. She shifted around on the mattress. As she watched Grymonde's rolling, top-heavy gait, arms swinging wide from his vast shoulders, his huge head, she saw why Estelle had called Grymonde 'the Infant'. From behind he looked like a giant child who had only recently learned how to walk.

Some twenty paces ahead the Rue Saint-Martin was blocked by a chain strung at waist height between iron hooks bored into the walls of the buildings on either side. Midway along this side of the chain a guard stood leaning on a spear. He wore a white band around his arm and a white cross pinned to his cap. His mouth gaped as Grymonde walked towards him. He lifted the spear across his chest, as one who didn't know what to do with it. He tried to conceal his terror. Grymonde held up his right palm and spoke some greeting she couldn't hear, but the man was not reassured.

Bigot headed for the farther end of the chain and Papin to the nearer. The guard glanced at both and thought he read their intention, but still could do no more than gawp at the monstrous figure rolling towards him. He didn't dare level the spear and he'd left it too late to run. Grymonde skipped forward and as he landed he punched the guard in the stomach and plucked the spear from his hands and tossed it aside. He shoved the winded man to his knees and grabbed the chain as Bigot and Papin unhooked it at either end.

Antoinette raised her head above the rim of the cart. Carla put an arm around her and pulled her face into her skirts. She didn't look away. She wanted to absorb all she could of Grymonde.

Grymonde looped a turn of the chain around the guard's neck and, with a wave of his hand, stepped back. Bigot and Papin took up some slack and each threw his weight backwards like men engaged in a contest of strength. The chain sprang taut and the guard was lifted from his knees as his throat was crushed, yet his arms barely fluttered. He hung there, limp as washing. The youths seemed to take his failure to struggle as proof of some failure of their own, for with oaths and grunts they doubled their efforts. The guard's skull canted over one shoulder and his cap fell off, and his face turned a darker shade of blue, but he remained as dead as before.

Carla felt nothing for him. She had nothing to spare.

Grymonde took the chain and gestured, and the lads eased off and dropped the chain on the ground. Grymonde unwrapped the iron noose and let the guard fall. He picked up the cap and the spear and returned to the cart. Bigot and Papin took the corpse by the ankles and dragged it behind them.

'Take his clothes, if he hasn't beshitted himself – they're not bad quality – and dump him in yonder cesspit. When you come back, make sure you hook up the chain.'

Grymonde put the spear in the cart, taking pains to conceal the blade beneath the baggage where it would not harm the passengers. He examined the inside of the dead man's cap, as if looking for lice. Finding none, he looked at Carla.

'No hangman could've done it neater.'

'That must take a great weight off your conscience.'

He laughed with such coarse gusto that Carla couldn't help but smile.

'Who is this errant husband of yours? If he's not very rich, he must be very gallant to deserve you.'

'I'm not sure Mattias would own to being gallant, though by instinct, and by fate, he is the most gallant man I've ever known. While he seeks riches, he does not count them the measure of a man, nor of woman nor child. I have seen him cast all he had into the flames, without hesitation or regret, to serve a friend. He is at heart a gambler, and life is both his game and his wager.'

She found her voice trembling and stopped.

'Then you're well matched,' said Grymonde.

'I don't know why he didn't come home. I don't even know if he's alive.'

'You were that friend, for whom he cast all into the fire.'

Carla swallowed. She nodded.

'At least that gamble he won,' said Grymonde.

Carla started crying.

She lowered her head and shielded her eyes with one hand. She fought the tears, for she thought them weak and unseemly when she needed to be strong. Yet still they came. Her yearning for Mattias tore through her. He was no longer near. She no longer felt his essence reaching out to her. She felt utterly alone.

She knew the feeling well enough. It had never really left her. It had dominated her youth and young adulthood. In youth her only companions had been music and the deserted shores of Malta, and the sea. Later, in her exile, there had been Amparo and more music; and then Mattias and her son, Orlandu, whom she had lost and in some ways never found, and who now was lost again. Inside her lay her baby, walled off since the last contraction by her own body. She could feel his head, bearing down through her pelvis, stretching her very bones, but she couldn't feel him, not as she had come to feel him and know him these last months. Only now did she see how deep and marvellous that strange companionship had been, and how much she treasured it now that it, too, was gone.

And yet in her power of loneliness, in the knowledge it had brought her of her self, she felt her greatest strength. In her power to be alone, to be utterly alone, lay her freedom. She dried her eyes on her skirts. She looked at Grymonde. He was twisting the cap in his enormous hands but had kept his peace, and for that she was grateful. She smiled.

'The price of belonging is high. I've never been good at paying it.'

He did not know quite what she meant, but did not enquire. He leaned into the cart and put the cap on Antoinette's head, and, though it was too big, he arranged it at so charming an angle, one would hardly know it. The cap was of dark blue serge, the sort an artisan might wear. The white cross was made of strips of paper.

'Today the price of belonging is death,' said Grymonde. 'But not if you belong with me. They won't mistake us for Huguenots. We're poor.'

'The decree is true, then.'

'The bourgeois militia muster in the Place de Grève. The Huguenot grandees are massacred already, down at the Louvre, but they entrusted that job to the Swiss.'

'They can't murder every Huguenot in Paris,' said Carla.

'They can try.'

'Will you?'

'Why?' asked Grymonde. 'Do you care for that crowd of hypo-crites? Or do you only think you should?'

'I'd be a fool to argue moral distinctions with a butcher of women and children, and it's a fool who'd expect me to do so. I will say I care for the company I'm forced to keep.'

'I kill only for profit and to keep what's mine. Does that make you feel better?'

'Slightly.'

'Splendid. Now we must move. We've work to do, and you more than any.'

He beckoned the waiting plunder train and went to stand between the shafts of Carla's cart and took one in either hand. The cart rolled forward a good deal faster than before. Carla felt a rising pang and braced herself on the timbers.

They stopped again at Rue Saint-Denis and Grymonde fell into a parley with two *sergents à verge*. Money was exchanged. One of the *sergents* studied Carla, her hair and fine gown. Should she ask them for help? Their corruption was plain enough. What help, at best, could they offer? An escort to the Louvre? Or a church? Her only contacts at the court were Christian Picart and Dominic Le Tellier. She had warmed to neither, yet could think of no reason they would refuse her; if she could find them. Surely there was some gentleman there on whose mercy she could throw herself. But the Louvre was the scene of a bloodbath and at any moment she might find herself laid low. She didn't know where to find Orlandu; in any case, he knew naught of childbirth or anyone who might. Would Grymonde let her go, as he had said he would, knowing she was witness to his crimes? The panic she most feared flickered to life.

Grymonde stepped away from the *sergents* and walked back along the caravan giving instructions. Papin and Bigot returned from their errand, the latter carrying a bundle of clothes, which he tossed into one of the carts. Two of the carts peeled away. One of the *sergents* went with them. Concealed in the last cart, she knew, were the bodies of those Altan Savas had killed. Grymonde came up to her.

'Carla, your thoughts are plain to see. Swear on your child that you'll not betray my name or this –' he swept a hand across his features '– and I'll tell Sergent Rody to take you where you will. Your baggage, too.'

The choice deepened her panic. She wished he had not offered it.

'Why?'

'Why?' Grymonde pursed cherubic lips. 'A king is entitled to his whims.' He hesitated. 'And perhaps because, even from the beginning, this –' again he gestured to his face '– did not appal you.'

'How would you choose?'

'My choice would favour the babe, which would mean my mother.'

Carla struggled. To choose as her refuge a den of beggars and thieves where, by all accounts, even the King's Guard dared not tread, seemed an act of madness. Yet inside her panic sat the trust she had already invested in this man, this grotesque Infant. Her fear was of abandoning that trust in exchange for the unknown.

'I can't say what other allies you might call on,' said Grymonde, 'or how close you hold them, but whoever they are – especially if they're at the palace – I'd think twice.'

'What do you mean?'

'Someone hired me to kill you and he knew where you could be found.'

Besides Captain Le Tellier and Petit Christian, there must have been a dozen people in the Louvre who had known where to find her; others could have found out.

She said, 'The Louvre.'

'This morning they slaughtered two hundred people after treating them to silk sheets and dinner with the Queen. My caution is well advised.'

'I don't dispute it. I've been too distracted to reason it out.'

She felt another contraction loom and tried to fend it off by an act of will.

'Who hired you?'

She pressed on her belly with both hands.

'Villains from the higher orders act through go-betweens, often several, so they'll not be held to account. I know the man who hired me – and I'll take an oath he holds nothing against you – but not who hired him.'

She wanted to know more but the pang was unstoppable.

She submitted to the pain.

'Take me with you.'

Their way led through a maze of alleys barely wide enough to take the carts. Even had she tried, Carla could not have remembered the way back.

She had entered the Yards.

She was, perhaps, the first of her rank, man or woman, ever to do so.

The Yards were a fabled land, known only by the myths that walled it off from the rest of the world. Myths of depravity and violence, of diseased and feral children, of licentiousness without bounds, a place where a man might be killed for the feather in his hat. Wealthy Parisians loved to boast of these benighted lairs, as if their notoriety somehow enhanced their own prestige, despite that they'd never dared explore even their borders.

As Symonne herself had declared, 'We have the vilest beggars in Christendom.'

The houses were built with no logic beyond the need to create more space in which to shelter from the rain. Each successive storey looked newer than the one below, though all were decrepit, each structure saved from ruin only by means of sagging against its neighbours. Some were absolute hovels, unfit for goats, made out of mud and turf. All stank of the humanity living as tight as bees inside them.

Bigot and Papin pulled while Grymonde walked ahead, driving away flocks of curious children. They climbed a hill. Here and there the alleys opened onto courtyards, and men walked out to stand with fists on hips as the carts rolled by. Their eyes lingered on the booty, and with something close to disbelief on Carla, and she saw Grymonde loosen his shoulders, as if trouble were afoot. He nodded curtly to this man and that, and hailed two of the more sinister by name, who hailed him back, though with little warmth. At length they passed them all without serious challenge.

They descended the hill.

In what seemed like the depths of the labyrinth but which, for all Carla knew, could have been its outermost edge, they swung into another yard and Grymonde stopped.

'Welcome to Cockaigne.'

In general this court was similar to the others, except for an odd house crammed into one far corner. The buildings surrounding the yard were four storeys high, but this one boasted seven, at least of sorts. The upper three floors, if such they could be called, were newer than the rest by centuries, and incomplete. The walls and frames had been thrown together from haphazard lengths of timber purloined from diverse sources. Their windows were glassless, irregular in size, and compressed into eccentric quadrangles by shifts in the structure. The whole of this new edifice had twisted and lurched forward at an alarming angle, prevented from collapse by a cable wound around its middle and anchored out of view, and additionally by a beam, cut from a ship's mast, wedged steeply across the angle to the roof adjoining. It looked as if a summer breeze would send it toppling. In a different circumstance Carla might have laughed at it.

'The tower needs a little work,' admitted Grymonde, though not without pride. 'But you won't be lodged up there.' He lowered the backboard. 'Let me help you.'

'Gladly. I felt like a felon en route to the block.'

'Perhaps next time I'll make you walk.'

'In truth I would have preferred to.'

'Why didn't you say so?'

'You had just murdered four adults and three children. I was your prisoner.'

'That hasn't stopped you flouting me whenever it took your fancy.'

His massive hands took her beneath the armpits and lifted her down.

For an instant her belly touched his. Their faces were close. She smelled his strange smell. His ugliness towered over her. He released her and took a step back.

'The mattress was thoughtful. You've been –' She stopped, for the statement seemed absurd; yet it was true. 'You've been very kind.'

Grymonde grunted.

'It's nothing. Now, I can't be seen bickering with a woman, so you'll excuse me.'

People had emerged from the houses and were swarming about the carts in great excitement. They were gaunt and begrimed, and tattered and tagged, and most stood shoeless in the filth, yet their vitality was immense. Carla felt it flow into her veins. The children, who were many, and the adults, too, stared at her as if at some exotic animal. The glances of the women were less than kind. Grymonde stood beside her and she felt safe. She stretched and though her thigh bones ached, her back pain eased. The crowd hummed with talk, yet none dared fall on the plunder as they wished to. She felt Antoinette take her hand and she squeezed it.

Grymonde raised his arms.

'All hail a mighty day for the people of Cockaigne.'

He was rewarded with rowdy hurrahs. He grinned.

'We have food and fiddles, and wassail and wine, and sugar and silks galore, and all of it to be taken today – for there may be no tomorrow.'

'No tomorrow!' shouted a woman.

The cry was taken up.

'No tomorrow!'

Grymonde turned to look at Carla, as if to say, *Now do you understand?*

She was strangely moved, in part by the joy of the people, in part that her feelings should matter to him. She nodded.

'What's the girl's name?'

'Antoinette.'

Grymonde turned back to the gathered.

'First make welcome these our new sisters. Carla, the lady from the south, though she needs nor pomp nor pride, so don't be timid. And Antoinette, another orphan to be fostered by our plenty. As Jesus himself said, *Suffer the little children to come unto me.*'

Carla wondered if this was a cruel jibe and looked at his face, but it was not. The man was quite able to marry viciousness and virtue with perfect inner harmony.

Grymonde clasped his hands and became grave.

'Some of our brothers will not be coming back. The teeth of the young lions were broken in the fight with a dreadful foe. We will wake their souls till morning; we will mourn them as we feast. Let laughter and full bellies bid them farewell. Thus, too, will we hallow our dead enemy, aye, for Solomon in all his glory ne'er faced so savage a beast. Let his name be spoken and heard, that he might become a legend among us. Carla?'

He turned to Carla and for a moment she was taken aback to be given the stage.

'Speak up. It's your champion we seek to honour.'

'Altan Savas.'

Her throat tightened. It was true. Altan had died for her. She raised her voice.

'His name was Altan Savas. Which means *Red Dawn Rising.*'

'You see?' Grymonde smiled at the crowd. 'Who but Fate could have sent such a man to test our mettle? Altan Savas. *Red Dawn Rising.* And a right bloody dawn it was, too.'

''Twas Grymonde who slew him with his own hand!' cried Bigot.

'Knee-deep in blood they stood!' added Papin.

Grymonde tapped his own chest with an enormous finger.

'This old cutthroat didn't stand alone or he'd have torn my lungs out.' He saluted his comrades. 'Not only was this Altan Savas a warrior of uncanny prowess, but, as you will see, his very hide was carved with devils and writ with secret charms and magic spells.'

Grymonde gestured to Bigot, who reached into the cart and brandished two broad strips of fresh meat. On one side the strips shone dull red with clotted blood and tissue. On the other they were inked with Arabic script and janissary tattoos. Mattias had such markings on his arms and thighs, as had Altan Savas.

The crowd gasped and murmured and some made the Sign of the Cross.

Carla turned away in revulsion. She looked at Grymonde.

He avoided her eyes in favour of his audience.

'But the telling of heroic tales can wait until our table is laid. We've a pig on the way to enhance these excellent viands, so save your appetites. Till then, we've much to do. So have at the plunder and clear the carts for we'll need them. But not this one.'

Grymonde pointed to Carla's baggage.

Carla, still disgusted, shook her head.

'No. Let them have it. The only thing I value is my gambo violl.'

'Well said, well said,' murmured Grymonde. His eyes were alive with the passion of his harangue, and again she questioned his sanity. 'Which is this gambo violl?'

'The largest of the cases.'

He plucked the case from the bunch and waved it aloft.

'Carla says make free with her riches. She, too, believes there is no mine or thine.'

'Can I keep my recorder?' asked Antoinette.

'Take it,' said Grymonde, 'before some other lays claim. But if they do, do not cry.'

The thieves' triumph seemed all but over and Carla would soon meet her midwife. She didn't want to do so both bedraggled and empty-handed. She needed a token of respect.

'Grymonde, let me see inside that valise.'

Grymonde stuck his arm among those already ransacking the baggage, swatting several aside. Carla turned and bent to lean against the cart as the next contraction began.

She felt a fresh trickle of fluid between her thighs. Her throes went unremarked as the people of the yard fell upon the spoil. The surge of pain, the relentless and ungovernable flexing of her own strength, encompassed her being. The pain unlocked something inside her and she was flooded with a love which was hardly less crippling.

She gave her love to her baby and hoped the pain was hers alone. At length the spasm passed but left her drained, breathless, close to a faint. She took a moment to collect herself. She was shocked. So early in the labour and already her energies were taxed. She had believed herself well prepared. She had done this twice before. But her body told her this time would be harder. She was older. She was weaker. All the more reason to concentrate on the birth and nothing else.

She straightened.

'Hugon,' said Grymonde, 'carry these for Carla.'

A gaunt, delicate lad who had not been on the raid ran over to her. He was naked to the waist, like many of the boys, and his skin was the colour of mother-of-pearl, his muscles vivid. He had two knife scars on his chest. Delicate was the wrong word. Perhaps she had landed on it because she found him beautiful.

Hugon bowed to her, his eyes on hers, and she acknowledged the courtesy. He took the violl and valise from Grymonde, and looked at her again, without any expression she could name. Yet while the other denizens were merely curious, from Hugon she felt something like a plea, as if he were stranded and hoped that somehow, against all reason, she could help him.

Grymonde offered her his arm.

'Come, I invite you to my home. There's no sounder haven in all the Ville.'

Carla laid one hand on Grymonde's forearm, but put no weight on it. Her strength rebounded. She had given up trying to walk with any semblance of grace some weeks before, but as they walked to the crazed house she held her chin high.

Hugon followed them.

The door was open. To her surprise she caught a breath of sweet scents from within. They reminded her of the great ward of the Hospital in Malta. Thyrus wood or something similar. Grymonde climbed the doorstep, then remembered his manners and turned, and stepped back down, and invited her with a sweep of his arm.

Carla stopped and looked for Antoinette.

The girl was engaged in a struggle for her recorder with a boy near twice her size. ·

'Antoinette, let him keep it,' called Carla.

Antoinette aimed a kick at the boy and missed and let go of the recorder. She shouted something at the boy and ran to Carla, on the verge of tears of fury. At the sight of Grymonde she clenched her lips. Carla squeezed her shoulder.

'I will get you another. What did you say to him?'

'I told him I would get it back later.'

'You were very brave.'

'Maman told us we must always be ready to face God.'

'She was right, we must, but not for the sake of a recorder.'

'Let her stay out here with them,' said Grymonde. 'She'll not come to any great harm, and she can always knock on this door.'

Carla rearranged the cap on Antoinette's head.

'What do you want to do?'

Antoinette looked back at the festive gaiety investing the carts.

'If I may, I'll stay out here for a while.'

'Very well. Remember, you can come to me any time you want.'

As Antoinette headed back to reclaim her instrument, Carla glimpsed a skinny, wild-haired figure, half-concealed at the mouth of the alley that gave onto the yard.

It was Estelle, the Rat Girl who had fallen down the chimney.

The girl was naked. Her solitude was pitiful. Carla was certain Estelle was staring at her, and for the first time since arriving in Cockaigne she felt afraid.

'Look, I believe that's Estelle.'

Grymonde turned. 'I knew she'd come.'

Of all the horrors of the morning, none had affected Carla more keenly than Estelle's humiliation and banishment. She didn't know why; only that it was so.

She said, 'You used her cruelly.'

'Heat of the moment. I had to set examples. As I recall, I was provoked to do so.'

Carla was too annoyed by the smirk on his face to contest this detail.

'Anyway, I didn't want her to see –' he shrugged '– the things we had to do.'

'I am amazed to hear you own to such scruples.'

Carla turned back to the yard. Estelle had gone.

'Call her back,' said Carla.

'She shouldn't have been with us anyway. Joco brought her.'

'Send someone after her.'

'She'll be back when she smells roasting pork. She knows I love her.'

'I don't think she does.'

'She's a dangerous little vixen when she wants to be. And she bears you no affection. I saw the way she looked at you.'

'I do not ask for my own benefit. The girl has thrown her lot in with rats, in preference to humans. That's how little she knows of your supposed love.'

Grymonde bristled but on this point could not contradict her.

'There's no one here could catch La Rossa, unless she wants to be caught.'

Carla's instincts were insistent.

'In her heart that's exactly what she wants.'

'Papin!'

Carla recoiled from the bellow. Papin almost fell from the cart.

'La Rossa lurks in the alley. Send someone to fetch her.'

'Estelle?' said Papin. 'What for?'

'Tell her we forgive her! Tell her we love her!'

'We do?'

'Send someone she doesn't want to stab, if such can be found.'

Grymonde turned back to Carla and bowed, not without mockery.

'Thank you,' she said.

'It is my pleasure to serve.'

A woman's voice rasped forth from inside the house.

'Get on in here and give us a kiss, you dirty devil.'

Carla looked through the door but saw only piles of rummage in the gloom.

A wild cheer erupted, prompted by the discovery of a barrel of wine.

'Hellfire, what've you been up to? Aside from evil?'

The voice from within was common, unvarnished and loud.

'Wouldn't you just like to know, Mam,' returned Grymonde in kind.

'If this old girl has to come out there she'll make you plant that kiss on her arse.'

Grymonde beamed with pride.

'And who's that you've got with you? Has she no better manners?'

Carla took a breath, smoothed her stained gown, and steeled herself.

'And now, with your permission,' said Grymonde, 'I will present my mother.'

CHAPTER TWELVE

On the Vertex

The nearest church was ancient and much neglected. Tannhauser had passed it on the way from the Place de Grève. Behind it he could see the spire of the priory of Sainte-Croix, but he was not in the mood to talk his way to the top of a ladder of monks.

The church was small and of plain rectangular design, without a transept or chapels. It was empty but for two old women praying. Two decrepit wooden rails either side of the nave separated the narthex from the pews. On the left of the narthex was a stone baptismal font, the sight of which sickened him. There was only one other exit, a door in the wall of the southern aisle just short of the raised chancel, where burned a red sanctuary lamp strung from a chain. He found the door ajar. He followed a corridor past a locked sacristy and through a second door, also ajar, into a small adjoining house. In the front room he found a priest bibbing wine for breakfast.

The priest wore nose-glasses. On the table before him were sheets of paper, quill and ink. He looked to be around forty, with nothing to cover the dome of his head but memories. His face suggested a bilious disposition. He was tall and thin, as if, apart from wine, life offered little to please him. He did not notice Tannhauser enter.

'Mattias Tannhauser, Chevalier Magistral of the Order of Saint John the Baptist.'

The priest's reaction was of such blind fear that he spilled most of the wine down the front of his cassock. He jumped to his feet and clapped one hand to his chest.

'Forgive this intrusion, but if you are the curé I must ask of you a sacred and urgent service.'

On the wall behind the priest was a portrait of a man in the red hat and robes of a cardinal, who sat on a gilded chair with an altar boy standing at his side. Despite the artist's efforts to flatter his subject, the cardinal's features evoked those of an ageing madam in a waterfront brothel. Though not explicit, the staging of the piece suggested that the cardinal was fondling the boy's arse, and the boy's expression lent credence to this interpretation. When he looked back down at the priest, Tannhauser noted a distinct resemblance to both cardinal and boy, as if the one had matured into the other.

The priest removed his nose-glasses and took in the fresh blood-stains on the Maltese Cross. He concluded that, despite general appearances, this brute was unlikely to kill him, mopped the wine from his chin and gave a short bow.

'Good morning, chevalier. Father Philippe La Fosse.'

Tannhauser stared at the priest for a while. His mind was blank.

'How can I help you?' asked La Fosse. 'Chevalier?'

'My wife has been murdered.'

'Your wife? I am horrified –'

'She lies not far from this church, indeed it's possible she attended Mass on recent occasions. She may even have discussed a baptism. She was in late pregnancy.'

The priest's brow furrowed with the bland compassion required by his vocation.

'I recollect no such woman, I'm afraid. And this is not the parish church, so I doubt she would have come here. Sainte-Cécile is a chapel attached to the priory of Sainte-Croix, though it is open to the public on Sundays and Solemnities.'

'Be that as it may, I'd be grateful if you'd rouse some servants to fetch her body here, at once. A woman with a strong stomach to wash her. I want a good stout coffin lined with lead. I'll be taking her home and it's far. A decent shroud, the appropriate sacraments, a requiem, so forth. To rest in a church would comfort her soul and keep her from further desecration. The rats. It would also comfort me.'

La Fosse fluttered his fingers. His sympathy was genuine enough, but not so deep as to encompass unforeseen labours. He produced a kindly but regretful smile.

'This is rather a shabby old place, and Paris hardly lacks for splendid churches –'

'Christ was not impressed by splendour. Neither was Carla.'

'As for a lead-lined coffin –'

'This is a fat parish in a fat city. There are dozens of such coffins to be had. The rich fancy it improves their chances of Paradise. I just want to avoid the smell of her rotting.' He dropped half an ounce of Spanish gold on the table. 'For that I could buy a coffin lined with silver.' He added a second double pistole. 'For the poor box.'

The difficulties vanished as quickly as the gold.

'I will see to it personally. For a modest donation the priory provides a most beautiful six-voice requiem. Exquisite boys. They would break the stoniest heart.'

Tannhauser's heart was broken enough.

'An honest man mourns without witnesses.'

'As you wish.'

Tannhauser thought of Carla's love for music.

'No. A chant may suit after all. I'll reconsider these details when I return.'

'Where will my servants find your good wife?'

'In a bedchamber on the first floor of the Hôtel D'Aubray.'

La Fosse turned a shade redder. He leaned one hand on the table.

'Your wife was the guest of Madame D'Aubray?'

La Fosse was shocked into frantic cogitation. Tannhauser could read none of it. Priests hid their thoughts as a matter of habit. La Fosse reclaimed his bland composure.

'May I ask why your wife was there?'

'She was invited to the royal wedding, by the Queen Mother. She was lodging with Madame D'Aubray, who was also invited.'

'This is tragic. Tragic. Please, accept my heartfelt condolence.'

'Carla is covered with canvas, in a bedchamber on the first floor. Your servants will find other bodies but they're not my concern. Nor yours, unless charity so moves you.'

'Others?'

'Madame D'Aubray is hanging from a window. Her children and a manservant are inside. Carla's bodyguard, too, but I'll deal with his remains.'

With these further details, La Fosse put a hand to his brow.

'Are you listening, Father?'

'Yes, forgive me. I knew Symonne D'Aubray. This is appalling. A perfect gentlewoman. Her children, too? God's mercy. When did this happen?'

'I'd say two hours ago, while I was detained by events at the Louvre.'

'The Louvre?' He reappraised Tannhauser's eminence. 'The Protestant conspiracy? The attempt to assassinate the King?'

'There was no such conspiracy nor any such attempt.'

'But they've tried more than once before –'

'Tonight we conspired against them.'

The priest's eyes revisited the blackening stains on Tannhauser's chest. He essayed an unctuous smile then abandoned it for fake woe.

'What a terrible loss you have suffered in the service of God and the Crown –'

Tannhauser clenched his teeth. He wanted to stab the priest.

'I serve neither God nor the Crown. I serve no one.'

'I see.' La Fosse stared down at his thumbs.

'I do not even serve any purpose.'

Tannhauser put one hand over his face and squeezed his temples.

His chest felt tight. He could hardly remember why he had come here, why he was talking to this black-frocked lickspittle. Rage filled him. The rage was a skin stretched thin over other, more painful, sentiments he was less well equipped to contain. His mind was at war. Yet even war had the illusion of structure and intent, of outcomes to be feared or desired. His mind had none. He did not know where his next step should take him, still less where it would. Thoughts crowded at the borders of the emptiness inside him, held at bay because any one of them might unman him.

'Is the babe doomed to Limbo?' Tannhauser blurted the question without the awareness of having conceived it. 'Our child had a soul. Surely the journey from the womb to the world does not in itself create the soul. Such a journey is long and dangerous. Only a soul would have the courage to attempt it.'

He dropped his hand. He clenched his fists by his thighs. He looked at La Fosse.

'I know the Church has little mercy on babes who die without baptism. I baptised our first child, for that reason. But if our new babe was killed before it was born, it must be innocent of the crime of being born, which – and here I will agree with Mother Church – is the greatest crime of all. And if our child was thus unstained by Original Sin, wherefore should she, or he, go to Hell?'

He felt the urge to take La Fosse by the throat and squeeze him blue.

'Would you send such a soul to Hell?'

'No, no. Never. Of course not. Please, chevalier, don't hurt me.'

'To bring Carla back – even to have arrived in time to die in her defence – I would sacrifice every human being in Paris. She would damn me for the deed, perhaps for the thought. Yet I would take the axe and drag them to the block one by one, just to see her smile again.'

La Fosse cowered from his bloodstained ravings.

Tannhauser reined himself in.

'Forgive me, Father. Thank you for taking charge of her remains. Adieu.'

He turned away. He felt obliged to give a reason.

'I'll be back later. I have to recover my guns.'

'Brother Mattias, wait.'

Tannhauser felt La Fosse's hand on his arm. He looked at him. His near departure had reassured the priest. He was no longer terrified.

'Make your confession and I will hear it, for it will lighten the load you are carrying. Then you may take Holy Communion. Let the Body of Christ salve your wounds.'

'Father, since I entered this city not a day ago I have killed six men who, in truth, I need not have killed at all. I advised the King's first counsellor, with powerful and subtle logic, to slaughter the Huguenot elite. Their blood is on my hands. I neglected my wife and our unborn babe and both lie butchered and defiled. And there are murders yet to be accomplished, whose victims are yet unknown to me, which await my labours. These sins and more I claim and confess, some with shame, some with bitter remorse. But while I would accept your blessing, I cannot accept absolution, because most of my sins I repent not in the least particular.'

'Do you think all sins absolved by the Church are sincerely repented?'

'Those sins are not on my conscience.'

'Such rare scruples do you credit.'

'Carla loved her Faith. She honoured its sacraments. In memory of her, so will I. I won't mock them in search of a comfort I do not deserve and will not find and do not need.'

'Then I will give you my blessing, but first, stay awhile. Take some wine.'

'I will take some information. The D'Aubray house was sacked by ruffians so low they stole a sack of flour as if it were saffron. They headed due west. I am a stranger here. From what district might such villains hail?'

'Brother Mattias, I beg you, spare yourself any thought of seeking justice for this horrible crime, for you'll never find it. Let God punish them, for His vengeance will be terrible. Mourn your wife. Take consolation in the works of Our Lord.'

'You must have some notion.'

'There are a dozen notorious enclaves of absolute lawlessness scattered all over the city, each a tangled knot of blind alleys and secret courtyards known only to its denizens and jealously guarded by the same. These wretches live like – well, one cannot even compare them to animals, for what vermin would peddle a boy's virtue for a flagon of parsnip wine? – and in conditions of unspeakable degradation, godlessness and violence.'

Tannhauser walked to the table and poured wine from a jug. He drank.

'As to the culprits you seek? No one would betray them to you.

Even if you had the villain's very name, as well might you plunge your hand into an anthill to find the ant that had stung you.'

'Which of these hellholes are best placed for commerce with the court?'

'You can't mean the Louvre?'

'We know who pays for the parsnip wine.'

'Whatever I know is gleaned from gossip and can't be trusted.'

'Gossip will do.'

La Fosse struggled, as if making a decision he felt was unwise.

'North of Les Halles – the market quarter – lies the worst such den in the city. The Yards, so called. It occupies the hill just south-west of Porte Saint-Denis, and more or less due west from the Hôtel D'Aubray.'

'The Yards.'

It sounded as good a place as any to shake hands with the Devil.

'No one from outside sets foot in the Yards, least of all the police. The children are as dangerous as the bite of a rabid dog. The women are worse. Two gentle Franciscans went into the Yards with nothing but love in their hearts, to spread the Word of Christ, to bring light into their darkness. They were never seen again. Within a day their robes and rosaries were on sale in the Place de Grève. Some say their meat was sold as pork in Les Halles. Can you imagine the implications for the resurrection of their bodies at the Last Judgement?'

La Fosse kissed the crucifix around his neck.

'These place names mean nothing to me.' Tannhauser indicated the scribe's tools on the table. 'Draw me up a map.'

La Fosse donned his glasses and chose a stripped quill from a jar. He dipped it and took a sheet of paper. He drew two well-spaced lines across the width of the page.

'Let this represent the River Seine. And in the river, the City.' He drew the island and marked a cross at either end. 'Notre-Dame. Sainte-Chapelle.' He dipped ink and drew bridges joining La Cité to the right bank. 'From La Cité to La Ville, we have Pont Notre-Dame, Pont au Change, and the Millers' Bridge, with the waterwheels.' To the south he drew two more bridges. 'And from La Cité to the Latin Quarter, we have the Petit Pont and the Pont Saint-Michel.'

'Marvellous. Go on, Father.'

'To the north of the river, the city walls of Charles the Fifth make a shape that we might compare to the shell of a duck egg.' La Fosse drew a semi-ovoid spanning the whole north bank of the Seine. He dipped his quill. 'But the older walls to the south enclose a space more proportionate to a quail's egg. Or perhaps a hen's.'

As the vast city acquired a shape in his mind, Tannhauser felt less at its mercy.

'Good.' Remembering that every artist craved undiluted praise, he added, 'Superb.'

La Fosse warmed to his performance. He exchanged the quill for a finer one.

'Here are the six gates of the north, which I will mark thus by letters. Porte Sainte-Honoré. Montmartre. Saint-Denis. Saint-Martin. The Temple. Saint-Antoine, which I will mark B, for the Bastille, which guards it. Now, here, we find Les Halles, west of the great tower of Saint-Jacques, which the butchers paid for. And they talk of the wealth of the Church. Here is the most feared building in France, the fortress of the Châtelet, where the police are quartered. If it's justice you seek, my brother, go elsewhere. And here is the Cemetery of the Innocents.' As if starved for acclaim he said, 'I hope this crude sketch is helpful.'

'It's a masterpiece of cartography.'

'As for the other churches of the Ville, where do I begin –?'

Tannhauser aimed a forefinger at the western edge of the map. 'The Louvre?' Then again, to the east of the Pont Notre-Dame. 'The Place de Grève and the Hôtel de Ville?'

'Correct. Very good. We are here, approximately.' He marked the map.

'And the Left Bank?'

'Personally, I avoid it. The students fill one with despair. Here is the Tour de Nesle. And the six gates.' He sketched. 'The gallows in Place Maubert. Ah, the abbeys. Outside the wall we have

Saint-Germain-des-Prés, and within we have, my word, Cluny, Sainte-Geneviève, the Augustinians, the Bernardines –'

'Excuse me, Father.' Tannhauser tugged the map away before it became congested. 'I'm in your debt.' He blew on the ink. 'Tell me more about Symonne D'Aubray.'

La Fosse repressed his discomfort so expertly that Tannhauser wasn't sure he'd seen it. La Fosse indicated the papers scattered on his desk.

'The D'Aubrays are Protestants. Her late husband was a radical but Symonne devoted herself to her family and her business.' He shrugged. 'She's on the list.'

'A list of Protestants.'

'An ensign sent by the Bureau de Ville dragged me from my bed to make sure it was complete. Their list is drawn from tax rolls and therefore wholly deficient. I know every household in the parish, even those who aren't Catholic. The Bureau is in a state of panic. Is it true a Huguenot army is at the gates?'

'No. Coligny and all his captains are dead.'

'Praise God.'

'Why does the Bureau need such a list?' asked Tannhauser.

'The city is ruled by the legal and financial grandees, 'Les Messieurs', who have been infiltrated by the Protestants. Marriage, kinship, conversion. Heresy is no longer even a crime. Money matters more than love of God –'

'Why does the Bureau need the list?'

'I'm told it's for their own protection.'

'The Huguenots?'

'Parisians are weary. Famine, high prices, plague. Taxes to pay for wars declared but not won. Taxes to bribe the mercenaries hired by the Huguenots to leave. Taxes to pay our own foreign hirelings. Taxes to raise grand buildings we can't afford to finish. Taxes to pay for this abomination of a wedding. Who believes in the match? Not the bride and groom. And now they want us to fight the Spanish? Parisians want these problems to go away, which means they want the Huguenots to go away, that's all. But some factions – the militant confraternities – are not weary at all. Hatred of the Huguenots is the principal enthusiasm of their lives.'

'Who will provide this protection?'

La Fosse said, 'I don't know.'

'Who polices the city? Who's in charge of order?'

'A dozen magistrates would give you a dozen different answers and none would swear an oath on his opinion.'

'Nor need you. Explain.'

'The King and the Bureau share, and compete for, the power to govern the city. The *sergents à verge* are some two hundred constables and bailiffs commanded from the Châtelet by two *Lieutenants* – *Civil* and *Criminel* – and their superintendents and inspectors – the *commissaires* and *examinateurs*. They investigate primarily by means of the rack, and spend most of their energies collecting the fines and fees that pay their wages. However, and I assure you I am not inventing this, they take no responsibility for the prevention of crime in the streets. That is the province of the Lieutenant of the Robe, who patrols the city by day with twenty archers.'

'A villain's paradise.'

'Well put, chevalier. Paris also has a military governor entrusted with the defence of the city walls. The Royal Watch is another company, of thirty men, which patrols by night, or when they can be dragged from the taverns. All these offices – civil, criminal and military – along with others whose names and functions escape me, overlap with each other at every point in authority, responsibility and jurisdiction.'

'So there's always someone else to blame.'

La Fosse frowned as if this had never occurred to him. 'Of course. Of course.'

'Who are the clowns roaming the streets with banner and drum?'

'The civic militia, or *bourgeois guet*. Each company of a hundred men is drawn from one of the city's sixteen *quartiers*. During the last war their captains proclaimed themselves Soldiers of Christ. They were, shall we say, very active during the Gastines riots, in which Roger D'Aubray died. The King alone can call them up. Beyond that, and legally speaking, no one is sure who controls them, or who defines the limits of their duties, or even what those duties might be. In practice, they are under the sway of the confraternities – groups of devout and, shall we say, militant Catholics.'

Tannhauser recalled the confraternities in Sicily. Foot soldiers of the Inquisition.

'So the militia is run by fanatics.'

La Fosse hesitated, uncertain of Tannhauser's leanings.

Tannhauser said, 'I was called a fanatic myself only yesterday.'

'I will put it this way. The people at large have no great affection for the city fathers, but when the civic militia hold a parade they come out in droves to cheer.'

Tannhauser took the nose-glasses from the table. Two convex lenses in silver frames connected by a C-shaped bridge. His own eyes were not what they used to be.

'May I?'

He put them on. The fit was too snug. He noticed the priest wince as he bent the C-bridge wider. Vanity had prevented him testing such glasses before. He was startled by their power. Various blurred details on the map sprang into focus. The ink was dry. He folded the map in four, wrapped the glasses in the map, and slipped both into his pocket. He wondered if he should leave Juste and Grégoire here, for safety. Some instinct rebelled against it. He glanced at the portrait of the cardinal. He scooped up the sheets of paper covered with names and rolled them and shoved them into his boot top.

He walked to the door.

'I'll be back to make further arrangements and approve the coffin.'

'Brother Mattias, you haven't received my blessing.'

'Just make sure the coffin will please me.'

'And my nose-glasses?'

The two boys had fashioned a collar of gold braid for the half-bald dog and were pleased with themselves. The dog trotted between

Clementine's forehooves like a little jinn, an arrangement with which both animals seemed content. When the sentinel jumped to lower the chain he gawped at the dog as if its bizarre appearance among the entourage were further evidence that Tannhauser was of unsound mind. In the gallows square beyond the chain, the number of armed men had swollen. More limp flags were brandished in the humid morning air. A bagpiper played a jaunty air.

'Greetings, good sire! Do you know there is a cur hiding under your horse?'

Tannhauser flipped a sou at him. The sentinel snatched at the coin and knocked it into the street. He set to scouring the ground with his head below his knees, his concentration compromised by frequent glances at the dog.

'That cur has something of the devil, sire. It's giving me the evil eye.'

Grégoire spotted the coin and picked it up. He handed it to Hervé, who began to smile but grimaced when he saw Grégoire's lip. He took the coin without thanking him and backed away. Grégoire was unmoved.

'What was this oaf's name?' Tannhauser asked Juste.

'Hervé the plasterer,' whispered Juste.

'Hervé,' said Tannhauser, 'Father La Fosse tells me the militia are in charge of maintaining the peace and tranquillity of the city.'

'Thus charged we are, sire. Peace and tranquillity will be maintained at all costs. Rebels will be punished with the harshest legalities.'

'He says the Bureau has ordered you to protect all Huguenot civilians.'

Hervé polished his coin. 'The militia takes its orders from the King.'

'I saw His Majesty not three hours ago, at the Louvre, during the harsh legalities we inflicted on the rebels with the edges of our swords.'

'God bless His Majesty for finally seeing the light! And God bless you too, sire.'

'Is the priest misinformed?'

'Their eminences in the Bureau de Ville like to think they run everything in Paris, by which they mean stuffing their pockets with gold. Whose gold? Why, Huguenot gold. Huguenot bribes. Huguenot taxes and tolls. That's why the Bureau protects them. Of course it's really our gold, squeezed, swindled and stolen from honest artisans such as myself, for when it comes to extorting money the Huguenots are second only to the Jews. But to answer your question, sire – and this is a strict legality – only the King himself can call up the militia, in matters of dire circumstance to the public good, *ipso facto*, whereby we assume with all due courage and honour, and while risking our lives, though seeing not a sol in payment, our civic duty.'

Hervé took a breath and jerked a thumb at the mob in the Place de Grève.

'And as you can see, the King has indeed called us up, has he not? We trust him and he trusts us. In respect of which sacred duties thereunto – and in so far as we are told – His Majesty's wishes could not be any plainer.'

Tannhauser recalled the words Guise had shouted in the Rue Béthizy.

'It is the King's command.'

'Right you are, sire,' agreed Hervé. 'Kill them all.'

Tannhauser further recalled his own words to Retz.

'Kill them all,' repeated Hervé with relish, mimicking what he imagined was a kingly tone. 'And leave not one of them alive to spit on my mother's grave, or rape our wives and cut the throats of our children.' He grinned toothlessly.

Tannhauser mastered an urge to kick him in the throat.

'I quote his very words, sire. As you know better than me.'

'Coligny and his captains are dead.'

'I'm surprised you didn't hear the cheer we raised when we got the news, sire. Coligny and the provincials were a very good beginning, but as Captain Crucé said: "Lads? The rest of them are up to us."'

'The rest of them?'

'The rest of the Huguenots, sire. I can see you're not a local man, sire, so let me tell you, there are more than you might think. Thousands and thousands of 'em. No man sleeps more than six feet from a prostitute or three feet from a rat, and such is the sorry state of Paris that Huguenots outnumber the whores.'

'You believe the King wants to kill all the Huguenots of Paris.'

'All is all, isn't it, sire?' asked Hervé. 'Anything less than all isn't all at all.'

Tannhauser rode on with Grégoire and Juste at his stirrups.

'You can count on us, sire! And gramercy for the contribution!'

The Place de Grève was so congested that Tannhauser was obliged to ride around the edge. Charcoal cook fires flourished, into one of which he tossed La Fosse's list. Hawkers did a brisk trade in food and wine. The number of whores had increased. As a military force the militiamen were a joke. They milled around their district pennants in ill-disciplined clusters. They made a lot of noise. Apart from the white armbands and crosses, no two men wore the same gear or bore the same weapons, which latter they tended to carry as if they were brooms. Fifty Swiss could have driven them into the Seine.

Tannhauser surveyed their faces. He doubted there were two score men among the lot who had ever deliberately taken a life. Hervé the plasterer may have dropped a pallet of bricks on a work-mate's head, but he'd never shoved cold steel into someone's gut. The militia looked like what they were – five hundred cobblers and candlestick-makers, gossiping in the square about the injustices of life and the particular evils inflicted by the Huguenots. It was Sunday morning, they'd been up half the night, they missed their wives and their beds, and they had no orders. They stank of fear, anger and hatred. They stank of stupidity and bad leadership. Like everything else in the city, they stank of shit.

Despite La Fosse's list and Hervé's enthusiasm, he found it hard to believe that a serious attempt could be made to kill the Protestants of Paris. Nothing he had heard from Retz or Arnauld suggested that the King had any such intention, or that any such order would have been conceived, let alone issued. The King had been squeamish enough about killing Coligny. Tannhauser was certain that no such notion had entered the mind of anyone else at the Louvre, any more than it had entered his own, for the simple reason that it would serve no useful purpose and would create a political and financial catastrophe. Retz and Catherine were as amoral as circumstance demanded, but their political guile was not in doubt. For a decade they had outfoxed the best diplomats of half a dozen countries and two empires. The idea of exterminating a large portion of the city's best educated and most productive citizens – for what? Something as stupid as a spite they didn't even feel? – would strike them and anyone around them, including even Guise and Anjou, as worse than madness.

Beyond that, the project, in practical terms, was unrealistic. It could be done, but to identify, arrest and execute so many would take days, even weeks. It would need real troops, not this self-glorified rabble. It would require the consent of the governor, Montmorency, a moderate Catholic, along with that of numerous lesser officers, military, civic and legal, who would be no keener than he to stain their reputations with the blood of thousands of decent citizens and their families. It would require that the rule of law be utterly abandoned, with the complicity of *Parlement,* the magistrates and the lawyers who outnumbered the soldiery. It would require the absolute corruption of an entire society. It would require the most civilised city in the world to embrace an extreme of savagery and shame that, for all the quotidian cruelty of its streets, had to be far beyond its ken. Such insane violence stood at the limit of even Tannhauser's imagination. And he doubted anyone in Paris had witnessed near as much bloodletting as he; though such ignorance had a double edge.

He understood the grievances of an Hervé. He saw the opportunities for criminals. There would be a rash of robberies and killings. Some private feuds, high and low, would be settled. Death cancelled all sorts of debts. There would be a lot of talk and bravado.

No more than that. The King had shown his teeth. He had slaughtered his political foes. He had established his authority. He had preserved the faith of his fathers. *Te Deums* would be sung, the city would heap him with praise and his subjects would go back to making money.

Applause erupted from the mass of men in the Place de Grève. Tannhauser looked back and saw the gallows. As if to confirm the pettiness of their ambitions, a lone figure convulsed at the end of a rope, his body a blotch against the newly risen sun. He swung back and forth, his legs flailing and his torso bucking, to the accompaniment of jeers. They hadn't even made a decent job of hanging him.

He despised the men in the square. Yet his only claim to superiority lay in his skill with arms. Like each of them, he was trapped in the squalid cell of his own feelings. The only moral high ground he might stand on was a blood-soaked dunghill.

Despair gnawed on his heart. He felt exhausted. His mind was dulled. Beyond his notion to recover his gear from the printer's house, he had no plan. Worse, he had no desire, no direction. Without Carla to fire them, such impulses had no meaning. Rage stirred within him but then subsided. There were riddles to solve and debts to settle, but he had no appetite for either. Her death had drained his spirit. He had taken enough revenge to know that, hot or cold, it was a dish that fed only the worst in himself and poisoned what was best. He tried to summon his hatred for her killers. But the square was a lake of hate already and he did not feel inclined to piss in it.

He wanted only to be far away.

Across the river, he saw the hulk of Notre-Dame de Paris.

He rode towards the high tower of Saint-Jacques. At the Rue Saint-Martin he turned south across the Pont Notre-Dame, whose guards watched him approach and lowered the chain without saying a word.

The road across the bridge was flanked on either side by identical terraces of narrow houses, each with a ground-floor shop and two upper floors. The shops were given over to luxury trades and goods. Their signs hung out above the street on long iron rods. Hatters, wig makers, art dealers, feather merchants; importers of Italian finery for women. Though the morning was well advanced, and this was one of the busiest thoroughfares in Paris, the street was deserted. He was sure all the houses were occupied, for while militiamen might leave their wives abed, no shopkeeper ever leaves his stock unguarded, yet of human life there was no sign at all.

Tannhauser found himself back on the island of the City.

Tight streets. Alleys that even Juste would have found a squeeze. Houses on the verge of collapse, some only prevented from doing so by ingenious buttressing. A splendid new townhouse would appear wedged into the midst of the ruling decrepitude. Inns abounded. Hereabouts there was more activity, though the tension was no less palpable. He smelled cooking from taverns and rotisseries. Several establishments had stationed an armed man on the doorstep, some wearing the jackets of the *sergents à verge*. None appeared very sure of himself. As Tannhauser passed, they nodded, as if in the hope he had come to tell them what was happening and what they ought to do.

The road continued south into what must have been the Left Bank. All that identified the end of the bridge was a squat fort, which Grégoire told him was the Petit Châtelet. At a cross street Tannhauser turned for the cathedral.

Notre-Dame de Paris loomed abrupt and massive, as much a fortress as a church, less a celebration of faith than a demonstration of power. A threat in stone. He would not have called it the most beautiful, but perhaps he had spent too much time in Italy. With the sun at its back, it did not fail to inspire his awe. But he had not come to pray. He craned his neck at the immense height of the two bell towers.

The cramped cathedral square, the Parvis, was the geographical centre of France, or so Juste assured him with the pride of a visitor who had garnered some notable facts. In defiance of the timid quietude elsewhere it was shrill and swarming with whores, beggars, hawkers, poets, jongleurs and buffoons, half of whom at least were thieves or shills. There were gangs of militia, too. They were fewer and less loud than those in the Place de Grève, but their members seemed bred from a nastier bone.

When they saw Tannhauser and his bloodstains, they gave him the nod.

The Parvis was flanked on the south side, along the river, by the hospital, the Hôtel-Dieu. Several Hospital Sisters moved among the throng of the maimed, the poor and the monstrously diseased that milled around the gate in the hope of acquiring admittance or food. With expert eyes they picked the truly needy from the many fakers, though even the most fortunate of the bunch were models of wretchedness. One of the latter such petitioners spotted Tannhauser, or the Hospitaller's cross on his chest, and detached himself. He appeared to have only one leg, though in Paris one could never be sure, and he moved at remarkable speed, his body almost horizontal to the ground, using a pair of short sticks in cankered hands. Before Tannhauser could swing Clementine to swat him aside, the stocky little dog exploded from between her hooves and went for the beggar's leg without a bark of warning.

The beggar scuttled away, his sticks clacking on the flagstones. The dog stopped, his chest puffed out, gold braid gleaming, and watched him retreat. He wagged his obscene pink tail. He barked in contempt. Grégoire and Juste looked at Tannhauser.

'As you see, he's extremely intelligent,' prompted Juste.

'Perhaps even more intelligent than Clementine,' added Grégoire.

'I doubt any of the three of us are that,' said Tannhauser. 'But in Paris, a dog that runs off beggars must be worth a tidy sum. I wonder how much the Hôtel-Dieu would pay? The Hospital Sisters would adore him. Imagine all the time and labour he would save them. Imagine all the soup they'd no longer have to boil.'

Grégoire and Juste exchanged glances of panic.

'Or,' said Tannhauser, 'we could donate him, as an act of Christian charity.'

The dog returned and halted between the two boys. He looked up at Tannhauser, tongue lolling, as if in expectation of some reward.

'But master, as you see,' said Juste, 'we cannot possibly sell him to anyone, or even give him away as an act of Christian charity, until all his hair has grown back.'

'It's true,' agreed Grégoire. 'The sisters would never take in a bald dog.'

'A fair point,' conceded Tannhauser. 'I can think of no religious order that would accept a bald dog. Until his hair grows back, then. Give him some affection so he knows he did us a service.'

The boys petted the dog and exchanged winks of triumph and relief.

'What have you decided to call him?'

Juste said, 'He's called Lucifer.'

'That would certainly dismay the gentle sisters.'

'You don't like it?'

'I worry I'm neglecting your moral education.'

'Master, I have never learned so much so quickly. Grégoire, too, I'm sure.'

'Master, it's true. You are a fine teacher.'

'You can learn a lot from a dog, too,' added Juste.

'Keep your eyes and ears open,' said Tannhauser. 'Much of what you hear will be rumour, fantasy and lies, but pick up what fact you can. Say little, preferably nothing. Today every step we take, every word we speak, might betray us.'

The dog yapped at Tannhauser.

'That's a big name for a small dog.'

'He is small,' agreed Grégoire. 'But he survived the fire.'

There was food to be had in the square and Tannhauser dismounted and bought a warm loaf for the boys. They tore it apart with such ardour he bought a pair of roast pigeons, still hot and threaded on sticks, to go with it. He watched them eat. The lads were so hungry it wasn't until the food was half gone that Grégoire thought to give a morsel to Lucifer, beyond which point the dog enjoyed the best of both their rations.

Grégoire pointed out a corral in a side street and there they left

Clementine. As they approached the façade of the cathedral, Tannhauser scanned the multitude of arcane figures and hieroglyphs with which the grand portal had originally been adorned. Many had been erased by hammer blows inflicted by priests who, though ignorant of their meaning, had learned that they spoke from the Hermetic rather than the Christian tradition. Other icons had been smashed by Huguenot fanatics.

Tannhauser entered through the portal of the Last Judgement.

He crossed himself with Holy Water but spared himself the misery of genuflection. After the bright sun it seemed dark inside and Tannhauser waited for his eyes to adjust. The first thing he saw was a wickerwork crib in which lay three babies, none above a month old. Tannhauser felt a lump of pain in his chest. He turned away.

The rearmost pews of the cathedral were colonised by prostitutes, of either sex and to suit every taste. At least two were currently *in flagrante*, bending over the benches in front of the panting clients while various of their colleagues watched, though whether this was out of boredom or because they had been paid to do so, he could not tell. At the far end of the church a service was taking place behind the rood screen, but the distance was so great that neither business interrupted the other.

'I was born in that crib,' said Grégoire.

'Your mother's loss was our gain.'

Tannhauser surveyed the vast and enchanted interior, in which each stone had been carved and placed to embody its own several and particular meanings. Petrus Grubenius had believed that the whole structure had been built, on the principles of sacred geometry, as a single gigantic alchemical vessel – that is, not only as a crucible, though it was that, or as a text which transcended words, though it was that, too, but as a cosmic ship on a voyage to the time beyond Time, and whose spiritual pilot was Hermes Trismegistus. Tannhauser felt that boys might by stirred by this notion.

He said, 'If we accept – as Petrus Grubenius did, and as do one or two adepts within the Hospitallers – that the Mass is a manifestation of the Magnum Opus, and that the seven sacraments symbolise alchemical processes, whose goal is at once the transmutation of matter into spirit and of spirit into matter, then Notre-Dame de Paris does indeed become our Mother, the sacred centre, the womb from whence we might be reborn into enlightenment.'

Grégoire and Juste looked up at him with perfect politeness. He appreciated it. He needed, for a moment, to feel that he was more than he knew himself to be.

'The mysteries of which the best of us once were masters will never be understood again, not in all the world's turning. We're doomed to grope in twilight, forever trying to persuade ourselves it is dawn. We come here in desperation, kings, killers, babies, whores, hoping to breathe some essence of the Divine, but the most we can take away is an inkling of how much we have lost. Yet, I'm certain that these babes see farther than the wisest man. That's the root of your distinction, Grégoire. Once, you too saw so far.'

'But, master, I can't remember seeing anything.'

'Your mind has forgotten but your spirit has not. Now, can you tell me how to climb the north bell tower?'

Grégoire took him to a door but the door was locked.

'Can I help you, my lord?'

Tannhauser turned to look at the speaker.

The speaker had done so over his shoulder, for he was a burly young brute and he was busy pissing against the cathedral wall. The general stench suggested he was no lone offender. As he finished and put himself away, Lucifer trotted over towards him.

Tannhauser tapped both boys on the shoulders.

'He's your dog. You look out for him.'

Lucifer sniffed with scorn and cocked a leg. The burly one took a half step backwards, to get a good swing into his kick.

'Sirrah! That's our dog!' shouted Juste.

'Don't hurt him!' added Grégoire.

The burly one looked at the boys and mimed his regret that they enjoyed protection. He looked at Tannhauser. Cherubic but brutal features, a face not merely shaped by, but born to, a world of vice. The corruption ran so deep he could have been as young as fifteen or ten years older. Tannhauser recognised him, and vice versa, but he couldn't place the face. The cherub smiled.

'If your Excellency wants a bit of privacy with his boys, in the stairwell there, I can arrange it. I can arrange all sort of things that might please you.'

Tannhauser considered himself within his rights to kill him there and then, even, given that he judged them within the narthex, inside Notre-Dame during Sunday Mass. But, as if the greasy tone of the pimp's voice were a trumpet call, two wretched children tottered from the shadows. Vermilion daub made harsh gashes of their mouths, and their eyes had been driven deep into their skulls by something more hurtful than pain, something more lasting than grief, something more degrading than terror. They were the same twin girls that the same pimp had tried to sell the day before. The pimp, whose business it was to recall both faces and predilections, held his palm out behind him.

The girls stopped dead.

'I want to get to the top of the bell tower,' said Tannhauser.

'The top of the tower?' Though he daily catered to grotesque sexual appetites, this request struck the pimp as bizarre. 'But there's four hundred steps. So I'm told.'

'If you have the key, open the door and I'll give you a sol.'

'You wouldn't want these two sweet girls to starve, would you, sire?'

'I don't want the girls. I want to get to the roof.'

'I know you don't want the girls, sire, what I mean is –'

'Open the door and take the sol. Or I'll take the key.'

The pimp was as tough as his trade demanded, which meant he could frighten women and girls and the kind of men who paid to abuse them. He grimaced as if swallowing vinegar. He wagged a key at the end of a cord around his neck.

'A sol for a minute's work?' He smiled. 'Better wages than most earn in a day.'

He opened the door. The twin girls fluttered over. With their painted smiles and hollowed eyes they looked like emaciated clowns approaching a torture chamber. Tannhauser wondered what it took to make them rush towards whatever vile ordeal they expected beyond the door. He wanted to stab the pimp. He didn't.

The pimp swung around and punched the nearest girl in the stomach.

'This gentleman isn't for you two, silly!'

As she doubled over, the other caught her and stopped her falling.

Tannhauser wedged the pimp's fist between his shoulders and bounced his face off the wall by the door. The pimp spat out tooth fragments and blood.

'You can't walk into Notre-Dame and treat a man like this. It's a cathedral.'

Tannhauser cranked the arm higher.

'What's your name?'

'Tybaut. It's Tybaut.' He grit his teeth. 'There's no need for this, sire. I've got my influences. I've got my value. I'm a nose. Well, a nose *to* a nose –'

'A nose to a nose?' Tannhauser glanced at Grégoire.

'He spies for a spy. A nose to a nose.'

Tannhauser hurt the pimp some more. Tybaut grunted.

'There are all kinds of spies,' said Grégoire.

'Your imbecile is right, sire. Police spies, court spies, palace spies. Brothel, tavern and street spies. Bedroom spies and kitchen spies. Spies for husbands and spies for wives. Not to mention spies for the colleges and spies for the Church. Every second servant in town is a spy, guaranteed. Some of the highest *messieurs* in the land are spies, but even you must know about them. We're all spying on each other, sire, aren't we? Spying is life.'

'Who is this grand nose you spy for?'

'I may have exaggerated his importance, sire. He's one of the deacons here. But I believe he will rise and I hope to ascend with him.'

'And you think you could be of value to me.'

'I guarantee it, sire. With respect, you don't seem to know the workings as well as you might. And everyone can benefit from knowing more than they know.'

'It would benefit the world at large if I broke your spine.'

'If you'll forgive me for saying so, sire, you don't strike me as a man who greatly cares to benefit the world at large.'

'Who's your deacon on the rise?'

'Have a heart, sire.' Tybaut grunted with fresh pain. 'Father Pierre.'

'Did he tell you to wear this white armband?'

'He didn't have to. I can see what I can see, same as you.'

Tannhauser let go of his arm. 'Tell me something else worth knowing.'

Tybaut turned around and pointed at Juste.

'Well, he's a red rag to a bull, should you meet a bull, and you will. I mean, most people are thick, you know that, and the police are even thicker. As for the militia?' He knocked his knuckles on the side of his head. 'But that's only most of them, not all of them. It's obvious he's a foreigner, and so are you, sire, though that's no crime. But that little white cross he's got pinned to his chest doesn't make him a Catholic.'

'Give him your shirt. That jerkin, too.'

Tybaut laughed. Tannhauser slapped him. Tybaut hit the wall again and slid down the stones to his knees. The sound of the slap echoed around the cathedral. Heads turned, then turned away. Tannhauser glanced at the twin girls. They were clutching each other and staring at Tybaut. They were concerned for him. They were scared.

They were scared of Tannhauser.

Tybaut collected himself, head down, thinking, still on his knees.

'If you draw that knife I will blind you and cut your thumbs off,' said Tannhauser. 'You can spy on the other cripples outside the Hôtel-Dieu.'

Tybaut stood up. He papered a smile over humiliation and rage.

'I'm used to getting a bit more respect than this, sire.'

Tannhauser slapped him with his other hand. Tybaut was far too slow. He went down again and heaved for breath on hands and knees.

'Get up, pimp. Give him the clothes.'

Tybaut clambered to his feet. There were tears in his eyes.

'You're a boy with qualities. You're wasting them.'

'Yes, sire,' said Tybaut. 'Nice to see someone making the most of theirs.'

He stepped back to avoid a blow that didn't come. He stripped off the jerkin.

'Try not to get blood on the shirt.'

'You might have thought of that before you knocked my teeth out.'

'What else have you heard today? What do you expect?'

Tybaut threw the jerkin at Juste. 'I've heard we're going to rob and kill a lot of heretics. And that's what I expect will happen.'

'You're no killer.'

'I meant we Parisians. It's the hottest day of summer, the hive's been kicked once too often, and the bees have had enough. If you weren't so bloody lofty you'd hear them swarming. You'd shit yourself.'

'You mean the militia.'

'See? You don't know what you're talking about.' Tybaut stripped off his shirt. 'Who are the militia? A crowd of cobblers. But there's militias within the militia. The leagues, the confraternities. Certain priests run their own militias. Certain captains. Certain noble gentlemen. Then there's the beggars, the thieves, the smugglers, the bravos. The pimps. Kingdoms within the kingdom. Kings and captains in deed if not in title. And then you've got the police, wherein you'll find every sort of faction, and each of them consorting with one or more of the rest. Each lot have their purposes. As do we all. What's yours?'

Tybaut balled his shirt and threw it at Juste.

'I hope that's not lousy,' said Tannhauser.

'I'm very fussy about fleas, lice and ticks. You won't find one on those girls, neither. I look after them, sire, and as you see, they're in blossom. They can still be yours for one white franc. Or your boys if they want to lose their chastity. I won't even charge the extra for the imbecile. That's a bargain. I've schooled those little lambs myself in every known depravity, plus some I invented fresh all by myself.'

'Give me the key.'

Tybaut handed it over. Tannhauser proffered some coins.

'Here's another sol. When I come back down I want to see your girls on that bench eating something hot. If I don't, I will keep the key.'

Tybaut took the coins. 'Bread and hot soup it is, sire.'

'Pigeon.'

'I don't believe pigeon soup is available, sire.'

Tannhauser slapped him. Tybaut picked himself up.

'The girls bless you, sire.'

Tannhauser climbed the spiral stair without stopping and without altering his pace. His shoulders scraped the walls. The faces of the twin child prostitutes stayed with him. They made him think of Carla. They would have moved her to pity. But the world would no longer be graced by Carla's pity. He stepped out onto an exterior stone walkway that ran between the two bell towers. He didn't look out at the city, nor down on the Parvis. He walked to the base of the north tower, where he saw a wicket. It wasn't locked.

He climbed a second, tighter, stair. His chest felt scorched. His back ached. His weapons snagged the stones. Sweat poured from him in pints. The exertion cleared his mind of everything except Carla's image. By the time he neared the top he felt empty.

A breeze caught his face. It was almost cool and smelled of burning charcoal. He rested his forehead against the stones and caught his breath. He mounted the last step. He climbed on top of the parapet wall, his toes treading on air.

He looked down.

The entire city swayed far beneath him.

For the first time he perceived a single entity, immense and crazed.

Paris.

He glimpsed her essence.

She had torn out his heart and left nothing in its place.

She would take that place for herself, if he would let her.

Her spirit would merge with his and she would never leave him.

And he would never leave her.

And in return she would fill the emptiness inside him.

But never with a heart.

And never with love.

Tannhauser found himself willing.

Love brought pain.

Lucifer skipped onto the parapet wall beside him. He surveyed the reeking metropolis below with the hauteur of one who owned it. He looked at Tannhauser.

'Have you come to make me an offer on my soul?'

The mutilated creature yapped once.

'I'm afraid it's already taken.'

'Master?'

Tannhauser heard the anxiety in the voice. He stepped down from the wall.

Grégoire sagged against the doorway with relief. Juste panted into view.

'Don't be afraid. I'll find some other way to die in due course.'

Tannhauser noted the useless red shoes hanging around Grégoire's neck.

'If I see those again I will throw them off the top.'

Grégoire removed the shoes and hid them behind his back.

'Here. Look at this.'

Tannhauser retrieved La Fosse's map and unfolded it. He donned his new nose-glasses. The paper was damp and the ink had run, but the quality of both was such that the map remained readable. It was accurate but could not convey a sense of distance. The city was small yet the moment one passed through its gates it became limitless, as if to enter Paris were to pass through some defect in the weave of material creation. Every mile seemed like ten. As seen from the tower, the city was a stain leaking out across the farmland that unrolled in every direction from its suburbs. Villages nested in grain fields ripe for harvest. As far as the blue and green horizon, the vista shimmered. If it seemed otherworldly, it was. The world was out there; within the walls there was Paris.

With Grégoire's help he traced on both the map and the living city below the route he had taken since his arrival at the Porte Saint-Jacques. No one section was far yet each had seemed a journey worthy of Ulysses. He also realised how small a fraction of the city he had seen. Even vacated of its inhabitants, it would have been unknowable. Seething as it was, it changed from moment to moment into something it had never quite been before and never would be again.

He located and fixed in his mind's eye various landmarks. The city was a sea of rooftops, and no two among the tens of thousands seemed to be the same height. Dwellings were stacked on dwellings, and others were stacked on those, as if the city had been built by an infant in the hope that it all should fall down. The moss that cloaked the roofs had been burned pale as jade by the sun. The bowed and tilting walls of the streets obscured all but two or three of the broadest roads, the latter themselves barely twenty feet wide. Gardens invisible at street level mapped the *quartiers* favoured by the rich.

Beyond the western wall of the Latin Quarter was the abbey of Saint-Germain. The other sprawling *faubourgs* that circled the walls and moats, north and south, were sorry collections of cheap huts to which the poorer artisans had retreated. So densely built was the island of the City below that even from this vantage the Seine could not be seen.

North-east of the Hôtel D'Aubray was the Grand Tower of the Temple, the headquarters of Tannhauser's Order. Its walls were white and its Donjon and corner turrets were capped with black conical roofs. The tower was surrounded by an enclosure of thirty acres within a high wall, and defended by ramparts, watchtowers and moats.

Tannhauser stowed the map and glasses.

'Can't we stay up here?' asked Juste. He was leaning over the wall. 'For a few days? We could bring food, water. Who would know? Who would care?'

'I need my guns. I need to see to Carla's body, at the chapel. She didn't die of bad luck. She was assassinated. I need to know why.'

'Tybaut is right,' said Juste. 'I'm going to be killed.'

He pointed. Tannhauser looked down towards the Pont Notre-Dame.

From this height a length of the north-west side of the street was visible. Sunlight winked on the sign of the Golden Hammer. A cluster of people dressed in black stood beneath the sign, their backs to the shop window, their hands raised in surrender. There were perhaps eight of them, a family group. A banner appeared nearby. A line of militiamen lunged into view. There was a pause. Then in a sudden flurry they speared the whole family, stabbing until what looked like a pile of black rags lay heaped before the window. At this distance the murders were strangely silent, but Tannhauser saw the mouths of the dying gape open as they screamed.

'Can I stay up here alone?' asked Juste. 'With Lucifer?'

'No. Put on that shirt and jerkin and keep the white cross.'

Tannhauser walked around the corner of the parapet for a better angle to the north. The Place de Grève had half-emptied. The regular troops and the artillery hadn't moved, but loose gangs of militia were dispersing in all directions.

'Master?' called Grégoire.

Tannhauser returned to find Grégoire pointing at a column of smoke that rose between the rooftops in the south-western quarter of the Left Bank. The smoke was fresh, hanging in the hot, still air, and it seemed to rise from a street, not a building. Tannhauser was distracted by the sounds of a commotion rising from the Parvis below.

The square was in confusion. The street entertainers and food peddlers were packing up and leaving with the organised haste of those with a nose for trouble. Even the beggars were vacating prime spots on the cathedral approaches.

The exodus was provoked by a gang of militia, advancing with three flags and a fanfare raised by a pair of drummers and a piper. They filled the street from wall to wall. A large bearded man in a steel helm walked in front, wielding a sword in time to the music. The rest of the armed irregulars formed a hollow rectangle stretching behind him. The hollow was filled by a mass of Huguenot prisoners in their distinctive black clothes.

They were of all ages and sexes, family groups rousted from their homes, and in all they must have numbered between three and four score. Some were singing and their voices sent pitiful scraps of the Psalms to soar above the drumming, until spear butts applied to the ribs shut them up.

The uneasy peace of the last two hours was over. The pack had decided to follow the scent of blood. All kings feared Anarchy more than plague. This king had opened the door of its cage. The beast was crawling out. He looked at Juste.

'I won't tell you again. Put the pimp's clothes on.'

'That fire in the sixteenth must be close to the printer's shop,' said Grégoire.

His attention was still focused near the south-western curve of the city wall.

Tannhauser looked. With a sudden billow the rising smoke became thicker.

Tannhauser pressed a coin into Grégoire's hand.

'Bring Clementine to the Parvis. Fast as you can.'

CHAPTER THIRTEEN

Alice

They sat across a table in the kitchen and drank rosehip tea. The kitchen was at the front of the house. The sun had risen high enough to shine into the yard and through the windows. In the rising heat, the tea was refreshing.

Carla could not take her eyes off the woman in front of her.

Alice was shapeless, heavy boned, once plump, now shrunken by hardship and years. The skin of her arms and jowls hung in wrinkled flaps. Her face was broad, her cheeks patched with purple. Her mouth was full, her lips the colour of liver and puckered over her gums where the teeth were missing. Her hair was a dark ruddy brown, wisped with white, and cut crudely just above her shoulders. Her eyes were winter-grey, yet in them Carla saw Grymonde. There was a deep tiredness in her, yet also the embers of a natural force that once must have been tremendous. In spite of all, she radiated largeness. Carla couldn't tell how old she was; sixty at least, perhaps seventy, or even more. Old as she was, diminished as she was, Alice seemed to transcend the notion of age.

'Time's a fairy tale, love,' said Alice, as if reading her thoughts. 'A gaol without walls. They were clever, weren't they, them as got us all to believe in it. Calendars, dates – the year of Our Lord, no less, that'll keep us quiet, won't it? But like most such craft and fancy, it's naught but another lash for our backs. Now they have clocks, so they can have us in shackles and chains as well.'

Carla was uncertain of how to contend with her. She was in a den of thieves, with the mother of a man prone to murder all and sundry without compunction. Alice laughed, a dry laugh that, had it been less warm, might well have mocked her.

'Don't be timid here, love, that would never do. Speak up. You'll be speaking up before this day's out, and this woman will be mopping up your slops, so let's not stand on ceremony.'

'I do appreciate you taking me in, madame, more than words can say.'

Alice flapped a hand in dismissal. Her palm was shiny and red.

Carla realised Alice was not merely tired, but far from well, and her heart went out to her. In all her life Carla had never known a woman for whom she felt awe, and few for whom she'd felt any great respect. Her own mother had been weak, docile, afraid of her husband, afraid of the Church, afraid of the opinions of her peers. In every sense she had lived on her knees, and had died in a welter of regrets. Her mother had betrayed Carla in just such a circumstance as this, when she had conspired in the abduction of Orlandu on the morning he was born. Her mother had stolen Carla's motherhood, and Carla had never found the goodness to forgive her.

Carla reached down for her valise but her bulge got in the way. She pushed her chair back and stood up and squatted. Inside the valise she found a bottle of perfume and wrapped it in a silk scarf the colour of the sky. She had bought the scarf because its blue was the same shade as Mattias's eyes. As she stood up a pang took her. She put the bundle on the table and leaned her hands on her knees. She breathed as deeply as she could and mustered her pride to stop her crying out. She felt Alice's eyes taking her measure. The old woman said nothing and Carla was not sorry. Her previous midwife had belaboured her with such a torrent of needless instructions she had had to tell her to be quiet. The pang passed.

She straightened and managed a smile, which Alice returned.

'That's another you won't have to go through again.'

'I wonder how many more.'

'Best not to, love. There'll be more than you dare imagine. Forget each one until the next comes along, and you'll sail through this like Cleopatra's barge on a river of ass's milk.'

'I sometimes fear I'll lack the strength.'

'There's naught stronger in Creation than a woman in labour. If Our Mother hadn't made us that way, none of us would be here.

If a grand to-do is called for, we'll have one, don't you worry. In the meanwhile, why not enjoy? At least as best we can?'

Alice's faith in their respective powers anointed Carla like a balm. She felt a great weight lift from her spirit. The very strength of her reaction prompted her to doubt if it was wise. She had no good reason at all to place her trust – her life, her child – in the hands of this strange old woman. No reason except her instinct; and the old woman's strength. The latter could not be in doubt, for Alice was here, alive, in Cockaigne. She'd endured. Carla reminded herself that she, too, had endured. She cast out the doubt. Doubt was fear in its most treacherous form and her worst enemy. She smiled.

'What a marvellous plan. Yes. Why not enjoy?'

She retrieved the bundle and offered it.

'What's this?'

'For you, madame. A token.'

Alice wiped her hands on her skirt and took the bundle and unwrapped it. She caressed the scarf against her cheek, and its quality was not lost on her. She studied the bottle and removed the glass stopper and wafted it beneath her chin.

'Oh my.' She dabbed the stopper under each ear. 'This is much too fine for this old girl. They'll mistake me for the Queen of Sheba.'

'Nonsense. This is the sweetest smelling house in Paris. It's the first time I've felt able to breathe. Please accept it.'

'Nonsense, is it? Very well. Thank you. But you must keep the scarf.'

'The scarf is yours, too.'

'No, no, enough is more than enough. It will serve to wipe your paps when you're feeding the babe. Isn't that why you brought it with you?'

Carla nodded. She took the scarf and draped it round her neck.

'You might have picked a darker colour for the job – one could say the same for that fine frock – but no one here will care. Sit back down and tell me what you wanted to say.'

'You said time was a fairy tale, but is time not a condition of our mortal existence?'

'No, it is not. Our Mother Nature takes no heed of time, though the spheres themselves fall like apples, as, mark my words, one day they will.'

Carla took a sip of rosehip tea. She thought of Mattias and his mystical notions.

'I'm not unsympathetic to such ideas. Yet the seasons turn.'

'Aye, they turn. As do the stars, like a wheel without cease. They know nor month nor year, nor beginning nor end, because there is no end. There's only what comes next. How much time is in a dream? Or a memory? Or an embrace? And if we can't answer that, how shall we say how much time there is in a life? Let alone in Life Her-own-self?'

'The Bible attests that God made the universe in six days.'

'And who writ the Bible? Fools. For what need would God have of days?'

Alice scoffed. Carla suppressed a smile.

'You make a strong point.'

'Then allow this old heathen to make a stronger one: God did not make us, either. Our Mother the Earth made us, just as she makes the leaves on the trees and the birds of the air. As she makes all living things, and always did. A rib, they tell us? Hellfire. Did God make a sow from the rib of a boar? And dare we even ask which part of the cock He used to make a hen?' She made an obscene gesture with her fist. 'No wonder He needed six days.'

Carla was laughing and Alice joined in, rapping the tabletop with swollen knuckles.

'That book's stuffed my son's head with all manner of bloodshed and crime, and in those trades his head needed no help at all. Not that he's a scholar, mind, he just has a taste for tall tales and peculiar ideas. If we must speak of time, the Bible was written yesterday, and on some tomorrow not so very distant, all the bibles ever struck will be swallowed by the dirt from which they came, aye, and their churches and their palaces too, be they ever so mighty. Now, let the buggers come and burn me.'

Again they laughed.

'Since I surely cannot refute you, they'll have to burn us both.'

Carla clapped both hands to a twinge in her belly, but it wasn't a true pang.

'Your pardon,' said Alice. 'This old woman is short of decent company. But anything she says is yours to take or leave, as you will.'

'I'll happily take it. I'm short of good company, too.'

'Perhaps not so.' Alice leaned her head back and squinted. 'Who's your angel?'

Carla answered without thought, even though she wasn't sure what was meant.

'Amparo is my angel.'

'Her essence glows, just behind you. Pale as dawn. And as fearless.'

'That's Amparo, yes.'

Carla felt tears rise. She blinked them back. She turned. She saw nothing. Part of her mind wanted to disbelieve Alice, but in her heart she did believe her, completely. She turned back and Alice saw that she believed.

'You're lucky to have such a guardian, especially for this work.'

'She was my dearest friend. She –'

'Amparo knows all that and so do you. This old girl doesn't need to. It's just good that we're mindful she's here.'

'Thank you for making me so. And it is good, so very good.'

Alice shifted in her chair to ease some stiffness. She clasped her hands.

'Let's hold our peace a while, so Amparo knows we cherish her presence.'

Carla closed her eyes and let Amparo's spirit fill her. She remembered the golden days they had spent together. A more unlikely pair could hardly be imagined, yet what music they two had made. Strange roads, as Mattias had once put it, strange roads had brought her and Amparo together; her and Mattias, too; just as strange roads had brought her to this table. In the usual course she would have questioned what was happening here; and the questions in their asking would have locked out all the answers worth having. She felt at home. She didn't know why. She had never known that feeling for a place before; not for the dark mausoleum in which her parents had raised her; not in the house she had lived in for almost twenty years. She had known it only in moments: when transported into music's realm; on horseback; amid the suffering and chaos of the Hospital in Malta. In Mattias's arms. Yet she felt at home in this squalid hovel.

Sorrow pierced her. Salt tears slid down her face.

'I'm sorry, madame.'

'Let the tears fall, love.'

'I am all in confusion.'

Alice reached a hand across the table. Carla took it. The hand was cool, yet the warmth of an immense love flowed into her, and with that flowing, the love became yet larger.

'Mattias is missing, Orlandu is missing. The children I kissed goodnight were butchered while I listened to their screams – and while I did nothing to help them. Everywhere is frenzy, cruelty, hatred, greed –'

'Not here, love, not here.'

Carla couldn't help glancing towards the door and the revels beyond.

'Leave them to their sport,' said Alice.

'They sport with trophies cut from a man's skin.'

'And one day my son's head will decorate a spike on the city walls.'

'No number of wrongs can make a right.'

'This woman didn't say they do. She was simply pointing out, in agreement with you, that barbarity and corruption are but the faces on the coin of man's kingdom.'

'But why so? There's more than enough for all.'

'Set no store in politic, love. Don't seek answers where you'll never find them.'

'Are we helpless then?'

'Not at all and to the very contrary. We can't stop their wrongs, much less should we avenge them. They're busy enough with all that as it is. There'll never be any shortage of heads and spikes. But they're the helpless ones. They're the ones who've mortgaged their souls to idols of their own invention. But we needn't catch their madness. We can invite their horrors in here, or we can not. We can live as our Mother intended, right here where we are, wherever we are, because we are here, and here is us: you and your child, and Amparo, and what's left of this old devil's dam.'

'My shoes are filled with the blood they spilled. It's not easy to ignore them.'

'This lowborn lass didn't tell you to ignore them either, still less that anything was easy. But we can pay attention to the things that will make us more, rather than less.'

'It was your son who –' Carla bit her tongue.

'My son has broken this old heart times without number. That's what sons do, and we mothers can only count the ways. They are men. They are monsters, even those who are reckoned – and especially those who reckon themselves – the glory of their race. But we can't hold that against them, no more than we can blame the rain for being wet. They fear life, even when they don't fear death, because they know in their bones they can never bring Life Her-own-self to heel, much as they're bent on trying to. So they make up their wondrous tales – for that talent, at least, let's give them credit – and they say, "This is the world as it should be", and they set out to dominate the worlds-that-should-be, instead of living in the world-without-flaw that already is. And thus they are always at war, with each other, and with themselves, and with Life Her-own-self. They call their doomed fancy "civilisation". Paris is its centre, so they tell us, and that makes the point far better than this old witch can.'

'I have a son.'

Alice said nothing to this. Carla looked at the table, into nowhere. Orlandu, in the moment of his purest innocence, and without any choice in the matter, had broken her heart before he had known that she possessed one. And he'd broken it again when he'd left her to go to Paris; and when he'd talked Mattias into teaching him how to fight with a knife, and when . . .

'And I am carrying a son.'

'The chances are always fair. We'll see. How much does it matter to you?'

'It matters not at all, of course not. Boy or girl, it's my child.'

'It matters a good deal to some. Women are drawn into the fairy tales, too.'

Alice squeezed Carla's hand and withdrew it and Carla felt an enormous sense of loss. Alice put her palms on the table and leaned forward to hoist herself up to her feet.

'The water in the kettle's still hot. We'll wash that blood off in a twinkling.'

'No, don't go, madame, please, stay. I've waded in blood before, I don't care about that. You're right, I know you're right. Truly I do. Please, let me have your hand again.'

Carla held Alice's hand and looked into the long, hard winter of her eyes.

'You have so little, yet you give so much.'

'We'll have no talk of that kind, thank you very much. We're not running a stall on the market, though we could. The house is stuffed with rubbish.'

'I didn't mean to offend you. I only intended –'

'We know what you intended, love, and none is taken.' Alice rolled the ache from one shoulder. 'As regards what you at least seem to mean by "having", you "have" rather less than a little yourself. For a certainty the things you've left behind aren't here, and may never be "there" again, so why lean on them?'

'I do not lean on them. If I did, I don't think I would be alive to be here.'

'Well said, girl. Whatever a person can't carry in their own arms isn't worth having. That's my book.'

Carla smiled and felt the tightness of the dried tear stains on her cheeks. In her mind's eye she saw Orlandu as ragged as he'd first appeared to her. She saw Mattias watching his life's work burn from the deck of a midnight galley. She saw herself, not in one place or moment but in many – perhaps those were the only moments when she was herself – with nothing of value but whatever lay within her. That was never more true than here and now.

'So, you're not hearing anything you don't already know.' Alice smiled, too. 'Mayhap you're a bit of a witch yourself.'

'Mayhap.'

'Grand. Grand. Now we can talk plain.'

Carla revisited her visions and found an error.

'I couldn't carry a horse, and I would have had little indeed without their companionship. But then, one never possesses a horse. At best, one is with it.'

'A delight these old bones have never known, so it's a joy to see it in you. And there we are: as far as "giving" goes, and by no means as regards only horses, we meet upon the level. And there I trust we'll stay, in confusion or otherwise.'

'You flatter me.' Carla saw Alice raise one brow in warning. 'Yes. I accept. On the level, there we meet and there we'll stay.' The brow fell. 'May I ask an odd question?'

'They tend to be the best kind.'

'You call me "love".'

'It fits well enough. But if it bothers you, I'll call you anything you want.'

'No, no, it's wonderful.'

Again Carla found herself smiling. Alice's smile was altogether more wry.

'Then your odd question has its answer.'

'And another? I may be mistaken, but I don't believe I've heard you say "I".'

'You're not mistaken. On the whole, this woman would rather not be fooled into thinking she's at the centre of much that matters, a fancy which saying "I" fosters, and which same fancy she sees everywhere about her, and which is prime among the many tales that fill our shoes with blood. It gives her a clearer view of the way things are, which is that she is but a thread, and not the tapestry.'

Carla took this in. Her reason hopped from toe to toe in consternation. Her soul understood in an instant: at this of all moments, she wasn't 'I', she was 'we'.

'She might also point out,' added Alice, 'that this is not a matter of false humility.'

'We had already gathered that much. A golden thread, then.'

Alice took this edged compliment with an inclination of her head.

'Besides,' she said, 'I have my angels, too.'

Carla studied her hunched, lumpy figure, so graceless yet so full of grace.

'I wish I could see them. They must be glorious.'

'No more than yours nor anyone else's. And when you open your eyes, you will.'

'May I call you "Alice"?'

'Hellfire, it would surely be an improvement on "madame".'

Carla felt another contraction arise. She stood up and leaned forward on the table. This time she groaned without inhibition and felt the better for it. As the pang in her belly waned, the pain in her back became so intense she feared she had done some injury to her spine. She pushed the heels of her hands into the agony, but couldn't push hard enough.

Alice lumbered to her feet. Her stoicism could not mask the effort it cost.

'Don't get up, Alice. It's passing now.'

Carla craned her neck and straightened and masked her discomfort. Alice shuffled around the table. Carla saw that her ankles and feet were so swollen they overlapped the edges of her slippers. Alice rubbed her hands together and stood behind her.

'No wonder. Drop your shoulders, and widen your feet and push your hips out, you're not here for an audience with the Queen.'

Carla did as she was told and felt some improvement.

'Now, let's see if these angels won't give us a bit of help.'

Carla didn't feel Alice touch her, and was sure she hadn't, yet a deep heat crept through her loins. Within moments the pain had subsided to a gentle ache.

'How did you do that?'

'We all have healing hands if we would use them.'

Alice limped to a dresser, favouring one hip, and into a wide, deep bowl stacked two smaller bowls, two spoons, all of wood, and a knife. She set them on the table.

'Let me help you.'

'Don't fuss. It's done.'

Alice returned to the dresser. From a cupboard she took an earthen jar and brought it to the table. A worn grass-green cushion lay on her chair. She adjusted the cushion and sat down with a groan of relief. The purple patches on her cheeks were darker. She breathed with strain, propped up by her reddened elbows, and it took her several breaths to recover. Carla was worried. She didn't want the effort of attending her labour to overtax Alice. Couldn't they recruit some extra help? Alice saw Carla's expression.

'You were told not to fuss.'

Alice cleared her throat into her fist and swallowed with a florid grimace.

'Now, open that jar and let's set to.'

The earthen jar was painted with pitch and sealed with plaited willow twigs coated in wax. Carla cut the lid off and a sweet aroma rose from the neck. She was starving. The jar was filled to the brim with liquid honey and halved pears. She loaded the small bowls.

'This smells delicious, but of more than just honey and pears.'

'There's some quinces diced up in there if you dig deep. They're choice. And don't skimp on the honey, pour as if our souls depended on it. We want to finish this jar before my son gets back. It's a miracle it's survived this long.'

'Where has Grymonde gone?'

'This old woman has learned not to ask.'

'But he'll be back?'

Carla felt safe here; but Grymonde would make her feel safer.

'That big bowl is for you, in case you puke.'

'I'm still leaking.'

'The floor's seen worse. Just let us know if it shows green or bloody.'

'May I stand to eat? It feels more comfortable.'

'Please do, it will help the babe along.'

'Really? That is, I would stand on my head if you so counselled, it's just that previous midwives instructed me to lie in bed all day.'

Alice confined her opinion on said practice to a grunt and a curl of her lip.

'Wait until the surgeons get their hands on us, as of course they're scheming to do. The gravediggers and priests will make a fortune.'

Alice grabbed a bowl and they ate, Carla passing compliments while Alice supped and sighed and smacked her lips. Carla felt a surge of deep tenderness for the old woman, so deep she didn't know what to do with it; so deep she again felt tears begin to trickle down her cheeks. Alice pushed her empty bowl across the table and Carla refilled it and poured more honey. A tear fell into the bowl and she apologised. She set the jar down and took a sip of rosehip tea.

'Our Mother welcomes all her children's tears, love. They remind her we're worth all that we've cost her. And happy tears most of all. Here, let's heat that tea up.'

'No, it's good cold, to wash down the honey.'

Carla drank again and composed herself. She wasn't used to so many sentiments.

'*Play for her*,' whispered Amparo.

Her voice was so clear that Carla turned around. She saw no light or emanation, and was disappointed, but her eyes fell on her violl case stacked among the rummage.

'What did she say?' asked Alice.

'She told me to play for you.'

'The fiddle's yours, not plunder? As if we needed any more.'

'Grymonde took nothing from me. I don't understand why. He's so –'

Carla hesitated. She didn't know how to continue.

'My son is mad, bloody and beautiful. His affairs are his, and yours are yours, this woman doesn't pry. But his dominion stops at that door, so if he troubles you, let us know.'

'I'm not his prisoner, at least I don't think so.'

'We'll leave it at that. Are you fit to play?'

'Until the next pang comes, yes.'

'You can't say no to an angel, love. And the rest of us would fain listen, too.'

As Carla took the violl case the next pang came and she was glad, for its passing would give her time to play. She leaned on the case and rode the spasm. Its strength was greater yet, and lights danced behind her clenched eyelids, but it took less from her than the one that had almost laid her low in the yard. She realised how frightened she had been, despite her bravado. She stretched. She undid the ties on the case and took the violl and bow and sat on the edge of her chair.

Her stomach bulged across her thighs and as much as she spread her legs the baby had shifted so far down, and her muscles were so tense, she could hardly bow at all. She lifted the instrument clear and closed her thighs, and rested the violl against the outside of her left thigh and twisted sideways towards it. The position was imperfect but easier.

'Amparo came from Spain. She brought this *Follia* with her, from the dances known to the bull drovers she grew up with. It isn't a piece in the usual sense. It has no fixed form or theme, though it belongs to the key of D minor. We never knew where it was going to take us. We never played it the same way twice.'

She felt suddenly bashful, which was unlike her. But though she had played for princes and rogues, she had never had an audience like this. She turned her head. Alice was watching her. She nodded. Carla took courage from the angel at her back.

'Amparo said it should be played as if you're trying to catch the wind.'

Carla's gambo violl was as much a part of her as the fingers that played it. And yet, as she bowed an arpeggio from treble to bass to prove the tuning – as she'd done ten thousand times before and more – the vast and bottomless sound that rolled through the room stole her breath away.

She heard Amparo sigh.

She heard Alice murmur.

The violl spoke from where Carla stood, teetering on the rim between death and life. The instrument was as close to her heart as any other living thing; and that it was a thing alive she knew as surely as she knew her own name. During her solitude – and not then alone but always: in love and in confusion, in grief, in gladness, in desperation, in shame – the violl had affirmed, and acclaimed, all that was most true in her spirit. Before the chord could fade she plunged after it, running pell-mell along the rim, chasing the wind.

Notes in abandon flew with her and came from she knew not where. They blew through her being in shifting gusts, like wasteful seas, like falling blossom, like hail, like startled doves; like peals of thunder. She wept. She smiled. She dissolved. She knew not who she was. And in that not-knowing she knew a oneness with all that she had never imagined. Wood; skin; strings; sound; child; quinces; woman. Pang. She leaned forward into the pang, into the violl, sawing the bow, faster, stronger, no longer chasing the wind but riding it. She threw her head back and cried out in ecstasy. The *Follia* cried out with her, and the rim itself dissolved, and life and death merged to avow the oneness.

The *Follia* had no end; that was its nature.

And so, when Carla at last stopped playing, she didn't know it.

'Carla, are you all right, love?'

Carla felt a hand on her shoulder and opened her eyes. She found herself bent over her lap, one arm cradling her belly and the other her gambo violl. She roused herself and looked up at Alice. The old woman's face was drawn.

'Alice, I'm sorry, I'm fine. If I alarmed you, forgive me.'

'Hush, now,' Alice's own voice was hushed. 'Let's not chase it away.'

She meant the *Follia*, and she was right. Its shade still lingered, like incense.

Alice took the violl. She tried to stoop to pick up the bow from the floor but had to pause halfway. She leaned on the violl for support. Carla retrieved the bow and they straightened up together. Their faces were inches apart. They had not been so close before.

Carla's condition had mewed her up within it, within herself and her need to birth her child. She knew it, because now she saw how frail Alice was. She had seen the signs but not felt the fact of it; and the old woman's fundamental force was so great it masked her infirmity. Carla knew too, that if Alice hadn't chosen to reveal it, she wouldn't have seen it.

Carla put her arms around her. Her belly pressed against her.

Alice laid her cheek on Carla's breast. Her voice almost cracked.

'All my days I waited to hear the Song of the Earth.'

Carla stroked her hair. It was thin and dry. Carla didn't speak. Alice raised her head and for the first time put a hand on Carla's belly. Her touch was unexpectedly delicate yet Carla felt her body giving up its secrets. Alice nodded and her former indomitability was restored. She stepped back and handed over the violl.

'He's well on his way. Or she's on hers.'

Alice lumbered back to the table, once again radiating largeness.

As Carla stowed the violl, she realised that Alice had said 'I'.

She closed the case and turned and saw Alice take a slim deck of cards from a shelf. She sorted through them, selected one, and laid it face-up on the table. She spent some moments in its silent contemplation. She closed her eyes and splayed the rest of the cards face-down and mixed them, moving her whole body back and forth as she circled and crossed her palms. She stopped and opened her eyes and gathered the deck back together and cut some from the top with her left hand, and set them aside. From the stack that remained she drew a card and laid it on the table, below and to the left of the one she had selected. Though its image must have been familiar, she absorbed it with the raptness of a trance. She turned another to the right of the second card, and studied this, too, and then a fourth to the right of the third to form a line. She set the deck aside, and put her palms on the table, and leaned over the cards for what seemed a long time.

Whatever Alice may have been reading in the cards, Carla could not read her.

Carla waited. Another pang came. She leaned on her knees and rode the wave. The power was intense, yet it no longer frightened her. The power was hers now. The birth was no longer something that was happening to her; she was no longer in Nature's fist; the birth was something she and Nature were doing together. The spasm passed.

Alice sat down in her chair and beckoned Carla to stand beside her.

The first card Carla saw was Death. She looked away.

'Now then,' said Alice. 'What shall we two witches make of these?'

CHAPTER FOURTEEN

Burning Man

A t the bottom of the spiral staircase Tannhauser locked the door
and hung the key around Juste's neck. The twin girls were
sitting on the pew he had specified and were drinking from wooden
bowls. There was no sign of roasted fowl. The girls waved at him
and smiled their tormented red smiles, no doubt as so ordered by
their pimp. The soup had smeared the paint on their mouths.
Marooned in the black circles daubed on their lead-white faces,
their eyes were full of fear. The fear had been there the first time
he had seen them at the Saint-Jacques Gate. Fear always. Pain often.
Humiliation without cease.

Tannhauser turned away.

Tybaut was not to be seen.

Tannhauser left the cathedral by the central portal and stopped.

Fresh blood shimmered on the Parvis in a large, irregular pool,
its surface as tense as a globule of crimson quicksilver. It crept
outwards, with sudden excursions along the joints between the
flagstones. Four men had contributed to the globule's creation,
their throats cut with unusual thoroughness and depth, as if by
someone who boned meat for a living. Their corpses were slung
in a heap from which their all-but severed heads lolled out at
extreme angles, their black garments gleaming wet in the morning
sun.

Tannhauser watched as the bearded captain he had seen from
the tower cut the throat of a fifth Huguenot, whose hands, like those
of the already murdered, were tied behind his back. He did so with
the kind of skill that makes a difficult job look simple: a single stroke,
rotating from the hips, using a knife sharpened so many times its
blade was worn to a crescent. A primeval moan erupted from the

collective belly of the assembled, Catholic and Protestant united, at least for a moment, in their awe of indecent death.

The captain was a man of enormous size, and when the brief but spectacular fountains of gore had spent themselves in the lake, he dragged the corpse away with one hand and hefted it by its belt onto the pile.

Tannhauser felt Juste bury his face against his back. He looked for Clementine but the big grey mare was not to be seen.

The audience for the murders was composed of militiamen and their prisoners, along with those beggars and civilians of a ghoulish nature who had elected to stay behind in surprising numbers. The bearded captain looked at Tannhauser. Tannhauser returned his gaze. The captain sucked his moustache with his lower lip. He wore red and white ribbons entwined around his arm, as did a fair proportion of his men. He looked down at Tannhauser's feet. Tannhauser knew the freshened tide of blood was about to lap his boots. As it did so, he didn't step out of the way. A murmur rippled through the militia.

The captain raised his arms for silence, as if resenting the loss of attention.

'We've promised ourselves that for once in their greedy, thieving lives the lawyers wouldn't get away with it. Nor will the heretics and traitors who deny the True Presence, and who'd sell our city to the English and the Dutch for a handful of double farthings. And so here we are with the first batch of vermin, though God willing it won't be the last.'

A hearty cheer went up from his men. From the sixty or so victims awaiting their turn rose a cacophony of lamentations. The captain grinned.

'Do they have to be Huguenots, captain? Or will any lawyer do?'

The captain frowned and he was good at it.

'Steady now, men, this is serious work. The King's work. God's work. And who are we but His strong and humble hands, we who have sworn to accomplish His will?' He crossed himself with the bloody knife. 'So. Who's next? Come on, come on, the sooner we get through this lot the sooner we'll be on to the next.'

A sixth man was shoved to his knees. The captain stared at him. His face distorted with recognition and malice. He leaned over, almost nose-to-nose.

'You remember me, don't you? Course you do. Bernard Garnier? Falsely charged with murder in sixty-three? And persecuted ever since for debts thus incurred? You should remember, you turd, you've pocketed enough of my money.'

Vulgar laughter. The bound man closed his eyes.

'No, no, no,' said Garnier. 'We're saving this bastard till the end. Set him over there where he can watch. And take his shoes off. If he closes his eyes, stab him in the feet, and if he keeps on muttering his Huguenot filth stick him again. Now, bring his wife and children up, so he may watch me bleed them.'

Tannhauser glanced to his left as Tybaut arrived, still shirtless. His breaths were fast and shallow, both his pride and his courage stretched to their limits. His cheeks were swollen and red. He held one hand behind his back.

'Take my advice, Tybaut. Go away.'

'I want my key back.'

''Tis a pity you're a pimp. I might've had use for you.'

'Give me my key or I'll turn your boy in for a dirty heretic.'

'Go away now, Tybaut, or I will kill you.'

Tybaut sniggered. 'Oh yes? These are my people, not yours, you pillock.'

Tannhauser drew with his left and stabbed Tybaut through the gut below the breastbone. Beyond skin and muscle, the resistance to the blade faded, then he felt an elastic tug as he pierced the aorta. He withdrew the dagger and returned it to its sheath. The move took hardly longer than it had taken to slap him. Tybaut grunted, winded and astonished. The wound appeared unremarkable, yet inside his abdominal cavity his life was rushing away, embalming his coiled entrails in his own blood. The colour stole from his face. A knife tinkled to the ground. Impending death filled him with a need for Tannhauser's blessing.

'There's thousands worse off than my girls. Why'd you pick on me?'

Tybaut's eyes swam with bewilderment.

Tannhauser spun him by the arm and grabbed the back of his breeches.

'Here's another godless traitor. He's no lawyer but he'll do.'

Tannhauser hoisted him into the blood. Tybaut's legs tangled one about the other in their attempt to keep him upright. He fell full length, his arms too weak to break his fall, and a groan went up from the gathered as a great shower of gore speckled their clothes.

Tybaut's jaw drooped open. His last sigh bubbled into the red swill. Tannhauser seized an ox-tongue spear from the nearest militiaman and spun it down and wedged the blade through the rear of Tybaut's ribcage by the spine. In a pinch the ox-tongue would have served as a shovel. Though Tybaut was long gone, Tannhauser stood over him and ploughed him with steel.

He stabbed for his mother. He stabbed for Amparo. He stabbed for the twins with vermilion mouths drinking soup in the cathedral. He stabbed for Carla. Not one of them would have thanked him. All would have found him repellent. He stabbed the dead youth from the lava of rage and pain surging up through his heart as if from the stones beneath his feet. He mutilated the pimp in a spasm of disgust at his own impotence.

And just like the Devil squatting on his back, and his guardian Angel watching from the bell tower, he could see himself all the while.

He paused to blink sweat and blood from his vision. He looked down.

The ox-tongue spear had chopped Tybaut's ribs from either side of his backbone, exposing his core through two gaping trenches. Even in the grip of blind rage, the skill was commendable. Even by the standards established on the Parvis that morning, the sight was obscene.

Among the spectators there was absolute silence, as if they feared that to make a sound would doom them, too, and in that instinctive calculation they were not far wrong. Tannhauser looked up. His gaze met that of a Huguenot who knelt bound and shoeless, waiting to watch the death of his kin, at the outer rim of the blood.

The Huguenot was silent, too.

Yet did he mouth the words '*Kill me*'?

Or did he merely say as much with his eyes?

Or did Tannhauser hear the pleading of his own deranged spirit?

Neither Devil on his back nor Angel on the tower knew for sure.

He waded through the gore, the blood riding up over his boots like red mud, and drove the spear through the Huguenot's heart. He heard a woman's cry from among the prisoners. The kind of cry torn from the inmost workings of a woman who has lost the man she loved. He put a foot to the Huguenot's chest and shoved him from the blade.

He turned and looked up at the cathedral and its vast and mysterious text. He heard the Green Lion roar and he wanted to roar himself, for he heard its message. Petrus Grubenius had tried to convince him to devote himself to its truth. A message so radical it could only be written in – and trusted to – an alchemical code so mysterial that few living men would ever read it and fewer still take it to their hearts. Tannhauser had merely taken it into his memory.

The only manifestation of wisdom that is worthy of the wise is compassion.

Compassion for the worthless and the forsaken.

Compassion for the victims of the strong.

All other paths, no matter how glorious, lead only to emptiness and folly.

He could have taken a dozen militiamen at least; given their quality, probably all thirty, though by ten or so even these donkeys might have the sense to run for their lives. Without looking, he positioned Garnier in his mind, for the captain would have to go first. And if they did not run, if they stayed to fight, then so much the better, for what more apt ground than here on the Parvis to admit his failure in the art of life, in the custodianship of his soul, thence to stake his claim on everlasting fire?

He thought: *I am going mad. And I love it.*

The clatter of massive hooves declared Clementine's arrival.

Tannhauser turned again. He saw Grégoire take in the blood-bath, in which Tannhauser stood ankle-deep, with gore running down the spear shaft and the dead heaped around him like the proof of unspeakable crimes. He saw Grégoire grin, his exposed gums shiny and snotty with the mucus from his nostril. Grégoire grinned because he was glad to see him and for no other reason at all. He did not care what Tannhauser had done. He loved Tannhauser. The grin restored Tannhauser's sanity.

He tossed the ox-tongue spear to its owner. The owner ducked and shielded himself with his arms and the spear clattered to the ground. Grégoire shoved the big mare into the perfect position for Tannhauser to step into the stirrup and mount. Tannhauser did so and looked down at Juste. Juste was pale. Tannhauser wondered how much more he could take. With a gesture he ordered him to hold on and Juste grabbed the stirrup.

Tannhauser looked at Captain Garnier, who had witnessed it all. The speed and precision of the kills; the berserk frenzy. Garnier blinked. Tannhauser ran a slow glance across the other spectators. If any of them recognised Tybaut, and it was at least as likely as not that they did, no one spoke up for him.

'Won't you stay to see off more heretics, chevalier?' asked Garnier.

Tannhauser didn't answer. He looked at the huddled doomed. He felt nothing for them. But he had heard the Green Lion roar. He turned back to Bernard Garnier.

'This ground was consecrate to God before men discovered fire. These stones are the sacred centre of Paris, of France, some say of the world. By the law of divine symmetry, and in the opinions of diverse philosophers, it is probable that beneath our feet is the vertex of the cone of Hell itself.'

This was rewarded with a general gust of dismay.

'The burning lake below is far from full. On this weird locus, we all should beware what sacrifice in blood we offer to gods unknown, for one thing is certain: if this sacrifice is meant for Christ, it will curdle His bowels.'

Many in the crowd retreated from the Parvis, step by step, as if from some poisonous swamp. Garnier groomed his beard with bloody fingers.

'As for these Huguenot women and children, I speak for His Majesty in person when I urge you to take them to the priests in the cathedral. Give them the chance to consider a Catholic baptism and if not, to claim sanctuary. If you deny them that small mercy, what mercy will you deserve come the Last Judgement? When we rise from our tombs and Michael takes a reckoning of our souls, and our eternal destiny is weighed on the balance of the love we showed, not only to God, but to all His Creation.'

He pointed out the apocalypse carved above the cathedral's central portal.

'Is it coincidence that Judgement Day is here writ above our heads?'

A Huguenot cried out: 'We would rather die than submit to popery.'

Tannhauser did not know which Huguenot had spoken, yet he answered him.

'Do you, too, crave more blood?'

'The good chevalier is right,' declared Captain Garnier, whose cravings were not in question. 'Let this windbag, whoever he is, demonstrate his piety by taking his right place at the front of the line.'

No one moved.

Perhaps, in fairness, the anonymous theologian was about to do so, but at that moment the scorched dog bolted forward and rolled in the blood in an ecstasy of abandon. His eyes bulged, his tongue lolled, he growled with satisfaction, the sound deep and sinister for an animal so small. It seemed to Tannhauser an excellent way to salve his blisters and burns, but the dog's exploit provoked more gasps and whimpers, from either side of the religious schism, than had the murders. The crowd retreated further.

'Lucifer, come here,' shouted Grégoire.

In case Grégoire's pronunciation had been lost on the dog, Juste added 'Lucifer!'

'The beast is possessed.'

'Satan speaks through him.'

'We'll fall down the cone of Hell.'

Tannhauser kicked Clementine into motion. Grégoire and Juste, more concerned with the cur than with the mob, almost let go of their stirrups.

'He'll follow his pack,' said Tannhauser.

So he did. Mantled and gleaming from ears to tail in the bright, comingled gore of lawyers and pimp, Lucifer righted himself in the wallow and scampered in pursuit, splattering those in range with globs of blood. The boys lavished him with praise. As the dog took his place between Clementine's hooves, Tannhauser reached the cross street beyond the Hôtel-Dieu. He paused to take his bearings.

Ahead, towards the spire of Sainte-Chapelle, members of Garnier's militia ransacked houses and conferred in urgent knots over the bodies heaped in the gutters.

The street to his right ran back over the Pont Notre-Dame, where more dead lay in reeking piles. Men were pillaging various of the fine shops on the bridge, carrying trunks and furniture from doorways, and pitching goods down from upper-floor windows. At the far end, where the chain blocked the thoroughfare, a confrontation brewed; between whom he could not say.

To his left, a shorter bridge spanned the narrow branch of the Seine. It was jammed by a similar uproar, most intense around the gaping arch of the squat stone fortress on the far bank.

'The Petit Châtelet,' said Grégoire. 'For the *sergents*. And a prison.'

Tannhauser continued west, past a row of public latrines and a narrow wharf of crude pilings that fell steeply to the Seine. Two boys, no older than eight, struggled to lug the corpse of a woman to the edge of the wharf, prodded to the task by the swords of two militiamen. The boys swung the woman into the river but their effort was ill coordinated and her head bashed the timbers as she fell. The boys turned around, blinking at the world in which they were stranded, and the militiamen stabbed them and shoved them off the wharf to join the woman in the turbid water. The men exchanged nods, as if to affirm a job well done.

Tannhauser pressed on.

The next bridge, Saint-Michel, was as chaotic as the others, he presumed for similar reasons. Those trying to leave the island were blocked by a chain across the end of the street. At the same time, on the other side of the chain, a second crowd sought to escape the Left Bank for the Cité.

In the middle of the two mobs a handful of archers in the jerkins and caps of the *sergents à verge* tried to impose their authority, though to what end was clear to no one, least of all themselves. So far their only success had been to stir the toxic brew of anger, confusion and alarm that characterised the general mood.

From certain upper windows of the houses lining the bridge, a gallery of citizens added taunts, laughter, threats and legal advice to the rising tide of altercation. By means of climbing on the shoulders of a taller comrade, and waving a green neckerchief, one of the *sergents* won an interlude of relative quiet.

'Gentlemen! Gentlemen! Even if we accept that this chain has no sound purpose at all,' he shouted, 'we can nevertheless be certain that the chain would not be here if its purpose was to be ignored! In short, gentlemen, it does not matter *why* the chain *is* here! What matters is that the chain is here! And in the unhappy absence of any known statute, principle or decree governing the movement of the public in relation to this chain, we are obliged to remain on one side or the other until some higher authority enlightens us!'

The mob absorbed this valiant attempt at quasi-legalistic reasoning as best it could, then erupted into catcalls, obscenities and a variety of learned refutations pooling case histories referencing the rights of the city's inhabitants, with special respect to the Sabbath, dating back to the time of Julius Caesar. There was pushing and shoving.

The *sergent* teetered on his perch.

Tannhauser judged the moment ripe to add Clementine's bulk to the argument.

'Lads, hold on to Clementine's tail.'

Once again Grégoire's choice of mount proved inspired. Clementine shoved her way through the press at a steady, merciless pace. Bodies lurched and in some cases flew to either side, accompanied by oaths and cries of pain. Clementine showed neither remorse nor favouritism for age, disability or sex. When they reached the chain, Tannhauser found himself a head higher than the elevated *sergent*. They conducted their conversation above the milling crowd.

'Mattias Tannhauser, Chevalier of Malta, military adviser to His Majesty the Duc d'Anjou, and diplomatic envoy at large to Albert Gondi, Comte de Retz.'

The *sergent* could not have been happier to see him. He saluted. His grin was distinguished by a single front tooth in his otherwise vacant upper jaw.

'Constable Alois Frogier, Excellency. You are Heaven-sent. Confusion reigns.'

'I've come directly from a meeting of the *commissaires* at the Châtelet. Who ordered you to block this bridge?'

'Excellency, Captain Garnier gave the order.'

'Are you telling me the *sergents* of the Châtelet now take their orders from the volunteer militia? Does the *Lieutenant* know you've allowed the militia to usurp his authority?'

Frogier's fear was as naked as any Tannhauser had seen all morning.

'No, Excellency, probably not, though no usurpation has taken place, and if any such error, through no fault of my own, appears to have been administered, then perhaps the *Lieutenant* should not know, that is with your kind permission and sympathy. The confusion, you see. The rebellion. Captain Garnier claimed that –'

'Bernard Garnier has no claim on the officers or resources of the Châtelet. Do you understand? Can we rely on you in this?'

Frogier saluted as he swayed like a sailor in the rigging. 'Excellency, you can!'

'The mass of these people are good Catholic citizens who want only to retreat to the safety of their homes, which is exactly where the King, the *Lieutenant* and the Bureau de Ville want everyone who lacks a useful role in the maintenance of order to be. A sound policy, you agree?'

'Excellency, I could not agree more sincerely.'

'Lower the chain so the street can clear. Have your men create two channels, one to flow in either direction. Then present yourself to me.'

Jostling provoked the *sergent* upon whose shoulders Frogier sat to launch a flurry of punches at the nearest citizens. Frogier wheeled his arms and toppled towards the ground. Tannhauser could have righted him but, to authenticate his status, chose not to do so. While Frogier picked himself up and began bellowing at his men – who set about the crowd with their maces – Tannhauser looked across the chaos to the Collège d'Harcourt.

Whatever Orlandu had been up to, it was connected to his mother's death. He could not imagine Carla provoking homicidal intent, but the possibilities for trouble inhering in youth were to all intents infinite. He wanted another chat with the old porter who had warned Petit Christian about Tannhauser. But the smoke worried him. His guns. The printer's daughters. The porter could wait.

Frogier presented himself at Clementine's shoulder, the great mare providing the rock around which the two opposing streams of humanity now flowed.

'Frogier, what's the situation in the sixteenth?'

'Excellency, we have been told to keep out of the sixteenth *quartier*.'

'By Bernard Garnier?'

'Yes, Excellency. We have clear orders from the Châtelet *not* to hunt, arrest or kill unarmed Huguenot citizens; though, as Captain Garnier pointed out, we have not been ordered to prevent anyone else from doing so.'

'So the militia have a free hand in the sixteenth?'

'Yes, Excellency, and to give credit where it is due, they are killing them wherever they find them. That is, killing heretics. Alley by alley, house by house, room by room. Elements of the student population are assisting them. After all, they live there. They know who's who and what's what and which rats might go to ground in which hole.'

'What were your orders before Garnier commandeered you?'

'To man our booth in the Place Maubert, as usual.'

'Then we both know your rightful place. If any other units have been illegally seconded to the militia, you have my authority to release them.'

'At once, Excellency.'

'That man of yours with a whited eye, order him to surrender his bow and quiver to me. Let him say it was expropriated by the militia. I will give you an *écu d'or*, which you can divide as you feel is just.'

'I wouldn't want your life to depend on his bow, Excellency, but for two *écus d'or* you may expropriate mine. As you see, it is a far better weapon.'

Tannhauser examined the bow for cracks and flaws and found none. While not as short as the Turkish weapon he preferred, it was short enough to fire from the saddle or in a tight space. The nocking point was served with red silk and hardly worn. He flexed the bow and reckoned its draw weight at around sixty pounds, enough to fell a stag, though Altan Savas, whose bow drew at over a hundred, would have laughed at it.

'It's a decent string at least.'

'Beeswax and linen, my own weave. Sixty strands of shoemaker's thread in three cords. Gives a kick this horse would be proud of. There's a spare in the quiver.'

'Let me see an arrow.'

Frogier offered a deerskin quiver of a dozen or so. Tannhauser took one. White birch, by the grain. Accurately fletched. The bodkins were the length of his forefinger and filed like stilettos. The nock was made of horn and sought the string of its own accord.

'Two years seasoned, double-varnished and perfectly matched for spine and weight to this bow. Those bodkins are charcoal-hardened.'

He glanced at Frogier's wrist guard. He wouldn't have got it over his knuckles.

'No broadheads?'

A broadhead was like shooting a man with a knife, and leaving it inside him. Each time he moved or breathed, it sliced him deeper.

'The Châtelet banned them, Excellency. They were obliged to spend too much money on surgeons – you wouldn't believe how often these lads hit the wrong criminal. But who needs a surgeon to pull out a bodkin? Don't despair, those will split a barn door at half a furlong.'

'The green and red paint between the feathers, is that your own livery?'

'Don't worry, Excellency, if a shaft were to be found in the wrong place, the blame would fall on the Huguenot who stole my gear this morning, in the confusion.'

'They are notorious thieves.'

'For the extra *écu d'or*, a man of vigilance might even be able to identify the culprit, among the dead.'

Tannhauser turned south past the Collège d'Harcourt and the Red Ox into the Rue de la Harpe. Just beyond the tavern, as if to demarcate a boundary beyond which decency could be abandoned, a dead man hung by his ankles from the iron pole of a shop sign. Tannhauser had crossed that frontier already. He steered Clementine well clear.

The inverted corpse was naked and a cross had been cut into his belly, though whether as a symbolic act or to facilitate his disembowelment could not be known. His entrails dangled in a twisted cluster that obscured his face. The pink and grey coils were streaked with yellow fat and had not yet lost their lustre, and some of them crawled between the others with slow contractions, as if fear clung to life when all other feelings were extinguished.

Tannhauser pressed on.

Bodies wetted the dust in the street. Five. Ten. A score. More. He stopped counting. Most of them were men, more or less fully grown. Axed, stabbed, bludgeoned, strangled, often a combination thereof. They lay in random locations, struck down on thresholds or at the mouths of alleys, caught outdoors wearing the wrong clothes, the wrong faces, the wrong names. Two hung by the neck from improvised nooses. Men who had ignored the warnings or who had not heard them.

No one was ignoring them now. After yesterday's teeming the

street was eerie in its emptiness. It was filled, as elsewhere, with a sense that a multitude huddled in concealment. Shouts bounced around between walls distant and near, the kind of yells of warning and pursuit as attend a hunting party. Street dogs yip-yip-yarooed. He heard screams. Screams pitched so high by terror even more than by pain that Tannhauser could not tell if they came from the throats of woman, man or child.

Thirty or forty thousand Huguenots lived in Paris. He still would not credit the civic militia with the wit, or even the spite, to execute a purge on such a scale. But hundreds of tiny massacres, conducted by a score or so of small, militant death gangs: that he could believe. Unrestrained, and with time, such gangs could rack up the numbers of an army claiming havoc.

Lucifer trotted to sniff each corpse they passed by. Informed by some logic of his own, he pissed on some but not on others. The blood in the fur on the front half of his body had congealed to leave the hairs stiffened and spiky, so that he looked a good deal bulkier than before. By contrast, on his bald rear half the coating had dried into a dark red sheath, with a strange matte texture, like the skin of some as yet unidentified reptile. The dog was increasingly alert to another smell, and so was Tannhauser. The cloud of smoke that drifted above the rooftops stank of charred paper, grey fragments of which floated earthward. It stank, also, of burning meat.

As Tannhauser rode by a cross street he saw a gang of men battering down the doors to a pair of adjoining houses with axes and pike butts. Youths, who Tannhauser took to be students, threw stones through the windows and yelled threats and taunts to those inside, alternately urging and daring them to open the locks. They glanced at Tannhauser, and he looked at them, and they turned away.

At the end of this street he could see the high rim of the city walls. The smell of burning intensified. He came to the corner of the street where the printer lived.

He stopped and dismounted.

He peered around the edge of the building and saw a bonfire

in the middle of the road. The best of the blaze was over. It was largely composed of books, whose ashes now formed a great black pile. As the embers caught a breath of air, sudden streaks of luminous red striated the blackness, and random bursts of flame erupted skyward. In the centre of the pile was a charred and trussed body, by its size probably a man's. A militiaman stood on the far side of the fire, downwind of the smoke, scratching himself. A second emerged from the open door beneath the sign bearing the name of Daniel Malan. He was carrying Tannhauser's wheel-lock rifle, which he examined in the sunlight with puzzlement.

Tannhauser turned back. He tied Clementine to an iron rail outside a shop.

He looked at Grégoire and Juste.

'I will be back shortly, but to you the time will seem long. If anyone comes by, especially militia or students, I want you to be prepared to escape. Keep your distance. Do not let them surround you. Do not let them get close enough to grab you. Do not trust anyone. Treat all as you would a poisonous snake. If they ask who you are, tell them you are guarding my horse, and that I am engaged on a mission of great importance for Captain Garnier. If you see that they intend to take Clementine, let them do so and run away. Do not worry for Clementine's safety, for no one will harm her even if they steal her. Unlike the rest of us, her value is beyond question.'

Tannhauser unlimbered Frogier's bow

'Can't we come with you?' asked Juste.

'No.'

'I am a very fair archer. In Poland I've shot hare, ducks, deer, boar –'

'Your job today is to avoid becoming the quarry. Now – see – you have three choices of escape from here, four if you count running towards the fire. Grégoire, you know this district well enough, don't you?'

'I see six choices,' said Grégoire.

'Good. You should be able to outrun and outfox any I've seen on the street. But don't try to be too clever. If you have any doubts or fears, I order you to run, even before they get close. Trust your instincts.'

'We're not cowards,' said Juste.

'I know you're not cowards so let me hear no more of such nonsense. Make Lucifer your guide – he will detect evil intentions before you do. And when you run, he will follow. Remember, Clementine is safe but Lucifer is not, for he is worthless. They will kill him for the fancy. You must run to protect him.'

The boys looked down at the wretched little cur and then at each other. They seemed agreed that the dog's life was worth more than both of theirs put together.

'I repeat, if you have to run – if you want to run – run. You can either circle back here to see if it's safe –'

He looked about the surrounding streets.

'See, you can spy from there, and there, or that alley there.'

They nodded, the notion gaining the appeal of a dangerous game.

'Or you can make your way back to Engel's stable. If either you or your bodies are not here when I return, I want to know where I can find you.'

Tannhauser pulled five arrows and nocked one to the bowstring. The others he held in the same hand as the bow, Tartar-style.

'We have no weapons,' said Juste.

'If you have weapons you will fight, and if you fight you will be killed. Your weapons are your brains and your feet.'

Tannhauser walked through a light blizzard of charred paper, the bow and arrows by his left thigh, his eyes slitted against the smoke, his stomach soured by the familiar smell of burning flesh. It always made him salivate, the worse so when he was hungry, as he was now. He felt a rising nausea. The burning man was most likely Daniel Malan. He was not the first man Tannhauser had seen roasted on a pyre of his own books. It was the kind of jape that appealed to certain minds. Thus had Petrus Grubenius met his end, at the hands of other fanatics, led by Orlandu's father. The body was face-down and only half-consumed. His hands had been tied behind his back and thence to his ankles.

The blackened skin of his back and his thighs had swollen and split. Rivulets of molten grease trickled into embers and crackled briefly into flame.

Tannhauser mastered his need to vomit. He hurried by.

The two militiamen were debating the workings of the rifle, but as the dog-arm remained locked back in the safe position, it posed no threat. Tannhauser heard shouts and screams, some of them female, though these were now so routine as to arouse no reaction in the two volunteers. Beyond Malan's house, several more doors – three, four – stood open on the same side of the street. He saw pole arms too cumbersome to use inside – pikes, halberds – stacked against the wall by each door. The butts and blades of some of them were blackened by soot. They must have used them to shovel Malan back into the flames, when he squirmed away. With luck, perhaps one had killed him.

A rough count: twenty weapons.

The two militia looked up as he strode towards them through the smoke.

'God bless His Majesty,' said Tannhauser. 'Where is Captain Garnier?'

'Garnier?' said the one with his rifle. 'I don't know, sire. He's not our captain.'

'Is that the printer?'

'That's the bastard in person, sire. We had timely information.'

Tannhauser let this pass. 'And his daughters?'

'Daughters, sire?' He looked at the second man. 'He has daughters?'

'They kept that quiet, the sly young dogs.'

'That rifle needs a key to wind the wheel, like a clock,' Tannhauser explained.

'I told you so,' said the second man, to the first.

'The key's usually stored inside the butt plate. Let me show you.'

Tannhauser smiled and stepped closer and drew his dagger from behind his elbow with his right hand. He stabbed the man with the rifle up and under the breastbone. The heart burst and he shoved him over and slashed for the throat of the second. The second was quicker than most and Tannhauser only cut his shoulder down to the bone before the man was running.

Tannhauser pegged the dagger in the dead man's chest and drew the nocked arrow with his thumb. At a range of five paces he shot the fugitive in the arse. The shaft pierced his left buttock halfway to the feathers as the bodkin threaded his pelvis and erupted from his groin. As the man was thrown to the ground, Tannhauser snatched his dagger and ran and fell on him from behind. He stabbed him through the root of the neck and with a stroke severed the vessels of the upper thorax. He sheathed the dagger unwiped.

He straightened amid the smoking debris and the silence of the slain.

He saw and heard nothing to suggest he had been observed. He put one foot on the end of the arrow in the dead man's arse and with a sharp tread he snapped the shaft off. He grabbed the feathered stump with its red and green livery and twisted it free of its splinters. He tossed it on the fire. He nocked a fresh arrow. He retrieved his rifle and slung it across his back by its strap. The shuttering had been torn from the front of Daniel Malan's shop. He looked inside. Bookshelves had been emptied and torn down, display cases pitched over. There was no one there.

He glanced inside the door. The hallway was empty. He grabbed the first militiaman by the collar of his jerkin and dragged him inside and dropped him. He listened. He heard vague sounds from the rear of the ground floor. He heard others, muffled voices, from up the staircase, which ascended from halfway down the hallway, on the left. The house was one room wide. Three open doors lay ahead, two on the right, the same side as the shop front; the last directly ahead at the corridor's end. From the third door came a dim light. One closed door stood to the left, under the stairway, which likely led to a basement.

Tannhauser dragged the second corpse inside. He grabbed a half-pike. He pushed the front door closed. The lock and upper bolt had been unseated from the door jamb. He shoved the point of the half-pike into the planking, and wedged the butt beneath the iron casing of the broken lock.

He headed down the corridor of the ground floor.

The house smelled of ink, turpentine and metals. Tannhauser glanced in the first doorway to confirm what he'd seen from outside. At the second door he listened, heard nothing and went inside. He found no one. The wooden frame of the printing press had been overturned. Tiny rectangles of type were scattered in heaps across the floor, along with job trays, tools and hand moulds. An ink-stained leather apron hung from a peg by a water butt. He took it and looped the neck strap over his head. The apron hardly reached his thighs but it covered the Maltese Cross on his chest. He moved on to the last room.

Short of the doorway he stopped. He could hear someone grunting with effort. He recalled that wherever three men are gathered, at least one is called Jean.

'Ho, there, Jean?'

'Both Jeans are upstairs,' came the reply.

Tannhauser stepped inside and drew and aimed his arrow at a man on his hands and knees at the far end of the room. The man had his back turned and he was engaged in rolling up a rug in front of a writing desk. Two candles guttered on an iron stand. The rest of the room was stacked with supplies. Malan's house was built directly onto the back wall of the next street. There was no rear exit.

Tannhauser relaxed the bow and drew his dagger and moved closer.

'Who else is up there? How many?'

'How would I know? I'm down here.'

The kneeler turned. Like many in the militia, he was a fellow in his twenties.

'Why? Who are you?'

'Is it true we've got two girls upstairs?'

'So they say, but who are you?'

The man rose to one knee and Tannhauser slashed his throat

from shoulder to shoulder. The fellow got a hand in the way and a finger flew. His blood surged massively and he fell into his own spillage. He made no sound that anyone outside the room could have heard. Tannhauser hauled him twitching into the corridor, where his neck wound would impress itself on anyone coming through the door. He stooped over the first two corpses, and stabbed each of them in both eyes.

He climbed the stairs. He heard distant screams from the houses next door but none from above. He did not wish upon Pascale and Flore any reason to scream, but the silence worried him. At the top of the staircase a landing bent back on itself. It passed two doors on its way to the next flight of steps to the top floor. To the left it extended to a back room with a doorless frame.

Tannhauser glanced back downstairs towards a noise. Already the front door rattled against the wedged pike. Someone hammered with a fist. A muffled shout came from the street. Tannhauser lunged at the open doorway of the back room.

As he got there a man appeared, roused by the hammering below. His hands were empty. His face showed no alarm until Tannhauser ran the dagger through his gut and opened him up to the breastbone. The man expelled a windy sigh that conveyed his self-pity. His breath was foul. He clung to a thread of life and Tannhauser hefted his weight on the blade, the breastbone hooked on the quillions. He shuffled backwards. The dying man staggered with him, blood and gall slithering forth down the apron, his weight collapsing forward with enough momentum to reach the top of the staircase.

Tannhauser turned and pitched him down the steps.

The man slid off the blade and toppled backwards in silence, his hands grasping in some final possessive spasm at the guts falling out between his legs. The assault on the front door was now pronounced and the butt of the pike was being jolted blow by blow from under the lock case. Tannhauser checked the back room. There was no one else in there. He strode to the second door. It was ajar. He shoved it open. There was no one inside. He heard the door to the street burst inward.

He heard stunned exclamations. He heard breathless oaths. He heard them ask each other if they were enough in number, or if they should not send for more.

Tannhauser kicked open the third door.

A kitchen. Two men.

The nearest had emerged from a pantry carrying a plate of apples and cheese. He was wearing a breastplate. Tannhauser stabbed him in the armpit and gouged him to the hilt. He twisted the blade but left it in place and let him sink wheezing to his knees. As the second man rose from a chair at a table, upon which lay a helmet and two short swords, Tannhauser drew an archer's yard and let go. The man cringed and threw out his left hand. The arrow went though his palm and nailed the hand to his chest. He fell back into the chair and stared at the shaft.

Tannhauser put the bow and three arrows on the table. He grabbed one of the swords. The bodkin-pierced militiaman bawled for help. He raised his right arm to defend himself and Tannhauser put both hands into the swing, and cut the arm off above the elbow. The sword had a better edge than he had expected. The bawling turned into formless screams. Tannhauser grabbed a dishcloth and stuffed it in the gaping mouth.

He seized the nailed arm and dragged the man from his chair and across the room. The first man was on his knees and elbows, panting for breath and staring at the pool of blood beneath his face. Tannhauser shoved the one-armed man into the wall by the door. The manhandling had dragged the pierced hand some six inches along the shaft towards the fletching. The iron bodkin was embedded near its full length in the upper chest. Tannhauser pulled out the dishcloth. Red foam bubbled out behind it.

'Where are the two girls?'

'Upstairs.' He saw his stump and sobbed. 'They're upstairs, sire. Upstairs.'

'With Jean?'

'Jean? Yes, I'm Jean. I have five children.' He swayed.

'How many men are upstairs with the girls?'

'Two, sire. Jean and ah . . . Yes, Jean is upstairs, but it's not me, it's another Jean. Jean and – give me a minute, sire, I'll remember, Jean and –' He coughed red drool. 'Students, sire. I didn't know 'em until this morning. I only came in for a bit of breakfast, sire. That's all. A bit of breakfast.'

'Is that why your clothes stink of smoke?'

'Please don't kill me, sire. I haven't even seen the girls. Please don't kill me.'

'Close your eyes.'

Jean did so. 'Jean and Ebert. Yes, Ebert. Please, sire, don't kill me.'

Tannhauser crammed the rag back into his mouth and stood back. He mustered a second swing and cut off Jean's nailed hand at the wrist. The blow knocked the bodkin loose but did not dislodge it. Jean took a deep breath to scream and sucked the rag down his throat. Tannhauser pulled the arrow from Jean's chest with the hand still impaled. The bodkin was not deformed. He slid the severed hand free of the shaft and pitched the arrow onto the table. The hand was sweaty and hot. He tossed it through the door and into the stairwell. Blasphemies erupted from those who saw it land.

Jean was strangling on the dishrag but had no means of pulling it out. Tannhauser pushed him out of the door. The ceiling of the landing was the full height of the stairwell, plenty of space for the third swing, which clove Jean's skull through the vault as far as his eyebrows. It was not a blow Tannhauser would use with his own sword; there were better strokes with less risk of damage to the blade, but the scalp bled to spectacular effect around the lodged steel. He left the sword in place and tilted Jean backwards over the rail. Tannhauser wasn't sure if anyone had yet dared start to climb the staircase. If they had, the bleeding body dropped on top of them.

The consternation below reached a new crescendo. He heard someone call for cannon and someone else for cavalry. If only they had armour. If only they were decently equipped. If only their heroic service were better appreciated. He heard the militia retreat as far as the street.

He returned to the kitchen where the man with the apples and cheese had died. Tannhauser recovered his dagger from his thorax and wiped and sheathed it. He pushed two apples into his doublet. The cheese was fouled with gore. He rolled the dead man flat on his back, dragged him out onto the landing and kicked his legs apart. From the kitchen table he grabbed his bow and arrows, and the second bastard sword. With a ditch-digger's thrust he planted the sword through the dead man's genitals, the tip biting deep into the wooden planks beneath. He renocked the bloody shaft to the bowstring and headed to the third floor.

At the top of the stair, which was narrower than the one below, he found a shorter landing and only two doors, both of them closed. In the ceiling at the rear a trapdoor hung open. An ingenious folding ladder, which was attached to the trapdoor, hung down from the loft. He looked up. All was dark and quiet. He couldn't see a way out onto the roof, but there had to be one.

He stopped by a large wicker basket filled with laundry. He heard two male voices from the farther of the two bedrooms, the one at the front of the house. Jean's screams had not disturbed them, nor had the shouting below; but they'd been ignoring screams and shouts all morning. He unslung his rifle and checked the pan. Since the day before, someone had primed it. The wheel was cocked. He laid the rifle in the laundry basket.

He imagined what to expect. A cramped bedroom, the same size as the kitchen. Furniture, beds, clutter. Obstructions of every kind. Two innocent parties. Two young, untested hostiles. A fair chance of panic. He hadn't found his pistols.

He unslung the quiver and put it with the rifle. He unbuckled his sword belt and added that, too. He drew the lapis lazuli dagger and took the bow and bloody arrow.

He stood at the first door and listened. Nothing. He turned the handle, threw the door open, drew the arrow. A ransacked bedroom. A man's shoes. The fragrance of orange water. Daniel Malan's room. He stopped at the final room.

He had let Carla die. In his mind's eye he saw her face.

Tannhauser kicked on the door.

'Jean. Ebert. Put your britches on and come out. The captain wants us.'

Silence fell. Then low, frenzied murmurs. Students, not militia. A debate. They sounded guilty, anxious. No sound from Pascale or Flore. But then silence was the usual response to violence and rape. A reedy male voice piped up.

'We can't come out right now. Our regrets.'

'Tell the captain we will join him later.'

'Regrets?' Tannhauser kicked again. 'You'll regret a good flogging.'

He heard a key turn in the lock.

'Listen here, sirrah,' a voice began, with a stab at lordly authority. 'We're not members of your militia and we're entitled to do as we please. Is that clear?'

At that, as if to dramatise the point, the fellow popped the door open.

Tannhauser was about to stab him when he recognised one of the two actors he had thrashed in the Red Ox the day before. The actor recognised him, too.

He almost screamed: 'No. No. We saved them. We saved them both.'

Tannhauser pulled the upstroke that was meant to gut him, and smashed the pommel of the dagger through the bridge of his nose. The bones gave way and rivulets of blood snorted forth. Tannhauser kicked the actor's legs from under him and shoved. The actor hit the floor as Tannhauser entered, the thumb of his dagger hand on the bowstring. He drew and aimed at the second actor, who rose from a chair by the window. He noted that both men had been gouged in the face by fingernails.

'Sit down or I will kill you. Put both hands under your arse.'

The youth obeyed, his eyes flitting back and forth from the gleaming leather apron to the wet red bodkin aimed at his chest.

'Are you Jean?'

'Yes and it's true,' said Jean, 'we saved them both —'

'Don't speak. Stare at your balls.'

Jean obeyed.

Tannhauser looked at Pascale and Flore.

They were alive. They were fully dressed. They appeared unharmed. To his shame he felt tears cloud his vision. He lowered the bow and sheathed his dagger. The room contained a double bed, two chairs, a table by the window; sundry jumble and clutter. Pascale and Flore sat on the farther side of the bed. Ebert lay face-down, snivelling blood. Tannhauser stomped on his left ribs.

'Ebert, crawl under the bed.'

Ebert moaned and snaked across the floor until his head and shoulders were crammed under the bed. He started crying. Ebert had a knife at his waist. Tannhauser took it. It was trash. He threw it out of the door. He stomped on Ebert's right ribs and felt the cartilages crackle under his heel where they joined the spine. He turned to Jean and took a long butcher's knife from Jean's belt. It was new and appeared unused. He held the edge under Jean's chin while he peered through the window into the street.

'Got yourself a butcher's knife, did you, Jean? Fancy yourself a butcher?'

The windowpanes were thick and blurred at their centres, but he could see enough. A mob of around a dozen militiamen were holding a conference upwind of the bonfire. There was a good deal of arm-waving and red-faced recrimination.

Tannhauser turned and looked at Pascale. She wore a red silk scarf around her throat. She looked back at him. For an instant it felt as if the whole world were frozen by her immense and unreck-onable woundedness. But he knew that it was an illusion and that the world was moving still, and moving against them.

'Where are my pistols?'

Each girl held a thin pillow across her lap. Neither of them moved. Tannhauser thought about the long and scalp-crawling terror they must have endured.

'Forgive me if I'm curt.' He hadn't shifted the knife at Jean's throat. 'You must be sore distressed, but only the practicalities are material. The pistols?'

From her lap Pascale produced the first of the wheel-lock pistols, holding it in both hands like a short musket. The dog was down on the pan cover.

Flore revealed the second.

'Are they primed and cocked?' he asked.

Pascale took a deep breath, as if it were the first she'd taken in a while.

'If they were not, there'd be no sense in having them.'

'Perhaps I asked a stupid question.'

'It was a good question,' said Flore. 'Papa showed us how to prime them this morning. They're loaded, primed and cocked.'

'May I take charge of the pistols?'

'Not this one,' said Pascale.

'I understand,' began Tannhauser.

'No you don't,' said Pascale.

'I intend to travel over the rooftops,' he said. 'We can't so travel with cocked guns. If you'd seen as many men shot by accident as I have, you'd take no offence.'

'I take no offence,' said Pascale. 'And I will not shoot by accident.'

She stood up and pointed the muzzle of the gun at Jean's chest.

Tannhauser stepped well clear of the bore.

'Pascale, don't fire. Let me explain.'

Pascale paused but held her aim. Jean began to shake.

'We came here to save you, Pascale,' said Jean. 'We did save you.'

Before Jean could talk her into shooting him, Tannhauser smashed out his front teeth with the butt end of the butcher's knife. Jean fell to the floor. He looked up at Tannhauser. His eyes were glassy.

'I told you not to speak.'

Tannhauser looked at Pascale. Pascale looked at him.

'Pascale, we are in a dire pickle. We have a long way to go before we'll be clear of it.'

'You think we can get clear?' said Flore.

'I didn't come here to die. As you've discovered, those pistols come in handy, especially if those clowns in the street don't know we have them.'

Pascale's eyes were dark tunnels drilled for the conveyance of pain.'

'Are you telling me not to kill him?'

'I'm asking you not to shoot him. We'd be deaf for the rest of the day. If you want to kill him, cold steel is more reliable. But killing is a bridge you cross in only one direction. There's no way back from the other side, not just in this life, but through all eternity. My advice is to keep your soul clean of murder. More likely than not, you'd regret it.'

'I do not consider it murder. I do not believe I will regret it.'

'Listen to him, Pascale,' said Flore. 'I believe Papa would say the same.'

'Father is dead.'

Pascale did not break her gaze away from Tannhauser's.

'He is dead, isn't he? That is what we've been breathing all morning. The smell of Father burning?'

'Yes. He's dead. They burned him on a pile of the books he had made.'

He heard Flore choke down a cry. Pascale didn't blink.

'But I said "more likely than not". I did not say for certain. I do not know you. Perhaps it is your destiny, to be a killer, whether you regret it or not. Or I should say: perhaps to be a killer is the destiny you will choose, for a destiny must always be chosen, despite that it lies in wait for you to find it.'

'Do you regret choosing yours?'

'I crossed that bridge so long ago I can't remember what lies on the other side.'

'I waited for you,' said Pascale.

Tannhauser was taken aback.

'For me?'

'For you. You told us you would come.'

Tannhauser didn't reply.

Pascale's lips trembled. She clenched them.

'I waited for you all night. I told Father you would come. I told Flore you would come. And you didn't come.'

'Pascale, don't say this,' said Flore. 'He did come, he's here now.'

'Then I waited for you all morning. And then they took Father. And they burned him on a pile of the books he had made.'

Pascale's eyes filmed with tears. Yet she did not let them fall.

Tannhauser felt his own vision blur again.

'He was the best man in this world,' said Pascale. 'He could sing and he could dance. He could speak and write in the ancient tongues. Inside his mind the universe turned ten thousand times a day, so he told me. And I believed him.'

'I believe him, too,' said Tannhauser.

'He was a better man than you.'

'I do not doubt it. He raised you and Flore.'

Without breaking her gaze, Pascale raised a hand and wiped one eye at a time.

'I'm sorry,' she said. 'This is a dark and bloody day.'

'It's a darker and bloodier day than you can know. But I am a dark and bloody man. Let me deal with the practicalities.'

'I want to deal with the practicalities, too.'

'There are six men downstairs whose souls already squirm in Hell, and who did their share of squirming as they died. As for these two, if they stand not high in your esteem – the contrary possibility being the only reason I spared them this long – I'd rather they didn't live to spread my name.'

'We don't know your name,' cried Ebert from beneath the bed.

'His name is Tannhauser,' said Pascale. 'Why don't you show him your cock like you showed us? Go on. Get it out again.'

Tannhauser looked at Ebert.

Ebert broke wind. 'We didn't mean any disrespect.'

'We came to help you, Pascale,' said Jean. He rose to his knees, gibbering through the fresh gaps in his teeth. 'And we did help, didn't we? We kept the others away from this door, didn't we? We protected you. We don't hate Huguenots. By my word, I admire them. We aren't like the others, we're not militia.'

'You brought them here,' said Pascale. 'You knew where we lived.'

'They knew your father,' said Ebert. 'They would have come anyway.'

'They wouldn't have come so early,' said Pascale. 'They wouldn't have come until later, until tonight, or even tomorrow. They wouldn't have come two hours ago. They wouldn't have come before Tannhauser arrived.'

'We didn't know Tannhauser was going to arrive,' blurted Ebert. 'Though of course we thank God that he did.'

'We came to take you home with us,' said Jean. 'And if you let us, we will.'

'You mean that dirty garret? Or to meet Mater and Pater in the grand chateau?'

'Pascale,' moaned Jean. 'Can't you see I adore you? I'm in love with you.'

Pascale hawked and spat on him.

'You're not going home,' she said. 'I'm going to murder you.'

'His Excellency is right,' said Jean. 'You're not old enough to kill me.'

'I'm old enough for you to squeeze my tits.'

Tannhauser should have killed both the students as soon as he'd come through the door. As he listened, he was confused as to the rights and the wrongs. He had taken great pains to steer Orlandu clear of killing. He hoped to do the same for Grégoire and Juste. But boys he understood. Of the hearts of girls he knew nothing. He was inclined to give Pascale what she wanted, but she wasn't much more than a child. He didn't want to help her damn her soul. On the other hand, her soul was her own.

And at her age he had reached the same decision.

'Is it true you brought the militia to this house?' he asked Jean.

'Yes, yes,' said Jean. 'Because we knew we could protect the girls.'

'How did you know?' said Flore.

Jean opened his mouth but closed it without speaking.

'You could have come alone and warned us,' went on Flore.

'You didn't need to bring the militia. But then Papa would have told you to go away and leave us alone. The militia got rid of him for you. You made a bargain.'

Jean stared at her. He didn't trust his voice to deny it.

Tannhauser looked at Flore, too, and she at him, and his view of her changed.

Flore had pronounced a death sentence on the youths; and she knew it.

Tannhauser looked down into the street again. The militiamen had stopped bickering and were listening to their leader. Tannhauser turned back.

'Pascale, give me the gun.'

Pascale pointed the pistol at the floor and with her ink-stained fingers she locked the arm of the dog into the safe position. She handed the gun to Tannhauser.

'You're wearing Father's apron,' she said.

'I hope you don't mind.'

'It's drenched with blood.'

'The blood is not mine, either.'

'Will you loan me your knife?'

'What you want to do is uglier than you think.'

'Nothing could be uglier than what I think, except what I feel,' said Pascale. 'I want to reek of blood. Like you do.'

Tannhauser went to Flore. He put the pistol and his bow on the bed beside her. He held out his hand and she gave him her pistol and he locked the dog.

'Do you have the saddle holsters? And the wallets?'

Flore pulled them from under the bed.

'Pack a clean dress for each of you in the wallets. Wear shoes you can run in.'

Tannhauser checked both pistols and holstered them.

'My father is a rich man,' said Jean. 'He could make you rich.'

Tannhauser went to Jean and cranked his right arm up between his shoulder blades and hauled him towards the door. A torrent of snivelling and bleating poured forth from Jean's lips at such speed, and with so choked a voice that Tannhauser couldn't understand a word, which was perhaps as well. When Jean grabbed the door-jamb and wrapped one leg around it, Tannhauser jerked the arm higher and snapped the bone just below the shoulder joint. Jean screamed.

Like all the other screams that had pierced the city that morning, it summoned neither help nor pity. Tannhauser tucked up Jean's other arm and bundled him out to the landing. He shoved him to his knees by the wooden balustrade above the staircase. He glanced back to make sure that Ebert hadn't moved from under the bed.

Pascale followed him to the landing.

Flore remained on her bed.

Jean wriggled like a bound sheep.

Tannhauser broke his other arm.

'You are dead, son. Try to leave this life with some dignity.'

Jean submitted, though, in his sobs, pain and despair were more evident than pride.

Tannhauser looked at Pascale.

'Pascale, are you ready?'

'I am ready.'

'We may both be damned for this, but I am damned already, so I risk nothing.'

'I want to cross the bridge and not come back.'

Pascale held her hand out for the knife.

'I don't want to remember what it's like to be on this side.'

'To kill a man quickly requires skill, commitment, attention to detail, especially anatomic detail. God did not design us to be butchered, despite that we are besotted with the practice. So, imagine the ribs are armour, front and back, which is not far from the truth. Here, see for yourself.'

He prodded Jean about the thorax with the tips of his fingers to demonstrate. Pascale followed his example. She nodded. Jean squirmed and sobbed.

'Oh my Lord God, I am most heartily sorry for all my sins –'

'Pray in silence,' said Tannhauser, 'like the monks.'

Jean relapsed into bloody snivels.

Tannhauser continued, 'To penetrate the ribs, then, is tricky, not to mention that the blade can get jammed between them, or even break. Besides which, you can inflict all manner of wounds without finding a vital organ. The world's full of stabbed men. I'm one of them. Consider also that it is harder to cut a man's throat, fatally, than is generally believed, for here – see the straps of muscle protecting the great blood vessels? You need a sharp knife, a determined stroke, to make a cut so deep. And cutting the windpipe itself may not be fatal at all, especially for a man who knows it.'

Pascale took all this in with great concentration.

'However, feel here, behind the collarbones.'

Pascale prodded the root of Jean's neck, cold to his tears.

'The skin and muscle are stretched as thin as a drumhead, even on the strongest man. Right below is a trove of vital organs – the great vessels as they rise up from the heart, the lungs, the heart itself. Get a blade in there and even the luckiest will be hard pressed to survive. But the thrust must be vertical – thus – with your weight directed down through the hilt, either from above, if attacking from behind, or, if attacking from the front, from below.'

He demonstrated.

'You understand?'

Pascale mimed the strokes with a clenched fist. She nodded. She looked up.

She said, 'This is shameful, isn't it?'

'I'm glad you said that. Go and join Flore. I'll take care of them.'

'That's not what I meant. I would rather be shameful than weak. I'm tired of being one of the weak people.'

Tannhauser nodded.

'You won't contradict me? Killing will make me stronger?'

'It often fosters that illusion. Sometimes it's no illusion at all.'

'Let me have the knife.'

Tannhauser put the tip of the knife to the root of Jean's neck, behind the right collarbone, angled obliquely, towards his heart.

'Exactly as I have the blade here, see? Push harder than you think you need to, and follow through all the way down. Then turn the hilt thus, like the lever on a printing press.'

'Pascale,' begged Jean, 'as I love you, please, in the name of Jesus, mercy.'

'When Father screamed you stuffed your fingers in your ears.'

'Don't let your victim distract you,' said Tannhauser. 'It can be fatal.'

Tannhauser handed her the butcher's knife. She took it. She grabbed Jean by the hair and pulled his head back. She studied his eyes, his tears, his mouth.

'Pascale,' said Jean. 'Pascale.'

'Most important of all, do not hesitate, for that is the very essence of a killer.'

Whatever Pascale felt, it was not hesitation. She put the tip of the knife to Jean's neck and drove the blade down through his chest as if she'd done it as often as Tannhauser. Jean sighed. She pushed the hilt, like the lever on a printing press, and severed his heart.

'Jean's gone. You felt it. You know it.'

'Yes.' Her lips curled. She licked them. 'Yes.'

'Draw the blade and step aside.'

Pascale pulled the knife out and stepped back.

'Never linger. The instant you've killed, be ready to kill again.'

'Yes.' She thought about it. 'Yes. I understand.'

'A fight to the death must be over in seconds. If a man has the skill to survive three of your attacks, he has the skill to kill you in one of his own. Don't get wounded.'

Tannhauser draped Jean over the rail like washing and wedged the corpse's feet between the balusters to anchor its weight. In the bedroom, Tannhauser kicked Ebert in his broken ribs until he wormed himself back out from under the bed and crawled to the landing. There, while he wept, and following Tannhauser's instructions as to the best approach to the great arteries of the neck, Pascale cut Ebert's throat.

Her fascination with the result, which was torrential, fascinated Tannhauser. Many a farm boy had baulked at his first pig. Pascale had just murdered two men as if she'd been born to the practice. Perhaps she had. She looked at him. He felt a dread kinship.

He hoisted Ebert and hung him over the rail. The blood of the two dead youths cascaded down the woodwork and onto the floors below. The drops danced and burst in tiny fountains. The stairwell filled with a humid red mist.

'Well? Were they students or actors?'

'They said they were both. Perhaps they were neither. I don't care.'

'We can at least applaud this final performance.'

Flore came to the door. 'I can hear someone walking on the tiles.'

Tannhauser listened. Flore was right.

There were at least two men on the roof directly above them.

'Can they reach the trapdoor and the ladder?' he asked Flore.

'The hatch has a bolt on this side but it's open. Papa sent us to the rooftops, but Pascale stopped to abuse the students, and they caught her. I couldn't leave her. I didn't think to throw the bolt shut again.'

'Sisters should stick together,' said Tannhauser.

'Will you stick with us?' asked Flore.

'I'll stick with you until you're safe.'

Tannhauser felt the heat of Pascale's eyes. He looked at her.

'Does that mean you're adopting us?'

Tannhauser almost laughed; then saw she was just as serious as she'd been when she'd driven a knife into Jean's chest. He went to the window in the bedroom and looked down at the street. He was in time to see the militia rush in a mass towards Malan's front door.

'Our luck has turned. They're going to try to take us by storm.'

CHAPTER FIFTEEN

The Madman Has No Master

C arla looked over Alice's shoulder at the four cards.
They were tarot trumps, in the Italian style, and had come
from different decks. Two were printed from woodblock and coloured
by hand, and were numbered XII and I; two were painted *a tempera*,
with great beauty, by different artists. These last had neither names
nor numbers and were slightly larger. She had seen similar used in
games, though she'd never played. She'd seen them used by sooth-
sayers on the streets in Naples, in the market on the waterfront in
Marseilles. She had never consulted them, being wary of Catholic
doctrine, though she knew Mattias had. The particular cards on the
table made her shiver.

'Do you read the cards?' asked Alice.

'No.'

'But you have a sense for them.'

'The Church forbids divination in all its forms.'

'For which we may be thankful, for they'd turn the practice to
wicked ends, like most else they've purloined. If you're averse,
speak up.'

'I trust in you.'

'You'll have to show more willing than that or you'll close the
doors to your own knowing, and that's where the cards speak
from.'

'But I know nothing of the cards. I don't even know their
names.'

'Divination hopes to catch the wind, too, as it blows through
your soul. Your *Follia* opened doors in this old pagan even she didn't
know were there, so the moment was meet. No doubt it is for you,
too.'

'I'm not sure I want to know the future.'

'No one can know the future, not in the way you mean it, not even God.'

'Surely God by definition knows all things –'

'No, only by the definition of them as appoint themselves his overseers, so as to keep the rest of us trembling. If God knew what we were going to do, don't you think He'd have the decency to stop us?'

'God gave us free will –'

'Whether He gave us free will or not – and this woman doesn't believe it, not least as everything the clever say of Him describes a being who would loathe the very notion – we have it, which is very much to the point. Like all that was, and all that is, the future is woven from boundless small threads, which is our Mother's genius. With each breath we take, we warp one thread rather than another, mostly without knowing which or why, because we take not the care to know. Divination is a means to better come to that knowing, and thus to take part in the divine, which is the way of Creation – the making of all that is, and all that will be, the dance of Life Her-own-self.'

'Her dance goes on inside me, right now.'

Alice smiled, as if proud of her.

'Yes, love. And never is Her dance more beautiful.'

'Please go on. How can I better take part?'

'If your soul is open to itself – and thence to you and all that you are, and thence again to all that is around you – the question becomes: how can you harvest some of all that knowing to help you warp a thread or two with care, instead of with blind groping? For all that knowing is too much for any mere mind – or its will, free or otherwise – to encompass. Too much from which to make a choice of thread or warp or knot. And so, no wonder we are so much in confusion.'

'Yes. I understand. But if you speak of blind groping, is it not so that the cards are selected by blind Chance?'

'Not so blind, though you put your thumb on the answer, which is: we invite Chance to take its right place in the doings. For not only does Chance encompass all possible knowing, it is, by its essence, the opposite of mortal will – to which it pays no heed at all, much as we might like it to. Thus, Chance knows not what it is to be in confusion, for confusion is part of its essence, too. Confusion, that is, as mortal will might see it.'

Alice took a slurp of cold tea to give Carla the time to absorb these notions, which were mighty, and yet which Carla heard as if she had known them all her life. She took a sip from her own cup, and nodded that Alice might continue.

'Since all things are connected – for how could they not be? – these cards, or rather their images, provide a meeting between the knowledge possessed, in confusion, by the soul, and the power of Chance to choose from among that knowledge. From that meeting, a divination can be made, which is not wholly blind, for we do direct its gaze, even if only seen as through a glass darkly. From amongst all that which we do know – but which by its abundance confuses us – our attention can be pointed towards that which we need to know.'

In its challenge to her prior conceptions, the conversation put Carla in mind of more than a few winter evenings she had spent sitting by the kitchen hearthstone with Mattias and a jar of wine; and before him, of other mystic moments with Amparo. But before she could respond, another pang came.

She leaned on the table and groaned, trying not to lose the thread of her deliberations. Alice put a hand on top of hers and watched keenly but without concern. Her unconcern was welcome. Both of Carla's previous labours had been carnivals of anxiety, most of it neither hers nor of her making. Carla opened her eyes and found the drawn cards lying inches from her face.

The row of three chosen by Chance and Alice's soul.

The first was the Hanged Man, reversed.

The second, a figure dressed all in red, also reversed.

The third portrayed a beggarman, shoeless, in patched rags. His golden curls were threaded with feathers and flowers, and on his right shoulder he carried a staff, as if not sure why he did so, or what he ought to do with it. He was young, and his mazed black eyes swam with pity, as if haunted by all he had seen on the long road. He stood alone with his back to the dark blue edge of yonder – an ocean, a river, an abyss – as if he could go no further. He seemed altogether lost.

The first two cards were woodblock prints. The beggar was an exquisite painting; as too was the fourth card, the one Alice had chosen at the start and set above the rest. Carla had avoided this last, being unable to deny its name; but now she looked on it full.

Death, his bones bedight with a robe of crocus-yellow finery, rode bareback on a black horse rampant. A long white ribbon was knotted round his leering skull, just above the sockets, and fluttered gaily behind him like a lady's favour. Above his head he wielded an enormous black scythe, its shaft embossed with gold.

Never had the Reaper looked more gaudy, more joyous and deranged.

His charger, with its bared teeth and crimson tongue and demon's eye, was nearly as horrible. It galloped towards the left-hand edge of the card. Trampled beneath its hooves – in a field of daisies – lay the corpses of a king, a bishop, and two cardinals, who flanked a dead pope, perhaps Peter himself, for a wound as if made by a nail scarred his right hand.

Certainly, thought Carla, as her pang ended, the artist had made his point.

'If these deep doings exhaust you, we can stop. My reading's done.'

'Not only do these doings keep fatigue at bay, they have enthralled me. But let me ask, if the future cannot be known, what is it that the cards tell us?'

'What will happen is not important – for what will happen is Life Her-own-self, and she dances to no tune but her own. What matters is how we take part in that happening, the way that we make of it one future rather than some other. If we listen to who we have been, and who we are now, our soul can show us what we can be, and thus make us better ready for what we will be – or not – in the future.'

Carla looked again at the beggarman.

'Where did you learn all this?'

'This woman didn't so much learn it, as learn that she knew it. No doubt the wise men are drawing up their rules, and no doubt they'd say she doesn't know what she's up to, but no one's obliged to listen to her. Whether anyone listens or not is their affair, not hers.'

'I'm listening.' Carla indicated the draw. 'What are these cards called?'

Alice pointed to each in turn.

'The Traitor. The Juggler. The Lunatic.'

'Why did you choose Death?'

'The card purposely chosen represents the quester and her question. It overlooks the whole tale and sees what lies beyond. Don't let it upset you. My question didn't concern you or your babe.'

'The tale these tell seems a grim one. What do they say?'

'Each card always speaks anew, for its purpose is to raise the unseen images hiding in the quester's soul, and lurking in the realm of the question, so that the reader might catch their meaning. Like a dog flushing birds to the wing. And aye, up to a point, these are grim doings.'

She indicated the three cards from left to right.

'This old woman sees these pictures whole, forward and back, arse over tit. She knows them as you know your fiddle. But a simple view, a beginning, is to see in these three images, past, present and future. How did we? How do we? How will we do?'

Alice picked up the Hanged Man and held the card the right way up. A man in green pantaloons dangled by his left ankle from a rough-hewn gallows supported by two posts. His arms were tied behind his back; gold coins tumbled from his pockets. His face was strangely unconcerned with this fate. It seemed as if he were almost about to smile.

When Alice spoke, her voice was bitter.

'The pelican feeds her chicks with her own blood. The worm eats his own tail. The Traitor's head sways over troubled waters and his mind sinks down, yet he knows it not, for he has despised all prudent counsel and lost his wits. He has not loved his life and never will, even to the loss thereof. He that he has betrayed is but his own self, and though he renounce the false path, though he expiate his sins, though he cut the bonds that bind him with the knife of sacrifice, he will drown. For he sees not his secret enemies, and he will never spend their coin.'

Alice replaced the card, reversed. She took up the Juggler, who was dressed in red. He stood at the table of a street gambler, on which were arrayed the tools of his trade: dice, a knife, a pea and three shells, money, a cup of wine. He held a thin stick, or perhaps a whistle for attracting custom. Alice plucked notions from some inner vision.

'A falcon winged by an arrow. A she-wolf, snared, chews on her own leg. A cry of hounds. A bull untamed. Falsehood. Sleight of hand. Ambition. Festering wounds. Subtlety rejoices in evil and wields in its name the warrants of a spiteful god. Yet among even the conspirators fear abounds, for the cup is poisoned and the poisoners will drink it to its lees.'

Alice waved the card as she put it back in its place.

'This Juggler is the enemy the Traitor does not see. No one yet sees him.'

'Then a card may embody a particular individual, a real person.'

'Of course, usually several. The cards capture the quester's quest, a drama that might well boast many actors. The particulars of this one needn't concern you, though you're right: the play so far runs on intrigue, avarice and lies. Yet all's not lost, for beyond all calamity, and beyond all fear, stands the madman.'

Alice took the Lunatic and regarded him with something like tenderness.

'Hark, hark, the dogs do bark, the beggar is come to town. His belly is as empty as his plate and he has no pockets. They punished him not for the errors he made, but for those that he did not: for over his brothers and sisters the Lunatic never sought power, nor did he seek dominion over Our Mother. The sea is made over to the crocodile, and the petals and the thorns to the rose. His journey has been from darkness to light and to darkness he must return home. He has walked every path worth walking, he has known every thing worth knowing, and now, at the last, he knows he knows nothing at all. The Abyss gapes at his heels, and he does not see it, and he will fall. It is deep beyond human reckoning but not without a floor; its bowels are strewn with the stones of ruined empires; of obelisks that once stood seven times seven tall. Yet, if the Lunatic started at nothing, and at nothing he now stands, we must ask: is his journey over? Or is it about to begin again?'

Alice proffered the card.

'Do you know? Does this old woman? Does he?'

Carla stared at the lost, bewildered outcast, whose pity extended to all but his wretched self. Feelings she could not name overwhelmed her. She sobbed.

'Amparo.'

'Yes, love.'

'And my child.'

'Yes, love. And you and I, too.'

Carla let her heart speak and Alice took her hands in hers. Just as Carla feared that her sadness was too infinite and formless ever to end, a new contraction began, and she was almost grateful for its unfeeling progress. It was remorseless, dwarfing in power and duration all its predecessors. At last, this pang passed, too, and Carla blew her cheeks and looked at Alice and Alice winked, and Carla gave in to a grim smile. She wondered why she did not need to sit down, or lie on her back; her thigh bones throbbed; yet she kept her feet.

'Don't some call the Lunatic "the Fool"?'

'Does he look like a Fool? You're right, that is how most call him, these days. But how could some jester with bells who cuts capers for kings – a slave whose daily bread is dirt – know what the Lunatic knows? The madman has no master. A fool crawls at his master's feet, and his pay is grubbing for table scraps with the dogs. How could such as he show us how to walk untainted through chaos and corruption and pain?'

Alice scoffed – that curl of purpled lips, which Carla had come to look forward to. She sighed and shrugged, forsaking anger for resignation and regret.

'The Lunatic will be robbed of all he has, of all that is most precious, not to him, but us. And what is most precious is Nothing. He'll be cast out from even his own rags, he'll be forgotten and damned, and in place of his truth we'll have bells. Lots of bells. But bells is popular and the long road to Nothing is not. It's no more than they've done to Jesus and plenty more. In the end, they'll take it all. But your pardon, the question was fair.'

'What was your question, that you had Death speak it for you?'

'It was a question fit only for an old woman to ask.'

'Thank you for telling me something of its answer.'

Alice gathered up the four cards and turned them face-down and slotted them back into the deck amongst the others. And they were gone. The void left by their going was so strong that Carla was shocked to find how real their presence had been.

Alice handed her the deck. Carla hesitated.

'I don't know enough about them.'

'If you don't want to ask, this woman won't mind.'

'Alice, I don't even know what to ask. I don't know how to.'

'Let your card do the asking.'

'But which card?'

'You'll know it when you see it. It's there, waiting, in the twenty-two. The right card for this here and this now. At another moment, another card, or the same card in some other aspect. Don't worry, don't think, don't dwell, don't compare. I'll tell you their names so you don't have to wonder. Just look. And when you choose, choose quickly.'

Carla accepted the deck and shuffled them face down. The sizes of the cards varied, and by the patterns on their backs they had come from at least four different decks; whether by necessity or design she didn't ask.

'You can mix them proper for the reading.'

Carla realised the shuffle wasn't required. She turned up the first card.

Alice said: 'Love.'

Carla blinked. She hadn't expected so powerful a subject to leap out. The image showed a blindfolded Cupid above a wedding couple.

But it belonged to some other time and place, not this. She put it face down on the table and turned again.

'The Wheel of Fortune.'

Carla discarded it and turned up a grim, battlemented tower.

'The Fire.'

'The Juggler.'

'The Emperor.'

'The Moon.'

'The Star.'

'The Devil.'

'The Traitor.'

'Strength.'

A woman closing the mouth of a lion. Carla paused. She discarded.

'The Sun.'

'The Chariot.'

Carla turned again and knew she had found her quester. A woman in a blood-red gown stood on top of a green circle, which floated on a mass of blue clouds. Inside the circle were mountains and on the mountains fortified towns. She held a sceptre and a golden globe, and behind her head was a scalloped silver halo. The woman's balance seemed precarious, as if the earth, which Carla took the circle to be, were turning beneath her feet; but she hadn't fallen off. Not yet.

'This is the card. I chose a red dress to wear when I met Mattias. The circle is a kind of womb. And she certainly has a good view.' She showed Alice. 'Who is she?'

'She is *Anima Mundi*. The Soul of the World. A bold choice.'

Carla heard note of warning; but the day had forced such choices.

'Hold your question in your mind and mix the cards as I did. When they get heavy, stop and let me gather them.'

Carla pooled the cards on the table and swirled them about. She closed her eyes to compose her question. Her mind swam with so many, but one theme dominated. Her baby. Orlandu. Mattias. Her family. Would they ever be reunited? Would Mattias ever hold their child in his arms? She let a vision of them all together form.

Other figures, mere shapes, joined the family. Mattias had tears on his face, she hoped of happiness. She felt the cards drag on the wood and stopped mixing. Alice gathered the deck.

'Cut with your left hand. We'll see what *Anima Mundi* sees.'

Carla's hand hovered over the deck as she felt a flutter of dread. Alice sat with her hands in her lap, her body slumped, her eyes on the Soul of World. She paid Carla no heed. Carla cut the cards. Alice took the remainder and drew the first card.

'The Judgement, reversed.'

Carla watched Alice take in the elaborate image, its many figures. She seemed to have emptied her mind, as if waiting for words to arise from the void. At last Alice spoke.

'Weighed in the balance and found wanting.'

She turned the card right way up and Carla, her dread rising, saw it clearly. Two angels, with green wings and crimson tunics, hung from the clouds and blew on silver trumpets. Below them, seven naked men and women clambered from the vaults of a red tomb. Some threw up their arms in joy; others covered their nakedness in guilt or doubt. Carla bit her tongue, not daring to break the mood. The card told her at least one thing she already knew: she should never have come to Paris. Yet if she hadn't, she would not be here with Alice, and here was the only place she wanted to be.

Alice drew again.

'The Fire.'

The dark, massive tower in the painting evoked Carla's memories of the Siege. She had waded those ramparts in gore-sodden skirts and given her heart to the dying. One side of the tower was falling, its slabs melting, sliding apart, and what Carla took to be flames leaked out from between the stones, though the artist had rendered them like streams of blood, as if such had mortared them together. A tall, black archway gave into the base of the tower. More red flowed from its threshold and pooled without. Carla was appalled.

'And so is Limbo rendered. And all our chains of brass in piecemeal broken.'

Carla almost told Alice to stop; she sensed who the next card would be; but he could not be stopped. Perhaps in so dark a drama as this, only he could come to her aid. Alice turned towards her and their eyes met. Her face was slack and dreamy.

She drew Death and placed the card without looking at him.

'I need nor gold nor riches, nor favour of princes nor popes, for the world is mine. And come I early, or come I late, all of you who live now will dance with me.'

Alice turned back to the draw. So did Carla. She waited for Alice to explain why the tale was not quite so terrible after all; but the old woman weighed the cards in silence.

'Judgement, Fire and Death,' said Carla. 'For a moment I was afraid I'd draw something dire. But I have a formidable champion. And he too rides a wild horse.'

She pointed at the skeleton, delirious in his white ribbon and bright yellow robe.

'See, he charges back towards the Fire.'

'Choosing *Anima Mundi* as your quester was bold enough – and she for her part hasn't minced the matter – but to claim Death as your champion might be rash.'

'I jest to ease my dread, and, please, forgive me for disturbing your muse.'

'Tell me your question.'

'I want to see my husband's face when he holds our child. I want to be with my family again. What must I do – how should I be – in order to get there?'

Alice looked at the draw. She pursed her lips. She raised and dropped one brow.

The pang seized Carla with no warning. Its power was immediate and it knocked the breath from her. The pain was excruciating. She held onto the table without a sound. She doubled over and the pressure on her hips was so great she sank into a squat. She heaved for breath. The contraction bent her to its will. She let go of the table and went onto her hands and knees. She let out a groan that rose from the ground of her being. She waited for the intensity to crescendo, but it continued to rise. Her elbows sagged and her belly touched the floor and she pushed her arms out straight again to raise it. She breathed and groaned again. She sensed Alice lumbering about. Death galloped through her mind on his crazed black horse, and his grin was so ridiculous she would have joined him in laughing had she been able. She groaned again. She imagined she sensed the pang waning, then realised it wasn't, then realised it was. She felt a rumour of nausea and readied herself to vomit. The nausea passed. The pang passed. She panted on all fours on the kitchen floor.

She heard Alice's breathing and felt her hand rest on her back. 'Stay where you are, love. All's well.'

Carla would not have believed anyone else in the world.

'Let's see how far we're along. Steady now, naught to be afeard of. Breathe.'

Carla nodded with gratitude and made herself breathe steadily. She felt Alice take the skirts of her gown and roll them up around her waist. She kept her eyes closed.

'You'll feel my fingers and a cooling lotion. Oils of almond and lilies.'

Carla felt Alice's fingers slip inside her. There was no discomfort, rather, she felt soothed. The fingers were strong, decisive; they knew their work. They probed more deeply.

'Grand,' announced Alice. She withdrew her hand. 'Life Her-own-self is proud of you, so let her be your champion. Are you able to get up?'

She heard Alice's heavy breaths, each itself a labour.

'Yes, perfectly, I'm fine. I don't need help.'

Carla felt a tug of embarrassment that she had succumbed so abjectly. She knelt upright and used her hands on the table to stand up. She brushed her skirts down.

'The matrix is taken up and dissolved entire,' said Alice. 'The womb gapes by a good two fingers and the head is well down. We couldn't hope for better signs. But don't be pushing yet, not for a good while. You need to preserve your strength. It's time we settled down in the birthing room. Can you climb a set of stairs?'

'Of course.' Carla was more concerned that Alice had to climb them, but didn't say so. She smiled. 'I don't believe we finished off those pears.'

'Carla, you're a woman after this old woman's heart, and being as it's a stony one, rarely has she found it in her to say as much. We'll make some tea and do for them pears, and then we'll birth a fine strong babe.'

'And the cards?'

Alice flapped a hand at the fateful draw.

'This old she-wolf couldn't have read them better herself. Claim Death for your champion. Charge towards the Fire.'

CHAPTER SIXTEEN

In the Land of God

T annhauser took four arrows in his left fist, along with the bow, grabbed two more in his right, and nocked a seventh arrow to the string. He listened to the militia clatter through the front door. He listened to the momentary quiet as they took in the sight of the eyeless, the limbless and the disembowelled. He listened to a hum of murmuring, their whispers concealing everything but their fear. The bold spirit with which their enterprise had begun had fled them as soon as they crossed the threshold. Tannhauser wondered if he had overplayed his hand, but after taking a moment to rally, and invoking the names of various local saints, the militia charged up the stairs through the bloody fog.

Tannhauser retreated into Daniel Malan's bedroom.

The bedroom was windowless and stifling. Tannhauser felt something drop on his boot and looked down. Clots of blood were draining from his apron. He wiped sweat from his brow. Their most aggressive men would be at the front, possibly one at the back to keep the rest honest. Their most dangerous should be on the roof. He heard them find the man whose privates were pinned to the floor. He heard oaths of vengeance. He heard one suggest they let the unknown killers be, for clearly they were barbarous and many. He heard that man shouted down, though the shouters were few. He heard their curses and prayers as they dashed through the shower of gore still draining from the actors.

The stairwell enjoyed good light from the windows overlooking the street. The militia were forced into single file as they started up the narrow final staircase. They could not see him. He was calm for there was nothing left to do except the things that were going to be done. At last, and for a moment, life in Paris was simple.

During his youth at the Enderun janissary school he had been trained in the Turkish bow style, using a thumb draw and loosing down the outer side of the bow. It allowed for a faster nock, especially for the second and third arrows in his right hand. Since he didn't have a thumb ring, the modest draw weight of Frogier's bow was a boon.

In the vanguard of the assault force was a heavy-set customer carrying a sword and wearing a helmet and breastplate. Behind him came a second man in helmet and cuirass who extended the shaft and winged blade of a *spontone* ahead of the first, as if in some primitive battle formation. The bodkins would more than likely pierce the plate, but at this distance there was no reason to gamble. When the first man reached the second step from the top and raised his foot, Tannhauser moved to the doorway and at a range of six feet from his knuckles he shot him in the face.

The bodkin bored through the inner angle of the first man's right eye and knocked off his helmet as it burst from the left rear quadrant of his skull. Sixty pounds of bow strength exploded through the holes in his head and threw him into the arms of the second militiaman, who dropped his *spontone*. Tannhauser shot this second man below the helmet, too, a right-cheek hit, angled downward, which erupted below his left jaw with such force that the arrowhead was buried in the plaster and lath of the wall beside him.

Tannhauser nocked again and stepped out to the wooden balustrade.

Below him there were seven men, crammed into a line that stretched from the landing by the kitchen to the two who blocked the top of the stair in a tangle of limbs. They were all of them bespattered with the blood of the slaughtered actors and they all knew they were cursed by it. In a poor position from which to attack, they were too afraid of cowardice to run, until it was too late; which very moment had arrived.

Tannhauser cocked the bow over the rail and leaned into the stairwell and shot the farthest in line – the seventh, by the kitchen – between the backbone and the right shoulder blade. The bodkins had greater penetration than a musket ball. The crimsoned shaft erupted from his chest. The shooting angle was so steep that to miss the vitals was difficult. His next arrow punched the sixth man through the breastbone and hammered him belching gore to his knees. He shot the fifth through the root of the neck at so vertical an angle that the shaft slid into his body as far as the fletching. As he nocked and drew again he heard the creak of the roof ladder behind him. The fourth man in line scrambled over the pierced and groaning bodies of his comrades. Tannhauser dropped him with another steep shot through the upper back, into which the arrow's feathers vanished altogether.

Tannhauser stooped towards the Italian *spontone* that the second man had dropped when his head had been skewered to the wall. The spearhead was a twelve-inch double-edged blade, much like a broadsword's, but at the base were two scalloped and sharpened wings for cutting and trapping. A kind of trident with truncated side blades. The shaft was hexagonal and shod with three strips of iron. The butt was socketed into a spiked steel counterweight, its narrow tip bevelled like a chisel. Tannhauser grabbed the shaft in a double overhand grip, still holding the bow and his last arrow in his left.

He saw the nearest of the three surviving militiamen wrestle to escape downwards past the man below him on the stair, who, to his credit, remained eager to reach the fight.

Tannhauser turned and marked the man coming down the ladder from the roof: another helmet and cuirass, and the creaking was no wonder for he was hefty. He saw Pascale slip from her room, her gap-toothed mouth twisted in a snarl. The man on the ladder jerked and bellowed and dropped his sword as she slid the butcher's knife between the rungs and under the rim of his breastplate and sawed the blade in and out of his lower gut. The man grabbed at Pascale's forearm and fumbled for his dagger.

His steel back plate didn't leave much choice. Tannhauser swung his hips into the rise of the spear, powering the blade of the *spontone* through the crack in the man's arse and up through the bone ring of the pelvis to rupture the bladder and bowels. Tannhauser hoisted and with a shriek to break glass, the gutted man toppled sideways into Daniel Malan's bedroom. Tannhauser freed the spear and looked over his shoulder.

The fighter on the stair had struggled up past both the escapee and the man still nailed to the wall by his face. He clambered over the corpse of the very first of the slain, a rapier poised to thrust, but yet out of range Tannhauser rammed the *spontone*'s spiked steel counterweight through his right eye. He dropped the pole and the fighter tilted sideways as his head was dragged down by the weight. The fighter grabbed the pole and tried to pull it from his skull but the blade snagged in the planking. He tried to jerk his impaled head from the spike, grunting and convulsing, his good eye rolling, but the skull bones gripped tight to the steel and he flopped from side to side like a gaffed fish.

'Christ, the captain's down,' called a voice from above. 'Where are the rest of you?'

Tannhauser looked up through the trapdoor and nocked the last of the arrows in his hand. Sunlight from the unseen roof hatch fell across the lower half of someone holding a sword by his leg. He didn't seem inclined to dare the ladder. Tannhauser shot him just below the buckle of his belt. The strength of the bow and the stiletto head propelled the arrow through a dozen coils of intestine and beyond all chance of revocation. The man clutched the feathers in his belly. He screamed, more with horror at the knowledge of what was inside him than with the pain that hadn't yet arrived. He staggered and his left foot plunged though the trapdoor and he hung there suspended and squalling, the point of his own sword now impaled through his thigh.

Tannhauser had three unused arrows in the laundry basket. He laid the bow alongside them. He grabbed the pole of the *spontone* and jerked the speared man up from his knees and levered him sideways over the balustrade, the shaft rotating in the wound, the cheekbones and the side of his skull cracking open as he screamed and the weight of his body plucked him from the spike. He fell to join the already damned below.

Tannhauser checked his rear before reversing the spear to be sure he didn't harm Pascale. She had armed herself with a sword.

He was about to warn her to be careful when she shot him a furious glance and he held his tongue.

The wounded and the dead were heaped in a puling, squirming pile that jammed the lower end of the stairway with their bulk, their spasms, their tangled limbs and groping fingers. There were only two unharmed militiamen left, hedged in between the blood-soaked barricades below them and above. The skewered wretch, choking on his swelling tongue, still clawed the blood-drenched plaster to which he was affixed. Tannhauser stomped on his face with his heel and the arrow that nailed him snapped off at the wall and the body flopped backwards.

Tannhauser trod on him, one hand on the timber rail that had proved so stout, and struck down and out with the full six-foot length of the *spontone* at the next man, who was pressed against the wall of the stairway, shaking from the knees with his arms clutched over his ears as if to block out the cries of woe that echoed around him. The weight of the pole drove the *spontone* through his armpit to the depth of its wings and breached the lungs as if his chest had been a wicker basket. Tannhauser hauled the *spontone* free and let the tip drop and used the pole to vault down across the corpse.

There remained only the runner. He was crawling over the morass of bloody bodies, his legs jellied with terror, shouting to the Holy Virgin for deliverance. Tannhauser stabbed him through the nape and detached his spine from the skull.

Tannhauser leaned on the pole. He wasn't breathless but he took a breath. While there was still a deal of writhing and groaning to be quieted, by his own strict reckoning he had brought down eleven men in less than a minute. He speared three bodies that still showed signs of life and a fourth who did not but who roused his suspicions. Then, for the sake of so little extra effort, he impaled the rest of them, too. He retrieved four arrows in usable condition and the fletched stumps of three more whose bodkins were too strongly lodged in sinew and bone. Male screams from above drew his attention. He turned.

Pascale stood at the foot of the ladder and was using a sword to hack at the leg of the man wedged in the trapdoor. Tannhauser feared a spasm or a kick might knock the blade into her face.

'Pascale, stop.'

She looked at him. He climbed the stairs and motioned her to step back and she did. He speared the man beneath the floating ribs, then manoeuvred the body until it dropped to the foot of the ladder. He retrieved the arrow from the dead man's gut and returned it to the quiver with the rest.

'Get rid of the sword.'

'I want to keep it.'

'You don't know how to use it and it would take you years to learn. None of these fools had learned either. If you must go armed – and I wouldn't give this option to many – take the captain's dagger.' He pointed to the gutted hulk. 'It's not too long and will suit your build. I'll show you some moves you can count on. Take those white armbands, too, if they're not too bloody.'

As Pascale bent over the captain's body, Tannhauser saw Flore in the bedroom doorway. Her eyes were on Pascale. As Pascale rose with the captain's belt and dagger, she looked at Flore and seemed to detect some censure, though Tannhauser saw none and wondered if it did not reflect some scruple within her own conscience.

'They killed Father. They were going to kill us, too.'

Flore said, 'I don't want you to hurt yourself.'

Pascal wound the captain's belt twice around her waist and buckled it. As if to emphasise her stand, she stooped by the two dead students and tipped them over the rail.

'Their blood's no use to us any more.'

'Hike up your skirts and tie them around your waist,' said Tannhauser, 'or you'll carry a gallon of the stuff into the street. If you want to spare your shoes, go down the stairs barefoot, but take care not to cut yourself on fallen blades. Pascale, bring the pistols. Flore, the wallets. And bring some cloths that we can use to wipe ourselves down.'

'What are we going to do?' asked Flore.

'Whatever comes next.'

Flore looked down into the stairwell at the sodden carnage. She stifled a sound in her throat. There was hardly a square inch of the floor not coated with gore and whole swaths of the walls were thus arrayed. The smell of blood had been overwhelmed by the stench of those who had befouled themselves as they died. A business of flies, convened from a variety of species and hues, snarled in rising number to propagate and feed.

'We were born here,' said Flore. 'We slept here every night and we woke up here every morning. All our lives. Mama died here and now Papa, too. And now here is gone.'

'Yes,' said Tannhauser. 'Here is gone. But we are not.'

'Will you carry me down the stairs?'

'Of course. Let me sort my gear.'

Tannhauser slung his rifle across his back, the bow and quiver over one shoulder. He was carrying too many weapons, perhaps, but he couldn't bring himself to abandon the *spontone*. Against the multiple foes in prospect, it was superior even to dagger and sword.

Pascale reappeared, skirts high, shoes in hand, and his wallets and holsters draped across her narrow shoulders. He held out his left arm and Flore swung up to sit on his hip with her legs wrapped around his waist and her arms around his neck. Pascale picked her way down the stairs in bare feet, showing an admirable indifference to the semi-liquid gore that splashed her ankles and calves. Tannhauser descended behind her, using the *spontone* to steady his steps.

There were no militia left in the house. He left the girls inside and checked the narrow street and saw no one. He stepped out and threw the three broken arrow stumps into the fire. He took off the leather apron and spread it over the body of Daniel Malan, still smouldering on the embers of his burned books.

He went back to the workshop and there he and the girls washed the blood from their hands and their feet and their weapons. The sisters did not speak and, though he was tempted to utter some reassuring platitudes, neither did he. Each girl in her way evinced a surprising calm, drawing on some inner well of strength as if both had been expecting so dire a moment their whole lives. Perhaps they were simply too stunned. The girls put on their shoes.

The street was still empty and Tannhauser hurried the girls past the fire. The sisters looked at the corpse beneath the smoking printer's apron.

'Thank you,' said Pascale.

There were tears in her eyes but she wasn't crying. Tannhauser kept them moving. They reached the end of the street, where Clementine was waiting but the boys were not.

The big mare had pulled the rein tight and was stepping this way and that and rolling her eyes and tossing her head, disturbed by her abandonment, and by the smells of blood and burning, by the sounds and silences of terror and death, by the great drifting fog of human madness and evil which, to her animal senses, must have permeated the whole of creation thereabouts. She was glad to see Tannhauser. He took the time to murmur endearments in Turkish, a language he believed all horses loved. Clementine was comforted, though no more so, and likely less, than her huge heart comforted him. He thought of his great Mongol horse Buraq, now enjoying his last years out to pasture at La Penautier.

Tannhauser said, 'Call her the most beautiful.'

'Yes, yes,' said Flore. She looked into Clementine's big blunt face. 'Yes, Clementine, yes, you are the most beautiful. Can I touch her?'

'Hold out your hand, so she can take your scent. Let her touch you.'

Clementine nuzzled Flore's palm. Tannhauser seated the wallets and pistol holsters on the mare's enormous back. The horse had dumped a pile of dung and the dung had been scattered. Some broken lumps lay several yards down the street, as if someone had thrown or kicked them. He worried about Grégoire and Juste.

He produced the two apples from his shirt. They looked delicious and reminded him he was starving. He handed them to Flore and Pascale, who misread his intentions and, before he could stop them, fed both fruits to Clementine. They called the better bargain. The horse's pleasure was so intense that the whites of her eyes bulged beyond their rims and the girls laughed with a delight that on that street ought not to have been possible.

'Do you ride?' he asked.

'No,' said Pascale. 'We never had the opportunity.'

'You're off to a bold start, then, for she's the tallest horse I ever sat on.'

He wondered how to mount them without soiling his hands on their feet.

''Tis a pity Grégoire isn't here.'

'You mean your lackey?' asked Pascale.

'His back would have served you for a mounting block.'

'Where is he?'

Tannhauser didn't answer. He climbed into the saddle and reached down and one by one helped the girls swing up behind him onto Clementine's back. Then he swung his right leg over her neck and dropped to the ground. Pascale shuffled forward onto the saddle and Flore held onto her waist. He gave the rifle to Pascale and showed her how to rest it across the pommel. He took Clementine by the bridle.

'Why don't you ride with us?' asked Flore.

'I can fight better down here. If trouble occurs, I'll set Clementine to a canter and she'll carry you clear. Anyone who gets in her way will regret it. Hold onto her mane and grip with your knees. Now, tell me, who will take you in? Who can shelter you?'

The sisters stared at him as if no betrayal could be more foul.

'You must know someone. Friends, relatives, neighbours.'

'Half the men you killed on the stairs were our neighbours,' said Pascale. 'They'd known us all our lives. Some were Father's friends. Perhaps you should have asked them.'

'Have you no Catholic kin? I can't drag you about Paris, not today.'

Flore said, 'On any other day we wouldn't ask you to.'

Their way was marked by more cadavers, now of every age and gender, heaped in the gutters and draped bleeding from windows and doorways, like merchandise in some improvised market of the damned. They passed blood-boltered bands of militia and students, who cast glances up at the girls, suspicion in their eyes and lechery in their balls; but none dared beard Tannhauser, and this was as well for them, for he was in the vein and keen to be provoked. They saw thieves emptying houses, frantic with greed. Some worked in the wake of the militia, plundering the recently slaughtered. Others committed their own murders, without regard to creed. Some streets were so awash with fresh spilt gore, so choked with ongoing butchery – families hacked in sunder, children before their mothers, fathers before their sons as they knelt and begged for the lives of their kinfolk – that Tannhauser dared not take them, and he had Pascale navigate some other route to their goal.

At moments an uncanny silence would fall across the *quartier*, and the girls would take deep breaths and believe it all done. But like much else, each silence proved itself false. The echoes would return, of looting, torture, dying and rape. Rats skittered back and forth in the spoil as if deranged by its sudden abundance. A pair of dogs, panting in the heat, made sport with the rats. And, as before, all this havoc in a city that seemed near derelict, for those who were not doomed stayed indoors; the limbless, the demented and the blind had flown; the whores had retreated to their cribs; and once the butchers had moved on, the streets were given over to the corpses of the newly slain.

The Écurie D'Engel was open. Tannhauser relieved Pascale of the rifle and helped the girls dismount in the outer yard. He closed and barred the gates to the street but opened the hatch in the upper half of the wicket door. He pointed to a water butt.

'Fill a bucket for Clementine.'

He went inside the building where he found Engel, if such was the hostler's name, hanging by his neck from a rope tied around a roof beam. The hostler was naked, his face turned away into the shadows. The blackened fingers of his left hand were trapped between the rope and his throat. His feet and legs below the knee were grossly distended and the colour of pickled beetroot. Tannhauser reckoned him dead since at least yesterday evening. The stable was silent and a quick tour revealed that all the horses were gone. There were any number of explanations for the scene but none of them concerned Tannhauser. The absence of Grégoire and Juste did, but the possible reasons for that were even more numerous and most of them were grim.

He mashed up a bucket of chaff, bruised barley and beans, and took it to the yard. Pascale and Flore watched Clementine eat. He went back inside and found a wagon sheet and spread it below Engel. He sawed through the rope and the body dropped and folded over stiffly without spilling any noxious contents. He rolled it up in the sheet and dragged it outside and unrolled it behind a heap of garbage down the street. When he returned with the sheet, the girls did not ask what it had contained. Despite the chaff, which he'd included to slow her down, the mare had made short work of the barley and beans. Tannhauser led her to a salt brick and as she licked it the girls pointed out small, amusing details of the mare's expressions and behaviour.

Tannhauser was touched by their smiles.

He had been wrong to let Pascale kill the actors. He wondered why so obvious a conclusion had eluded him at the time. His capacity to reason was impaired. He tried to reason now, to make a plan, but a plan required some notion of an outcome that was plausible and desirable, and such he was incapable of formulating. All that was clear to him was that since his arrival in Paris every decision he had taken had been in error. He felt as if he was standing at the edge of the world, with nowhere left to go but over its rim.

He sat down on a bench and put his head in his hands, like a man who had come to the end of something he once thought had no end. If he had not sat down, he would have been crushed to his knees by the measureless weight of his despair. He had mourned before. He had mourned many he had loved. This black humour was more than grief; or failure or guilt. He squeezed his skull as if he might expel the poison. His hair was clogged with crusts and clots that broke down into a paste beneath his fingers and released a thin fluid that trickled down his neck. He was a man of blood in a city of blood in a world of blood. He trembled from his core. He waited for the fit to pass, not knowing if it ever would.

The sisters came and sat down on the bench beside him, Pascale to his left and Flore to his right. He did not look at them. They had been orphaned and exiled from their own lives. They had been plunged amongst sights and sounds that should be reserved for the damned. Each girl folded her hands in her lap and said nothing. They were good girls. After a moment, and in the same moment, they both started to cry. They cried quietly, without fuss, as if they didn't want to disturb him, but needed to be near.

Tannhauser wanted to be alone. He did not want to have to care for them. Their muffled tears scalded his conscience. He wanted to invite Carla's spirit into his mind and his heart – her image, her face, the sound of her voice – for she would know how to comfort them and he did not. He did not dare. His own grief stirred, shifting down inside the void within him like some stunned beast threatening to awake, and he was afraid. More than any of the men he had killed, more than all but a tainted handful of men in the city, this bloodbath could be laid to his account. So could the murder of Carla and their baby.

He had an urge to tell the girls his troubles, to use them as his confessors, but he quelled it for the weakness that it was. It would undermine their faith in him, and they needed it. Fragile though it was, such faith was all they had. He forced himself to speak; to say anything.

'In the desert –'

He sensed the girls lift their heads and look at him. He tried again.

'In the desert, south of the Atlas Mountains, is a desolate region that the tribes thereabouts call *Mur n Akush*, or the Land of God. I travelled with a band who are forever on the move, who are born and suckled on the move, who die and are buried on the move, who live and love and write songs on the move, who have been moving thus for generations without number, and who will do so for generations without number to come. They chart inexhaustible variations on the same prodigious journeys, along the same ancient yet invisible routes, and no sooner have they completed one vast arc across the surface of the earth, than they turn about and begin all over again.'

He carved illustrative figures of eight with his soiled hands.

'In their tongue they call themselves "*the free and noble people*".'

The sisters wiped the tears from their cheeks.

'In a sense the band, or their clan, has always been, and will always be, on the same one journey, whose beginning is lost to memory, and whose destination will never be reached. Each night they make a new camp, beneath a new arrangement of stars, and each morning they set off in a new direction, for even though the routes they follow may be ancient, the deserts are never still but always changing, and no foot ever falls twice on the same road. In one sense, then, these travellers are always at home, for they never leave that place in which they were born. In another, they find themselves arriving – always – at a place where no one has ever been before.'

The sisters thought about what he had said, each for a moment lost within herself.

'Were they good to you, the free and noble people?' asked Flore.

'Without them I would have died.'

'Did you find God in the Land of God?' she said.

'I always find God in the wilderness. All right men do. Girls, too.'

'I'd love to go to the wilderness,' said Flore.

'We are in the wilderness,' said Pascale. 'And God is not here. Only the Devil.'

Tannhauser said, 'Then it's the Devil's tune we'll dance to.'

'If you'll let me, I'll dance it with you.'

Tannhauser scratched an armhole.

'Why did you tell us about the desert?' asked Flore.

He felt their eyes on him. He didn't answer, because he didn't know.

Flore said, 'Is it because you think we should keep moving, like the tribesmen?'

'We need to find a safe place.'

'Isn't it safe here?' said Pascale. 'Clementine likes it.'

'Sooner or later the militia, or the police, are going to shove on that door.' He nodded towards the street. 'If it's barred on the inside, they'll want to know who is here. If they don't get an answer, they'll take the door down to find out.'

'They'll listen to you,' said Pascale.

'I can't stay. My son is across the river, in the Ville. He's gravely wounded, why or by whom I don't know.'

'Then let's go to him,' said Flore.

'The white bands on your arms will persuade only those who want to be persuaded. There are no Catholic girls on the streets. The only reason for you to be at large is because you're not who you claim to be.'

'Yesterday we were girls carrying water,' said Pascale. 'Why are we so important today?'

'We've become fast friends since then, you and I. That's why.'

'I mean why are we important to the militia?'

'You're not.'

'Then why do they want to murder us?'

'They've a grand plan for the purification of the world, to which end you must die.'

'But they don't even know we exist.'

'Such riddles have baffled greater philosophers than we. Our task is to survive and, if we can find the appetite, start life afresh.'

'You said "a safe place". That means somewhere you can leave us behind, doesn't it?' said Pascale. 'Even though you say we're friends.'

Tannhauser stood up. He went to the water butt and dipped a bucket and bent forward from the waist and emptied the tepid water over his head. He scrubbed the blood from his hair. He rubbed his face. He rinsed again. He wanted a bath. He straightened up.

'Is it true you're going to leave us behind?' asked Flore.

'The city is no longer governed by the King or his servants, nor by Church or state, nor by any law, religious or profane, nor even by the militia, the police, or any of the other gangs sharpening their knives. Madness governs the city. A blood fever in every sense: bred in the blood, felt in the blood, for the joy of spilling blood.'

He looked at Pascale.

'Have not you and I been inflamed by this delirium?'

Pascale didn't blink. 'All the more reason not to leave us.'

Tannhauser took a deep breath. Boys were so much easier to handle.

'Even if the will to extinguish the madness exists, which I doubt, the means to do so do not. The killers won't stop until the fever exhausts itself, or they run out of victims. Every hour will see more men catch it and rave. The many – the bulk of the populace – will not succumb at all, but they will say little and will do very much less. What they say will be said in whispers, behind locked doors, which they'll be too afraid to open to the likes of you, or anyone else they don't know. In this they will play no more than the part expected of them. But the few, the ravers, will be more than enough to slake the fever's thirst. Our problem is, that in a city of this size, that could take weeks.'

'We're with you,' said Flore. 'We want to stay with you.'

'We love you,' said Pascale. 'Do you not love us?'

Their desperation appalled him. He turned away.

It took a moment to find what he was looking for.

He turned back and held out his arms and beckoned them. They ran towards him and threw their arms around his waist. He put his hands on their shoulders and they pressed their faces against him and wept, this time without restraint. He patted each girl on her back. They cried harder. He rubbed their backs instead.

'I've not always given love its due,' he said. He sensed it was not the best of beginnings. 'But yours is more precious than rubies. Whatever happens, I love you too.'

He felt some strength flow into them. He waited and they caught their breaths.

'We found a place to shed our tears. Now let's smile at them and keep them in our hearts. I must do what's best for you, as you would for me. If I have any allies in Paris, which is uncertain, they're on the far bank of the river, and today that is far indeed. The bridges will be defended by militants and like any predacious beast they will scent their prey, which is you. But the Saint-Jacques

Gate is close and most anywhere outside the walls will be safer than anywhere within them. I noted an abbey – a stone's throw to the west?'

'Saint-Germain-des-Prés,' said Flore. 'They're Benedictines.'

'I know the Order. Their word to me will be honest. Now, in case you are questioned, I found you here at the stables by chance. You fled from thieves to protect your virtue. Invent an imaginary past. Imaginary names. The shambles we left behind us will be delved into, and soon. Militia are not soldiers, they don't expect to be killed. If they did, there'd be a sight fewer of them. Two or three dead volunteers might not raise much uproar, but the nineteen rotting in your father's house will. You mustn't be known as the daughters of Daniel Malan.'

The girls looked at each other.

Flore said, 'It would be best if we pretended we're not sisters.'

'Very good,' said Tannhauser.

'How will we get through the gate?' asked Pascale.

'With lies and gold.'

Flore said, 'Will we ever see you again?'

Tannhauser thought about the Temple manned by his own fearsome brethren – the great white tower, and the security it guaranteed beyond the reach of all but royal authority. Was it only two miles distant? The streets alone he would have dared, with the girls. The bright side of this labyrinth was that there was always an alternative route to be found. But the City was not the printer's staircase. Men were killing on the merest whim. The wrong word, glance, inflection or gesture, could, at any moment, provoke a frenzy, and the girls would be dead.

'Taking you across the bridges is too reckless.'

'You've already explained that,' said Pascale.

'Even if we never see you again, we'll still love you.'

Flore spoke softly and with all the truth of her heart, and she cut to the quick of what remained of his honour. But madness had no respect for honour, and honour was no friend to reason.

'When Orlandu's fit enough, I'll bring him to the abbey. We'll be reunited.'

The girls' enthusiasm for this indeterminate plan was not great but they could find no reasonable objection. Before they could muster some other variety thereof, Tannhauser went to tighten Clementine's girth strap.

'You said you would show me some moves I could use.'

Pascale held the short dress dagger she had taken from the captain.

'I use tools all the time in the shop. Father says I'm as deft as Apollo.'

He reckoned she wanted the fellowship more than the knowledge. It seemed little enough to give. He held the dagger flat against his forearm.

'The body is a map of death but much is stony ground. The kill is hard to find, the quick kill most of all. You must know the landmarks.'

'The bones.'

'Those and more. Two moves, both simple. Both require extreme close range and nerve, but of that you have plenty. First. Here, inside the thigh, is an artery as thick as my finger. Sever that and a man will bleed to death before he's worked out that he hasn't lost his tackle, which is what will alarm him most. Speed is all, both in and out. Conceal the blade against your forearm, thus. Charge in, calling something womanly – for mercy, for help, or his name if you know it. That will give even a hard-hearted man a second's pause, and in that second you kill him. Push your head in his gut, bent over, so he can't see, then make a deep, strong cut through the inner thigh, below the groin, here, as if you're cutting through a wheel of hard, stale cheese. Then get out, run away, get your distance, let him bleed, he'll be in no state to follow.'

'Don't hesitate. Don't linger.'

'Excellent. Second, the same approach, a vulnerable girl seeking help. If he's not too tall, throw yourself against his chest, your left palm outward as if to caress him – perhaps even touch his cheek. With your right hand, the blade flat as before, you come up and drive the tip down into the root of the neck, behind the collarbones, as with Jean. See?'

Pascale nodded, her eyes bright. 'Yes, I see.'

'Then, as before, at once get out and run. In all this be fast and sly. As a fox. Escape is the best defence. Do not get wounded. Decide. At every instant, deciding is everything. Deciding is more important than what you decide to do. If you decide, you can do; if you don't, you can do nothing but die. But choose combat only in the direst of straits. You don't see me taking risks I don't need to.'

'You just killed seventeen armed men.'

He noted how meticulously she had subtracted Jean and Ebert from the sum.

'Half as many geese would have been harder. I was never close to getting a scratch. And you'll recall I was set on flight across the roofs, not a confrontation.'

'But you weren't afraid. How do you not be afraid?'

'I am afraid. Fear lives in the body, naturally, like hunger, not in the mind, as most believe. And knowing that, a fighter can harness it, for fear is a mighty power. Fear makes his mind clearer, faster; it makes him move faster; it doubles his strength, his daring; and so it becomes courage, which is but another point on the self-same natural circle. If we see fear and courage as opposites, as contraries, we're setting ourselves a magician's job to turn one into the other. But if, in essence, they are one, like good luck and bad on Fortuna's wheel, one can learn how to give the wheel a spin.'

'I see. I see.' Her eyes near bulged. 'But how do you spin the wheel?'

'Wherein lies the joy of, say, riding at the gallop, or diving into deep water?'

'It's scary.'

'For many it's pure terror, and they get thrown, or they drown.'

Pascale thought about it.

'So you find the joy in the terror.'

'I correct myself. Terror has no contrary, except perhaps death.'

'So terror isn't on the wheel.'

'Terror hunts alone and swallows you. Let those jaws shut and she'll not let go until she's finished, or you are. But if you're quick, you can jump on her back.'

'I'm quick.'

'Learn to ride that she-wolf, and you become terror.'

'I can see the wolf, but how do you know it's a she?'

Tannhauser laughed. Why was he telling a child such things?

'Are you laughing at me?'

'You're keen, girl, I'll give you that. And to answer, it's just my fancy. If I can give some material form to a force that has none, I can better grasp it.'

'Yes.'

Pascale reached for the dagger in his hand. He gave it to her.

'Can I practise? Just once?'

'Sheathe the blade first.'

'But then it won't be real.'

'That's my intention.'

'I'm not going to hurt you.'

'Slowly, then. Very slowly.'

Tannhauser gritted his teeth. She was swift and accurate. It took all his nerve not to cringe as the blade came close to his crotch. He nodded, to convey his approval. Over her shoulder he saw Juste's head appear beyond the sliding panel in the wicket.

'Can I try again?'

'Later.'

'Master? Are you there, master?'

As Tannhauser opened the wicket he heard Juste mutter something about mice. When he stepped back, Juste herded Tybaut's twin girls inside. They were holding hands and didn't let go of each other. Juste followed, alone. Tannhauser looked up and down the street. There was no sign of Grégoire. He closed the door.

Juste stood staring at Flore. No master painter could have better portrayed the effect of Cupid's arrow, and likely as not would have chosen not to do so, for the lad looked as slack-jawed and witless as a young ram. Tannhauser reassessed Flore. She was pretty, though in such matters the contribution made by beauty was unpredictable. Amparo's face had been half bashed-in, and she had won his heart.

Flore's bedraggled and tear-stained appearance may even have increased her allure. By the way she returned Juste's gaze, Tannhauser guessed that the same arrow had pierced her, too.

'Flore, Pascale, this is my good friend Juste. He's a Pole of noble lineage and newly, if sadly, heir to his family's holdings in that illustrious land. He's brave but not rash, and he doesn't insist on the deference and formalities that are his due. Isn't that right, Juste?'

Juste roused himself from his stupor to bow to each of the sisters in turn.

'The honour is mine,' he choked.

'Does he always travel with prostitutes?' asked Pascale.

'I saw them all alone near the Hôtel-Dieu,' blurted Juste. He looked to Tannhauser. 'I knew you'd want me to help them.'

Tannhauser looked at the twins. Their fingers were knotted together and seemed encrusted with purple mud, as did their arms to the elbows. The white lead, charcoal and beet juice with which their faces had been painted was smeared into antic patterns. They were shod in sandals woven from straw and so caked in congealed gore that their feet appeared twice their true size. They stared at the floor with a wretchedness that could not be imagined. He had provided them with soup and murdered their keeper, and then he had forgotten them. They increased his burdens, but only in degree and not in quality.

'Well done, Juste. Do they know about Tybaut?'

'When I found them they were trying to drag his body to the hospital.'

Tannhauser recalled the state in which he had left Tybaut's corpse.

'Do you know their names?'

'They won't speak to me and they haven't said a word to each other. I've been calling them the Little Mice and it seems not to offend them.'

Tannhauser found this nickname a sight too dainty but didn't quibble. He looked at the older pair of sisters. 'Make these Mice look presentable for the Benedictines, and be gentle.' He looked at Pascale and she blushed. 'I'll stand no more mean talk.'

He beckoned Juste to examine a two-wheeled cart tilted on its shafts at one end of the yard. The cart was open at the front, where a driver could sit or stand. At the rear was a hinged tailboard. It was shabby but the wheels were tight and the bearings greased.

'Well? Is Grégoire alive?'

'Yes, forgive me, I should have told you at once. Lucifer, too.'

'Where is he?'

'He followed the two men but I don't know where they've gone. Lucifer went with him.' This seemed to disappoint Juste. 'We decided I should come back to find you, and then I found the Mice near the Hôtel-Dieu –'

Tannhauser pulled him to the tack room.

'Who are these two men he's following?'

'Grégoire isn't easy to understand, but I think he called one "Petit Christian". He made a pantomime of a monkey, so you'd know who he meant.'

'I know who he means. Who was the other man?'

'He rode a marvellous sorrel horse with four white socks. He wore black with a gold chain across his chest. He was older, older than you, but not as old as the porter.'

'The porter from the college? A withered insect in a wig?'

'Yes, that porter.'

'So you saw three men: Petit Christian, the porter and the notable.'

'Yes.'

A gold collar suggested a knight of some order of chivalry.

'Can you describe the links of the gold collar, or its medallion?'

'No, I didn't really look. We didn't want to get too close.'

'You did well. Here, carry this.'

Tannhauser dug out a breast collar with its traces and breeching. He piled them into Juste's arms. They returned to the yard to harness Clementine to the cart.

'Go back to the moment I left you in the street. Tell me everything.'

'First of all we threw horseshit – no, first you killed the two men at the fire and dragged them inside the shop, then we threw horseshit at the men, well, very young men, almost boys, but they had knives and axes, and they chased us through the alleys, but Grégoire knew a hole into a tunnel by a church, where they stack the bones and where the lunatics live. The smell made me sick, and after the sunshine it was dark, I admit I was very frightened, but –'

'Why did you throw horseshit at the boys with knives?'

'Lucifer barked at them and I said, "They're going to follow Tannhauser into the shop!" and Grégoire grabbed the dung. He's used to it, you know, but horseshit really isn't so bad, I think it's better than any other kind, for throwing.'

He nodded, as if to reassure Tannhauser on this point.

Tannhauser quelled an urge to chastise their recklessness.

'I'm sure it is. And you were brave. Go on.'

'Well, the lunatics were furious when we ran over them – we trampled on their pallets, smashed jugs of wine, the tunnel was full of strange rubbish – and they screamed at us, and their dogs were barking, Lucifer was barking, some of them were women, hags, and some were naked, the men, too, it was like Hell, but Grégoire grabbed my arm and pulled me. We didn't stop until we got to some steps. I heard the boys start shouting behind us, fighting with the lunatics and their dogs, I think, but I didn't turn around. We ran up the steps to a graveyard, very small, behind the church, and Grégoire threw Lucifer over a wall – he didn't like that, I must say – and we climbed over. We didn't see any of the boys coming up the steps. And then we kept on running through the alleys. I was lost, but Grégoire wasn't.'

Juste paused to take a deep breath.

'May I have some water?'

Tannhauser tightened a harness buckle. He filled a dipper at the butt. Juste drank.

'What happened next?'

'We made a big circle, because we wanted to get back to Clementine, but as we passed the hanging man, near the bridge, Grégoire saw Petit Christian, and we stopped to watch. Well, in fact we first stopped to look at the fine red horse, and Petit Christian came out of the college with the porter, and the notable questioned them both. Then the porter went back inside and the other two crossed the bridge to the City and we followed.'

'Why?'

'Grégoire said that's what you would do, that is, if you didn't kill them. You did tell us to gather what facts we could.'

'They didn't spot you trailing them?'

Juste shook his head. 'The island was still in a tumult. There are boys everywhere, they love the excitement.' With a note of accusation he added, 'Though most of them have knives, or at least a stick.'

'You've survived without either. Continue.'

'Grégoire also said something about "Le Tellier", I think.'

'The captain of the Scots Guard. Dominic, you remember him.'

'Of course I remember him. But he wasn't there. I'm certain.'

'Dominic is in league with Petit Christian.'

'That's what Grégoire was trying to explain, I suppose. We followed them towards the cathedral and they turned across the Pont Notre-Dame, to the Ville. That's when we decided I should find you, so you wouldn't worry, and Grégoire told me how to get here. From the cathedral it's straight up the hill and —'

'You crossed the Petit Pont?'

'*Audentes fortuna juvat,*' said Juste. 'Which means —'

'*Fortune favours the bold.* And let us hope it is so. But how?'

'We – the Mice and I – tagged along with a gang. I let them think I was like Tybaut. Isn't that what you would have done?'

'What will Grégoire do when he's done with his bold quest?'

'You said you were going back to the chapel of Sainte-Cécile, so he will wait for you in the Hôtel D'Aubray.'

'A grim choice. Why?'

'There's no one left to kill and nothing left to take, so there's no reason for anyone else to go in there.'

'You lads will soon be outfoxing your master.'

Tannhauser hooked the last of the traces to the swingletree and stood back. He had left the saddle on Clementine's back as he intended to donate the cart and harness to the abbey. Some gold pieces on top and the Benedictines would sing a weekly Mass for his soul.

'I hope you don't expect us to ride in that manure cart,' said Pascale.

With scrubbed faces, the Mice seemed even younger, their inner scars more visible. They still held hands and stared at the ground. Tannhauser gave Pascale a stiff smile.

'The cart's been used for fodder and it's cleaner than most plates. You will all ride in it. If you're so particular, get some blankets from the tack room to cover the floor, but be quick. And see if you can find some gloves to cover those ink stains. Flore, will you fill that goatskin with water? Juste, see if there's anything else worth taking.'

Juste glared at Pascale's dagger. 'Can I have a knife, too?'

'You won't need a knife at the abbey. Neither will you,' he said to Pascale. 'Put the dagger in the wallets.'

'You're going to leave me with these girls?' Juste was unsure as to whether the prospect was unwelcome or not. He stole a glance at Flore.

'They'll need a brave gentleman to protect them,' said Tannhauser.

Pascale's laugh was less than kind.

'Did you find your wife?' asked Flore.

Tannhauser was bemused. 'Carla?'

'You told us you came all this way to find her and we haven't asked if you've done so. You must think us selfish and thoughtless.'

'We've all had a lot on our minds,' said Tannhauser.

'Well, did you find her?' asked Pascale.

Tannhauser did not have the stomach for expressions of sympathy, and the girls had no need of more woeful news. He glanced at Juste, who stood silent.

'Yes. Carla's on the other side of the river, in the Ville.'

He set about stowing his weapons in the cart.

The children stood looking at him in a kind of silent mutiny.

'Do as you were told,' said Tannhauser. 'We're on the move.'

CHAPTER SEVENTEEN

More Shameful Than Murder

Tannhauser's scheme survived as far as the Porte Saint-Jacques, where a crowd of fugitives, thirty or so, huddled before the gatehouse. Its entrance was barred by a portcullis. Soldiers loitered behind the grate, indistinct in the gloom, and a wall of darkness beyond meant that the leaves of the great gate itself were closed. The fugitives conversed in a cowed murmur while their children cried, fractious in the heat of high noon.

They put Tannhauser in mind of blind ants fleeing from a stomped hill. The spectacle made his skin crawl. He realised it was because he was one of them.

He was standing at the front edge of the cart bed, holding the reins. He had draped the wagon sheet over the cart and the children were sheltered beneath, though imperfectly concealed, for at close range the bobbing of their heads betrayed them.

A postern opened and an officer of the guard appeared. His livery was unknown to Tannhauser; the defence of the walls was in the hands of Montmorency. A soldier brought out a mounting stool and the officer climbed on top and raised one arm for attention. The murmuring stilled. The officer made his announcement with the air of one who had performed the duty several times before.

'In preparation for the impending threat of the Huguenot army or armies, the Porte Saint-Jacques has been closed and locked. All the gates of Paris, north and south, are closed and locked. The keys to all city gates, north and south, have been taken into the physical custody of the Hôtel de Ville. In short, the gate is locked and no one here has the means to open it. I myself cannot leave the city. My men cannot leave the city. You cannot leave the city, nor can anyone else, regardless of rank or eminence. The city is sealed.'

A groan escaped from the gathered.

'If you wish to petition the Bureau de Ville for use of the keys, you may do, but I grant you no hope of success. In the meantime, you must move away from the gate, which must be kept clear for military purposes. If you do not leave immediately, I will be obliged to instruct my men to disperse you. I hope I have made myself clear. God bless the King.'

Tannhauser began to wheel Clementine about.

'That means we're not going to Saint-Germain after all,' explained Juste.

'We're neither deaf nor stupid,' said Pascale.

The officer pushed through the crowd, ignoring questions. He saluted Tannhauser.

'I am sorry to disappoint a Knight of Malta, sire. I'd gladly let you through, but for now Paris is a prison.'

'I want to get these orphans to a safe haven.'

'The Abbey of Sainte-Geneviève took in some people this morning – you can see the Tower of Clovis, just yonder – but I'm told the militia have it under blockade, the swine. I don't know how much one can trust the churches for sanctuary, or if such is being respected. Why not take them to the Temple? Surely you'd be welcome there, though it's likely they've blockaded that, too.'

'It's good to meet a gentleman. Thank you.'

'Did you fight in the Great Siege?

'I did.'

'I am in awe, sire. Was it as terrible as they say?'

'It was worse. Yet not as bad as this.'

'I think I understand. I fought the Huguenots at Jarnac, under Tavannes, but that was war. Our duty was laid out clear, and duty keeps death honest.'

'Death is always honest. His is the only promise we can count on.'

'Surely we can count on Christ's promise of salvation.'

Tannhauser made the Sign of the Cross.

'Let's hope so. *Dominus vobiscum.*'

Tannhauser started the cart back down the hill.

'Pascale, do you know the Place Maubert?'

'Of course I do.'

'Clementine and I await your directions.'

They turned east into a *quartier* of colleges and abbeys.

As they rode, Juste, in his appointed role as their guardian, tried to entertain the girls with a variety of gallant tales but found himself defeated by Pascale's tongue. Squabbles ensued beneath the canvas but they seemed as good a diversion as any and Tannhauser did not intervene.

His mind roused itself. He wanted to get his hands on the lousy old porter, but not while hauling this cargo. He considered the officer's suggestion, of an abbey in the Latin Quarter, but if he had to negotiate the militia he preferred to do so on the bridges and stow the children somewhere in the Ville, closer to Orlandu, and where the ultimate answers to the riddles would likely be found.

They passed Sainte-Geneviève where armed louts did indeed guard the gate. He could have brushed them aside, but that would only reveal the children's location to others, and if carnage stained their threshold, the monks might well not make them welcome. They drove down a steep hill.

In this *quartier* evidence of slaughter was less flagrant and as they passed various colleges of the Sorbonne the streets became rowdy with students swilling wine and groping whores. The revelry was in no way inhibited by the smell of burned flesh. As Tannhauser reached the Place Maubert, the smell grew stronger. Here the festivities were general, served by the same entourage of hawkers, cooks and entertainers that had earlier grubbed for coppers on the Parvis. A malodorous haze lingered in the stifling air. A permanent gallows was sited in the square and its greasy ropes creaked under the weight of six fresh corpses. Nearby, an iron stake arose from a bed of coals, its chains supporting the charred remains of a double execution.

On the north side of the square Tannhauser spotted what he had come for.

'Tell me,' he said to his hidden passengers, 'if a duck quacks and a dog barks, what sound does a rabbit make?'

Various solutions to the riddle were discussed, but none were deemed worthy.

'Exactly: none. I want you to behave like a crate of rabbits.'

In the shade of their wooden booth five *sergents à verge* lounged around a table, picking at the remains of their dinner. They were working on a glazed earthen demijohn of red wine, and it appeared that Alois Frogier had done his share of the labour for he was dozing, elbows on the table and chin on his chest.

Tannhauser stopped the cart just out of earshot. The wall-eyed *sergent* saw him and gave Frogier a nudge and a muttered warning. Tannhauser stepped down and waited for Frogier. Frogier rubbed at a stain on his tunic and mustered an overwarm smile.

'Frogier, I'm happy to find you both sated and refreshed.'

Frogier bowed. 'Thus can I better discharge my responsibilities, your Excellency. As you know, they are many and grave.'

'I could do with a nap myself. I'm here to return your bow.'

Frogier's brow rose in happy surprise, then furrowed.

'I don't want any money back. It's best for us both if I'm not seen with it.'

'I am your loyal servant, as always.'

'Walk me to the Petit Châtelet.'

Tannhauser led the horse and cart towards the spire of Notre-Dame and the river. Frogier tugged at his lip, then signalled his comrades at the table and trotted after him.

'His Excellency has acquired some new companions.'

'That needn't concern you. What might is that you are missing four arrows.'

Frogier thought about this and turned pale as a cheese. 'Four?'

'The bodkins will point the curious towards the Châtelet's archers, but I broke off the butt ends and burned them, so they can't be traced to you.'

'Who would trouble to trace four arrows in a bloodbath?'

'It's a matter of where they'll be found. Events will warrant investigation, so you might consider losing the whole quiver. The confusion, Huguenots, thieves.'

'Events?'

'The less you know, the more sincerely will you be able to feign surprise, or more properly shock, when, in the course of your duties, you first hear the details.'

'And I will hear these details, Excellency? Even on a day as grim as this?'

'Without a doubt. Up to a point, though it's a sharp one, we're in this together. Accomplices, you might say. So unless we have an audience, you can drop the formalities, they grate on my nerves.'

Frogier was either a born philosopher or a veteran of many a risky and nefarious intrigue, for he absorbed these revelations with neither self-pity nor reproach.

'Should I lose the bow too? No, to lose both would be harder to believe. I'll leave the quiver – I'll cut the strap – where some vagabond will find it. He'll sell it on for the price of a drink and by dark it'll be at least two steps removed.'

Tannhauser knew he was inviting more expense, but he wanted to cede Frogier a small victory to bind him tight.

'Are your comrades sound?'

'No man can be trusted in every circumstance, but, as you know, nothing strengthens the temper of any man's soundness like a taste of gold.'

'I'll pay for the demijohn.'

'You think we pay for wine?'

Something caught Frogier's eye.

'Let me have the bow and quiver.'

'In the cart.'

Frogier retrieved the weapons. He blinked at the sight of the blood-soaked shafts. He looked at Tannhauser, but said nothing. He darted down an alley. He returned with the bow over his shoulder. The quiver was not to be seen. He nodded at the cart.

'Unless that sheet is to shade them from the sun, it serves no purpose, other than to proclaim them fugitives.'

Tannhauser peeled the sheet back and bundled it.

'Why, those are Tybaut's girls,' said Frogier.

'I'm Anne Durant,' volunteered Pascale.

'And I'm Geneviève Lenoir,' added Flore.

Frogier tugged on his tooth. 'What are you doing with all these brats?'

Tannhauser had to detach himself from these children. They encumbered him, and he endangered them. Frogier was at least a devil he knew.

'Escort us through the barricades to the Ville.'

'The Ville?' Frogier might have been asked to dip his head in a bucket of vomit. 'Why?'

'I need a safe haven for these youngsters, somewhere they'll be fed and watered for a day or two, and guaranteed protection from all harm.'

'In the Ville?'

'I'd hoped to keep them nearby, but it's their security that matters.'

'I suppose they're heretics.'

'They're of no significance to anyone but me.'

'My older sister, Irène. She lives in the City, on the quay at Saint-Landry.'

'A husband?'

'I arranged to have him hanged.'

'With Irène's approval?'

'At her request. He was too fond of using his belt, and he was a Scotsman, so there were two good reasons to see him swing.'

'What's her occupation?'

'The unkind might whisper, indeed they did, that there was a third and even better reason. This Scotsman, with whose tragic fate you are acquainted, owned a small hostel. Under the new ownership of my sister, the business has flourished. She caters to lawyers from the provinces, but as of this morning, there's a room or two unoccupied.'

'No one but she and we must know the children are there.'

'My sister drives a hard bargain.'

'Here's my bargain with you. If I find them safe when I collect them, I'll pay you well. If I don't, I'll strangle you with your own bowstring.'

At the Petit Châtelet, Frogier left Tannhauser in the wide, arched passageway and he went to report the theft of his quiver by villains unknown. The *sergents*, present in some force, seemed unhappy with their lot, tense and resentful on what should have been a dozy Sunday. Like Frogier they were too habitually steeped in corruption to burn with the blood fever. They cast glances at Tannhauser and his passengers, but made no approach.

Tannhauser looked through the northern arch of the passageway. On the short street occupying the bridge lay a pyramid of corpses, glazed in their own gore and left to bake as if by some homicidal pastryman. Apart from that, it was deserted. At the far end he saw why, and why the *sergents* were out of sorts. A section of militia stood guarding their chain with the look of men who believed their mission had been etched in stone by the finger of God.

Tannhauser chanced a glance at his young charges. All five were arrayed behind one side of the cart, staring at him with a bleak unanimity of reproach. He attempted a warm smile, which felt more in the way of a grimace, and turned away.

Frogier returned, adjusting the sling on a new quiver.

'One of our men wounded one of the militia in some dispute over God knows what. Everybody hates the police. Who knows why? He'll live, unless the wound putrefies, but until they receive orders from higher authority than any they recognise here, they claim jurisdiction over the bridge. In short, I cannot take you across.'

'Fall in behind me.'

Before the *sergent* could object Tannhauser led Clementine out onto the bridge. The militiamen roused themselves. Eight of them, some bearing the stains of the day's work. In the normal course, they wielded little power over their own lives and none over anyone else's. Now that the town was theirs for a day, they were making the most of it. All eight wore red and white ribbons tied around their arms.

Their evident leader sat with his legs dangling from the top of a large cask, perhaps with the purpose of lending a good six inches to his height, for even by local standards he was uncommonly short. He wore a helmet adorned with a goose feather and across his lap he held a stock whip. A man who cherished his hate and felt the better for it. The cask was placed behind the centre of the chain. A band of ragamuffins roistered about beyond the militiamen. They stopped to watch as Tannhauser approached.

He stopped halfway across the bridge. He took his rifle from the cart and made a display of checking the priming and lowering the dog onto the pan cover. A shuffling of feet spread through the line of militia.

'Stay here. If I shoot, get the children to the gatehouse.'

Tannhauser cradled the rifle and walked to the man on the cask.

'Mattias Tannhauser, military adviser and diplomatic envoy to His Highness Henri, Duc d'Anjou. The correct form of address is "Excellency". Who are you?'

The man shifted on his seat with unease, unwilling to face the humiliation of climbing down yet sensing that it might be wise. He ventured a seated bow.

'Ensign Jean Bonnett, Excellency, for God and His Majesty the King.'

Some of the louts repeated this last phrase. Tannhauser stared them down.

'His Majesty didn't order the militia to defy the Châtelet. Nor did he order this butchery.'

'That's a rumour spread by Protestant spies,' said Bonnett.

'Watch your tongue. And "Excellency" will do.'

'I meant only that perhaps his Excellency had been misled by –'

'I want to speak to Bernard Garnier.'

'He's not here, Excellency. In his absence, I speak for the captain.'

'I will speak to him in person.'

'He was called to the sixteenth, across the river, there's been a most horrible massacre of our valiant comrades –'

'Send a man to fetch him.'

'That could take some time, Excellency.'

'We will wait.'

'We're under siege, Excellency, I'm not sure I can spare a man.'

Tannhauser stabbed him in the chest with the barrel of the rifle. Bonnett grunted and tumbled head-first over the rear of the cask and disappeared. From the gatehouse behind him, and a variety of spectators in the windows of the overlooking houses, came squalls of laughter. The ragamuffins took this as leave to join in.

'Send a man,' repeated Tannhauser.

He turned and strolled back to the cart. He smiled at the children. Frogier gaped.

Pascale said, 'Isn't it dangerous to turn your back on them?'

'If I stayed to face Bonnett I'd be back where I started. He now has an easy choice: he can send for Garnier. His other choice is to cross the chain and confront me. If the latter, I'll see it in your faces.'

'What if he just sits back on his barrel and does nothing?' asked Pascale.

'Let's bless our good fortune you're not in the militia.'

'Bonnett is sending a man,' reported Juste.

'Why didn't you just tell him to let us pass?' asked Pascale.

'I want a pass from Garnier. If he spares you once, he'll likely do so again should your paths cross.'

As Tannhauser made the rifle safe he noted they had stopped by an eating house. It was closed. A man watched the scene on the bridge from an upper window.

'How much to feed five children and two loyal servants of the King?'

'What price to a man's soul if he honour not the Sabbath –?'

Frogier said, 'Jean, don't make us break the door down.'

They went indoors and Pascale forced Juste to change his seat twice, first when he claimed a spot next to his sweetheart, whereupon she elbowed her way in between them, and again when she insisted that Tannhauser sit between herself and Flore. The freeing of the necessary space banished Juste to the opposing bench with the Mice, at as far a remove from his love as the table permitted. Pascale peeled off the kidskin gloves she'd found in the stables. Flore stared at the ink on Pascale's fingers. She started crying. Juste stood up as if to comfort her, but Tannhauser shook his head in a signal to let her be.

Frogier pulled up a stool at the head of the table and polished his tooth. The cook, belying his qualms about the Sabbath, had already been busy, and probably short of customers, for in addition to a cold flesh pie made of minced pork, small birds and gobbets of rabbit, he laid out a tray of cheese tartlets, a charger of stuffed eggs, a blankmanger of rice with dark chicken meat, and a pottage of sundry beef innards that Tannhauser sniffed and rejected on behalf of all for fear of the flux. Jugs of wine arrived.

Tannhauser crossed himself. The children sat on the benches with their hands clasped in their laps, beset by a shared melancholy and showing no appetite for the spread. Frogier began to shovel blankmanger onto his platter. Tannhauser felt obliged to raise the table's spirits.

'I'm glad of the chance to enjoy this unexpected dinner with you —'

'Because it will be the last chance we ever have?' said Pascale.

Flore stifled a sob.

'Nonsense,' said Tannhauser. 'It's the first of many, or, in our case, the second. There, you see? We'll have all manner of dinners. And one day we'll look back and say "Remember when we ate stuffed eggs on the Petit Pont, on Saint Bartholomew's Day?"'

'There'll be too much else to remember,' said Pascale.

'Much, but not too much. We've each lost someone dear —' He grimaced. 'We've each seen things that shouldn't be seen.'

Frogier, his mouth bulging with rice, grunted his agreement.

'It's a bad day but it will pass,' said Tannhauser, 'as all days do, good and bad both. And even on a bad day you can find good moments, if you look hard enough.'

He dredged the bloody images in his mind, in a vain search for a suitable illustration of this cheery principle.

'Such as saving the dog? Lucifer?' ventured Juste.

'Exactly, Juste, exactly.'

'Or feeding the apples to Clementine?' said Flore.

'Indeed, Flore – Geneviève – even better.'

Pascale said, 'And when you covered Father with his apron.'

The memory was offered sincerely, but the table fell back into its former gloom.

'Please don't leave us, Mattias,' said Flore.

His chest felt as if it was encased in armour made for a much smaller man.

'It won't be for long,' he said. 'Frogier's sister will take good care of you. Who could be more reliable than a woman who sent her husband to the gallows and made it pay?'

The humour was lost on all but Frogier, whose mouth was too full to laugh.

Tannhauser poured a beaker of wine and drained it. It was good.

'Now, with Frogier's permission, I'm going to eat.'

Tannhauser sat down and took a halved egg from the charger. As he raised it to his mouth the ensemble proved too dainty for his coarsened fingers and the stuffing popped free. It cascaded down the front of his shirt to embellish the bloodstains.

Tybaut's girls broke their long silence by exploding into laughter.

Tannhauser doubted a sweeter sound had been heard in Paris all day.

And for all he knew, since the Romans left.

On impulse he grossly exaggerated his surprise, then his dismay, then he gasped in horror at the damage to his shirt. He must have made a passable clown for the giggles were redoubled. Juste joined in. Tannhauser pitched the empty hard-boiled white through the door to the street and took a second egg.

With painstaking slowness he brought it towards his lips. Silence fell as they watched its progress. Tannhauser parted his jaws to their maximum extent. At the last moment he squeezed the white and the lightly browned glob of yolk, chopped parsley and butter tumbled down his chest to join the first. Flore lent her voice to the renewed mirth and Tannhauser turned to his left and winked at Pascale, who shook her head but rewarded him with the light of a begrudging smile.

'These eggs are jinxed,' he said. 'Anne, darling, pass me a slice of pie.'

To the delight of all, Pascale passed Tannhauser a third egg.

The meal progressed in a light vein and when Pascale began flicking grains of rice at Juste, and Tybaut's girls joined in, Tannhauser did not chide them. He blunted the edge of his hunger and took more wine. He kept Frogier's beaker brimful, and in return Frogier kept him busy refilling it. He ordered dessert. The cook served up a batch of small fig pies basted with honey, and a dish of candied orange peel and a pitcher of cow's milk, and while the youngsters were thus occupied he questioned Frogier.

'If you were to see a man of middle years, dressed in black, with a gold chain on his chest, and riding a sorrel horse with white feet, who might you be looking at?'

Frogier was hovering over his stool as he watched the decimation of the fig pies, which his young companions had kept beyond his reach. He sat back down and his expression changed to one that Tannhauser recognised from that morning.

'I'd be looking at Marcel Le Tellier, with the hope that he hadn't seen me, though it's likely he would have done so before I noticed even the horse.'

The name caught Tannhauser unawares. Grégoire must have recognised the man and told Juste. And Juste and Tannhauser between them had misunderstood him.

'Why would you want to avoid him?'

'He'd ask questions I'd rather not answer and set chores I'd rather not do.'

Tannhauser smiled at the delicacy of this rebuke.

'Tell me all you know about him.'

'What can a humble constable know of the doings of the mighty?'

'Consider yourself the one-eyed man in this kingdom of the blind.'

Frogier cast a maudlin glance at the last of the fig pies.

'Geneviève, give him the pie,' said Tannhauser.

'But we saved it for you,' said Flore.

'Frogier's need is greater. Perhaps it will loosen his tongue.'

Pascale, who was seated between the two men and considered herself their equal in the discussion, intercepted the pie. She smiled unkindly at Frogier as she answered.

'Marcel Le Tellier is the *Lieutenant Criminel* of the Châtelet. He stands above all the *commissaires* and has the powers of a judge.'

'What does Le Tellier's chain look like?'

'It's made of gold cockleshells,' said Pascale.

'The Order of Saint Michael,' said Tannhauser.

By tradition, the membership was limited to fifty but in recent years Charles had created hundreds of knights in return for cash and political support.

Tannhauser said, 'If he didn't buy it, which I would guess is beyond the means of even the *Lieutenant Criminel*, he must wield a good deal of influence at the court.'

Frogier stared at the pie, still hoping to earn it.

'Le Tellier was knighted while he was still *commissaire* of the seventh *quartier*, in Les Halles. The honour helped him to usurp his predecessor, who retired under the threat of various indictments. Marcel is a great schemer. He had to be. He's not the first to rise to his office from a mere *sergent*, but no one can remember the last. His father was a *prud'homme* appointed by the royal cook to buy fish from the market for the King's table. You speak of kingdoms, Les Halles is Le Tellier's kingdom. He was born in the shadow of the Châtelet with the threefold stench in his nostrils – the fish, the abattoirs and the Cemetery of the Innocents.' Frogier rubbed his single tooth. 'Do you know how much a cow shits when it stumbles into Paris? No less than we will on the day we enter Hell.'

'So Marcel is a great solver of crimes,' said Tannhauser.

'No, no, no,' said Frogier, again eyeing the pie. 'Solving crimes – which could not be easier, thanks to the rack – is not the Châtelet's purpose. Our purpose is to gather money for the King and to pay our own miserly wages. This money, on the whole, derives from the law-abiding. Almost anything you can do – run an inn, sell a pair of shoes, operate a wagon – requires the payment of fees. To sell a salmon you must pay four different duties. For infringements of the regulations governing such activities, which are many, and designed to be easily broken, there are fines. In addition we serve summonses, and we –'

'What do the law-abiding get in return?'

'In return we execute an enormous number of criminals, mainly thieves, but also blasphemers, sodomites and murderers. The solving of a crime requires only two things – an accused and his confession, and since the torturers of the Châtelet are the most experienced in the world, neither is hard to acquire.'

'We're still waiting to hear something useful,' said Pascale.

This was too much for Frogier. Tannhauser saw his eyes withdraw like a lizard's. He assuaged the *sergent's* dignity by pushing the fig pie towards him. Frogier crammed it between his gums as if he feared it might be taken back.

Pascale scowled at him. 'Marcel served in a *quartier* where most of the food that feeds Paris is bought and sold. More money runs through there than through the treasury. He extorted a fortune for his masters, and himself, and climbed the ladder.'

Crumbs spilled from Frogier's open mouth. 'That's exactly what he did.'

'Is he a violent man?' asked Tannhauser.

'He has no need to be. In Les Halles brawn is cheaper than fish guts.' Frogier stabbed a finger at the contents of his mouth, which he opened his jaws to reveal. 'You could buy a broken leg with this fig pie. Marcel always had stout lads with him, his bailiffs, a Norman called Baro. Some rose with him. In fact, he's famous for his weak stomach. He can't abide torture or executions, though, I should say, only as a spectator. He's sent thousands to the Place de Grève, and more to the dungeons, without a single Amen.'

'Spies,' said Pascale. 'He's known for that, too.'

'True.' Frogier glared at her. 'From the beginning he had his noses. Drovers peaching on the butchers, wives on their husbands. Even lawyers on their clients, would you believe?'

'Why should that be a surprise?' said Pascale.

'That's why they raised him to the rank of *commissaire*. He knew more than any three other *commissaires* roped together – any six, for after all what's a *commissaire*? A man who wants to sit at home while his *sergents* gather fees to buy jewels for his wife. Now Marcel runs whole chains of spies that reach so far most don't even know they serve him. If five men gather in a tavern for a drink, one will be in Marcel's pocket.'

'Maybe you work for him yourself,' said Pascale.

'And maybe you too, for you're a bold enough young –' Frogier caught Tannhauser's look '– lady. I have my own masters, and whose parsnips they're buttering I can't say, though I will say, Excellency, that few are as kind as you.'

'I wouldn't have given him the pie,' said Pascale.

Tannhauser nodded, his thoughts elsewhere. He was tangled in the web of Marcel Le Tellier. Both instinct and logic insisted. The several riddles were becoming one. The porter, Petit Christian, Dominic Le Tellier, Orlandu, his own arrest: that thread at least was certain. The sacking of the Hôtel D'Aubray at a time when little other mischief was afoot beyond the Louvre. Marcel's reach embraced it all. If so, it was a large and intricate design, even for him. What would justify such an effort?

It was a fair bet that Marcel was acting for someone else. In the squalid context of the Châtelet he was a great man; but the Louvre was full of grandees to whom he would never be anything more than the son of a fishmonger. They could buy a *Lieutenant Criminel* for a false smile. Beyond the court, Paris was crawling with men rich in money and power.

Tannhauser massaged his eyeballs.

The riddle still had a thousand possible solutions. The key could only be Orlandu. What had he got himself into, and why would it require the assassination of Carla? Love, politics or money. A common crime, even murder, would hardly be worth so much effort, unless it had provoked some extreme lust for revenge, the potent elixir Retz had extolled. Killing Orlandu's mother was a sure and cruel way to cause pain. He had to ask Orlandu. Or better still, Marcel Le Tellier.

'Where does Marcel live?'

'In Les Halles,' answered Frogier. 'He bought an old *hôtel* with a view of the river, west of Saint-Denis, near Crucé's abattoir. Anyone there will know it. He could've done a lot better, but we reckon he can't sleep without the smell.' Frogier's anxiety emerged from the fog of wine. 'You're not going to beard Le Tellier?'

'God forbid. I was already warned against the man by friends in the Louvre, discreetly, you understand. I'd simply forgotten his name.'

Juste was bursting with his own question. Tannhauser prompted him.

'Juste, you were at the Louvre.'

'Yes, sire. I saw a captain of the guards there called Dominic Le Tellier —'

'Marcel's son,' slurred Frogier. 'Though some do wonder, for he hasn't the wit of this empty jug. Marcel was so much devoted to his wife he never took another. A great beauty, I saw her once, but she wasted away and died. Melancholia. Her brother — she doted on him, they say — came to a bad end. Broken on the wheel, they say. Le Tellier wears the black for her, that is the wife. Has a Mass said for her every Friday, at Saint-Jacques.'

A *sergent* appeared at the doorway. 'Alois? Garnier's at his chain.'

Tannhauser hauled Frogier to his feet. He looked at the others. 'Stay here until I call you. And put those gloves back on.'

Ensign Bonnett cringed against the cask as Bernard Garnier, his enormous fists knuckled on his hips, bent forward from the waist and lathered him with insults.

Frogier leaned on the sideboard of the cart as if he might fall without it.

Tannhauser propped his rifle against a wheel and draped the holsters over the rim. The *spontone*, its blade sleeved in a leather feedbag, was ready to hand. Tannhauser took two steps towards the chain and stopped and waited. While he waited he took the measure of each militiaman, and knew he could kill them all, and in what probable order, bar the fleetest of foot. Garnier caught some murmured warning and straightened up. He sleeved spittle from his lips and turned and glowered. He was huge and full of rage. Tannhauser sensed a man who felt that the world had not recognised his quality with sufficient gratitude or honours.

'Captain Garnier. Let us parley in private.'

Garnier flicked a hand and his men lowered the chain. He walked over.

'At your service, your Excellency.' He managed a bow.

'The formalities are appreciated but we may drop them. I've a favour to ask.'

'Those fools have no right to hinder such as you. They'll be chastised.'

'They look chastened enough to me. Commendable.'

Garnier was taken aback by the compliment.

'I do my best with what I've got. These aren't trained soldiers. They don't know how to give this rebellion its due. But if they saw what I've just seen they'd know it. They'd shit their Sunday breeches.'

Garnier played the plain, gruff sort, the brute. The role fitted him so well that Tannhauser wasn't sure how sly a fox hid within.

'The Huguenot army is leaderless and miles away,' said Tannhauser.

'I'm talking about a massacre in the sixteenth *quartier*.'

'I rode through there myself. The riot was murderous and general.'

'A massacre of stalwart militiamen. Good and true citizens, serving God and King. Ambushed and slaughtered like cattle. A murdered captain. Mutilations to turn the stomach of a Turk. At least twenty men dead.'

Tannhauser heard some muffled oath from Frogier.

Garnier threw the *sergent* a filthy look. Tannhauser didn't turn.

'I am a butcher by trade and I never saw an abattoir so bloody. They were still carrying bodies out when I left. The printer had two daughters, they say.'

'The printer?'

'You were seen down that way, on a warhorse, they said. Some say with two boys, others swore it was two girls. You're not an easy man to miss. Or to forget.'

Tannhauser looked Garnier in the eyes. After a moment, Garnier looked away.

'We must find the murderers before they strike again,' said Garnier, 'and since, as you say, you rode through, you might have seen something suspicious.'

'I saw gangs of criminals stripping houses and killing children. I saw streets as lawless as those of the cities of the plain before Gabriel razed them. I saw the same things you saw. Do you think Catholics are killing only Huguenots? It's a free for all, man. A day to murder anyone you fancy. Your dead men had enemies. Who does not? Cast your suspicions where there's a chance of finding the guilty. Unless you believe I killed twenty men with the help of a carthorse and two boys. Or two girls.'

Garnier tried to appease him with a short laugh.

Tannhauser didn't smile.

'Your Excellency, these are deeper waters than I'm used to. I beg your pardon.'

Tannhauser nodded.

'Your counsel is wise and welcome,' Garnier continued. 'The militia does indeed have enemies, for we're the King's men, body and soul, and the Pope's, too, and there's more than one high lord as would drag them both from their sacred thrones. The dark times have only just begun. So, please, tell me how I may serve you.'

'Pledge that these children will not be subject to persecution.'

Tannhauser turned to the eating house to call the children out.

They were already crammed into the doorway, watching every move.

Tannhauser turned back. He looked at Garnier.

'I won't deceive you, captain. The lad there is my lackey. The girls came upon me as they fled in fear of their lives. Perhaps they were raised in the Protestant faith. I don't know. I didn't ask. I don't care.'

He leaned into Garnier's face.

'I am a religious man.'

Garnier took a step backwards.

'I am a Knight of Saint John the Baptist. My scars were carved by the Turks in the war to save Christendom. Jesus Christ suffered little children to come unto Him, but these have come to me. And while you may not need me as friend, you do not want me for an enemy.'

Garnier wrung his hands in atonement.

'Chevalier, for you, I'll have them guarded in my own home.'

'I'm moved by your offer, but I've made my own arrangements. Just spread the word that they're not to be threatened or harmed in any way. Are the white armbands sufficient to preserve them?'

'Yes. I'll make doubly sure my men understand, on my oath.'

'Good enough. Now I must go, to interview Marcel Le Tellier.'

Garnier teetered on the verge of another step backwards. His eyes narrowed.

'Can I put in a good word for you, with the *Lieutenant Criminel*?' asked Tannhauser.

'Not today,' said Garnier. 'Perhaps some other day.'

'Between you and I, conspiracies abound.'

While Garnier grappled with these sinister innuendos, Tannhauser glanced at the militiamen. They were clustered by the cask, casting poisonous looks in his direction.

'Like you, I've commanded men in the field. Morale walks on the edge of a knife.'

Tannhauser waited for Garnier to nod.

'Don't turn around just yet,' said Tannhauser. 'As the rankers watch us confront each other, we appear to them as giants, making the great decisions that ordain their fate. They're desperate to have faith in us. They crave it. You are a leader of men. You understand.'

Garnier was enthralled. 'Faith. They crave it.'

'That faith knows no better encouragement than the faith that their captains demonstrate in themselves. And not just in themselves, but in each other. My suggestion is that you clap me on the back and turn to your men with a broad smile on your face – in which expression of camaraderie I'll join you – and they'll see two giants unperturbed by the perils of the world about them, which perils they themselves fear.'

As Garnier absorbed this, the smile that grew on his face was not just sincere. He had become Tannhauser's dog and didn't even know it.

Garnier clapped his master on the back and turned with a grin, and Tannhauser laughed a manly laugh, and the militia transformed before their eyes from a crowd of sullen idlers into something that at least resembled men. They straightened their backs. They marshalled their line. They righted their weapons. They smiled; even Ensign Bonnett. Garnier, buoyed by renewed prestige, gave Tannhauser a formal bow. Tannhauser gritted his teeth and returned it. Garnier's pride was almost pitiful.

Tannhauser waved the children to the cart. He stowed his guns.

Frogier stared at him. His voice was a hiss.

'Twenty?'

'The captain gives me too much credit. The precise tally is nineteen.'

Once they'd crossed the bridge, Tannhauser had the children lie down and swore them to monastic silence. Their way led through a thicket of streets, emptied by fear and death and the stagnant heat of the afternoon. The hostel lay due north of Notre Dame and backed directly onto the Seine. The timber building was four storeys high and one room wide. According to Frogier the upper rear windows gave fine views of the gallows on the Place de Grève. The journey had been short but when Tannhauser looked in the cart, all but the stalwart Juste had fallen asleep.

He didn't disturb them. He followed Frogier inside and found just the kind of inn that would make a provincial lawyer feel secure: too prim to make one want to stay overlong, but uncluttered and cleaner than most.

Frogier's sister, Irène, was a petite woman in her forties, dapper as a crow, with a quick blue gaze that took Tannhauser's measure with a shrewdness polished by her trade. He mustered what was left of his charm, announced only his legitimate titles and apologised for his unkempt – he hoped not too alarming – appearance.

In response, and with a hint of censure, she noted that this was no ordinary Sunday. The militia had searched the hostel that morning and taken away two guests, who hadn't returned. He sensed that what disturbed her was the effect on future business. For himself he was glad to hear that the militia had purged the street, thus leaving themselves no cause to visit again. When Frogier asked Irène where the missing guests' baggage could be found, she gave him a vexatious glare with which her brother seemed familiar.

Tannhauser laid out his needs. Bed and board for five exhausted youngsters, who were not to leave the building until he returned, which he hoped would be that night. They were protected by the warrant of Bernard Garnier. One room would do for them all. For the first-floor room facing the river, he would pay whatever her Christian conscience could bear. He'd reserve a second room on the same floor for him to share with his son, Orlandu. If this arrangement required other patrons to move he would compensate them, via her. If a barefoot boy with a harelip called Grégoire should turn up, he was to be given every courtesy and installed with the others.

A bargain was struck, as expected a stiff one, but he didn't haggle.

He checked the first room and found it satisfactory, its two beds more than ample. From the open window he saw that the rear wall fell to a small vegetable garden. Beyond that lay a narrow, paved quay and the River Seine. He noted that while the sand of the far bank was crammed with beached boats, this bank and its quays were vacant but for two barges moored thirty yards or so to the east.

Across the river he could indeed see the Place de Grève, where knots of armed men milled about to no apparent purpose. Two wagons were pulled up on the edge of a wharf, both heaped with corpses. Two pairs of men, stripped to the waist and shiny in the sun, slung bodies into the water. Some were small enough to need only one pair of hands.

He roused the children in the cart to the degree that they could take off their shoes at the door, as Irène insisted, and stumble up the stairs to their beds.

Tannhauser pulled Juste and Pascale to the privacy of the parlour. They sat at the table and kept their voices low and he explained their situation, which he assured them seemed to him a good one, in the circumstances.

He told Pascale to wear her gloves in public, even at table, and to excuse it by claiming a dry inflammation of the skin. He decided on a matter that had troubled him: he would once again leave his guns in their keeping, but emphasised at length their dangers and the need to keep them secret from Irène who, he was certain, would either disapprove or extract another fee.

He gave them some money in small coin.

He told them about the slabs of opium in the wallets, which they could sell in small pieces to apothecaries for no less than thrice whatever price the latter first offered them.

He gave them all but one of his double pistoles: four each.

'Keep these secret, too,' he said. 'Sew them into your clothes. Each is a half-ounce of pure gold, worth four hundred sols, but unless you're buying horses they're too big to spend. To change them into *écus d'or* or smaller, anyone able to do so will take advantage of your youth, and you may have to go as low as three hundred and sixty, say six *écus d'or*.'

'Why would we need to change them?' asked Juste.

'Because he might not come back,' said Pascale.

'That's true,' said Tannhauser. 'I've paid your room and board for three nights. If I'm not back by then, I will be dead or in a prison I'll not soon get out of. Either eventuality is unlikely, for I'm in the vein.'

'In the vein?' said Pascale.

'The killing vein,' said Juste, ever helpful.

'In such an unlikely case, assuming you have no powerful allies of whom you've kept me in ignorance, and assuming also,' he gave Pascale a pointed look, 'that you've wisely taken pains to win her respect and affection, you should trust Irène before anyone else, even in matters financial.'

'What about Frogier?' asked Pascale.

'Frogier has parsnips to butter. Rely on Irène. He's scared of her.'

'So we'll be on our own,' said Juste.

'Others have flourished from stonier beginnings. So can you.'

'What would you do, if you were us?' asked Pascale.

'I would leave Paris. There's nothing for you here. They'll seize your father's property. Sooner or later they'll discover you're the printer's daughter and they'll hang you.'

She nodded, as if this reflected her own calculations. He looked at Juste.

'If I were you, I'd take the printer's daughters back to Poland.'

Juste's mind was momentarily benumbed.

'It's a long way.'

'And many would be the hands raised against you,' agreed Tannhauser. 'But at your age I travelled further and I wasn't going home. You could flee to some Protestant stronghold, as will many others. La Rochelle. The Netherlands. But all of them are bonfires waiting to be lit. The English aren't as barbaric as is widely believed, at least on their own soil. My best friend was an Englishman, though he was from the northern lands and as a true barbarian as ever I knew. Or you could get baptised.'

Pascale said, 'Why join a Church that would rather burn us?'

'We could make it to Poland if we had Grégoire,' concluded Juste.

'He would be a mighty asset, but you'll have to ask him. One last caution. If you do find yourself alone, and facing the long road, leave the Mice here with Irène and give her a double pistole. By the time they've eaten that, she'll have had them working here for years and be loath to lose them. They're trained to please. They'll get by.'

326

Juste couldn't contain his dismay. 'But aren't they in league with us?'

'Yes, they're leagued with us, but without me you'll be a different us, and if you take the Mice, none of you will survive.'

Pascale did not need convincing. Juste dropped his chin.

'The Mice will never live in the world we do,' said Tannhauser. 'They've known horrors no living soul should ever know, not even those condemned to the bowels of Perdition. They've been used as receptacles for all that is most vile in the human spirit. Their timber has been warped, and it won't be straightened anywhere this side of Paradise. Despite all that, they have endured. Despite all that, they still have it in them to laugh.'

Juste pondered on this. He didn't raise his head. Perhaps he was picturing the Mice as they dragged Tybaut's corpse to the hospital at the Hôtel-Dieu. Tannhauser pictured it. When such a picture made perfect sense, the world was desperate indeed.

'Let the courage of the Mice be their gift,' said Tannhauser. 'To you, to me. We'll never see it cast in purer form.'

Juste looked at him.

'You are right. They are the bravest. I take their gift and I will treasure it. But that's why it feels wrong to leave them behind.'

'Loyalty's a fine quality, but if its practice kills the loyal, its virtue is dubious.'

'Like my brothers.'

The example hadn't occurred to Tannhauser. He nodded. Since Juste had raised the unhappy subject, Tannhauser asked him the question that it prompted.

'Did Dominic Le Tellier play any part in provoking them to the duel?'

Juste thought about it.

'The guards were laughing at Benedykt and we went over to shut them up. Dominic silenced the guards and told Benedykt that his real dispute was with you. Yes. He assured us that he and his guards wouldn't interfere in an affair of honour. He said he didn't know Poland, but that no gentleman of France would allow such an insult to pass.'

Juste fell silent, as if revisiting the outcome of their pride.

Tannhauser asked no more. Dominic had tried to get him killed, within minutes of meeting him, and when this failed he had locked him up. He had prevented him protecting Carla. Christian had tried to do the same, by proposing various delays to his journey to the Hôtel D'Aubray. Tannhauser's arrival had threatened a scheme already in motion. Yet all this was half a day before the King had given orders for the massacre. In the blood and chaos of the dark and the dawn, he had connected the events at the Hôtel D'Aubray to the massacre. Ill-informed logic had entwined the two in his mind. It was clear to him now that the massacre need not be connected to Carla's murder at all.

Before he could dwell further, Pascale tried to lift the sombre mood.

'I'd go to Poland. Or England. I bet they both need more printers.'

'Everywhere needs more printers,' said Tannhauser.

'My father said that that depends on what we print, and that to make a false book is a deed more shameful than murder. I would never print anything that wasn't true.'

'Well, we know that,' said Juste.

'On that noble note.' Tannhauser stood up.

They showed brave faces but he saw their dread.

'Embrace me and wish me good luck, for I shall need it.'

They did so and he was replenished.

He disengaged and walked to the door.

'Earlier you said we'd all lost someone dear,' said Pascale. 'Who did you lose?'

Tannhauser stopped. To tell her was no longer an indulgence. It was the mortar tempered with sorrow and blood that would bind them. He turned.

'Carla, my wife, and our child, who was almost full-grown in her belly. They were murdered in the dark before dawn. As with your father, I got there too late.'

He felt Pascale's affection deepen. His own, too.

Juste said, 'You said you had to find the culprits. Is that where you're going?' He tried to sound encouraging but his anxiety could not be concealed.

'I'll come with you,' said Pascale. 'I worked with my father, I can work with you. You know I can.'

Tannhauser felt a wave surge from the turbid ocean of feeling, uncharted and seldom navigated, in his chest. He had lost too many he had loved. He had lost too much of what was best in himself. Yet not all of it: for he realised that he loved these children, as truly as he had loved anyone. Even Carla. Even Amparo, and Orlandu, and Bors and Sabato Svi. He turned his face from the burning eyes that adored him.

'A girl can do things you can't,' said Pascale, 'go places you can't.'

If he could get Orlandu and these precious friends out of Paris, what need had he of solving riddles? Carla was dead. Justice was an illusion; revenge no elixir, but a poison. To hunt and punish her killers would comfort only him, and then but briefly. Could he live without that comfort? His chest and neck and fists tightened. His belly told him the truth: comfort was a small price to pay for these precious friends.

He turned back to look at Pascale. He saw her love. He saw her need. Her need was not to live; she cared not a fig to merely live, and in that he was with her. Her need was to belong. Though it stung the heart of his pride to admit it, he was with her in that, too.

'Culprits without number will go unpunished today,' he said, 'and the worst will be richly rewarded, for such is the way of the world. The best of us must rise above these affairs, for we won't change them.'

Pascale saw that he believed this, and she saw that it was true. He was glad, for he did believe it, and it was true. Yet the pull of hatred was strong. He saw that she saw that, too. Pascale could see many things in and through him. How strange for such as he to look at a girl as if she were some blurred and distant mirror. Let her see something worth seeing. She needed that, too. So did he. He sensed Carla's spirit. She agreed with him. He smiled. Pascale smiled in return. With her smile, his chest and neck and fists relaxed, and his mind was settled on what was right.

'I'm going to see that Carla's remains are secure. I'm going to bring Orlandu here. Grégoire, too. We will work together. The best revenge is to stay alive and flourish.'

On the street he had a word with Frogier.

'Now that we are known associates, sooner or later Marcel will arrive at you. Tell him nothing of these children. He's after me, not them, and they have no part to play in our game.'

'What game?'

'I haven't been apprised of the rules, though the likeliest umpire is Death. Tell Marcel I took the children to the Ville. Tell him he and I will meet in due course. If these children come to harm –'

Frogier rubbed his tooth. 'Yes, you will strangle me.'

'I will burn this house down with you and your sister roped face-to-face inside it.'

CHAPTER EIGHTEEN

The Magdalene

E stelle awoke in stifling gloom and saw rows of human skulls staring from the shadows. They didn't upset her; she'd seen them too many times before; and compared to what she'd seen in her dreams they gave her comfort. At least they weren't moving. Her other comfort, her rats, had scattered and gone, scared off by the gravedigger who had shaken her awake. She knew him, too, a kindly sort. His mates would have woken her with a kick. They lived knee-deep in the huge death pits outside, and were a harsh breed. Her back was to the wall by the charnel house doorway. She stumbled out into blinding sunlight without speaking.

She rubbed her eyes as she tottered to the gate of the Cemetery of the Innocents. Her feet were heavy, the sleep still clinging to her bones and the insides of her head.

She'd been up all night. Her face ached from Gobbo's slap. She felt more exhausted now than she had when she'd fallen asleep, with the rats in her lap, watching their black eyes and quivering noses. Everywhere, they took her for one of their own. One had put its mouth on her nipple for a moment, which always pleased her. She had never seen meanness in the eyes of a rat. She didn't believe they had any meanness in them. Perhaps that was why people hated them. She knew she had a lot of meanness in her. She'd tried hard to put it there; to put in more and more and more. As far as she could tell, that was what people did to rise. The meaner you were, the higher you rose.

She was starving. She was naked. But starving, naked children were common enough, and she didn't expect anyone would care.

She wandered around Les Halles with no destination in mind. She passed the folly of Saint-Eustache. They'd started to build it before she was born – Grymonde said before even he had been born – but it had never changed: a gigantic slab the size of a field, and a big arch without any walls, or only bits of walls, started but not finished. People used it as a jakes and for rutting, like they did the charnel houses, and for beatings and slashings, and other mean things. Grymonde said they couldn't pay for the stones to finish it. He said they'd spent all their gold on the wars instead. Enough gold to turn the whole land into Cockaigne, he said.

Grymonde had carried her on his shoulders down every street and every alley, and through all the galleries of Les Halles, and through all the markets and wharves, and past all the palaces and fountains and churches, and through fields where horses grazed, and even across the bridges to the City and the University, and everywhere, everywhere, whenever they had met, he had carried her on his shoulders, and he had never tired.

They would meet secretly, like spies, at some rendezvous, and she would run to him and turn her back to him and she'd hear him laugh, the deepest and most beautiful sound she ever heard, and she'd feel his enormous hands encircle her waist entire, and then: ecstasy. Her breath would be stolen and she'd scream with excitement and she would shoot up into the air, and her head would spin and the whole world would change and then she'd drop, and her stomach would jump as she landed on his shoulders, her hands grabbing onto his curly hair lest she fall.

The warmth and hardness of his muscles, his neck, his chest had filled her up inside. The long drop to the ground thrilled her. The fact that she, Estelle, herself, was the tallest creature in Paris made her giddy with triumph and pride, for it never felt as if she were riding him, as folk rode horses. She flew on Grymonde's shoulders. She swooped. She soared. She gave these flights a good deal of thought. No bird she had ever seen or heard of could have carried her, even though she was small. Lying by the hearthstone one night, she realised that only a dragon could.

Grymonde was her dragon.

When she told him this, he laughed his roaring laugh, and his delight made her hair feel as if it were streaming in the wind.

'I will be your dragon, La Rossa, if you will be my wings and my fire.'

Estelle loved the idea of being his wings; but she knew his fire was his own.

This conviction was only reinforced by the fact that Grymonde inspired fear and respect wherever he trod. No crowd packed for hours at the Place de Grève, waiting to watch for the executions, was too jealous to part like a field of barley when Grymonde and Estelle flew through it. He would nod at the gallows and shout up to her past his ear: 'One day you will see me ride that pale mare. And when you do, I want you to be proud of me.'

She had never believed him.

Dragons were killed in fables, it was true, but they never hanged.

The first time she had ever seen him had been at the fish market in Les Halles, with her mother, Typhaine. Typhaine, as always, had lingered over the pale red crayfish, as always without buying, before cursing and moving on to the eel. A huge hand had shovelled up three of the crayfish at once, and another had tossed a coin at the fishmonger, then the crayfish fell with a clatter into Typhaine's basket.

Estelle had stared up with awe at the giant whose hands had performed this deed. She had found him, at once, magnificent. She did not find his face ugly, though she came to understand that others did. She only saw that his face was more. More than any other face she had ever seen. More jaw, more brow, more cheekbones, more lips. He had looked down at her and grinned, with more grin than she had ever seen. He had great gaps between his teeth, which was common enough, except that only one of his teeth was missing. She could tell, because that gap, near one edge of his mouth, was much bigger than the rest. His nose was like that of the lions carved on the fountain. His eyes were the colour of gold. He winked and she grinned back.

Typhaine had uttered a stream of curses at the giant and he

had backed away without a word. As Typhaine dragged Estelle from the fish market, Estelle looked back, but the giant had gone. When she'd asked her mother who he was, her mother had told her he was a monster and she should forget him. Typhaine ate all three crayfish by herself, except for one claw, which she gave to Estelle.

Typhaine, and the brothers she lived with, Joco and Gobbo, taught Estelle to be a cutpurse and a burglar. Sometimes she wondered if the brothers wanted her to get caught and hanged; but she was good at it. She invented her own tricks.

One morning in Les Halles, just outside the cheese market, she picked a woman in fine black silk with a covered wicker basket over one arm. Concealed behind a clever pleat in her skirt, Estelle saw the bulge of a purse tied about her waist. She drew her knife from the sheath sewn into her belt and dashed into the crowd as if to pass the woman by. She grabbed the hem of the woman's skirts and circled her like a greyhound and trussed her tight. She shouldered her in the thighs and as the woman toppled backwards into the muck, Estelle slid her left hand into the pleat and seized the purse. She flashed the knife and the woman covered her face, and in a second flash the purse was severed free.

Estelle ducked the grasp of a do-gooder and with a third flash she cut him across the palm and felt the bones. She hooked the fallen basket over her arm and ran through the usual to-do for the alley. Shouts, gawking faces. A fat man blocked the narrow passage ahead. She feinted left and twisted right and felt his fingers in her hair. Fast as a dog bites she punctured him twice and slashed the hand and again felt the scrape of bones. He let go of her hair but grabbed the basket.

Estelle let him take it and ran with the purse. She ran like a rat. Her heart was pounding and she could hardly breathe, but her eyes were everywhere – looking for escapes – and her feet were ready to take her in any direction.

Two more men loomed before her, one behind the other.

As she stopped to twist and turn, the first man grunted and arched backwards.

As he fell, she saw that the second man was Grymonde.

'Run, La Rossa, run. Behind me. To the cemetery.'

So had begun her flights with the dragon. Grymonde had told her to stop the cutpurse trade, for at best she would end up in a slave shop for incorrigibles far from Paris. He promised to give her enough booty to keep Typhaine happy, and he did. He made her promise never to tell Typhaine where the booty came from. She didn't see him as often as she wanted to; but he was her light. The Grande Truanderie was home to villains enough, but the Yards were feared there. At least the Truanderie could be found. There was nothing to be found in the Yards but a deeper pit of poorness and a better chance of dying, from all sorts of things; yet for Estelle, Cockaigne had the allure of a magic kingdom in a tale. Then someone told her that Cockaigne *was* a magic kingdom in a tale, and this made its allure all the greater.

When she followed Grymonde from Les Halles, north through the Yards to Cockaigne, he chided her, and always sent her back to Typhaine. But more and more he let her hang around his doings, though he never took her into his house. She had thought Typhaine had known nothing of her secret life; until just last week, when she had persuaded Estelle to ask Grymonde to give Joco and Gobbo some work.

'If he's such a true friend of yours, why wouldn't he?' said Typhaine. 'It's money in your pocket, too. Food in your belly. Clothes on your back. And he's got something coming up. Ask him. If he wants to say no, he will.'

Estelle had asked Grymonde.

'So Typhaine won't stop you from seeing me?'

'She couldn't stop me if she tried.'

Grymonde had talked to Joco and Gobbo. He had given them the job.

Last night, Estelle had climbed the roof and gone down the chimney.

Grymonde hadn't really wanted her to, and neither had Estelle.

335

It was Joco's idea, though Estelle knew it was a good one. Grymonde had given her the choice, and because she knew it would help her dragon, she had said yes.

Now she was cast out, because of the lady from the south.

Carla.

Estelle didn't like to cry. She had learned not to, unless it served some purpose, which was rare. But as she circled Les Halles and drifted north up the Rue Saint-Denis she cried. She heard other cries – screams – echoing down the streets, but she didn't care. Here and there she saw piles of dead bodies, and bands of men with axes and spears, but she didn't care, and they paid her no mind.

Carla had not been mean; even though Estelle had been mean to her. Carla had been tender. She had told Grymonde she was brave. And if not for Carla, Altan would have killed her, she knew. Yet, she also knew that, somehow, Carla had caused her banishment.

She couldn't hate Grymonde. Grymonde was the king, so he had to be mean; sometimes, even to her, she supposed; even though he had never been mean to her before. She had failed, it was true. But if bravery wasn't enough, what was? She didn't have anything else to give. She thought about it. That was true, too. She had nothing at all.

What tormented her most was that Grymonde had taken Carla inside his house.

Why?

He'd never taken Estelle inside his house. Never, ever.

Estelle ran out of tears. Her belly ached and she felt dizzy.

She went home.

Typhaine and the brothers rented two rooms on the second floor. The brothers hadn't always been around, but this was at least the third summer Estelle could remember having to bear their rages and their smell. As she got to the door she heard her mother and Joco bickering. Estelle knew how to sleep through bickering.

'They cut his cock and balls off,' whined Joco.

'That's no loss to the world and neither is he,' said Typhaine. 'I should've got rid of you bastards a long time ago. Look at me. A count once had me in his bed, and more than once, too.'

'Don't we know it? The whole street knows it. Christ!'

Joco broke off in a prolonged groan. Estelle walked in and saw Joco gasping on the bed. His back was arched rigid and his hands clawed the mattress in agony. Uttering a series of short whimpers he lowered himself back down as if onto broken glass. He took shallow, timid, breaths, as if each plunged a knife in him.

'He must have broken five ribs, on either side. Or broken me back.'

'And you didn't get a sou? Arsehole. Did they cut your balls off, too?'

'They couldn't, could they, 'cause you got there first.'

'That poxed bastard did it to flout me. No, he's too stupid to think that far.'

'I need to piss. Oh Jesus!'

Joco whimpered through another spasm.

'Grymonde made Joco eat a dead dog,' said Estelle.

'Don't you start, rat face. Typhaine, pass me the pot.'

'Get it yourself.'

'I can't even sit up. Do you want me to piss the bed? Give me that jar.'

Typhaine emptied wine from the jar into two bowls and dropped it on Joco's stomach. While he fumbled with himself and moaned, she turned on Estelle.

'And where've you been? I've been worried to death.'

Estelle didn't believe this for an instant. Typhaine was still slender, still very pretty; her dark red hair was still lush and wild. Estelle had once thought her beautiful; she didn't know what had changed. Typhaine had often told her she was descended from Irish kings and Estelle believed it. Once, when giggling drunk, she'd told her that Estelle had royal French blood, too; but she'd never said it again, and Estelle doubted it.

'And where's your smock? Christ, put something on.'

'I'm hungry,' said Estelle.

'There's bread and cold soup in the kitchen. It's too hot for a fire.'

Estelle ate while Typhaine taunted Joco. She found her eyes closing between spoonfuls. There was an urgent knock on the front door. It roused her and she ate more soup. A third voice joined the squabble and Estelle started to feel sick.

She knew the voice.

Nasal, high-pitched, not like most people's.

Petit Christian.

She felt afraid. She went to the doorway and listened. He was asking questions about the raid on the Hôtel last night. How did he know about that? He was a toady, the kind who knew lots of things about lots of things. She was glad he was talking about the raid and not about her.

One night last winter, Typhaine and Joco had taken her to Petit Christian and told her to go with him. He'd taken her to a grand *hôtel* near the Louvre, far bigger and more splendid than the one they had attacked that morning. When she went inside, it was a place such as she'd never imagined existed. Petit Christian and a woman had bathed her and washed her hair with perfume and dressed her in a beautiful blue gown, such as she'd never worn, with a gold star on the front, which they told her was the Star of Bethlehem. Then they'd told her that she was to play a game, in which she would pretend to be Mary Magdalene. Estelle knew the name, but not what it meant, and they told her the Magdalene was a special friend of Jesus.

They took her into a huge bedroom. In the bedroom was a man in a long white robe and wearing a crown of thorns, though the thorns weren't real, in case they might hurt his head. He looked like Jesus in some of the paintings in churches. He put his feet in a silver bowl of water, and they told Estelle to wash his feet with her hair.

Estelle said no. He could wash his own feet.

She didn't remember the rest, though she sometimes had dreams. She had never told anyone. Typhaine had never asked what happened. Estelle sensed she knew. She could never tell Grymonde.

They'd taken her to Christian a second time; but she'd run away from him and lived with the rats for three days.

She heard Joco say: 'They were all of them alive when I left, except the Turk, so what more can I tell you? Ask Estelle, she was still there.'

Estelle was so scared she couldn't move. Christian came to the doorway. He was all in green, like a toad. His face made her sicker than his voice. His smile was even worse.

'How is our little Magdalene? Pretty as ever. Though a bath wouldn't hurt.'

Estelle retreated across the kitchen. She felt her belt for her knife, but she'd given it to Grymonde, so she wouldn't stab herself going down the chimney. She took a carving knife from the sideboard. Its hilt was so big she had to use both hands.

'Put that down,' said Typhaine. 'He just wants to ask you about this morning. Tell him and he'll buy both of us a new frock.'

'I don't want a new frock.'

'She has sentiments for Grymonde,' Typhaine explained to Christian.

'I have only one question, my little hedgehog.'

Christian was trying to charm her. Estelle's stomach hurt.

'I'm not a hedgehog. And I'm not a nose.'

'I'm glad to hear it. No one likes a nose. But noses harm their friends, and this is a matter of helping your friends. Joco says there was a fine lady at the Hôtel D'Aubray, named Carla. Do you remember?'

'Grymonde made Joco eat a dead dog.'

'I'm sure he enjoyed it. But tell me, what happened to Carla after Joco left?'

'I was sent away, too, and it wasn't fair. I was brave. Even Carla said I was brave.'

'Carla was right, you were very, very brave. Where was she?'

'She was sitting in a chair in the street. Then I ran away, from the boys.'

Christian pouted. He was frustrated.

'Why do you want to know?' asked Estelle.

Christian studied her. Estelle squeezed the knife.

'Carla is a special, sweet lady,' said Christian. 'The people who love her want to know what happened to her. They're very worried for her.'

'What people?'

'Well, her husband for one. He's a great chevalier, you know. He would pay a lot of gold to find her. He would pay even more to get her back. It's called a ransom.'

Estelle struggled. She didn't like Carla being in Grymonde's house. Wouldn't Carla rather be in her own house, with the chevalier who loved her? Petit Christian did work for *Les Messieurs*. And Grymonde liked gold. It all made sense, yet her stomach still hurt her.

'Would the chevalier give the gold to Grymonde?'

'Of course he would, lots of gold, if Grymonde knew where she was. The chevalier would be happy, Carla would be happy and Grymonde would be happiest of all.'

'Estelle,' said Typhaine. 'Where is she?'

'Carla is with Grymonde, in Cockaigne, in his house. She has a baby inside her.'

'How do you know this?' asked Petit Christian.

'I followed them. I saw her go into the house.'

'Grymonde didn't hurt her?'

'No. He was kind to her. He told everyone she was their new sister.'

'What did I tell you?' Joco's voice wavered in from the bedroom. He whimpered with pain. 'That's why he tucked me up. The Infant's ardent. She charmed him.'

'Don't make me laugh,' said Typhaine. 'He was only ever ardent for one and that was me.'

'Hold your filthy tongues,' said Christian.

He turned back to Estelle and smiled. Her skin crawled.

'Do you think Grymonde is fond of Carla? Does he like her?'

Estelle hated these questions. She was sure Grymonde liked Carla.

'Well, who'd have believed it?' said Typhaine, staring at her.

340

'I said keep quiet,' snapped Christian. 'Estelle? Does Grymonde like Carla?'

'I don't know. I suppose so.'

'Good girl,' smiled Christian. 'You shall have two frocks.'

'I don't want your frocks.'

'Then I'll have all three,' said Typhaine. 'I'll buy them myself if you don't mind.' She held out her hand to Christian. 'We didn't make a penny today so we want our share, three shares for the job, and the rest for this one. After all, it was me who put you onto that monster –' she glanced at Estelle. 'It was my idea in the first place.'

'Indeed. Look how it has turned out.'

Christian left the kitchen, with Typhaine in pursuit. Estelle ran to the door and spied. Petit Christian gave Typhaine an *écu d'or* and before she could protest put a finger to his lips.

'There'll be more, later, much more. Stay here until I return. All of you.'

As he shut the front door behind him, Estelle's relief was so great her legs trembled. She went to curl up on her sheepskin by the hearth. She still had the ache in her stomach but didn't know why. She wasn't a nose. Grymonde would get some gold, and Carla would go home to her chevalier. What was wrong with that? Estelle could fly with the dragon, like before. As she drifted to sleep she heard her mother complaining to Joco.

'Who does that little bitch think he is? Never any pleasing him. If the boys aren't too old, the girls are too young. He asked me if I knew anyone mad enough to do it and I told him. What in Christ's name did he expect? What fool would hire a madman and not expect him to act like one?'

When Estelle woke up a heavy rain was falling outside the open windows and the light was grey. She got up from the sheepskin. She wanted to go out before the shower passed and run around under the drops. She felt hot and dirty, and the rain would be cool and clean. She heard Typhaine ranting next door and didn't bother to listen. It was another good reason to get out. She found a dirty smock in a basket and pulled it on. She went to the bedroom and found that Petit Christian had returned.

'He'd kill me on sight,' said Typhaine. 'Anyway, the police have never been up the Yards. You couldn't pay 'em to go.'

'If no one has ever been there they won't be expecting us,' said Christian. 'We'll be in and out in half an hour. You'll be perfectly safe. Besides, we're talking about the Soldiers of Christ, and a contingent of Swiss Guard, not a gaggle of chicken-hearted *sergents*.'

Estelle saw that two *sergents* stood inside the front door. The insult didn't bother them. One she recognised because he was known not to take bribes: he was called Baro, and unlike most he was a real killer. The other *sergent* yawned and polished his single front tooth on a knuckle. The tooth was brown. Christian continued.

'If you don't want him to see you, you can leave as soon as you get there.'

'Speaking of cowards,' said Typhaine, 'are you going with them?'

'I'm not sure that will be necessary and in any case it's irrelevant.'

From the bed, Joco said, 'I'll take you there, if you make it worth my while.'

'You couldn't walk to the door,' sneered Typhaine. 'Anyway, I wouldn't miss this for a solid gold pisspot with the King's head graved inside. In fact, you can put the same on my bill.'

Estelle felt sick again, like Petit Christian had made her feel before. They were going to do something bad to Grymonde. They weren't going to give him lots of gold to take Carla home. They hadn't said, exactly, that that was what they were going to do, but she knew spite when she heard it, and the sound of plots and lies and treachery. The spite was deep in Typhaine's heart. Why did she hate Grymonde? The spite was in Christian's eyes. He hated Grymonde, too.

Estelle had to warn Grymonde.

'Very well,' said Christian. 'Come with me, now, and you'll see it all.'

'I can't go like this, I've got to get changed,' said Typhaine. Her look warned Christian not to argue. 'It'll give this thunder shower a chance to blow over.'

Estelle crept to the door. The two *sergents* looked down at her.

'Where do you think you're going, madame?' said Typhaine.

'I want to go out in the rain. I'm hot.'

'Your arse'll be hot when I've finished tanning it. Get back in the kitchen.'

'This good *sergent* will make sure no one leaves,' said Christian.

He nodded at the one with the single brown tooth. Christian smiled at Estelle, as if he saw a chance to be cruel to her instead of to Typhaine. He reached in his purse and took out a silver franc between finger and thumb.

'Do you know why you were the perfect little Magdalene?'

Estelle didn't answer. She retreated from the horrid green toad.

'Because you have red hair,' said Christian. 'Judas had red hair, too.'

He flipped the coin. It hit Estelle in the chest and fell to the floor.

She sobbed and ran into the kitchen. She climbed onto the bench beneath the open window and stuck her head out. Rain splashed her face. She looked down into the alley and saw what she already knew: there was no way to climb down; and the drop was much too high. She had betrayed Grymonde. She was a Judas. There was nothing worse. Her tears ran down her face with the rain. Should she jump anyway?

The one-toothed *sergent* reached from behind her and shut the window.

'Don't fret little Magdalene. This isn't our affair. And, by my oath, isn't that onion soup I can smell?'

One-Tooth sat her on the bench and she watched him taste the cold soup and smack his lips. He filled two bowls. Estelle didn't want to eat. She wanted to warn Grymonde that Petit Christian and the Soldiers of Christ were coming to get him.

'*Sergent!* Quickly!'

Petit Christian's voice was a frightened hiss. One-Tooth took a huge slurp of soup from his bowl and went to the doorway. Estelle followed him to watch. In the bedroom, Baro was holding a cudgel and had flattened himself against the wall by the front door.

'Arm yourself,' said Christian. 'There's someone at the door.'

One-Tooth shrugged his bow from his shoulder and nocked an arrow. He retreated into the kitchen, ready to shoot. He looked down at Estelle and put a finger to his lips. The door rattled with a heavy knock. Christian stood back and nodded to Typhaine.

'Who's there?' called Typhaine.

'It's Papin. Let me in, I'm wet as a boiled frog.'

'One of Grymonde's lot,' whispered Typhaine.

Christian bit his lip and hesitated.

Estelle's heart raced. Papin could warn Grymonde. But would he hear her through the door? He might hear her scream but, here, screaming was usual.

'Invite him in and smile,' said Christian. 'You know what's at stake.'

Christian made a hammering gesture to Baro, who raised his cudgel.

As Typhaine smiled and opened the front door, Estelle squeezed past One-Tooth. Papin, dripping, lumbered over the threshold. Estelle shouted, loud as she could.

'Run, Papin! They want to kill Grymonde!'

Papin looked at her. Baro's cudgel smashed him across the nape. Estelle didn't see him drop. The back of Typhaine's hand cracked her across the face and for a moment she couldn't see anything at all. She found herself on her hands and knees, staring at One-Tooth's shoes. She heard groans and shouts behind her but none of that mattered.

She had failed Grymonde.

She was a Judas.

She would never fly with the dragon again.

CHAPTER NINETEEN

The Birthing Room

The birthing room seemed located in some mythic realm where time did not so much stand still as repeat itself, end on end. A pang would roll through her and she would ride the wave; then the next would come, always before she expected it. The monotony taxed her almost as much as the pains. There was a bed in the room, covered with a piece of ship's canvas, stained but not putrid, and on the canvas a sheet. Dry rushes covered the floor.

She paced, she squatted, she leaned over the back rail of a bench. She resorted to the chamber pot half a dozen times, but usually failed to pass water. When fatigue became too much she lay down and turned this way and that, without finding any comfort. She groaned and was aware that she sounded like a cow. Sometimes a contraction would awaken her with her mind still clinging to the fragments of some dream, but she could not have dozed for more than a minute or two. Fairy tales. Dreams.

How much time was in a minute? Or in two?

Though Alice assured her that foul language of any extremity was welcome in her house, Carla did not complain. Not complaining was her last hold on the dignity which she had otherwise abandoned without a qualm. The curtains were drawn against the sun but the heat was inescapable. Thyrus smoke lingered in the air, invisible except where it curled in blue wisps through the shafts of light. The boy she had found beautiful, Hugon, ran errands at Alice's command, fetching water, linens and tea. Carla heard him ask after her welfare, and twice she saw him at the door, but Alice didn't allow him to enter the room.

Carla had changed into a white nightgown, which was saturated with sweat, as was her hair. She decided that she was the Fire and

345

her body the tower under siege, melting, gaping, splitting apart. The prolonged confrontation left her racked, bedraggled, exhausted; as if she and Life Her-own-self had each other by the throat. She recalled Bors holding forth on the nature of glory, the elation, the delirium, which arose from the struggle with pain, fear and death. Was this how Mattias felt in battle? She doubted it, but if so, and if this was glory, its charm eluded her. Yet the experience had brought Alice into her life. That was glory enough.

Carla was lying on her back at Alice's request, or, rather, instruction. The old woman had examined her and declared her progress well and happily advanced. Now she wrapped a damp linen cloth over Carla's belly. The cloth was soaked in a lotion of boiled sorbe apples, egg whites, powdered hart's horn and frankincense, which she claimed would help mitigate stretch marks and wrinkles. Whether or not this end would be achieved, it felt good.

'Alice, what will happen to us, after this is over?'

'Even with the cards, we can't know that.'

'I'm not my usual self, yet I believe that in any circumstance we'd find things to admire in each other. Speaking for myself, very many more things than I can say.'

Alice laughed and coughed and swallowed phlegm.

She slid the linen cloth in cooling circles.

'Hellfire, this woman has never met another like you, and will confess it's been a grand lesson in the manners of the on high, one to put her to shame.'

'Whichever might pass for "on high", I'm far from any such state today, and my manners are no one's but my own.'

'This woman meant only to return your compliment. Here in the Yards we're not used to giving them, so forgive her if she missed the mark.'

'No, I'm the one who should apologise. You've shown me nothing but kindness.'

'Now, now, let's not plough that field again. If you are asking shall we remain joined – once the babe is born and you're both fit to go on your way – then of course we will. Our fates have entwined, we've shared – we are sharing – the most sacred of cups. Best not to put a collar on these things, or we'll choke them. For now, now is more than enough. Hell, this old girl hasn't left the yard in a dozen summers, and rarely this house. Next time she leaves, she'll be going a ways farther than the fish stalls, and come to that, the cemetery, too.'

'At least I'll know where to find you.'

Alice put her hand on Carla's breast. 'You'll find me in here. Always.'

Carla put her hand on Alice's. She looked into the winter eyes. The love that shone there, through the mist, was unlike any Carla had known. It seemed founded in something more than human. She realised the contrary was the case. The love in Alice was all that being human was meant to be. Carla began to cry. She choked her tears back.

'Always,' she said. 'Always.'

'Let them fall, love.'

A fresh commotion arose from the yard beyond the curtains. Alice glanced towards the noise and hoisted herself to her feet and lumbered away.

Carla clenched her fists as a contraction lifted her shoulders from the mattress. She bellowed. She rode the wave. She wiped the sweat from her eyes with her blue scarf. Alice returned holding a stiff sheet of paper, roughly the size of a large quarto.

'Few there are have ever seen this. My son believes it was burned long ago, but this old she-fox forgives herself for fooling him.'

Alice sat on the edge of the bed and handed the sheet to Carla. Carla took an involuntary breath. It was a portrait – a shirtless, bust-length, three-quarter profile, drawn in black, red and white chalk – of a stunningly gallant young man. His features were so fine yet so rugged, the curves and angles of cheekbone, brow and jaw, fixed in such perfect harmony, the musculature modelled with such right proportion, that one might have wondered if the artist were striving for some allegory of masculine beauty. Yet, so exquisite was the work in its subtle mingling of colour, its sureness and ease, its intensity of expression, its tenderness and empathy, that she did not doubt a true artist had captured a true likeness. The youth stared from the frame with a lofty ferocity, his eyes those of a man who knew that the world lay at his feet. The curl of his lip he could have learned only from his mother.

Carla said, 'Grymonde.'

'The bonniest lad that e'er I saw. Now a doomed and tormented man.'

Carla looked at Alice and saw the sorrow that she nursed deep inside. Carla had many questions, yet in the face of Alice's sorrow they seemed trivial. The old mother had a tale to tell, perhaps one she had never told. Carla took her hand and waited.

'You've seen what my son has become. Ten years it's taken, one day stacked on another, since that picture was made. He lives under a curse that slowly consumes him. What we see on the outside is the blossom of the sickness in the tree, in the growing timber, in the sap. And I it was who cursed him. I cursed him because of a woman, and the child they two had made, and because I was jealous, and because evil hid in my heart, awaiting its moment to claim me.'

'I don't believe that. As this babe fights for life inside me, I don't believe it. Grymonde has some unknown malady – a slow ague, or some poison he ate –'

'This mother thanks you, and mayhap you're right, but all things are connected, and I did – again I say "I" – I did curse my son, which is a wound to any mother's soul. The moment it flew from my tongue a molten arrow pierced me, and Our Mother cried out from the stones beneath my feet, for some things once said cannot be unsaid. He took his whore, for such she was and is, and he took his babe, a daughter every bit as bonny as he, and he left this old fool alone to sup on her regrets.'

Tears fell down the purpled cheeks. Carla swallowed on a great sorrow of her own. Her womb clenched and she squeezed Alice's hand as the pain spiralled through her and she made no sound.

'This was wrong,' said Alice. 'You're in no fit state to listen to my follies.'

Alice reached for the portrait. Carla shook her head and held onto it.

'I'm glad you told me. Alice, I know what it is to betray a son. The cards spoke of that plain. Weighed in the balance and found wanting. Such was I, as a mother. I feel foolish telling you anything, but is this not our burden? Is it not the hardest to bear?'

Alice wiped her face on the back of her hand. For an instant she looked like a child. She nodded and Carla smiled at her, and Alice smiled, too, and shook her head.

'He was in love, you see. And this old woman feared what it would cost him. He could have had any girl, there were plenty willing and not just in the Yards, and he'd had his share, too. It wasn't that. It wasn't losing him, it was losing him to her. She was a bad sort. The Devil's blackest whore. But there's no rhyme or reason to love, we don't need the cards to tell us that. She cut his heart out soon enough, as I knew she would. She was a beauty, of sorts, it must be said, and there were gold trinkets and gay times to be had elsewhere, among the better sort. He made a fool of himself, as men will in such straits, but in the end he found his way home and licked his wounds, and he made himself King of Cockaigne, over the bodies of many a stern foe. His enemies called him "The Infant".'

'I have heard that name. Why?'

'At first it was meant as an insult. He was scarce nineteen. The veterans thought he didn't know what he were doing, that he should've been working for them. By the time they learned different, they were dead. You see, my son values his life no more than a flower values its petals, and his enemies reckoned their lives were worth much more.'

There was pride in Alice's voice, as well as pain.

Carla almost said: *I know such a man. I married him. I love him.*

But she didn't want to interrupt Alice's reverie; her sharing of a mother's burden.

'He never wooed another, lost all feeling for love – refuses to speak of it – but this old woman won't credit the whore for that.

His heart mended as hearts do. No, he lost his desire. That was the fruit of his mother's curse, too. And who knows what else? For he's grown into the darkest of men.'

'You say Grymonde has a daughter?'

'He never recognised her, for which, among much that he can, he can't be blamed. He never knew his own father, though that was no tragedy. This grandmother hasn't seen that little love since she was born, right here in this room.'

If these events were about ten years ago, Grymonde was much younger than Carla had imagined, only thirty or so. She couldn't help but think of Estelle. She recalled the fierce, sooty face, and could find no resemblance, though, as she knew too well, that meant little. It was the girl's look that struck a bell, the molten arrow of jealousy she had loosed at Carla. Whoever the granddaughter was, the wound her loss had left in Alice had never healed.

'My son was taken from me the day he was born,' said Carla. 'He was raised a bastard, an orphan, in a world not unlike these Yards. He was twelve before I saw him again. It took me that long to find the courage to look for him. And now he is lost again. This child, I swear, I will never let leave my arms.'

A pang arose of such tremendous intensity that Carla felt that her hips would be rent in two. It passed and she felt purged of emotion. She asked for some cold tea and Alice gave it to her and she drank. The drawing lay on the bed and Carla picked it up and studied it, again marvelling at the work. The blacks had been sketched in powdered slate with a metal stylus. The red flush that made the subject throb with life was in rusty clay. The spark of light in the irises was caught with brown pencil. It was a masterpiece. She contained her curiosity. Alice smiled.

'There's a fine story to go with that picture, if you want to hear it.'

'Please, I'd love to.'

'So, my lad is eating breakfast outside a tavern in Les Halles one day, when a most distinguished gentleman walks up and asks him if he would object to having his portrait drawn. Now, a person runs into all sorts in Les Halles, but even there this request was without precedent, and my son took him for a sodomite – the gentleman would not have been the first such to approach him – and he told him to be on his way while he could still walk. But the gentleman persisted, offering to pay him handsome for an hour of his time. For what? Well, the gentleman sees in my son an irresistible challenge to the practice of his art, whereupon he declares himself the most famous painter in France.'

'I knew it: Monsieur Clouet. He is painter to the royal family.'

'That's the very fellow. The name means nothing to my son, of course, but his vanity is now piqued and, having nothing to fear, he finishes his sausage and follows him to a splendid apartment in the Louvre, where – as good as his word and without any tricks – Monsieur Clouet makes this splendid picture in no more than a trice. Quite a performance, by all accounts, and very pleased with himself he was, too, the monsieur.'

'I should think so, it's superb. But how do you come to have it?'

Another pang of great intensity intervened. Carla bore it with impatience. The birth was close now, she sensed it for the first time, and then no distraction would suffice.

'Go on.'

'So, Monsieur Clouet thanks him and hands my son five gold *écus* – a sum so far beyond his expectations that he wonders if they were not counterfeit. But before he takes them, he gets his first sight of the picture. What do you think happens next?'

'Tell me.'

'"No, monsieur", says my son. "I'll take my picture as my pay, thank you very much, for it will please my mother. And since you've had your challenge and met it square, the bargain is straight." You can imagine the to-do.'

'If I wasn't in such straits I would laugh.'

'When my son's mind is set, it's set, and there's an end to it. So by the time the palace guards are called, the monsieur is in quite a tremble, and my lad threatens to tear the picture in pieces and use the shreds to mop up their blood. "But since t'would be pity to spoil this elegant trifle," he says, "– and if you're giving me five *écus d'or* it must be worth five hundred to you – I'll stand while you make another picture, and we can have one each." And so it was and there it is.'

'From the look in his eye, this must be the second drawing.'

'No, love, that's the first. During the second the monsieur's hand shook so much my son didn't reckon the quality to be good enough.'

For a moment Carla's delight overrode her caution and she laughed. Her body responded with another wrenching throe. While she lay groaning, Alice retrieved the picture and stowed it away. She returned and removed the linen cloth and dried her. She dipped her hand in the pot of lotion.

'Let's see how we're doing.'

Carla opened her legs and Alice explored inside her.

'Grand. There's naught but a lip left, the head is full down. But don't push yet.'

A moment later they heard heavy footsteps below

'Mam! I'm coming up!'

'You wait down there until you're told different!'

'I've news.'

'You heard me.'

Carla was too engaged with the next pang to be much alarmed. Alice waited.

'My son grew up in this room, watching his mother's work. Since her strength's not been what it was, he's helped out more than a few times when the baby's been awkward. Far more likely than not we'll have no need of him today, but on my oath, you can trust him more than any surgeon. That said, if you'd rather he didn't come in, he won't.'

Mattias had been with her through most of her last labour, except at those points where his anxiety had so taxed her she had sent him out to chop wood. All that mattered was the baby. Her concern for its welfare surged through her. If she'd been standing before a crowd it would no longer worry her.

'If he might help, he's welcome, I don't care. But I need to stand, or squat, I feel too feeble lying on my back.'

She clambered to her feet without letting Alice help her. Her vision went black for a moment, then returned. There was no frame to the bed, so she went to the short, stout bench that she'd used earlier. She grabbed the backrest and felt calm enough. She breathed evenly. She heard Alice and Grymonde talking outside the door, some dispute conducted in murmurs, on Alice's part with quiet ferocity. She didn't try to eavesdrop. She wasn't curious. She was more tired than she had realised; the heat had sapped her. The pressure on her pelvis was immense, greater than when lying down, but on her feet she felt at least the illusion of greater control. Her thighs were heavy but after years in the saddle she had no doubts as to their strength. For the first time she felt the inclination to bear down building inside her.

'Alice, I want to push.'

'Wait for the next pang.'

Carla waited but the next pang didn't come. Her womb felt less tense than at any time since she'd got here. A kind of physical silence had fallen. Her mind struggled in a vortex of rogue feelings and emotions. She took deep breaths. She knew that at this stage the dangers were greatest. Was the baby's head too big? She dismissed the thought. Were her muscles exhausted? Was the baby in distress? She was, after all, a week or two early.

'The pang isn't coming.' She didn't hide the tremor of panic in her voice.

'Don't fret, love. That's common enough when you get to the brink.'

'Your body is gathering its strength for the real work,' said Grymonde.

Carla turned her head and looked at him. She had forgotten quite how grotesque his face was. Monsieur Clouet's portrait flashed through her mind. Sweat ran into her eyes and she wiped it with her scarf. In as far as she could read the crude features, Grymonde seemed troubled, but not by her. As far as she was concerned, he showed not a trace of diffidence or embarrassment. He roused a broad smile. While the situation seemed unremarkable to him, its absolute strangeness was not lost on Carla, despite the vortex, and yet his massive presence did lend her confidence.

'Carla,' he said, 'you've done us all proud.'

'Thank you. You're most welcome.'

'Have you washed, you big ox?'

'Of course I've washed.'

As Grymonde brandished his huge hands for inspection the contraction came in a great surge and on instinct Carla squatted and bore down. For the first time she felt the actual movement of the baby. Her skin began to burn. She groaned and pushed until the long wave waned. She breathed deeply and looked down but her nightgown covered her thighs. She pulled it up but it still obscured her view.

'Tie it up for me, please.'

She tucked the front edge of the nightgown beneath her breasts and Grymonde gathered the skirts up behind her and tied them snug behind her back.

'No need for shame,' he said.

'I feel no shame.'

She bent her head over her belly to look between her thighs, but still couldn't quite see. She took a hand from the rail and felt herself. She was swollen and bulging apart. She heard both Alice and Grymonde utter soothing encouragements, but hardly noticed their words. She was alone in this now. The thought redoubled her strength. This was her baby. The baby was counting on her.

'I won't let you down.'

The next surge roared through her and she moaned and pushed and the burning intensified. Again she felt the movement, enormous and inexorable, peeling her open. The pain flooded her imagination. She shifted her feet on the dried rushes. Her legs were strong. She gave herself to the opening, she willed herself open. She pushed. She groaned.

'I love you.'

The pang faded. She stood up for a moment, bent forward, caught her breath. The burning raged at her core. She wanted to push but breathed and waited. Again, the wait seemed endless, harder to endure than the pangs, for they required only submission, not restraint. Grymonde spread a linen towel on the floor between her feet. She realised the effort that so simple a task would have cost Alice, and she was glad he was here.

'I'm glad you're here.'

'The honour is mine. I'm going to open the curtains, so that the babe might emerge into sunlight.'

She nodded. Her back was to the window, yet after the relative gloom to which she had become accustomed, the light was blinding. She closed her eyes. She squatted. She felt Alice's hand squeeze her shoulder and she reached back to stroke it.

Another pang.

She pushed and moaned.

Another.

Another.

Another.

Another.

With each surge the burning reached a crescendo that seemed impossible to exceed, yet with each following the intensity was greater. Grymonde knelt beside her.

'With your permission.'

'Yes, yes.'

He peered between her thighs. He took her hand from the rail.

'See. The babe is near crowned.'

She put her hands between her legs. She felt wet hair. A warm, hard head.

'Oh God.'

Her elation at touching her child vanquished her pain; but only for an instant.

She felt Alice squeeze her shoulder again.

'You're almost done, love. On the next throe don't push too violent or sudden, but strong and steady, so you won't tear.'

'Like pulling a cork,' offered Grymonde.

The pang rose and she bore down, strong, steady. The burning peaked.

'I am the Fire.'

She let out a moan of ecstatic release as the head passed and turned.

She released a rush of water, more than she had thought still in her.

She heaved for breath.

She reached down.

'Is he all right? Tell me.'

Grymonde sat on his heels, ducking low, indifferent to the fluids.

'Pink as a ripe peach and already blinking.'

Her fingertips touched skin of exquisite softness. A cheek. She sobbed.

'Don't relax just yet, love. A couple more throes and you're done.'

'Should I wait?'

The pang came before Alice could answer and Carla closed her eyes and bore down. The burning rose again, though she hardly noticed and cared not at all.

In a final torrential rush her baby's body slithered out of hers.

In that instant she felt loss pierce her, then it was gone amid a wave of relief so complete she swayed on her heels. She squeezed on the rail to keep her balance. She opened her eyes and looked down.

The babe sat gleaming in Grymonde's enormous palms. The damp head flopped this way then that in venturesome movements, eyes blinking through pearls of fluid, which also sputtered from its lips. Limbs flexed in seeming delight at discovering such freedom. A torn sheet of translucent white membrane, still attached to the cord at one end, clung around the babe's shoulders and encased the flexing legs.

'Born in the caul,' said Grymonde with pride. He glanced at Alice. 'As near as matters to me. It's a good omen.'

Carla hardly listened. She let go of the rail and Grymonde offered up the babe. Carla took the babe under the arms. Her hands encircled the warm body, smeared in creamy grease, and her heart flooded with rapture. She felt the delicate ribcage heave, and life and hope and courage throbbed between her palms.

With great gentleness, Grymonde peeled the caul away.

Carla supported the babe's head with her fingertips and sat backwards on the floor.

She held her new child up before her face.

Carla was overwhelmed by her beauty.

Her beauty.

Carla's heart flooded again with pure love.

The babe was a girl.

Carla cradled her and put her mouth to the little girl's lips and sucked out the remnants of fluid. The baby girl blinked and waved tiny hands and looked at her. Her eyes were as pale and lustrous as opal. Carla knew she had given birth to an angel.

'Amparo.'

Amparo uttered a short, sweet cry.

Carla put her cheek to Amparo's. She whispered in her ear.

'You will be a singer of songs.'

She felt Alice at her shoulder and turned to see her joy.

She loved the old woman.

'Thank you, Alice. I will never –' she swallowed. 'I will never forget.'

Carla looked at Grymonde. How could such a man contain such darkness? She thought of Mattias, of whom she had asked herself the same question. She had a terrible urge to see Mattias hold his baby girl in his arms, for she knew it was a girl he had hoped for. But Mattias wasn't here, and she and their daughter were. Before sadness could overcome her, she mustered a smile for the monster kneeling before her.

'Thank you, too, Monsieur Grymonde.'

Grymonde displayed the unnatural gaps between his teeth.

'I did nothing, Carla. You did it all.'

'You've both been generous friends to me. To us.'

Emotion overwhelmed her and she felt tears fall.

'Let's move to the bed,' said Alice. 'There's a few chores yet undone, not least giving Amparo her first feed. The sooner the better, the *colostra* will help the afterbirth.'

Grymonde stood behind Carla and put his hands around her waist and lifted her to her feet as if she weighed no more than the baby. The absence of the load she had carried for so long unbalanced her. She steadied herself. She found she could walk well enough but was happy for the bed when she got there. Alice spread two clean towels and Carla sat on them and reclined against the pillows. She put Amparo to her nipple, who at once took it in her mouth and suckled in absolute bliss.

Carla's happiness was near as complete as her baby's.

'My daughter. My lovely daughter. And all this time I thought you a boy.'

She smiled at Alice. Alice inclined her head towards her son.

'In this woman's view you got the better side of the bargain.'

'I believed her to be a boy because she kicked me so hard.'

'This old girl predicts you'll be far from the last she kicks. Here, love, feel the cord, while your two hearts still beat, the one to the other.'

Carla took the blue coil in her hand and felt her own blood pulsing through it.

'It feels strange, but beautiful. Should we not cut it?'

'We cut it when it stops its beating. Is it not still a living part of you both? What fool would kill it before its natural end?' She scoffed and held up her palm. 'Don't tell me. Now, while you're both content, let's see how the afterbirth goes. And you, you big ox, clear up those wet reeds before they go sour in this heat. And draw those curtains, we're roasting.'

Grymonde laughed. 'The big ox will tend to the caul, then the slops.'

'And tell Hugon to make us some fresh tea.'

Grymonde spun, quick as a wild beast, his hand on his knife, as a strange sound, itself deep and raw enough to have come from the throat of some fabled creature, echoed up the stairs. Carla knew the sound. Someone had bowed her gambo violl, crudely but well.

'Don't be alarmed. It's my violl.'

'Your violl?'

Grymonde bellowed down the stair.

'Who's that? Get up here now!'

Hugon appeared at the door, shamefaced and afraid. Grymonde glowered.

'Is it true, knave? Did you tamper with the violl?'

'Please,' said Carla. 'He did no harm. Don't chastise him.'

'Your pardon, madame. I heard your music. We all did. It made me cry.'

'I'll make you cry, boy.'

Grymonde raised a hand and Hugon waited for the blow. It didn't fall. Hugon looked at Carla without remorse; but with the yearning she had seen before.

Hugon said, 'I wanted to know how the sound was made.'

'You made a fine start,' said Carla. 'You attacked the strings with a spirit that few ever dare.'

Hugon blinked, amazed. He avoided Grymonde's glare.

Carla smiled. 'You should learn how to play.'

'Me? Could I? It's possible?'

'I could give you your first lesson.'

'Now?'

The boy lit up with such hope that Carla almost said yes.

'Enough,' said Alice. 'Bring us some tea and all will be forgiven.'

She flapped a hand to drive them away and they left.

'Hugon is an outsider, but a decent soul. He's different from the rest, but too young to know why or how. He suffers for it. When he becomes a man, he'll suffer more.'

'I wasn't being kind. The violl spoke for him.'

'This woman heard it, too. But there's many can speak who will never be heard.'

Shade cooled the room. Very gently, so gently Carla felt nothing inside, Alice tried the tension on the cord, but didn't pull on it.

'Grand. When you feel the urge, a push will help, but no hurry. There'll be a bit of bleeding, or what might seem more than a bit, but that's usual. Then, when you're ready, this old girl will give you a bath – and you can bathe that little treasure.'

After some time the pulsing in the cord stopped and Carla's throat tightened. The toils of the pregnancy, the throes of the labour, were already memories. She would have endured a thousand times worse to cradle her daughter for even a moment. She let go of the cord. One connection had ended and others had begun, too many and too deep to be imagined, yet already known in her every fibre. She stared at Amparo's face as she suckled. She wondered if she would ever want to look at anything else. She felt a strong cramp in her belly; after what she had been through, it didn't deserve to be called a pang.

'I'm ready to push.'

Alice lumbered over with a bowl of water, linen cloths draped over one arm, and set them down. She caught her breath and leaned over and nodded and Carla bore down. A membranous reddish-blue mass bulged from inside her, accompanied by trickles of blood. Alice massaged Carla's belly and guided the afterbirth with a gentle tug on the cord. Carla pushed with another contraction. As the mass emerged further – a large flat disc nearly an inch thick at the centre – Alice rolled it up and over on itself in her hands. The manoeuvre made its passage easier and the afterbirth slid free. More blood drenched the towels, a cupful or so, but, as Alice seemed unimpressed, neither was Carla.

'Did I tear?'

'No, you're sound as a bell. Do you want to see this?'

Carla leaned forward as Alice laid the afterbirth on the towels. It was the size and shape of a dinner plate and the side through which the cord entered was white, like the caul, and marbled with blood vessels. Alice turned it over to display the inner face, which was raw in texture and the colour of red wine. She pored over it with a finger.

'We must examine this maternal face of the cotyledon exactly, to make sure all the lobes are intact. If one or several are missing, they are still attached inside the womb and may bleed or turn putrid. But as you can see, this afterbirth is unbroken, the surface even, each lobe complete and fitted to its neighbours without a flaw.'

Carla nodded. She had not examined an afterbirth before. She was amazed that she could have generated so peculiar a thing and that it had been her connection to her baby.

Alice blew her cheeks.

'And with that we may declare the miracle it performed complete, and yours, too, and give all due thanks to our Mother Nature, for it's her genius we honour here. That said, you may pray to any God or idol that you wish.'

Carla looked at Alice. Her features were drawn. The day had taken its toll on her, too, more so than Carla had been able to see; or than Alice had allowed her to see. The grey winter of her eyes shone with the bloom of another spring; yet conveyed, too, some knowledge that this would be her last. Carla opened her mouth to speak but could find no words to convey what she felt. Alice curled her lips, as if to fend off displays of excess sentiment, but Carla needed to make some gesture.

'Here, hold Amparo.'

Carla made to offer the babe and saw that she was asleep, her open mouth still at her nipple, her lips yellow with the first milk. Once gain, Carla was entranced.

'Let Amparo nap on your breast, the little treasure needs it. You don't think she slept through all that to-do. My joy can wait while we've seen to the cord and so forth. And then we'll call for a jug, for this old girl is parched something terrible.'

She put one hand on her thigh and the other on the bed and shoved herself to her feet. She stood still for a moment, her breathing crackly. She spoke without turning.

'You couldn't have chosen a lovelier name. Your other Amparo is shining.'

Alice checked that the cord was done and tied it with string and cut it with a knife. She smeared some ointment on the stump and Amparo slept through it all. Alice cleaned up the blood and gave Carla a sponge bath, which almost sent her to sleep, too. The pleasure of giving Amparo her first wash they shared, and still she did not awake, though she moved her lips and her eyes shifted beneath their tiny lids, and her hands fluttered, as if she were dreaming her first dream in this new world.

'Shouldn't she cry more?' asked Carla.

'We've given her nothing to cry about, yet. But we will.'

Grymonde returned from below with a loaded tray.

'Tea for the Countess of Cockaigne and a jug of fine wine for its Queen.'

'Keep your voice down, the little one's napping.'

Grymonde had brought honey to put in the tea and Carla took some. Alice quaffed a large cup of wine without taking it from her lips. She gasped. Grymonde refilled it.

'They're roasting a pig in the yard,' he said. 'Can you smell it?'

'Did Estelle come back?' asked Carla.

'La Rossa? I haven't seen her. There's too much other game afoot.'

'Whatever's going on in the yard – or anywhere else in civilisation – interests us not in the least,' said Alice. 'And we'll thank you to have that rabble mind their noise.'

'I think she should be told,' said Grymonde.

'If there's something ought to be done, then go and do it. If not, keep your peace, and let us have ours until it's worth interrupting.'

'There's something you think I should be told?' asked Carla.

Her state was such that she was pressed to think of much that might disturb her. The sounds of revelry rose from the yard. With a stab of guilt she remembered Antoinette.

'Is it Antoinette? I've neglected her all day, is she –'

'Antoinette is thriving,' said Grymonde. 'If she stayed a week she'd be running the place. No. This wayfaring husband of yours, Mattias? Is his name Tannhauser?'

'Speak of the wolf and he will come,' said Alice.

Carla held Amparo closer. She didn't know what to feel.

'Yes. Mattias Tannhauser. He is a Chevalier of Saint John the Baptist.'

'That drives the nail home.'

'What do you mean?'

A rumble of summer thunder rolled across the Yards.

Grymonde ignored his mother's glower and shrugged his black brows.

'I've strong reason to believe the man is here. In Paris.'

CHAPTER TWENTY

Pope Paul

T he raid on the Hôtel D'Aubray had been contracted five days before, through the mediation of Pope Paul at the Blind Piper. Thirty gold *écus* and all the plunder they could carry, not for simply killing all who dwelled within – though the deaths of the two ladies had been emphasised – but for leaving a gaudy show behind them.

'Cut their tits off,' Paul had said. 'Something bold and bloody, let your lads off the leash. Give *Les Messieurs* some tittle-tattle. Make them sweat in their fine silk sheets.'

Paul had admitted that so public and vile an outrage made the venture more than usually dangerous, which was why the Cockaigne Infant had been his first call. The hazards were reflected in the price.

Grymonde had knocked it up to fifty, a sum which told him that the malice footing the bill festered somewhere far beyond the Yards. The money answered all other questions and Grymonde hadn't asked them. It was to claim the last twenty in gold, and to try to learn more from the fat bastard, that Grymonde went to visit Paul now.

As he strode down the hill in the wane of the day, towards Les Halles and the Blind Piper, he reflected that, for the first time in memory, the Yards comprised the safest streets in Paris. There were no Huguenots here, nor was there aught worth stealing but for that which had been stolen from elsewhere, and which no man who valued his life would dare even covet. Furthermore, the gangs of villains and vagrants, the beggars and feral children, whose usual haunts were any shadow dark enough to hide them, had deserted their posts. They had flown in search of pickings, which, thanks to the King, could be found all over the city, regardless of creed. A chance to forget their station at the bottom of the manure pile.

Strange, but though Grymonde had been born here, and slept most of the nights of his life here, and had never even had cause to go outside the city walls, he always believed his own station lay elsewhere, above and beyond the manure pile altogether.

Today had taught him otherwise.

Today he'd been gnawed from within, as if by La Rossa's rats.

Now the cards on the table gnawed at him too.

The irony was that Grymonde was well used to being gnawed from within. He was poxed to the core. There were bodies in yonder pits sporting better-fettled insides than his. He'd been dying for years. The vast weight of his bones, his head; the gross corrugations of his scalp; his disfigurement; the pain in his joints and hands, his swollen tongue; all these he could endure, or ignore, or even use to advantage. Even the fact that his cock had long since failed to serve any purpose other than pissing had its benefits. The price of fornication had always been a piece of his soul, a fact all whores could thank for the existence of their trade, for money could be replaced. These things he could grasp: deformity and wounding were part of Nature's way; he'd seen enough babes fall blighted from the womb to know that. His horror of this morbid affliction, be it malady or evil spirit, lay in the things he could not grasp but even so knew.

His heart was getting larger, like some great black crab growing inside his chest. He could feel it clatter against his ribs where once it had not. Sometimes the crab stifled his breath. His kidneys were corrupt; they cramped on him; in the middle of the night he would rise to piss like a horse. Headaches; bellyaches. Lately some new ague had infected his eyes, for at times they'd quake in their sockets and he would see double. Men believed him mighty; but he was not.

He was a dead man in handmade boots the size of charcoal barges.

This slow rot was familiar enough; but the rats that had worried his insides today were not, for they ate at an organ he had forgotten he possessed. His conscience.

He had tried to glut their appetite with barbarity and had failed; and then, when blood had all but choked him, by lending a hand to his mother, and to Carla and the babe. As always, Alice had been right, and as always he had not listened, for the gnawing had returned with a vengeance since he had raised with Carla the name of Mattias Tannhauser.

Grymonde heard distant thunder.

Summer rain started to fall, but the street got no cooler.

He padded by the Cemetery of the Innocents, its stench a challenge to even his filth-hardened nostrils. Paul's tavern, the Blind Piper, lay on its far side.

Inside the great necropolis, Gobbo and the others Altan Savas had killed were already rotting. Though they had enjoyed no such ceremony, a funeral here meant a drop of variable depth, through the hinged floor of a coffin, into one of the huge pits – each sixty feet deep and over a thousand corpses-strong when full – through which the burials rotated like crops. There the deceased would rest until his flesh had putrefied and settled, along with that of his thousand companions, into a fatty potage through which his bones would rise to the top. In principle, these bones would then be dredged and stacked in the charnel houses that lined the cemetery walls, and which afforded a degree of privacy to fornicating couples and sodomites; in practice they went for bone flour, and the fat to scented soap for *Les Messieurs*, whose power to profit from the poor reached even beyond the grave.

Not for the first time, Grymonde thought: *We're killing the wrong people.*

He saw the Blind Piper through the rain.

He paused before crossing the street.

It was easy enough to pretend he knew nothing; it was close to the truth. As for seeing what stood before him, he didn't need his gut to tell him that the Piper was a den of treachery. The Blind Piper was to treachery as the Vatican was to the Laws of God. What his gut knew was the gnawing, and what stood before him was his conscience; which Carla had awakened over the corpse of a demon Turk.

Return to the Hôtel D'Aubray? Go back to the beginning?

He sensed that he should. When the bear wanted to hunt the

hounds, he started from the site of their last kill. This hound might find the bear sniffing there. But why should Grymonde go? The justification was too thin. He owed nothing to anyone. But owing had naught to do with it.

He wanted to serve Carla.

He had never served anyone. It felt good.

Grymonde craved information. If Paul wasn't always the first to know whatever was worth knowing, he was always the second. Paul had sent a runner with word of the Louvre massacre before it had happened. Claiming his gold gave Grymonde a reason to be here.

The Lunatic be damned.

Grymonde crossed the street and pulled open the tavern door.

That morning, after his mother had banished him to give her and Carla some peace, Grymonde had led his young lions back out to the richer *quartiers* of the Ville.

The King's general order to exterminate the Huguenots he had learned of only while on their journey to the Hôtel D'Aubray. If the Swiss Guard had recently slaughtered the Protestant nobles, the environ of the Louvre would still be too hot, so he headed east again towards the *quartiers* of Saint-Martin and Sainte-Avoye, where merchants and nobles alike had lately been feathering new nests.

Anarchy appealed to Grymonde, in principle.

'*The unlawful liberty or licence of the multitude*' was how the on high defined it, excluding, with characteristic cunning, their own vile liberty and licence, having taken care to enshrine the latter in statute. He did not blame them for their rapacity, nor even their mindless wars for which all and sundry were forced to pay in anguish and coin; but he did resent being called a criminal – a title he otherwise bore with pride – by the most corrupt and pitiless criminals alive. But such was life. It was a fool who hobbled his stride with notions of good and evil; only the deluded ever tried to live by them. Mother Nature took account of neither. In her timeless ledger good and evil counted less than the rains and the winds that bore them. For him, as for wind and rain, the day was the thing.

By the time they reached the walls of the *Fille-Dieu*, his regulars had been swollen by so many new volunteers that they numbered forty or more. Most were adolescent, some even younger; most boys, but with a sprinkling of bold girls. He stopped them in a mass and climbed on a cart.

'Listen close, my young lions. The King has decreed that all the Huguenots of Paris must die. But unless their pockets be heavy and deep, Huguenots be damned.'

He saw perplexity in the faces of even his lieutenants. He grinned.

'The King and his lordly counsellors have delivered the sword of confusion into our hands.' He flexed his massive fingers in a mime of wielding such a weapon. 'And we will use it to cut their bollocks off.'

A ripple of uncertain laughter, which Grymonde encouraged with his own.

'Our purpose is to take whatever we want from whoever's got it – from them as don't know what it's like to go to bed hungry, from them as never thought there'd be a price for their greed. None of these swine are friends to us. In famine and siege we do their starving. In their wars we do their dying. When their debts fall due we pay them with our toil. Should we live the lives of saints we'd die as villains in their eyes, and so, let us prove ourselves more villainous than their direst fears. Bare your teeth and let them feel your bite.' He sniffed the air. 'Can you smell their money?'

The tatterdemalions answered with a fierce and reedy cheer.

They loved him. Grymonde loved them.

'Let your hearts be stone. And on that stone sharpen your knives.'

'Kill the cunts! Kill 'em all!' cried Papin, as another hurrah was raised.

'Fall upon their lives with the spleen of tigers.' Grymonde clenched a raised fist. 'Let their lamentations be your music. Let us fill our horn of plenty with their blood.'

'All praise to the Infant!' shouted Bigot.

'No, lads, no. Bigot's been spending too much time in church. Do not praise this man but, rather, praise us all. For Cockaigne is us and we are Cockaigne and together we'll abide in plenty. Now. Band yourselves in groups of seven, a magical number. From each band let one declare himself its captain – or if a girl hath the necessary temper let herself so declare – and let that captain appoint a fast runner. Let these bands be as swarms of stinging bees that swoop and gather honey, and should one band fall into a hard encounter, let the runner be sent to summon new strength. The bourgeois militia are out there and they're no friends of ours either, so beware. If you must fight, sting and run, sting and run. We come to prosper not to die. And steal only the finest stuffs, else we'll scarce have room enough to freight it in our carts. Are you feeling nimble?'

A wild roar of 'Aye!' and obscene boasts.

'Are you feeling cruel?'

The cries grew even wilder.

'Share and share alike!' roared Grymonde. 'No tomorrow!'

Grymonde doubted that the King's decree was genuine. The country was ruled by imbeciles, true; but any dumb beast could see that killing forty thousand citizens would gut the city. When they reached the Rue Saint-Martin, his doubts were removed.

He stopped and his followers halted behind him, and they stared up like witnesses to some shared hallucination as, on the parapet of a four-storey building, militiamen shoved a family from the roof.

The children went first, one by one. Saint-Martin was one of the few paved streets, and three small bodies already lay on the flagstones, stunned and shattered, or dead. Four more followed, whimpering, bewildered, terrified as much by the shouts of the Sunday soldiery as by the prospect of the drop. The speed at which they fell perplexed Grymonde's senses: at the same time much slower and much faster than he expected. They fell in silence, perhaps that was it; as if holding their breaths; as if it were some daring game with a jolly outcome. Their clothes fluttered briefly; their legs broke;

their heads bounced and split apart to discharge their brains. It occurred to Grymonde that their end, ghastly as it was, was swifter than that which his own victims had met at the Hôtel D'Aubray.

The women were next, three of them. They filed from the low doorway of a garret with their hands clasped before them, praying as they sobbed, and they went to their deaths with a dignity that put their murderers to shame, though of shame the latter showed not a trace. The women believed in something Grymonde did not, and he thought of Carla, and the shame became his, and the rats inside him bared their teeth and started to gnaw.

He looked back at his tatterdemalions. The diversity of their feelings could only be guessed at, but many eyes turned to him, as if for guidance, and he could not give it. He turned away.

Two Huguenot men holding bibles plunged from the roof; then the militia ducked into the garret and the roof was empty. Piteous groans drifted from the tangled pile.

Grymonde chewed his tongue. He looked up and down the street. Other groups of militia – four, five – were breaking down doors with spear butts and axes, and dragging folk outside, where-upon they slaughtered them.

A great confusion overwhelmed him. His heart banged on his ribs like the knock of some infernal bailiff on the gatehouse of his soul. He heard the sound of his mother's voice but not her words. He had spent his life in loving her and not listening; and though she had loved him through all, she had not listened either: to his rage at not being the man he might have been; though what that man was, he himself had forgotten long ago.

A weight lay in his gut like a sow of lead; he had carried it all day. He had borne that same burden only once before and, there was no mistaking it, for nothing else on earth was so heavy. He was in love with Carla. On the part of whichever demon played such pranks, it was a good one; not least because this time, unlike the last, he had no doubt as to the woman's true worth.

'Chief?' said Bigot.

Grymonde flapped a hand to silence him; but Bigot was right. There was the business in hand. The militia emerged from the house opposite, empty-handed but for their half-pikes, and they stabbed the broken and scattered bodies in the street. The groans of those yet alive ceased. The militiamen moved on to other atrocities.

Grymonde had never felt more like a king. He had roused his people to action with a confection of fine fancies that served his own vanity and which would damn their souls. He could have ordered them to turn back and go home. He could have spun some other fancy to justify it. Like the people of any king, eating shit was the one thing they could be counted on to do. But that decision would inaugurate the beginning of the end of his reign. A true king would have laid down his crown, though which king had ever done so, except at the point of a knife? His kingdom was miserable and fleeting, though which was not, even should it encompass the world?

He loved Carla, and in that cause, and without a qualm, he would have laid down all he had. But there was nothing that could serve that cause. Carla would consider it no decision at all, but only that which ought to be done on the instinct of decency.

Rage could lighten the weight that oppressed his entrails. He knew that. The practice of evil could dull the pain of love better than any physic. He knew, too, because Alice had taught him, that evil was not some eternal essence on its own account, but merely a craft – a practice, a tool – designed like many others by the race of men to advance their power. And like any other king, what else could he lay claim to but the power to do wrong?

Perhaps that was a king's duty. Their habits suggested so.

The king turned to his army. Some had made their own decision and were scuttling away. He didn't stop them. He looked at Bigot. Bigot took a step back without knowing it and stared at Grymonde's chest.

'Elect one band to yonder house to reap the pillage,' said Grymonde. 'Another to follow the militia and scavenge their droppings. Tell 'em to keep it sly. We're going on.'

Bigot nodded. Grymonde looked at his rabble. His spell had waned. He was king not of lions but of crows. They needed to spill some blood. The weight inside him was heavy. His heart kicked his chest. He waved them on.

They got their blood. The streets were soon awash with it. It filled the iron-hard wheel ruts in the mud; it brimmed from doorsteps; the noonday sun baked it into enormous glazed platters that crackled underfoot. Killing for kings, killing for duty, killing for gold, killing for pleasure, killing for creed, it was all much the same; and much of it there was to be had, and much was done. Grymonde had never been for a soldier; he preferred to die for his own crimes than be gutted for someone else's; yet here he was doing a soldier's work, killing his enemy's enemies for money he would never spend, turning boys into murderers and worse. Like dogs gone crazed in a field of sheep which slaughter without eating, they forgot they were here to profit, and the carts remained half-empty. On and on it went in the foetid heat, house to house, street to street, family to family, the beggars competing in atrociousness with the militia they despised, and grease and sweat ran from Grymonde's pores, and he lost his mind. He had no purpose of his own in all this; yet he stayed; he exhorted; he inspired. And he was not alone. Here, two priests wandered the carnage, sprinkling the butchers with Holy Water from buckets plated with gold. There, a bevy of armed nobles sat their mounts and watched as if at a tourney, until boredom drove them on to other pleasures. A herald rode up in a uniform that must have cost more than his horse and blew a trumpet, as if God were a comedian and this a bold satire He Himself had writ upon His Judgement, and in the King's name the herald told them all to stop, and they pelted him with rocks and turds and drove him away, for here Death was king and god both, and all of them his loyal subjects, the living and the slain alike.

Grymonde's army dwindled.

They stuffed their shirts, mostly with bright trash, and sneaked away.

Grymonde didn't stop them.

He lost track of the carts and didn't care.

The weight in his gut got heavier. His vision blurred and the images crafted by evil multiplied in his brain. He clapped a hand to his eyes. He no longer needed to see the depravity; he was no longer even part of it; rather, he contained it: all of it, the blood, the vomit, the tears, the shit, the screams; it was all of it awash and reeking in the cesspit of his being. He stumbled through an open porch to escape the carnival, but in this deplorable home no escape was to be found.

Bloody bodies littered the hallway in puddles of gore. From the parlour came coarse grunts and piteous whimpers. Conscience had been hatched to keep the poor at heel, for the rich never jumped to its sting, and so he had always disdained it, blunted it, silenced it. He told himself to find some other refuge. He drew his twin-barrelled pistol from under his shirt and lowered both hammers to their wheels.

He barged into the parlour.

Papin held a young woman face-down over a table, while Bigot grasped her buttocks in his meaty, bloody hands and raped her. His face was bright red with sunburn and the strain of trying to pump out his seed, for this victim was not his first. They both looked at him, startled.

'Leave her be,' said Grymonde. 'We're going home.'

'What, now?' gasped Bigot. His thrusts became more frantic.

Papin stepped away from the table.

'Marshal the carts and the crew. And leave her be.'

'Papin's already taken his turn.'

'I said leave her be.'

'You said share and share alike –'

Grymonde shot him in the face. Bigot flew backwards and hit the floor without a twitch. Grymonde looked at Papin through the powder smoke. Papin stared at Bigot, panting with shock. He spun towards the door without facing Grymonde.

'Papin.'

Papin stopped on the threshold, too afraid to turn.

'The carts. The crew. Take them home.'

Grymonde pointed the pistol at the head of the girl and fingered the second trigger. She raised her face up and recoiled, more at the sight of him than at that of the gun bore. He hesitated. What was he doing? The girl looked at him again. Her eyes pleaded for mercy, but whether that meant life or death he couldn't tell. He locked the hammer back, returned the pistol to his belt. He took the girl by the arm and pulled her to her feet.

'Can you walk?'

He didn't ask her name and the girl didn't give it. She said nothing at all, and neither did he. As they threaded the maze towards Les Halles the streets became quiet, if not peaceful. Too much dread infested every building to leave any room for peace. A knot of militia approached them, heading for the killing grounds. Grymonde gave them the stare and they looked at their feet and trotted on by. His mind cleared. The pressure behind his eyes eased and his vision steadied.

He stopped at the Church of Saint-Leu and turned to the girl.

'You'll find sanctuary here, if you want it.'

'Must I be baptised?'

'Father Robert is no zealot. We'll ask.'

The girl nodded without looking up at him.

The interior was gloomy and he heard a swell of fearful murmurs and cries of alarm before he saw them: the church was packed with refugees. The terror his entrance had inspired in their throats was reflected in their faces. Wounded lay on the floor and an old priest stooped among them with a jug, and he must have been deaf for he didn't turn. A second priest, much younger, pushed his way down the aisle. He was appalled and he was angry, and he made no effort to hide it. Grymonde knew his reputation: devout, but a man of true charity. He did not reflect on the priest's probable opinion of him.

'Father Robert, I'd be grateful if you'd shelter this girl.'

Robert bowed to the girl. He gestured towards the aisle. She hesitated.

Grymonde said, 'She's afraid you'll make baptism the price of her safety.'

'Mademoiselle, you are welcome here without any conditions.'

The girl burst into tears. Robert beckoned to some women. Two hurried over, attempting to mask the disgust they felt at approaching Grymonde. They escorted the girl away to join the rest.

'She's been ill used,' said Grymonde.

'I will not ask by whom. She'll be handled gently here.' Robert glanced at the bloodstains on Grymonde's shirt. 'You're the one they call the Infant.'

'My name is Grymonde.'

'The one is as black as the other. Now you may leave. You frighten them.'

Grymonde found himself unhitching his purse.

'Keep your blood money,' said Robert. 'Satan's coin will not buy your salvation.'

'I seek no salvation, least of all from this house of lies. I'll pay the Devil his due in whichever coin he wants, though I dare say he's in my debt by now. Keep your scorn for the next time you kiss your bishop's ring, and hear me out. This madness – this Catholic madness – will go on for days, and where and how far it will go, no one can foretell. The door of this church is held safe only by words –'

'God's word.'

'Few are marking His word today, and among those preaching a different gospel are a number of your own Roman brethren. So mark a word of good sense. Hire a *sergent* to stand watch. I'll send one over. I needn't tell you none will do it for free.'

Grymonde shoved the purse into Robert's chest.

'Christ will forgive you for paying in Satan's coin,' said Grymonde, 'even if your pride won't. Besides, you've got mouths to feed, and none will do that for free either.'

Robert took the bag. Its weight surprised him. Grymonde turned to leave.

'I will say a Mass for your mother –'

'My mother doesn't need your gibberish.'

'Then I'll pray for your black soul –'

'Just hire the *sergent*.'

On a Sunday Les Halles was like a heart that had stopped beating. The rest of the week, it pumped the lifeblood of the city: the vast tonnage of food that Paris shovelled down its gullet between one dawn and the next. Each night thousands of beasts bearing flesh and organs to suit every pocket were driven down the Rue Saint-Denis to the reeking abattoirs, and to the shambles where the animals were butchered in the open street. With them came scores of wagons loaded with fish, fowl and game, greengrocery, wine, and above all grain, for Parisians loved bread more than God.

With a shrewd eye for making a fortune, King Francis had ordered the rebuilding of the whole neighbourhood in '43, the year that Grymonde had been born. They'd been rebuilding ever since and still weren't done.

He'd learned to run and talk and steal and sell in an enchanted land of demolition and construction. He'd watched buildings he loved torn down, and buildings he loved rise up in their place. He'd mixed mortar and dug footings and hauled bricks and timber and lead; for pennies. If they'd knocked it all down and started all over again, Grymonde could have told them how to do so as well as any other living man, and would have made a better job of it than most. But he was from the Yards and a bastard, and his mother some villain's doxy, so digging was all he was fit for.

Even so, he loved it all.

Les Halles, as locals loosely marked it, was bounded on the north side by the Truanderie, on the east by Saint-Denis down to the Châtelet, on the west by the cheesemongers, and on the south by the old salt works near the river. It was at once vast and intricate. The new markets were covered galleries devoted to every variety of produce, and not foodstuffs alone, but leathers and furs and fabrics, cutlery, shoes and exotic birds. Above the galleries were dwellings, and interspersed among them were churches, houses and *hôtels*, the public fountain, the octagonal tower of the pillory, and the remnants of the old market and its workshops.

On a Sunday the roar of multitudes, human and animal, surrendered to the relative quiet of watchmen, promenaders, young lovers and delinquent children. Today only the watchmen were left, reinforced by a larger than usual contingent of *sergents à verge* from the Châtelet. The Huguenots en masse, and sundry unlucky

Catholics, might be dying in their thousands in their own homes, but nothing could be allowed to threaten the markets.

Grymonde nodded to various of the sentries as he passed by. They knew he paid the bite when it was proper; they knew his interests lay elsewhere; indeed, various of their employers sold his goods, often more than once if they were willing to let him know to whom they had sold them. They were all partners in the neverending crime that was Paris.

Grymonde spotted Sergent Rody outside a cutler's shop.

'We're in for a spot of rain,' said Rody, nodding east.

'A dry post awaits you. Father Robert needs a watchman at Saint-Leu. He'll pay whatever you're drawing to stand here. If you can't claim both wages, you should retire.'

'I heard he was harbouring heretics.'

'You don't care if they live or die, so why not?'

'I've got orders not to care, but when did you become a samaritan?'

'If you don't want the job, I see three from here who'll take it.'

'Oh, I'll take it,' said Rody. 'The militia won't violate the church. They've too much else to do. I wouldn't trust them to shovel shit without getting it stuck between their teeth, but they've strong stomachs, I'll give 'em that.'

'The Châtelet's keeping its nose out?'

'When this is over the militia will go home. We can't. We'll be back to collecting fines next week. Wouldn't do for us to be seen as a gang of murderers, even by murderers.'

'Men of principle, then.'

Rody laughed. 'We kept the militia away from the market or they'd have left it covered in corpses. We moved out all the Huguenot tenants ourselves, quietly like, and handed them over to Garnier and Crucé. Le Tellier's orders. Meek as lambs they went. Thought they were going to prison, the Conciergerie. Well, they were, but when they got there they were butchered, underground. And they threaten us with Hell, eh? Garnier said he'd sworn an oath to Saint-Jacques that he'd send a hundred to the Devil by his own hand. We gave him a good start.'

Grymonde had ordered the pig roast from Garnier's abattoir that morning.

Rody winked. 'It's an ill wind but it'll blow good for some. The Crown will auction off the empty premises. The goods inside won't last that long – if you're interested.'

'I know where to find you. I've had my drink of havoc up and down.'

'It's a quiet day, for us, funnily enough,' said Rody. 'The city's tight as a drum. All the gates are locked.'

'All the gates?'

'All of 'em. They'll open just the Porte Saint-Denis at midnight. Can't leave a thousand cattle to strip the *faubourgs* clean. Besides, they can butcher Huguenots, but we can't eat 'em.'

'Anything else on the wind?'

'The King wants the rioting to stop, if you want to spread the word.'

Rody smirked. Grymonde didn't smile.

'There is one sniff worth a few francs,' said Rody. 'A peculiar item, given, as you say, havoc up and down. A man someone wants to find.'

'I'm no nose.'

'Even so, you've got one, and this has naught to do with your lot. This man's a Chevalier of Saint John. A big man, white cross on his chest, bold as you please. He killed three Huguenots, in a duel yesterday evening.'

'Is that why he's wanted?'

'Why would that give warrant? The Châtelet can't arrest one of the Religion like some street thief. They'd need the Parlement, the King, maybe the Pope in Rome.'

'The Religion?'

'The Knights of Saint John. A law unto themselves. Everyone lets them be. Anyway, we weren't told he's wanted for a crime, just that his whereabouts are sought.'

'Who seeks him?'

'I don't know, and neither did the man who told me, nor whoever told him, and so on, unto who knows where or who? He is needed for some weighty matter of high urgency. Who knows, perhaps the chevalier has a big cock and the Duc d'Anjou is feeling penitent.'

'I'll keep an ear open, what's his name?'

'Mattias Tannhauser.'

Grymonde twisted his lips as if the name meant nothing. One advantage of his face was that any expression he cared to make was so extreme it served to mask whatever he was thinking. What he thought was that the name didn't mean much; but more than nothing. His gut told him it meant much more.

'Anything else to mark this man out?'

Rody squinted skyward to rack his brain and Grymonde was relieved. Rody swam like an eel in a sea of lies, as did they all, but had he wanted to deceive he'd have tried a little harder than that. It meant that Rody knew of no connection between the woman he had seen that morning in Grymonde's cart and Mattias Tannhauser. Rody shook his head.

'No.'

'So the big cock isn't a certainty.'

'Only in my wife's dreams.'

'I'm off. You can tell your wife Father Robert pays in gold.'

'Why would I want to tell her that?'

Grymonde stopped at the Fontaine des Innocents and washed his boots under the spouts. There might well be no connection, but Mattias was hardly a popular name; except, Grymonde presumed, among Saxons. The lead weight still lay in his gut. He loved the woman, so the choice was simple. He could act upon the sentiment; or he could not. He reminded himself to change his shirt before he went to the birthing room. Whether the Saxon had a big cock or not, it could not be denied that it worked.

Grymonde glanced at the sun, still hot and high but advanced in its decline to the west. He'd lost the run of time. He pressed on to Cockaigne.

Tannhauser would be looking for his wife; he wouldn't find her. Others might, once they found out she was still alive; and find out they would, if they hadn't already. He muttered random of his thoughts out loud in the hope of making more sense of them.

'A murder isn't a ribbon for your sweetheart. Nobody buys one on a whim.'

The risk. The expense. The courage. The crime was cowardly, but the idea alone would turn most guts to pisswater. And not just a murder but a plot. Plotting took practice, though there was plenty being had. This wasn't the buyer's first purchase on the murder market. He thought of the Louvre.

'Bastards.'

Why were the Châtelet looking for Mattias Tannhauser? To tell him, help him? Warn him, protect him? Perhaps the same malice that had paid Grymonde to kill Carla was reaching out for Tannhauser, too. Who would want to kill either of them and why? In a life spent with miscreants high and low, Grymonde had never met anyone more unlikely to provoke murderous hatred than Carla. Then again, murder solved a wide range of problems. On a day that the royal family had painted their own palace with blood – the blood of wedding guests, relatives and lifelong friends – anything was possible.

'The babe,' said Grymonde.

Was the babe the reason?

Was Tannhauser the secret villain?

'He wouldn't be the first husband to rid himself of a wife.'

Who knew how long Tannhauser had been in Paris?

Grymonde swatted grease and sweat from his eyes.

His brain hurt.

This was why it didn't do to ask questions. Or break a contract.

He stopped to piss. The *sergents* wouldn't come into the Yards; the price now and later would be too high. They didn't need to. The Yards appeared as a unity to outsiders, but like much of the world it was patchwork sewn together with envy and spite. Grymonde was not short of rivals and they could be hired as easily as he had been, and probably cheaper. It was a better time than most to fight a gang war; but not for him.

He walked on.

He shouldn't have killed Bigot.

The entire city had gone from celebration to bloody chaos in less than two days.

Events could move swiftly.

He had to get sly.

He quickened his stride.

He had to get Carla out of Paris.

On his return, Alice forbade him to mention the chevalier to Carla.

The birth of the baby girl wiped the slate of his cares, at least for a while. Carla won his heart more completely than ever. He relied on his face to conceal the fact. He wondered if his mother knew.

To see her work, to see her be, had lost none of its power to entrance him. She knew what he was. She refused to profit from his doings down to the loaves of bread she ate. She had taught him her way, but Grymonde had been unable to live it. And such was her way that she did not condemn him; as she had once told him, that was his burden to carry.

Alice's skill with labouring mothers and their babes, in joy, in grief, sometimes in horror, he had witnessed since boyhood. But the bond she had forged with Carla he had not seen before. He wondered what had passed between them. Their bond reignited his fears for Carla's life.

A horse and wagon could easily be had. Grymonde had gold, despite his rash donation to the priest. The Saint-Denis gate was close. The customs officers made half their income in bribes. They could leave just before the cattle and sheep came in. The plan eased his mind.

He told Carla he believed Mattias was in Paris.

Carla was exhausted by her throes and already under the sway of strong emotions. Whatever she felt about this news was swaddled among them, held in check by that rare composure which had roused him from the moment they had met. For a short time she said nothing and studied her sleeping babe. She looked at Grymonde.

'Please, bring me pen and ink, and paper. I must write to him.'

'Write? Write what? Besides, we have no such tools.'

'When Mattias finds you, he will kill you. I'd rather he did not.'

Grymonde's dignity was piqued. He had formed a vague image of this husband as, well, the kind of gallant who might win a woman like Carla. A fine fellow, and no doubt brave to boot, but hardly one to chill Grymonde's blood.

'I'm touched by your fears for my safety. Mine are for some well-bred gentleman who is at large, and by all accounts lost, in the Devil's sweatshop.'

'In the senses you intend, Mattias is neither well bred nor a gentleman. In combat he is the equal of Altan Savas; I'll not say "better" only out of respect for Altan's memory. In every other art that war and survival might demand, Mattias has no equal at all.'

Grymonde recalled the three Poles killed in a duel, a detail he had chosen not to dwell on. The Poles had a reputation for being hardy. He felt his lips purse.

'I'll take your word on his audacity. But finding this man is another matter.'

'He would find you were you entombed in the hottest chasm of Hell.'

The calm of her conviction unnerved him. Perhaps he could unnerve her.

'I have a question that may offend you, but I have to ask it.'

Carla nodded.

'Is it possible that your husband wants you dead?'

'No.'

Grymonde said, 'You may have to stake this child's life on it.'

'I wagered everything I am on Mattias's love a long time ago.'

Alice gave Grymonde a look. 'For once in your life take heed of someone else. Carla doesn't want her man at your throat – where he's more than well entitled to be – nor you at his.'

'Mattias has never been in Paris before,' said Carla. 'While I believe he would find you, I equally believe that you might find him sooner. A letter from me could protect you both from injury.'

Grymonde nodded, appeased by this tardy tribute to his own fighting prowess.

Alice said, 'Carla, let him take some word of mouth that could have come only from you. Something he'll know could not have been wrung from you by force.'

Carla looked at her baby; then into some inner distance.

She turned to Grymonde.

'Tell him: *A new nightingale awaits your thorns.*'

'A new nightingale awaits his thorns?' said Grymonde.

'Yes. Just as you have it.'

'A riddle.' Grymonde shrugged his brows. 'Let's hope his wits are sharp.'

'It's your wits we're worried about,' said Alice. 'You've got your duty clear, now go about it. And don't be taken in by false shadows. The Juggler's afoot.'

'You've been at the cards.'

'They'd have stood your curls on end.'

'You're right about the Juggler,' he said. 'Anything else?'

'The Lunatic points the way out, if there is one. The edge is closer than you realise. Whatever you're up to, you know a lot less than you think you do. And if you can't know it all, it's better to know nothing. Then you'll see what's right in front of you.'

'More riddles.'

'I know you. Don't try to be too clever. Think with your stomach, not your head.'

Grymonde looked at Carla for more material guidance.

'What does this husband look like?'

'Mattias is forty-four years old, two inches taller than you, and his hair is the colour of bronze. When he looks at you –' in the same gesture he had used, Carla swept a hand across her features to indicate his own, '– this will not appall him. The other things I've said of him you will see in his eyes – which are blue.'

'Good enough.'

'How did you come to know he is in Paris?'

'We've heard all we need to for now, love,' said Alice. 'What you most need is sleep.'

Carla thought about this and nodded.

'Can I bring you meat or drink?' asked Grymonde

Carla shook her head. Grymonde walked to the door.

'Grymonde,' said Carla. 'Thank you. And good luck.'

Grymonde nodded. 'A new nightingale awaits his thorns.'

In his room next door he reloaded his pistol and concealed two extra knives, one strapped to his left forearm, the other in his left boot. As he descended the stairs he saw the cards on the table. His gut told him to keep going. They weren't his cards. But then, Alice had surely been questing on his part, and he already knew the better part of the spread, the Juggler and the Lunatic were in play. Which card was in first position?

He went over and looked.

The quester card was *Anima Mundi*.

He was sure that was Carla.

Her spread hit him in the throat.

The Judgement. The Fire. Death.

Grymonde headed south for the Blind Piper.

'Do you know,' said Paul, 'how much money is waiting to be made out of shit?'

In his way, Pope Paul was no less grotesque in appearance than Grymonde. He dressed in a purple robe of fine spun silk, which was drenched in equal measure with perfume and sweat. He must have weighed thirty stones and his fat made his arms bulge like sections of colon from a newly butchered pig. More fat bulged from beneath his armpits in rolls of increasing curvature, and his belly draped his thighs – each large enough to bear a saddle – in a wide, obscene apron. On his belly sat enormous splayed teats. His jowls spilled onto his chest and shoulders. Sunk into the jowls was a head of normal dimensions, but which seemed tiny in relation to the monstrous corpus beneath it. He must have been over fifty, but fat stretched his features into a youthful sheen. He was largely bald; the remainder of his hair was bunched in lank coils over his ears.

Grymonde waited for the performance to play out.

'It's all in the numbers,' continued Paul.

'And you're a numbers man.'

'Numbers alone hold sway above the flux. Numbers is the future. So let me show you how to arrive at a big one. The city will soon be buried in shit, as we all know, so the Bureau de Ville is going to start paying for its removal. Out there in the wilderness, farmers will cough up more cash to spread it on their crops. Let's be parsimonious and say we clear just one white franc per wagonload. Who'd move all that shit for a franc? A good living for some, but for such as we? But hear the numbers. A scholar – don't ask me how he did it – has reckoned that in one single day enough shit to fill a wagon will be shat by three hundred people. Again, let's not be greedy. For the city as a whole, let's call it eight hundred, no, halve it, four hundred wagonloads a day. Knock off feast days, Holy Days, plague days, and call it three hundred days a year. Do you have any idea how many francs that would amount to?'

'Enough to keep you in wine and victuals for a week.'

Paul laughed and wobbled. He reclined on a large couch, which was underpinned with blocks of timber and upholstered in rough-napped silver plush, now much the worse for a multitude of rancid stains. At either end of the couch stood one of the stable of muscular brutes that Paul kept on hand, in principle as bodyguards, in practice to enable him to get to his feet, get out of bed, get into and out of his robes, and to tend all the other duties required for the care of what was, in effect, a gigantic baby.

In this their size and strength were vital; but they also served to lend Paul's court an intimidating air; at least for some. Rowdiness and violence were almost unknown at the Piper; such pleasures could be reliably had in a hundred other dens. The Piper was a place of business and Paul was a rich man. He owned pieces of Les Halles, an abattoir, other taverns, and much else that few knew of. He could read a contract as well as any magistrate, in Latin, Italian, English and French. All the major villains of the Ville, on either side of what passed for the law, sooner or later found they had need of Paul, and their word kept the Piper peaceful. No one trusted Paul but everyone had to. His treacheries were uncommon and, without exception, unproven. Whoever he had betrayed, none had survived to exact revenge.

The brighter of the two brutes raised a hand, to answer Paul's question.

'Maurice would have you think him a mathematician,' said Paul. 'But he's heard this scheme before. That's very dishonest of you, Maurice.'

As Maurice lowered his hand, a refined voice piped up from behind Grymonde.

'A hundred and twenty thousand francs per year.'

The tavern was a long narrow room. The bar ran down one side in front of gantries of wine casks. Paul's couch stood at the rear and Grymonde sat in one of the chairs reserved for audiences with the Pope. Grymonde turned and saw a short, vain fellow at a nearby table. He was expensively dressed, for the Piper, in bottle-green velvet. He had a white band tied round either arm and, lest the point be missed, a white cross was pinned to his hat. He regarded Grymonde with undisguised repugnance; and a certain spite.

'Yet another mathematician.' Paul's lustreless eyes turned on the visitor. 'And an eavesdropper into the bargain. I told you, monsieur, I'll hear you when I've a mind to.'

The visitor opened his mouth to say something petulant, then shut it. He turned back to his wine and played with some coins on the table.

'Looks like they're bagging the shit already, in little green velvet sacks,' said Grymonde. He turned to Paul. 'The only number that interests me is twenty in gold.'

Paul wagged a hand and Maurice filled it with a purse.

'I expected you sooner.'

'Busy day, Paul.'

'I hear it's been right lively.'

'You should have these lads knock a wall down and carry you out to see it.'

Paul laughed and tossed the purse. The coins clinked in Grymonde's fist.

'What happened to the second woman?' said Paul.

'You mean the third. She's in a cesspit, back of Saint-Martin.

We took a little girl, too. Let's say we adopted her, call it a whim, or the Hand of God, I don't care, but adopted she will stay.'

'You were paid to make an example.'

'We left examples that would make you puke.'

'The job was particular, Grymonde. Two particular women were specified. In further particular, a lady from the south.'

'You specified kill them all and kill them all we did, all but for the little girl. And how were we to know which women were particular?'

Grymonde sensed that this was a poor excuse. He kept talking.

'My boys were entitled to their sport and time was pressing. The Turk was a fiend, which you neglected to tell us. We lost six and it was still cut fine. So no apologies. If you want the lady from the south I'll show Maurice where to find her. He can fish her out of the cesspit and drag her back here.'

Maurice shuffled with dread. Paul studied Grymonde at length.

'I can't afford to be at odds with you, Paul,' conceded Grymonde. 'I'll refund five *écus d'or*, not more. For that you could pay this little green turd to get the body.'

'It's not my money,' said Paul. 'It's them as spent it won't get what they wanted.'

'Who's to tell 'em? As to a show, Hellfire, no one's counting bodies today. You yourself could parade the streets naked and no would notice.'

'Fair point. And I can't afford to be at odds with the mighty Infant. The day we hang will fetch the biggest crowds the Place de Grève as ever seen, and we can't deny them that.'

Paul smiled and Grymonde grinned. He felt he'd brazened it well.

'I've a morsel or two you might savour,' said Grymonde. 'Fresh to me at least.'

'Fresh and tasty morsels are my trade.'

'The Châtelet moved some heretics out of the market and they won't be coming back. There'll be an auction for the deeds, but the goods are available tonight. Rody's the man.'

'Tasty enough. But where's your appetite?'

'We've filled the carts twice already. And Mam's feeling sickly.'

'Never trust a man who doesn't care for his mother.'

'This next is small beer, but Rody also said the Châtelet are looking for some chevalier of Saint John. I forget the name. Mattias. Something foreign.'

Paul studied him again, then said, 'That matter's been taken well in hand.'

Grymonde didn't feel so brazen any more. Here it was, at his feet, but he didn't know how to pick it up. Don't be too clever. Aye. Clever alone would do. His gut urged silence. He ignored it.

'Anything in it for me?'

'It's in hand. And your mam is sickly.'

There was a movement behind Grymonde. He turned.

The little green turd was walking away down the bar.

'There'll be music later!' called Paul. 'Superior harpist with a lovely voice!'

The visitor left by the door. Grymonde chewed his tongue. He wondered if the minstrel was real or some kind of cipher. With Paul you could never tell.

'No more patience than manners, that sort,' said Paul. 'You missed a good purse.'

Grymonde turned back. 'For what?'

'The chevalier's head. No small matter to kill a member of the Religion. They'd take it to heart. And they're vengeful. I'm not sure it's ever been dared. But they reckon this chevalier can be tarnished, his name blackened, so his brethren couldn't act.'

Grymonde stared at him. He didn't know why Paul was telling him all this.

'Blackened?'

'Tannhauser – that's his name, by the way – went mad, it seems. Murdered his wife and half a dozen witnesses. He may well have dumped her body in a cesspit.'

Grymonde's brain felt hot. It throbbed in time to his heart.

The Juggler was more than afoot. He was all but dancing on Grymonde's grave. Pope Paul did not gossip. His every word – his tales of shit, his every quip – had purpose. He moved pieces around a chessboard with a thousand squares. The heat surged to a boil inside Grymonde's skull; but his gut was clear. For Carla he'd bring the roof down on the lot of them. Without turning he recalled the room behind him. A dozen men or so; three, four, who needed to be taken seriously. No women. Paul couldn't abide their wheedling and their chatter. Grymonde's skin sensed the locations of his pistol and his various knives. Maurice and his mate first. He rolled his shoulders. Even before he spoke, he saw something in Paul's eyes that he'd never seen before. Fear.

'Don't play with me, Paul. Or I'll end the game now.'

It occurred to Maurice that for the first time in his career as Paul's arse-wiper he might have to risk his life and that, if so, would lose it. He shifted and glanced at his mate.

'Maurice, keep still,' said Paul. 'Od, you too. You'll get us all boned like codfish.'

The guards stood rigid. Paul looked Grymonde in the eye.

'Peace, Grymonde, peace. Of course I play with you. I couldn't sing a lullaby to a babe without making a play. You might as well tell me to lose weight. And you are playing, too, my friend. You didn't come here for gold. You came to learn what I am telling you.'

'Why are you telling me?'

'That's my business. Other pieces, other plays.'

Paul leaned closer, as best he was able.

'You can kick our board over, and I know you'd do it. That's what makes you the Infant. When you decide to stamp your feet, the earth trembles. But the game never ends. The others will just play on without me. And without me, you'll lose.'

'And with you?'

'You still might lose. That's what makes it a game.'

'And your wager covers either winner.'

'That's what makes me the Pope.'

'Then tell me what you will tell me. But tell me no lies.'

'I can't remember the last time I told a lie. I can't remember the last time I had any use for one. A dull blade at best and always brittle. That's the beauty of living in a world of lies: my blades are so keen you don't even feel the edge when it cuts your throat. And it's true: three hundred people will fill a wagon with shit in a single day.'

'So the assassins are out in cry, for Tannhauser.'

'The best I could find. War veterans. Five of them.'

Grymonde blew his lips.

'I know,' agreed Paul. 'Money's no object. Take no chances, they said. They want the chevalier alive, if possible, they said, but that's a chance I doubt those lads will take.'

'Depends on how big a bonus they're paying.'

Paul sat back and smiled, to indicate that there was such.

'Where will they take him? Or his head?'

Paul jerked a thumb over his shoulder.

'They'll keep him in the backyard until he's collected.'

Grymonde waited without saying more.

'They do want that woman with a passion,' said Paul. 'They didn't say why, but whatever the reasons they had this morning, they've got even more now, haven't they? This is how intrigues come unravelled – when heads that didn't expect to start to fall. Who knows what stones this lady from the south might upturn? They can't let her get away. And now they know you've got her.'

'How?'

'When her body didn't show, there were questions. Rumours. My faith in you didn't wholly reassure them. Your cesspit tale confirmed their suspicions.'

Grymonde felt rain and sweat and grease slide down his brow. He didn't wipe it.

'The little green turd. You staked me out for him like a goat.'

'Not so, my friend. You didn't have to take Carla home. You didn't have to come here now. You didn't have to tell lies that even Maurice might have smelled. And I did warn you quite loudly he was an eavesdropper.'

Grymonde's gall rose. Pope Paul's truths were sharp indeed. Grymonde felt his own knives, the ones he better trusted, tingle afresh against his skin.

'Who've you sent against Carla?'

'No one,' said Paul. 'They didn't ask me to. I wouldn't have known who to send if they had. No one good enough to stand a chance would be fool enough to dare Cockaigne. Hirelings don't like risks; that's why they get paid to take them. And I don't know where your woman is, so how could I tell 'em?' He read Grymonde's expression. 'I don't know how to find Cockaigne. I never needed to. My Land of Plenty is here.'

'You know people who do know.'

'Very likely the little green turd knows, too.'

'What do you mean?'

'Well, he didn't ask me where to find her,' said Paul. 'They must have other resources besides me. Considerable resources, too.'

Truth, lies, intrigue. Grymonde stopped trying to think. Listen to the gut.

'Rody.'

'A collector of fines.'

Grymonde shook his head. He made clear his meaning.

'The Châtelet.'

'I don't know for certain, so let's say I'll field no conjectures.'

Paul had no love for the Châtelet and its commissioners, their greed and hypocrisy, their insatiable bite. His game became clearer. If Grymonde could hurt the Châtelet, with no fault attaching to Paul, the fat pig would quiver with delight. If Grymonde went down, Paul had done his bit to help them. They wanted Tannhauser alive; and they were still in pursuit of Carla, despite the general riot.

'You and five assassins don't add up to an official investigation.'

'Since when were most of the Châtelet's antics official?'

'Cut their tits off, you said. Someone's squatting on a dunghill of hate.'

'There's an abundance of that to go round. Even more stupid than lying.'

'Who's the turd?'

'A lickspittle. Christian Picart, a functionary in the Louvre. A writer.'

'A writer?'

'He once penned a play that no one ever saw, now he turns out hate tracts for one of the militant confraternities. The Pilgrims of Saint-Jacques. Petit Chris, they call him, on account that his cock will fit into a thimble and still leave room for his thumb.'

'So it was the turd who hired me.'

Paul shrugged, always the lawyer he'd started out as.

Grymonde pondered his dilemma in like manner.

If he kept all this knowledge to himself, he could tell Carla – without a lie – that he knew not where her husband was. A lawyer's truth. And perhaps the five assassins would get lucky; and that would leave him alone to be Carla's protector. Yearning rose through his bloated heart. He didn't need to share her bed; wouldn't even try to. Carla would accept him, if he foreswore evil, and he would. He already had. His mother's face swam into his mind, her eyes, grey as the wind, looking into his. He saw her love. He saw the pain of her boundless disappointment.

Grymonde clenched his fists.

'Are any of the yard gangs paid to turn against me?'

'No,' said Paul. 'But in the circumstance, I'd reckon that small comfort.'

The Châtelet. The confraternities. The Louvre, too.

He had to get Carla out of Paris.

He remembered her wager.

He realised she wouldn't go. Not without Mattias.

He stood up. Maurice and Od jumped.

'Where's Tannhauser?'

Paul pursed his lips.

'The game's late,' said Grymonde. 'Would you play me as a rook or a pawn?'

'The five carry my commission.'

'From what I know of this chevalier, I'd be saving their filthy lives. And your reputation with 'em. Maybe your fat skin, too.'

'The Infant is scared of him?'

'Not yet. But I'm not relying on these two to keep me alive.'

Paul flapped a hand and Maurice bent low to hear his whisper.

Maurice left by the back door. Paul smiled.

'I've always wanted to see my Infant prosper, and you have. I've

392

pulled more than a few strings for you, without you knowing it. I even suggested you might step around this particular job. Remember?'

'Twas you who offered it.'

'You were requested, particular. I don't know why. I didn't ask. Clients don't like to be asked. But I knew these were deep waters. Deeper than any the Infant has waded before.'

'Better to drown in deep waters than a pool of piss.'

'There'd be good money in it,' said Paul. 'To turn Carla over.'

'For me?'

'For both of us. Petit Chris would pout, but he's not paying. These people ransom each other all the time. That's why they don't get killed in all these battles: there's money in it. It's no crime to squeeze your assets. I thought that was your ruse in taking her – I thought "my Infant's learning" – until you asked for the whereabouts of the husband.'

'Where is he?'

'Let me utter a word I utter rarely: why?'

Grymonde couldn't tell him the truth. He groped for an answer.

He said, 'In the place where there are no men, be a man.'

For the first time in their long acquaintance, Grymonde saw shock in Paul's eyes. He hadn't thought the man capable of even so much as surprise, except when faking it.

'You didn't find that pearl lying in the Yards. It was her, wasn't it?'

Grymonde didn't answer him. Paul leaned forward again.

'As you say, my Infant, the game runs late. The hirelings have been out since early afternoon, lying in ambuscade, at a chapel. Sainte-Cécile, on the Rue du Temple.'

'How can they be sure Tannhauser will come?'

'The chevalier believes he will find his wife at the chapel. In a coffin.'

Grymonde sucked on his tongue.

He recalled the obscenities he'd left behind at the Hôtel D'Aubray. By instinct, he understood. Tannhauser believed Carla was dead. He had seen enough of the carnage to assume it was so, but hadn't dared look for her body. The thought of seeing Carla thus spoiled turned Grymonde's stomach, too. No husband would choose to look at that.

Grymonde turned to leave.

'What happened to my mighty Infant?'

Grymonde walked towards the door. Paul's voice followed him.

'Hate? Power? Greed? Why not? But love?'

Grymonde kicked open the door and stepped into the street.

The rain had stopped.

To the east the sky was dark as gun metal.

To the west a day of damnation waned red as shame.

A night of damnation would rise with the full of the moon.

The hounds would bay for Carla's blood.

He hesitated.

He cared for her, not some damned knight who'd left her in peril.

They couldn't take Cockaigne. No one had ever even tried to. The name alone was a bulwark. He had time. And Carla had drawn the cards and made her wager.

The Judgement. The Fire. Death.

Grymonde headed east towards the chapel of Sainte-Cécile.

CHAPTER TWENTY-ONE

The Symbol

Tannhauser found a stable near Irène's and there he stowed the cart and harness, and had Clementine watered and fettled. He was tired. He ached. For an hour on the heaped straw he would have paid a ransom. He thought of Grégoire.

He remounted and took up the *spontone*.

He rode past the plundered shops and the reeking pyramids of dead on the Pont Notre-Dame. He crossed the Place de Grève, where wine flowed and a jongleur turned cartwheels. Where shade was to be had militiamen stuporose with heat and drink sprawled on the ground by their weapons. He saw little sign that they'd been active in the killing. The militants would be elsewhere, stalking the labyrinth, beyond all discipline short of running out of hate. As if to assert that they were doing their best, a wagon stacked to the raves with recent victims clattered towards the Seine. Blood leaked through its seams and brimmed in intermittent gouts from the flatbed, fore and aft. Method had been applied to the stacking, for the upper layers were largely composed of infants and children.

Tannhauser pressed on.

At the Rue du Temple, Hervé the plasterer was not to be seen, nor was any surrogate. The chain hung coiled from its iron hook in the wall. Pillaged houses stood where this morning they had not, and bodies in bleeding stacks lay awaiting the dead wagons. Perhaps La Fosse had drawn up a fresh list. As he approached the chapel of Sainte-Cécile the burden of his next duty added its weight to that of the afternoon heat. The thought of being civil to La Fosse disheartened him further. He was glad to have a reason to delay the chore. The dead had patience. Carla's body could wait.

The doors of the chapel stood open and as he rode by he slowed and glanced inside. Candles burned in two rows at the top of the aisle. Between them, trestles draped with a white sheet supported an open coffin. The gloom was otherwise empty. Tannhauser felt numb and was glad of it. He rode on to the Hôtel D'Aubray.

The only change in its shattered façade was in the state of Symonne D'Aubray's corpse. She still hung by her ankle from the golden cord, her flesh the colour of candle wax marbled with blue. Her arms and fingers had swollen into purple tubers. Colonies of flies shimmered green on her wounds and orifices. Her head looked like that of a bedraggled Gorgon. Tannhauser urged Clementine closer to the door and bent to peer across the threshold.

The black pudding that coated the hallway was ploughed by footprints and seethed with winged insects laying eggs. Altan Savas had not been moved. Rats were feeding on the exposed grey meat of his limbs. Tannhauser saw no means to soon bury him. A warrior's grave would have to do.

Tannhauser dismounted.

He recited the *Salat al-Janazah*.

By the time he had finished, he was still alone. He called out. 'Grégoire.'

He called a second time. He got no answer. He walked down the alley to the garden at the rear. The stains on the back door were baked to the texture of pitch. He called again, in vain.

At least three hours had passed since Grégoire had parted from Juste. Tannhauser did not believe the boy had abandoned him, despite he had every right to. Beyond that, any explanation for his absence was possible, most of them grim. Tannhauser's mind felt filled with mud. He couldn't think of a reason to move. A woman's lamentations drifted through the rank humidity. He wished them silenced and at once they were gone, as if her voice had escaped from a dream only to be recaptured. Had Carla screamed thus? Of course she had. He'd heard such screams all over the world; they would never stop. He was sick of grief. Grief was as common as dirt and worth even less, his own included.

He was tired.

He saw Altan's palliasse.

He left Clementine to graze the cabbage and dragged the straw mattress to the rear wall of the garden. He lay down in the shade and his body groaned its thanks. There was a thin chance he'd get his throat cut, but as long as it was done neatly the prospect was not without allure. He closed his eyes.

Tannhauser awoke because Clementine had stopped eating. He rolled to his hands and knees, dagger clenched, and looked across the garden. There was no one there. He followed Clementine's gaze to the mouth of the alley.

The grotesque dog emerged in his gold braid collar. Grégoire followed. His bare feet and legs, and the once-red breeches, were caked in Paris mud, as was his shirt. He grinned and his face gaped open and Tannhauser mastered his urge to turn away. He returned the grin and meant it. He stood up.

'Welcome, Grégoire, back from the wars.'

Grégoire ran and stood before Clementine's chest. She nuzzled his head.

Tannhauser carried the *spontone* to the house and propped it against the wall.

'How goes Juste?' asked Grégoire.

'He's bronzed and he's fit and living in luxury with four girls, one of whom he is in love with. Not only that, but I fancy the charm is mutual.'

While Grégoire absorbed this shock, Tannhauser took the lid from the butt and scooped warm water into his face. He scrubbed the grit from his eyes.

'Not one of Tybaut's girls?' said Grégoire, with justifiable dismay.

'No, another sister of more or less his own vintage. He needs you to help them get to Poland, if that's any consolation.'

'I don't know where Poland is.'

'That problem can wait on another day. Spin me a tall tale while we walk to the chapel.'

'No, not the chapel.'

Tannhauser looked at him.

'There's a lot to tell,' said Grégoire.

Tannhauser sat on a stone bench. The sun was now hidden by the streets yonder. His ear had to reacquaint itself with the grunts and growls of Grégoire's voice but with the boy's repetitions and mimes, and by probing for details, Tannhauser understood it all.

After crossing the bridge, Petit Christian and Marcel Le Tellier had gone directly to La Fosse's house, next door to the chapel of Sainte-Cécile. While they were inside, Grégoire had looked inside the chapel and found it empty.

When the two men reappeared they went to the Hôtel D'Aubray and Petit Christian was sent inside to investigate. When he came out, he puked, then gave his report to Le Tellier in a state of marked agitation. Marcel gave instructions then rode north towards the Temple. Grégoire followed Petit Christian west, into Les Halles.

'Why did you choose Christian?' asked Tannhauser.

'He's the errand boy. I wanted to see the errands.'

Christian entered a tavern near the Cemetery of the Innocents, the Blind Piper, and stayed some while. On leaving he walked to a shabby house in the Grande Truanderie and went inside. This visit was shorter; Grégoire didn't know who was in there. On leaving, Christian went to Marcel Le Tellier's *hôtel*, near the river, west of the Rue Saint-Denis. Grégoire watched the house in the hope that Christian would come out again, but he did not. Two *sergents* guarded the front door. Messengers and officials came and went. Time passed. Grégoire was on the verge of leaving when a wagon drove up.

He recognised the driver: Sergent Baro. Le Tellier's man, Le Tellier's fist. Everyone knew Baro. The wagon turned by the south side of the *hôtel*, and Grégoire saw Stefano, of the Swiss Guard, sitting on the back.

Grégoire circled the *hôtel* by its northern side and watched the wagon enter the rear courtyard, past another *sergent*. He walked by the gate, toying with the dog, and looked in. He saw Stefano help

Orlandu from the wagon. Orlandu was unsteady, as if he were still drowsy. He leaned on Stefano as they walked into the Hôtel Le Tellier.

Grégoire sensed that Christian's errands were not done. He paid a street boy a penny to watch at the rear, for a man in green, and returned to watch the front door. Some time later, Christian emerged and Grégoire followed him back to the Blind Piper.

There were the usual comings and goings, but no one Grégoire knew. He waited so long he fell asleep, sitting against the cemetery wall. When he awoke, he poked his head inside the Piper and Christian was still there, sitting with the boss, Pope Paul.

Grégoire then decided it was time to go and find Tannhauser.

'Does Orlandu still have both his arms?'

Grégoire nodded.

'Did Stefano look friendly?'

'If they want to hurt Orlandu, they won't do it there at the Hôtel.'

'How would Marcel know I went to the chapel? Help me, lad.'

'His noses are sniffing. People trust priests, and not just in confession.'

Tannhauser had trusted La Fosse only that morning. Yet the priest's shock – his surprise at the news of the murders – had seemed genuine.

'Why would La Fosse contact Marcel?'

Grégoire shrugged. 'More likely he sent for Petit Christian.'

'If La Fosse expects me to return to deal with Carla's remains, so does Marcel.'

Grégoire nodded, as if this was obvious.

'The coffin in the chapel is bait,' said Tannhauser.

'Yes. I've just been to the chapel. There are men inside.'

'Did they see you?'

'No, of course not. And I didn't see them, or hear them, but I smelled them. They were eating cheese just inside, behind the doors. At least one on either side.'

'How did you come by all this guile? You didn't pick it up in a stable.'

'I didn't grow up in a stable.' Grégoire bit his tongue. 'What are you going to do?'

'When I walk in I'll be lit by the candles and looking at the coffin, or so they'll expect. My back will be lit from the street. An easy kill. Guns or arrows, or both.'

'Assassins like the crossbow.'

No matches, no smoke, no noise. Less skill than a bow; and no draw.

'Marcel must know about the duel,' said Tannhauser. 'If he's cautious and prepared to pay for it, he may have as many as four men, two behind each door.'

They had probably seen him pass by. He had almost put both feet in their trap. He recalled telling La Fosse that he was going to recover his own guns, another piece of foolishness, compounded by not having them. He retrieved the *spontone* and took out his whetstone and spat on it. He began to work the edges of the blade and wings.

'Marcel will also be prepared for me to pay La Fosse the courtesy of visiting his house first, before going to the coffin. La Fosse will be there on his orders, to usher me to the slaughter through the church doors. If I were Marcel, I'd have one more man, hidden in the house, to keep La Fosse honest and to warn the others as soon as I arrive.'

'Marcel will use good men, not *sergents*. Assassins. I think that's why Christian went to see Pope Paul. Paul can arrange anything. But five to kill one man?'

'Let's hope I flatter myself and there are only three.'

'You don't have to take the bait, do you?'

'La Fosse is a piece of the riddle. And if I don't turn up, the assassins may search elsewhere. I don't want to have to imagine them lurking round every corner in the city. But I can't walk through those doors.'

Tannhauser pulled a dagger and scratched a map in the dirt.

'Crossbows, space and distance give them all the advantage. If just one stays beyond the reach of my spear, I'm done. Here, there's a corridor from the church, it runs past the sacristy to this inner door, into the house. That's the choke point. If I can get La Fosse to lure the others into the corridor, they'll block each other's fire and be close to my blades.'

Grégoire listened with the air of one used to such discussions.

'To use the priest you'd have to get to the hidden man first. But how?'

Tannhauser studied him for a moment. Grégoire shuffled.

'You were a thief, weren't you?' said Tannhauser.

Grégoire opened his mouth. He dropped his eyes.

'Don't be embarrassed, lad. What am I missing?'

'The lookout will warn them as soon as you enter the house, or even if I go in, or Lucifer. If anything changes at all he will warn them. He'll be gone.'

Lucifer was examining the sun-shrivelled remains of the severed genitals. He cocked his head and panted, as if relieved to be excluded from the scheme.

Grégoire pointed to the map.

'If they know you're in the house, they will not come down that corridor for La Fosse, except maybe one man, or, if there are five, maybe two. They know a choke point, too, I think. They know the tricks.'

Grégoire was right. Tannhauser considered alternative designs, but all of them depended on seizing the lookout in silence, and therefore on the lookout being a fool. He stopped thinking about the lookout.

'I'll show those scabs some tricks.'

'Five Paris assassins?'

Tannhauser pointed at the plan in the dirt.

'I can't lure them into the corridor. But if these bravos believe that I want to lure them into the corridor – and that I'm waiting for them there – some of them will leave the chapel by the street. They'll come through the front of the house to get behind me.'

He pointed to either side of the choke point.

'They'll have me back and front.'

'How can you be sure they'll come out?'

'When they hear La Fosse scream, they'll have to do more than sit in the chapel and pray for him.'

Tannhauser gave Grégoire his last double pistole and told him how to find Irène's hostel. He told him to take Clementine and find a circuitous route to the crossroads south of La Fosse's house. He was not to pass in front of the chapel. From the crossroads he could spy on the outcome. If it went badly, he was to join the others if he wanted to, and, if not, to make his way as he would, with the gold he had more than well earned.

'And before you ask,' said Tannhauser, 'in this you have no role to play.'

Tannhauser walked down the street with the *spontone* at port.

At the entrance to the chapel he stopped where he reckoned he could be seen through the gaps at the doorjambs. The arch was recessed behind the step by some eight inches and framed by twin stone architraves. Two men coming out abreast would scrape their shoulders. Two wielding crossbows would not try. He looked inside at the coffin. He made the Sign of the Cross. He did not have to fake the sadness of a man bereaved. He heard not a sound from within, but above the foetid reek of the city he detected fresher odours. Rotten teeth and gut wind. Cheese. He lowered his head and closed his eyes and murmured an *Ave*, to reassure them he had no suspicions and to give them the chance to spring. They didn't take it. Their discipline was good.

A dull peal of thunder rolled from the east.

Drops of rain bounced in the dust.

Tannhauser crossed himself again and walked on to La Fosse's door. He propped the *spontone* on the wall. He banged on the door. La Fosse answered. He looked as if he'd been bibbing to soothe his nerves, but the wine only rendered his attempts to mask his fear more pitiful. He stepped back.

'Ah, Brother Mattias. Praises be to God.'

'Praise be to Jesus Christ and all His Holy Apostles.'

The words drowned the sound La Fosse made when Tannhauser punched him under the breastbone and shoved him to his knees. He walked past the priest to the doorway on the far side of the room. He looked to the left. The door to the corridor and the chapel was just ajar. He fancied he saw the last quiver of its movement. As he had remembered, it opened away, towards the chapel, and was hinged on the left.

He pulled La Fosse upright by the throat and threw him into a wall.

'How many bravos are in the chapel? I know the answer so don't lie.'

'Four,' said La Fosse. 'No, now there are five.'

'Crossbows, knives, swords. What other arms are they carrying? Think.'

'Crossbows, knives, swords,' repeated La Fosse. 'I saw nothing else.'

'All five carry crossbows? Think hard.'

La Fosse closed his eyes. He thought hard. 'Yes.'

'Armour, breastplates, helms?'

'Three wear helms. I saw no plate, unless it's well hidden.'

'No guns?'

'No, I saw no guns at all.'

'And your job is to murmur pieties and send me through the doors. Yes?'

'Yes. Forgive me. God forgive me.'

Tannhauser assumed he had a few minutes for the pieties before his assassins had cause to get too nervous. He aired some conjectures as if he knew them to be facts.

'You arranged for my wife to stay with Symonne D'Aubray. Why?'

'Christian Picart asked me to approach Symonne, on behalf of the palace. I introduced them. He charmed her. He gave me no reason to suspect a malign purpose.'

Petit Christian had explicitly denied that he had lodged Carla with Symonne.

'Symonne was Protestant, why would he ask you, a Catholic priest?'

'Symonne was a convert. I baptised her as a child. She converted when she married Roger. He was a known radical, a Huguenot militant.'

'Why did Christian pick her?'

'Symonne was a noted musician. Your wife, too, or so Christian told me. The notion was to mirror the royal wedding with a musical symbol of reconciliation between the two Faiths –'

'When did Christian first approach you with this scheme?'

'After the wedding was announced. Late April, perhaps early May.'

Over three months ago.

'Symonne readily agreed?' asked Tannhauser.

'After her husband's death she was a strong advocate for peace.'

'Why didn't Christian approach Symonne himself?'

'I don't know. He asked if I knew her, knowing it was likely. It's my parish. It's part of our work to grease such wheels.'

'Why was Christian aware of Symonne?'

'Perhaps he knew of Roger. Roger was murdered in the Gastines affair.'

'Christian was involved in that?'

'His confraternity was involved – the Pilgrims of Saint-Jacques.'

'Fanatics.'

'Devotees of the Blessed Sacrament, from Saint-Jacques, the butchers' church near Les Halles. They wear red and white ribbons to signify their motto: *One bread. One body.* For most it's an excuse to throw banquets and get the best seats at Mass. But some are militant leaguers – politicals, militia captains.'

'Bernard Garnier.'

'Garnier, Thomas Crucé –'

'And you.'

'No, no, I don't share those interests at all.'

'You share others.'

Tannhauser grabbed him and turned him to face the portrait of the cardinal fondling his own bastard. He spoke from behind La Fosse's ear.

'Christian pimps for the lordly. What dainties does he procure for you?'

'Please, Brother Mattias –'

'You whisper secrets gleaned from confession in his ear and he pays you with boys. Christian sells boys and you buy them. Isn't that what he holds over you?'

'The eminences in Rome proved that nowhere in Scripture, nor in the writings of the Doctors of the Chapel, is carnal knowledge of a boy deemed fornication.'

'That can quiet your conscience when I cut your throat.'

'My God, my God.'

Tannhauser threw him back at the wall.

'You sent a message to Christian. You told him I'd been here.'

'I had to tell him what happened at the Hôtel D'Aubray, which, as you can testify better than anyone, came to me as the most horrible surprise.'

'Tell me this. If there'd been no riot today, but the events at the Hôtel D'Aubray had still taken place, how would those events have been received?'

'Murderous burglaries are hardly unknown.'

'And if the victims were a Protestant family with a radical history, how many tears would be shed? That is, outside the Huguenot community?'

'Any general outrage would be difficult to imagine,' said La Fosse.

'The police are hand in glove with the Catholic militants, so any investigation would be perfunctory, the crime neglected and forgotten. Yes?'

La Fosse nodded. 'More than likely.'

The knot of the riddle loosened.

'They didn't need this massacre to disguise Carla's murder,' said Tannhauser. 'It was already disguised, as the death of an unfortunate bystander. And as a Catholic woman in a Protestant home, she wouldn't even get much pity.' He thought of Bernard Garnier on the Parvis. 'Some would even welcome the crime, not only as one more warning to the Huguenots at large, but to any Catholic inclined to show them friendship.'

La Fosse sagged as if some bleak revelation had dawned.

'More than just a warning.'

'Explain,' said Tannhauser.

'Don't you see? If all were as usual – if Admiral Coligny had not been shot, if the week of wedding celebrations had reached the happy climax so intended, and if the Queen's Ball, and its musical symbol, had gone ahead as planned – then the assassination of Carla and Symonne would be seen as a singular repudiation of religious tolerance. That is, a violent expression not simply of militant hatred for the Protestants at large, but of their contempt for the royal wedding, for the Peace of Saint-Germain, for the Edict of Toleration, for the Queen's entire policy –'

'Murder the symbol.'

At last, Tannhauser understood.

'Precisely,' said La Fosse. 'The Huguenot nobles would have insisted on justice – and not just a few thieves sent to the gallows. They would never have believed it was the work of mere criminals. Symonne wasn't even that rich. Admiral Coligny would have put tremendous pressure on the King to find and punish the conspirators, but would the King have dared? Not just the militants, but Paris itself was against the wedding. Rome was against the wedding. The Pope's dispensation was never even acquired; it was forged to trick Cardinal de Bourbon into agreeing to the ceremony. Thus, the crime would have forced the King to choose between alienating Coligny, or alienating – indeed humiliating – the strongest champions of the Catholic cause. And while the latter may not approve of Charles, they are more than eager to fight for him.'

'Another war.'

The greater crime now consuming the city had provided the perfect screen for the lesser one of Carla's murder; or so Tannhauser had believed until now.

In fact, and to the contrary, it had buried it.

The murder of the symbol – of two musicians who embodied conciliation between Catholic and Huguenot – had been lost amid the murder of thousands. It was unlikely that this muting of their voice would disappoint the conspirators. By chance their intrigue had collided with a larger one, but in place of a promising stratagem they had the war of annihilation they craved.

The performance at the Queen's Ball was to have been on Friday night. Carla had been safe until then. There was no sense in murdering the symbol in advance of it becoming one. Carla and Symonne had been killed on the night following, Saint Bartholomew's Eve.

The D'Aubray outrage had been prepared, not in hours – to exploit the unforeseen opportunity provided by the massacre – but over months. The wedding and its celebrations had been the opportunity. And of all the many such amusements laid on, none was more apt to purpose than the gala devised by the Queen, she who, more than any other figure, was seen as a traitor to the Catholic cause. Catherine would have understood the message, and its political implications, in an instant.

Tannhauser admitted the scheme's brilliance. Retz had told him Coligny had threatened civil war only last week. The murder of the symbol could have tipped the balance with ease. Previous wars had blown up over much less.

Carla's assassination had not been personal. It had been political. She and Symonne were pawns, sacrificed in an attack on Catherine de Medici and the policy of tolerance.

No one had expected Tannhauser's arrival, not even Carla. Unwittingly he had threatened their scheme, long planned and prepared for that very night.

Orlandu, as Carla's only potential defender in the city, had been spied on by the porter, who had indeed known who Tannhauser was. The porter had alerted Petit Christian, who had followed him to the Louvre and alerted Dominic Le Tellier. Dominic, improvising, had tried to get him killed in the Duello, and having failed, had arrested him.

Orlandu must have got wind of the intrigue, and been shot before he could warn or protect his mother. Why was he imprisoned, not killed?

The riddle was unravelling entire.

And the assassins next door would soon be itching.

Tannhauser looked at La Fosse. La Fosse cringed.

'On the blood of Christ I played no knowing part in this conspiracy, let alone a willing one. You must believe me.'

'I do. Who is your go-between?'

'Boniface, the porter at the Collège d'Harcourt.'

'Boniface, is it? Tell me, who is Orlandu?'

'Orlandu? I don't know. I have no idea. Truly, on my –'

'What is Marcel Le Tellier's role in all this?'

'I didn't know he had a role until he came here today with Christian. I'd never met the man, though I know his reputation.'

'Is he a militant? One of the Pilgrims?'

'I don't know. Many conceal their convictions for fear of the Queen. In his position, obviously, he would be wise to do so.'

'What did Marcel say?'

'He questioned me on our conversation, which I related. I spoke of you only in the most respectful and fraternal terms.'

'He told you exactly what to do with the coffin.'

'Yes. I'd started making provision for the coffin as soon as you left. He told me to continue, precisely as you had asked, even though the body –'

'He told you to expect these assassins and to do their bidding.'

'Yes, exactly, though I didn't know they were assassins until they arrived.'

Tannhauser considered the time had come to let the bravos earn their pay.

'Is there anything else you can tell me about these men?'

La Fosse hesitated. Tannhauser leaned into his face.

'If I die, they won't know you helped me. If I live, you will need my charity.'

La Fosse said, 'I believe Le Tellier wants you alive, if possible.'

'Did he say that?'

'No. I heard his men talking, about how to shoot to cripple you, not to kill.'

'They'll soon be forced to abandon that ambition.'

Tannhauser unrolled the cuffs of his boots to cover his groins.

'If they succeed,' said La Fosse, 'they intend to take you to the

Blind Piper, a villains' den, I believe. If not, they will take your head for proof.'

'You're sure there's five. You saw them. You saw them into the chapel.'

'Five, yes, I'm certain.'

Tannhauser put a dagger to La Fosse's throat. La Fosse farted.

'You wouldn't be the first priest I've killed.'

'Please, brother, please –'

'If you try to warn them, you'll be the first to die.'

'I swear. And the body. I've something else to tell you about the body –'

'The body can wait. Come with me and keep quiet.'

Tannhauser pushed him from the room to the door in the corridor. On the far side he reckoned it twenty feet to the chapel. On this side, it was ten feet from the room.

Tannhauser spoke softly at the nape of La Fosse's neck.

'Stand with your face close to the door. Good. Now lift both your hands above your head. Place one on top of the other and both flat against the door. But do not push.'

La Fosse's arms and hands shook as he obeyed. He whispered. 'Why?'

'I want you to stay in this exact position until I return. Understand?'

La Fosse's shoulders sagged with partial relief. 'Yes.'

Tannhauser grabbed the iron handle of the door with his right hand. The door was still a little ajar. He held it firm. He drove the dagger through the priest's hands and nailed them to the timber. La Fosse screamed with a passion that curdled the blood. Tannhauser pushed the door half open, towards the chapel, and La Fosse shuffled with it. Beyond the priest's pain-stiffened frame, he caught a shadow of movement at the end of the corridor.

Tannhauser turned and ran for the street.

The street was empty but for the rain. He grabbed the *spontone* and ran to the arch and stopped short of the double stone architrave.

He held the *spontone* as a woodsman does an axe, his right knuckles almost grazing the wall, his left foot forward, eyes peeled for the arch. The *spontone* was a foot of winged steel blade, socketed on five feet of ash. Its weight soothed him while he waited. He heard voices in conference. They were strained but steady. There were no prayers for La Fosse, whose screams echoed within.

The sound tactic was to send three men out while two stalked the corridor.

The voices fell silent. Footfalls slapped on stone approaching the door.

No one running with a crossbow held his fingers on the trigger lever; it was too easily tripped. When the first of the bravos burst forth, his crossbow was at half-port, his right hand on the tiller. His speed carried him two paces clear before he saw Tannhauser, by which time the second bravo was looming in the arch.

Tannhauser stepped forward a pace and severed the first assassin's left arm through the elbow. The crossbow fell. Tannhauser swivelled towards the archway.

The second bravo teetered on the threshold as he halted his charge. His bald pate was peeling from the sun. As he brought his crossbow to bear Tannhauser sidestepped its path and slammed the flat of his blade down hard where the stirrup met the curve of the bow. The crossbow dipped and the blow tripped the lever and the bolt was shot. As it buried itself in the baked dirt of the road, Tannhauser whipped the blade back up and stabbed the bravo in the throat. He felt the tip bite into the pulp of the spine and he stepped back and heaved. The bone clung on as the blade plucked free and the bravo was dragged from the threshold to fall on his face. His peeling head convulsed atop the flaccid body and he gargled on his blood as it spilled from his mouth.

Through the archway, a shape stepped in front of the candlelight.

Tannhauser lunged to the wall to clear the arc of fire and a bolt hissed forth from the gloom and split the timbers of a house across the street. Tannhauser looked through the arch.

The third hireling had one foot in the stirrup of his bow and was drawing the string, a bolt clamped between his gums. Tannhauser's concern was the other two bravos, whose weapons were already loaded. Either might still be behind the door. He turned.

The one-armed man knelt on his heels, two yards behind him in the rain, staring at the torrents gouting from his sleeve. Tannhauser hoisted him by the stump and shoved him to stumble through the arch. His entrance flushed no hidden danger. As Tannhauser followed him the third bravo freed his jaws of the bolt and called back over his shoulder, towards the sacristy door.

'He's here! He's here!'

He seemed not to realise that his voice was hoarse with terror.

Tannhauser let him slot the bolt between the fingers of the nut, then embossed him though the chest unto the wings. He swayed from the waist to avoid the spray that blurted black and foamy from the sundered gullet, and he held the fellow skewered against the rail while he stole an extra bolt from his belt and put it between his teeth. He tugged the crossbow from the slackened hands and let the corpse slide from the blade to befoul the narthex. He flipped his right hand to take the *spontone* in a javelin grip, in case he was called upon to throw it. He lanced the one-armed man through the liver and kicked him free of the blade to splash in the shambles.

He strode towards the sacristy door.

The door stood open, just short of the chancel, in the wall of the right hand aisle. It was hinged on the left and opened into the corridor. Tannhauser checked the crossbow. The lath was steel, the bolt holder shaped from a strip of antler. The bolt head looked like a giant horseshoe nail. It was small as crossbows went, as befitted an assassin's needs, but at forty yards it would punch a hole through plate steel.

He heard the priest begging the last two hirelings to free him, with the desperation of one not ashamed to repeat himself. They had not done so. La Fosse's bleating must have drowned what little noise the first three had made in meeting their end. Tannhauser craned his left eye around the doorjamb.

The fourth bravo stood in half-crouch, some fifteen feet along the corridor. His back was to Tannhauser. Just beyond, La Fosse stood on his toes, his face tilted up between his pinioned arms, and pleaded with God. His body on the door blocked a good half of the passageway. As Tannhauser had calculated, the geometry had forced the fourth man into a cramped position on the left, requiring cumbersome footwork to turn and fire. Judging by the skittish movements of his head and shoulders, he was trying to see what was going on beyond the priest.

'Munt! By the shit of Jesus, where are you?'

A muffled shout was returned from his unseen confederate.

Tannhauser strode down the passageway, his javelin arm cocked, the priest's anguish once again a boon. At his fourth step the assassin heard him but the walls were too narrow to allow him to spin with the crossbow levelled. He had to point the bolt upwards as he shifted both feet to step and turn, then lower it to aim. He reacted with admirable speed but before the vertical arc was half-complete, Tannhauser had rammed a foot of steel through his armpit. The damage to the lights and heart was so instant and so vast, the only sound to mark his death was a bubbling wheeze. Tannhauser booted him from the blade and advanced as far as the shield provided by La Fosse. He nudged him with a shoulder and La Fosse howled.

Tannhauser spoke through the bolt between his teeth.

'Pray louder.'

La Fosse clenched his eyelids and did his best.

Tannhauser stepped past the priest and was back in the house. He stopped short of the doorway to the main room and stacked the *spontone* by the jamb. He hefted the crossbow. He called, his voice disguised by the bolt and La Fosse's Latin.

'Munt? Where are you?'

'Get out! He's in the chapel! Schmidt's dead!'

Tannhauser stepped into the doorframe and levelled the crossbow.

Munt was standing in the rain outside the front door.

He fled south.

Tannhauser strode to the door and used the jamb as a bench to steady his elbow. Munt had dropped his weapon to aid his flight but the target would hardly have taxed a lesser marksman. Tannhauser shot him between the shoulders and saw the bolt vanish. It kicked up water from a puddle thirty paces down the street. Munt arched his back and veered aslant on buckling legs. He slithered to his hands and knees. He looked up towards the crossroads, as if some miracle might be found there. His arms went and his face hit the mud and he stirred no more.

Tannhauser laid up the crossbow on its stirrup and took the spare bolt from his mouth. He stepped from the doorway and waved, even though, apart from Munt's corpse, he saw nothing of note. Sure enough, and conjured as if from nothing more material than sunlight, Grégoire appeared and charged through the rain towards him.

Grégoire hurdled Munt and clapped his spade-like hands. He laughed as he ran with the strange halting laugh that had first so taken Tannhauser's fancy. The bald dog cavorted by his ankles, sheathed in a scaly black carapace of human blood. Grégoire spread five fingers. Tannhauser nodded.

Grégoire cocked an ear. 'Who's that?'

'It's La Fosse thanking God for our deliverance.'

Tannhauser remembered the coffin.

Despair dimmed the afterglow of combat.

'Fetch Clementine. Haul that body to the chapel.'

Tannhauser dragged Schmidt into the narthex. He searched all three and found twelve *écus d'or* and some silver between them. A doubloon apiece.

He went to the corpse in the corridor and found four more *écus*. La Fosse was trembling and muttering like a man who had lost his mind. In an attempt to persuade the Almighty of his worth, he appeared to be comparing himself to the Thief on the Cross.

'The Good Thief joined Christ in Paradise, not the good pederast.'

Tannhauser searched him and recovered both his double pistoles. He braced the priest's hands to the door and pulled the dagger free. La Fosse groaned and slid to the floor. It didn't seem necessary to tell him not to move.

Tannhauser dragged the fourth corpse to join the others in the chapel. Grégoire appeared, soaked. In Munt's purse he had found a bowstring with short iron rods attached to either end for grips. By garrotting Munt's feet with one hand, and wrapping a turn of Clementine's tail around the other, he had delegated the bulk of the effort to her. He showed Tannhauser four *écus*.

'At least we're making a profit,' said Tannhauser.

'This is yours, too.'

Grégoire gave him a fistful of small coins, mainly coppers.

'I sold the shoes. I hope it's enough.'

The sum was a small fraction of what Tannhauser had paid the day before.

'You drove a hard bargain. Well done.'

Grégoire nodded.

'And I commend you on your honesty.'

'I'm not a thief any more.'

'We may yet call on that talent, but you're right not to steal from your mates.' Tannhauser nodded towards the street. 'Fetch the crossbows. Remove any bolts and pull the triggers before you pick them up. Watch your fingers.'

Tannhauser laid out Munt alongside his four accomplices. Their blood slaked the floor of the narthex and their mouths and eyes gaped up at Heaven, as if struck down by a peevish god while caught in some arcane ritual of penitence. He wondered if he shouldn't decapitate them and leave their heads on the altar for Marcel. It was no bad thing to have one's enemies think one deranged. But Carla's remains were not yet desecrate, for he had killed them all outside the bounds of the chapel proper, and so it should stay.

He glanced at the coffin. Guilt and grief intermingled in his gut.

He sought further practical diversions.

In the corner behind one door he found a leather satchel. It contained rope and a pair of leg irons, lead-weighted cudgels, spare bolts, half a loaf and a heel of cheese. He discarded the cudgels and leg irons. Grégoire returned and they examined the five crossbows. All were trued and fettled. All were small and could be cocked by a stout back and a strong pair of hands. One was made all of steel and dressed with ivory and silver. The draw weights were double that of Frogier's bow.

'If you didn't grow up in a stable, where were you raised?'

'Here in the Ville,' said Grégoire. 'In Les Halles.'

Whoever had adopted Grégoire from the crib in Notre-Dame had done so not out of charity but to use him as the pawn of a gang of beggars. Beyond a certain age his face had been so repellent that his earnings in disgust far exceeded those in alms. After that he had been used as a decoy and a tout for a variety of cutpurses and snatchers. He chewed soap and feigned fits. He trailed rich men to their homes to furnish burglars. He watched his comrades disembowelled and hung in the Place de Grève. One day he saw some thieves about to steal a horse and cart filled with supplies. He warned the owner, who discovered his own boy was their accomplice. In a fit of gratitude that proved to be uncharacteristic, Engel had given Grégoire the job.

'So you'd made good,' said Tannhauser, 'until I came along.'

'A new boy means more work for Engel. He'll take me back.'

'I doubt that.'

Lucifer trotted in from the street, panting with the air of a dog which, despite its scorched condition, had found a female of the species willing to be mounted. He inspected the dead bodies and selected two to piss on.

'If you're going to take him home, he'll have to be better trained.'

As a matter of fact, not of self-pity, Grégoire said, 'I don't have a home.'

'I mean my home, in the south. Will you come?'

Grégoire stared at him. He blinked his eyes, as if at some inner vision.

'Yes, master. If we can get there.'

'I'm not going to die in Paris. And having a varlet seems to suit me.'

'A varlet?'

'It's a nobler version of a lackey, with better wages.'

These details seemed to make the prospect more plausible. Grégoire brightened up. As if eager to be on the road he said, 'Have you seen your wife yet?'

'My next duty, and one I've put off long enough.'

'I am sad for you.'

'Take the satchel and these weapons to the kitchen. Get something to eat.'

Grégoire reached into his shirt and produced a crumpled mass of fabric saturated with sweat and water. He held it out. It wasn't until Tannhauser made out that it was tied with a sodden ribbon that he realised it was the christening robe.

Tannhauser crossed himself and walked up the nave to the coffin.

The head of the body was pointed towards the altar. He stopped short.

The body was the wrong size.

The wrong shape, length and build.

He lunged forward. The corpse was wrapped in a white sheet with a flap covering its face. He pulled the flap aside. The face was a woman's, the features waxy, grey, indistinct in the way that death has of erasing character.

But the face was not Carla's.

Tannhauser dropped the christening robe on the floor.

He had been prepared to feel pain, not absolute confusion. He was relieved that the corpse was not Carla's, but the relief was abstract, a thought, not a feeling. He had grieved for her. The weight of his grief had almost crushed him. No weight he had ever carried had been so heavy. No substance, not steel, nor stone, nor even love, had ever been more true. And he had carried it. His grief had become him. He had become the man who carried it. It had not destroyed him. It had not driven him mad. Had he had no right to it? Was it gone? How could something so material vanish? Yet in an instant it had and he was emptied. Into the emptiness, he felt fear creep out.

Carla's death had banished fear.

He turned his back to the coffin wherein Carla did not lie.

Where was she?

Was she alive?

The fear came.

If Carla was alive, he might have to lose her – and mourn her – all over again. He did not know if he could. If he couldn't, he wouldn't be a man worth being.

If Carla had not been murdered in the Hôtel D'Aubray, it was certain she had not escaped. Altan's body proved that. Only death could have forced him to abandon her side. At that point she had been theirs to do with as they pleased, and Tannhauser had seen what pleased them. The only reason to take her alive was for sport. That she was pregnant could appeal to any number of appetites. And they'd had all day to go at it; at her; at her unborn child. Whether Carla was still alive or if they had tired of such amusements and killed her, Tannhauser had wasted the day that might have saved her from either.

That lay at the doors of his guilt and his fear. It had not been grief that had stopped him from climbing those stairs, let alone a weak stomach. It had been guilt, for guilty he was: of failing as a husband; of selfishness and vanity and misguided loyalties; of leaving her alone with child; of every wrong decision he had made since entering Paris; of not getting there in time. It had been fear, for he had been afraid: of fatherhood and its obligations; of the freedom he would lose; of another dead babe. That was why he had lacked the courage to climb the stairs; to face the accusations of her corpse and his conscience. By that act of cowardice he had abandoned her yet again, to monsters, while he grovelled in bloodshed and self-pity.

He had known nothing of guilt and nothing of fear.

But he knew them now.

He would know them forever.

Enough.

Enough of fear and guilt and self-disgust.

All that and forever, too, could wait until tomorrow.

He looked up at the crucifix above the altar. He had believed his soul to be dark; but had known nothing of darkness either. He said no prayer. Light he did not need. Night was falling and only darkness would get him through it.

He summoned cold rage.

Tannhauser strode down the corridor, where La Fosse sat cradling his wounds. He clasped his hands around the priest's skull, thumbs wedged under the cheekbones, and hauled him aloft against the wall. La Fosse's eyes rolled like those of a roped cow. As the nerves in his face were compressed, he screamed.

'Where is my wife?'

'I don't know! I tried to tell you she wasn't in the coffin –'

'Is she alive?'

'I don't know!'

La Fosse's pain was so extreme he dared in his writhing to grab at Tannhauser's wrists. Tannhauser kneed him in the pubes. He increased the pressure with his thumbs.

'Where is my wife?'

'Do you think I'm keeping it secret? Do you think I fear anything more than I fear you? I fear you more than God. I pray I knew where to find your wife. Christ on the Cross, even they don't know. Please stop hurting me. Please.'

Tannhauser let go. La Fosse sagged over. Tannhauser shoved him upright.

'What do you mean, "even they don't know"?'

'Something Christian said when he saw the body. He's a man of tantrums. He was incensed. He told me I had the wrong woman, as if I didn't know it was Symonne.'

'What did he say?'

'Please, let me explain. I can't breathe.'

Tannhauser took his hand from La Fosse's chest.

'I hired servants to recover the body of a woman in the bedchamber, just as you instructed. They brought back Symonne D'Aubray. They swore there was no other such body in the building.

Reliable men, simple men. I explained all this to Christian and Le Tellier, and that's when Christian said to Le Tellier, let me get it exact, yes, he said, "*The commission was clear. What's that animal done with her?*"'

'What was Le Tellier's reaction?'

'He silenced Christian with a look. Christian said not another word.'

'But they both expected Carla to be dead, at the Hôtel.'

La Fosse nodded. 'Without a doubt.'

'Was Le Tellier troubled, perplexed?'

'He was calm as a dead carp throughout the whole meeting.'

'Was anything else said about the attack? Any names?'

'No, no names, nothing. I told Le Tellier I was certain you would be back – he pressed me on that – though I didn't know when. He told me to continue with the arrangements just as you had instructed, as if the body were your wife's. The rest you know.'

'There was another woman strung from a window. She's still there.'

'Symonne's housekeeper, I believe she was called Denise.'

Tannhauser ordered what he knew.

Christian had recruited the villains. The general massacre had rendered the murder of the symbol meaningless, therefore Carla, if she was alive, had no such political value and posed no immediate threat to the conspirators, of whose identity she was ignorant. There was no reason she should much trouble Marcel Le Tellier.

Le Tellier's problem was Tannhauser.

Why did he want him alive?

Le Tellier also had Orlandu hostage, and good reason to keep him alive, at least until Tannhauser was taken or killed. But all that was secondary.

Carla could be anywhere in the vast and demented city.

Some 'animal' had taken her. Petit Christian knew who the animal was. So must others. He doubted that Christian, busy little bee though he was, had dealt directly with the dog-burners. He would be one go-between among several. Perhaps even Marcel

Le Tellier was no more than that. Tannhauser would climb to the top of that ladder in due course, no matter how high it went.

If Carla was alive, she was at its bottom, with the animals.

He had to drop the 'ifs'. Carla was alive.

He dragged La Fosse to the kitchen.

'How do you get messages to Boniface?'

La Fosse indicated the grounds of the abbey through the window.

'Brother Anselm, from Sainte-Croixe.'

'You creatures like to work in teams, don't you?'

La Fosse did not defend the monk's honour. But a monk would be able to cross the river unhindered. Tannhauser called Grégoire and sent him to fetch Anselm.

'Where are your finest gloves?

'Gloves?' asked La Fosse.

Tannhauser plugged the priest's wounds with flour and told him to be thankful it wasn't salt. He helped him thread thin liturgical gloves knitted from silk over his fingers. He let La Fosse pour a cup of wine down his throat, then sat him at his desk with paper, quill and ink. He found a sheet already covered with his handwriting.

'This is your last chance to preserve your life. If your script isn't as perfect as this sample, you'll have squandered it.'

'I'll need my nose-glasses, if you still have them. You can take them back again afterwards. In fact you can keep them. Consider them yours.'

Tannhauser dug out the glasses. La Fosse donned them. He flexed his fingers, wincing in hope of sympathy. Getting none, he dipped the quill.

'Open with your customary greeting to Petit Christian.'

La Fosse scratched at the paper. Tannhauser squinted over his shoulder, missing the glasses. A blot besmirched the paper.

'My God, my God,' moaned La Fosse.

'A few blots are forgivable. Continue as follows: *The Chevalier knows everything.*'

Desperation guided La Fosse's quill. The handwriting was unsteady, which Christian would find natural in the circumstances, but it was clearly the priest's.

'*I am fled for my life. You will not find me.*'

This provoked a whimper of hope. La Fosse dipped his quill. He said, 'May I suggest: *Not even Le Tellier will find me . . .?*'

'Good. It had better be believable.'

'There are a hundred religious communities in the Ville that owe him nothing.'

'Then add: *Let the boldness of that statement alert you to whose wrath I fear the most.*'

'Very good, Brother Mattias. Very true. But consider . . . *Let the boldness of that statement proclaim the revised hierarchy of my loyalties, priorities and fears . . .?*'

Tannhauser nodded. La Fosse scribbled.

'*Le Tellier's complot is trumped entire by superior powers at court. He will not survive.*'

'May I embellish with: *The Chevalier's allies are illustrious indeed . . .?*'

'Good. *The Chevalier swears by the Blood of Christ that he will spare your miserable life on one condition.*'

La Fosse paused. '*. . . spare your miserable life, as he has so nobly spared mine . . .?*'

Tannhauser nodded. He considered the next passage. He was not relying on this stratagem to succeed and did not intend to wait for it to do so. Five or six hours would give him time to try others; if they failed, he would see what the letter had produced. Open space would allow him to watch for perfidy, and, if it came to it, give him a chance to fight his way out.

'*You must wait, alone, by the gallows on the Place de Grève, at midnight.*'

La Fosse dipped, wrote.

Tannhauser continued, '*Any sign of treachery and your death is certain.*'

'*On that you may take him at his word.*'

La Fosse wrote this without waiting for consent.

'If you fail to keep this appointment,' dictated Tannhauser, *'the Chevalier will hunt you down and kill you slowly. I urge you, for your own survival, to reconsider your current allegiances.'*

'Superb. Shall we add . . . *as, from time to time, so must we all . . .?'*

'I like the authenticity. Suggest a conclusion in similar vein.'

La Fosse stroked the quill against his chin.

'I pray that you act upon this heartfelt advice, in order that our amity might flourish anew, in happier and more tranquil circumstances.'

Against his better judgement, Tannhauser had almost decided to let La Fosse live. This talk of flourishing amity, and what it meant for the city's boys, altered his mind. He retrieved his glasses from La Fosse's nose and read the letter. It hadn't been written by a man who expected to die. At the least it would drop a scorpion in Christian's pocket. If Christian dropped it in Le Tellier's, nothing was lost.

'Add your signature, so forth. Your usual seal.'

Grégoire called from the kitchen, announcing Brother Anselm.

'Boniface must act with all urgency,' said Tannhauser.

La Fosse rose and swayed and fell back onto the chair.

'Forgive me. My hands. The pain gets worse.'

'I carry opium in my belt. You can have some later. Now get up. I'll be listening and my lad will watch you.'

The letter was despatched to Boniface.

Tannhauser clapped La Fosse on the back.

'Tell me, Father, does this old chapel have a crypt or some such?'

'Some of the order's first luminaries are buried below. Why?'

'My gold is heavy. I want to secure it, if I can trust you not to steal it.'

La Fosse began to protest his honesty. Tannhauser smiled.

'A jest. Show me the crypt. Then we all can be on our way to our just havens.'

La Fosse took Tannhauser down to the crypt and helped him shift a slab on a tomb. Tannhauser doubled the priest over the rim and slew him without ceremony. He shoved him in the tomb and replaced the slab and it was done.

He collected the *spontone*. The rain had stopped. He found Grégoire in the twilight with the scarred grey mare, feeding bits of cheese to the bald dog. He wore the assassin's satchel across his back and had bundled the crossbows by their stirrups with the garrote.

He did not ask after La Fosse.

Tannhauser mounted Clementine.

They walked to the crossroads and he stopped.

'The Yards. Do you know them?'

'No, master. I only know where they are. I'm sorry.'

The air was damp from the shower, heavy with the day's heat. The long street to the west offered a rare prospect to the farthest edge of the Ville, where the sky smoked with streaks of cinnabar and ochre, as if polluted by the fires that razed Sodom. The light of sundown glimmered through the soaring stained-glass windows of a lofty church tower, their beauty enfeebled by shame, the virtues they glorified mocked by all they looked down on. Screams bade farewell to the dusk as they had greeted the dawn. Night would embolden criminals, fanatics and degenerates. Chaos would enfranchise their vilest whims.

Somewhere in this flux, Carla was looking death in the face. He imagined her gaze and that dark green fire which could chill even him to the bone. Carla saw a different world from the one he saw; even when the world was this ugly. She saw possibilities to be seized; he saw limits to be breached and torn down. If anyone could survive, if anyone had the grace, it was she. If not, he would grieve her again. He did have it in him. It was the only thing in him worth having. He believed in her.

He had to, not for her sake, for his own.

He closed his eyes.

He could feel the babe's heart beating. His little girl.

He had lost her, too, today. He had missed her.

She was back, inside him. They both were.

'I knew she had a great heart,' said Grégoire.

Tannhauser opened his eyes.

Grégoire was stroking Clementine's enormous chest. He looked up at Tannhauser.

'She didn't let you down.'

'She's not the only one, lad.'

Grégoire's acumen did not extend as far his own worth.

'You had another horse?' he said.

'No. Clementine was stalwart all the day long. We should bed her down.'

'I know all the stables, the good from the bad.'

'You also know where to find your own bed. Go and claim it.'

'If you send me away, I'll follow you. You won't see me.'

'I've much to do and more to hazard.'

Grégoire snorted a cheese fragment into the dirt.

Tannhauser reached down.

'Give me that bundle.'

He took the crossbows and held them in his right fist with the *spontone*.

He reached down again with his free hand.

'Sit up here, behind me.'

'You want me to ride with you?'

Grégoire seemed to find the notion improper. He mooted an explanation.

'As your varlet?'

'As my friend.'

Grégoire blinked, as if out of all the day's happenings this was the only turn that truly astounded him. He looked away to hide a tremble in his lip.

'I've had some stout ones,' said Tannhauser, 'but none I'd hold higher.'

Grégoire sleeved his eyes and turned to look at him.

'And I never needed one of them more than I need you.'

Grégoire took his hand and swarmed onto Clementine's back.

'Can Lucifer come with us?'

'Why not? Where we're going a hellhound might prove handy.'

Tannhauser watched the creature take its place between the huge front hooves.

'Where are we going?' asked Grégoire.

Tannhauser wheeled towards the crimson death throes of the sun.

'We're going to pay the Piper and call the tune.'

PART FOUR

AS FAR FROM HELP AS LIMBO IS FROM BLISS

CHAPTER TWENTY-TWO

The Minstrel

With a price on his head and the noses sniffing like drabs on the tout for the pox, Tannhauser had Grégoire guide him through the backstreets. Near the corner of the Rues Trousse-Vache and Saint-Denis he sent him to stable Clementine without going in himself.

In a dank alley he unravelled the ivory and silver crossbow from the bundle, and cocked it but didn't arm it. When Grégoire came back with the satchel, Tannhauser selected five bolts fletched with tin. Each was twice the weight of an arrow with a kiss that would make the boys cry. He tucked them in the back of his belt and returned the bundle to Grégoire.

The Blind Piper stood near the south-west corner of the cemetery. They worked their way towards the stench. Outside various shops and galleries, *sergents* and watchmen waited for looters. Grégoire guided him around them through slits in the city that rarely caught the sun and which in twilight were almost dark. An occasional figure lurked in the gloom but Tannhauser let them see the *spontone* before they saw him, and each beheld some vision of his own disembowelment and slithered away.

'That's the backyard of the Blind Piper.'

Grégoire ran over to two wooden gates in a high brick wall.

'Padlocked on the inside,' he said.

Good. Escape would difficult.

'No dogs,' said Tannhauser.

'Paul doesn't like dogs.'

Tannhauser beckoned with his head and they circled the building. They stood in the shadow of the graveyard. The tavern was twenty feet across. Yellow light behind thick glass panes; a heavy door. The upper floors were dark.

'Where is the bar?' asked Tannhauser. 'How many serve behind it?'

'The bar is on the right. Usually, one man serves behind.'

'Does the door open in or out?'

'Out.'

'How sure can you be that the Pope's in there?'

'Paul's the fattest man in Paris. He never leaves. He sits on a couch at the far end of the room. He has two guards, to help him stand up.'

Tannhauser had dealt with Paul's sort from Istanbul to Tangiers. Patience was usually in order; tonight he had none. The tavern would be no rough house. Men who liked to fight, and were good at it, didn't drink together. For a brawl they'd go elsewhere. Tannhauser didn't expect much to worry him; except women. He had never killed a woman; none had ever given him sufficient cause. He wasn't sure that sitting in the wrong tavern on the wrong night fitted that bill. He drew a dagger.

'Hold up those crossbows for me.'

Tannhauser sawed through the strings of the four bundled crossbows.

'Does Paul run whores?'

'No. Paul doesn't like women.'

'Boys?'

'Paul doesn't like children either. Only business and food.'

Tannhauser sheathed his dagger and slotted a bolt into his crossbow.

He heard music. Strings. Singing.

Grégoire said, 'Paul likes a minstrel of a evening.'

'He does, does he?'

A minstrel. Tannhauser thought about it.

A man ran up the street. Tannhauser shrank back.

The runner dashed into the Blind Piper, without seeing them.

'Let's hope our luck is better than his. Give me that bundle.'

Tannhauser held the armed crossbow in his left hand and took the other four by the handles of the garrote in his right, along with the *spontone*.

'Open the door for me, but don't come in. Wait there. I'll be a while.'

'No one ever touches Paul. That's why he's the Pope.'

'It's time he was unfrocked.'

Grégoire hauled open the door of the Blind Piper.

Tannhauser saw straight down the bar.

The beamed ceiling was low. He would have to mind his head.

At the far end a purple mass, topped by a small pink dome, reclined on a couch, flanked by two human oxen. The runner was bent to Paul's ear.

Halfway down the room a minstrel sat on a chair and plucked the strings of the harp in his lap as he sang. He had a beautiful voice. His back was to Tannhauser.

Tannhauser stepped inside and the door closed behind him. He propped the *spontone* by the jamb. At a glance: nine customers at the tables.

They were all of them scum of one kind or other, some finely dressed. Several pairs of eyes took note of the Maltese Cross on his chest. Two of the pairs knew what it meant and who he was. They were expecting him, placed to be behind him, if necessary. Good. If Paul had feared he was coming, Paul had tales to tell. He didn't let his gaze linger; theirs did. He spotted a senior villain who recognised only the abundance of his weaponry. The villain's companion looked like a courtier; paying for a frolic on the dark side. The villain alerted two toughs, seated at the next table, with a wag of one finger: wait and see. The toughs didn't need to be told; they had seen the armed crossbow and hoped to see no more. Three other bravos, seated in the corner, knew Tannhauser, too. When he looked at them, they stared at their beakers of wine.

Tannhauser took two steps and swung the bundle high and let go. The four crossbows landed with a clatter and skated across the flagstones towards Paul. Their severed strings snaked back and forth. If the particular significance of the gesture was lost on most, its general meaning was not.

431

The minstrel stopped his song. Silence fell.

The two oxen looked at Paul, as if hoping he might produce a thunderbolt. At this distance, Paul's face was too bloated to betray his fear. His voice did the job.

'Welcome, chevalier! News of your bold deeds has just reached me.'

Tannhauser tossed his chin at the minstrel.

'Sing.'

The minstrel turned away and struck a chord. He sang.

Tannhauser drew his sword and held the crossbow clear.

He threw his hips into a backhand and decapitated the minstrel in one.

The severed head hit the flagstones with a dull crack. Gore erupted from the neck stump in all directions. The body remained seated, cradling its harp.

A more profound silence fell. They watched the eruption subside.

Tannhauser turned and walked back to the front door.

'Christ, he beheaded the minstrel.'

A lively murmur broke out.

Some discussed what the minstrel might have done to deserve it.

Others the morality of allowing the killer to escape.

Tannhauser threw the bolt and locked the door.

The sharp thud brought all speculation to a halt.

Tannhauser turned back round and looked at them.

'Oh my God,' said the courtier.

The villain's toughs read it best. Their only chance was to draw their daggers and charge. He shot the first in the chest as he rose from his table. The quarrel threw him into the wall like a bag of manure. He used the second tough's momentum to broach him through the upper gut with the sword, then hammered the ricasso with the stock of the crossbow and carved him open to the bladder on the outstroke. The tough groped at his sundered entrails and reeled away.

Their chief made a dash for the door, or perhaps even for the *spontone* there propped, but his choice would never be known. Tannhauser chopped him through the hamstrings and sent him down, then ran him through beneath the left rear ribs, perforating kidney and bowel. He left him to squirm and looked at the two hired to brace him from behind.

Paul had wasted his money. They hadn't moved from their stools. Neither had the three scabs in the corner; nor the gawping courtier whose frolic was proving more lively than he'd bargained for. The sense of panic was intense; yet almost silent as each man weighed his options and found them all wanting.

Tannhauser laid the bloody sword across the counter top.

He grounded the stirrup of the crossbow and slotted in his foot, and grabbed the twisted sinews with both hands and drew. He saw the larger of the oxen lumbering down the bar towards him, bellowing and wielding an axe. The second ox advanced behind him, his lesser zeal but little roused by Paul's high-pitched exhortations.

Tannhauser set the crossbow on its stirrup against the counter. He turned and grabbed the *spontone*, and turned again and levelled it, right foot forward. He lunged and gored the charging ox so deep beneath the sternum the tips of the wings pierced his ribcage. He let go of the shaft and stepped aside and around the perforated hulk. The ox staggered onward, his axe falling only by virtue of its own weight. To spare damage to the *spontone* blade, which jutted out between the ox's shoulders, Tannhauser grabbed him and turned him as he toppled, and the hulk crashed to the floor on his side.

Tannhauser turned to see the second ox in full retreat towards Paul. A wine jug sailed through the air and Tannhauser swayed backwards from the waist. The jug smashed against the counter. He retrieved his sword. To his left the young courtier had drawn a rapier. Terror gave him the courage to use it. He advanced as taught by his fencing master, the long blade poised with admirable elegance. As the predicted thrust came, Tannhauser stepped across and in, and hacked the courtier's neck unto the spine. The courtier fell and convulsed and gargled in the minstrel's slops.

Tannhauser stepped back to the counter.

He exchanged the sword for the crossbow and slotted a bolt to the nut.

The second ox, ignoring his pope's frantic commands, dragged the luckless runner away from the back door, and assumed the latter's task of trying to open it.

Tannhauser took aim and shot him. The bolt struck the ox below the nape and to the left of his backbone. It flattened him into the door and nailed him choking thereon, his hands swatting the timbers in feeble spasms.

Tannhauser drew the crossbow and laid it up. No else came at him. No one else would. If any had imagined they had a chance, they knew they hadn't taken it. They had reduced themselves to their last chance, which was to hope that he would have mercy. He took his sword and flicked the blood from the blade and sheathed it. The villain by the door was still moaning with the pain of his wounds. Tannhauser put a foot on the dead ox and stooped and heaved the *spontone* from his thorax. He spiked the villain through the temple with the counterweight.

He surveyed the room.

Aside from Paul and the runner, who was trying to get past the flailing bulk of the second ox to unbolt the back door, there were five men left.

The two bravos who had spotted him still sat rigid at their table, as if hoping this might make them invisible. The other three stood in a group against the rear wall. They were all gibbering at Tannhauser in great earnest, but he didn't hear them. Two of the three separated themselves from the third, whose terror increased. They identified him as the jug-thrower, and swore on the souls of their mothers that they had only dropped into the Piper for a quiet drink. Their several unsheathed knives and the maces propped by their stools argued otherwise, but it would have made no difference. There was nothing left but butchery.

One by one, Tannhauser lanced all five with the *spontone*. He did it cleanly; one thrust apiece through the heart, and where necessary the hands clasped thereto. First the two bravos at the table, who had favoured their own skins over Paul's. They kept their seats until the end, as if survival might be won by good manners. Then those who claimed unto the last to be peaceable drinkers and devout

Catholics; then the alleged jug-thrower. He found another man on the floor behind the bar, hiding beneath a gantry of wine casks.

Tannhauser lanced him, too.

He collected the crossbow and walked to where Paul sat quivering on his papal throne. He propped the *spontone* on the wall. He fitted a bolt to the crossbow and laid it, trigger up, on a table. He marked the runner, who had crammed himself into a corner. The man held a knife for comfort, though it brought him none. His eyes were wide, his brain boiling with too many thoughts to think, and none of which would profit him.

Tannhauser looked at Paul. He had seen fatter men, in Egypt, but only one or two. Paul's face was shiny in the lamplight. His eyes were fixed on Tannhauser's chest and he was taking fast, short breaths through pursed lips, as if he were trying to whistle and making a poor job of it. The boil in his brain needed to be cooled, too.

'I'm Mattias Tannhauser. I take it you're the local pontiff.'

Paul didn't respond. He wasn't able to respond. Behind him, the nailed ox wheezed his master's name like a frightened child. He sprayed blood on the door with each gasp.

'Paul . . . Paul . . .'

Tannhauser stepped around the couch and looked at the runner.

'Drop the knife.'

The runner dropped the knife.

'You've been to the chapel. Apart from the dead, what did you see?'

'I saw the Infant. I followed him there. Paul told me to. Sire.'

'The Infant?'

'Grymonde.' The runner panted on every other word. 'Grymonde went in the chapel. He stayed inside, it seemed like a long time, then he came out of the priest's house and stood in the street. You can't read Grymonde. I can't. He headed north, towards the Temple. Then I looked in the church and saw the dead men, all laid out like hares, and I ran back here.'

'Good. Now stand behind Paul and put your hands on his shoulders.'

'Paul . . . Paul . . .'

The runner ignored the ox, as did they all, and did as he was told.

Tannhauser drew the lapis lazuli dagger and put a hand on the nape of the messenger's neck. It was clammy. The man was trembling. Tannhauser thought about Carla. And what criminals like these had done to her.

'This isn't necessary,' said Paul. 'This isn't how things are done round here.'

'Have a heart, sire,' panted the runner. 'I'm deaf in one ear.'

Tannhauser cut the runner's throat and held him upright while he drained onto Paul's head. Paul squealed and spluttered. He vomited on his great purple belly.

Tannhauser let the body drop.

'Paul . . . Paul . . .'

'For God's sake, man, could you at least keep Maurice quiet?'

Tannhauser looked at the ox, still exhaling blood onto the door. The tin fletchings were twisted, wedged between his upper ribs. The head of the bolt was buried in the wood but had missed the lethal vessels and organs. Tannhauser stabbed Maurice behind the collarbone. Without his legs to support his weight, Maurice broke off the shaft at the bolt head and slid to the floor.

'Thank you,' said Paul.

Tannhauser took the chair facing Paul. Paul's face was a glistening red mask. Blood trickled down the great rolls of fat that enshrouded him. He wiped his eyes and blinked.

'Did you have to kill the minstrel?'

Tannhauser saw his intelligence surface through his fear.

'Where's my wife?'

'I will gladly tell you where to find Carla when you understand why killing me would run against your interests.'

'What state is she in?'

'I assure you she hasn't been harmed. At least, not yet.'

'Is she held for ransom?'

'If only she were,' said Paul. 'A piece of the purse would be mine. But don't despair, you've come to the right man. If we pool our respective talents, which in sum would be a most remarkable power, I'm certain a happy outcome can be achieved.'

'Your vanity exceeds your intelligence.'

'It's takes neither vanity nor intelligence to say that you need me.'

'I'm told you love business, so here's the bargain.' Tannhauser nodded at the crossbow. 'Tell me what I want to know, and I'll put that bolt through your skull.'

'I've entertained better offers.'

'Fat doesn't bleed overmuch. I could carve off two or three stone and it would still take a week for the putrefaction to finish you. I'd add your tongue and your fingers, too, though by then you'd be too crazed to speak my name.'

'Your name's already spoken, all over town,' said Paul. 'Carve away if it will please you, as seems likely. I'd answer your questions and you'd learn the things you want to know. But you wouldn't learn the things you need to know, because you don't know how to ask for them.'

'I've known men who can defy pain. You aren't one of them.'

Tannhauser stood up and drew his dagger.

Paul raised his bloody hands.

'Wait. We all know the legend of the knight who played chess with Death. Well, I may be playing for my life, but you're playing for Carla's. You can't afford a wrong move at this stage of the game.'

Tannhauser didn't sit down. He nodded at Paul to go on.

'This affair had a bad smell from the start —'

'When did Christian hire you?'

Paul licked the blood on his lips, as if he'd just lost one of his pieces.

'This afternoon.'

'For the D'Aubray murders, not mine. You're the murder man, aren't you?'

'A week ago. Christian only told me the particulars of what they wanted, not the why. Perhaps the lickspittle didn't know himself. But I could see the why right off.'

'Light the fuse. Start a war.'

Paul reassessed him yet again.

'Very good. Naturally, I was tempted. There's a lot of money to be made from a war, especially if you're one of the few who knows it's coming. I asked a princely fee to test their ardour. They didn't quibble. By then, I couldn't back out, they'd have lost trust in me. These aren't your usual criminals, though I'm not certain who they are. My sources in the Louvre are weak, I admit. And militants aren't my clientele.'

'The Pilgrims of Saint-Jacques. Marcel Le Tellier.'

Paul was even more impressed.

'I suspected as much. Plenty would like to see that Caesar fall.'

'He will. And your game goes badly. You've told me nothing worth knowing.'

'I can tell you how and where to hide, you and your wife. When these riots are over, when Le Tellier has been ruined, I can still the troubled waters. I can get you safely out of Paris. Better still, you could stay and get rich with me.'

'Hiding doesn't suit my temperament. Carla's neither.'

Tannhauser stabbed Paul sideways through his fat. The sensation was peculiar. Paul shrieked. Tannhauser shoved the dagger in up to the quillions and left it in place. The blade was a good foot from anything vital. He sat down and watched him quiver.

'You sent Grymonde to the chapel to bolster your bravos.'

'Nobody sends the Infant anywhere. He went to warn you that they were there.'

Tannhauser chewed on that but couldn't swallow it.

'Why?'

'Because he is mad, as are you.'

Tannhauser stood up again.

'Grymonde is in love with your wife.'

By the time Tannhauser took this in, he realised it didn't much surprise him. Carla was pregnant, and very far from being a seductress; she despised such wiles; but the power of her allure ran from depths that could not be fathomed. She had tamed the lion. Grymonde had spared her. Carla had sent him to find Tannhauser. It would not win Grymonde his life, but Tannhauser felt some affinity with the man. He knew the kind of love Carla could inspire; even if he himself had lately proved unworthy of it.

'You hired Grymonde for the murders.'

'Christian asked for him, in particular. The job was meant to draw attention and he'd been told the Infant wouldn't care, which he didn't. The Infant would never have worked out that he was going to start a war. On the other hand, if he had, he would have been glad to.'

'Grymonde is a fanatic?'

'Only in his own cause, which is destruction, though he doesn't know that either.'

'So Carla is in Grymonde's hands. Where?'

'Up in the Yards, on the hill near Porte Saint-Denis. He calls it Cockaigne. You'll not find it alone, Theseus himself couldn't. Neither could I. And for Carla, time runs short.'

Tannhauser pulled out the dagger. Paul whimpered. He was on the edge of complete submission, yet still clung to his fantasy that this was a game.

'The minstrel was the most harmless man in the room,' said Tannhauser. 'When I killed him, every other man knew he was going to die too. And here is a strange fact. Most men, once their doom is revealed, find it easier to die than to fight. The fighters were flushed, but even they were resigned to the outcome. All of them, except you. Not because you are a fighter, but because you believe that the world needs you. But the world needs no one. It doesn't need Carla. It doesn't need me. Here.'

He stabbed Paul in his fat a second time. Paul howled.

'That's for sending your scum to murder my wife.'

He stabbed him again.

'That's for sending your scum to murder me.'

Tannhauser stropped the blade on the sole of his boot.

He let Paul see the street shit coating its edges.

'That should be sufficient of Paris to poison you slowly.'

He stabbed Paul a fourth time. Paul sobbed and wobbled.

'Now your doom is revealed.'

'You're a bloody lunatic.'

Tannhauser stabbed him again and left the knife in to soak. Paul twisted and whimpered, his eyes bulging from the bright crimson mask that coated his face.

'How do I find my wife?'

'Joco knows, in the Truanderie. He knows Cockaigne.'

Grégoire had seen Petit Christian visit a house in the Truanderie.

'Joco or Typhaine, a redhead,' said Paul. 'Her daughter knows it, too.'

'I know the house. Which floor?'

'They're on the second floor.'

'And if they're not there?'

'Joco's laid up in bed. Grymonde broke his ribs. He'll be there.'

Tannhauser stared at him. The Pope clenched his eyes shut. He was still trying for some final, secret victory. Petit Christian. Christian knew about the Truanderie. Grégoire had followed him there. La Fosse had said that they didn't know where to find Carla; but that had been some time around noon. Now they did know.

'How long has Christian known where to find Carla?'

Paul stared at him with the fury of utter humiliation.

'I was waiting for you to walk through that door, man. I was waiting to tell you everything. I wouldn't have charged you a single copper penny.'

'I know that. Do you want me to start on your thumbs?'

'Christian left here over an hour ago.'

Tears swam into Paul's eyes and rolled through the gore on his cheeks.

He sobbed. 'In the place where there are no men, be a man.'

Tannhauser said, 'Hillel.'

From Hillel to Sabato Svi.

To Tannhauser.

To Carla.

To Grymonde.

'Grymonde quoted the rabbi. Didn't he?'

Paul's tears stopped. He looked at him.

'He said that was why he wanted to find you. That's why I told him how to.'

'Are you a Jew?'

'Do you think they'd let a Jew sit where I sit? I once knew a Jew. He taught me some things worth knowing, the best of which I chose to forget.'

'Then we share something in common.'

Tannhauser pulled the dagger from Paul's fat. He wiped and sheathed it.

'We share something more,' said Paul. 'We love not Marcel Le Tellier.'

Even as he sat putrefying, Pope Paul was making moves that would outlive him. Tannhauser grinned, in admiration. He sat down.

'How do you know Le Tellier?' asked Paul.

'Never set eyes on the man. Today was the first I ever heard of him.'

'Marcel wants to get his hands on Carla, badly. I don't know why.' Paul nodded at the slaughter that engulfed his tavern from front door to back. 'Though, as you appear to appreciate, to wipe a dirty slate clean is always prudent. To that end, he is spending a good a deal of money and taking a good deal of risk, but he can't use the resources of the Châtelet, not directly. He couldn't conceal that from those who would step into his shoes, and they would use the fact to bring him down. Catherine de Medici will turn this war to her son's advantage, even if she didn't want it. But she will not tolerate a chief of police who uses the Châtelet to aid her enemies. No man is more enslaved to the state than a policeman. Her dwarves would be using Marcel's head as a footstool within a week.'

Tannhauser said, 'The Pilgrims.'

'Garnier, Crucé, Brunel, Sarrett – perhaps other confraternities, too.'

'The Pilgrims would murder Carla for Le Tellier?'

'Not a murder, a mission of mercy. To rescue the Catholic damsel from a notorious fiend. The Cockaigne Infant. After today they'll be feeling like the Life Guards. The captains will leap at the chance. And then she'll be in Le Tellier's hands. He has a son –'

'Dominic.'

'He will have sly resources, too, guards for hire. In sum, more than enough to take her, dead or alive. Grymonde doesn't merely not expect it. He doesn't believe it. He's the King of Cockaigne. The mighty Infant. He's mad. But, in truth, it's just another beggars' den, a patch of weeds that no one cares to rip up.'

'Will Marcel lead the expedition in person?'

'Marcel is no warrior. And he won't steal the Pilgrims' glory. The glory will be their only reward, and they're pious enough to think it a rich one.'

'Your bravos were told to take me alive.'

'There was a generous bonus in it,' said Paul. 'Le Tellier must have some other use for you.'

'Unless he seeks his own executioner, I can think of none.'

'In his shoes I could think of plenty,' said Paul. 'For instance: I'd leave you chained in a dark hole for a day, dispose of Carla, then rescue you. I'd prove to you, and whomsoever else, that some other party was responsible for this conspiracy – child's play, by the way – and let you, and the Religion and the law, in whatever combination, take their course. The other – guilty – party being one of Marcel's enemies, of course. Two birds with one stone. It would be a fine piece of treachery, but Paris has seen better. Believe me, no one will ever know who had Admiral Coligny shot. I doubt the man who pulled the trigger knows.'

'Le Tellier has proved all he needs to, to me.'

'I speak of the possibilities in his mind, which yet can know little of what is in yours.' Paul spread his hands. 'Alternatively, he could have your throat cut in the same dark hole – if only you were in it, which I suspect is still his fond hope.'

'Assassinating a Knight of Malta without their consent is a risky move.'

'Not if the knight in question murdered his wife and half a dozen innocents. He'd paint you up a regular Gilles de Rais. It worked on Gilles, didn't it? And from what I know of you, it would be no challenge to make the deception convincing.'

'What's the case now – as far as Marcel knows it?'

'You're either dead or tied up in my backyard,' said Paul. 'Or you never went back to the chapel, and you're drunk in a brothel, waiting for some *sergent* to find you.'

'Why would I be drunk in a brothel?'

For the first time, Paul appeared to find him stupid.

'Because you'd allowed your wife to be murdered by beasts.'

Tannhauser allowed him his morsel of spite.

'That was beneath me. I apologise,' said Paul. 'You'll find a purse on Maurice with the bonus, if you want it. Thirty *écus d'or*.'

'The King's head is always welcome.'

Paul leaned forward, despite his wounds, as if scenting something tasty.

'There's plenty more. More than you'd think. But it's not here.'

'Then it's no use to either of us.'

'You do know such as we could make a fortune together.'

'Yesterday, perhaps. Today the only ledger I'm keeping is writ in blood.'

Paul glanced at the crossbow on the table. He looked Tannhauser in the eye. Tannhauser saw the nerve he had needed to make himself the Pope of Les Halles.

'Grymonde is no great thinker,' said Paul, 'though he is a philosopher of sorts. He is cursed, as you will see. You won't mistake him. And he has a shrewd gut, when he has the sense to hear it. He said, "someone is squatting on a dunghill of hate".'

'War will turn the dunghill into a mountain.'

'He wasn't talking about Huguenots or fanatics. He meant something personal. Something to do with Carla. If not her, someone close to her.'

'What does your fat gut say?'

'It agrees with Grymonde's.'

'Do you know Orlandu?'

'No.' Paul grasped at this last straw. 'But I can find him for you.'

'I know where to find him.'

Tannhauser stood up.

'Don't you want to know more about Marcel Le Tellier?'

'Unless you can get me close enough to kill him, I don't need to know more.'

There was no sense wasting a bolt. Tannhauser chose the *spontone*.

Paul started shivering. 'If I've a last request, Chevalier, it's that you believe this –' His voice trembled. 'I swear that when Grymonde left, it was to try to save your life.'

'There's only one who can save his, and it's not you. Why do you care?'

'Let's say I like to think of Grymonde as a wayward son.'

Tannhauser looked at him. Paul dropped his eyes.

'A pope who sired a king. You could have done worse.'

'I hope your *gambito* pays off, you black-souled bastard.'

Tannhauser levelled the *spontone*. Paul raised one finger.

'Have you any idea how much money there is in shit?'

Tannhauser stabbed Pope Paul through the heart.

He collected the purse. He took the crossbow. He turned.

His way to the door was awash with the gore of the slain. Those few flagstones left unpainted were grouted with the run-off. The dead in their stillness rendered a silence that had nothing to do with sound. The headless harpist hadn't moved from his chair.

Tannhauser felt no scruple and wondered at himself.

He concluded that it was just as well.

The dirty slate was far from clean.

Carla needed him.

He needed her.

He walked the length of the bar and threw the bolt.

He shouldered his way out into the street.

He left the Blind Piper behind him.

Or tried to.

It was almost full dark. He couldn't see Grégoire. A nearby butt collected rainwater funnelled from the roof. He laid up his weapons and peeled off his shirt, which was plastered to his skin with blood and sweat. He plunged his head in the water up to his

shoulders. It was cooler than he expected and welcome. He drank.
He rinsed the shirt and swabbed himself down. It felt good. The
boy ran across the street with his dog.

'You were gone a long time.'

Grégoire stared at the janissary symbols inscribed on Tannhauser's
arms.

'I told you, I'm not to going die in Paris.'

'What happened to the minstrel?'

Tannhauser wrung out the shirt. He didn't answer.

'The music stopped. I heard the noises. Then I saw that.'

Grégoire pointed. Blood flowed under the door and down the
step.

'Then all the noises stopped.'

'I couldn't talk to Paul with a dozen knives at my back.'

'Did the minstrel have a knife?'

'The minstrel didn't suffer. He died singing.'

Grégoire threw his arms around Tannhauser's waist and sobbed.
He was a child. Worn out with fear and toil. The one man he
looked up to had murdered a minstrel.

Tannhauser slung the shirt over one shoulder and put his hands
on Grégoire's back. He felt the ungainly body shudder against him.
If God at the moment of Creation had held the essence of goodness in His palms, and in the spirit of curiosity stacked the pain of
confusion on top of it, Grégoire was what He might have made.

Feelings that Tannhauser did not need to feel rose inside him.
He was one of the men who had made this world into the world
that it was. He searched through the shame for something worth
saying. For something he had the right to say; something that was
true, and not some evasion. He could tell Grégoire he was not a
good man; that he was not a wise man; that in pursuit of his woman's
safety he was content to employ any evil, at any cost to his spirit.
He could tell him many such facts. But the boy wouldn't understand. He would not find in such truths any grain of the comfort
he needed and deserved. He should never have taken the boy from
his stable. He remembered sitting with the printer's daughters, in
that same stable. It was worth a try.

'Grégoire. I love you.'

The boy looked up at him, his gums covered with snot, as if he'd never heard the words before, which, on reflection, Tannhauser thought was likely enough.

'You have saved my life. You may yet save my soul. Should I lose them both, I will love you from the fires of Hell. Now, wash your face.'

Grégoire scrubbed his face with water.

Tannhauser took a piss against the wall. He tied the shirt around his waist by the sleeves. The shirt had served him well, but it marked him a wanted man.

Grégoire relieved himself, too. Tannhauser laughed.

'A wash and a piss and a man feels ready for anything.'

Grégoire grinned and nodded.

Tannhauser needed Grégoire to take him to the house in the Truanderie. Joco. Red-haired Typhaine. After that, he could place him in some hostel, and, despite the boy's protestations, he could bully him into obedience. That was the right thing to do. Yet Tannhauser could not find it in himself to expel the boy from this dark quest upon which Destiny had called them.

'Grégoire, I have more bloody work to do. I will do it.'

Grégoire nodded.

'Dire hazards lie ahead. I will set you somewhere safe if you want me to, but if you'll join me, I'd be grateful for your help. Without you, I don't much fancy my chances.'

'What do you want me to do?'

'Take me to the house you saw in the Rue de la Truanderie.'

CHAPTER TWENTY-THREE

Crimson Apron

C arla awoke to find Amparo looking into her eyes. Their noses were almost touching. Carla wondered what the babe saw. She seemed to be bathing in her mother's breath. Carla didn't move. She was spellbound by her radiance. She felt the embrace of eternity. The world was one and it was forever. Amparo uttered her sweet, piping cry. A greeting, a question, a song of life. Carla smiled.

'She's ready for another feed,' said Alice.

Carla looked up and saw her by the lamplight. The old woman sat by the bed, absorbed in the spectacle, as if seeing it for the first time.

Amparo cried out again and Carla sat up and put her to her nipple. The curtains were drawn back to let in the air. The sky was mauve, streaked with red tendrils. Fires crackled in the yard below and sparks flew upwards in the gloaming. Voices and laughter. The smell of roast pork. Grymonde's feast. Carla felt hungry. Alice had an iron tripod warming over a candle. When Amparo was fed, Alice brought over a bowl of broth and set it by the bed.

Carla wrapped Amparo in a shawl and held her out. She was surprised by the tug in her heart at handing her over, even to Alice, but the joy in Alice's face banished the feeling. Carla swung her legs over the side of the bed and sat up. She needed to use the pot. She asked to be excused and Alice walked to the window, murmuring to the babe. Carla stood up, amazed at how light her body seemed. She was unsteady but felt strong enough. Her stomach cramped in a late contraction. She left some clots in the chamber pot but not enough to worry her. Alice returned and sat in her chair and Carla sat on the bed and ate. The broth was good.

'Should we swaddle her?' asked Carla.

'It's up to you. Most do. But this woman doesn't believe in swaddling bands. What young living thing would want her arms and legs bound tight? It makes no sense. There's plenty bonds in life without having to start off in them. A nicely tucked shawl is enough, and as much of your skin as she can get.'

'Show me how you would do it.'

Alice produced a white linen clout and demonstrated the knots and folds that would keep it round the baby's waist without chafing her. She stood back to let Carla practise. What delight. They swaddled Amparo in a shawl from Carla's valise. Sounds came from downstairs: the front door opening to a waft of festive noise, which was muffled again when it closed.

Carla said, 'Grymonde?'

Alice shook her head. 'The house didn't shake.' She stood up and shuffled to the door. 'Who's there? Speak up or we'll have your guts for garters.'

'I'm looking for Grymonde,' called a small, bold voice.

'He's not here.'

'Where is he?'

'I think it's Estelle,' said Carla. 'Call her up.'

'Come on up.' Alice looked at Carla. 'Estelle?'

'One of Grymonde's gang, I think.'

Alice frowned, as if she thought this unlikely.

Estelle appeared in the doorway and stopped. She was, if anything, even more filthy than when Carla had first met her. She was smeared from head to foot in damp soot. Her hair was matted with the stuff. Her arms and legs were covered with scratches and scrapes. Her eyes shone white from the black mask, fierce as ever. She didn't enter the room.

'Hellfire.'

'Estelle,' said Carla. 'Did you come down the chimney again?'

'No, I climbed up a chimney. Where's Grymonde?'

'He's out,' said Alice. 'And if you're coming in here you'll not escape a wash.'

Estelle submitted while Alice removed her belt and pulled her smock over her face and used it to swab up the worst of the loose soot from her long ringlets. Alice bundled the smock and threw it out of the window, ignoring the protest from below. She took a linen towel used earlier and wrapped the girl's hair in a turban. Most of the fallen soot was confined outside the door.

'This is a special place, so mind your manners,' said Alice. 'Now, save this old woman's back and put that basin of water on the floor, go on. Don't spill it.'

Estelle tiptoed into the room. She saw Amparo in Carla's arms and stopped.

'Is that your new baby?'

'Yes, she's a little girl.'

'What's her name?'

'Amparo.'

'I never heard that name before.'

'When you're clean, you can say hello to her. You'll be her very first friend.'

'Her first friend ever?'

'Her first friend ever, in all the world.'

Estelle lifted the wide pewter basin from the table and set it on the floor. The water wasn't fresh, but that hardly mattered. Estelle stood in it with great solemnity. As Alice prepared to struggle down to her knees, Carla stood up and offered Amparo.

'Please, let me do it, I feel fine.'

Alice didn't resist. She took the baby and Carla knelt by Estelle and washed her from the neck down with a soaped cloth. It was the first bath the girl had had in some time. There were sores on her skin, as well as the new scratches. When her hands were clean, Estelle leaned on Carla's shoulders for balance. The hands felt good.

'You'll have to find a better way of coming and going than by the chimney.'

'I hate the chimney, but the *sergent* was sitting by the front door and the window was too high. He ate all our soup and fell asleep. I hate him, too. I hate them all.'

'Well, there's no one to hate here. We're all good friends.'

449

'Is Grymonde your friend?'

'Yes, Grymonde has become my friend. He's a good friend to have.'

'He takes me flying.'

'That must be wonderful,' said Carla.

'It is. But you like the chevalier better than you like Grymonde, don't you?'

Carla stopped and looked at her. She remembered the jealousy in Estelle's eyes, the pain at her expulsion. The jealousy was gone; in its place was a terrible need. Carla's heart clenched. There was no doubt in her mind. Estelle was Grymonde's daughter.

It was not because she saw Grymonde in Estelle's face, but because she saw Alice in Estelle's eyes. Wild and grey as the sea, and as deeply wounded. The urge to cry rose in Carla's throat. She swallowed. She wanted to look at Alice, but didn't. The chevalier? She wrung out the cloth. She wanted to wipe her brow, but cloth and water both were now so filthy she used the back of her arm. Her thoughts were blurred by emotion. She took refuge in practicalities.

'Step out of the basin, Estelle. We'll use fresh water for your face.'

Estelle stepped out of the basin and Carla used the bed to lever herself to her feet. She stooped to pick up the basin but Estelle reached it first.

'I'll do it.' She carried the basin to the window. 'Below!'

Estelle dumped the water, provoking more oaths. She carried the basin back and Carla put it on the table and poured fresh water from a jug. She looked for a clean cloth.

'You said the chevalier. Do you mean my husband, Mattias?'

'You do like him the most, don't you?' nodded Estelle, afraid of Carla's answer.

'Yes, of course I like Mattias the most. I love him. But how do you know of him?'

'Petit Christian said the chevalier would give Grymonde a lot of gold if he would let you go home, so I told him you were here.

But he's a liar, they're all liars. He called me a Judas and I'm not a Judas, so I escaped to tell Grymonde, and you.'

'So you didn't see Mattias, the chevalier?'

'No,' said Estelle. 'They just talked about him.'

'They? Who else was there?'

'My mother and Joco.'

'Joco from this morning?'

Estelle nodded. 'You made Grymonde hurt him, without saying so.'

'Does Petit Christian work at the Louvre, for the Queen?'

'I don't know. The people he works for are bad. He's a poison toad.'

Carla found the cloth and twisted it in her hands. She wasn't safe any more, but the feeling was distant because so much else was close. Her body. Her fatigue. Her joy. Her baby. Alice.

'Carla? Let this old woman wash Estelle's face, if you please.'

Alice offered Amparo. Carla took the babe and hugged her. Amparo was asleep. Carla's breasts ached. She saw Alice study Estelle with great intensity, with her essence as much as her eyes. Estelle shrank back. Alice sat on the bed and beckoned her.

'Don't be frightened of this old girl, Estelle. You want your beautiful face to be nice and clean for when Grymonde gets home, don't you?'

'Is he coming home?'

'Grymonde always comes home. He's my son.'

'He's my dragon.'

Estelle smiled. Carla couldn't remember seeing her smile before. It was Grymonde's smile, a little mad, and as big as her heart. Alice sighed, all her pain and all her stolen joy in that sound. She patted her lap for Estelle to sit on it. Estelle did so, her blackened face alive beneath the soiled white turban.

'I didn't know Grymonde had a mother,' she said.

'Everyone has a mother, love. Even a dragon.'

Alice soaped and dipped the cloth. She hesitated. For one to whom flesh gave up its inmost secrets, she seemed almost afraid, as if Estelle might disappear if she touched her. Carla understood.

She held Amparo to her cheek and watched as another moment of eternity unfolded before her. Alice began to wipe the soot from Estelle's face. She touched her skin with tenderness and passion, rinsing after each stroke, as if each stroke were a treasure worth a lifetime of anguish, as if with each stroke that anguish, like the soot, was wiped away.

Carla's fears were banished by something more potent, more enduring, than earthly woes. Something mystical. Amparo opened her eyes and cooed and Carla turned her around so that she could watch, too.

'Grymonde lifts me on his shoulders and we fly,' explained Estelle, between wipes. 'His shoulders are the highest place in Paris, higher than everyone, and he takes me wherever I want. I pull on his ears to tell him which way to go and he roars fire out of his mouth. And everyone gets out of our way and they all wish they were me, because I'm the only girl in the world who can fly with the dragon. Is my face clean yet?'

'Not yet, love.'

'Why are you crying?'

'Because I'm happy.'

Estelle looked at Carla. 'Are you happy, too?'

Carla realised her own tears were falling. She nodded.

'I only cry when I'm sad,' said Estelle.

'Sad tears are good. Happy tears are better,' said Alice.

Alice wiped the soot from Estelle's lip, and from her nostrils, and from her ears. She told her to close her eyes and wiped her eyelids and lashes. She looked at her.

'You are her. You are you. Can I put my arms around you?'

Estelle looked at Carla for reassurance. Carla nodded.

'If you like,' said Estelle.

Alice embraced her. Carla saw her searching within the great realms of her knowing, questioning herself, searching for the truth, for the right. She was ready to deny herself her own just claim, despite that that claim – that recognition – would have healed every wound she carried. It was with the wisdom of that denial that she struggled. She was trying to see beyond her own desires to what Estelle most needed. She looked at Carla.

'The other, you know, lady, told him the babe wasn't his. That's how she got rid of him. Said it was some high-born gentleman, who would give her money, though, if he did, no one ever saw it. By then he was starting to change – his teeth, his for'head – and she was ashamed of having anything to do with him. Perhaps for him it was easier to believe it than not. But this woman knows one thing, he loved that babe from the moment she was born.'

'He loves her still,' said Carla. 'Would you like me to tell her?'

'This woman drew a card for the babe that day. The Twilight of the Morning. The circle and the square, the red and the white, the past and the future, Hope and Faith. The stillness after the storm.'

'The Star,' said Carla.

Estelle had listened to every word. If she didn't understand what had been said, she knew she was the subject. Her gaze was on Carla.

'You saw the spread this morning,' said Alice. 'She might not have him long.'

'Perhaps that's a reason to be truthful.'

'Perhaps he is wiser than we are. A parent is just a parent. But a dragon?'

Carla remembered something Mattias had told her about Orlandu. When he had first told the boy, in the inferno of Saint Elmo's, that he had come to reunite him with his mother, Orlandu had been so hurt, so angry, that he had forsaken Mattias's friendship, for a while. Orlandu had believed the mighty Tannhauser had chosen him as a friend for his own qualities, not because he was someone's son. That there was another reason for that choice, a dull, practical reason, had robbed him of his pride.

'The one abandoned her,' said Carla. 'The other chose her.'

'What are you talking about?' asked Estelle.

'We're talking about you, Estelle,' said Alice. 'You are the Morning Star, the brightest in the sky. That's why Grymonde chose you.'

Estelle searched Alice's face for a long time.

'Grymonde calls me La Rossa. Can we wash my hair for him?'

Washing and perfuming Estelle's hair cost Alice more effort than Carla's childbirth, but every moment was a delight to both participants. Carla confined her contribution to fetching the pails of water that the silent Hugon brought to the door, while Amparo lay on her back on the bed. By the end Carla was soaked.

She fed Amparo again and changed back into her pale gold frock. It hung about her hips in baggy folds. She put her hands on her stomach. She was sore down below and her insides were tender, still prone to short pangs. She was very tired. Moments of near ecstasy alternated with deep sadness.

She started to worry about Petit Christian.

She paced with Amparo in her arms.

In searching for her, Mattias would have started with Christian. While rewarding her abductors would offend his principles, he would pay any price to get her back. Where his principles would not have bent was on being there in person, to control such negotiations. Why was Christian discussing ransom with the likes of Joco? Don't trust the Louvre, Grymonde had said. He didn't know who had hired him to kill her.

She realised Petit Christian had hired him. Not on his own account, but on behalf of some powerful other. Nausea rolled through her. The invitation to the wedding. The long journey to Paris. The music. It had all been a sham. They had brought her all this way to kill her. And then they had waited almost two weeks and butchered a whole family.

Why?

She felt her legs shake. She stopped by the window and leaned on the sill. And watched the gaiety around the cook fires below. Did Christian's master have the power to come here, to the Yards? They were talking to Joco. About money. Grymonde would not betray her. But anyone else in the Yards could be bought for a clean shirt.

She could not take to the streets. Grymonde might return any moment; he might even bring Mattias. As the strange dreaminess of her labour wore off, she yearned for him more and more. She had been right, that morning, to feel that he was close.

He was close.

He was coming.

She saw his face in her mind's eye. The face of a Mattias who knew her to be in peril. His blue eyes. More than they gave comfort, the eyes frightened her. She thought she had known what he was capable of. She had fallen in love with him while watching him torture and kill a helpless priest. The picture in her mind was of a man who was capable of deeds she could not imagine; who would violate any boundary of morality or honour, even his own; who would scar his soul to its core; for her. She loved him. She wanted him. He frightened her. She turned away from the window, confused.

She looked at Amparo. At the perfection of her absolute innocence. How could the man in the picture have helped to make her? She turned to Alice. She needed her counsel. But she could not bring herself to sully Alice's joy. And because, in some sense, Alice had entered her, and had awakened things she had always known but never dared know, she knew what that counsel would be.

The room is full of love.

Here, now, is love.

The choice is love or fear.

Alice looked at her and Carla smiled.

A frock of sorts was fashioned for Estelle from a blue silk chemise that Alice had not worn in twenty years. Carla found a pair of combs in her valise. Estelle basked in the admiration with which she was showered, and which Carla sensed was foreign to her experience. Carla picked up Amparo and felt faint and stepped to the windowsill to steady herself. She felt Alice behind her, her hands around her waist.

'We've put you through too much, love. Come and lie down.'

'A dizzy spell, let me wait until it passes.'

She closed her eyes and shook her head. Her strength returned. She looked down from the window and caught a glimpse of Antoinette. The girl was blindfolded and chasing among a gang of children, trying to catch one. She was laughing. She seemed to have changed all her clothes except for the beret with the white cross. Carla felt less guilty for neglecting her all day.

The feast was well advanced. There must have been over fifty people in the yard, milling around the remains of a pig spitted above a bed of coals in a brick fire pit. Other braziers burned. Lamp-lit trestles were laid with bread and dishes of beans, rice and tripes. A barrel of D'Aubray wine had been tapped. Puddles of water shone on the ground.

'It's been raining.'

'What troubles you, love?'

'We're not safe here any more.'

'I know.'

A burly figure shouldered his way through the crowd to the house. He looked up and saw her and stopped beneath the window. It was Papin. He was sweating and breathless. He was scared. He called up.

'Is Grymonde in there?'

Carla stepped back. She didn't want him to see Amparo. Her legs felt weak again, but not with dizziness. She wanted Mattias. She wanted Grymonde. Alice leaned out.

'What do you want?'

'Is Grymonde there?'

'He's busy. Eat some pork.'

'Can I come in, Mam?'

'Don't you dare. You know the rules.'

'There's trouble, Mam.'

'Take it elsewhere.'

'I can't. It's coming here.'

'Wait down there.'

Alice stepped back from the window. Her face was waxen.

'The bad men come,' said Estelle.

It was the phrase Altan Savas had used.

456

Carla and Alice turned to look at her.

Estelle was as fierce as she had been that morning in Carla's room.

'Christian talked about Guards and the Soldiers of Christ. They want Grymonde. They want you, Carla. They still want you.'

'Estelle,' said Alice, 'go downstairs and bolt the front door. There's a high bolt and a low bolt – the low one will do. And a plank that bars the middle.'

Estelle ran from the room, tossing her damp red hair behind her.

'And close the windows and the shutters.'

Alice leaned on the bed and stooped and picked up the pewter chamber pot. She went to the window and emptied it and banged it on the sill like a gong.

'Cockaigne! Cockaigne! Hear your mother!'

Her voice was made weak by time and fate, yet all her inner power flew on its wings. Carla's blood ran cold. The voice resounded from the walls of the yard and fell upon the revelry like the curse of some Devil-haunted dam. Alice let the pot fall from the window and leaned both hands on the woodwork. Her head dropped between her arms and she wheezed in deep breaths. Carla put her hand on her back. She felt the bubbling in Alice's chest. Amparo blinked and stared up at Carla. Alice rallied and rose up again, and by now the yard was silent but for the crackling of the fires.

'Can you hear them? Them as hate us? Them as always hated us?'

Carla listened. She heard the distant sound of feet marching in double time.

'To the tiles my children. Judgement is here. To the tiles. Make them rue the day they dared to set foot in Cockaigne.'

Alice sagged, spent.

The crowd started to move.

Voices rose: in dismay; in doubt; in rage.

Youths broke away and ran for the doorways.

Carla took Amparo in her left arm. She ducked her right shoulder under Alice's armpit and wrapped her free arm around her. She carried her to the chair and sat her down. She poured a cup of wine and put it in Alice's hand. She went back to the window.

The feasters, leaderless, had broken up into knots of uncertainty. Darkness was almost complete, its shadows made blacker by the glow and flicker of the fires. Carla couldn't see Papin, or Antoinette. She saw Hugon shout at some lads and they followed him as he ran into a doorway. She couldn't see Grymonde.

The whole yard lit up to a volley of musketry.

Plumes of powder smoke rolled into the crowd and bodies hurtled into their fellows and splashed into the puddles, men and women both. Panic swept the courtyard. A rush for every doorway and alley. The musketeers ran to deploy in two lines across the southern and western sides of the yard, eight of them in all, and began recharging their pieces. Each musket was defended by a militiaman with a pike. From behind this first wave came a fanatic horde howling the name of Saint-Jacques. They wore white and red armbands, steel helms. With sword, axe, halberd, spear, they fell upon the yard folk crowding the doorways without discrimination, hacking and stabbing at adults and children alike.

Carla saw figures appear on the rooftops on the south side of the yard. They stood and watched, unnerved by the gunfire and the savagery.

Amparo started crying and Carla held her closer.

She saw Grymonde loom from a black slit, his enormous head and shoulders unmistakable. He cut the throats of a musket man and his flanker from behind before they knew they were dying. He ran to the fire pit and raised his arms, bloody knives in either hand.

'Fight for your very souls! For Cockaigne!'

A pikeman lunged at him and Grymonde stepped aside and stabbed him with both blades and hoisted him and rammed him face-down into the coals amid a fountain of sparks. The spit and its roast tumbled over. Flame whooshed from the pit as the pikeman's hair caught and Grymonde let him go. Tiles and slung stones began to hurtle from the roofs along with jeers and oaths of hatred. The pikeman staggered away, lumps of glowing charcoal embedded in his face, his head ablaze. Grymonde took the fallen pike and spun and launched it overarm at a clutch of militia. They scattered and one was impaled through and through, and as the weight threw him down the pike impaled a second through the legs. The lamed one dragged himself clear and crawled, and a woman darted from the shadows and stabbed him in the neck.

Grymonde looked up at Carla. He tossed his chin at the front door.

Carla walked to Alice and kissed Amparo, who still cried, and though it tore at her innards she put the babe in Alice's arms and hurried from the birthing room.

Her belly cramped and she ignored it. The stairway was dark; a yellow glow from below. Her hips were stiff and she had to lean on the wall. Towards the bottom she lost her footing and slid down the last few steps on her arse. She thrust herself to her feet and staggered across the kitchen.

She saw Estelle who stood looking at the cards still spread on the table.

'Grymonde is here. Help me open the door.'

Gunshots boomed outside, individual fire. Estelle sprinted ahead of her and drew the lower bolt. Together they lifted the heavy bracing timber. Carla wondered how the child had managed it alone. She pulled open the door and Grymonde barged in as a musket ball threw splinters into his neck. As he shut the door, Papin threw his shoulder against it and stumbled inside. Grymonde restored the bar to its hasps and threw the bolts.

'I didn't find Mattias,' said Grymonde. 'Only the bodies he left behind him. Then I got wind of this.' He turned and saw Estelle. 'La Rossa? My, what a beauty you're becoming.'

'I'm not a Judas,' said Estelle.

'How could you be a Judas? You're the dragon's wings.'

He grinned and stroked her hair.

'Can I have my knife back then?'

Grymonde returned her small knife and she put it in her belt.

'Now, to the roof, all of you. Papin, the sledgehammer there, fetch it.'

Grymonde grabbed a satchel from a peg and shook a purse to show them it clinked and stuffed it inside.

'Papin, stop trembling, these girls shame you. Take the sledge to the roof.'

'How did you get away, Papin?' Estelle stared at him.

'From one *sergent*? Easy. How did you?'

'No more talk,' said Grymonde. 'Action. Action.'

Papin took the sledgehammer and lumbered to the stairs.

'Estelle,' said Carla, 'will you go and tell Alice to wrap Amparo snugly?'

Estelle ran after Papin. Grymonde put a powder horn and a pouch of balls in the satchel. He took Carla's arm and walked her to the stair. He stopped at the table to look at the cards.

'The Pilgrims of Saint-Jacques are here to rescue you. There's no other reason those fanatics would come. If it were they alone I might let you go, for I believe their motives are gallant, for once. But Petit Christian is out there, too.'

'It was he who hired you.'

'Aye. I still don't know why. He also hired five bravos to capture or kill Mattias. If his master wanted you dead this morning, he's even keener now, though of all that business I'm sure the Pilgrims are ignorant. So, please, to the roof.'

Grymonde scooped the cards from the table along with the rest of the deck.

'I don't think Alice can get to the roof,' said Carla. 'I don't think she'll try.'

'Tell me what was the first card in the earlier spread?'

'The Hanged Man, reversed. Alice called it the Traitor.'

'The dragon bites its tail.' He nodded. 'I've destroyed Cockaigne. And the quester?'

'Death.'

'You're right, Mam won't try, so let her be.'

The windowpanes beyond the shutters smashed. Fists hammered at the door and voices demanded it be opened in the name of the King.

Carla climbed the stairs. She felt something shift inside her.

She pushed herself upwards against the walls on either side. She reached the top and felt something slide down her leg. She ignored it. She shook off a wave of faintness. Her baby.

In the birthing room, Alice sat on the bed with Amparo on her lap. Estelle sat beside her, studying how to swaddle the babe in the shawl. Carla went over and Alice held out Amparo and Carla took her.

'Can I hold her?' asked Estelle. 'I'm clean now.'

Carla overcame her instinct and put Amparo in Estelle's arms. Alice clucked her tongue in gratitude. Estelle took a sharp breath and a great wonder flooded her fierce grey eyes. As if she sensed the immensity and the mystery of her own destiny – her own beginnings and her own future – she and Amparo seemed to dissolve into each other, joined by a love without boundaries, for it had no purpose to explain or define its existence. Carla knew it was a bond that Estelle would never relinquish, for nothing had ever been so truly and purely her own. Estelle looked up at her with a piercing sorrow.

'I was bad, this morning. I said I'd kill your baby. I'm sorry, Carla.'

'You were frightened. So was I. Don't think about it any more.'

'She's so small.'

'You were born in this room,' said Carla. 'Just like Amparo.'

'I was?'

'Yes you were,' said Alice. 'A right little devil from the start.'

Estelle thought about this.

'So am I one of us?'

'One of us? Of course you're one of us. We'd be a pretty poor us without you.' Alice put an arm around her. 'All daughters together. Carla, sit down here, love.'

Carla thought of the roof, the assault below. She sat down and Alice put her other arm around her. Carla felt the warmth of the old, lumpy body; its pain; its joy; its strength. Emotion overwhelmed her.

'Some say living is harder than dying, and you can see their point,' said Alice. 'But not when the living's as good as this, eh?'

She laughed her coarse, hag's laugh. Carla and Estelle laughed, too.

Grymonde appeared at the doorway. He looked at them and his brow furrowed, and, whatever he saw, and whatever it made him feel, it stopped him entering the room.

'We must hurry.'

'There's no hurry here,' said Alice. 'Wait outside.'

Grymonde retreated into the dark.

'Carla?'

Carla looked at her, their brows almost touching, and in Alice she saw no fear.

She saw peace.

'You bore great horrors to come to this home. You brought great beauty with you. You brought life. You brought love. You even brought out the goodness in this mother's son, and that's a feat no one else ever managed.'

Carla looked at the bony girl who cradled her babe.

Carla said, 'No one except Estelle.'

Alice looked at Estelle. She nodded. She turned back to Carla.

'This woman blesses you with all her heart.'

'Oh Alice.'

'May I call you my sister?'

'You are my sister. My mother. My angel.'

'Amparo is still here. She watches over her namesake, now. And fear not, this old girl will be there to see you endure. And you will endure, so don't despair. Mattias will find you. You summoned the pale horseman. He will come.'

'I love you.'

Carla cradled Alice's head and kissed her on the lips. She kept her eyes open, and so did Alice. The world retreated as they filled each other's spirit to the brim. They parted.

Alice turned to Estelle.

'Can this old girl get a kiss from you, too?'

Estelle hesitated. Perhaps she wasn't used to kisses. Perhaps she was overpowered by the blotched, purpled, drooping face that loomed over her.

'Ah, go on, you little devil.'

Alice pursed her lips and Estelle kissed her.

'Now, you'd better go with his majesty.'

Alice gave Carla one last squeeze.

'Charge towards the Fire.'

Carla took Amparo and held Estelle's hand. She looked at Alice.

She couldn't do it. She couldn't leave her. Alice turned her face away.

'Estelle, be a love. Take Carla to the roof. Don't look back.'

Outside the door they found Grymonde leaning against the wall, his eyes pressed into the bulk of his forearm. He carried Altan's horn bow and its quiver of arrows across his back. He heard them emerge but didn't move.

'Well, is the coven over?'

'Tell us what to do,' said Carla.

Grymonde sniffed and swallowed and drew his arm aside. He pulled his double-barrelled pistol from his belt and levered one of the hammers back and forth. He looked at Carla and she saw the pain in his gorgeous brown eyes.

'Do you know how this works?'

'I'm not going to kill with my baby in my arms.'

'I know how it works,' said Estelle. 'You showed me, remember?'

'Of you, La Rossa, I remember everything.'

Grymonde gave Estelle the pistol. She held it against her narrow chest in both hands. The gun appeared huge, but she seemed unimpressed. Grymonde took a cord from around his neck and looped it around hers. The cord was threaded through a winding key. He tucked it inside her frock. Below, the front door rattled with what sounded like the bite of an axe.

'You're going to take Carla to the convent of the Filles-Dieu.'

Estelle nodded. Grymonde looked at Carla.

'As long as no one knows you're there – and you don't tell them who you are – you'll be safe until Mattias finds you. Or I do.'

'I'll have a kiss from you, too, while we're at it,' called Alice.

'Is Alice coming with us?' asked Estelle.

'We'll meet her later on. Wait for me on the roof.'

Carla could not help but steal a final glance.

As Grymonde walked over to his mother, she held out her arms to him.

The climb up two dark flights took more out of Carla than she had reckoned on. Her joints had stiffened since the labour, her stretched tissues felt tight. Each step was clumsy, heavy, uncertain. Estelle came behind her. At the top was a door that gave out into the last of the twilight. Carla leaned against the jamb. Her head swam. She closed her eyes and held Amparo tight. Her pelvis was a mass of dull pain. The pain she could take. The fatigue she could overcome by an act of will; the damaged sinews she could not.

She opened her eyes.

The roof sloped gently to a sheer drop, beyond which raged the madness in the yard. She saw youthful shadows on the other roof-tops, ripping up tiles and hurling them down. A musket boomed and a mass of skirts plummeted earthward. The sound of the axe from below was steady. Carla saw Papin.

He huddled in the shade of Grymonde's tower and didn't look at her.

The tower at close quarters was even more bizarre and ramshackle than it appeared from below. It looked more like something built for the amusement of children than a monument to Grymonde's glory. The three storeys were no more than three huts in a precarious stack, each smaller than the one below. The lowermost was built almost to the edge of the roof, and the whole had twisted and sagged under its own weight. It strained against the ship's cable tied about its middle, which in turn was lashed to an iron ring bolted into the base of the chimney stack.

Carla stooped to Estelle.

'Estelle, do you know where we're going?'

Estelle pointed east and Carla's stomach sank.

Grymonde's roof shortly gave way to a much steeper ridge which

464

connected in turn to other such ridges of various heights and inclines, and with no more logic than the cracks on a broken plate. Generations of improvised building that shared more in common with the works of Nature than those of man. Carla felt a thin carpet of moss underfoot. It was soaked and slippery with rain.

'Have you been this way before?'

Estelle shook her head, unperturbed.

'Then how do you know how to get down?'

'There are always ways down from the roofs. Garrets, windows.'

'You mean we break into a house.'

Estelle shrugged as if this was obvious.

Grymonde arrived. He took off his satchel and tied a knot in the strap to shorten it, and hung it around Estelle's chest. It was heavy but the girl didn't flinch.

'I don't think I can get across these roofs,' said Carla.

'Then I'll carry you. Don't worry. Papin!'

Grymonde went to Papin and gave instructions. He pointed at the section of ship's mast that propped the tower up against the adjoining roof. Papin nodded. Grymonde returned and drew a knife from his boot. He began to saw through the cable.

'Stand back.'

Carla and Estelle retreated. Severed fibres curled from the edge of the blade.

'Now, Papin. Make me proud.'

Papin stepped out and swung the sledge with all his might. The head smashed into the mast where it was fixed to the tower. Nails squealed and the mast shifted. The tower creaked. Grymonde grabbed the almost sawn rope and heaved backwards. Another creak as the pressure eased on the prop.

'Again, Papin. One more for the Infant.'

Papin swung the hammer and the mast shunted again but still held. Papin snarled and put his back into a third swing. The prop splintered free and fell. Grymonde let go of the cable and slashed through what was left with a stroke and covered his face with his arms as the rope snapped and whipped and the tower lurched towards the yard. He charged forward and thrust his fingers beneath the rising edge of the lower wall and sank to his heels. With a single heave of his haunches and back he powered himself upright and toppled his tower from the roof and into the yard.

The crash and shatter of wood swamped the wider uproar.

Grymonde looked back at Carla and grinned and she could see it in his eyes. His moment of triumphant destruction was too great to resist. She beckoned him.

'Grymonde, let's go.'

Grymonde dashed to the edge like a child to see the result.

Papin lunged from the dark and shoved.

The head of the sledgehammer caught Grymonde in the back.

Carla's breath caught in her throat.

Grymonde plunged from the roof without a sound and was gone.

Papin stared over the edge, stunned by what he had done.

Estelle bared her teeth and ran at Papin.

Carla choked off the cry of caution that might have warned him.

Papin sensed Estelle and turned. He raised the sledgehammer over his head. Estelle rammed the gun into his belly and fired. Papin screamed as ball and sledgehammer threw him back into the bloom of his own blood. He vanished into the yard.

Carla turned and looked again across the wilderness of tiles.

A faint mist hung above the moss.

She did not lack the courage to try. It wasn't a matter of fear; from that there was no escape. And though she might find the strength, she did not believe that her body had the agility to navigate the slimy ridges. Pursuit was certain. Her progress would be slow and treacherous. She took two steps and felt the slime break apart and slither beneath her shoes. She didn't think bare feet would be much safer. If she fell with Amparo in her arms; worse, if she dropped her –

She swallowed on a surge of nausea.

Had the fallen tower blocked the door, as she assumed had been Grymonde's intention? How long would it take for strong men to drag away a pile of wood? Had they already got in? Would they dare the mossy tiles? And would they not patrol the streets below, looking for her? Was the convent of the Filles-Dieu not an obvious haven?

Estelle came back. 'Papin was the Judas.'

'You were brave. Put the gun in the satchel.'

Carla closed her eyes. She didn't dare think what she thought.

Amparo – her angel, her daughter's angel – spoke from behind her.

'*Do it. I will go with them.*'

Carla took a deep breath. She had to be passionless. She had to act with the coldness, the boldness, of Mattias. If the Pilgrims had been recruited to save an abducted Catholic noblewoman, Christian couldn't kill her here. She had to do it.

She covered Amparo's face with a flap of the shawl. She didn't dare look at her. If she had, her nerve would have failed. She didn't dare frame in her mind what she was going to do. If she had, she could not have done it. She kissed Amparo's head through the fabric.

'Tell me, Estelle, can you carry Amparo across the rooftops?'

'Yes.'

There was neither doubt nor bravado in Estelle's eyes.

'You won't fall?'

'Of course I won't fall.'

'Will you take her to the convent for me?'

'Yes.'

'Do you have any sisters?'

'No. And no brothers.'

'Neither do I. But we are sisters now.'

'Me and Amparo and you?'

'Yes. You and I and Amparo. And Alice, too. We four girls.'

Estelle's eyes filled and she started to cry. Carla took the hem of her gold frock and wiped Estelle's cheeks. She realised she was crying, too.

'They're happy tears,' said Estelle.

'Mine, too. Leave the satchel here, it's heavy.'

'No, I need the satchel. I can carry it. I'm strong.'

'I know you are.' Carla saw that the argument would take some winning. She abandoned it. 'Take care of your sister. Take her to the convent. Don't tell them what happened here. Say you found Amparo on their step. Do you understand?'

Estelle nodded, as if she were used to much more intricate deceptions.

'Then come back here, but be very careful of the soldiers.'

'They won't see me. If they did, they'd never catch me.'

'Wait for a big man called Mattias Tannhauser. Can you say that?'

'Mattias Tannzer. Is he the chevalier?'

'Yes. He is Amparo's father. He will come. His hair is almost your colour, but not as long. He is fierce and brave, like you, but don't be afraid. Tell him what happened.'

Carla put Amparo in Estelle's arms. Amparo cooed beneath the scarf.

'An angel will come with you. Alice saw her. She'll keep you safe.'

Estelle took all this in with an aplomb that amazed Carla; and gave her hope.

'I'm going to stay here with Alice. Can I kiss you?'

'You're my sister.'

Carla kissed her on the cheek. She kissed Amparo again.

The worst of it was done.

'You're the best sister in all the world,' said Carla. 'Now go.'

Estelle ran away across the roof and Carla could hardly watch, though she did. Estelle took short, quick, light steps on her tiptoes, her bare feet as sure as a squirrel's. She skipped up onto the ridge and kept going at the same pace, Amparo in her left arm, her right hand steadying the satchel behind her back, leaning forward into the motion, flying above the mist.

Carla was flooded with disbelief at what she had just done. She almost called Estelle back. She almost tried to follow her. But the girl's speed was proof that the decision was right.

Carla was about to give in to the sobs that were waiting inside her, when she realised that the night had fallen quiet. Random shouts from the soldiery, but no gunfire, no cacophony. She glanced across the yard. The other roofs were empty. With Grymonde's death, the kingdom of Cockaigne had died, too, and its subjects had melted away into the Yards.

She turned back to watch Estelle. The girl was still running, her wild hair streaming above the wilderness of tiles. Then, as if they had passed through some warp in the smoking night, Estelle and Amparo were gone.

Carla heard footsteps on the stairs.

Carla drew a breath and held it. She let it go. She found her steel. She thought of Mattias. The pale horseman would come. Like her, he charged towards the Fire.

The door crashed open behind her, as if kicked. She turned.

Dominic Le Tellier stopped and looked at her. He held a bloody sword. He glanced to the edge of the roof, and in her gut she knew he was thinking of throwing her off. She heard other, heavier footsteps mount the stairs, the clatter of armour. Her contempt wasn't difficult to summon.

'Captain Le Tellier.'

Dominic shuffled, as if condemned by the sound of his own name.

'Better use your sword, or I promise I will take you with me.'

Dominic's mouth drooped open and he looked at the edge again.

'I already know you for a clown. Now I see you are a base coward, too.'

A huge, breathless figure struggled from the doorway and shouldered Dominic aside. He was a brute, thick in the chest and tall, taller than Mattias. His sword was clean. In his other hand he held a lamp. He saw her and sheathed his sword and pulled off his helmet. He bowed.

'Lady Carla de La Penautier? Captain Bernard Garnier, at your service.'

Carla curtsied and Garnier's brows rose with joy.

'Captain Garnier, you have saved me from a beast too vile to deserve a name.'

Garnier's pride added another inch to his enormous height.

'It was nothing, my lady. You do me an honour too great to be named.'

'Such is the honour you have won. I am weak. Would you help me?'

Garnier was far from refined, but his mind was practical and quick.

'With your gentle permission, my lady, I will light your way ahead of you down the stair, and though I am in no sense worthy, if you feel the need, and with all respect, I invite you to take what support you may deem proper and fitting from my back.'

Carla swayed with fatigue. She had him. She bound him tight.

'A broader back I could not wish for. Please, take this as my token.'

Carla pulled the blue silk scarf from around her neck and held it out.

'My lady.' Garnier looked close to tears. 'I can't, I am not of noble blood –'

'Nobler than most who claim to be so. Take it, captain. It would please me.'

Garnier took the scarf as if it had graced the shoulders of the Holy Virgin. He held it before him, uncertain of how to treat it. Carla took the scarf from Garnier's hand and holding either end she tossed it over his head and across his shoulders. Garnier sank to one knee. Carla clasped her hands, lest he should try to kiss one. She sensed Dominic, dumbfounded, close by, but didn't look at him.

'Now, Captain Garnier, you may guide me down the stairs. I shall need to ride. A wagon, a cart. My ordeal. I am weak.'

'My lady, yes, we have carts, the beggars' carts.'

Carla put a hand on his arm as she walked to the door, and was glad of it. She followed Garnier down the stairs. At the door of the birthing room she stopped.

'I have a lady companion who must come with me, to tend my needs.'

Carla stepped into the birthing room.

As if her very womb screamed in protest, she was pierced by the most awful pang she had known all day. She clutched herself with both arms. She couldn't breathe. Though her heart almost burst inside her chest, though her anguish could not be measured and threatened to dissolve her steel, she determined not to let them see her grief. That was what Alice would have wanted.

She heard a coarse, hag's laugh, just behind her.

That was what Alice did want.

Carla had a new angel at her shoulder.

The old woman sat in her chair, by the bed upon which she had helped so many sisters to bring forth life. Her shapeless body seemed almost peaceful. Her hands were laced across her stomach. Her chin sat on her chest. Her full, purple lips were bowed almost in a smile, as if she were only napping, and dreaming of honeyed quinces and wine. Thus had Alice met Death, with an embrace.

A crimson apron of blood draped her, chin to lap.

Carla turned and looked at Garnier.

Whatever he saw in her eyes drove him backwards.

'Who did this?'

Her voice surprised her. Garnier raised his hands and brows. Clearly, he was not guilty. He looked back at Dominic Le Tellier, who clearly was.

'This woman was my mother.'

Dominic scoffed. He started to speak. Carla cut him off.

'You base cesspit trash. I will see you hanged for this cowardly murder.'

Dominic essayed a smirk of defiance. Carla saw his fear.

'Believe it, knave. If I have to kneel before the Queen and pledge her my soul.'

'My lady,' said Garnier, rising to his part, 'would you like her body taken to church? I can have her rest in Saint-Jacques itself, if it should console you.'

'No church stands that is worthy to house her bones. Leave her as she sits.'

Carla swept past them and down the stair.

She paused in the kitchen where she and Alice had sipped rosehip tea. She saw the deck of cards on the table. She went over and took them and slipped them into the pocket of her frock. She saw her gambo violl in its case and told Garnier to fetch it. For a moment she almost insisted on staying, though she knew they wouldn't let her. She had felt more at home here, she had learned more worth the knowing than in all the fine abodes she had ever dwelt in. She didn't want to leave its spirit behind. But she didn't need to. Alice was with her.

On the doorstep she stopped as a terrible sound cleaved the night. Her body checked her with a visceral dismay. The sound was a roar of outrage more than of pain, for to the latter he would no more admit than would have Prometheus as the eagle ate his liver. A woman's spite echoed from the walls of the yard.

'There's your Samson for you, you ugly bastard.'

The rage that split the darkness had erupted from the throat of Grymonde.

CHAPTER TWENTY-FOUR

The Yards

The stairwell stank of such noxious filth that Tannhauser worried for the calluses on Grégoire's feet. He set down his weapons by Joco's door. Grégoire knocked.

'Who's that? Jesus wept!'

A cry of pain and self-pity identified Joco and his ribs.

'News from his Excellency Le Tellier! Le Tellier!'

Grégoire did his best and, whether or not the words were comprehensible, his voice wasn't one to evoke alarm. When Frogier opened the door, his sword held down by his thigh, Tannhauser stabbed him through the forearm and twisted and the sword dropped. Tannhauser knocked his tooth down his throat with an elbow strike. Frogier's cap flew off. Tannhauser kneed him in the bladder hard enough to lift him off the floor. He pulled and sheathed the dagger and threw the *sergent* face-down. He took Frogier's knife, and the sword, and checked the kitchen and found it empty and tossed the knife inside.

Frogier regurgitated a copious swill of grey liquid but was too stunned to lift his face from it. Tannhauser stood on his left wrist to splay the hand and stomped the edge of his heel through the base of his thumb. The knuckle popped like a walnut. Frogier screamed and squirmed. Tannhauser bent over him.

'Your archery days are over. The rest of your days are yours to win or lose.'

Lucifer trotted in and busied himself with a frenzy of sniffing and pissing. Frogier's bow and quiver lay at the foot of the stinking mattress. Tannhauser slung them across his chest.

'You, Joco, get up. Take me to Cockaigne.'

Joco, with many groans to demonstrate his valour, propped

himself up on his elbows. 'Sire, I can't walk, it's my back. I believe it's nigh broke.'

Tannhauser swiped his left ear off. He misjudged the keenness of Frogier's sword and cut Joco's shoulder to the collarbone. The wound was nasty but not lethal.

'Get up or I'll hack your feet off and find someone else.'

Joco hauled himself upright and stood with his hands on his knees, wheezing and bleeding. A watchman's lantern hung on the wall: a candle in a glazed case attached by a chain to a stick. The stump had a good few hours in it. He told Grégoire to light it from the candle on the table. The lad had been warned to expect some violence; he handled himself well. Tannhauser told Frogier to get to his feet. He told Grégoire to give the lamp to the *sergent*, and to take the *spontone* and wait for him in the street. He threw the sword in the kitchen. He retrieved the crossbow and let Frogier see the bolt.

'You told Le Tellier everything.'

'Excellency, what else could I do? Please, don't kill me.'

'You can't be blamed for buttering the wrong parsnips.'

'Excellency, I pray that in your wisdom you see it that way.'

Tannhauser heard a dull crackle of sound, muffled by countless buildings but unmistakable. A short volley of muskets, perhaps half a mile to the north.

'Put your cap on. Don't let Joco fall down the stairs. Hurry.'

Tannhauser took the lantern from Frogier and gave it to Grégoire in exchange for the *spontone*. Again he heard the distant pop of guns; individual fire. He kept count while he gave orders. He told them not to speak. He had Joco throw his right arm over Frogier's neck; the *sergent* held Joco around the waist. Joco's rib injury was real; if pushed too hard, he'd curl up and wait to be killed.

'I don't care if either of you live or die,' said Tannhauser. 'Get me to Cockaigne and we'll see how tender I feel. As the *sergent* knows, I'm given to whims.'

The gunfire had ceased. Seven muskets. In the dark, with near twenty steps to reload, there'd be four minutes before the next round.

He set the pair off in front of him and had Grégoire walk behind him with the lamp. They headed due west.

The pace was miserable. Joco moaned with each short step he took. At the first corner they turned north. The musketry crackled again. They seemed hardly any closer and were still on city streets. Tannhauser fought an urge to pursue the gunfire alone. He knew what the Yards represented; he had encountered such warrens in Naples. Their denizens built them into labyrinths as a defence against the law. Sound might take one to within a stone's throw, yet leave one trapped in miles of blind ginnels and winding alleys. The moon wouldn't be high enough to help for an hour or more.

He dropped back a pace and rested the tip of the *spontone* against Joco's back. By means of judicious pricks, and at the price of heightened bleating, he doubled their speed.

They passed rows of shuttered shop fronts and four watchmen, each of whom found it prudent to mind his own business, especially as the *sergent* made no complaint. They passed several taverns and two cross streets. The muskets started to fire again, closer but still too far for Tannhauser's liking.

Seven guns. How many Pilgrims? There was vanity in numbers as well as safety. Forty? There could be twice that; more. Too many to beard, with Carla at risk. He had left Garnier on good terms. Why not join them? Convince Garnier to take Carla to the Temple, and hobnob with the brethren. It would be a sight more glorious than the Hôtel Le Tellier. Dominic would object, but, as Tannhauser would point out, the great Garnier was answerable to no one but the King. Had Marcel told Garnier about the militia slaughtered at the printer's? The story would hardly help persuade the Pilgrims to rescue Carla, and Marcel had a strong reason not to tell it: if Marcel wanted Tannhauser for his own purposes, he wouldn't want Garnier muddying the water with his rage.

'Frogier, what orders did you *sergents* receive concerning me?'

'Excellency, we were to report any sighting and if possible keep a watch on you. It was my sworn duty to –'

'I was not to be arrested?'

'For what, Excellency?'

'Killing nineteen militiamen?'

Frogier laughed with fear.

'No, no, there was no suggestion your Excellency was a felon. Rather that you were urgently sought for high matters of state. Which is the only reason I did my sworn –'

'What do you know of this attack on the Yards?'

'Nothing, Excellency. I was ordered to guard the hovel where you found me.'

'So where is the redhead, Typhaine?' asked Tannhauser.

'Forgive me – I'm addled by pain. She agreed to take Christian to Cockaigne.'

The street began to slope upwards. The gradient was mild but Joco seized the excuse to slow down. Tannhauser jabbed the spear into the dark stain on his shirt. The street narrowed. Three men stepped from a tavern, a few steps beyond Frogier. Their bulk blocked the way. They turned to study the strange procession and saw Tannhauser, naked to the waist and festooned with weapons. They'd had their share of wine but Tannhauser sensed no belligerence. He let Frogier feel the spear point.

'Good evening, lads. The *sergent* here will pay an *écu d'or* to any man can guide us to Cockaigne. Are any of you willing?'

Two of the men looked at the third, who wiped his mouth on his wrist.

'No man here knows the way.'

'Will you step back into the tavern while we pass?'

Tannhauser didn't want them behind him. He prodded Frogier.

'The *sergent* will buy you a jug. A deep one.'

Frogier fumbled in his pocket with his good hand. He produced two coins and held them out and the third man took them. The men went back inside. Tannhauser told Grégoire to watch their backs and pushed on. They crossed another street and beyond it the hill became steeper. They headed east a short way, then turned north into an alley too cramped to permit two men abreast. The stench worsened.

They were in the Yards.

'Joco,' said Frogier, 'hold onto the back of my belt.'

Joco did so and they continued upwards. The alley wound about, east and again north. The next round of musketry was overdue. Was the engagement over? Tannhauser's impatience intensified. He had to reach Cockaigne before they left.

Joco stopped with a grunt up ahead of him. Tannhauser jabbed him. The instant Joco squealed, Frogier made his move: he spun and shoved Joco backwards with all his weight. As the spear tip slid in between the ribs, Tannhauser pulled it back, but the body was falling, down the slope, head arched backwards with the force of Frogier's charge. He let go of the shaft and stepped back and the counterweight spiked into the mud. Joco impaled himself through the lung.

Tannhauser raised the crossbow as Joco twisted and fell and shot the black shape lunging for the gloom. Frogier sobbed and dropped. Tannhauser pulled the *spontone* from Joco, who was racked with wet coughs. He stepped over him and beckoned Grégoire to follow with the lamp.

Frogier was doubled over on his side, weeping. The bolt had disappeared through his lower back. Tannhauser shoved him supine with the spike. The tip of the bolt stuck eight inches clear of his stomach. Tannhauser propped the *spontone* and the crossbow on the wall of a mud hovel. Tannhauser stooped and took Frogier's cap from his head. He wrapped the cap around the bloody bolt head and ripped the shaft free of his entrails. Frogier screamed. Tannhauser unbuckled Frogier's belt and stripped it off.

'Grégoire, where's your hellhound?'

Gregoire lifted the lamp and pointed. Lucifer stood with his ears cocked, watching Joco's liquid gasps as if awaiting the chance to lick the blood from his beard.

'Leash him with this. Let's hope they set fire to their own dogs.'

Tannhauser gave Grégoire the belt. He righted the bent tin fletchings and found them serviceable. As he drew and reloaded the crossbow, he looked at Frogier.

'Did you tell Marcel the children were important to me?'

Frogier sobbed. 'I told him you loved them.'

477

'And what did Marcel say?'

'He said: "Good."'

Squatting on a dunghill of hate.

The hatred was Marcel's.

The hatred was for he who loved the children.

He who loved Orlandu. And, above all, Carla.

Tannhauser took up the *spontone*. He looked at Grégoire.

'Let's see if Lucifer can guide us through Hell.'

He stepped over Frogier, pallid and shivering in the lamplight.

'Excellency, don't leave me here. In ten minutes they'll have my clothes.'

'You lived like a pig. Die like one.'

They followed the alley until it widened and forked in four directions near what seemed like the crest of the hill. There had been no more gunfire, but, above the prevailing stench, Tannhauser at last smelled powder smoke. Down two of the forks, he sensed as much as saw wider spaces, the courtyards of lore. The dimmest of yellow lights glimmered here and there. It was quieter than it should have been, perhaps on account of the battle. He sensed they were being watched. There wouldn't be many guns out here, if any, but there'd be arrows, stones, roof tiles. The lantern would give them a target.

'Grégoire, give me the lantern. Go out in front with your dog.'

He took the stick of the lantern in the same fist as the *spontone* while Grégoire murmured encouragement to the cur. The cur lunged off down the left-hand fork. They started across the yard. Within paces Tannhauser heard a dull hiss and he jumped forward, ducking his head, and half-turned his back towards it. The slinger was either lucky, or good enough to lead his target. The stone hit Tannhauser in the outer wing of his back muscle, just below his left armpit. He had taken musket balls that had stung less.

'Run, Grégoire. Hold your arm over your ear.'

They ran as more stones sang and cracked into the walls beyond them. Jeers came, too, boys doing their job, defending their ground.

Tannhauser heard a thump and Grégoire staggered but didn't fall and kept on running.

They reached the alley on the far side without further injury. The yard boys would pursue; for such were the joys. With the alley to funnel their sling stones, the prospect was uninviting. Tannhauser halted, propped the *spontone*. He felt a trickle of blood down his loin. He gave the lantern to Grégoire.

'Were you hit?'

'Only the satchel,' said Grégoire.

'Keep going. Wait around the next bend.'

Tannhauser watched the boys howl across the yard in a pack, seven- or eight-strong. He could have let them crowd the alley, and there have slaughtered enough to send the rest home; but at twenty feet he stepped out and let them see the steel of the crossbow.

The gang were good. Instead of stopping in a bunch they scattered like deer. In a twinkling he could see not a one of them. He retreated into the alley.

'Go back the way I came,' he said, 'and on my honour you'll find a dying *sergent* with a pocketful of gold.'

'On your honour?'

'Why not bend over and we'll kiss the back of your bollocks?'

Laughter.

Tannhauser joined in. They heard him and theirs stopped.

'The low-hanging fruit lies yonder, lads, and its taste will be sweet. Take a dainty profit before some other does. Come this way and you'll harvest only pain.'

He heard whispers. An aimed stone skirred from a wall and into the alley, but its force was spent and it missed him. Even so, he admired the intention.

'Your spleen is manly, so here's another bargain. I seek my friend Grymonde, the mighty Infant, in Cockaigne. Take me there and I'll pay you well.'

'The Infant's dead.'

'No he's not, not for sure.'

'They said he was shot and fell from the roof.'

'So what do they know?'

'To Cockaigne will do,' said Tannhauser.

'How do we know this *sergent*'s there?'

'He left his black guts on this quarrel. Take a sniff.'

Tannhauser stuck the crossbow out into the lesser dark. He heard quick steps.

'It's bloody all right! Fresh as paint!'

'Why didn't you take his gold, then?'

'I'm in haste and I've gold of my own,' said Tannhauser. 'But the *sergent*'s will spend easier than mine, and the prize is not to be counted in gold alone, for he's still alive. You can peel him like an apricot and spin the tale round your kitchen fires for the rest of your lives.'

Bare feet slapped the mud. Two shadows dashed away along the wall. Their comrades gave chase. Down the alley, Tannhauser found Grégoire.

They pressed on.

Lucifer led them with confidence through a bewilderment of twists and turns, pausing here and there to sniff or void. No passage they took deserved the name of 'street', but for the Yards such they were. The firework tang of gunpowder got stronger. Beyond the next row of dwellings Tannhauser saw a pillar of smoke. Flares of sparks flew up into the night. He caught another smell and realised why Lucifer's progress had been so unerring, whether the cur was a native or not. Roasting pork. Then a more acrid whiff of burned hair. Perhaps it wasn't pork. At the next corner he told Grégoire to restrain the panting dog and wait. A short alley gave onto the south side of another courtyard.

He had found the Land of Plenty

There were plenty of bodies. Men, women, youngsters. Some lay crumpled where they had dropped from the rooftops; others were heaped in doorways or sprawled on the open ground. All appeared to be denizens of Cockaigne. None moved or groaned; but the militia had been practising on the wounded all day. Several braziers burned and a brick fire pit glowed. Trestles; a barrel of wine; spilled dishes. A feast interrupted. Of the militia themselves there was no sign beyond the slaughter they had left behind them.

Tannhauser had missed this chance.

His purpose had not wavered since he entered the city. He wanted to be reunited with Carla. He wanted to make sure that she was safe. He had been in no hurry to kill Le Tellier, and, had it proved the price of her safety, he would have foregone the pleasure altogether; or at least until he could return to Paris alone. But Le Tellier had just changed from a dog snapping at his heels to a citadel standing in his way. Now he would have to take it by force of arms. He wondered if the riddle, to which Frogier had supplied the key, might guide his assault.

Marcel Le Tellier wanted him to suffer.

He aimed to punish Tannhauser's loved ones as the worst way to punish him.

For the moment it did not matter why; so Tannhauser wasted no thought on speculation. If he didn't know already, Marcel would want to find out if Tannhauser was alive. His minions would find the headless harpist; the chapel of dead assassins.

And then Marcel Le Tellier would be afraid.

Le Tellier had expected to savour his vengeance at a distance of half a thousand miles. He had expected Tannhauser to get the news of Carla's death in some weeks' time. He did not even need to set eyes on him; he did not need to see him suffer, but simply to know it. For Marcel it would have been enough to know that Tannhauser, faceless, would grieve until the day he died, tormented by the knowledge that his wife had died alone, and in pain, and in terror, and without him.

The wheel of the riddle had turned yet again.

Tannhauser didn't doubt that the plot to murder the symbol and start a war was real, and an element of Le Tellier's intention. The man was a Catholic fanatic. The political logic grasped slowly by La Fosse, and instantly by Paul, held true. Two birds with one stone; but the second bird was not the one Paul had imagined. The second bird was Tannhauser's heart. The political and the personal. His instinct that morning had been both right and wrong. The plot to assassinate Carla had been personal; but the reason, and the target, was not Orlandu, but Tannhauser.

Marcel liked his revenge packed in snow. Tannhauser preferred it piping hot, but, perhaps for that reason, he understood and was impressed. The patience. The foresight. The discipline. A tick lived for years on the tiniest drop of blood, clinging to a blade of grass until a bear or a dog walked by, whereupon it struck and glutted itself, bloating its being with enough to sustain it for a lifetime. Thus had Le Tellier survived on his drop of hatred; thus did he intend to feed on the thought of Tannhauser's pain.

A man, then, who placed his faith in design; in reason; in cleverness; not in boldness or passion. A politician; not a warrior. Not a barbarian; a chief of police.

Marcel Le Tellier didn't live on hate alone. A Caesar adored his empire. In both the personal and the political intrigues he had taken every precaution to protect his position. Much as he might feed on his various hatreds, he needed power even more. Most of all he wanted to live. A man who truly loved power – or hate – would risk his life for either, and Le Tellier, with efforts strenuous and scrupulous, had not.

Tannhauser looked at the bodies of those who had died on Le Tellier's behalf; he thought of the many more who were decomposing all over the city.

Marcel Le Tellier was a coward.

When he found out that Tannhauser was alive and at large, he would keep Carla in pawn, as he had Orlandu. He would use them to manipulate his foe. To bargain with him. To play on his love and his fears. But if Le Tellier won, both Carla and Orlandu would be killed anyway, as Paul had said, to wipe the slate clean.

As a matter of both temperament and logic, Tannhauser scorned all such bargains and such fears. He had nothing to lose. Marcel Le Tellier had gambled everything, and a man who went into a fight with that much to lose had already lost.

Tannhauser studied another figure in the yard. As far as he could see, the only one still breathing. He was a big man: big in the shoulders, big in the skull, big in the thighs; big in his pride and big in his fall.

He knelt in the red glow thrown by the fire pit, his hams on his heels, his arms bound behind his back, his head bowed down on his enormous chest like some chastened and penitent boy.

The Infant.

Grymonde, King of Cockaigne.

The yard was scattered with fragments of broken roof tile and up above there yet lurked a lithe shadow or two. In one far corner sprawled a vast heap of wooden wreckage.

Tannhauser raised his weapons aloft in what he hoped would be read as a sign of peace by the lurkers. The sling stone lodged in his back tugged and he felt a fresh trickle. He walked into the yard.

A dead woman knelt at one end of the fire pit, the upper half of her body burning on the coals. She was the source of the smoke. He could see from the shape of her begrimed ankles that it wasn't Carla. The smell of charred flesh and bone was nauseating. He lowered the *spontone* and pitched her from the pit with a hiss and crackle of fat. The corpse fell on the far side and lay smouldering. Beyond her lay the remains of a roast pig.

Tannhauser turned to the kneeling giant. On his back was a quiver of arrows and the horn bow that had belonged to Altan Savas. His scalp gaped open and oozed black gore. A shard of timber jutted from his outer thigh. He seemed near insensible.

'I'm Mattias Tannhauser.'

Grymonde mumbled into his chest. Tannhauser stepped closer.

'I've come to parley with the Infant.'

'All you have found is the Traitor.'

The voice rumbled with anger and shame. He didn't lift his head.

'Is Carla alive?'

'She was hale the last I saw of her.'

'I'm told you love her.'

Grymonde gave a coarse laugh.

'Aye, we've both of us had our hands between her legs.'

Did the man want to die? It was hard to tell; he hadn't yet looked up.

'Can I catch the Pilgrims before they reach the Hôtel Le Tellier?'

'No. They were keen to get back to civilisation, where their victims don't bite back.'

'Why did they spare you?'

'Spare me what?'

Grymonde raised his face towards Tannhauser.

His eyes had been bored out with something hot. The roasting skewer. His cheekbones, and the rims of the empty sockets, were blistered and deformed, the lids puckered and shrivelled like melted wax. They must have scooped out the burned eyeballs, for of them there was no trace. In places the orbits were charred to the bone. His pain must have been extreme, though his shame seemed to grieve him more.

'Did they enjoy themselves?' asked Tannhauser. 'Did they have a good laugh?'

'Does it please you, too, to mock me?'

'I seek to gauge the depth of your rage.'

'How deep is the ocean wide? How deep run the bowels of Hell?'

'I came in hope of finding my wife. I'll settle for finding a comrade.'

The grotesque features twisted in confusion. He choked a grunt of agony.

'You came here to kill me.'

'If revenge is not your balsam,' said Tannhauser, 'I can do you that favour.'

The Infant grinned. His teeth were hugely gapped.

'She promised me the Devil's own. She knows her man. As to balsam, give me my knives and cast me amid the throng, and see what riot a blinded bull can run.'

Tannhauser turned. Grégoire stood at the mouth of the alley, battling to restrain his dog. He beckoned him. He saw a line of youths, girls and boys both, holding slings, cudgels and blades. He glanced up and saw the shapes of others cut out against the stars.

'Your friends suspect my intentions, and they look staunch.'

'Children of Cockaigne!' the man's voice was thunder. 'We have a new brother!'

'This is my young friend Grégoire.'

'Two new brothers! Brave Grégoire! And Mattias Tannhauser, of grim and murderous repute!'

Grymonde turned his face towards Tannhauser.

'These bonds gall me more than the burns.'

Tannhauser laid the *spontone* on the ground. He removed the bolt and laid the crossbow by the spear. He grabbed the thick splinter in Grymonde's leg and braced the thigh with his left hand. He hauled the shard free and tossed it in the fire pit. Grymonde made no sound. The wound leaked a thick black ooze.

'The tower broke my fall. The only good use it was ever put to, apart from smearing a brace of Pilgrims into the mud.'

'That bow belongs to my friend Altan Savas.'

'They left it as a jest. Petit Christian. He said the image of the blind archer was poetic. It wasn't that turd's idea to take my eyes, but he gave the order.'

'How many did Altan take with him?'

'Six.'

'You got off lightly.'

'Another heartbeat and he'd have done for me. Strange, eh? Another heartbeat, and all these hearts would still be beating.' Grymonde tossed his chin at the dead he could no longer see. 'How many hearts have you stopped, today, chevalier?'

'Today isn't over.'

'You're not the type to leave the count to God.'

'I can think of only one with a chance to reach His gates.'

'Indulge a blind archer.'

'Since I got out of bed, call it forty-five.'

'Hellfire. Poor Paul.'

Tannhauser slit Grymonde's bonds. He handed the dagger to Grégoire.

'Go and cut us some fat meat, then help yourself.'

Grymonde rose to his feet, allowing himself some groans at the stiffness.

'I'm taking the bow and quiver,' said Tannhauser.

'They're no use to me.'

'Hold still.'

Tannhauser manoeuvred the weapons over Grymonde's head.

'I'll have the thumb ring, too. It's on your finger.'

'I don't remember which hand.'

Grymonde fumbled, found the ring, handed it over.

'Have you a woman handy with a needle?' asked Tannhauser.

'For a man whose wife is in the hands of swine, you don't seem overly troubled.'

'We could both use some stitches.'

'What thorns await that little wren indeed. Hugon! Are you alive?'

Heads turned this way and that. A bent man of middle years answered.

'He's not here. Some as got shot on the tiles are still up there.'

'Who's that? Andri? Tell Jehanne she has some needlework to do. And bring me some knives. And some chairs. And don't tell me that barrel is empty or there'll be woe.'

They filled their bellies with pork and a wine of exceptional quality. Courtesy of Grégoire, the bald dog ate as well as they, while a pack of curs emerged from nowhere and petitioned the hare-lipped deity without satisfaction.

'You said Carla was hale the last you saw her.'

'Just before they cored my right eye.'

Tannhauser flinched at the thought that Carla had witnessed it.

'Her face was the last thing I'll ever see,' said Grymonde. 'Given I've cheated the pale mare for more years than I deserve, it was worth getting blinded for.'

'Beyond basking in her gaze, did you note aught else?'

'I'd say she had Bernard Garnier on a tight leash.'

Tannhauser considered the politics. An excellent stratagem.

He said, 'I'll drink to that.'

'Aye. Who'd have thought we'd have something in common with that big fart?'

Tannhauser laughed and so did Grymonde, until the burns stalled him.

'Did Carla say anything?'

'She said, *Alice is with me.*'

'What did that mean?'

'It means they killed my mother.'

Tannhauser said nothing, his own memories stirring in the dark.

'I'll thank you to keep your pity,' said Grymonde.

'None was felt nor offered, nor will be.'

'Good. After that, they ran. They'd won, but they knew they hadn't conquered.'

Every facial gesture, every word, caused Grymonde's seared nerves to jump in agony. Apart from muted gasps, the man made no complaint, but Tannhauser could see the burns were driving him to distraction. He had known many men thus scourged, such as Le Mas on the blood-caked rubble of Saint Elmo's. Even such as he, the stoutest who ever wielded steel, could find their senses overwhelmed, and of those Grymonde was short already. From the pocket sewn into the inner face of his belt, Tannhauser dug out a pill of opium. It was wrapped in a patch of oilcloth, which he peeled and discarded.

'Swallow this, with some wine. The taste is bitter but worth the bite.'

He put the soft black pill flecked with gold into Grymonde's palm.

Grymonde rolled it between finger and thumb.

'What is it?'

'It is a Stone of Immortality. A physic of my own confection but devised by Petrus Grubenius, after the discoveries of Paracelsus.'

'Yes, yes, I'm sure. What's in it?'

'It will give you a glimpse of what it's like to exist as pure spirit.'

'My mother gave me such glimpses all my life. I ignored them. What's in it?'

'Brandy, lemon oil, flaked gold –'

'Pah.'

'But mostly it's a ball of raw opium –'

Grymonde popped it down his throat and swilled wine.

'Is one enough? For a man of my constitution?'

'We'll see.'

A brisk woman called Jehanne turned up and dug an oval pebble from Tannhauser's back and closed the wound with a sail-maker's needle and thread. She did the same for Grymonde's scalp and thigh, the bone of which appeared sound, and for some gashes over his ribs. Jehanne dabbed the burns to his face with a calamine salve, the white streaks of which augmented the unnaturalness of his features and filled his vacant orbits with a ghostly glow. No artist ever painted a more demoniac visage.

'What do you know of the Hôtel Le Tellier?' asked Tannhauser.

'Naught worth stealing in there, naught worth the effort. Fifteen rooms, cellar to roof. Marcel lives alone – but for his valet, his cook, his housekeeper, Sergent Baro, and sometimes his son, Dominic, who's a –'

'I know Dominic.'

'Dominic left my house with Carla and Garnier. Likely it was he killed Alice.'

Grymonde clawed his fingers.

'The Hôtel Le Tellier,' said Tannhauser.

'Of custom there's a lit lantern above the front porch, where a *sergent* stands watch, not to defend Le Tellier's person – for anyone grand enough to assail one so grand would use more subtle means, and what's a *sergent* but a sack of yellow shit? – but to ward off beaten wives and drunkards, and other rabble fool enough to seek justice at his door. The Châtelet's three minutes at a run, ten to get help. At the back stands a high wall and an iron gate, and a door stout enough to stand a cannon shot. The door to the cellar matches it. The ground floor windows there are barred. What strength protects him tonight, I don't know.'

'Marcel can't imagine the strength it would take to stop me, and so it won't be there.'

'No one's ever dreamed of sacking a *commissaire*'s *hôtel*, except me, and even I could see no point to it.'

'We have a point tonight,' said Tannhauser. 'As to doors, I understood this was a den of thieves. Have you not yet learned how to pick a lock?'

'I can pick any lock in Paris, blind. Andri! What if the door's bolted?'

'The city's in chaos,' said Tannhauser. 'Marcel is the chief of police. There'll be comings and goings. The inner guard won't bolt the door between every knock, and what's a guard but a man looking forward to his bed? You say an attack has never been dreamed of. He's not expecting the Mongols. At worst, he expects me.'

'I doubt even that. Unless he knows, as I do, that you're brain-cracked.'

'Marcel has risen high,' said Tannhauser, 'but there are plenty stacked higher above him, and he has reason to fear their displeasure. He committed many treasons today. He stained his office. He betrayed the will of the Crown. He exploited the Pilgrims' honour and blood. These wrongs he has concealed and must continue to conceal lest he lose his head. He won't ask the Governor to call out his troops, let alone the King his Swiss Guard. And anything less won't be enough.'

'The Pilgrims –'

'He can't ask the Pilgrims to guard his *hôtel*. Against whom? He daren't even call out his own police in any number.'

'Marcel is wily,' said Grymonde. 'You don't know him.'

'I've known many like him and they're all the same. He's grubbed for power and believes that it serves him, but power has no master, only slaves. His power is the cage in which I will butcher him.'

Grymonde pursed grotesque lips but said no more.

'Where is his office?' said Tannhauser.

'On the first floor of the south wing, overlooking the river.'

'Is there a separate stair?'

'No. A landing and a corridor from the main staircase.'

Grymonde sent Andri to fetch his tool bag.

'What if he's prepared to kill Carla, at any intrusion?' asked Grymonde.

Tannhauser was surprised by a surge of cold rage.

He leaned towards Grymonde's scourged face.

'Is Marcel not the sort to pay someone like you to do it elsewhere?'

Grymonde flinched. 'You gamble with her life.'

'Don't claim concerns you have no right to, blind archer, or I'll leave you to bleat for your mother in the dark.'

Grymonde clenched his fists. His eyeless grimace was monstrous.

'She's your wife.' He nodded. The fists relaxed. 'I meant no disrespect.'

Tannhauser swallowed a mouthful of wine and watched him.

Grymonde's scorched, painted and misshapen face twitched. He seemed assailed by many thoughts and many feelings. Tannhauser reminded himself of the man's vile deeds. If all the men he had killed that day were to pool their crimes together, they would unlikely equal the crimes of Grymonde. Strangely, even so, he felt for him. And not because of the man's dire afflictions. If his own path had been dark, Grymonde's had been darker. What they had in common, Tannhauser realised, was that each of them knew that it need not have been so; and that it was not so because of the choices each, on his respective road, had made. Grymonde came to some conclusion and revealed what fragment he felt proper. He grinned.

'You would have liked my mother, Alice. She spoke up for you.'

'I'm honoured.'

'Alice loved Carla.' Grymonde shook his head. 'And Mam guarded her affections, excepting babes. She knew, she'd learned, that to spend that treasury was to exhaust it. Carla's coming was the sign she'd been waiting for. The sign that she could go in peace, because she knew there was at least one other to bear the flame. She was right, as always. There was no hurry. Carla loved her, too.'

Tannhauser did not question these riddles. The Stone of Immortality was working on the Infant's brain. Tannhauser was undecided on the best course to take, after he had settled his affairs at the Hôtel Le Tellier. He and Carla would not be safe at the Louvre. There would be too many lies to tell, too many liars. To claim sanctuary at the Temple would likely require more bloodshed, with her in tow. A different set of lies, too, and there they would stick harder in his throat, though he would swallow them. His decision must wait on Carla's needs. Pregnant as she was, he didn't know how hard she could travel. For himself, he would rather get out of Paris.

'The gates of the city are locked,' he said. 'Do you know any other way out? A smugglers' tunnel or some such?'

'Smugglers don't dig, they bribe,' said Grymonde. 'But the Porte Saint-Denis will open at midnight to let in the meat on the hoof, the grain for the mills. Thousands of animals. Wagons. The Châtelet doesn't control the gates. The Governor's troops and the tax collectors do. Collectors like to collect, if you can pay.'

'I've been gathering wages all day.'

'Aye, I didn't find a sou on those bravos in the chapel.'

'Marcel may have stationed a *sergent* or two, not to arrest me – to take word back, with a view to catching us out on the open road, which would be easy enough. But by then I'll have sheathed my sword in his bowels. It's the Pilgrims' part I can't foresee.'

'You said they aren't his dogs.'

'Garnier is his own dog. The danger is, he may want to bite me.'

'Why?'

'This morning I killed seventeen militiamen.'

Grymonde laughed. He cursed as his blisters excruciated him.

'This afternoon, when Garnier suspected as much, I made myself his friend.'

Tannhauser took out his whetstone and dipped it in his wine.

'Marcel knows I killed the militiamen. If he wants to play out his blood feud in private – as he's so far contrived to do with great care – he'll keep that dagger up his sleeve. If he has to, he'll draw it and tell Garnier, and Garnier is a leader of men in a way that Marcel is not. Garnier is a butcher and he is proud, a man of passion. He believes in himself, and in his purposes. His men believe in him, not in his rank. Garnier is not constrained by politics, and today they are all giddy on the taste of blood.'

Tannhauser refreshed the edges on his weapons. In the light of the coals the people of Cockaigne tended their dead. Lamentations broke out as this or that loved one was discovered.

'When are we going to move?' asked Grymonde.

'When the Pilgrims have had time to get their pat on the back from Marcel. Then he'll dismiss them. He might like them to camp on his doorstep, but it wouldn't be politic.'

'I'm tired of thinking. The cards are in play, so at best it's vanity.'

'The cards?'

'Carla drew them. She drew you. *Anima Mundi* saw you coming.'

The tarot. Carla had been suspicious of the cards, he knew, but for that very reason he was not surprised that she might have a gift for their mysteries. He didn't ask which card she had drawn to represent him.

'I want to kill,' said Grymonde. 'And then die a violent death.'

Tannhauser saw no reason to dissuade him of these ambitions.

'Strange as it may be,' said Grymonde, 'I feel quite cheerful.'

He did not attribute this happy fact to the opium; but that was no surprise.

Distant cries drifted across the sky.

There were still thousands of Huguenots to root out. The streets crawled with murderers. The murder gangs worried Tannhauser a good deal more than Le Tellier did.

'You could hide,' said Grymonde. 'There's places no *sergent* ever heard of. And one or two even Paul never knew.'

'As I told Paul, hiding doesn't suit my temper.'

'Paul likes a good parley. He must have loved you.'

Tannhauser let that one lie. Grymonde had a revelation.

'I need another of your Immortals. This one seems weak.'

His grin, rendered demonic by the whited sockets, suggested the contrary.

'You want a violent death. You don't deserve a painless one.'

'When Carla sent me to find you,' said Grymonde, 'she feared you'd kill me on sight. She gave me a charm to protect me, a sort of spell.'

Tannhauser laid down the *spontone*. He drained his beaker.

'Spit it out, my Infant, or you'll have need of it.'

Grymonde laughed and flinched. He scratched the stitches in his scalp.

'What was it now? A tiny bird. Andri! More wine! A wren. A crown of thorns.'

Beyond Grymonde's bulk, Tannhauser saw a small, slender girl creep into the yard from the east. Damp, curly tresses cloaked her almost to her elbows. A heavy satchel hung at her hip. With both arms she carried a small rag bundle.

'Aha, I have the spell exact,' said Grymonde. '*A new nightingale awaits your thorns.*'

Tannhauser spoke her name without needing to think.

'Amparo.'

'My, my. Indeed it works like magic.'

Tannhauser felt a chill. Amparo was dead. She had died alone, in pain and terror and worse; for he had abandoned her. He had surrendered his weapons in the hope of protecting her; and he had been wrong. Carla knew it all. No. She hadn't found Amparo's corpse. She would never know what it had cost him. Carla had loved Amparo, no less than she loved him. Only Carla knew the meaning of the nightingale.

He grabbed Grymonde by the forearm.

'A new nightingale?'

'Another Immortal, I say. So strong a charm must be worth at least that.'

Tannhauser's fingers dug into the densely muscled flesh.

'Grymonde?'

Tannhauser looked over at the wild-haired girl. Her voice rose.

'Grymonde!'

The girl seemed too overjoyed to dare believe that it was him.

'La Rossa!'

La Rossa's smile was radiant.

Grymonde's joy equalled hers. His smile was horrific, though he could not know it. With his gouged and painted visage he looked like some gigantic and deranged harlequin. He lunged to his feet and turned and threw his massive hands wide. Tannhauser stood up and grabbed his shoulders to stop him; to turn him back; away from her.

'My Infant, let me prepare the girl –'

La Rossa saw Grymonde full-on.

She screamed.

Her badly nourished face was gored by pity.

'Where are your eyes?' sobbed La Rossa. 'Where are your eyes?'

Tannhauser dropped his hands as a sound took him by the throat.

The little bundle that La Rossa carried in her arms had started crying.

CHAPTER TWENTY-FIVE

Mice

P ascale dreamed of Tannhauser.

She had thought of him while she lay on her pillow in the hope that she would, and she did. In certain wild flights, which even in sleep she strove to prolong, the dreams were erotic. Other flights were bloody, the two of them in league, and she loved those, too. In yet others, Tannhauser was wounded and alone, beset by monstrous beasts whose strength, though only thanks to number, exceeded his.

When she awoke, she remembered that his wife was dead. She thought: *I'm almost old enough to marry.* She kept her eyes closed and pictured the battle he had fought on the stairs outside her bedroom.

When her father had experimented with his drawings and carvings for a new typeface, for he thought most barely readable, he would give himself entirely to the moment. Everything he was. Tannhauser did the same – only more quickly, and intensely – when he killed. There was nothing in him but the killing. Thoughts, yes, but all those, too, devoted to that purpose. No fears, no doubts, no pity. Just movement – decision – flowing wherever it needed to, the way a swallow used its wings. It was that beautiful. How could he not love it? How could a swallow not love flying?

He said that seventeen men hadn't stood a chance, and she felt she understood why. It wasn't just that he knew more about fighting. They had brought too much that they didn't need, including each other, and each other's fears. They thought being together was enough. They'd decided what was going to happen, not what to do. Not one of them knew how to decide; not really. They knew only how to get killed.

She opened her eyes on the Mice, who sat facing each other on the second bed, playing some game with their fingers. Pascale lay on her side, watching them, waiting for the heaviness to leave her limbs. She had seen the twins before, on the streets, and had never paid them any mind, any more than she had to the thousands of other children living wretched lives. She recalled what Tannhauser had said, about their courage, and their timber being warped by men, and she felt ashamed. She wondered how a man so steeped in blood might see so much in two so small and so forlorn.

'What are your names?' she said.

They stopped their game as if caught doing something wrong. They didn't speak.

'Do you know how to talk?'

They looked at each other and came to some mutual but invisible decision.

'What do you want us to say?'

'We'll say anything you like.'

'You could tell me your names,' said Pascale.

'Our real names or our work names?'

Pascale remembered. They were trained to please. She didn't like the idea of being pleased, at least, not just because someone felt that they should please her. But she didn't expect she could change them if their timber was warped.

'Your real names. My name is Pascale, my sister's name is Flore.'

'We know,' said one. 'I'm Marie.'

'I'm Agnès. Tybaut said they weren't very pretty names.'

'He was wrong,' said Pascale.

She remembered what Tannhauser had said about Clementine. It was the moment she had known that it was right to love him.

'I would call your names the most beautiful.'

The Mice looked at each other.

'Now you ask me something,' said Pascale. 'Anything.'

'Is the funny man coming back?'

'What funny man?'

Pascale remembered the eggs.

'Tannhauser. Mattias. Yes, he'll come back.'

Pascale tried to sound more certain than she was. And yet, how could he not?

'He always comes back.'

She stretched and rolled onto her back. Flore wasn't there. She felt alarmed.

'Where's Flore?'

'She's working in the other room, with Juste.'

Pascale leapt to her feet and opened the door. The palliasse laid out for Juste was empty. She stepped to the door opposite and grabbed the handle and stopped. She was breathing hard. Flore was her senior by a year, yet Pascale had always taken the lead. Usually, she would not have hesitated, but this was not usually. She felt betrayed. Working? Flore? They'd trifled with boys, rather Pascale had trifled for both of them, but they had never considered more than that. She squeezed the handle and hesitated again.

She was in charge. Tannhauser had left her in charge. He had taken her aside, not Flore, and though he had taken Juste, too, she knew he put his faith in her, not the boy. Juste was too tender hearted to be in charge. But not too tender hearted to be in the bedroom with her sister when he should have been on guard in the corridor. Against her instinct to charge in, she knocked. As she did so, she thought she heard another knock come from downstairs.

'Flore it's me. I'm coming in.'

She opened the door and charged in. Flore and Juste were asleep in each other's arms on the bed. They were both fully clothed. Pascale held her tongue. They looked at peace. They looked lovely. Pascale took some deep breaths. She was about to turn and leave them alone when she heard voices from the street. Rough voices, impatient.

The window was open.

As she walked over she heard Irène say something about Captain Garnier. Her voice was stern; but theirs were harsh. Irène mentioned

Frogier. So did they. Pascale stopped short of the casement and peered down over the edge of the sill.

At the front door stood three *sergents*. None was Frogier.

Frogier had turned them in.

They'd be killed like the rest.

Pascale closed her eyes. Fear filled her chest. Her mind raced. Be clear. Be quick. She was quick. She knew she was. Her stomach convulsed. Her limbs felt like skins of water. She took more deep breaths. Make the fear into strength. Turn the wheel. A fighter's power. But thinking it didn't make it happen. She had to act. As Tannhauser would act. She had to decide.

That was all.

She could do it. She would do it. Because Tannhauser had believed she could do it. That's why he had told her these things. He hadn't told Flore. He hadn't told Juste. He had told her, because he knew she was a fighter. Who in the world would know a fighter better than he?

'I am a fighter.'

Decide and do. Do anything.

She ran to the bed and shook Flore awake and clamped a hand over her mouth. As Flore woke, so did Juste, mortified. He opened his mouth to utter some explanation or apology but Pascale shushed him. She kept her voice low, but she kept it fierce.

'There are three *sergents* at the front door. We're leaving by the back window.'

Pascale ran back into her room, where the window was closed to block out the sound of the drunks across the river. She saw the saddle wallets and the holstered pistols. She saw the rifle propped against the wall. She took the rifle and lowered the hammer to the wheel and laid it on her bed. She wrapped her belt and dagger around her waist.

Her limbs were not watery any more.

'Stand up, now,' she said.

The twins obeyed.

'I'm going to drop you from the window into the garden. It's a game. First Marie, then Agnès. Stand by the window.'

Pascale opened the window. The river was tinged red by the dying sun. On the other side, they were still throwing corpses into the water from the wharf. *That's why they need to be drunk*, she thought. On this side, the banked quays of the Port Saint-Landry were deserted. The two moored barges were deserted, too. She looked down. The drop was further than she thought. She turned to the twins, who stood side by side. She took the first girl under the armpits.

'Close your eyes until I say open them. Agnès, you watch to see how it's done.'

'I'm Agnès,' said the girl Pascale already held. She closed her eyes.

'Then you'll go first, Agnès.'

She sat Agnès on the sill. The girl was even lighter than she looked.

'Tuck your legs up and swing around, outside. Good girl. Now turn over on your belly, I'll hold you, don't be frightened.'

Agnès did as she was told without a murmur and didn't open her eyes. Pascale was glad, yet her gut turned as she sensed why the girl was so unnaturally pliable.

'Good. I'm going to hold you out of the window by your arms. Don't be afraid.'

She held Agnès over the sill by her upper arms and leaned out herself on tiptoes. She lowered the girl one arm at a time until she held her by both wrists.

'Now open your eyes and look down. Can you see the ground?'

'Yes. It's a long way.'

'Not really. If the funny man were there, you could stand on his shoulders. Ready? I'll count to three and let go. One, two, three.'

She let go. Agnès landed like a cat, her hands dipping to the ground, and stood up.

Pascale turned and picked up Marie and sat her on the sill.

'Close your eyes, Marie. Agnès did it easily.'

Flore ran in. She was afraid, very afraid, but had resolved to be calm. She made Pascale remember their father, just before the militia had dragged him away.

'Pascale, we think we should talk to them. They're police, not militia –'

'Take a pistol and give one to Juste. Lower the hammers.'

'But they might only want to talk –'

'If they come up the stairs, shoot them.'

Marie had followed Agnès's example without needing instructions. Pascale held her out of the window and worked her grasp down either arm to the wrists.

'Pascale?' said Juste.

'Now open your eyes and look down. Are you ready?'

'Yes,' said Marie.

Pascale let her drop and she landed as lightly as her twin had. Pascale pulled her head back in and grabbed the wallets. Powder and ball, but there would be no chance to reload. Opium and gold. Better the Mice give it to thieves than the police get it. There was more chance a villain would take pity on them.

Juste stood in front of her.

He was a good man. He was gentle. He was brave. He was the most beautiful. She understood. Perhaps he was right. But she was the fighter.

She was in charge.

'Pascale, think,' urged Juste. 'Tannhauser would talk to them.'

'They'd be afraid of Tannhauser. Take a pistol.'

'Listen, we could bribe them.'

Pascale dropped the wallets into the garden and leaned out after them.

'Marie, Agnès, take these and go and hide by the river. If you see a man come to this window, or the back door, run away. Go home. Do you have a home? Tybaut's home?'

The Mice nodded and picked up the wallets. They staggered across the garden.

Pascale took a breath. She saw the not-far-distant dead wagons.

She was right. Juste was wrong.

'If we run they'll come after us,' said Juste.

'Not if we shoot them.'

'They're *sergents*.'

'I don't care.'

'We can't kill all three.'

'We have three guns,' said Pascale. 'And they think we're children.'

'We are children, aren't we?'

'Why is Irène trying to keep them out? They mean us harm.'

'Then you and Flore go, and I'll talk to them. At least I can delay them. Go.'

Pascale started past him to take the rifle.

Juste pushed her back. He grabbed Flore by her shoulders.

'I love you,' he said.

He hugged her and Flore choked. Juste pushed her towards Pascale.

He walked to the door. Heavy footsteps echoed below over Irène's protests.

Pascale rushed to the holsters for a pistol.

'Flore, take this, like Papa told us.'

Flore ran through the door after Juste.

Pascale reached for the rifle, which was ready to fire. In the gloom of the corridor a blur of motion and noise swept past the doorway, from right to left. Coarse oaths. Juste yelled as he stumbled backwards. A *sergent* pursued him, swinging an iron-bound cudgel overarm. Flore cried out from the corridor.

Pascale couldn't see what was happening.

As she lifted the rifle, the *sergent* staggered back into view, crashed into the doorway, grabbed the jamb for balance. Juste had both hands around the *sergent*'s throat.

Terror pounced.

Pascale was stunned. It sprang from inside her pelvis and howled out of her eyeballs and shredded her entrails on the way. She swayed and dropped the rifle.

Picture it. Picture it.

The she-wolf had her. Pascale closed her eyes and saw her. For a single instant, the she-wolf waited for her. She was magnificent. She peeled back her lips. Slaver spilled through her teeth. Her eyes were blue.

Jump now and I might let you ride.

Pascale drew her dagger and charged.

She ran and ducked as the *sergent* cudgelled Juste on the shoulder and Juste reeled back. She saw only the *sergent*'s body, half-turned towards her, his left side closest. She drove the blade into the gap between his legs below the groin and pierced his inner right thigh and carved outwards with all her might, as if cutting through a wheel of hard cheese. She felt the edge scrape on bone. Blood spurted down her arm and she got out, she ran backwards. The swing of the cudgel missed her head by a foot or more.

She realised why Tannhauser had told her to cut as if the flesh were a stale cheese. In practice, the flesh felt no more resistant than a boiled egg; but had he told her that, she would not have slashed with such strength.

The *sergent* looked down at the waves of blood pulsing over his knees. She was amazed at the speed of it, the sheer liquid life of it, as if it had always yearned to be so free. The *sergent* looked at her. He took a step to the door and stopped and swayed. He tried to raise the cudgel and failed to get it as high as his chest before it fell from his fist. He seemed bewildered that his will now counted for so little. He leaned into the jamb like a drunkard.

Pascale dashed over and stabbed him in the belly and pulled with both hands to slice him sideways. It was tougher than the leg. She screamed to give to herself more strength and she felt the tug and give on the edge of the blade as it arced downward. She dashed back out. The *sergent* slid to his knees.

Sheathe the dagger. Sheathe the dagger.

His bulk blocked the corridor and he turned his head towards the shouts of a second *sergent* trying to get past him. His head flopped. He folded backwards into his comrade's legs.

Pascale grabbed the rifle and fingered the trigger.

The second *sergent* saw her as he started through the door. He was quick enough to spin and rush for the stairs. She charged for the door. As the *sergent* slithered down the stair Pascale levelled the rifle and shot him in the back. The recoil stunned her and a blast of flame blinded her in the same instant. She had held the butt tight against her hip with her elbow, and the rifle hurtled backwards from her grasp. The fingers of her right hand felt numb. The sound deafened her and smoke choked the stairwell. The rifle hit the floor behind her.

She stumbled back into the bedroom, itself polluted, and pulled a pistol from its holster. Her ears rang. She heaved for breath. She felt sick with the firework smell; her legs were unsteady. She blinked and drove herself to focus on the hammer. Her right-hand fingers felt like thumbs, but didn't seem broken. She lowered the hammer to the striking wheel. Pascale pictured the she-wolf. She was still between her thighs.

Pascale decided to kill the third *sergent*.

She dashed back to the door.

She held the pistol in her left hand, supporting the barrel with her right. The smoke was still dense. She leaned against the wall with her right shoulder and started down the steps, the pistol held out before her, each step light and quick and steady. As she neared the bottom the smoke was lighter, swirling away into the house. She saw the hump of a body, unmoving. She heard muffled screaming. Not screams: shouts, as if from a distance.

'He's gone! He's gone!'

It was Irène. She was backed into a corner on the far side of the parlour. Pascale's head stopped ringing. She looked at the front door. It was open. She stepped over the body and dashed out into the street. She saw a figure running west, or waddling. She didn't think she could hit him from here. She couldn't trust the recoil. Decide. Do.

Pascale sprinted after him. She wanted to howl but the she-wolf between her legs was silent and she lengthened her stride to match her. She felt strong. She had never known a strength like it. She bore down on him. Her teeth clenched.

She felt pure. She felt ecstasy.

He didn't hear her coming. She shoved the muzzle of the pistol into his back and before she could fire he turned to look over his shoulder and tripped to the ground. Pascale skipped around him and turned. He was scrambling onto his hands and knees. Cold steel was more certain. She skipped around him again and drew her dagger and laid the gun on the ground behind his feet. As he raised up on one knee and put a hand on his thigh to push, she stabbed him, in and out, in the armpit, and as he clenched she reached over his shoulder and braced the back of his head and sliced the right side of his neck as if it were cheese. Upwards and deep, behind the ear, as with Ebert, until she felt the scrape of the bone.

She stepped back from the spray and shoved him forward.

He quivered and flapped one arm, splashing in the wide black puddle that his blood made, and she took deep breaths as she watched him die. Don't linger. She wiped her dagger on his back and felt the death in him. She sheathed the dagger. She loved her dagger. She needed to learn how to sharpen it. She looked about. They were almost at the edge of the market. The body was too easily seen. A stable. She grabbed the dead man's wrists to drag him to the stable alley. He was too heavy. She squatted and found she could roll him over. Four rolls and he hit a mound of manure by the side of the road. Pascale felt dizzy and closed her eyes. The she-wolf had gone.

She leaned over between her knees and vomited. She felt better. She wondered why she had been sick, for she felt no disgust. She felt glorious. She shook her head to clear it. She had needed a lot of spleen to do what she'd done, but she didn't need so much now that it was. That was why she had puked. Her hearing had returned.

It would soon be dark. They had to run.

She recovered the pistol and ran to the house. She went back inside and saw the second body. She almost stopped herself from looking at it, but made herself not stop. This was her work. She ought to check it. The rifle ball had bored through the *sergent's* upper back and somehow blown apart his jaw. It hung from his face like a piece of broken carpentry. They hadn't come to talk. They had come to kill them. She wanted to spit on his body. Would Tannhauser? He wouldn't waste the effort. And her mouth was dry.

She looked at Irène. She let her see the bore of the pistol.

Should she kill her, too?

Irène saw it in her. She pointed at the door and spoke carefully.

'I can't tell anyone anything he can't tell them.'

'Who?' said Pascale.

'The one that got away.'

'He didn't get away. He's dead.'

Irène took a deep breath.

'I tried to keep them out. I swear it. I told them –'

'Bring us some food. In a sack. Be quick. If you leave, I'll come after you.'

Pascale locked back the hammer of the pistol and climbed the stairs.

They had to run. Where could they run to? The Mice had a home. A room. A street. An alley. Scabs. Pimps. Whores. Let them try. Would Tannhauser find them there? Yes. She'd tell him. The smoke still swirled. She heard Juste crying. She wondered how badly he was hurt. Could he get through the window? They could use the door, but how soon would others get here? *Sergents*, militia.

She saw why Juste was crying.

He was on his hands and knees by Flore's body, staring at her face.

Pascale walked over. Flore was utterly still. Pascale could recognise that stillness now. There was no other stillness like it. A heaviness. A silence. She didn't feel the anguish or shock that she felt she ought to. Perhaps the sound of her father screaming as he burned had drained her of such feelings for ever. They were all walking tombstones. At least Flore had died quickly. If they had captured them, they would have raped her, one after the other. It was better not to feel too much. The feelings didn't achieve anything useful. They just made you weak.

Juste turned his face up towards her. He was stricken.

Pascale said, 'Flore's dead.'

'Are you sure?'

505

Pascale looked at Flore's face. It was half-concealed by locks of bloody hair. She squatted down and put a hand to Flore's cheek. There was nothing inside her, just death. Pascale's heart turned in her chest. She felt her jaw tremble and she clenched it. Flore was gone. She could feel sad later, if she was alive. She looked at Juste.

'She's dead.'

Pascale remembered the melee, the *sergent*'s cudgel.

'She should have taken the pistol when I told her to.'

'What?' said Juste.

Juste stared at her. He had stopped crying. She stared back at him.

'I'm in charge. If you don't want to come with us, you don't have to.'

'I don't want anything.'

Pascale put the pistol on the floor and stood up.

'Let's put Flore on the bed. I'll take her legs.'

Flore was lighter than Pascale expected.

'Flore was a beautiful sister to have. I was lucky.'

They laid her on the bed and Juste took Flore's hand and sat beside her. Pascale looked at the wound. There was a soggy depression in the left side of her head, behind the eye. The blood oozed from rips in her scalp.

'Get the sheet from the other bed. Cover her up.'

Pascale went to fetch the rifle. The corridor was awash with the blood of the first *sergent* she had killed. She took the rifle into the bedroom and wiped it on a pillow and propped it by the window. Juste hadn't moved. Pascale stripped the sheet from the second bed and threw it on Juste's lap. She returned the pistol to the saddle holster. She took the holsters to the window and leaned out.

'Are you still there?' she called.

Agnès and Marie appeared from the dusk. They waved. Pascale waved back. She dropped the pistols to the garden. She got the rifle and lowered it from the window by the muzzle. Its heat surprised her. She dropped that, too.

'Agnès, Marie, do you know how to get home from here? To Tybaut's?'

They nodded.

'Wait for me.'

She turned. Juste hadn't moved.

She went to the corridor and yelled down.

'Irène? Where's our food?'

Irène appeared with a flour sack, about a quarter full. Tannhauser had paid her well. There wasn't time to argue. Pascale held out her hand for the sack. Irène climbed the stairs. She saw blood trickling down and stopped. She looked at Pascale with hatred. Pascale splashed down the steps. Irène flinched as drops flew into her cheek. She held out the sack. Pascale didn't take it.

'Tannhauser will be back. If you tell anyone about us, he will know and he will kill them, and then he will kill you. I'd kill you, only I don't know if he would.'

Irène still hated her; but she was scared, too. Pascale took the sack.

'Go back downstairs until he gets here. Tell him we'll wait for him.'

'Where?' said Irène.

'He'll know.'

Pascale returned to the bedroom and dropped the sack through the window.

Juste had covered Flore with the sheet up to her chin. He still held her hand.

'Juste, let's go. They came to kill us all.'

'I know. I was wrong.'

'I didn't mean that. I mean they only got one of us, instead of all five.'

'I'm staying here, with Flore.'

'Others might come. We don't know.'

'I hope they do.'

'I love Flore, too.' Pascale almost said *more than you do*. 'She

was better than me. Just as Papa was better than Tannhauser. Flore
and Papa are dead. You're better than me, too. But I need you, so
you mustn't die.'

'I was meant to die last night, in the Louvre.'

'You didn't. Flore was meant to die this morning. She didn't.
And in all this –'

Pascale wanted to cry and decided that she wouldn't.

'In all this you fell in love and so did she.'

Juste choked. He turned away.

'Come with me, Juste. Tannhauser will find us. He won't give
up. But until he does, I need you. The Mice need you. Your
Mice.'

She took the cap from the dead *sergent*'s head and dipped it in
his blood. Papa had taught her how to print in black; Tannhauser
in red. She went back into the bedroom.

She painted a word on the wall: MICE.

She went to the window. She saw militia on the far bank
peering towards her in the failing light. They must have heard
the rifle shot. She put one leg over the sill and then the other.
She twisted around onto her belly, weight on her elbows. She
could have made the drop. But if Juste would let go of Flore,
perhaps he could leave her.

'Juste, I hurt my hand. Help me get down.'

She waited.

Juste bent over and kissed Flore. He covered her face. He walked
away.

He took Pascale's hands and lowered her and let go. She landed
safely. She retrieved the rifle and holsters. Juste jumped down. He
took the sack and saddle wallets.

They joined Agnès and Marie.

They ducked low and headed east along the river bank.

Pascale stopped in the lee of the second barge, where the
militia on the Place de Grève couldn't see them. It was stacked
with sacks of charcoal from the forests upstream. She gave the
rifle to Juste and rummaged in the wallets for powder flask and
ball.

'Can you reload it?' she asked.

Juste nodded. He was deep in melancholy and seemed glad to have a task.

'The pistol, too?' he asked.

'I didn't fire it. Are you hurt?'

Juste rolled one shoulder and shook his head.

Pascale sat on the gunwale and covered her face with her hands to think.

Tannhauser would come back to Irène's. He would find Flore. He would see the message. He would see all that had happened and how. He would follow. He would try to think as she, Pascale, thought. And if he saw what had happened, he would know that she was thinking like him. The rifle was a burden. She had to leave it. The pistols, the opium, the gold, she would take. They would go to Tybaut's. Tannhauser would read the message. No one else would understand it. He would find them there; wherever it was.

She pulled Agnès and Marie close.

'Can we share your room with you? At Tybaut's?'

Agnès and Marie looked at each other, as if they found the idea odd.

'Yes. If you like.'

Pascale took the rifle and stowed it between the gunwale and the sacks of charcoal. The other barge was clean, but the filth hid it better.

'We'll hide in the Terrain until the moon is up.'

'What's the Terrain?' asked Juste.

'Cathedral land. Fields, orchards. It's close.' Pascale turned to the Mice. 'Do you know any secret ways home? By the alleys?'

'Yes.'

The Mice exchanged another puzzled glance. They looked at Pascale.

'But we have Tybaut's key,' said Agnès.

'Good,' said Pascale.

She reckoned it dark enough to move. She slung the holsters

over one shoulder and the sack with their meagre provisions over the other.

'What if he doesn't find us?' said Juste.

'Then we'll be on our own,' said Pascale, 'which is what we already are.'

CHAPTER TWENTY-SIX

Sisters

E stelle liked the roofs. They were a lot cleaner than the street and she didn't meet any people up there. Sometimes other children who could be mean, especially boys, but usually she saw them first, and if she didn't she was usually faster than they were. Or meaner. One time some boys held her over the edge by her ankles, just to make her scream, but she didn't scream, and they didn't drop her. She knew one of those boys and she had told Grymonde what he had done. The next time she saw the boy, he had no ears.

When she thought about Grymonde falling from the roof, she wanted to cry, but she had to look after her new sister, Amparo, and if she cried as hard as she wanted to, she wouldn't be able to keep hold of her, so she didn't.

Amparo seemed to like the roofs, too. Her little eyes were open, looking at the stars, and looking at Estelle. Amparo didn't cry, either. She hadn't seen Grymonde fall, too, and didn't understand what was happening, but it helped Estelle not to. Estelle wondered if they should stay on the roofs all night; there were plenty of nooks up here; but she'd promised Carla. At least, she'd said yes, which was a kind of promise. People broke promises all the time, every day, every hour. Promises were a way to get you to believe a lie. Estelle didn't want to break her promise, because she didn't think Carla would break a promise to her, unless she couldn't help it. Even so Estelle didn't really want to keep it either.

She didn't like nuns.

She found herself a long way from Cockaigne. She found two doors that were locked; then a hatch that was propped open to the air. She peered inside. She heard sniffs and scratches, and saw dark shapes lumped on pallets. Some of the shapes were big enough to be grown-ups and one of them murmured in his sleep. She moved on and found a third door with latch. She opened it and crept down a pitch-dark stair. Every few steps she stopped and listened for anyone coming up from below. All she heard were sounds from the rooms she passed. Down and down they went. On what she hoped was the last flight she stopped as the sole of her foot touched something soft.

She pulled her foot back and listened and heard breathing. She stared down into the dark until a darker shape emerged. Someone asleep, she hoped drunk with wine. She went back up the stair to a small window on the landing. She felt under the sill and found a nook where the slop bucket was stored. The bucket felt empty. She took the bucket halfway up the next stair and left it on a step. She crouched down in the empty nook. She couldn't squeeze all the way in, but far enough. In the dark, he would go right past her, and trip on the bucket. She pulled out her knife and held tight to Amparo.

Estelle crept back down the stair and stabbed the sleeper, in a lump that looked like a shoulder, and darted back for the nook.

She stopped as the sleeper didn't move or make a sound. She couldn't have killed him; it wasn't a deep stab. Maybe he was trying to trick her, but it was hard to ignore a stab, just to trick someone. She went back down and poked him with her foot, and he grunted but still didn't wake up. A lot of wine. Estelle climbed over him, leaning on the rail, and skipped to the front door.

After the stairwell the alley seemed almost light. She wasn't sure where she was. To the left was a real street, which was even less dark. She ran to it and peered around the corner. She was on the edge of the Yards, on the slope of the hill. Below she could see the square tower of Saint-Saveur. The convent of the Filles-Dieu was even closer. The strap of the heavy satchel cut into her shoulder. She climbed a low stone wall and sat behind it and took off the satchel and cradled Amparo and looked at her face in the shadows.

'Amparo? You were very brave.'

Estelle unbuttoned the top of her chemise. Her chest was as

flat as a boy's but the rats sometimes suckled her and maybe Amparo would like to. She put the baby's mouth to her nipple. Amparo sucked it at once and she seemed to like it. Estelle liked it. She loved her new sister more than anything in the world. More even than Grymonde, especially now that he was dead. She cried for a while. She couldn't lose the dragon and her sister, not all at once. Keeping Amparo didn't feel wrong. It felt right. So there had to be a reason.

'You don't want to live with the nuns, do you?' said Estelle. 'I wouldn't. They all wear the same clothes and you can never trust people who do that. It means they'll do what they're told, even if they're told to do something bad.'

Amparo took her mouth from the nipple and cooed and this seemed answer enough. Estelle was sure Carla would understand. She wondered what Petit Christian would do to Carla. He was nasty and did things for people who were even nastier, and they had a lot of men. Carla had sent an angel with them, with her and Amparo. Perhaps Carla should have kept the Angel with her. Estelle wondered if the Angel had made the sleeper stay asleep. She wondered what the Angel was called. Perhaps Angels didn't have names.

Estelle whispered.

'Are you there?'

She felt a shiver. A warm shiver. The Angel was there. She felt better.

'What shall we do?'

She listened very carefully. She heard distant voices, the kind of shouts and screams she had heard all day, but nothing nearby.

'Can you talk? Or do you just watch over us?'

'*Tannzer*,' said the Angel.

Estelle turned. She didn't know if she had heard it inside her or outside, in her ears. A thin ray of moonlight gleamed down from above the Yards. It shimmered.

'You mean Tannzer the chevalier?'

She felt like the Angel nodded, though she could only see the shimmer.

'Carla said Tannzer would come to Cockaigne. Will he?'

'*He'll come,*' said the Angel.

Estelle lifted Amparo and kissed her on the head. She put the satchel back on, this time on the other shoulder. She stood up and looked over the wall. She saw and heard no one. She smiled at Amparo. She kissed her again.

'Don't be afraid, the Angel is with us. We're not going to the nuns. We're going to find Tannzer. He's your papa.'

First she saw the burning torches, then the soldiers, then the carts.

The soldiers were pleased with themselves, Estelle could tell. They had flags and wore red and white ribbons. They thought they were right. They thought they were good. They thought they had done something good. They thought they were better than her, and the people of the Yards, and Grymonde. Maybe they were better. Everyone and everything said so. She knew she wasn't better than anything, even than rats. But if the soldiers were better, better wasn't something she wanted to be. Typhaine, her Mama, wanted to be better, and she blamed Estelle because she wasn't. Estelle's head hurt. She stopped thinking about it.

One of the passing carts was stacked with dead soldiers, and she was glad about that, too. In the second cart were wounded men. In the last cart was Carla.

Carla looked very poorly. Her head was down, as if she was asleep, but she wasn't asleep. Perhaps she was crying, though she didn't think Carla would let the soldiers see her cry. She had hated Carla, for a while, and she shouldn't have done, but Carla didn't seem to mind. Carla was better than anyone she'd ever met, except Alice. Carla and Alice didn't care who was better. They said Estelle was one of us. But who was us? It wasn't most of the people Estelle knew. Even though Estelle loved her, Typhaine wasn't one of us. In a strange way, she didn't think even Grymonde was one of us. Estelle didn't know why she herself was one of us, but she was, Alice had said so; and in some ways, that was even better than flying with the dragon.

The dragon was dead. She didn't want to think about that.

She rocked Amparo against her breast and whispered.

'Don't fret, Amparo. We're one of us.'

She saw that Carla had her arm around the same little girl she had brought with her that morning. But the little girl wasn't one of us, and Carla was, so Estelle didn't mind. Carla was kind, that's why she cared for the little girl. It wasn't the same. Somehow, being kind made Carla stronger; it had made Alice strong too. Was Estelle just being kind to Amparo? It didn't feel that way, because Amparo was her sister, and Amparo was one of us, and the Angel was, too, she was sure of it.

Estelle saw Petit Christian and wished someone had killed him. She wished she had killed him herself, like Papin. Petit Christian wasn't just better, he was evil. She hid in the dark and rocked Amparo and hummed to her until all the soldiers had passed by. The carts turned south into the Rue Saint-Denis and Carla disappeared.

Estelle hurried through the alleys to Cockaigne.

When she poked her head around the corner she saw the fire pit and the braziers, and the shadows of people moving about in the smoky yellow light. Bodies lay on the ground. She heard women crying. She saw boys and dogs.

She saw two big men sitting on chairs.

The one facing her was bare to the waist and he had long hair. His skin shone in strange patterns in the glow of the pit and he had dark pictures carved on his arms, like Altan. His body was splashed with blood. That was why the patterns were strange.

It was Tannzer. She didn't know why she knew it. She just did.

Tannzer talked and listened while he sharpened a huge spear.

Estelle was frightened of him. He was sharpening the spear because he had blunted it with killing and because he was going to kill more. He sat on the chair as if he was the king, not just of Cockaigne, but of anywhere he might be. And not like a king, because she knew he didn't care about Cockaigne or anywhere else. He made her think of Alice, but she didn't know why.

Tannzer had an angel, too, but it wasn't like theirs. It didn't shimmer by the light of the moon but by the red coals of the fire.

Tannzer's angel had black wings. She wondered how he could be the father of Amparo. But how could Alice be the mother of Grymonde? Estelle didn't know who her father was; but lots of girls didn't. Did Tannzer have a father? And a mother? Sisters were easier to understand.

She turned Amparo to face Tannzer.

'Look, Amparo, that's Tannzer. Don't be afraid of him. He's your papa.'

She thought Amparo might cry, but she didn't. She cooed. Estelle wondered what their angel thought of Tannzer, and Tannzer's angel. Tannzer put the spear down and drank from a beaker. The second big man shifted in his chair and waved an arm. Estelle stepped out so that the second man was outlined against the glow. He scratched his head. She knew that head. She knew the feel of the strange ridges beneath its curly hair. No one else had shoulders like that. She had flown all over Paris on those shoulders.

'Grymonde? Grymonde!'

Grymonde stood up and turned around and opened his arms and smiled.

Tannzer tried to stop him, she didn't know why.

She saw Grymonde's face. His smile.

He had no eyes.

Instead of eyes, he had big white dark gaping holes.

Grymonde stroked her hair and held her to his chest and said sweet things in his great rumbling voice, but his words she didn't hear. She smelled his strange smell, the only smell she liked. Amparo cried in the gap between their bodies and Estelle cried, too.

They two sisters cried together, for the chestnut-brown eyes that once had had a light inside them brighter than the sun and fiercer than fire and richer than gold and softer than down. How could such eyes be gone and not be somewhere else? Had the soldiers taken the eyes away with them? Could they be put back? No. Estelle knew no one could do that, except God; and God wouldn't. The white dark holes would never be filled again.

Not even with tears.

No eyes had ever looked at her the way the brown eyes had. When the brown eyes looked at her she felt like the only girl alive. The brown eyes made her feel like the world, and all the rotten things in it, were gone, and that all that mattered was her, and that she was good. The brown eyes made her feel the way she had felt when Alice put her arms around her and Amparo and Carla. So Grymonde must be one of us after all. He had his arms around her, and Amparo, the sisters who cried for his eyes. One of his hands covered her head like a bonnet made out of gentleness, and the other covered her back like a coat made of love. She loved being covered. But she wanted the eyes to be back in the holes.

Amparo stopped crying and so Estelle stopped, too.

They were sisters.

Estelle turned her head to breathe.

She saw Tannzer watching her.

His eyes were shrouded in shadows, but she knew they weren't brown. Even though they were shadowed, they were hard as jewels. And yet they were sad. Grymonde's gone brown eyes had never seen anything but her. But Tannzer's eyes saw everything. They saw her. They saw Grymonde. They saw Amparo. They saw people, and things, and happenings, that weren't even here. Things that had been. Things that would be. Things that might have been, but never would. Perhaps that was why he was so sad.

She knew Tannzer knew who Amparo was.

And because Tannzer was sad, and because he knew that Amparo was his daughter, she wasn't frightened of him any more.

Tannzer didn't move and he didn't speak; he just stood there and looked and knew the things that he knew. Estelle wished she knew them, too, and yet she was glad that she didn't. She knew being lonely. Her friends were rats; and a dragon. But Tannzer was the loneliest person she had ever seen. Tannzer wasn't one of us.

Tannzer wasn't one of anybody.

Estelle felt sad, too.

She felt sad for Tannzer.

She pulled away from Grymonde. The satchel was cutting her

again. She took it off and put it on the ground. Grymonde bent towards her, as if trying to see her, but without his eyes it didn't matter how far he bent down; he couldn't. He couldn't ever see her ever again, and it hurt him inside. It hurt Estelle, too. She looked up into the white dark holes and she saw the bits that were burned black, and the blisters that trickled as if his skin was crying because his eyes could not. She realised it must hurt, very, very badly. She felt deep pain, deep in her stomach, for Grymonde.

It was strange. Tannzer and Grymonde were so big, and she was so small, and Amparo was much smaller still, yet she felt sad for the two big men, and so did Amparo.

'La Rossa, don't go away. I'm still here, I'm still me, inside.'

'I'm not going away, don't be afraid. I can still see you, in the white dark holes.'

Estelle hadn't wanted her mama for a long time. There wasn't usually much to want. But she wanted her now. At least Typhaine could see.

'Did Mama come?'

Grymonde ducked and twisted his head in a circle, like a bull. He scowled.

'I haven't seen her for a while. Don't worry about her.'

'I was afraid she might be a Judas, like Papin.'

'She was a Judas all right,' said Andri. 'Now she's dead, God curse her soul —'

'Be quiet, fool, and be gone,' said Grymonde.

His head lunged this way and that, trying to find her.

'La Rossa? Where are you? Are you there?'

Estelle felt as if her body was empty inside. She hugged Amparo. 'I'm here.'

'Your mama is dead, La Rossa, my darling, yes, but she was no Judas. She was murdered by the same swine as took my eyes. She was a mad and fiery beauty, and she did what she did for love and for hate, not for silver, and for that and all, we must love her.'

Estelle was glad Typhaine wasn't a Judas. She was glad Grymonde loved her.

'Are you there?' said Grymonde.

'I'm here.'

'Don't leave me.'

'I won't. Can I give Amparo to Tannzer?'

'You have the wren? For the thorns?'

Grymonde laughed. Estelle didn't know why. He seemed brain-cracked.

'I have my sister, Amparo.'

'You brought her down from the tiles?' said Grymonde. 'Alone?'

Estelle felt Tannzer's eyes on her. She didn't dare look at him.

'The soldiers didn't see us.'

'My love, my darling, my beauty, yes, yes, give the little wren to her thorns. She is waiting for them.'

'You mean to Tannzer?'

'Yes, La Rossa.'

Tannzer had watched everything in silence.

Estelle turned and showed Amparo to him. She looked at him.

Tannzer came closer. The moon had come up. It shone bright and craggy behind him. He made the Yards seem small. He bent over and looked at the babe.

She saw his face.

She had never seen such a face.

It wasn't that it was strange, in the way that Grymonde's was, yet it had things in it, invisible things, that made her tremble inside, things that made her wish he was her friend. He was wiser than Grymonde and at the same time more wild. He wasn't as brawny as Grymonde, yet he was stronger. He was finer than Grymonde, yet even more like a demon. As Tannzer looked at Amparo his face changed, and the things that had made her tremble went away, as if they had never been there, and Estelle knew she was seeing things in that face that no one else had ever seen before. Because Tannzer's eyes were seeing something Tannzer had never seen before. Only Estelle and her sister could see these things, because Grymonde was blind.

'Tannzer?' said Estelle.

'Aye.'

'This is Amparo.'

Tannzer took a mighty breath and held it. He sighed. He smiled. Some of his teeth were broken. He nodded, as if he had been on a journey for a long, long time, and from a long, long way away, and had finally reached the place he had been looking for. He made a sound and his throat choked. He coughed. When he spoke, his voice amazed her. It was as gentle as he was big.

'Amparo.'

Estelle had never heard such love in one word. Or in many. Tears filled her.

'Amparo.'

Estelle didn't cry the tears. She held the babe out towards him.

'You can take her if you like. Carla said she's yours.'

Tannzer didn't move, for a long time.

He didn't take Amparo. Estelle was confused.

Tannzer straightened up. He seemed taller than before. He looked at her.

'La Rossa, is it?'

'Grymonde calls me La Rossa. My name is Estelle.'

'Estelle.'

She was sure she heard love in that word, too. But how could she?

'You were named for the stars above,' said Tannzer.

'The Morning Star.'

'Call it the most beautiful.'

Estelle's arms shook and she pulled Amparo back to her chest.

'Shall I tell you what Amparo's name means?' said Tannzer.

'Yes.'

'It means *Shelter from the Storm.*'

The name took Estelle's breath. She looked down at the babe in her arms.

'We find ourselves in a world of blood and thunder,' said Tannzer. 'Do you think that little nightingale can shelter such as we? From such a storm?'

Estelle thought about it. She remembered how she had sat on the bed with Alice and Carla, and how safe it had made her feel to be one of us, even though it was a world of blood and thunder. And they wouldn't have been sitting there at all if not for Amparo.

'Yes. She sheltered me and Carla. And Grymonde, too, I think.'

Grymonde made a painful sound. The white dark holes in his face glowed.

Tannzer nodded, as if he had expected as much. He stared at Amparo.

Estelle didn't think that Tannzer needed shelter, but she said, 'I know she'd shelter you, too, if you wanted her to.'

'She has already sheltered me.'

Tannzer looked at Estelle. He didn't look at her as if she was a girl, but as if she was as big as he was. It was a strange feeling. It made her feel stronger.

'Did you know, Estelle, that even in the darkest storm, by day or night, the stars – most of all the Morning Star – still shine above it?'

'No.' She thought about it. 'Because the stars are higher than the storm?'

Tannzer's brow rose. 'You have a rare mind.'

'Is that good?'

'It is marvellous. You are right, the stars are always higher than the storm. And so, if Amparo gives us shelter from the storm, and you, the Morning Star, shine above that storm, what have we to fear?'

'Nothing?'

'I am very happy to know you are Amparo's sister.'

Estelle stared at him. She felt Tannzer had given her something precious, but she didn't know what it was. She didn't feel sad for him any more. He didn't need that either.

'I love my sister more than anything in the world. But don't you want to hold her in your arms?'

'I do want to hold her in my arms, Estelle. More than I want to breathe. But the storm, of blood and thunder, isn't over. Those upon whom it must fall do not even know that it comes. And Amparo will not shelter them. Shall I tell you why?'

'Yes, tell me.'

'Because Grymonde and I are that storm.'

Grymonde let out a roar of violent ecstasy.

'Heaps upon heaps shall I slay. Give me another Immortal.'

Tannzer didn't stop looking at Estelle.

'And because I am the storm, I can't hold Amparo until the storm is done.'

'Because the storm might hurt her?'

'You are a clever girl. Will you hold Amparo for me, then? A while longer?'

'I'll hold her forever if you want me to. I like holding her. I only thought you would want to hold her, too.'

'I do, Estelle. I do. But if I held her, even once, the storm might rage less fierce. And if we are to return Amparo to Carla, as we must, the storm must be terrible.'

'That's what your angel told you, isn't it?'

'My angel?'

'The Angel with Black Wings.'

'Her grandmother had a gift,' said Grymonde. 'She saw what most of us can't.'

Estelle didn't know she had a grandmother. She wanted to ask about her.

'I understand,' said Tannzer. 'Special gifts often skip a generation.'

'We have an angel, too,' said Estelle. 'Carla sent her, with me and Amparo. She has wings of moonlight. The Angel told me to bring Amparo to you, instead of to the nuns at the convent. I hope Carla won't be angry.'

'I agree with you and your moonlight angel. Better Amparo take her chances with us than with those black crows. Carla will be proud of you, as am I. I thank you both.'

Tannzer turned away and picked up the sharpened spear. It had three points, for extra killing. He took hold of Grymonde's right hand and put the spear in it. Grymonde planted the spear and Estelle could see that it made him feel steadier. He touched the longest blade and sucked blood from his thumb and nodded.

'What's in your satchel?' asked Tannzer.

'A pistol.'

'And powder and ball, a purse of gold,' added Grymonde.

Tannzer took out the double-barrelled pistol. He examined it. 'This is a Peter Peck. It's worth a fortune.'

'Perhaps it was,' said Grymonde, 'to the swine I stole it from.'

Tannzer sniffed the barrels. 'It was recently fired.'

'Not by me.'

'I shot Papin,' said Estelle. 'He fell off the roof, after you did.'

They looked at her and didn't speak. She waited to be chastised.

Grymonde started laughing, like a cracked-brain. Tannzer winked at her. She felt good. Tannzer took out a flask, and a ball and a patch, and recharged the barrel.

'Can we come with you?' asked Estelle.

'No,' said Grymonde. 'Wait here for us. You'll be safe.'

Estelle looked at Tannzer.

'I can still fly on his back. I can be the eyes of the dragon, instead of the wings.'

Tannzer studied her. She saw the invisible things that made her tremble. He looked at Amparo. Estelle trembled more. Tannzer poked Grymonde with an elbow.

'What does Estelle mean?'

'I've carried La Rossa on my shoulders, many times, all over the city.'

Tannzer packed the powder flask. He untied the knot in the strap and hung the satchel across Grymonde's chest. Estelle pulled out the key hanging round her neck.

'Can I wind the Peter Peck?'

Tannzer looked at her again, then held the pistol while she wound it.

'Grymonde, in what casket of treasure did you find this girl?'

'That's a tale now known only to me, and I'll never tell it.'

Tannzer beckoned a boy with a harelip. The boy held a bald dog by a leash.

'Grégoire, this is Estelle, and her sister, my new daughter, Amparo.'

Grégoire smiled and bowed. He was ugly, uglier than the dog, but seemed nice.

'Grégoire, I see a kidskin on the table there. Empty it and bring it over.'

Tannzer stuck the pistol in Grymonde's belt.

'The pistol is for Estelle,' said Tannzer. 'If she asks for it, give it to her.'

'What madness is this?' said Grymonde.

'My daughter comes with me,' said Tannzer.

Tannzer looked at Estelle. She held her breath.

'If it is her desire, her sister, Estelle, will come with us, too.'

'No,' said Grymonde. 'She will not.'

Estelle wanted to go with them. The idea made Grymonde suffer, but why? Why did he want her to stay here, with the dead, and without her sister? She didn't dare speak.

'Can children make such decisions?' asked Tannzer.

Estelle almost said, *Yes!* But although the two big men were talking about what she wanted to do, she knew she would have to do what they wanted. She bit her tongue.

'Clearly, they can,' said Tannzer. 'Should we let them? Or should we reckon their wisdom less than ours, here, in the Hell that the likes of you and I have slaved to build around them? I do not know. What say you, my Infant?'

'The Infant does not say.'

'This day has taken me beyond all knowing, short of what I know of the worst, that is, the worst I know I can do. That limit I hope not to reach, though if I have to breach it, I will not hesitate. Such crimes aside, I can only blunder forward, as blind as you are, with naught but my heart and my gut to guide my way.'

Estelle watched Grymonde's burned face twitch. She loved him.

Grégoire returned, shaking drops of wine from the kidskin.

'I say this only as a fact, not as a threat to sway your mind,' said Tannzer, 'but if Estelle stays, you stay, too. Without her, you are a stone in my boot.'

Estelle was proud that Tannzer wanted her to come, but she didn't want to leave the dragon. That choice scared her.

'If your purpose holds,' said Grymonde, 'and you pick the Devil's pocket, and you and your wife and child escape Paris, will you take La Rossa with you?'

Estelle tried to imagine what this meant. She couldn't. But she wanted to go.

Tannzer smiled, like she imagined a wolf might smile. He took the kidskin from Grégoire and cut away the neck and spout. Estelle was confused.

'What future awaits her here?' said Grymonde. 'Plague and the brothel.'

'Estelle, if you want to stay here, say so,' said Tannzer. 'It would be the brighter call. I am going to wade a river of blood and there's no telling who will reach the far side bank. But Amparo is coming with me, even should the red tide drown the both of us.'

'Oh, I want to come with you. So does Amparo.'

'What say you now, my Infant?'

'The dragon can't fly without La Rossa. He never could.'

Tannzer pulled the kidskin inside out. He held it open in front of her.

'Put Amparo in here. This will be her cradle. You will carry her home.'

Estelle understood: of course Tannzer would take her with him.

She slipped Amparo inside the kidskin. She filled it quite snugly and her little face peered over the top. Estelle laughed. She looked so sweet. Tannzer stooped and tightened Estelle's belt a notch. The top buttons on her chemise were still undone. He unbuttoned another. Estelle wasn't confused any more. She was going with them. She smiled. Tannzer smiled, too. Estelle put Amparo and her cradle inside her shirt, her little face poking out at her throat. The wineskin was wet and cool against Estelle's skin. The cradle felt strong. Tannzer buttoned the chemise up and stood back to judge the result.

'A baby's tougher than you'd think. Just make sure she can breathe.'

'I will.'

Estelle's heart was pounding. She was going to fly.

'Grégoire, give me the *sergent's* belt.'

Grégoire unleashed his dog and Tannzer coiled the belt around Estelle's chest, across her shoulder and under her armpit. It held Amparo more strongly. Tannzer manhandled Grymonde into position. He reversed the spear in Grymonde's hand.

'The blade's grounded so watch your toes. If you fall, I will leave you.'

'Fall? Give me another Immortal, man. And take one for yourself.'

Tannzer stood behind Estelle and picked her up under the armpits and hoisted her high. Her stomach dropped. She kicked her legs up and landed on Grymonde's shoulders.

'Don't touch his face,' said Tannzer. 'Is Amparo set right?'

Estelle shifted the kidskin to ride on one thigh, and circled it with her arm.

'She's right.'

Estelle saw that a gang of the yard lads and girls had gathered.

'We'll come with you, chief!'

'We'll take the bloody palace if you ask us to!'

Tannzer turned his back to the gang and spoke to Grymonde.

'Bold but sly is our game. They'll only be meat for the butchers.'

Grymonde faced the gang and raised his arms.

Estelle looked down on them. She had never been so excited or so scared. Her legs gripped the huge neck. She sucked her forefinger, to make sure it was clean, and put it to Amparo's lips. Amparo suckled the fingertip. Grymonde's war voice rocked the Yards.

'Children of Cockaigne. The time has come for me to bid you farewell.'

'No!' cried the lads and the lasses.

'Yes. I am resolved to drown in the bath of blood I will spill from the veins of our enemies. Do not mourn me, but keep me alive in your hearts, for there I shall be. Always. Listen for the weeping of their women in the days to come. Listen for the tales that will be told of the Infant's passing, for they will fill you with awe. And let that weeping and those tales be your warrant to rebuild the Land of Plenty. Will you do that for me?'

'Aye!'

'Will you give me your oath on it?'

A rowdy and heartfelt din filled the yard with promises.

'No tomorrow!' roared Grymonde.

Estelle watched Tannzer shoulder two bows and two quivers. He picked up a crossbow and walked away. The hare-lipped boy followed him. The hairless dog with the golden collar followed the boy. They were going to the river of blood.

Estelle and her sister, Amparo, were going, too.

And then they would all go home, together.

She pulled on Grymonde's ears. He laughed. He was brain-cracked.

'La Rossa, now you are my wings and eyes both.'

Estelle said, 'Let's fly.'

CHAPTER TWENTY-SEVEN

The Blackness

He could manage without the eyes. In Paris after sundown, and in the Yards above all – and those hours had taken up a fair slice of his life – eyes weren't much use anyway. Neither, given the stench, were nostrils, which was as well, for the only smell his own could detect was of his charred cavities. A sixth sense was what you needed in the Yards in the dark. His sixth sense had always been as sharp as a flesh fly's, elsewise he'd have been dead long ago. Tonight it was blurred by pain. Not the pain of the wounds sustained in his fall from the roof. Those he couldn't even feel. The burns. The pain of the burns had no focus: it shifted and warped from one instant to the next; it was never still; it was never one thing but many; it was never in one place but in many; it flickered and flared and whispered and blazed. It was everywhere, yet he couldn't point to it, couldn't draw a ring around it and set it aside, as he might have done with the hole in his leg. The fire pain surrounded his skull and everything in it, as if his head were sealed in a giant glass bottle filled with wasps. He could eat the pain as pain. Pain was life. But it galled him that he was more than merely blind. He needed another Immortal.

He needed to play his part.

His part, if nothing else, he could see, even through the pain. He pictured it in his mind. His mother's draw came to him. No longer would he play the Hanged Man, a traitor to himself. No more would he play the pigeon plucked in the Juggler's game. His part was now the Lunatic, his heels on the crumbling edge of the abyss; stranded at both the beginning and the end; knowing all and knowing nothing; with his staff and his rags and two pretty feathers in his hair. He did not need his senses. He needed only to be. And to walk on the paths that had heart.

His big feet were a boon. He pounded each one down as if to stamp holes through the earth, slow and steady, waiting to feel the earth protest before committing his weight and pounding onward again. He paired each pace of his left foot with a stab into the dirt of the spear he held in his right hand. It felt natural. He would not fall.

He carried on his shoulders, light as two wisps of fancy though they were – so light he could hardly feel their material weight – the two most precious spirits in Creation. One of them a Star to guide him; the other a Lunatic, too. A tiny Lunatic, she also teetering on the rim where end met beginning, knowing all worth knowing yet knowing nothing at all. Through the burning he felt the flutter of her brave new heart against the back of his head, while his own heart battered hugely into his ribs. How strange. How marvellous. To walk such paths as none had walked before. He felt a sharp tug on his right ear.

'We're turning south,' said Estelle.

'Into the jaws of the foeman. Good.'

Grymonde stopped and turned on the spot. He would not fall. He set forth again, stomping and stabbing the earth. The dirt underfoot was more even here and sloped slightly downwards. They were out of the Yards and walking parallel to Saint-Denis. He felt for Estelle's ankle dangling on his chest and gave it a squeeze.

'How are my darlings?'

'There are bodies on the ground up ahead. Huguenots. Tannzer is dragging them aside for us. Grégoire! Lend Grymonde your shoulder while we pass.'

Grymonde felt her slap his left arm and he let go of her ankle and reached out. A hand took his, stronger than he might have guessed, and he placed his palm on a thin shoulder.

'Thank you, lad.'

Grymonde stomped on. He held the spear vertical, out to one side, for fear of stabbing the boy. He detected a heat, a glow. It was faint, so he supposed, but his burns felt it and writhed.

'Grégoire, is that a lantern you carry?'

'Yes, sire.'

'Sire?' Grymonde felt a laugh bubble through him. 'Be ye as wise as serpents. Tell me, lad, is it the virtuous man you seek with your lamp? Even on this Devil's highway?'

Grégoire stopped. Grymonde almost knocked him down. He held him upright.

'Tannhauser'sfightingupahead.'

The lad garbled through his nose. Grymonde heard a doleful cry.

'Tannzer shot a man,' said Estelle. 'Now he's running. He's stabbed a second man.'

'Guide me to his side.'

'No. We are your eyes and wings. We'll tell you when it's time to breathe fire. Anyway, he's killed all three.'

'Three?' Helplessness and envy scourged him.

'They were robbing bodies. Tannzer's dragging them. Now we can go on.'

'Tannzer!' called Grymonde. 'Another Immortal, man. Or let me fight.'

'Be quiet.' Estelle slapped him on the head. 'Do as you're told.'

His feet splashed through pools of what must have been fresh blood. He ground his teeth. He hadn't been the one to spill it. The clenching scalded his blisters. He blinked, but couldn't, for he had no eyelids; a peculiar sensation. He started as Tannzer spoke close by. Even weighted with gear the man moved like a leopard.

'A murder gang is emptying a house, half a furlong hence.'

'Take these cherubs from my shoulders and let's have at them.'

Fingers hard as oak clasped his arm. Grymonde wasn't used to feeling comforted; the very notion was long lost to his memory; yet comforted he was.

'Killing them's no exploit, but there's enough that some might run and raise the alarum. Les Halles is full of *sergents*. I propose to cross Saint-Denis. Is there a spot from which we can size up the Hôtel Le Tellier without being seen?'

Grymonde shoved at the agony clouding his thoughts, like a

man pushing mist, and tried to picture the *hôtel* and its surround-
ings. He heard a stream of gibberish from the boy.

'A stockyard, says Grégoire.'

'He's right. Back of Crucé's abattoir.' Grymonde saw it. 'It should
be empty until they open the city gate. A drover or two at most,
who'll go and get drunk for pennies.'

The hand let go and he missed it, and felt foolish. Estelle kicked
his chest with both heels and he stumped on. He felt the oaken
fingers again. They pressed a small, soft globe into his palm. He
clenched his fist on an Immortal. He bridled at the suggestion he
was less than stout.

'I can get by without it.'

'As you will, but you're twitching like a madman's puppet.'

'I'll not be addled for the fight?'

'You're addled with the pain. The pain and the opium will abate
each other, like bitter and sweet. But you may have visions, so
Estelle, you keep him sharp.'

Grymonde threw the Immortal down his gullet. His tongue
turned as bitter as repentance but he liked it, because it was bitter,
and because the prospect of visions was sweet.

They crossed the Rue Saint-Denis without incident and made their
way south through the narrower streets. The odd gunshot cracked
in the distance, east and west, but no volleys. Another murder gang
prompted a second detour. Grymonde did not fall.

The obstacle they couldn't avoid was the profusion of Huguenot
corpses that littered their way. The spoor of hate, of greed, of
stupidity and power. He had played his part in that, too. It shamed
him. He had not killed for religion, for his own had neither name
nor priesthood. But what difference was that to the slain? He
remembered the nameless girl, ruined among the ruins of her family.
He had spared her. He remembered his own words to Tannzer:
spared her what?

He heard Tannzer question Estelle on the events of her day.
He half-listened, his mind drifting. He heard Typhaine's name,

and flinched at the memory of the expression on her face when she had mocked him as Samson and suggested they blind him. The intensity of her hatred baffled him, but he had lived with it too long to wonder. As to the blinding, he had taken money to cut a woman's tits off, and many a time had cheered with the crowd at the disembowellings on the Place de Grève. He heard 'Petit Christian'.

'That green turd is mine,' he said. 'I claim him.'

Estelle slapped him on the head.

'Stop here,' she said. 'And be quiet.'

'Chevalier? Where are you? Will you let me have him?'

He felt the flat of a large hand against his chest and stopped.

'If I can, I will. But patience, my Infant. Pay heed to Estelle or you'll fall.'

'Did you hear him?' said Estelle. She was cross. 'Pay heed to me.'

'I will, my darling, I will, I'm sorry.'

Grymonde waited while bodies were cleared from his path, but the real obstacle was the fact he had no eyes. A distance that, just that afternoon, he had strolled in ten minutes seemed to take hours. If he had murdered Carla that morning, or had left it to Papin and Bigot, he would still have his eyes, and Cockaigne would not be razed, and his mother Alice and many more would be eating roast pork by the moonlight. Aye, and the wren would not be flying on his back and he would never have felt her heart beat, and La Rossa would have no sister to defend, and he himself would have lived and died without ever finding the courage to admit to love.

How strange. How marvellous.

He wanted to cry, but he had no eyes to cry with.

He heeded Estelle and stumped on.

He saw his mother's face; purpled and worn; a vision beyond the dreaming of the seers of old; and in that face a woman who had had no equal, until she had anointed Carla her sister. Yes, he had listened outside the birthing room door. He had never taken Alice's counsel, though he'd listened to her every word and had never doubted its wisdom. He had never once told her that he loved her. Rather, he had brought her gifts, which she had scorned because they were stolen. And he had brought her more, and she had scorned those too, down to the meat and drink he had heaped on her table. Every mouthful she had ever swallowed, she had purchased with her own small earnings.

The one piece of his mother's counsel he had taken, without her ever having given it, was to spare Carla's life and bring her home. And yet, that counsel, too, she had given all his life, had whispered to him in her womb, had fed to him with her blood before he was born. Yes, he had listened outside the birthing room door. He had heard the secret that those four sisters shared, even if he could not put it into words.

How marvellous. How strange.

In his vision, Alice was smiling.

And other potent cards were in play.

Judgement. Fire. Death.

Their images rose a hundred feet tall, and painted in a hundred colours, before his eyeless gaze. The silver clarions of Armageddon. The burning, bleeding Tower. The pale and delirious horseman on his black and delirious horse.

He squeezed the lad's shoulder. The lad yelled and wriggled free.

Grymonde stopped and leaned on his spear and gaped up at the images.

Carla had chosen *Anima Mundi*.

And the Soul of the World had guided her hand towards that implacable draw.

And such were the cards now in play.

Death rode rampant.

He charged towards the Fire.

And beyond the Fire, the Judgement.

Grymonde soared in the grip of the talons of ecstasy.

A tide of fear watered his bowels.

Perhaps he would not die.

Perhaps Death would not reach him through the Fire.

Was that his Judgement? And his sentence?

To live? Like this?

'Where are you, lad?'

He sensed feathery blows on his head and the voices of cherubim.
Sounds, as of a drum, echoed in his chest. His hand was seized and
his palm was placed on a bone and he squeezed. He heard a yell
but the bone didn't move. Good bone. Brave bone. The strange and
marvellous boy. Grymonde relaxed his grip. His bowels steadied.
His feet steadied.

The talons carried him higher.

In the images, Grymonde saw the Many Faces of God.

The Soul of the World. The Judgement. The Fire. Death.

Carla. La Rossa. The Wren. Alice. Alice?

God was not there. God was here.

And God was not God.

No gods here. Only Our Mother, the Earth. And us.

Agony wiped his revelation clean in a white flame. Scoured it.
The vision, the images, the knowing. Gone. He gazed upon blackness and less than that. The agony waned.

'I said pay heed,' said Tannzer. 'Keep sharp.'

Grymonde had felt no force, short of, he now realised, the blows
of La Rossa's hands and heels. Tannzer had stroked his burns. The
oak hand grabbed his arm.

'We're close. Stay sturdy. I need the mighty Infant.'

'The Infant is sturdy. Guide him unto the battle.'

'Bold but sly. Favour the visions without, over the visions
within.'

Grymonde tried to blink. A white flame steadied him. He
nodded.

'Estelle, Grégoire,' said Tannzer, 'you did good work.'

'Amparo, too,' said Estelle.

'Aye, Amparo, too.'

The less than blackness returned and Grymonde held onto it.
Golden lights flashed like shooting stars and he let them fall. He
stumped on. Sturdy. Bold but sly. Tannzer? Tannzer. Yes, La Rossa
was right. The sound of it cut to the bone, as did the man.

He loved the man.

Grymonde leaned on Grégoire's shoulder. Grégoire stopped and so did he, without collision. Visions within. Visions without. Yes. Without, Grymonde sensed Tannzer stacking the slain with the passionless phlegm of a man who had stacked them before, in number well beyond reckoning. Tannzer's blood was colder than any Grymonde had ever heard tell of; yet a limitless passion drove him. And that knowing was no vision from within. Tannzer sought Carla. He had found the babe that they two had made. He had found the wren in a place that was designed to be unfindable, a place no one man had ever even dared to seek. He would gamble all, even wife and babe, to bring they three together, be they living or dead. And this, at least, was not strange.

Not strange at all. It was right. It was true.

It was marvellous.

Yes.

He loved the man.

He loved them all.

Enough of the marvels within.

Grymonde raised his hand and stuck his finger in the hole where his left eye had been. The finger pierced his entire skull like a hot nail. He seized on the scream he wanted to loose and strangled it into an elongated grunt. He was alive. He was without. He was needed. They moved on. He would serve Carla. He would serve the sisters on his back. He had never served a man in his life, and would have cut his own throat before doing so. But he would serve Tannzer. No. A man among men had the right to call his own name.

Grymonde, the mighty Infant, would serve Mattias Tannhauser.

Yet why did Tannhauser need his service? Grymonde was a fistful of stones in the man's boots. La Rossa could have carried the wren by herself at five times the speed. No. He was going within again. He poked himself in the hole where there was no eye. The interior of his skull was drenched in blue flame. He grunted. He swayed. He stumped. With his grunting and stumping he served, for he knew not what else he could offer.

A smell distilled from decades of manure, shat from the guts of cattle which sensed their doom, fought its way through the liquid charcoal dribbling down his nose.

'Hoi! You lot! Be off with you! Or I'll call the watch!'

Grymonde turned his head towards the voice. The voice choked on terror.

'God's blood.'

The man made no sound more but for that of his corpse hitting the shit.

Tannhauser had paid him in steel rather than coppers.

'Wait here, my Infant, and keep quiet.'

Grymonde waited. He felt a deep patience. Alice had said there was no hurry, and she had been right. She had seen her end coming and had spent her last moments on love instead of fear. The woman had always had an eye for a good bargain. Could he do the same? He was amazed to find he had love to spend in plenty. Where had it been stored all these years? In what lost vault had he hidden it? Sadness rose inside him. He wanted to cry again, and was glad that he couldn't. Pay heed. Keep sharp. He had rage to spend, too. He'd never had trouble finding that. But he had not time enough for both. This bargain wasn't so easy to call. He felt Tannhauser's hand.

'Garnier just left the *hôtel* with four of his men. A *sergent* guards the door.'

'What next?'

'I'm going to lift Estelle from your shoulders. Estelle, don't kick him in the face.'

The wisps flew away. Grymonde missed them. He was alone. He felt a wave of self-pity. He raised his finger to his eyehole to right himself, but Tannhauser's hand seized his wrist. Grymonde was comforted. Tannhauser's voice was calm, strong, as if hoping to make himself clear to such as a child.

'Grymonde, I am going to put the stock of the crossbow in your left hand. Your left hand only. You will take the weight, but lightly so, in order that the crossbow may turn, and that the strength of your hand may follow it. The weapon is not yet armed. You must not touch the tiller or the trigger. I am going to show Estelle how to aim it and shoot it, from your hand. The weight is yours, but the aim, and the decision, is hers. If she shoots, you will draw the sinew, that she may shoot again. In this, she will be your mistress. Are you with me, my Infant?'

'Yes. Yes. I'm with you.'

Grymonde had thought himself mad; as such had prided himself. Yet with madness such as this he might have ruled Paris.

'But where is La Rossa?'

'I'm with you, Tannzer,' said Estelle. 'Amparo is with you, too.'

'I know you are,' said Tannhauser. 'You shot Papin. You carried your sister from the tiles. You saved her from the nuns. You united her with me. You flew the blinded dragon. There is no one I trust more, girl, and only Grégoire do I trust as much.'

'What do you want me to do?' said La Rossa.

'I will show you. First you will practise with me, then with Grymonde. But there's another task I must ask of you. A greater one.'

'I'll do it,' said La Rossa.

A flame of love hotter than the skewer that had bored his skull seared Grymonde's heart. She was his daughter. But he was her dragon. He fought to stay without.

'In this world of blood and thunder, of which we spoke,' said Tannhauser, 'anything can happen. My task is to find Carla, so that the sisters and their mother might be together, and go home. In that task I might fail. But whether I fail or whether I win, the attempt demands that I leave you here awhile, and I must ask brave Grégoire to leave you, too, on other business.'

The lad garbled what Grymonde took to be his consent.

'I know you will, lad,' said Tannhauser. 'Estelle, Carla trusted you to take care of Amparo. So do I. I give all my power of judgement to you. You are a clever girl. The men who blinded Grymonde and killed your mother might come here. If you think Amparo is in danger, I ask you to take her back to Cockaigne. Will you do that?'

'Yes.'

'If I live, I will find you. If I die, you will have to find a woman who will give Amparo milk. Can you do that?'

'Yes. You don't want me to take her to the nuns?'

'I'd rather you raised her in Cockaigne than have her adopted by the Pope himself. I dare say Carla would agree. If you take her there, you must leave Grymonde to die in battle. Can you do that? Can you leave him to die?'

Grymonde listened to a longer silence. A silence he longed to break for there was nothing he wanted more than thus to die. He felt a hand slide into his, a small hand, and he held it so softly that he felt her fingers squeeze his.

'Yes,' said La Rossa. 'I can leave him to die.'

'Good girl. Now, come here, and let me show you how to shoot this crossbow.'

'Why do you carry two bows?' she asked.

'A good question. The arrows made for one bow will not fly true from the other. For one bow the spine in the shafts is too soft, and for the other too hard.'

'How do you know?'

'I learned it. Some things are made to work in harmony, like you and Amparo, and Grymonde, and Grégoire and I. And some things are not.'

Grymonde smiled. Perhaps it was the Immortals, though he did not think so, but he had never known such harmony in his life. La Rossa's hand slipped away and Grymonde was alone again, but he did not mind. An image rose and filled his blackness.

He had not yet thought to wonder what Tannhauser looked like.

He had never seen the man.

Now he did.

Tannhauser was Death.

Grymonde laughed.

It must have been catching, for Tannhauser laughed, too.

Perhaps a laugh was just what was needed, for the lad, Grégoire, joined in, and so did La Rossa, and the sound of their laughter conjured a vision sweet indeed.

'Four men are coming,' said La Rossa. 'One has a lantern.'

'Are they armed?' asked Grymonde.

'Two have crossbows, like ours, and swords and clubs and knives.'

'Helmets?'

'All of them, and two have breastplates.'

'Do they look like villains? Bravos?'

'Yes. The *sergent* at the door waved at them. They didn't wave back.'

Grymonde felt serene, which was as well, for he had no idea what to do. Tannhauser had gone to scout the rear of the Hôtel Le Tellier. He had sent Grégoire to procure a horse and wagon. He had left Grymonde and La Rossa behind the stockyard fence, by the gate.

'If they go inside,' said La Rossa, 'Tannzer will never get to Carla.'

Grymonde wasn't so sure, but no doubt the bravos were a handicap.

'I can shoot one,' said La Rossa, 'and they'll come after us. We've got the pistol, so I can shoot one more, at least. Then we can run, the way we came, and they'll follow us.'

In more usual circumstances, Grymonde would have considered this plan reckless even by his standards. In his serenity, he could almost believe in it.

'I can't run,' he said. 'But you and the wren can. Promise me you will.'

'Quickly,' hissed La Rossa. 'They're going to climb the steps.'

He felt her pull on his belt and he took a step forward and held out the crossbow in his left hand, sideways to his body, the tiller level across his hips, as he had practised. He felt her shoulder against his belly as she took control. He heard a cooing sound from the wren. Fathers and daughters, he thought. Were there ever two such pairs as they?

'I'm as proud of you as Tannhauser is of his wren. No, I am prouder.'

'Quiet. Tannzer's shot one. Hold strong. The door's opening. He's shot another, no two, with one arrow, it went through one and into the next, but he's not dead. Hold strong!'

Grymonde gripped the stock and gave to the pressure of a final adjustment in her aim. The bolt flew. Beyond the slap of the sinew he heard yells of alarm and pain.

'Pull the string, quickly, pull the string.'

Grymonde stooped and found his toes with the stirrup.

'Tell me what you see.'

'Tannzer charged, he's stabbed the last bravo in the neck, the one wounded by the arrow, and the *sergent*'s run into the door and pushed it open to get inside, and Tannzer's killed him, and they can't shut the door, the body's in the way. He's charging in, there are men in there, I don't know how many. I can't see what's happening any more.'

Grymonde drew the string with both hands and felt the click of the nut. He resumed his former stance and felt La Rossa slot home a fresh bolt. The last bravo?

'You hit one of the bravos?'

'Yes. But he's crawling away. I'm going to shoot him again.'

'Wait, he's out of the fight and you might need the shot.'

'Yes. He's stopped crawling. Now, he's crawling again, but slower. I think he's going to die. There's Tannzer! Tannzer's come back out.' She giggled. 'He's hit the crawler on the head with an iron club. He's dragging two bodies up the steps and through the door.'

'He is a reliable hand with a body, we must give him that.'

'He's come back out. He walking away, back to, no – he's picked up a bow, he must have dropped it. He waved the bow at me.'

'Call it a salute. You saved his neck.'

'He's dragging the last two bodies. They're all inside. He's shut the door.'

Grymonde felt her let go of the tiller. She put her arms round his waist and he felt her head against his belly. He raised the crossbow high. He felt her trembling. He felt the pressure of a small lump.

'Watch out for the wren. Are you crying?'

She stepped back. 'No.'

He groped with his free hand. 'Where are you?'

'There's a *sergent* coming, from the river. He's going to the house.'

Grymonde thought about this. La Rossa's thoughts were faster.

'Get ready. When he gets near the lantern over the steps, I'm going to shoot him.'

Grymonde lowered and levelled the crossbow. La Rossa took the tiller.

'It's Sergent Rody.'

'Rody? The stupid bastard.'

'He's got someone with him, by the arm. A boy. Wait, it's Hugon.'

'Our Hugon?'

'Tell him to run. Shout loud. Quickly.'

Grymonde inhaled and bellowed.

'Hugon! Run! Run for your very soul!'

His burns exploded across his face.

'Hold it steady!' said La Rossa.

He clenched the stock. The sinew sang.

'I got Rody in the top of the legs, in the balls I think. He's fallen on the steps.'

'Take me to Rody, hurry. Good shot, La Rossa, good shot.'

'Hugon's coming.'

Grymonde swung the crossbow and struck the fence, and propped the weapon against it. He felt the pistol disappear from his belt. He heard clicks.

'Don't shoot him.'

'I won't.'

Estelle grabbed his index finger and tugged and he followed her.

'Rody, eh?' he said. 'Little fish taste sweet.'

'Grymonde?'

Hugon's voice was threaded with horror. Grymonde wondered why.

'Are you hurt, boy?'

'No.'

'Take Rody's knife, and his bow, and be careful. Set me over him.'

La Rossa placed him. He heard gasps of pain. He stuck out a toe and hit a leg.

'Jesus Christ Almighty on the Cross.'

Rody's terror seemed excessive even for one facing death. Grymonde remembered the holes in his face. Quite a sight, he imagined. He grinned and Rody cried out.

Grymonde dropped to his knees and felt bones crunch inside the flesh that cushioned his fall. Fingers grappled for his throat and he grabbed a wrist and plucked it away and took the hand attached to it and crushed it and wrung it like washing until it felt like a purse filled with gravel. Flames burst over his face and carried him upwards in a spiral of ecstasy, and of the next moments he knew little, only the vague impression of something like a wicker basket giving way beneath his knuckles, and of something like a pewter vase cracking on stone and turning soggy, and of hair and blood sticking to his hands. He heard La Rossa's voice and the ecstasy spiralled back down into mere serenity, though a more gratifying species thereof than he had felt before.

He stood up and swayed.

'Hugon? Are you there? Put Rody's ankle in my hand. La Rossa, guide me.'

He hauled Rody into the stockyard.

Estelle gave him the crossbow and he drew it.

'Hugon, explain yourself.'

'I followed Carla and her violl from the Yards.'

'And you let Rody catch you?' Grymonde laughed, he felt in a kindly fashion. 'But well done, and don't fret, Tannhauser's gone in to get Carla back.'

'Gone in where?' said Hugon.

'Hugon, why are your clothes wet?' asked La Rossa.

'In Le Tellier's *hôtel*, where else?' Grymonde felt serene but confused. 'Wet?'

Hugon said, 'Carla isn't in the *hôtel*.'

Grymonde laughed. The lad was entitled to poke him back.

'Be quiet,' said La Rossa.

'Hugon jests.'

'He does not jest. Hugon, if Carla isn't in the *hôtel*, where is she?'

CHAPTER TWENTY-EIGHT

The Angel

The Angel watched Tannhauser close the door of the *hôtel* and she knew he would not find within what he needed to find, the grail for which he quested, the mystery whose solution he had sought all his life, and which he would not find anywhere except in the last place he might look, which was in himself. In the Hôtel Le Tellier he would only find reasons to inflict more horror. He would so do without hesitation, but not without cost.

The Angel was sad.

His life he held cheap by virtue of the fact that he possessed it. It offended him that he should possess it while others nobler and gentler than him did not; when others nobler and gentler than him had been robbed of life's beauty in front of his eyes. This injustice, this flaw in the logic of being, was the sin he would carry to his grave; and maybe beyond.

Yet he also gambled the lives of those for whom he would die. He gambled the lives of those for whom he would destroy the world, and those same lives with it. This other flaw in the logic of being, if such it was – for the Angel claimed no authority in such matters – did not offend him, for he knew, somehow, that being was more than mere life.

He would let his daughter, Amparo, ride through a Hell that only men of all living things, mortal or immortal, could make, in the arms of a tatterdemalion girl, on the shoulders of a blinded monster, because he knew, though he could not say how, that his daughter, not yet half a day breathing, had already known perfection of being, and of ecstasy and of beauty and of love, and of Life Her-own-self, even if she knew nothing at all of the world.

These wagers on the Wheel of Fortune, and the direful deeds

in whose metal those wagers were minted, tortured him, as if to that wheel his limbs had been bound and broken. Yet of that pain no one would know, for he would let none know it. To reveal it would earn him no more than sympathy, and that meagre coin he scorned, for it would only weaken him. No one knew but he and the angels.

In this squalid realm no other dared such knowing, or such wagers, as dared he; and it was this power to dare, more than his skill in arms or his understanding of men, that made him so appalling. No other could see and stand and face the cost to his soul without losing not just his soul, for souls were lost carelessly enough, but his mind.

The Angel was Love. All angels were love, the risen and the fallen, those winged with black, those winged with white. That was their purpose. It was not their purpose to see what will be. But this Angel knew Tannhauser was right.

He would not die in Paris.

The Wheel would not be that kind.

She knew the black-winged angel who watched over him. She loved him, the Angel with Black Wings, and he loved her, and they both loved Tannhauser and Carla, not just because they were angels and could do no other, but because they had loved them both, each in their way, since the moment they each had set eyes on them. Both of them. All of them. This Angel could only know but not explain. Perhaps the Angel with Black Wings could explain, for he was brilliant and she was not. This Angel knew that Tannhauser had loved her, and loved still, and yet he had never told her so.

This Angel had been many things. She had frolicked in the mountains with fighting bulls. She had made music with Carla where music was more precious than rubies. Naked she had swum through powder smoke and blood to feel the joy of him inside her, and to give him the joy of being inside her. She had been the road down which Tannhauser had walked to find the power to love Carla. Down such strange roads had Carla walked to love Tannhauser. And here sat the nightingale, cooing in her kidskin, in the thin, brave embrace of the tatterdemalion girl, a girl such as this strange Angel, once, herself had been.

How beautiful.

She wondered, this Angel, if Tannhauser were not some kind of angel, too, for he was engaged in the same task as she, of trying to guide these children through Hell. If so, what colour might his wings be? She laughed and Estelle turned in the stockyard and looked at her.

He's my blood-red rose.

'Who is your blood-red rose?' said Estelle.

Tannhauser.

'Of course,' said Estelle.

Red is the colour of my true love's wings.

'Oh, I would love to see them.'

One day you will, but not today.

CHAPTER TWENTY-NINE

The Juggler

I n the hall of the *hôtel*, Tannhauser checked the bodies for life by the light of the chandelier. He found none. A breathing *sergent* might have been useful, but he had erred on the side of inflicting lethal wounds. He listened and heard no sounds. The slain had died with a variety of sighs and prayers, but no screams; desperate men in a brawl didn't scream, unless killed badly, and these had been killed well. They'd had no reason to call out for help; they had been the help. No more of a din, then, than might attend the arrival of four bravos.

He bolted the front door. He went to the back door and opened it. He dragged in the body of the *sergent* he had shot in the chest before he'd happened on the bravos in the street. He retrieved the bodkin.

Nine men in all.

Le Tellier must have been feeling insecure; and likely now felt safe.

Tannhauser could have used his own watchman, in case of chance arrivals, but he didn't want Estelle and young Amparo in the house. He took Altan's horn bow from his chest and hung it, with the quiver of broadheads, on the baluster at the foot of the stairs. He doubted there was another man in the city able to draw it. The bowstring dripped with blood where it had crossed his chest. He ran his fingers down its length and flicked away the gore. He took the crossbow he had dragged in with one of the bravos. He drew it and armed it and shoved four spare bolts in the back of his belt. He kept Frogier's bow on his left shoulder.

He made a quick search of the rooms on the ground floor.

All were empty but one, which was locked and showed no light underneath. If anyone had had the sense to lock it from inside, in the dark, they would be glad to stay that way. He let it be. He retrieved the flanged steel mace he had used to brain the dying bravo.

He climbed the staircase.

More doors. No lights within. No sounds. He let them be, too.

He headed south across the landing and down the corridor. The corridor opened into a lamp-lit ante-room. The door to the office was gilded with a cockleshell emblem. He listened. He heard a thin voice, a whine. Petit Christian. He paused.

In Le Tellier's shoes, he would have at least one bodyguard with him. Two? Two would be undignified, and a second would be better placed below; but two at most. If he were cautious, he would send Petit Christian to answer the door. The door opened inwards, hinged on the right. The bodyguard, were he worth his station, would be ready with gun or crossbow. If the guard answered, all the better.

Tannhauser propped the mace by the doorjamb. He unhitched the bow and quiver and left them, too. He couldn't do much about his accent, except raise the pitch half an octave and muffle it with feigned deference. He held the crossbow upright by the stock in his left hand. He knocked twice, lightly, and tried to sound timid.

'Excellency, with your permission, the new men are here.'

He stepped back a pace, his left foot forward and outside the edge of the door. He put a spare bolt between his teeth. A pause. The door opened. Tannhauser kicked Petit Christian through the pubic bone and felt it give way. The toad flew back to reveal a *sergent* levelling an arquebus at the far end of the room.

'Baro!'

Tannhauser presented a target until he saw the match flick down. The priming flared as he swivelled back behind the wall. The blast must have deafened those within. He felt the wind of the squandered ball and spun back into the doorway and lowered the crossbow.

He followed Baro as he fled his own smoke and shot him in the right loin.

He toed the stirrup and drew the string. He fitted the spare bolt.

He ducked his head in and out of the room. Christian squirmed on the floor. A bald man wearing a collar of gold cockleshells sat behind a polished oak desk, both hands over his ears. No second guard. Only Baro, clinging onto a window sill. He checked the space behind the door. He stepped back to collect the bow, the quiver and the mace.

He walked around Christian, who was coughing on vomit, and past the bald man, who sat as still as a bust of Nero at his polished oak desk. He stood the crossbow on its stirrup against the far wall, and the bow and the quiver by it. He swung the mace above his head from the back foot and clubbed the bleeding bodyguard through the nape. He felt a steel flange bite into the root of the upper spine and cranked the handle to split apart the bones. Sergent Baro dropped, his upper limbs quivering in a fit. Tannhauser turned.

He was in a room with Marcel Le Tellier.

Considering the trouble he had caused, the man was a disappointment.

Tannhauser found nothing in the face to interest him. A certain intelligence, a certain vanity, a certain gravity, affected or acquired. Nothing he hadn't seen before in a thousand such functionaries: those who had bartered their lives for an authority that as men they would never have owned. If there was a shadow of hatred in the eyes, it was bleached by utter disbelief even more than by fear. He did not meet Tannhauser's gaze. His hand reached towards a cup of wine; then stopped. He seemed stunned that the citadel not merely of his *hôtel* but of his prestige had been so violently breached. He stared through the drifts of powder smoke at the gore that painted Tannhauser's torso from throat to belt buckle.

Tannhauser opened the window to vent the smoke. He stripped the smouldering match from the arquebus and smashed its lock with the mace and threw the match outside. He was three floors above the street. From this wing no view of the stockyard was to be had. Screams and jeers, and wavering voices singing psalms, drew his attention.

He looked towards the Seine.

The buildings that lined much of the river parted here for a series of wharves. Below the bulk of the Conciergerie on the island, he could see a strip of the moonlit bank. The river was swollen by the recent summer storm. On the strand, with their banners and burning torches, Christ's militias were murdering Huguenots and slinging the corpses in the foam. Here and there groups of two or three knelt around some victim splayed in the mud and rutted like pigs. The doomed were herded down to the beach at spear point in pathetic clusters, family upon family, the nature of their end stark before them.

Tannhauser was sickened. The suspicion taunted him that all killing was much the same in the end, and that those who embraced death without making a contest of it, who chose to defend their souls over their lives, were the truly wise. The longest life was a morning dream as measured by the turning of the world. Tannhauser didn't have the temperament to live by such a creed; his dream was too compelling to be thus constrained. He loved his dream. He loved it now. Or perhaps he loved death, and in order to love death you had to be breathing. More likely, he just lacked the wisdom.

'How dare you, monsieur? Don't you know who I am? This is my house.'

Le Tellier sounded like a plucked crow.

Tannhauser stooped and picked up Baro by his jerkin and belt, and hefted him three paces and slung him on his belly across the desk, where he continued to twitch.

'I know who you are,' said Tannhauser. 'And the house is mine.'

He wielded the mace high and staved in Baro's skull. The scalp tore like lace and the vault burst apart along its sutures. Blood and vile jelly soused Le Tellier's face. He gagged and recoiled and covered his eyes.

Petit Christian stirred to his hands and knees and eyed the door. Tannhauser laid the mace down. He hoisted Baro's corpse and dumped it on the toadeater's back like some limp and cadaverous sodomite. He turned and leaned on the desk.

Le Tellier's beard was pickled in the brains of his last defender. He broke wind as his entrails loosened. His mind was either vacant or teeming with futile calculations. He dared not look at his captor. Tannhauser cracked the desk with the mace. Le Tellier flinched as he was splashed again.

'That's a knight's collar. It sits ill on the breast of a coward. Surrender it.'

'I have borne the Order of Saint Michael with honour.'

'You shat on it. Take it off.'

Le Tellier lifted the chain over his head as if its weight near defeated him.

Tannhauser hadn't expected so feeble an adversary. But then, the last time Le Tellier had been this close to violence was likely some brawl in the market twenty years before. With fresh blood he had never been this intimate at all. Its primal force neutered his will. Like most who sat on gilded chairs and sent others to kill and die, his liver was as white. Tannhauser took the collar and hung it around his own neck. The solid gold cockleshells slithered in the gore on his chest.

'Your counterfeit honour is gone,' said Tannhauser, 'along with everything else you ever bought or extorted. You've failed, in every particular. You've ruined yourself entire. And all these misfortunes for my sake and in my name.'

Le Tellier met his eyes for the first time. He spoke as if invoking some apparition whose spirit had long infested his inmost mind.

'Mattias Tannhauser.'

'This feud was over some wrong you believe I've done you.'

'In matters of indisputable fact, belief is not required.'

'A personal matter, then, not a matter of politics or law.'

'Of man's law, no,' said Le Tellier. 'Of natural justice, yes –'

'So there are none higher than you who are aware of this wrong.'

'None but God and the Devil.'

That was all Tannhauser needed to know from Marcel Le Tellier.

'Neither ever lost a wager they placed on me.'

He took the mace and walked around the desk to the chair.

'I made you grieve for her,' said Le Tellier. 'I made you weep.' The hatred had finally struggled to the surface of his terror. Tannhauser nodded.

'So you did. I suffered a day of pain that I wouldn't exchange for all the gold in Paris. I won friends for whom I would die. I learned things I would with gladness have given my life to know. I walked into the bowels of perdition and was greeted by the face of my new daughter. And Carla? You gave me the chance to fall in love with her, all over again.'

Le Tellier took this in. The hatred melted into some deep sorrow of his own, and for a moment he was some man other.

'For that and all,' said Tannhauser, 'I am in your debt.'

He clamped a hand around Le Tellier's mouth and smashed the mace through the top of his left shoulder. The flange snapped the bony roof clean away and the ball of the humerus popped loose and the arm dangled in spasms. Le Tellier bucked on the fine red velvet as his nerve strings were plucked from their roots. Phlegm sprayed from his nostrils over Tannhauser's knuckles. The police chief tried to rise to his feet but was no match for either the agony or Tannhauser's strength.

Tannhauser withdrew his hand and flicked the slime. He circled the back of the chair while Le Tellier sucked for breath. He unmade Le Tellier's right shoulder in similar fashion and clamped the gaping mouth as it opened. He wondered why. Screams abounded tonight. Who would imagine that this one came from the city's foremost procurer of torture? He maced Le Tellier through the knee. Le Tellier rocked around on this throne. Tannhauser put the mace on the desk. Le Tellier wore a linen ruff about his throat. Tannhauser ripped it off and crammed a length between Le Tellier's teeth.

He retrieved the crossbow.

He returned and took Le Tellier's left hand and slapped it palm-down on the desk. Le Tellier choked at the grinding of his shattered joint but could offer no resistance. Tannhauser held the hand in place by trapping the wrist against the oak with the outer rim of the crossbow stirrup, vertically applied.

'When I leave I will forget you. Within weeks, so will all who ever knew you.'

He stacked the right hand on the left, and fixed both by the stirrup.

'Within days, some other will sit in this golden chair, for when a chair is the prize the chair is all that matters, not the man who sticks his arse on it.'

Tannhauser corrected the angle of the crossbow and triggered it. With a flat crack the bolt pierced the hands and a good two inches of the oak underneath them. Le Tellier's pain was likely swamped by greater pangs, but the look in his eyes was compensation.

'I don't need a chair.'

Tannhauser tilted the gilded throne until it toppled over. The bolt held firm as Le Tellier plunged to the floor. He hung from his socketless arms and twisted like some half-slaughtered beast in an abattoir of pain.

Tannhauser recharged the crossbow and left him to his paroxysms.

He scouted the ante-room and landing. He listened at the foot of the stair to the next floor. Fifteen rooms. Apart from the obscene grunts drifting from Le Tellier's office the house was silent with the silence of those who wished not to be found. If they hadn't yet run to the gunshot, they weren't going to. If they were going to kill Carla at such a provocation, she was already dead. But so blind an order made no sense and without it no one would dare.

He went back down to the lobby and opened the door and checked the street. It was quiet. He waved towards the stockyard gate to indicate all was well. A thin arm waved back. He bolted the door and went to the kitchen. He found a basket and filled it with what he could see: the better part of a haunch of mutton, cheeses, a smoked ham and sausages hanging in the pantry, jars of pickles and preserves; bread. He left the basket by the front door and went back to fetch a tapped kilderkin of wine.

He returned to the office.

Le Tellier wallowed behind the desk, trying to rise to his one good knee but defeated by the need to throw his weight against diverse and appalling injuries. Christian panted beneath the corpse. His head was soaked in the leakage from Baro's skull.

'Get up.'

'Please, sire, I can't breathe.'

Tannhauser rolled the corpse off him with his boot.

Petit Christian crawled to Tannhauser's feet as if he might kiss them. He struggled upright against the miseries of a fractured pubic bone. He had pissed himself.

'Take me to my wife.'

'Please, sire, Excellency, I can't. She isn't here.'

'Where is she?'

'Sire, when we brought her here, she refused to get out of the cart. She reminded Captain Garnier that he was her protector, that she was a free woman, accused of no crime, and that if he had not the courtesy to offer her sanctuary, she would rather he at least take her some good distance from this foul place and leave her in the street.'

Tannhauser absorbed this unwelcome news.

'Fetch my bow and quiver. Carry both on your left shoulder.'

Christian waddled off to obey.

Tannhauser imagined Garnier cringing under Carla's disdain. It was the intelligent move. But no matter how sharp her wits, the throes of labour had to have left her exhausted and frail. Her feelings he could not imagine. Her peril had been so extreme she had surrendered Amparo to the care of a ragamuffin girl. That could only have been because she had expected to die. Without her babe, her torment must be immense.

He swallowed a knot in his throat.

Petit Christian returned and saw his face. He took two steps backwards.

'Don't be afraid, little playwright. Give me no good reason and I'll not kill you. Where has Garnier taken her?'

'Sire, he has a fine house on the north bank of the City, near the Pont au Change. He promised her every comfort that his wife and servants could provide.'

'Security? Guards?'

Christian was distracted by a gargle of distress from his former master.

Tannhauser slapped him, lightly. Christian staggered.

'Security was not discussed, sire. A militiaman or two, perhaps, for her peace of mind. No one would dare invade Garnier's house. No one has any reason to.'

'Does Garnier know I'm Carla's husband?'

'There was no reason to tell him. Only Dominic knows, and we three here.'

Tannhauser slapped him again. Christian fell over and writhed.

'Do not include me in any "we's" of yours.'

'Forgive me.'

'Dominic wasn't happy, was he?'

'He had no grounds to protest, though he tried. I stopped him myself, sire.'

'Where is Dominic, his musket men?'

'I don't know.'

Tannhauser didn't believe him but that, along with other questions, could wait.

'Is Stefano still here with Orlandu?'

Christian blinked.

'Stefano refused to leave Orlandu's side. They've been treated well, sire.'

'Are they otherwise guarded?'

'No, sire.'

'Any guns in there? Bows?'

'No. The Swiss has a sword.'

'There must be ready money in this room. Fetch it.'

'The keys are on his Excellency's belt, sire.'

Christian indicated Le Tellier. He had abandoned his master with no more scruple than a drunk would an ugly whore. He crawled around the desk and searched the wretched villain, flinching at the groans he provoked. He unlocked a drawer in the desk and lifted out a cash box.

Tannhauser walked to the window. The killing by the river continued. By the clock on the tower of the Conciergerie it was twenty minutes to ten o'clock. He could get Carla to the gate at the Porte Saint-Denis by the time it opened at midnight.

'The day was expensive, sire. About thirty pistoles, over half in *écus d'or*.'

Christian was looking inside two open sacks.

'Bring both sacks with you.'

Tannhauser closed the casement.

In his mind he saw Pascale.

'What were Le Tellier's orders concerning the children at Frogier's sister's?'

'Frogier?'

Christian retreated and cowered as Tannhauser walked to the desk.

'You were with Frogier this evening.'

Tannhauser shoved Le Tellier with a boot. Le Tellier howled into his ruff.

'Le Tellier sent three *sergents* to hold Anne in custody, at Irène's,' said Christian. 'In case you returned.'

'Anne?'

He remembered. Frogier knew Pascale as Anne.

'The girl with raven hair. Le Tellier asked which one you were most fond of.'

Tannhauser looked down. Le Tellier's eyes were marbled with terror.

'And the others?'

'He said Anne would be enough, and that the rest would just get in the way.'

Tannhauser remembered the Mice laughing at the spilled eggs. Juste eating fig pies. Flore. His right hand closed around Le Tellier's throat. The skin was papery and sweaty against his palm. As he lifted him from the floor he felt the tug of the anchored bolt against tendon and bone, the spasms in the unsocketed shoulders. He sensed the policeman's excruciation. And that excruciation wasn't enough.

'I had nothing to do with it.'

Christian's whimpered disavowal restored Tannhauser's wits.

He didn't want Le Tellier to die just yet. He dropped him to squirm.

'Take me to Orlandu.'

Tannhauser aimed to leave no one to tell of his doings in the *hôtel*; but he didn't want to kill Stefano. Christian laboured up the stair on his broken pelvis. Tannhauser pushed past him and grabbed him by the scruff and dragged him to the second floor. The domestic staff had been dismissed for the night and wouldn't emerge unless summoned. They stopped at a door. Tannhauser knocked.

'Stefano of Sion, Mattias Tannhauser.'

The big Swiss opened the door, holding a sword. He took in Tannhauser's blood-boltered corpus, the gold collar, the crossbow. He sheathed the sword and saluted.

Tannhauser spoke in Italian.

'How went the day?'

'My lord, since last I saw you, my hardest battle has been not to fall asleep.'

'How is Orlandu? Is he fit to travel?'

'If no forced march is required. He's poorly – hot chills – but his head's clear. I've had him walk up and down the room for a quarter of every hour.'

'Excellent man. Now, with regret, we must part again.'

'If I may, my lord, I've seen that collar before –'

'If it were still around Le Tellier's neck you'd be dead by morning.'

'That's why I didn't nap. I've sniffed ill will since we got here, though Orlandu was content. If you need me further, only ask.'

Tannhauser was tempted. But Stefano could have no idea what might be required. Tannhauser didn't want the Swiss Guards on his back, which, if he led one of their corporals that far astray, they might well be.

'I want everything you've seen and done since you left the Hôtel Béthizy with Sergent Baro – who is dead – to be your fastest secret. Spin some tale to cover your absence. On a day like this what tale could not be spun? Will you do that, on your word?'

'On my word, my lord, the secret is fast. May I know why?'

'We both of us were drawn into a conspiracy not of our making. The conspiracy began, and ends, with Marcel Le Tellier, and his end stands before you. Whatever investigation there may be of his conspiracy – or of his end – it would spell your doom to have played any part in it. At the same time, in no possible circumstance could playing any such part bring you any benefit.'

Stefano glanced at Christian. He looked at Tannhauser.

Tannhauser said, 'There will be no witnesses as to your presence here.'

'I understand, my lord. And I can spin tales.'

Tannhauser took the lighter of the sacks from Christian and handed it to Stefano.

'I'd keep this secret, too. Spend it in Sion.'

The sack's weight caused the Swiss's eyebrows to rise.

Tannhauser clapped him on the back.

'Some other day, then, some other battle.'

'I hope so, my lord. As long as we're on the same side.'

'If not, strike hard, for I will.'

Stefano saluted. He started down the stair.

'Stefano, use the back door, or a girl might shoot you in the chest. And be warned, down in the lobby you'll find –'

'I already found them, my lord, while you claimed the collar. *Buona fortuna.*'

Tannhauser heard Orlandu's voice.

'Mattias?'

Tannhauser removed the bolt and propped the crossbow. He pushed Christian into the room ahead of him. Orlandu sat in a chair, his tanned complexion waxy, but he was hale enough to rise to his feet and stand up straight. His eyes were as dark as his father's, to all intents black. Tannhauser grinned; an effect the sight of the lad had always had on him. Orlandu didn't smile.

He said, 'You're covered in blood.'

'Don't worry, it's not mine.'

Still Orlandu did not smile.

'Let me embrace you,' said Tannhauser, 'or at least shake your hand.'

Orlandu's left arm was bound across his chest in a sling. He held out his right hand and Tannhauser took it in his. His joy was tarnished by the sight of the porter.

The porter shrank back into the shadows.

'This is Boniface,' said Orlandu.

'We've met,' said Tannhauser. 'Can you walk down the stairs?'

'Yes.'

'Good. Sit on the steps in the lobby, I won't be long. If anyone knocks, call for me, then ask them who they are.'

'Please, my boy,' said Boniface. 'He's going to murder me in cold blood.'

'Be thankful it's not hotter.' Tannhauser looked at Orlandu. '"My boy"?'

Orlandu twitched. He looked at the gold collar on Tannhauser's chest.

'You've killed his Excellency?'

Tannhauser was more disturbed than Orlandu was.

'His Excellency prays for death, down below.'

'Mattias,' said Orlandu, 'I don't understand.'

'Neither do I, but it can wait. Carla is in danger. Go and watch the front door.'

'Boniface is my friend. I lodge in his home.'

Tannhauser's stomach turned. He looked at the porter.

Boniface lowered himself to his knees and clasped his hands.

'Yesterday,' said Tannhauser, 'this friend told me he couldn't remember the last time he saw your face. Are you mates with this degenerate, too?'

Orlandu glanced at Petit Christian, and Tannhauser saw that it was so.

'These clowns schemed with Le Tellier to kill your mother.'

'That's not possible.'

Tannhauser stared at him. 'Are you still delirious?'

559

'Le Tellier is a great man,' said Orlandu. 'A brilliant man. He's taught me many things about politics. Thanks to him, I was to be ordained into the Pilgrims of Saint-Jacques, which is a –'

'I know what they are. Soon, so will you.'

Tannhauser closed his mind to the pain he felt. Orlandu's father, Ludovico, had been a fanatic, an inquisitor. Did it run in the blood? He took a breath.

'Le Tellier's only claim to brilliance is as a deceiver. And you have been deceived.'

'Is it true?' Orlandu directed the question to Petit Christian.

Tannhauser backhanded Petit Christian to the floor.

'You ask this sack of filth to vouch for my word?'

Orlandu stepped back from his rage, as well he might.

'To what degree are you in league with these beasts?'

'Not against you, Mattias. Nor my mother. How could you –'

'Then against who?'

Orlandu retreated further, no longer unreadable. He was terrified.

At this moment, Tannhauser could summon no sympathy.

'You've not been here,' said Orlandu. 'You don't know the radical Huguenots, or what they're like or what they intend to do, to the Crown, to the country –'

'Who shot you?'

'I don't know,' said Orlandu. 'It was dark. They came from behind.'

Tannhauser trod on Christian's head and compressed his skull into the planks.

'Who shot him?'

'Dominic shot him,' said Christian. 'Dominic and Baro.'

'Why?'

'We couldn't let Carla leave,' panted Christian, 'or the scheme would fail. I saved the boy's life. Dominic would have finished him but those weren't the orders. I reminded him. I said he might yet prove useful.'

'"Couldn't let her leave"? What do you mean?'

'Orlandu tried to move his mother out of the Hôtel D'Aubray.'

Tannhauser looked at Orlandu. In the dark eyes lurked something terrible.

'You found out about their scheme,' said Tannhauser.

Orlandu didn't speak. Perhaps he couldn't.

'Answer me, lad.'

Still Orlandu didn't speak.

'Christian, how did Orlandu learn of your scheme?'

'I don't know.'

Tannhauser leaned more weight on his heel and felt the cranium underneath it change shape. Christian's eyes bulged. He flailed and gibbered.

'I don't know. I don't know. Oh God, stop, I don't know.'

'Yes, yes, stop this, I beg you,' cried Boniface. 'I told him.'

Tannhauser lifted his foot. He looked at the porter.

'Not all of it, but enough,' said Boniface. 'I grew to love Orlandu, long since. Then his mother came to Paris. When he would return from his visits with her, I witnessed his joy. He was so beautiful, more beautiful than ever, though I'd not thought that possible. I didn't care about her. I've never seen her. I kept silent. But when the day neared, I couldn't bear to see that beauty ruined. I told him I'd heard, from a reliable source, that assassins had been hired to kill Symonne D'Aubray, and that in her home his mother was in danger of her life.'

Boniface fell to weeping.

Tannhauser looked at Orlandu. Clearly the lad had no conception of the nature of Boniface's love, and so it should stay. The tale begged other questions, but Tannhauser didn't ask them. He had had enough of answers. He drew his dagger and walked to Boniface. The withered pederast grabbed at his boots.

'The old fear dying more than do the young. You'd think it would be otherwise.' Tannhauser glanced at Orlandu. 'If you don't want to watch, wait below.'

'Mattias –'

Tannhauser stooped and knifed the porter in the right lower quarter of his skinny gut. He slit him to the upper left ribcage and left him to convulse in his own entrails.

'You want to know if I would have saved the D'Aubrays, too.'

Tannhauser wiped the blade. 'I don't need to hear it.'

'You've never concealed your truth from me.'

'You would've left the D'Aubrays to die. Fine. Now let's be on.'

'No, Mattias. You must hear it.'

Tannhauser braced himself and sheathed his dagger. He nodded.

'I came here and told Le Tellier what Boniface had told me. I told him I had overheard the rumour in a tavern.'

Tannhauser grunted. What passed for cunning on the docks in Malta was something less than subtle in Paris. Le Tellier had done as he would have done himself; mark Boniface as unsound but keep him working.

Orlandu mistook him. 'You've lied, when you needed to.'

'It's a fine art. Go on.'

'He showed every surprise and concern, and said he would arrange the safest lodgings for my mother. He said more.'

Tannhauser waited.

'Admiral Coligny had been shot just that morning. The Huguenot nobles were in uproar, threatening retribution in the streets. Le Tellier explained that in a mood of such outrage, the murder of the widow –' Orlandu swallowed gall '– and the children – of Roger D'Aubray would be sure to incite the Huguenots to war. Even Coligny. He said we could not know the origin of this stratagem – which I took to mean the palace – but that its genius could not be denied. I understood. I agreed. I did not deny it.'

Tannhauser couldn't think of anything to say to ease his self-disgust.

'I knew those children,' said Orlandu. 'I played with them in the garden. I made them laugh. Do you know what happened to them?'

Tannhauser thought of the polished oak table, the gilded chair. In such rooms, no less than in perfumed carriages, the lives of children counted for nothing.

'They're dead.'

Orlandu's mouth trembled.

'You must never tell your mother this tale. She saw them die.'

'What?' Orlandu's confusion was appalling. 'How?'

Tannhauser shook his head.

'When I woke up, here, Le Tellier told me he'd sent her to the Louvre.'

'He's a better liar than you are,' said Tannhauser. 'And tell no lies to Carla. Never lie to a woman. They only believe you if they want to, and even then, they know.'

'Then what should I tell her?'

'The truth. You were on your way to see her, you were shot and drugged, you woke up here. You were as much a victim of their conspiracy as she was.'

'Where is she?'

'She's waiting for us. Come here.'

Orlandu stumbled over. Tannhauser took his head onto his shoulder.

'When I was your age I butchered Shiites for the Sultan and thought the work holy. So take my advice. If you must commit mortal crimes, commit them for yourself alone, not for some other, nor for his creed, nor his crown, nor his favour. Then at least we might be damned as men, not as whores.'

'I'm sorry.'

'Let's be on.'

Tannhauser held him at arm's length and grinned. Orlandu couldn't.

'How can I help?'

'Carry the bow and quiver, be ready to feed me.'

Tannhauser dragged Christian by his collar and belt and pitched him down the stairs. Moans drifted up from the bottom. Tannhauser dragged the mattress from the bed and threw it after him. He retrieved the crossbow and armed it.

'Why did Le Tellier plot against Carla?' asked Orlandu.

'He nurses some private blood feud against me.'

'Why?'

'I don't know,' said Tannhauser. 'I haven't asked him.'

The *Lieutenant Criminel* of Paris balanced on his one good knee behind his polished oak desk. His eyeballs vibrated in his brain-slaked face. The blood-and-mucus-wetted ruff dangled from his mouth like some obscene tumour. He swayed and uttered a medley of muffled cries. With his crossed hands he might have been engaged in some bizarre form of prayer. Perhaps he was.

Orlandu made some sound in his throat.

'Save your pity,' said Tannhauser, 'and if it be disgust, swallow it.'

Tannhauser had moulded this gruesome clay with little feeling. Now he was angry. He questioned the rightness of none of what he had done. It had been necessary. But it affronted him that such grim labours had been set by so base a hypocrite; and that such trash should have corrupted his son. He laid the crossbow on the desk.

'You, policeman, look at me.'

Le Tellier tried. It was beyond him. He dropped his eyes.

'Your former acolyte wants to hear your confession, though since neither of us have the power to absolve you, you will shortly join the damned.'

The Catholic fanatic was not unaware of his eternal destiny.

'You will answer me by nodding,' said Tannhauser. 'Nod.'

Le Tellier nodded.

'You paid for Carla to be murdered in order to torment me.'

Le Tellier nodded.

'When you learned I was in Paris, you hired bravos to deliver me to you.'

Le Tellier nodded.

'With Carla captive, you hoped to make me watch her die.'

Le Tellier started to sob.

'You knew she was pregnant,' said Tannhauser. 'Answer.'

Le Tellier nodded.

'You did this for revenge.'

For the first time, Le Tellier looked at him. He nodded.

'And before you had me killed,' said Tannhauser, 'you were counting on the pleasure of telling me why I deserved a punishment so vile.'

Le Tellier nodded. Squeezed tears dribbled into his beard.

'If I take the rag from your mouth, will you tell me what it was I did to earn your hatred?'

Le Tellier didn't need to nod. His desperation to accuse the guilty of his crime blazed brighter than hope. He nodded thrice.

'Good,' said Tannhauser. 'Because I don't want to know.'

Le Tellier didn't believe him.

Orlandu did. He walked around the table and reached for the gag.

'Leave it where it is,' said Tannhauser.

'I want to know,' said Orlandu.

'You have no say in this.'

Orlandu confined his pain to the blackness in his eyes.

'There are many with cause to curse the day I was born,' said Tannhauser. 'I need no more cause to remember this one.'

'Won't it haunt you?'

'If I were the type to be haunted, I would be insane.'

Le Tellier garbled. Tannhauser looked at him.

'Whatever I did to you or yours, I feel no morsel of regret. Your revenge and your reasons mean nothing to me. Your anguish means nothing at all.'

Le Tellier struggled to take this in. His eyes became deranged.

Tannhauser leaned forward and stared into them.

'And before I leave this city, of which you believed yourself master, I will butcher your son.'

Le Tellier mewled through his gag.

Tannhauser drew his sword.

'Let me kill him,' said Orlandu.

Tannhauser swallowed on something sour.

'In Malta, as brothers, we faced honourable foes, and I took pains not to let you take a single life. There is no honour in taking this one.'

He took Orlandu to the window and opened it.

'Nor in taking these.'

He let him see the shameful doings on the gore-blackened strand.

'There are your Pilgrims. There's your war.'

Orlandu held onto the sill with his one good hand.

'Our war,' said Tannhauser, 'for I'm guiltier than thee.'

He left Orlandu to make of it what he would.

He returned to Le Tellier.

He lifted the policeman's chin with the sword for a clear stroke.

'And so,' said Tannhauser, 'to the burning lake below.'

Le Tellier's eyes brimmed with a final vision of horror.

Tannhauser swung two-handed and cut him clean through the nape.

Le Tellier's bald head bounced across the desk and rolled at Christian's feet. A tide of blood swept the oak and set papers to floating. The broken corpse dropped and dangled from the bolt.

Tannhauser took the cup of wine and drained it. It was excellent. As he put it down, one of the papers caught his eye. He recognised the handwriting.

La Fosse.

In the turmoil above he hadn't grasped the significance of Boniface's presence.

He looked at Petit Christian, who was leaning against the wall by the door.

'Playwright, you gave the letter I sent you to Le Tellier.'

'No, no, sire, that is, it was not my intention to do so, but Boniface –'

'You have one last chance to save your life. Tell me their stratagem.'

Petit Christian was an animal of the sort that is quite unable to believe in its own doom, no matter how compelling the signs. While he lived, he thought he would survive.

'You ordered me to meet you at midnight, sire, under the gallows in the Place de Grève. Dominic and Captain Garnier, and of course their men, are lying in wait, dispersed around the square among the other militia, and the streets thereabouts. They believe you'll be there early. The letter was the first news we had of you.'

'So Garnier knows about the printer's house.'

'I knew nothing of that, sire, until Frogier, well, in fact it was Le Tellier who told Garnier that you'd massacred nineteen militia. I myself played no part in –'

'What time are you to take your place beneath the gallows?'

'Eleven thirty.'

'Are you to go alone or escorted?'

'Alone, in case you were watching me.'

They'd give Christian at least five minutes to be late before sending for him.

'Orlandu,' said Tannhauser, 'tell me the time by the clock tower.'

'It's just after ten.'

Tannhauser turned back to Petit Christian. 'Are the Pilgrims on foot?'

'Dominic, Garnier and Thomas Crucé are mounted.'

Three minutes to get here, five to recover their wits, three to get back to the Place de Grève, ten at least to rally the troops and move them out. Call it midnight. Move out where? He had to assume that they had more wit than they'd shown so far.

The Porte Saint-Denis was still Tannhauser's best option.

The Temple, and the protection of the knights, lay beyond the Place de Grève, or at the end of a long detour. That problem hadn't changed: persuade some night guard to open the gates while he conducted a broil in the street, for the Temple was the one place the militia were sure to blockade. They could hide, as Grymonde had suggested, but could he hide so many? And for how many days? By which time Dominic might have the Châtelet, and worse, on their track.

He had to find Carla and Pascale and get back to the Porte Saint-Denis by midnight. Any later and the torrent of traffic would be against them, perhaps even impassable. They had to be first through the gate. The livestock would slow the militia; but Garnier would be no more than half an hour behind them, and unencumbered by a wagon. Should he go and pick off the mounted men now? No. Pursuit would be immediate. They'd flood the *quartier*. Whatever his own chances, in a running street fight the wagon would have little or none. Garnier would pursue him beyond the city; that, he didn't doubt.

He flicked Le Tellier's blood and sheathed his sword.

He had to make sure that Dominic would join the pursuit. With those two dead, along with as many more as he could cut down, there'd be few among the survivors who cared enough to continue to hunt him. If any were feeling spiteful, there were still plenty of Huguenots left in Paris.

Tannhauser considered his resources for a fight on the open road.

His resources were him.

Under a full moon? Find a spot, strike from their flank. Scatter them like quail. He could double back towards the city and ambush what was left of the covey.

He picked up Le Tellier's head by one ear and drew his dagger. 'Orlandu.'

Orlandu turned from the window. His face was paler than ever.

'In the lobby you'll find two cuirasses. Collect them and wait. Helms, too. Take that mace with you. Playwright, give me your belt.'

He laid Le Tellier's head on the desk and cut two parallel incisions in the top of the scalp. He worked the blade through one incision and out of the other, and scraped the strap of skin so formed away from the surface of the skull. He lifted the flat of the blade and the skin strap became a kind of handle. Christian proffered his belt. Tannhauser threaded the belt through the skin strap and buckled it. As he lifted Le Tellier's head, the wrinkled brow smoothed. Christian gagged.

'Your master looks ten years younger, wouldn't you say?'

Tannhauser took the crossbow and herded the pimp through the ante-room and along the landing. He stopped.

'Garnier escorted Carla to his home.'

'Yes, sire, precisely, in person.'

'You told him. In the street below, before he left.'

'Told him what, sire?'

'That I'd slaughtered those scabs at the printer's house. That's how you got him to come back here so promptly.'

'No, sire. I told him only that we knew who had killed his men, not that it was you. That's why he hurried back. Marcel told him it was you.'

Tannhauser kicked him down the main stair.

He followed, dragging the mattress.

He flipped the loop of the buckled belt over one arm of the main chandelier that hung in the hallway. He steadied the suspended head on the tilted apparatus. The neck drained as it gyrated back and forth. The whole face was hauled upwards, the eyes whited, the mouth stretched up around the bloody gag in a crazed smile. The shadows thrown by the candles gave it the aspect of a comedic mask sculpted by a maniac.

It would be the first thing anyone entering the house would see.

Tannhauser stepped back and collected Altan's weapons from the baluster.

He saw Orlandu, holding the armour with one arm, looking at him.

'Will that make Dominic scream and run? Or fill him with rage?'

'First one, then the other,' said Orlandu.

Tannhauser hefted the cask on his shoulder.

'Playwright, pass me the mattress, and bring that basket.'

'You want Dominic to come after you?' said Orlandu.

'Dead men settle no scores.'

As Tannhauser reached the foot of the steps – as if to do so were to cast a spell – Grégoire pulled out from some invisible nook large enough to conceal a horse and wagon, and rolled down the street towards him. He grinned and Tannhauser grinned back. Clementine snorted in the traces. Lucifer trotted between her front hooves.

Tannhauser regretted not telling Grégoire to bring some other horse. Yet who better than Clementine to drag a cartload of demons through the halls of Hell?

'Is it good?' asked Grégoire.

'High sides and thick boards. I've never seen a finer war wagon.'

He loaded the cask and the mattress. Grymonde emerged from the stockyard, using the *spontone*. His other hand was held by a boy Tannhauser hadn't seen before. The boy was wet. Estelle came behind them. Amparo sat inside her shirt in the goatskin, cradled against the tiller of the armed crossbow Estelle carried in both hands.

Tannhauser saw Orlandu take stock.

'Orlandu, my crew. Grégoire, Grymonde, Estelle, and her sister, Amparo.'

'Amparo?' said Orlandu.

'They're your sisters, too.'

'My sisters?'

'Carla gave birth to Amparo this afternoon.'

Tannhauser wanted to dwell deep on the tiny face peering over the rim in the moonlight, but he couldn't dawdle. He took the bolts from his own crossbow and Estelle's.

'Load as you need to. If there's shooting, hold that breastplate over Amparo.'

He stacked gear and food in the wagon.

He lifted Estelle in after it. He looked at the damp youth.

'Who're you, boy?'

'That's Hugon,' said Estelle.

'I take it the city needs a new chief of police,' said Grymonde.

'Le Tellier was just another obstacle,' said Tannhauser. 'There are plenty more.'

'Where's that little green turd, Petit Chris?'

'I told him I wouldn't kill him.'

'That'd better mean what I hope it means. Let me have him.'

Christian shuffled closer to Tannhauser.

'He's going to take us to Carla,' said Tannhauser.

'Well, I can take you to Carla,' said Hugon.

Tannhauser looked at him. Hugon looked back.

'Hugon followed her,' said Estelle. 'He swam across the river, while the soldiers took Carla over the bridge. Then he swam back and Rody caught him, and I shot Rody.'

Tannhauser took off the gold collar. He hung it round Hugon's neck.

'Don't go swimming in this. Don't try to sell it as it is.'

'I'm not a fool. I'll melt it down.'

Hugon slid the shells inside his shirt.

Tannhauser took a rope from the wagon. He coiled it round Christian's chest.

'Hugon, which bridge should we take?'

'They're all chained, except for the Millers' Bridge, which isn't for public use. A covered road runs through the mills, for the grain wagons. It's guarded.'

Tannhauser cinched the rope. He dropped the ends and turned away.

Killing to cross the river, killing to cross it back. The gate. The road.

For a moment, at the very moment he could not afford to be, Tannhauser felt crushed. By all of it. The blood. The atrocity. The madness. The love. And all of it his. He loved these people. These children who looked to him for a safety he couldn't provide, a wisdom he didn't possess. He was a man looking for his wife. That was all. Yet that was no longer true. He looked at the children. The street was deserted, but for them.

'Go back to your lives,' he said. 'You'll stand a better chance.'

'No,' said Estelle. 'Our life is with you. We don't want to come with you so you can look after us. We can do that for ourselves. We just want to be with you.'

He looked at her.

'Don't be afraid, Tannzer.'

She meant it in the simplest way but she was right. He was afraid, not just of their dying, but the guilt he would feel if he survived them.

'We could wait for you here, they won't find us,' said Grégoire.

'No.' Estelle shook her head at him. 'Carla needs the wagon, and she wants Amparo back, and I won't leave my sister, and neither will Tannzer, and the dragon can't leave me, because I am his eyes. But you don't have to come, Hugon.'

'Oh, I'm coming,' said Hugon. 'For Carla, and the violl.'

Tannhauser's spirit was restored. He resolved to be cheerful.

'Aye, let's make some music. Orlandu, Hugon, get aboard.'

Grymonde, unaided, loomed over Petit Christian. Christian gaped up into the monstrous face. Even he knew that his life and his dreams were now done.

'I know you. Blinded and with my nose clogged with cow shit. You're a hole in the material of the world.' Grymonde stopped. 'You're the Juggler.'

'He gave me to a man,' said Estelle. 'A rich man, in a rich house, in a rich bed.'

'I saw him tell the soldiers to burn out Grymonde's eyes,' said Hugon.

'He let the monkeys die,' said Grégoire.

Grymonde turned his head towards Tannhauser.

'Give him to me. Give him to us.'

Tannhauser said, 'Feel the rope around his chest.'

Grymonde did so. He grunted.

'We may still need his tongue, to tell us things he knows that we do not. But he won't ride with us. He'll crawl.'

'Crawl?'

'I'm going to tie him under the wagon, to the axle-tree. Think about it.'

Tannhauser watched Christian think about it.

'Let him crawl,' said Estelle.

Grymonde saw it, too, borne aloft by pain and opium. He started laughing.

Christian stared at the filth coating the street. 'Excellency, please –'

Tannhauser threw him beneath the wagon. He held his breath and squatted. He ran the ends of the rope around the front axle and knotted them. He stood up and breathed. Lucifer gave Christian a sniff and pissed on his head.

'My Infant,' said Tannhauser.

'I am here.'

Tannhauser took his arm. He guided the blind giant backwards onto the rear of the wagon bed. He took the *spontone* from his hand and laid it on the boards.

'Sit here, in the breach, my Infant. Our children are behind you.

If anyone tries to enter this breach without calling his name, he is yours.'

'He is mine.'

'You said the cards are in play.'

'I did. They are. Carla drew them.'

'Which cards?'

'That's for her to tell. But I have better. You know what she said to me?'

Tannhauser's shoulder ached as the biggest hand he had ever seen grabbed it.

'*I wagered everything I am on Mattias's love a long time ago.*'

'Thank you, my Infant.'

'We've all taken our throw. Now the dice are yours.'

Tannhauser took up a position by Clementine's head.

He looked at Grégoire. He thought of Juste.

'*Audentes fortuna juvat.*'

Grégoire snapped the reins and the war wagon creaked into motion.

As they rolled towards all peril and the River Seine, Grymonde roared.

'Bring me the jawbone of an ass.'

PART FIVE

DIREFUL SLAUGHTERING DEATH

CHAPTER THIRTY

If This Be Paradise

The Millers' Bridge lay barely a hundred paces from the torture chambers and prisons of the Châtelet. Tannhauser saw no activity at the fortress gate. The police had kept their distance from the massacres. The intelligent move. If they took no responsibility, they couldn't be held responsible, whatever the political outcome. The militias had assumed control of the bridges. Should the police see one unguarded, they might not care to get involved; such might even be their orders. The incompetence of their rivals could only please them.

The Millers' Bridge was closed to the sky by the upper floors of the watermills that were built along its length. Near the entrance he saw a brazier, figures in outline. Three. A hanging lantern revealed no more. Nightwatch in a city where no one but their comrades dared to step outside the door. A dull duty, to which would be assigned dull men. He couldn't give them the chance to flee to the Châtelet. Nor could he let them escape down the tunnel to the City.

He had left the wagon in a side street. As he walked back, he looked west down the river. Level with the tower of the Louvre, he saw two distant boats on the water.

The river would take him farther and faster from Paris than the road north. Carla would be more comfortable. They could sail all the way to the English Channel. Better, they could hire rowers out of Elbeuf to take them up the Eure to Chartres. Let Carla get her strength back. A day or two on horseback to the Flèche, and hence the mighty Loire, and Saint-Nazaire, and a ship to Bordeaux and home.

The vision gripped him.

Garnier and Dominic likely wouldn't know where he had gone – or how – before morning at the earliest. Beyond morning, with tempers cooling and the political realities closing in – and with the price that it might cost them written in blood across the walls of the Hôtel Le Tellier – they might not pursue him at all. Once he was away from Paris, their power shrivelled, along with their reach. They would need to call on the power of other authorities, whose questions might prove awkward; or even fatal. Tonight they had the city to themselves; he would be just another body; but to ask the Crown to arrest a Knight of Saint John, on nothing but their word, at the dawn of a new religious war, would be a folly beyond even Dominic's stupidity. The risk of exposing their own criminality and treason would be extreme. The wise move, though he didn't count on it, would be to forget him.

He would not forget them.

But he could return some other time to collect those debts.

He recalled the barges moored at the back of Irène's. Hide Carla and the children on board. A bargeman and his blind slave. Grymonde's face alone might repel the curious. If not, Tannhauser had fought on the water; he doubted whoever was patrolling in those boats had.

'Hugon, those boats I see yonder, do they guard the river traffic?'

'No. It's a boom.'

'A boom.'

Tannhauser's vision dissolved, as those of beauty will.

'The boats are chained end on end, all the way across the river,' said Hugon, 'from the Tour de Nelle to the wharf of the Louvre.'

Grymonde grunted. 'They had that boom up by noon. Tonight it's either the gate at Saint-Denis or some room that smells of piss.'

Tannhauser armed the crossbow he'd used on Baro.

'Hugon, watch at the corner for my signal. Grégoire, bring the wagon up steady, as if you've got business at the mills. The rest of you, lie low.'

Tannhauser drew his sword and walked towards the bridge.

Naked to the waist and boltered with gore, he no longer bore any resemblance to the wanted man the militiamen might have heard of. He looked like no knight, ever seen or ever imagined. Make them think him one of them, gone mad with blood. The moon was behind him. The noise of the watermills buried his footsteps. The brazier had dulled their eyes, a day of dominance their wits. He could have fallen on them before they knew it, but he wanted to flush all five. He smelled roasting meat. Pigs' ears. Or cheeks. He waved his sword in greeting.

'What news, mates, what news?'

Tannhauser now saw four.

Their first reaction to the sight of him was fear. Two grappled for halberds.

'Those viands smell good. Pigs' ears?'

'Aye. Not much to go round, as it happens.'

'I've plenty to trade.'

Their spears drooped. The wolf was among the sheep. Tannhauser chose the order in which to kill them. The fifth man appeared and stuck his head over the shoulder of the fourth from behind. Tannhauser changed the order. He smiled.

'All this killing has given me an appetite.'

The fifth smiled back. Tannhauser's lunge took him well inside the length of their spears. His weight drove his sword blade through the gut of the fourth man and a good six inches into the gut of the smiler behind him. He panicked the others with the crossbow while he booted the dying from his blade. One ran. Tannhauser shot him in the back at close range, triggering with his right forearm. The pole of a halberd swept towards his knees and he blocked it dead with the stock of the bow. He ran the second guard obliquely through the throat; on the pull he severed the veins and arteries of his right neck. The first, and last, was the one who had tried to sweep him. Tannhauser dropped the bow and grabbed the spear shaft, and jerked him in and stabbed him in the belly and twisted. He let go of the pole to lend more weight to the ricasso with his left hand, and sundered him to the pubes and let him fall.

Tannhauser beckoned to Hugon.

The smiler was still crawling. The one he had shot was panting blood on his knees. Tannhauser cut their throats. He flicked his sword and sheathed it. He heaved the bolt from the dead man's loin. He reloaded the crossbow and propped it against the wall.

He dragged a pair of the dead down the passageway. Their bodies slithered through the flour dust, grease and water that coated the bridge. Lanterns burned at regular intervals, but he could not see the far end of the bridge. The noise of the wheels resounded from the ceiling. He reached the first of the watermills. In a gap between the buildings the bridge was open to the river. A chain windlass permitted the wheel to be raised or lowered, depending on how high the river ran. Ladders gave access to the gears that caused the water to turn the stones. The gears were uncoupled, or the cacophony would have been greater. He saw the paddles churn below. He slung the corpses in the water. They were tossed and battered in the spume like bloody dolls and disappeared.

He repeated the chore.

He collected the last guard, and dumped him.

He paused and leaned against the windlass. Sweat trickled down his face and through the blood that stiffened the hairs on his chest and belly like manifestations of some scabrous disease. He was close to worn out. His feet and knees ached, his back. His fingers were stiff. Too many bodies. He thought of Carla. She had to be more exhausted than he. He rolled his neck.

As he turned away he saw a miller in a dusty apron, staring at him from the wings of a double door. Tannhauser stared back and the doors closed.

The wagon rattled onto the bridge.

Tannhauser stopped it out of sight of the street. He stacked the militia's pole arms on the wagon bed, shafts first. He added the lamp. Tannhauser expected at least three more militia at the far end. The lanterns above meant that they would see him before he'd see them.

'Grymonde, I'll take that pistol. Grégoire, the pigs' ears are done. Bring the bread and the skin of wine, too. Wait for the signal. Come fast, but beware the grease.'

Tannhauser checked the priming pans and armed both barrels of the pistol. The waterwheels would muffle the shots. He stuck the pistol in the back of his belt with his left hand. He took the skin from Grégoire and poured half a pint down his throat and gave it back.

'Hugon, you come with me.'

He took his crossbow and drew his sword. He walked down the bridge.

At the next gap he took a better look down the river and saw a section of the boom. Mainly cargo lighters; the masts of the two fishing boats. He saw the continuing enormities on the beaches of either bank. Rape and murder gangs. A pity about the boom. He pressed on through pools of yellow and black. The bridge vibrated beneath his feet.

'Hugon, how many waterwheels?'

'Twelve. Two of the arches are empty for the boats to pass.'

'Stay here. You can still see the wagon. Wait for my signal to call them.'

Tannhauser walked on. He saw no guards. He entered the last dark spot. Up ahead, a lantern hung above the exit and a torch burned near the ground, stacked in a bucket.

A figure appeared, his half-pike planted.

'What news, what news?' called Tannhauser.

'If there's news, you're the one who's bringing it.'

The voice that reached him above the din sounded young.

'They left hours ago, or so it feels like. Did they send any word for me?'

Tannhauser saw his face: an eager lad, no older than Orlandu, and, like Orlandu, seduced by the folly of his elders. He had a white ribbon tied around his forehead to soak up the sweat, or mark him a Catholic. There was no one else behind him. Three guards at each end; two gone to drink and eat with the others. At the sight of Tannhauser, the lad seemed more overawed than afraid.

'So those buggers left you all alone. Which one was in charge?'

'Oudin.'

'Oudin? I might have known. All quiet this end?'

'Apart from the miller, you're the first I've seen all night.'

The lad smiled. It was a pity he had chosen to stand with scum.

Tannhauser stabbed him in the heart. He let him drop.

He turned and found Hugon, closer than he should have been, watching the bleeding youth. He looked at Tannhauser. The boy was hard to read.

'That'll teach him,' said Hugon.

'Fetch the wagon.'

Tannhauser checked the narrow street. It was empty in either direction but for a cart stacked with corpses and aswarm with nocturnal insects. Dockside warehouses. The Conciergerie; the clock tower. He could see the hour hand. Half past ten. He made the pistol safe. He dragged the slain youngster and his pike to the nearest wheel. He ditched the pike and stripped the white ribbon. He tied the ribbon round his own brow.

He threw the body in the Seine.

As the others arrived, Tannhauser took the torch from the bucket and set it in an iron ring bolted to the wagon for that purpose. He bridled at being on this side of the bridge. On an island. The Left Bank was a prison wall. With luck, the Millers' Bridge would not be reinforced before he returned with Carla.

And Pascale. If he could afford the time.

The warehouses were lightless. There'd be a quiet spot somewhere. After he found Carla he could bring the wagon back, hide it and its cargo, and then go for Pascale. Carla would have Amparo. A fight would be easier fought without the wagon.

'Won't that let the soldiers see us?' Estelle pointed at the torch.

'Well said. But they'll see us anyway, and since a wagon should have a light, a wagon without one will arouse their suspicion sooner. Hugon?'

'We go left.' Hugon indicated a turret, not far away. 'Past the Palais.'

Tannhauser wanted to see Amparo's face. He unloaded the crossbow and stowed it in the wagon. He looked at Estelle. Amparo was asleep in her kidskin cradle. His love was a strange feeling, real as the timber under his hand. He turned away, then turned back.

'Where's Orlandu?'

'He jumped from the wagon, just back there,' said Estelle.

She pointed across the bridge.

'He said, "Mattias will understand".'

Tannhauser reached into the wagon and grabbed Le Tellier's sack of pistoles. He ran back down the bridge. One pool of yellow, one of black. The waterwheels churned. More light. He stopped. If Orlandu was gone, he was gone. If not, he was waiting, watching.

'Orlandu. I do understand. Come with me.'

Orlandu emerged, from the edge of the darkness. He called out above the roar.

'I can survive in Paris.'

'That's no trick for the likes of us. Come with me.'

'I can't face Carla. Not yet. Or you. Tell her –' His voice broke. 'I promise I'll come home. Soon. Tell her I love Amparo. Goodbye, my brother.'

Tannhauser skated the sack underarm across the grease.

'Enough to live like a duke for a year, if you stay clear of the brothels.'

The sack stopped at Orlandu's feet.

Orlandu stooped and picked up the sack. He skated it back.

'I don't need it. You will.'

Tannhauser retrieved the gold.

Orlandu shook his head. 'I'm sorry, Mattias. I'm sorry.'

'Cheer up, man. We met in darker days than this one.'

Orlandu said, 'Not near so dark.'

Tannhauser recalled the Guva.

And the head of Sabato Svi. And Bors.

The weight of Amparo's corpse.

Those days had been darker for him.

He gave Orlandu a grin.

'See you take that arm to Monsieur Paré. Tomorrow.'

Orlandu made an honest attempt to grin back.

Tannhauser almost turned and left, for there wouldn't be a better moment; but it was Orlandu's leave to take, not his. He waited. A damp gust set the lamps to flickering.

Orlandu wiped his face on his sleeve. He saluted.

Tannhauser raised his hand.

Orlandu turned away into the shadows and was gone.

Tannhauser returned to the wagon.

Petit Christian coughed and heaved between the front wheels. His feet were shoeless and bleeding. His breeches had been dragged down to his ankles. He was covered, blinded – choked mouth and nostril – with dirty white paste.

'Hugon, take us to Garnier's house.'

'We'll pass by the militia at the Pont au Change,' said Hugon. 'You might have to teach them, too.'

'Grégoire, can we go around them?'

'It's a long way. I think we'd pass even more guards.'

The Pont au Change was lined with shops that dealt in gold and jewels. Private watchmen. Off-duty *sergents*. But the militia's job was to block the bridge, not the street that ran past it.

'We don't look like Huguenots,' said Hugon.

'Nor like militia, but bravos will do. Lower this sideboard, take those spears, and drop them in the river, but not mine. Shift that cask to this back end. My Infant.'

'Am I due another Immortal?'

'We may both need one. Come on.'

Tannhauser took Grymonde's arm and led him to the dead cart. It sang with flies. Tannhauser held his breath and found a pair of male ankles and heaved the body free. He put the ankles in Grymonde's fists. He took the arms.

'Follow the weight.'

'These must be from the Conciergerie. I heard a whole crowd of heretics surrendered to arrest and were slaughtered in the cells like sheep.'

They loaded the body face-down, head to the back of the wagon.

'You're going to trick the guards,' said Estelle.

'Very good. It's vile, but it won't be for long.'

They collected a second corpse and loaded it by the first.

Tannhauser reckoned it enough. He left the sideboard down. He guided Grymonde to sit beside Grégoire on the bench. They made quite a pair. Tannhauser armed the pistol.

'You three youngsters, if a fight breaks out, jump down and run. Hugon, take both satchels. Make a safe distance, look back. If it's gone badly, go home to the Yards. My Infant, hide your knives and keep your head down. They might know you.'

'I should hope they do.'

'Grégoire, unhook that chain. Wrap a turn or two around his wrists. And give anyone we meet a big smile. Estelle, Hugon, put those helms on.'

'It's too big for me,' said Estelle.

'All the better. My Infant, I might call upon you to laugh, so keep sharp.'

'Laugh? Laugh at what?'

The mouth of the Pont au Change, a main thoroughfare, was a lot more exposed than the Millers' Bridge. He had crossed it with Retz. A chain; three militiamen. Like those he had buried in the Seine, they wore only white insignia, not the red and white of the Pilgrims. As Tannhauser strode past, alongside the cart, one hurried over and motioned him to stop. Tannhauser signalled Grégoire to do so.

'Hold there, hold. Where've you been?'

'Add "monsieur" and you might get an answer.'

A shopkeeper, Tannhauser guessed, used to shouting at draymen, of which he seemed to suppose him an example. Tannhauser stood where the torch burned about a yard behind his right shoulder. The shopkeeper took in the blood and the weapons.

'Monsieur, where have you come from?'

'Les Halles, where there's a sight more to do than here.'

The shopkeeper looked at the children in their massive helmets. At the slumped giant on the seat and the hideous grin of the driver. The corpses and the bald dog. At the creature caked in flour and excrement, vomiting raw sewage beneath the wagon. He had no idea what to make of the tableau, though self-importance shielded him from alarm. He frowned.

'You crossed the Millers' Bridge. That's not regular.'

'Take it up with Oudin and the rest. They thought it regular enough. So did Bernard Garnier, who sent me that way to avoid your chains. They delayed his expedition, you'll remember.'

The shopkeeper did remember.

'The captain will be back shortly. As will I, to return across the Millers' Bridge.'

'There's a curfew. It's dangerous to be out. What's your business?'

'Garnier's business. I'll wait, if you so order. But you must ask him yourself.'

The shopkeeper looked him straight in the eye and at once regretted it.

Tannhauser smiled to stop him turning away.

'The captain's testy tonight. So am I. But he can afford to be, he's the captain. Call your mates over. Mates! Here!'

The shopkeeper didn't like this, though he had no more instinct for danger than his companions. They propped their pole arms by the chain and hurried over. They were sturdier types. Artisans. By the look of his hands one of them was a dyer.

Tannhauser nodded and they nodded back.

'Let's try this wine,' he said. 'I have high hopes for it.'

Tannhauser squatted and opened the spigot and drank. He stood up.

'I've tasted better. At least, I did once, and long ago.'

The artisans didn't wait for the shopkeeper's approval.

'You want to know why Garnier's in such a mood?' said Tannhauser.

The shopkeeper's manner changed. A gossiper offered some gold.

'He lost some Pilgrims tonight. The Confraternity.'

'Is that so? We heard a rumour he went up into the Yards.'

'So did we and horrible it was,' said Tannhauser. 'Even the girls are more dangerous than the bite of a rabid dog.' He winked at

Estelle, her eyes agleam in the dark beneath her helmet. 'But you know Garnier. He got what he wanted, and those beggars won't soon forget him. You've heard of the Infant?'

Tannhauser heard Grymonde shift his weight on the bench.

The shopkeeper shook his head. The dyer straightened up from his second helping of wine, while the other ducked to his third.

'The Cockaigne Infant? Grymonde? Who hasn't? He'd cut your throat for a shilling and give you eleven pence change.'

Tannhauser heard Grymonde sigh.

'I'll not ask where you tasted better wine, my friend, for it wasn't in Paris. This goes down sweet as cow's milk.'

'We've spent our lives drinking pickle juice, and never even knew it.'

'Take the cask, mates,' said Tannhauser. 'It's yours.'

Two jaws dropped. The shopkeeper shook his head.

'We're here to serve Christ and the King, not bib wine.'

'They're not drinking pickle juice in the Louvre,' said Tannhauser, 'or in the monasteries, which, by the way, is where I once tasted better. Are we Calvinists?'

Tannhauser laughed. The two joined in. They eyed the cask.

'There's more where that came from and it didn't cost a sou,' said Tannhauser. 'So drink and be merry. Or, if that's against regulations, take it home for your wives.'

The artisans seized the cask between them before their comrade could object.

'Monsieur, tell me,' said the shopkeeper, 'what happened to the Infant?'

'See for yourself,' said Tannhauser. 'There he sits.'

His voice was swamped by a bellow of crazed mirth.

The artisans fled with their cask. They stowed it and grabbed their spears. The shopkeeper slid behind them and they gathered at a safe distance to gape at Grymonde.

Grymonde rolled his head in their direction. In the shifting torchlight, the moist white bores of his eye sockets yawned without expression above the huge bared teeth, as if created to give the watchers a glimpse of Hell's ante-room.

'Give me an Immortal, you bastards!'

'As you see,' said Tannhauser, 'he's lost his mind.'

Grymonde rattled his chains. The militiamen took a step backwards.

'The movement of the wagon seems to soothe him,' said Tannhauser. 'But if you reckon we ought to wait for the captain, we could drug him with a few pints of wine.'

'Chevalier!' roared Grymonde, into the shopkeeper's face. 'A cup of wine!'

'You be on your way, friend,' said the dyer. 'And gramercy for the cask.'

The shopkeeper did not countermand this suggestion.

'I've probably told you more than I ought to,' said Tannhauser, 'so if Garnier asks, tell him Petit Christian has the matter well in hand, and leave it at that.'

Grymonde guffawed with such violence the guards fell back further.

'If he doesn't ask, it's a sleeping dog you can let lie or not as you choose.'

'Christian?' said the dyer to Tannhauser. 'What's he saying?'

The genuine Petit Christian was wheezing some word, over and over, as if in a chant. Faecal matter sprayed from his lips and nostrils, as if his inner organs were coated with the stuff. When he blinked, the whites of his eyeballs could not be seen, for they were coated, too.

'Ordure!' whined Petit Christian. 'Ordure!'

'Perhaps it's the title of his next play,' said Tannhauser.

The wagon shook with Grymonde's laughter.

'Rough way to travel,' said the dyer. 'What did the poor bastard do?'

'He was the lover of Marcel Le Tellier –' began Tannhauser.

Grymonde's laughter pealed towards the sky.

'Whom he murdered in a jealous rage.'

The guards stared at the befouled writer with heightened disgust.

'Who would have thought?' said the shopkeeper.

'Aye,' said the dyer. 'Murder's one thing, but fucking a policeman?'

'Why was he jealous?' asked the shopkeeper.

'Who knows what our betters get up to?' said Tannhauser.

The second artisan hefted his pike. 'Do you mind?'

Tannhauser was about to tell him they didn't have the time, but he caught Estelle looking at him. She pushed her helm back, so he would not mistake her meaning.

Tannhauser turned to the artisan with the pike.

'As long as you don't kill him, or vex the horse, help yourself.'

The artisan squatted down. Bone crunched as he stabbed Christian in the ankles and feet. Christian stopped chanting and screamed. The shopkeeper borrowed the dyer's halberd and slashed at the playwright's buttocks. Probably their first blood, but it would give them something to brag about.

'Well, mates, I'm on my way. God bless the King and the Pope in Rome.'

The blessing was returned with enthusiasm. They all but cheered him off.

Tannhauser walked on. The wagon creaked into motion behind him.

'Christian!' called the shopkeeper. 'Who are the children?'

Tannhauser called back over his shoulder.

'The children are mine.'

They swung south, away from the river. Garnier lived on the first street to the east. In case their new friends were watching, Tannhauser kept going south to the next street before he turned. The City was quiet. They'd been cleansing it all day. He disarmed the pistol. At a pile of trash heaped behind a tavern, he rolled the corpses off the wagon. They turned north, back towards the river and Bernard Garnier's.

It had to be getting close to eleven o'clock.

If he took Carla and the wagon to the warehouses, and hid them there, he was sure he could return past the shopkeeper's crew on foot without being seen. The moon was in the west. The shadows were as black as the North Sea. From the warehouses he could get to Irène's in ten minutes. That meant leaving Carla alone for half an hour; or more. That much time didn't sit well with him. The longer the Millers' Bridge was unguarded, the more likely it was to be guarded when they returned. If he took Carla across right now, they'd be back in the Ville in twenty minutes, instead of fifty.

In that case, if he wanted to fetch Pascale, he'd still have to leave Carla alone, for even longer. He could leave her in Cockaigne. No one else was going back there tonight. But if he returned for Pascale, with another double crossing of the river in his way, midnight would be long gone before they reached the gate, and the Pilgrims would be waiting. To bring Pascale to Cockaigne would cost him an hour. An hour could cost his wife and child their lives.

He had it in him to leave Pascale behind. Not because he had known her for only a day; some bonds were forged from metals even more mysterious than Time. He just knew that his ruthlessness stretched that far, that his will held that much sway over his heart and his stomach. Yet what directed that will if not heart and stomach?

His will waited to be told what to do.

He wished he could ask Carla; but he knew what she would say. And she wasn't going to get the chance to answer, for he'd never have the chance to ask. If he put Carla on that wagon, he wouldn't go back for Pascale. If he saw Carla's face, if he held her in his arms, if he saw her cradle Amparo, he wouldn't be able to leave her. Anywhere. His plan was an empty fantasy.

Neither Carla nor anyone here had ever set eyes on Pascale. She would be lost among the nameless slain; unknown and unremembered by all but him.

That notion didn't sit well, either. Pascale possessed something he had felt in no other, except himself. A purity of knowing, a clarity, which she hadn't had to learn. All she had to learn were the means to express it. Something to do with death.

He could go to get Pascale first.

Before Carla.

If Carla was at Garnier's house, she was safe. If she wasn't there, getting to the Porte Saint-Denis by midnight was a lost cause. He could hide the wagon and the others right here. Get Pascale. Gather up Carla and the others on the way back. They could be in the Ville in half an hour, all of them. But it would mean leaving Amparo. Estelle was likely a better protector for her than he was, he had said he wouldn't leave her, and he had meant it. He couldn't.

The dice had been rolled, the cards were in play, Amparo's life – all their lives – were already on the table. He had danced with Fate too often, at her most extravagant balls, to turn down her invitation. If he did, she'd dance with someone else, and he wasn't about to surrender the floor so late in the party.

'Grégoire, choose a place to hide the wagon, near here.'

Grégoire nodded, as if he already knew the spot.

'Keep the torch alight if you can, but it's the hiding that counts. I'll take the lantern. If I'm not back in an hour, you and Hugon should take the satchels and make of life what you will. Leave the mighty Infant behind.'

'Leave the Infant?' said Hugon.

'He'll make of death what he will, for he's a dead man already.'

'Dead I may be,' said Grymonde, 'but I'll make sure they go.'

Estelle stood on the wagon bed, cradling Amparo. Tannhauser looked at her.

'You've flown with the dragon, Estelle. Do you dare to fly with a devil?'

'Can Amparo fly, too?'

'This devil can't fly at all without both sisters.'

'Can we bring my crossbow?'

He saw what it meant to her. He nodded and she smiled.

He took the mace and pressed the haft into Grymonde's fist.

'How will I get a chance to use this?' said Grymonde.

'Let them see it in your hand and you'll be using it.'

Grymonde fingered the flanges. 'I'll charge for the sound of their bowels.'

Tannhauser had Estelle stand backwards on the edge of the wagon bed. He took her by the waist and hoisted her onto his neck. She settled and he felt Amparo against his right ear. He slung Altan's bow and the quiver of broadheads over his left shoulder.

'Where are we going?' asked Estelle.

'To the quays a little north of Notre-Dame.'

'That's not far,' said Estelle.

Grymonde said, 'Why are you going?'

'I'm going to fetch Pascale, a friend. Le Tellier's *sergents* have her.'

Tannhauser remembered he was taking Grymonde's daughter, as well as his own. That such she was had been evident to him in the Yards; as was the fact that Estelle didn't know it. He wondered why Grymonde hadn't owned her, but he didn't ask.

'Do I have my Infant's blessing?'

'La Rossa is your blessing. The Infant is dead. But if this be Paradise, it will do.'

'Hugon,' said Tannhauser, 'show me Garnier's house.'

Garnier's house was prominent enough without the two guards who slept on the steps outside. Tannhauser could have killed them as they dreamed. But his other calculations would remain unchanged, and killing them later, asleep or not, was no labour.

'Hugon, when Grégoire's placed, come back and watch the house for me.'

He gave him a slap on the back. He couldn't remember a man or boy who didn't like it. Hugon seemed not to. He rolled his shoulder, as if infringed.

'I'll watch the house for me,' said Hugon. 'And for Carla.'

'Even better. Watch for our return, too.'

Tannhauser fancied he could feel his daughter's heart beat against the back of his head. It couldn't be so, not through a wine-skin, but the fancy roused his spirit. He headed east towards Irène's through pitch darkness.

'Tannzer?' said Estelle. 'Do you like the name, "Pascale"?'

'Yes.' He sensed that his answer was flawed. 'But not as much as "Estelle".'

'Do you think Pascale would be a good name for a sister?'

'I do. I do.'

'So Pascale's one of us.'

'Yes, I should say she is.'

Tannhauser found he could keep a fair pace, despite his passengers. The lantern's light was puny and he couldn't have moved much faster on his own.

'Tannzer? What does "Pascale" mean?'

Tannhauser thought about this for a while.

The escape of the Israelites from Egypt.

He said, '*The Road to Freedom.*'

'Oh. Yes.'

Estelle thought about this for almost no time at all.

'With a star and shelter and a road, we can get all the way home.'

Tannhauser laughed. 'We're as good as there.'

'What does "Tannzer" mean?'

'That I don't know. Why don't you give it a meaning?'

They had reached the street that ran across the island from the Pont Notre-Dame to the Petit Châtelet. He glanced north. A brazier. Militiamen lingered by the chain that marked the entrance to the bridge. To the south, the street took a bend, and was empty. He crossed without being seen and pressed on.

Estelle bent to his ear and whispered.

'*The North Wind Blows.*'

CHAPTER THIRTY-ONE

The Judgement

C arla's exhaustion saturated her bones, seeped through her every fibre, and damped the last flames of her spirit to the merest embers. Even while working in the Hospital at Malta during the worst days of the Siege she had not felt so depleted. Mingled with the exhaustion was the blackest melancholy. Yet she couldn't sleep.

She lay on a decent bed in a guest room on the first floor of Bernard Garnier's house in the City. Awful sounds drifted through the window from the banks of the river, where the atrocities inflicted on the Huguenots continued. She lacked the will to get up and close the casement. The cries of the women and children, the desperation of the psalm-singers, rammed the obligation to listen into her belly. She doubted she would have slept in any circumstance. How could she, until she had Amparo back in her arms?

She should never have given the babe over. The image of Estelle disappearing across the rooftops swam about her mind. She couldn't have known that Garnier would be there to protect her. Dominic would have killed both her and Amparo if he'd had the chance. She had had no choice; or, rather, her choice still made sense. Amparo had been safer with Estelle. Yet her remorse was bitter, her anguish a crushing weight on her chest.

Her body was not used to the emptiness which so recently and for so long had been filled by new life. While Amparo had been with her, she hadn't noticed that emptiness; the babe in her arms had filled it, had filled not just that emptiness but the universe itself. Without her, the universe seemed emptied of all but despair.

Even thoughts of Mattias failed to console her. She was lost and he would not find her. The evil that had infected Paris to its core was too potent. She had seen that evil in the mutilated bodies scattered about the streets, in the butchery she had seen from the wharves. She had known the worst of war, but this was too appalling to name. Lurking within that greater evil, Marcel Le Tellier wanted her killed. She felt strangely uninterested in him. She had never felt so alone or so afraid. She wanted Amparo, who had been born amid human darkness and made it bright.

Antoinette had fallen asleep lying against her. The small solace of her presence was allayed by Carla's worry for her. She was a D'Aubray and presumably marked for death, as had been all her kin. If not, being with Carla made her so. They were not safe here, not for long. When Garnier had promised to lodge her, he had been at the head of his men. The power on the spot had been his. Le Tellier had the powers of a judge; not so immediate, but more inexorable. He hadn't given up all day; he was unlikely to do so tomorrow.

When she and Antoinette had arrived here, Madame Garnier, roused from her own bed, had absorbed her husband's instructions in some confusion but without demur, whereupon the captain had left. Carla feared he had returned to the Hôtel Le Tellier. She declined food, as did Antoinette. She expended the last of her energy on the courtesies required to close the door of her room as quickly as she could.

Antoinette fell to sobbing. Carla held her in her arms but couldn't comfort her. She sobbed, too. They might have sobbed all night, but Antoinette's fingers, with a child's genius, found the shape of Alice's cards in the pocket of Carla's frock, and curiosity overcame sorrow.

'What is this?'

'They're playing cards.'

Carla took them out and sorted through them. She removed Death and the Devil and returned them to her pocket. She showed Antoinette the rest.

'Can I play with them?'

'Of course you can.'

'How do you play?'

'You make stories with them.'

'How?'

'You put them next to each other. Like this.'

Carla laid out the Emperor, the Empress and the Lovers on the bed.

'See, this knight falls in love with this lady, and they get married.'

'What happens next?'

'Look at the pictures. You decide.'

Antoinette spread the cards around on the sheet.

'I don't like being here,' she said. 'I want to go back to the Yards.'

'When you've had a nice sleep you'll feel better.'

'Look, the lady gets a dog, to protect her and the knight.'

Antoinette put the card named Strength beside the others.

'A wonderful story, Antoinette. I think that's meant to be a lion.'

'A lion? Isn't that even better than a dog?'

'Much better. Take the lady and her lion, and you can all three go to sleep.'

The cards lay by the candle on the table next to the bed.

Carla thought of Alice. She had known the woman only a day, yet she missed her as if she had known her all her life. She had never looked up to another woman. She had never had a woman to look up to. Alice had given her back to herself. Alice was in her. She hoped that she was with her. Carla collected the Strength card, from where it lay on Antoinette's pillow.

Was the little girl's choice meaningful? She had picked it for the lion, tamed by the lady. Yet Alice would say that she should take the card not as a prediction but as an invitation to the resources of her own spirit. The card pointed to what she needed to know, first and foremost, of herself. Strength. Carla had never felt weaker. The challenge of the card only made her more aware of it.

She was weak. To acknowledge that and accept it, to see it and not be afraid of it, that was strong, wasn't it? She was weak and she was in the home of a man who was leagued with her worst enemies. Her babe's worst enemies. Was she so weak that all she could do was wait here, lying in bed and weeping, until they came to take her away? She swung her legs from the mattress and sat up. The movement provoked another of the late pangs, but she paid it little mind. She stood up.

She walked to the window. She could walk well enough, if she had reason to. The room was at the rear of the house and the window overlooked the river. To the left stood the houses on the Pont au Change, from beyond which came the sounds of the massacres. Overshadowed by the houses on the Right Bank, the strand was covered with empty boats. In the moonlight reflected from the water they seemed to be chained in clusters, but she couldn't be sure. On this bank there were no boats at all. To the right she could see the backs of the houses on the Pont Notre-Dame. She was on an island.

Where could she go?

She had seen the chains and militiamen blocking the bridges. Garnier had left two men on the front door, to ease her mind. One had already been stationed there, to reassure his wife. The new post he had assigned to his lieutenant, Ensign Bonnett, who had not been pleased to be given so lowly a commission, not least because the choice was Garnier's way of flaunting his chivalrousness. Bonnett had volunteered to hold the spit that blinded Grymonde.

She flinched at the memory. Grymonde was a monster. She had never forgotten that, even when she had seen her newborn daughter seated in his huge hands. Yet something in his heart had won her over, something more than the fact that he loved her. He loved her, though she had not known it until he lost his eyes.

The scene of his blinding had almost destroyed her composure. She had seen the red-haired beauty taunt him, the woman who could only have been Estelle's mother. She had seen the smirk of Petit Christian. The jeering of the soldiery. She had seen the first hole smoking in Grymonde's bone-cragged face.

Her outrage had been about to find its voice when his one remaining eye had pierced her; with the look of love. Grymonde had shaken his great curly head, despite that two men held it firm from behind. He had shaken it at her. And she had understood and known he was right. She couldn't save the eye. By defending the infamous criminal who had abducted her, and in whose conquest many had died, she would only undermine her status and her influence. Carla had kept her silence, had uttered not a cry and shed not a tear. Opposed by her shame and her pity, that silence was a battle her will almost lost.

When the second eye was gone, they left him, bound, on his knees, and Petit Christian explained to Dominic why – for such as Grymonde – it was a punishment worse than death. The red-haired woman provoked a furious dispute over money, and Dominic slaked his bloodlust by stabbing her and dumping her body in the fire pit. As Carla was driven away from Cockaigne, in the same cart she had arrived in, she looked at Petit Christian; just once. Her mind seemed empty of all thought or feeling, yet whatever was writ on her face, it wiped out his smirk, and filled him with dread.

Carla glanced from one bridge to the other. They couldn't get back to Cockaigne, though like Antoinette, she could think of no place in Paris she would rather be. She could not get to the convent of the Filles-Dieu and claim Amparo. The streets crawled not only with killers, but with those bent on indulging their vilest appetites.

She turned from the window. She took the two cards from her pocket. The Devil was indistinct in the candlelight. A winged beast who stuffed bodies into his mouth. She slipped it behind Death. The sight of the reaper and his horse trampling the mighty gave her comfort. Alice had chosen the card as her quester, and now Carla knew why. Alice had known it was her time to meet the pale horseman, and had embraced him and sought his counsel. In Carla's draw, Death, in an alternate incarnation, had charged towards the Fire. But how could Mattias find her here? Garnier's house was imposing but it was no tower.

Carla collected the rest of the deck from the table. She sorted through them until she found the Judgement. The first card she had drawn. *Weighed in the balance and found wanting.* Daniel in the lion's den. The lions did not eat him because they saw the strength of his spirit. And Death had charged not only towards the Fire, but towards the Judgement. She looked at the card more closely. She studied the image without thinking, without trying to understand what it might mean.

Angels with silver trumpets summoned the dead from crimson tombs.

The Last Judgement.

She recalled a carving in stone of the same scene.

Above the central portal of Notre-Dame de Paris.

The cathedral was but a few hundred paces from here. The degenerates crawling the street would never dare breach that sanctuary. If piety didn't stop them, fear of the gallows would. Even Marcel Le Tellier would need time, and all the influence he could muster, to evade the law of sanctuary. By then, she could prove herself – to every priest in the building – as devout a daughter of the Church as ever they'd met. A daughter such as she had been, until she'd met Alice. And for all that she had absorbed Alice's philosophy, she believed that Mother Nature could embrace a child who yet found in the Church's corrupted corpus a heart made of love, and in Christ a philosopher with whom she would not much disagree.

Most importantly, the nuns at the Filles-Dieu would be subordinate to the eminences of Notre-Dame. She was sure she could win over those eminences, their sympathy and support; and they had the power to reunite her with Amparo.

Carla put the cards back in her pocket. She didn't feel weak any more. Her body was drained but it would serve her. Her strength begged a question. Was she mad to act on the inspiration of pictures painted on cards? Women could go mad after childbirth. Yet if so – if she were mad – she found herself in a world of madness. She reviewed her design, and it made perfect sense.

She woke Antoinette.

There was a pitcher of water and a bowl on the dresser. Carla wetted a cloth and washed Antoinette's face. The girl submitted; and revived. She looked at the pillow.

'Where's my lion?'

'Safe in my pocket. You were right. This isn't a good place. We're leaving.'

'Are we going back to the Yards?'

'Tonight we can't get across the river. Will you do something brave for me?'

'What?'

'Creep to the stairs, very softly. See if there is anyone below, by the front door.'

Antoinette shrugged and nodded, as if such a task was nothing to a girl who had conquered Cockaigne. Carla hugged her. She opened the door. Antoinette left.

Carla washed her own face. Her hair was still in a braid and she smoothed down the loose strands. Her frock bore numerous stains, but few men noted such things.

'There's no one there,' said Antoinette.

In the hallway stood her gambo violl. Carla picked up the case. Its weight made her feel stronger. Had she been required to push it inch by inch up the street on her knees, she would have done so. She opened the front door.

Both guards sat dozing on the steps, their lanterns and weapons at their feet. They did not wake. Carla prodded Bonnett with the case. He scrambled up, as did his fellow.

'Ensign Bonnett, Captain Garnier will be happy to hear that his wife and his guests enjoy such vigilant protection.'

'I humbly beg your pardon, my lady. The day has been long, I was up in the dark −'

'So was I. We are going to Notre-Dame for matins.'

'Matins?'

'The midnight office. Psalms, readings from Scripture and the lives of the Saints.'

'Yes, my lady. Matins. But, it can't be much past eleven o'clock.'

'You keep good time for one who sleeps on duty. I am entitled to pray. Must the captain also know that you refused to accompany his ward to church? Or do you fear to walk in the dark? If so, we will walk alone, for we do not.'

Bonnett saw the violl case. He looked up at Carla.

She looked back down at him.

'Do they play music at matins, my lady?'

She stared at him without speaking. Bonnett bowed.

'My lady, please let me carry your baggage.'

Carla was glad to get outside. Though she took short steps and her pelvis was a bruised mass, she was glad, too, to be walking. Antoinette held her hand as they headed east towards the Pont Notre-Dame and its chain and its contingent of militiamen, who toasted chestnuts on a brazier. They headed south past Saint-Christopher's and then east again towards the towers of the cathedral.

Some of the houses and businesses had hired watchmen to stand outside. They nodded to Bonnett and, though she despised him, she was glad to have an escort so well known. They passed the Hôtel-Dieu. Unlike the streets of the Ville, these were free of corpses but she didn't doubt they had been here. The groundwater left by the shower that afternoon had dried out, apart from that collected in the deeper potholes, but the rain hadn't washed away the black stains that clung to a wall here and a door there. The island was a death trap. The hush she had felt that morning was intensified by night. It lay everywhere like an invisible fog, thickened, now, with horror, and even shame, though she saw little of either in the faces of the soldiery.

They reached the Parvis and she recognised the clutch and slither of congealed blood beneath her feet. She had trodden in such before. They had desecrated even the Parvis. The moon was behind them and nearing its height and the cathedral's intricate façade formed a vast mosaic of silver and absolute black. The Last Judgement was hidden in shadow but it was there, and so was she. The great doors beneath the frieze stood open. A dim glow shimmered within, thrown by scores of candles yet unseen. Three militiamen loitered around the entrance, she presumed to weed out Huguenots seeking shelter, and again she was glad of Bonnett's presence. She bent down to the girl.

'Antoinette? We'll be safe here until we're sure we will be safe somewhere else. It was your story that brought us here, so I thank you.'

'My story?'

'The story you made with the cards, the lady with the lion.'

Bonnett stepped back suddenly – leaving Carla, she could not help but notice, in the path of whatever danger threatened – and drew his sword.

A slender figure dashed towards them from the north side of the square. With one hand she held her frock up around her thighs; in the other she held a sack. She stopped a few steps short of Carla, and dropped her skirts and held the sack in both hands, or, rather, with the fingers of one hand slipped inside the sack's mouth. She stood tensed for quick movement. She glanced at Bonnett, and Carla had the curious sense that he was in more danger than the girl.

Bonnett snarled to cover his embarrassment.

'Who're you, slut?'

The girl ignored him. She looked at Carla. She was perhaps fourteen. Her hair was cut short without much regard for style and shone as blue as Turkish indigo under the moon. Her face was smudged with what looked like, but could not have been, powder black. Her eyes were grim but determined. Carla sensed she had seen worse things that day than even she had witnessed.

'Can you take us inside, madame?'

'Heretics, is it?' said Bonnett.

'Be quiet, Bonnett.'

'If you don't,' said the girl, 'they will try to kill us.'

'Try?' said Bonnett.

'Ensign Bonnett, I said be quiet.'

Carla nodded to the girl.

'Of course I'll take you inside. How many are you?'

'Four. Can you trust him?'

'I trust his fear of his captain, whose favour I enjoy.'

The girl turned and beckoned. Three more figures emerged from nowhere and ran towards them. In the middle was a boy, around the same age as the girl. A pair of bulging saddle wallets were slung over his shoulder. They flapped as if heavily loaded. Two small girls, identical in feature, clung onto his hands.

'I don't know about this, my lady,' said Bonnett.

'Ensign Bonnett, I had hoped to spare Captain Garnier the humiliation of hearing that his wife's defenders fell asleep on her doorstep. Accompany these children through the doors with me, and I will.'

'Are you looking to be baptised into the One True Church?' Bonnett asked the girl.

The girl shifted her weight and eyed him up and down. Carla was sure, though Bonnett, his sword lowered, was oblivious, that the girl was ready to pounce on him.

The girl said: 'No.'

'Enough,' said Carla. 'Take us inside. You go first. And put that sword away.'

Bonnett sheathed his sword and drew himself up to his full height, which was some inches less than either Carla's or the girl's. He puffed his chest and led the way, accepting slovenly salutes from the men on the door. Carla gestured for the children to go ahead of her and all but the girl did. The girl walked beside her, lithe as a tomcat.

They passed beneath the Last Judgement.

The cathedral, which she had expected to be empty, was half-full of refugees, all of them women and children as far as she could see. Their misery filled the immense space like incense. Carla turned to Bonnett and retrieved her violl.

'If you wish to stay and pray for forgiveness, you are welcome. If not, I free you from your charge. You may tell your captain I am safe and well.'

Carla was indifferent to his decision and left him to it. When she turned back to ask the girl her name, she found that the four fugitive children had disappeared.

Carla didn't dwell on them. The service she had done them was small; they had a lot of company. She took Antoinette's hand and walked up the nave. She had to find a priest, explain who she was.

She would speak Italian. Most priests here would have at least a smattering. It would mark her out at once from the Huguenots.

She felt faint. A cramp. Her legs threatened to give way. She was some way down the nave. If she passed out she might well be ignored, as many lay prostrate on the tiles. She set down her violl and slid into the nearest bench and pulled Antoinette beside her. Her head swam. She lowered it to her knees. It was the emptiness inside her. It was consuming her. She had to have her baby back. She saw Amparo's face. What if she never saw Amparo again? The nuns would rename her. Someone would claim her, adopt her. How soon? A wet nurse would feed her. Tonight? She'd be hungry. She'd be alone. The memory of the warmth and love into which Amparo had been born brought a great sob from Carla's heart. Estelle. Alice. Her mother.

How could the babe not know all that was gone?

What had she done?

The priest. She had to find a priest.

She tried to stand but couldn't. She felt something slide out of her.

This was sanctuary.

She covered her face with her skirts and cried, too empty to call upon God.

CHAPTER THIRTY-TWO

A Very Particular God

Tannhauser threaded his way across the market by the Port
Saint-Landry. He saw no one. He set the lamp by the stable
gate and lifted Estelle from his shoulders. Amparo was asleep. She
was a little miracle. He took Estelle's hand. They skirted a body
dumped by a midden with its neck cut nigh to the spine below the
ear. They slipped through the dark towards Irène's.

He stopped at an alley several houses short.

He saw no sign of a lookout. Le Tellier would have sent at least
one killer stony enough to murder three children, a Baro not a Frogier,
and two degenerate enough to hold them and watch. They were
expecting him. They'd been sent to capture him alive. They had made
thousands of arrests and would expect this to be just another. Irène
would answer the door. She probably lied well. One man in hiding,
below, or two? At least one would remain upstairs to threaten Pascale.
He armed the pistol and the crossbow.

'Estelle, will you wait here and look after my bow?'

She nodded.

'What will you do if I don't come out again?'

'Run with Amparo and make of our life.'

'You're a clever girl.'

'But you will come out again.'

'Of course I will.'

He stepped out from the wall. He could see no lights in Irène's
house. He went to the window and pressed his nose to the glass. A
dim glow came from the kitchen. He hammered on the door three
times, returned to the window and watched the candle approach
through the blur. A woman's shape. He shouted through the door.

'Madame Irène? Sergent Baro here.'

The door moved and he shoved it open and barged past Irène, lowering the crossbow. The smell of powder. A dead man lay on his belly at the foot of the stairs.

'They're all gone.' Irène's face was gaunt. 'Except for the bodies.' Tannhauser took the candle from her hand.

The *sergent*'s lower face had been shot away. There was a large-bore hole not far below the nape of his neck. A rifle ball. The range had been so close as to incinerate a good swath of shirt and hair. Tannhauser looked up the stair. Blackness.

He went up quickly. Thickened gore greased the upper steps and shone across the landing in a burgundy jelly. A second body lay folded backwards from his knees, his thighs and belly similarly caked.

Pascale had killed two *sergents*. Juste might have shot one; but his gut didn't believe it. She hadn't just wanted some fellowship. She had wanted the knowledge.

The front bedroom was empty. In the rear bedroom, the moonlight was enough to see a body under a sheet. He pulled it down. Flore. He had liked her. Juste had loved her. So had Pascale. He replaced the sheet. There were no other dead.

Juste and the Mice were alive. Pascale had killed Le Tellier's men before they could carry out their orders; by the looks of it, before they'd had a chance to speak.

He set the candle on the empty bed and went to the window.

He saw no blood on the sill. He saw the two barges. Across the water, torches moved and braziers burned on the Place de Grève. The militia's numbers had much thinned since this afternoon, but there were still at least three score of them, presumably as a reserve. There would be scores more in the surrounding streets.

Where would the children go?

He remembered Estelle. He turned to go and fetch her.

A word was smeared in blood on the wall above the candle. 'MICE.'

Tannhauser brought Estelle and Amparo indoors.

Irène grimaced at both of them.

'I'm thirsty,' said Estelle.

'We'll go in the kitchen,' he said. 'Irène, fetch us some water.'

Irène held her tongue. She provided water. Tannhauser propped the crossbow by the door. He and Estelle drank. Amparo would soon need a breast.

'Mice,' he muttered.

'Little swine. My floors are ruined, too.'

'Buy a mop. What happened to the third *sergent*?'

'Anne ran after him down the street. When she came back, she said he was dead.'

The body in the midden. Tannhauser felt a surge of admiration.

'So she killed all three.'

'She almost killed me, too.'

Tannhauser wondered why she hadn't. Irène read him.

'She said she didn't know if you would.'

'Then you're in my debt. When did they leave?'

'Just as it turned dark.'

Almost three hours ago. A long time to hide; enough to get elsewhere. Tybaut the pimp. 'MICE' meant they had gone to Tybaut's. Wherever that was. Time scourged him. A nose to a nose. Father Pierre at Notre-Dame.

Irène hugged herself. 'I've been here all night, alone with that corpse, waiting for Alois. Or you.'

'No one will come from the Châtelet tonight.'

'What are you going to do to me?'

'Stay indoors. I'll put the body in the street.'

'Very thoughtful, I'm sure. What do I tell Alois?'

'Frogier is dead.'

Irène put a hand to her mouth.

Tannhauser emptied the water down his throat. He set down the jug.

'How did he die?'

'In agony, in the dark.'

'You bastard.'

'Frogier promised the children safety. You took my gold for the same.'

'I'll see you hanged.'

'I am no Scotsman.'

'You're all the same. Bloody bastards. You make me sick.'

Tannhauser felt a twinge in his back. He thought twice about the body.

Irène screeched, 'I'll see all of you hanged.'

'Beware, Irène. The waters Frogier drowned in are deep enough to take you under, too. If questions come, claim you know nothing.'

'I'll have the lot of you. Your bloody children, too. I'll go to Le Tellier.'

Irène folded over and flew back into the sideboard and twisted as she fell. The dull snap of the crossbow's sinews accompanied her death, which was instant.

'I think I got her in the heart,' said Estelle.

More likely the aorta, given the rate she was bleeding, but Tannhauser didn't quibble. Estelle bore the look of one who had swatted a wasp. She expected no censure. He had none to offer. In Irène's death, he could only see the advantages, not least to his back. He checked on Amparo. She was blinking, but seemed unperturbed by the missile just released beneath her.

'I made sure you weren't in the way,' said Estelle.

'Good. The first rule of shooting at anything.'

He took the crossbow from her and recharged it.

'She said she'd hang the children.'

'Well, we couldn't stand for that, could we?'

She followed him from the kitchen. He took the spare quiver from the corpse.

'Where are we going now?' asked Estelle.

'To see a nose in Notre-Dame. Do you know a quiet way?'

'Can we fly again?'

'Fly? We'll have to.'

Estelle took him through the Cloisters. They were deserted. Amparo began crying, with a surprising lustiness for one so tiny. Tannhauser was charmed. What spirit. Estelle murmured to her. She was still crying when they reached the front edge of the cathedral. He set down his gear and the candle and lifted Estelle from his shoulders.

'I think she wants to face me,' said Estelle.

She loosened the buttons on her shirt and turned Amparo around. She crouched against the wall in the candle light and murmured to the babe and she quieted.

Tannhauser took the crossbow and scouted the Parvis. All was quiet but for two militia guarding the central portal. Their pikes were propped against the archway. A lantern stood at their feet.

He returned and took Estelle's hand and raised her up.

'I'm going to send you into the cathedral. Wait for me near the font. Walk ahead of me with the candle.'

He followed two paces behind her, where even the small flame would blind them to his presence. The guards saw Estelle and roused themselves, though to curiosity rather than alertness. Another pair of stalwart citizens recruited to a giant evil.

Tannhauser stepped out, well to Estelle's right, and levelled the crossbow.

'The first to touch a weapon takes it in the cock. So does the first to speak.'

Both stared at the bolt. Neither moved.

'You don't have to die tonight. Think of your wives and a soft bed. You, take the lantern. Both of you, turn around and hold hands.'

They obeyed. Their hands grappled for each other as if seeking comfort.

'Estelle, go inside.'

He watched Estelle through the portal. He took a pike.

'Walk round the side of the church.'

He stopped them in the shadow of the south transept.

'Ditch those helmets. Put the lantern down. Noses to the wall.'

They obeyed without letting go of each other. Tannhauser propped the crossbow and piked the first where his neck met the base of his skull. The second didn't dare turn. As his comrade slid down the wall without a sound, he didn't let go of his hand.

'My God, I am most heartily sorry for having offended Thee and I –'

Tannhauser piked him. He stacked the pike and collected the lantern and the crossbow and returned to the Parvis. He left the lantern inside the portal and entered Notre-Dame.

Tannhauser scanned the cathedral for armed men and saw no men at all. Both aisles this side of the transept were more than half full of women and children, most gathered in clusters, some in pairs or stranded in lone anguish. Others, especially the children, slept on the benches or the tiles. There was a good deal of crying, crying that had been stripped down to its bones. While each voice was its own, the whole was strangely harmonious, like some choir of woe singing from an infinite choice of hymns.

He found Estelle by the font. Amparo was sucking a nipple on her flat, narrow chest. The sight took him aback. But both seemed content with the arrangement and neither seemed to find it unnatural, so he let it be.

He retreated to a dark alcove and disarmed the crossbow and stowed it with his two spare bolts and the *sergent's* quiver. He stowed Altan's bow and quiver in a darker spot. He disarmed the pistol and hid it with them. He unfastened the sleeves of the shirt tied about his hips. The sleeves were beslimed with gore and he stripped the clots from shoulder to wrist and wrung them out. He'd take Estelle and Amparo with him. Not the most apt of escorts when asking how to find a pimp's den, especially Tybaut's, but Father Pierre was used to squalid company.

The rest of the shirt was damp but not too bloody. He gave it a good flap. The white cross on the front was dark red, but Father Nose could make of that what he would. He pulled the shirt on. It was corrugated with gore and mocked his attempts to smooth it. He was as presentable as he was going to get. No, not quite.

He went to the baptismal font and crossed himself, then scrubbed his face in the Holy Water. From the change in its colour, he considered it well done.

Blood and Holy Water.

Carla would want Amparo baptised. The Church was uncom-
promising on baptism; one could say harsh. The babe's soul could
be whipped off to Limbo at any moment, doomed through all
eternity never to see God, and all for want of a handful of water
and words. What a very particular God He was. But who was he
to argue?

'Estelle, let me have Amparo.'

'You want to hold her?'

'I'm going to baptise her.'

He took the kidskin cradle from Estelle's shirt. Amparo seemed
to weigh close to nothing. Yet no weight so absolute had ever fallen
on his heart. He raised her high in both hands and looked up at
her face.

Hundreds of candles burned in the church behind her and
filled its enormous vault with ochre smoke. What a beauty she
was. Only pure love could weigh so much, and yet fill him with
ecstasy. He had been right. Amparo did gentle the storm. He could
have stood there for an hour. Amparo was not so patient. She
started howling.

Tannhauser laughed. He lowered her and kissed her on the
nose, or as nearly as he could without piercing her new skin with
his bristles.

'Ah, little Amparo doesn't want to get wet. She wants her
breast.'

Amparo was not consoled. He tilted her over the mouth of the
font. He scooped a handful of murky water and poured it over her
head.

'*Ego te baptizo Amparo, in nomine Patris, et Filii, et Spiritus Sancti.
Amen.*'

Tannhauser took the crying infant to his chest with one hand.
He smiled.

'We have saved her from Hell. Now we must save her from
Paris.'

'Tannzer? Will you baptise me?'

His smile widened. He looked down and Estelle beamed.

'With pleasure. Lean over the font.'

He palmed water over Estelle's tangled locks. They were clean. He was surprised.

Ego te baptizo Estelle, in nomine Patris, et Filii, et Spiritus Sancti. Amen.

'Am I saved from Hell?'

'The Devil will be disappointed, but yes, you are saved.'

The babe howled herself red, but he was loath to give her up so soon. He murmured to her, as he might to a fractious horse. Estelle grabbed his free forearm with both hands as if to stake her claim to his attention.

'Hold tight,' he said.

He lifted her feet from the floor and swung her ahead of him and started to walk. Estelle shrieked with pleasure and landed and clung on tighter.

'Again!'

With one child thus entertained, he continued to mutter to Amparo in Turkish as he strode up the nave. The tiny screaming face was entirely captivating, but part of his mind turned to the practicalities. If Tybaut's hovel wasn't on the island, it was more likely on the Left Bank than the Right. It was unlikely he could reach either without bloodshed. Unless he took the priest with him. They'd lower the chains for a priest. A priest who consorted with pimps he could bend to his will.

'Mattias?'

Tannhauser stopped and lowered Estelle. He didn't dare turn.

His mind doubted the sound, that voice, for he wanted to hear it so badly he feared he must have imagined it. But his eyes filled with unmanly tears, and those he believed.

'Carla! What are you doing here?' Estelle let go of his arm. 'We've been looking for you all over, and now we've found you.'

Still, Tannhauser didn't move. He had mourned her. She had given birth to his child. Dungeon, fire and sword had stood between them, yet here they were, both of them, in the crucible of Hermes Trismegistus. All that stood between them now was his guilt.

'Tannzer, look!'

Tannhauser's heartbeat felt as fast as the babe's. He suddenly felt conscious of his dire appearance. It was nothing she hadn't seen before. At least he had washed his face; if he'd known she was going to be here, he'd have rinsed his mouth out, too. He turned.

Her gaze struck him to his inmost core.

Carla.

He held her stare for a long time.

She had always known him better than he knew her. He claimed few mysteries; hers were numberless. Her green eyes glittered, fire and tears. They were like wounds. He had been one of those who had inflicted them. The deepest of them. He loved her. With intense pain he loved her, and he knew he was unworthy of the honour. But she didn't need his shame. What did she need? What could he give her?

A smile couldn't hurt, could it?

A spirit too wild to be known or named flashed between them, the quintessence that bound their improbable and reckless union, and the hurt in her eyes retreated so completely he wondered if he had seen it at all.

It was all right then.

She still loved him.

His pain abated, but his love had never felt so tender or so fierce.

He took in her face, her body.

His heart squeezed and he took a deep breath.

She stood in the nave, trying not to sway in her bloodstained frock. She wasn't exhausted. He'd seen her endure exhaustion for months at a time. She was frail, a state he had thought her incapable of attaining. The blood was hers, shed for their child. Her hair hung over her breast in a braid. He had never found her so beautiful.

He stepped towards her and opened wide his arm and embraced her and pulled her to his chest. She looked at him, with her jaws clenched, in the way she sometimes did. He felt her nails dig into his chest until it hurt, her private way of telling him he was hers.

Not so frail, then. He offered her the babe. Amparo's wailing subsided to a tremble of the lip.

Tannhauser smiled.

'Carla, love, our nightingale is hungry, and not yet the worse for my thorns.'

CHAPTER THIRTY-THREE

Just Another Child

C arla realised it was the first time she had ever heard Amparo cry.

Yet despite the lamentations that echoed about the cathedral, some of them the cries of infants, she knew the instant she heard it that the voice belonged to her daughter. The sound penetrated her despair and shocked her out if it. No sooner had her most passionate wish been granted than she was afraid that she was wrong. Reason said she had to be wrong. It was mere desperation that recognised the voice, not her ears.

The cries came from the back of the church.

Amparo couldn't be here. No one knew that Carla was here, except Bonnett, and why else would anyone bring Amparo, and who would dare this bloody night with a baby, and how? She tried to stand up too quickly and her vision went black and she sat down again. She couldn't let herself faint. By the time she came round, Amparo might be gone. She put her head between her knees and breathed steadily. Her head cleared. She could still hear the unique cry, now louder than ever, and clearly outraged, but no closer.

Carla sat up slowly. She reached out and found Antoinette's hand.

'Antoinette, come and sit on my left side.'

Antoinette slipped past Carla's knees and sat beside her. Carla slid along the bench and lifted her legs over her violl to sit on the outer edge. Her pelvis had stiffened. The pain was considerable. She felt another trickle between her thighs. She turned to look down the nave. She forgot the pain.

A barbaric figure loomed from the rearmost shadows of Notre-Dame.

Her heart soared so fast, it almost broke.

She wanted to blink but didn't dare.

Mattias strode up the nave towards her with Amparo yelling from the bight of his arm. He was murmuring and pursing his lips at her with great absorption. His neck was black with blood, as was the cross of Saint John on his chest, and the gore pooled in the creases of his boots was still wet. He looked as untamed as ever. She had never seen him filled with such joy. He had found her. He had found them both. She noticed the white ribbon tied around his brow. The pale horseman to the judgement had come, carrying her baby. And he had brought the Morning Star with him.

Estelle clung onto his arm with both hands, repeatedly lifting both feet off the floor, whereupon he swung her in the air, and her red locks flew out behind her, and she laughed. Carla smiled. As a spectacle it made the royal wedding, which had taken the same route the week before, seem utterly drab. They drew closer. She was almost reluctant to spoil so lovely a picture. She felt a flutter in her throat and wanted to cry with happiness. She didn't. She didn't want his first sight of her to be a woman in tears.

Carla put her hands on the bench and pushed herself up. She didn't fall. Without thinking she smoothed her frock and realised she was almost as bloody as Mattias. She smoothed her hair and arranged her braid.

Mattias, entranced as he was by his daughter, walked right past her.

Estelle, giggling in flight, didn't see her either.

Carla almost laughed, but she needed all her might to step into the nave.

Mattias's back blocked out the high altar.

He was haloed with golden candlelight.

'Mattias?'

Mattias stopped. Estelle let go of his arm and turned towards her with delight, and said something she didn't quite hear. They had searched for her. They had found her.

Mattias's head bent forward and his shoulders heaved. He raised his head.

He turned and looked at her.

Of the things she needed most from him, she could only have named Amparo, and his love, which, long as he had been gone, she had never doubted. Had she doubted it, she could not have endured. Yet he gave her something more: his tears. Though he did not let them fall, they made his eyes shine, and she drank in the sight of their gleaming for a long time. There was no hurry. Mattias was always ready to die, as any blaze of fire must be. So was Amparo, cradled as she was against his blood-soaked chest. Her daughter. Their daughter. Yet in this moment his. Mattias and his daughter.

Nothing had ever stirred her more deeply.

Carla was ready to die, too.

If they were together, she was ready for anything.

Her flame leapt towards his and in an instant they were one.

Mattias looked at her whole and the sight knifed him. Her appearance must have been more sorry that she imagined; yet what was a frock? The last thing she wanted was for him to think feeble. She willed him to hold her so she could show him it was not so, and he stepped forward on the very instant and grappled her to his body and took her breath away. Desire surged up through her exhaustion and she dug her nails into his chest until her fingers hurt. He was here and he was hers.

He gave her something else that she needed and hadn't known it. He grinned the broken-toothed grin that had enchanted her when first they had met.

'Carla, love, our nightingale is hungry, and not yet the worse for my thorns.'

Amparo was cocooned in animal skin. Her lip trembled. Whatever her adventures had been, she radiated good health. There was no hurry, at least not to feed her.

'Kiss me.'

Mattias made a sound in his throat. He kissed her on the lips. She felt him flow into her. She poured herself into him.

She opened her eyes, her lips still on his, and he sensed it. She looked into icy pools. How strange was his love. It cascaded from places where love did not belong. He was altogether mysterious. Well as she knew him, and his instincts and reactions, at this range she always felt that she did not know who lurked inside him at all.

He withdrew and his expression changed.

'My intention was to leave Paris, tonight, but it will be perilous. This is the safest place in the city, especially for you. I've a bag of gold that would keep you as the cardinal's private guest for months. The intelligent move is to stay here. I think you should.'

Her stomach turned over. 'Are you telling me you can't stay?'

'The longer I stay in Paris, the closer I am to a noose.'

'Would Garnier violate Notre-Dame?'

'When he calls me out, and he will, I can't hide behind the priest's skirts.'

'I'd never ask you to.'

'If I did hide here, they would simply wait for me. This is their city, not mine. If I'm still here when this feast of blood is over, the crimes of which they will accuse me, and of which I am guilty, will be harder for those who matter to ignore. I'd be the fiend who lurked in their cathedral. But if I'm long gone, then it's a few dozen corpses among thousands, and their suit becomes a tale they'd be wise not to tell, for they're guilty, too.'

'How could you imagine I would let you go without us?'

He studied her. He had the respect, and wisdom, not to argue the case.

'The Porte Saint-Denis opens at midnight. We have time but I've a wagon to collect. Wait for me by the font. By the way, I baptised Amparo. It's valid – doctrine of dire necessity, Council of Trent, so forth. I didn't know you were here or I'd have waited.'

'You did right. What else troubles you?'

'Naught that need trouble you.'

He took her around the waist and led them to the rear of the cathedral. He spotted a stray chair and scooped it up as he passed. Carla leaned into him and lost herself in Amparo's face. When they reached the shadows, he had Carla sit down. She unbuttoned the top of her frock and put Amparo's mouth to her nipple. She began suckling at once. The sensation induced an ecstatic drowsiness. Carla threw her head back and shook it to rouse herself. The ochre glow beneath the vault augured some enormous conflagration.

'Charge towards the fire.'

'Carla, are you well?' asked Mattias.

'Yes. I'm well. Go.'

Carla saw Estelle watching her.

'I didn't take Amparo to the convent.'

'Thank you, Estelle, with all my heart.'

Estelle grinned. 'Now all we have to do is find Pascale.'

Mattias turned. Carla saw that this was what so troubled him.

'No,' he said. 'Not tonight.'

'But when?' said Estelle.

'Who is Pascale?' said Carla.

'She's one of us. She's a sister.'

'We don't have time,' said Mattias.

'You had time until you found me,' said Carla.

'My word is final.'

She saw the pain it caused him. She did not need to know more.

'Mattias, go and find Pascale. We'll wait here.'

Mattias walked away, towards the portal, not the altar.

'Mattias.'

He stopped. 'She's just another a child. Of those the world has plenty.'

'I don't believe you.'

'She has as good a chance without us as with us, maybe a better one.'

He continued and stopped again as an ungainly boy ran into the cathedral.

He spoke to Mattias in great earnest but Carla couldn't make out the words. He had a harelip. At his ankles trotted a small, grotesque dog. The boy mimed putting something over his own head, like a collar or a necklace.

Mattias turned and rushed past her, she couldn't see where.

He returned in yet greater haste and ran through the portal with the boy.

Carla gave in to the drowsiness without sleeping. As her milk filled her babe, her babe filled her. There was no hurry.

She opened her eyes and saw Grymonde.

He shambled towards her, his either arm held by Mattias and the boy. His face was painted white and the skins of broken blisters hung down his cheeks. His head roved back and forth in sudden jerks as if in search of his lost sight. His tawny brown eyes.

She felt Alice draw back with a deep breath of pain.

Whether behind her or inside her, Alice was here.

Carla turned back to Amparo and began to cry.

CHAPTER THIRTY-FOUR

The Crucible

Tannhauser would have left Pascale behind but for Grégoire's news. He would have left Juste and the Mice, too. He would have swallowed the guilt, though he would never have digested it. He glanced across Grymonde's bulk at Grégoire and nodded, in the hope that some particle of his gratitude would be conveyed. Grégoire grinned. They stopped by the door in the alcove and Tannhauser set down the lantern and found the tool pouch in Grymonde's satchel. He opened the neck and pulled out a handful of flat iron rods with tips of diverse shapes at their either ends.

'If you can't make good on your boast, tell me, and I'll find the priest.'

'Give me the pick filed like a scimitar. Guide my fingers to the keyhole.'

Tannhauser did so. Grymonde knelt and put his left hand on the lock case to gauge its size. He explored inside. He spat, as if on the locksmith who had provided so puny a challenge. He removed the pick.

'Let me feel the others.'

He selected one of several picks with L-shaped ends. He explored again.

'Give me another of the same.'

Grymonde inserted the second pick. He was reaching past the wards to trip the lever and the bolt. Tannhauser had seen his father forge lock parts, though he'd never picked more than a padlock. Grymonde inserted a third pick. He twisted the rods and the bolt scraped and clicked.

'No rust on that one.' Grymonde stood up and pushed the door open and sniffed. 'Have you found the priest yet?'

Tannhauser climbed the spiral stair. Since morning the number of steps seemed to have doubled and the walls become narrower. He pushed himself. He reached the exterior walkway and crossed to the wicket at the foot of the north tower. He set the lantern at his feet. Sweat had long since overwhelmed the ribbon and he took it off and used the ends to wipe his eyes. He rolled his neck. He opened the wicket and shouted up the stairs.

'Pascale! It's Mattias!'

He waited. The timber staircase was pitch-black. Would he have to climb the damned tower? He didn't think he could and still have the energy for what might come. He bent from the waist to loosen the knots in his back. He straightened and stared into the bore of a horse pistol. The sweat on his back ran cold.

Pascale lowered the pistol and stepped into the light.

'You're the first to make the chance to have me,' he said.

'The chance?'

'Come here, girl.'

Pascale skipped down the last of the steps and into his chest. He put an arm around her. She seemed so small. In his mind, she had assumed a much greater stature. He thought of what she'd been through. He gave her a moment. She didn't take more. She stepped back. Her eyes, like her hair, shone like obsidian.

'I saw Flore,' he said. 'I'm sorry.'

Pascale nodded for answer.

'Are the others fit to travel?'

'Yes. Where are we going?'

'Home.'

Pascale smiled.

'The risks are as bad as staying here, maybe worse, but the prize better.'

'I don't give a damn for the risks.'

She was ardent. She was alive. Her vigour raised him.

'I found my wife and our new baby. They're waiting for us below.'

Pascale blinked and there was an instant of bitter disappointment before she hid it behind another smile. He understood, though the understanding surprised him. To him she was a girl, at least as far as that went. She was entitled to see herself otherwise.

'When I told Estelle I was going to find you,' said Tannhauser, 'she asked if you were one of us. I wasn't sure what she meant, but I said you were. What I meant was that you're one of me.'

'I hope so.'

'You shouldn't.'

'I wouldn't change any of it, if it meant changing this.'

She made a gesture that encompassed them both and he saw the mixed stains on her hands. Ink, gun black, blood. He felt he had opened the darkest door in her soul; a door that should have stayed closed; yet the light that blazed through it to illuminate the obsidian dazzled him.

'A few minutes ago, before I knew you were here, I decided to leave you behind.'

She took it without a flinch; but the light flickered.

'For your wife and baby. I would have done the same.'

'Carla told me to find you, despite the peril to her babe.'

Pascale thought about it.

He said, 'Carla believes in what's best in me.'

'I believe in it all.'

'Call the others.'

Pascale reached for the dirty white ribbon in his hand. It seemed a poor token of aught but bloody toil. Perhaps that was why she wanted it. He gave it to her. She made the gun safe and noted his approval. She skipped back up the stair.

'Pascale.'

She turned. He had hurt her. She didn't want to let him know it.

'I was not much amazed to find the first two *sergents* afloat on their own gore.'

Pascale wasn't sure how to take this.

'That's how hard I reckoned the iron in your soul.'

Her spirits lifted.

'But running down the third in the street? Call it the most beautiful.'

Pascale beamed. She sped up into the gloom. He heard her call to Juste.

Tannhauser stood on the prow of the cosmic ship, a hundred feet above the Parvis. The still point of the turning world. The cork in the neck of Inferno. Beyond lay the sea of Time and Fate, its surface lent a false serenity by night and the moon. He leaned on a gargoyle and looked out across the city.

The rooftops formed a geometric fantasy in black and luminous greys. Lamps in the watchtowers burned along the rim of the enormous city walls, but within the latter's ambit few windows dared a light. Hundreds of thousands hid in the dark and wondered at the world they thought they had known and which, like that, was gone.

He saw faint yellow blurs, randomly dispersed on the Right and Left Banks. The torches of the murder gangs. He saw a much brighter glow, closer and moving this way, on what he reckoned was the Pont Notre-Dame. On the Parvis below he saw Grégoire conversing with Clementine. He picked up the lantern.

The Mice emerged, philosophical as ever. Pascale was behind them.

'I left your rifle on the charcoal barge. I'm sorry.'

'It was the right move.'

'I left you the wrong message, too. Tybaut's rooms are on the Left Bank. I didn't know about the key until Agnès and Marie said Juste had it.'

Tannhauser had hung the tower key around Juste's neck. If he'd remembered, he might have saved himself a decision he regretted making.

Juste appeared, loaded with bags. When he looked at Tannhauser, he tried to conceal the pain in his heart, but couldn't. He wouldn't let Tannhauser take the wallets. Tannhauser squeezed his arm.

'Is Grégoire here?' asked Juste.

'How would we get out of the city without Grégoire?'

'I don't expect we could,' said Juste.

'I'd not have found you if not for him. Nor my wife and babe.'

'Carla's alive?' This news moved him. He seized Tannhauser's hand. 'I told Flore, about the *hôtel*, about this morning. I didn't see any baby. I think I knew she wasn't your wife. But she was cut up so badly.'

'You've nothing to answer for. The failing was mine. And if not for that turn, we'd not have found Pascale or Flore alive.'

Juste looked down and nodded, the scars of his sorrow reopened.

'Whatever that encounter has cost you,' said Tannhauser, 'I'd say it was a bargain you'd strike again.'

Juste swabbed his nose on his sleeve. 'I'd pay anything.'

'Then no more woe until we're done.'

Tannhauser herded them across the walkway.

'Tell me, how did you get past the guards on the cathedral door?'

To acknowledge the thanks of the children she had brought into sanctuary, Carla could manage no more than a distracted nod. When Tannhauser helped her up from her chair, the weight she laid on his arm was heavy. Feeding Amparo seemed to have drained her, though she smiled a dreamy smile as she looked at the babe.

Such bliss alarmed him. He had seen something like it in men on the verge of dying. How much blood had she lost? Doubt assailed him. The wagon; the streets; hours – days – on unknown roads. Here he could have her in a bed in the priest's quarters in ten minutes; and a surgeon summoned, though they'd probably try to bleed her more.

'Tell me, love, are you bleeding?'

Carla shook her head.

'You're not fit for the road. We'll stay, all of us.'

'No. We must go, while Death is on our side.'

'Death takes no one's side but his own.'

'If we fear him, he'll turn on us, you know that better than anyone, and the judgement will go against us. Alice says we must go.'

The cards again. Alice says? He put the back of his hand to her brow. It was cool, clammy, not fevered. The madwoman's quilt of his own philosophy embraced her points readily enough, yet the moral logic bore down on him. He was proposing to hazard the lives of his wife and baby in order to save his own neck; yet he would have died for them on the instant to give them a single breath. It was a riddle. Carla seemed to have solved it, but he had not.

'Carla, if you stay here, you and Amparo will survive.'

'We didn't need you to survive,' said Carla. 'Our survival wasn't the reason you did what you've done. You did it to be with me. With us. I left Amparo with a beggar girl on a roof. Yet here we are. And here you are, with us. You can't leave us, because we won't leave you.'

Tannhauser looked up into the vast hull of the cathedral, the ship built by those who knew for those who are. The arcane wonders writ deep through its fabric, and married to the smoke and dance of hundreds of flames, filled him with the Primordial Awareness it was raised up to contain. That awareness was of pure confusion, its terror and its beauty. Being was Confusion. The Humid Way and the Dry Way in simultaneity. Blood and water, stone and glass, the crimson and the white; the knowing and the not-knowing; the Wrong and the Right; Christ and Satan; the Mass and the Magnum Opus: one, all one, here in Notre-Dame de Paris, simmering in the flux of its sacred crucible.

Yet whatever metal might be melted into oneness from the ore of their souls, its quality could only be proved when it was cast. The substance born in the crucible was always in doubt; doubt was its very essence. The only certain yield was the worthless slag into which it would boil down if left untested. These songs of woe would be in the alloy, too, and sacrileges and sins beyond number; but who would have known that charcoal can turn iron into steel? The doubts and the riddles could never be resolved within the crucible; only with its emptying. Confusion was eternal and embraced it all.

He looked at Carla.

Carla stroked the bristles on his cheek.

He kissed her. He turned to the ragged crew.

'Juste, see the Mice to the wagon. Lower one side and lay the mattress.' Tannhauser saw Hugon, who clasped Carla's violl case across his chest. 'Hugon, guide the Infant. Estelle, show Pascale to my weapons. Bring them. The lantern, too.'

As Grymonde lumbered by he turned his eyeless face on Tannhauser.

'Can you make good on your boast and get us to the Porte Saint-Denis?' His smile was horrible. 'Or should I find a priest?'

His chuckles drifted up into the vault as he shambled on.

'Carla, hold our nightingale tight.'

Tannhauser slipped his left arm behind Carla's thighs and picked her up.

'So it's the fire,' she said.

'A good husband knows when to do what he's told.'

Carla started to laugh and winced as her insides clenched.

'Are you comfortable?'

'I will be if you don't make me laugh and continue to do as you're told.'

'I'll do my best.'

'Take us home.'

He carried her towards the portal.

'Grégoire said Hugon followed you here. What happened to your escort?'

'Ensign Bonnett? I don't know. I told him I didn't need him.'

Tannhauser's mind saw a runty blackguard fall backwards from a barrel.

Bonnett would know him in an instant; one of few. If he'd abandoned his orders to escort Carla, he would report to Garnier to explain himself, at once. Garnier had bigger troubles than the fact that Carla was praying in Notre-Dame. But it was possible Bonnett had seen Tannhauser, either before or after he killed the guards. Tannhauser reached the portal as Hugon manhandled Grymonde outside.

'Hugon, did you see Carla's escort leave?'

'No. I went back for the wagon, didn't I?'

The Parvis and the square were empty.

Tannhauser sat Carla on the mattress.

'Lie behind the board, at least until we cross the Millers' Bridge. Pascale, Juste, the Mice, you must lie down, too. Juste, put that armour plate between Carla and the board.'

Carla lay on her side, her back to the sideboard. Tannhauser bolted it up.

'Front or back?' asked Grymonde.

Tannhauser chose Frogier's bow.

'The back. This time I'm riding. Estelle, my crossbow, three bolts.'

He ran his eyes over the crew. A woman, seven children and two infants.

Petit Christian puked shit onto the Parvis. He was naked from the armholes, half-flayed by stones and potholes. Some species of animal bone jutted from his gut.

Tannhauser could think of no further use for him

'The playwright stays here. Who wants to kill him?'

Grymonde hopped back down.

A crossbow's sinews thrummed.

Petit Christian bucked and writhed. His last cry sprayed Paris with its own filth. He slumped on the rope like some obscene blood sausage hung out to cure.

Estelle retreated on her heels from between the back wheels.

'I think I got him right up the arse.'

Grymonde laughed from the belly.

'The bolt completely disappeared.'

Grymonde flapped a hand for Hugon to seat him.

'Quickly, boy, while I can still stand.'

The sight of a giant face with no eyes, and no lids or brows thereto, howling at him with laughter, kept Tannhauser entranced for a moment. Estelle handed him the crossbow and four spare bolts. He took them. He almost told her not to make a habit of this, but judged the moment for it wrong. Carla would teach her comportment and other wiles. She'd be a proper lady in no time. He smiled at her.

'Good shot.'

Estelle took this as a permit to join Grymonde in his abandon.

So did Hugon. One by one, so did the others. The Mice. Grégoire. Pascale, too. All except Juste.

Tannhauser glanced at Carla. She was watching the Mice. The sound of laughter seemed to do her good. It did them all good. He ducked and cut the playwright down. When he stood up, Carla was laughing, too, a hand on her belly. Juste was still sombre.

Tannhauser armed the crossbow and stood it by the front wheel. He dug Frogier's bow and quiver from the back of the wagon.

'Juste.'

Tannhauser offered him the weapons. Juste took them.

'That's a sixty-pound pull. If you can't make a full draw don't let it throw you, you'll have power enough. If it comes to shooting, the range will be close. Aim at their balls, before you raise and draw. Loose quickly or you'll shake. Don't shoot with any of us in front you.'

He saw Carla watching him. He grinned.

'Set an example, love, lie down. Estelle, Hugon: helmets on. The rest of you: lie down. No armed weapons. No shooting unless I say so. Where is that hellhound?'

'We have a hellhound?' said Pascale.

'A real one,' said Juste. 'He's called Lucifer.'

'He brings us luck,' said Grégoire.

The scorched dog emerged from a study of Christian's corpse. He trotted to his station between Clementine's front hooves.

'I think I know that dog,' said Hugon.

'Well, he's ours now,' said Juste. 'That's the bastard who set him on fire.'

The accusation stoked Grymonde's mirth anew.

Tannhauser took the crossbow and climbed onto the bench beside Grégoire. Tannhauser noted that the big grey mare was saddled as well as harnessed. The boy was entirely undaunted, but when had he been anything but?

'To the Porte Saint-Denis?' asked Grégoire.

Tannhauser hesitated. Notre-Dame might have been the safest place in Paris, but it was also the centre of the labyrinth from which they had elected to escape. He heard giggles and glanced back at the press of bodies. To take any distraction into combat was an error. To take ten was demented. He found Carla looking at him.

She seemed to read his mind. She nodded.

Tannhauser turned back to Grégoire.

'Aye. Let's find out what metal we have made.'

CHAPTER THIRTY-FIVE

Short Weight for the Blind

H e told Grégoire to get him a glimpse of the Petit Pont on the way west. When he did, he saw that its brazier and chain were unguarded. The militia were in motion.

They rattled into the maze of the old city.

Bonnett would expect him to stay with Carla, in the cathedral; he would bring Garnier there, from the Place de Grève and across the Pont Notre-Dame. They could stay ahead of them – unless Bonnett had used the missing guards as messengers, to alert the other bridges; or the killers plying their knives on the strand.

Grégoire turned north towards the Pont au Change.

Tannhauser saw only the same three guards as earlier. He canted the crossbow on his left hip. If he didn't get a smile and a wave, he'd kill them. As they rumbled past, the shopkeeper and his men waved and smiled. Tannhauser saw them take in the new passengers. He didn't believe the smiles. The wagon skirted the Palais and the warehouses loomed.

'Grégoire, stop. Have you room here to turn the wagon round?'

Grégoire sized up the junction. He nodded. Tannhauser climbed down.

'Turn and wait back there, by the warehouse wall, so we can take either route.'

Tannhauser ran towards the river.

He stopped at the last turn and peered towards the Millers' Bridge.

The dead cart blocked the street. Men stacked sacks of flour either side of it, from warehouse to river bank. He heard a deal of belligerent rowdiness brewing up beyond. He chanced two paces of moonlight to grab a glimpse of the Conciergerie clock tower.

It was twenty-five minutes to midnight.

They still had time to reach the gate.

Tannhauser strode back towards the wagon in the shadow of the warehouse.

Fight them here; unknown numbers; win.

Drive to the other side of the covered bridge.

But there would be no fight there; only a wall; a blind cave and them in it.

The shopkeeper appeared in the wedge of moonlight permitted by the meeting of the streets. He was six feet from the tip of the bolt when Tannhauser shot him through the pubic bone. He dropped the crossbow. He drew his sword as a second shape silvered in the moonbeam. An archer, arrow nocked, peering into the gloom.

Tannhauser broached him through the left gut, two-handed but not too deep, and carved him wide on the pull. Lantern light. He stepped wide of the corner and evaded as the halberd came down at his head. Four men loomed at the junction. Five.

'Tannzer! Look out!'

The weight of the halberd's axe head took it nigh to the ground. As the artisan leaned back on the shaft to control it, Tannhauser closed and severed his windpipe with a back stroke under the chin. He bore down on the others without watching him fall.

The lantern was already moving away, back towards the Pont au Change. Its faint light betrayed the shapes of the three men left behind. Tannhauser raised the sword two-handed and feigned a head strike at the nearest. It was the dyer. Two stained fists raised the halberd shaft broadside to ward him, as expected. Tannhauser whipped the blade back down in an oblique arc, putting his back and chest into the hip swing. He chopped into the dyer's left leg and cleaved the bone where it was narrowest, two inches north of the knee. He cut clean through the thigh on the pull.

He stepped around the dyer to put him in the way of the next man, who was young and brawny enough to be keen to have at him. The brawny one wasted a blink on the severed leg and Tannhauser was on him, swatting the halberd across the man's body with his left hand, and running the sword beneath the left ribs. He pulled short and palmed the ricasso from above and sliced down through the colon. He swept his ankles with the sole of his boot and the brawny one fell with a brawny wail of dismay. As Tannhauser turned he saw the third shape stagger backwards and land on his arse. An arrow projected from his belly and rose and fell with his groans.

Juste stepped into the moonbeam and nocked another shaft to his bow.

Tannhauser strode over and slipped the bow from Juste's hand and shoved the handle of his sword in its place. The arrow was laid to the left and he took the string with his fingers. He marked the shadow that accompanied the jerking lantern.

'With a bow the right weight you wouldn't miss, but let's be sure.'

Tannhauser drew and shot the shadow in the back, from the way it arched and dropped likely in the lower spine. He handed the bow back to Juste and cleaned his sword and sheathed it. He nodded at the archer by the corner, who knelt on his head and elbows and stared at the coiled mass that squirmed from the gash in his gut.

'See if that bow suits you, Juste. Broadheads into the bargain.'

'My God,' said Juste. 'He's still alive.'

'Good. See if he wears a wrist guard.'

Tannhauser went to retrieve the bodkin Juste had shot. Its victim clung onto the shaft in his belly as if loath to part with it. Tannhauser slapped his hands away and yanked out the arrow.

'They're all still alive,' said Juste. 'All six.'

Juste stared at the diversity of wounded, each bemoaning appalling injuries or choking on the attempt. The dyer was the only one standing. He leaned on his halberd in lieu of his leg and cried out questions to God that received no answer.

Tannhauser collected the crossbow and two halberds.

He slid the bloody arrow into Juste's quiver.

They returned to the wagon. Tannhauser slid the poles by Grymonde. He drew the crossbow. He looked at his mates. They all looked at him. Their laughter was a memory difficult to recall.

Their eyes shone in the lantern light, full of fear and hope. He saw them as they were, tags and rags tossed adrift on an ocean of madness. He met Carla's eyes in the shadows. She gave him all he needed. The children needed a bright face, too.

Tannhauser clenched his shoulder blades and grimaced and smiled.

'The bridge is blocked.' He sustained the smile. 'We can't get across the river.'

Grymonde pursed his enormous lips. Burned muscles twitched.

Tannhauser said, 'We're going to sail down it instead.'

'Have you forgotten the boom?' said Grymonde.

'We're going to break the boom,' said Tannhauser.

'How?'

'Can my Infant handle a barge pole?'

'Your brain has cracked. Cracked at last.'

'Pascale.' Tannhauser looked at her. 'You said charcoal.'

'Yes. The other barge was empty. Why?'

'We're going to run a fireship ahead of us.'

He let Grymonde think about it.

'We need a pilot. Juste? Hugon? Can you can steer a boat?'

Hugon shook his head. Juste drew the string of his new bow as far as his ear.

'I never tried, but I will.'

'Shooting three bridges is no work for a novice,' said Tannhauser.

'I can handle a pair of oars,' said Pascale.

'I am no novice with a boat,' said Carla. 'As well you know.'

Tannhauser had hoped to spare her the chore. He nodded.

'Good enough. Lie down, all of you.'

He climbed up beside Grégoire and stowed the crossbow behind him. He saw the luckless dyer lose his balance and topple backwards. He nodded to Grégoire. The wagon rolled forward through the shambles.

'There's a man there missing a leg. Trim the one he has left with the wheels.'

Before they reached the dyer a feeble scream quavered up from below. The wagon was too heavy to transmit much of a bump. The back wheel excited a second anguished protest and no more pity than had the first.

'That's their governor's ankles gone,' said Hugon. 'Chase us now, you cunt.'

Tannhauser turned. Hugon was jeering back at the shopkeeper, whose feet were separated from his shins by two strips of wet stocking mired in a pool of blood.

'Hugon, lie down.'

The dyer screamed twice as bone and muscle gave way beneath the wheels.

'Why didn't you kill this lot, like you killed all the others?' asked Hugon.

'He wants them to die slowly,' said Pascale. 'When the militia come up from the river and find them screaming, they'll waste time. And they'll puke with fear.'

As if to make her point, the dyer screamed again.

'A fire barge?' scoffed Grymonde. 'It's a fool's errand.'

'Then we're well suited to the job,' said Tannhauser.

'We'll be under the guns of the Louvre.'

'The King didn't want his capital turned into an abattoir. The militia have run riot on him and it's their boom, not his. The palace guard won't intervene without direct orders, and if we're not out of Paris by the time they get them, we'll be dead.'

Tannhauser grabbed a stanchion beneath the seat and stepped down backwards onto the swingletree. As they passed the fallen lantern, he stooped and seized it.

'That boom will take an age to catch and burn,' said Grymonde.

'I know.'

'But you propose to put me aboard a hell ship with nothing but a pole.'

'Don't fret, my Infant. We'll both be on the hell ship.'

'Is another Immortal part of the bargain?'

'Perhaps it will improve your morale.'

Tannhauser unwrapped an opium pill and bit it in two. He stored one half and rolled the other into a ball. Bitterness suffused his mouth. He passed the pill to Hugon. Grymonde watched its progress with empty eye sockets.

'Can I try one?' asked Hugon.

'You're not hurt,' said Estelle. 'Give the Immortal to me.'

'La Rossa, my darling, please don't drop it.'

The Immortal reached the Infant's throat. He scowled at Tannhauser.

'Short weight for the blind, is it? How well you have taken to Paris.'

The chain across the Pont au Change was unmanned. They still had time to reach the Porte Saint-Denis. Had they reinforced the north end of the bridge?

'Grégoire, stop. Juste, give me Frogier's bow and bring your own.'

He stripped his shirt off. The dried gore was chafing his armholes. And when it came to instilling fear, a bloody hide was second only to armour; perhaps not second at all. He put the shirt in the wagon. Tonight the Devil's livery was more apt than Christ's.

He swung down and took four arrows and the bow in his left fist. As he walked to the chain he nocked a fifth. To all intents the bridge was a street; the street of money. It must have been the best-lit street in Paris. About every fifth shop on either side boasted a private watchman, and each had a lantern. He'd have to pass five or six and leave his back to them before he got sight of the far end. He looked Juste in the eye. The lad was sound.

'Juste, stay out of sight. If any man moves after I pass him, shoot him.'

'In the back?'

'Wherever you think you can kill him.'

Tannhauser unhooked the chain and dropped it. He wondered if he, in Juste's shoes, would have shot *him* in the back, in revenge for his brothers. He thought not, at least not at that age. He strode down the middle of the street between the watchmen.

He was within easy range of their pole arms. He let them take in the crusted detritus left streaked across his body by those who had tried before. He kept his face front. He didn't trust his eyes not to provoke a man who might be in the mood. They looked too seasoned to do more than they'd been paid to do; but if it looked like he was losing, and to them it might, they'd pile in.

He reached the summit of the bridge's gentle camber. The end of the bridge was blocked by two carts, the shafts crossed and roped together. He saw the pan flash and turned sideways on the spot and thumbed the bowstring as the musket boomed ahead.

Two guns, one per cart. He heard the ball pass but didn't feel it. He drew the bow and aimed at the second cart through the smoke rolling out from the first. The sight of him provoked the second muzzle to waver as the pan flashed. Tannhauser let loose at the head behind it. The ball sang by. The musket clattered from the cart on this side of the barricade. He put a second bodkin through the side of the first cart and nocked again as a figure vaulted clear in panic, short of his gun.

They would scatter before he could kill them all. By the time he moved the carts, they'd be back with help. A street fight all the way to the Porte Saint-Denis.

The river it was, then. He turned back.

The second watchman to his left lowered himself to his knees with the help of his spear and keeled over. One of the musket balls had found a mark. The watchman nearest the chain on the same side of the bridge dashed towards his fallen companion. Juste shot him in the back, just below the armhole. Tannhauser drew and shot the third watchman in the chest at fifteen feet. The man hadn't moved but it cleared the east side.

Tannhauser nocked and covered the men now shrinking into the doorways along the west side. One threw down his pike. The others thought it wise to do the same.

Juste levered the shaft of his arrow back and forth with both hands as he tried to pluck it from the ribs of his floundering victim. The victim choked up blood with every cry. Tannhauser clapped Juste on the shoulder.

'A good habit, but leave it. Come on, we'll get to Poland yet.'

'Are we going to Poland?'

'Not tonight, but Poland will still be there tomorrow.'

Tannhauser pulled him back to the cart.

'Grégoire,' he said, 'avoid the next bridgehead.'

'We'll have to cross the street that cuts the island. They might see us.'

'That will be their bad luck.'

Tannhauser climbed aboard.

'Take us to the quays at Saint-Landry.'

They headed south and turned east into the street they'd taken earlier. Halfway down, Tannhauser saw torches pass south through the crossroads up ahead. The dark shapes of men marched by. Column of twos. More torches. A red and white banner.

The Pilgrims of Saint-Jacques.

Tannhauser retrieved the crossbow.

'Grégoire, is there a choke point between that street and the quays?'

Grégoire consulted the map in his brain. 'No.'

'Will Clementine charge through them?'

'If I tell her to.'

The Pilgrims would need minutes to reorganise. Clementine's speed would give him several more by the time they reached the quays. Tannhauser slotted a bolt.

'Then tell her. The rest of you hold on tight.'

Grégoire rose to his feet and emitted the kind of snarl that only those who work with horses learn to master. Coming from his malformed palate, it scared Tannhauser, too. He leaned back on the bench as the wagon lurched after the huge grey haunches.

The shapes up ahead heard the hooves. Shouts. They leaped back.

Clementine thundered through the crossing.

Tannhauser faced left. The column stretched back over the Pont Notre-Dame for as far as he could see, a mounted man among them. Tannhauser turned and got a glimpse to the right. Another score or so. A church on the corner. Tannhauser turned back on the bench and sighted down the length of the crossbow. A torch. A cluster of the curious surged into the street behind the wagon. He shot the torchbearer in the chest. The street cleared. Tannhauser turned and toed the stirrup. Clementine faltered and snorted.

'Faster, Grégoire.'

Grégoire snarled and snapped the reins. As Tannhauser hauled the sinews to the nut he saw the lance dangling and bouncing from Clementine's flank, just forward of the stifle. She raised herself to Grégoire's call and strained against her collar and something burst inside her. She veered rightwards and Grégoire leant back on the reins to straighten her up. She straightened. The right wheel gouged splinters from the corner of the next row of houses and Tannhauser tossed the crossbow and grabbed the bench and threw his spare arm around Grégoire's waist as the boy fell.

The back of the wagon sheered left and they tilted on two wheels and screams erupted behind him. A heave from Clementine's mighty chest righted them and they crashed back down and she pulled on, trying to recover her stride, the wagon now faster than she, the swingletree chaffing her hocks. Grégoire still held the reins and Tannhauser grabbed them short and hauled. Whether from panic or courage, the great beast drove onwards. If she ran herself till she fell she'd upend them. He found the brake with his heel and threw his weight on it. Filth sprayed and the wheel smoked and the wagon slowed.

Clementine foundered in the traces and toppled onto her side with a groan.

Tannhauser let go of Grégoire and the reins and vaulted down. He unbolted and lowered the sideboard. Carla swung her legs down and stood up, the nightingale in her arms. Pascale pulled the Mice to their feet one by one and pushed them towards him. He lifted them down as Estelle jumped by herself. She reached back for her crossbow.

'Leave it, take this lantern instead. Hugon, fetch the satchels and wallets.'

Pascale had slung the saddle holsters over one shoulder. She

639

took the double-barrelled pistol and the larger of the food sacks and sat on the mattress to swing down.

Tannhauser saw Juste jump from the rear and run back into the dark.

Grymonde had disappeared.

Tannhauser spotted a damp black patch on the mattress where Carla had lain.

'Can you walk, love?'

'Yes.'

He didn't know if she could. She couldn't know either. Her body had taken more punishment than all but the dead. He guessed the quay at three hundred yards.

'Pascale, with me. Drop the sack.'

They ran towards the back of a massive figure who stood in a swath of moonlight at the crossroad that had doomed the wagon. Grymonde bellowed defiance into the night, shaking the mace above his head. An arrow skipped from a wall. Juste stood ahead of Grymonde, in the same moonbeam and well within range of the mace, as he loosed a broadhead at the torches in the distance. Tannhauser clapped Grymonde on the back and grabbed the wrist that held the mace while shouting in his ear.

'My Infant, are you feeling stout?'

The mace came down without disaster. The whited holes turned.

'Have we reached the hell ship?'

'Not yet. Give me the mace. Go with Pascale to the wagon.'

'Will you teach me how to shoot a bow?' asked Pascale.

'On my word. Keep to the dark. Get the others ready to move.'

Tannhauser dropped the mace. Another arrow passed, better ranged. He grabbed Juste and pulled him from the moonlight to the wheel-splintered house this side of the crossing. He unslung his own bow. He grabbed four shafts and nocked. The torches ahead had retreated but there was moonlight at the main crossroads, too. He picked a black outline and winged a bodkin into it. Other shapes fled as it reeled and fell.

'Stay in shadow. Pick your man. They will try to flank us down this street to your left. Keep them scared and let me know as soon as you see them.'

Another arrow sped by. Their archer was using the dark, too.

'I'm going forward,' said Tannhauser. 'Don't shoot me.'

Tannhauser ran low through the blackness. Shouts and oaths floated about the labyrinth, distance and location difficult to judge, consternation not so. None of the Pilgrims counted on dying tonight. Between this row of houses and the church was an open space. The archer stepped out thence and drew, his aim already chosen. Tannhauser pulled and shot him in the gut and knocked him onto his back.

Twenty feet more. Worth the trouble.

He nocked as he ran to the archer. He stooped to the quiver and snatched a fistful of arrows and the archer reached up for his throat. Tannhauser stabbed him in the face with a dozen broadheads. He turned left as a man ran at him from the church space, sword committed to a lunge. He let him come, sidestepped, warding lightly with the bow, and plunged the bundle of broadheads into his neck and left them there. A third man ran away and Tannhauser stepped aside and drew. The runner ran head-first into a fourth Pilgrim who rounded the corner of the church with a torch. As the arrow flew, the runner clasped the torchbearer's waist and the bodkin drilled his face, cheek to cheek, and nailed him to the other's chest. They shuffled from sight like apprentice dancers summoned to some ballet of the crazed, and Tannhauser turned to the erstwhile swordsman who knelt on his heels and gargled on his own gore. Tannhauser recovered the broadheads with the feeling of uprooting rushes from boggy ground.

He dashed back towards the wagon through the shadows by the wall.

'Mattias coming in,' he called.

Juste loosed. The arrow passed wide. Tannhauser heard a distant cry behind him.

The boy was panting and his eyes were wild.

'Easier than ducks, eh, lad?'

Juste nodded without conviction. Tannhauser divided the

dripping bundle and recharged Juste's quiver and shoved the rest into his own. He spotted the crossbow he'd dropped. The fall had triggered it. He toed the stirrup and drew the sinew and loaded it. He stacked it by Juste. Tannhauser squeezed the lad's shoulder to calm him.

'You are our rock. Watch for the flankers. If they rush you, fall back.'

Tannhauser ran back to the wagon. Hugon had loaded himself as told and added the violl to his burdens. The boy was calmer than he was. The Mice held hands, impassive as two matched pearls. Pascale had reclaimed the sack. Estelle had set down the lantern to hug Carla round the waist, it seemed for the latter's benefit.

Carla had propped her hams against the wagon, as if it were all that kept her upright. In her face was an anguish he hadn't seen before.

'I left Antoinette,' she said. 'I forgot her.'

Antoinette? Who was Antoinette? It didn't matter.

'Left her where?'

'In the cathedral.'

'She's a sight better off than we are, so be not fretful. My Infant.'

'The Infant is stout,' said Grymonde, 'so you be not fretful either.'

'Mattias,' said Pascale.

Pascale pointed at Grymonde. He was holding onto the wagon bench. The feathers of an arrow jutted from his right flank and rose and fell with each shallow breath. If the broadhead had cut any vessels worth cutting, even he would have been down; but another ten paces would do the trick. The blade would slice his innards with every move.

Tannhauser looked at Carla for an opinion.

'If the arrow stays,' she said, 'so must he.'

'Will I get it out?' he asked.

'Find the head. If you can feel it, you can expose it and cut it off.'

'My Infant, very slowly, turn to face me.'

Grymonde did so and Tannhauser pulled his shirt up and tugged it down through the neck to anchor it. The belly was thickly muscled.

'Hold fast. Pascale, bring the lantern, watch.'

Tannhauser judged the angle and the length and put his right palm on Grymonde's belly and his left on the nock of the arrow. He pushed. There was no easy give, as there would be through entrails. He chanced more pressure and felt the tip against his palm.

'The tip is in the belly muscle,' he said to Carla.

'Good,' she said.

'Excellent,' said Grymonde.

'Don't speak,' said Tannhauser.

He pushed harder still and the skin tented against his hand. He marked the spot with a finger and released the nock and drew the dagger on his left hip.

'Pascale, push the nock of the arrow, as I did. Hold when I say so.'

She did so without a squeam. The skin tented again.

'Hold there.'

Tannhauser cut an X across the bulge, two inches to either arm. The leaves of skin bulged like a split fig and bled.

'Why don't you just push it right through?' asked Pascale.

'He'd resist. The shaft would likely snap short. Ease off a little. There.'

He put a finger in and felt the tip of the broadhead in the other side of the muscle. He cut alongside the finger. The steel head popped forth and the muscle retracted around the neck. He gave the dagger to Pascale.

'Use both hands. Put the flat of the blade near the hilt against the nock. When I say so, give it a good shove. Two inches. Don't snap the shaft. Don't cut yourself.'

Tannhauser put both palms flat on either side of the wound to anchor the belly.

'My Infant, lean on your arms and let your belly sag, as if you want to piss.'

'I do want to piss.'

'Excellent, then piss.'

'I'll not piss in my boots.'

He lowered a hand to release his cock. He sighed as he let go.

'As before, Pascale,' said Tannhauser. 'Push just a little.'

He didn't want to get stabbed. The arrowhead poked out between his hands.

'Now shove.'

The broadhead slid three inches clear.

'Enough. Give me the dagger. My Infant, stop pissing.'

'Am I a dog?'

'Is it beyond the King of Cockaigne? Try.'

Grymonde, so far mute through his ordeal, groaned with the effort.

The stream abated.

'Harden your stomach tight and hold fast.'

'What now? Do you want me to beshit myself?'

'Only if you must.'

The arrow stiffened as if in a vice. Tannhauser gripped the head, finger and thumb, and whittled the shaft, above and below, deep into the fixing. He cut the head off.

'Finish your piss.' Tannhauser went behind him.

'With pleasure. Does that mean we're done?'

Tannhauser scrubbed his hands clean on Grymonde's back, then braced one palm against Grymonde's ribs and gripped the shaft beyond the fletching. He waited to hear the splashing and heaved. The shaft came eight inches clear before the muscles clenched and his hand slipped and the feathers scorched him.

Grymonde grunted. 'That stopped my water quick enough.'

'One more.'

Tannhauser stepped back and went for a foot and both hands. The muscles didn't relax at all. He hauled the shaft free and dropped it. Grymonde sighed and put his cock away. Tannhauser scooped axle grease from the bucket hung under the bench and plugged the wounds back and front. He swabbed his hands on Grymonde's shirt.

'That was a song and dance from a man with three Immortals on board.'

'Two, and a crumb that tasted like you plucked it from your nostrils.'

'Your entrails leak from half a dozen holes. So answer me true.'

'I could walk to your bloody hell ship on my hands.'

'Can you carry Carla?'

He felt Carla's hand on his arm. He held it but didn't turn.

'I'll carry her to Heaven's Gate if she wants me to.'

'The hell ship will do for now.'

'I want my eyes. My wings. I want La Rossa.'

Tannhauser looked at Estelle. She lifted her arms. He doubted the extra weight would tip the balance. Tannhauser took her by the waist and hoisted her onto Grymonde's shoulders. His smile was horrible.

'Can Amparo fly with me?' asked Estelle.

'Not this time,' said Tannhauser

He turned and opened his arms to Carla. She hesitated.

'If you fall, love, we all fall.'

The wildness passed between them. She nodded. He picked her up.

'My Infant.'

Grymonde extended his enormous hands.

Tannhauser put Carla in his arms. He grinned at her.

'They look more comfortable than mine.'

Carla smiled. 'They are.'

'Pascale, take them to the quays. Get them aboard the empty barge.'

'Why don't you come with us?' asked Estelle.

'They're too close and too many not to come after us. Go.'

Tannhauser turned away so as not to delay them. He glanced at what was left in the wagon. Altan's gear. A loaded crossbow. The armour. A skin of wine. Three pole arms. He took the two halberds and the skin of wine and turned to watch them leave.

The Infant stumped into the dark with his children and the woman he loved. Carla watched him from over the giant's shoulder. She knew what he needed.

She turned away.

Tannhauser looked for Grégoire.

The boy had pulled the spear from Clementine's flank and cut the traces, and dressed the wound with axle grease. He was trying to hoist the collar from Clementine's neck. Tannhauser went over and set down the gear and helped him. Clementine laid her head down with a sigh. Shivers trembled beneath her hide. She was gored through the gut. Grégoire started sobbing. Tannhauser pulled him away.

'Go with Grymonde and the others. Take these halberds.'

'Will she suffer?'

'No. Now go.'

Tannhauser turned and saw Juste running towards him with a Pilgrim in pursuit, a javelin cocked above his shoulder for the throw. Tannhauser ran to the wagon and snatched and levelled the crossbow. As the Pilgrim brought his arm over, Tannhauser shot him through the armpit. The spear faltered; but it flew.

Pilgrim and boy went down at the same time.

Tannhauser dropped the crossbow and ran behind the wagon. More men emerged from the side street and yelled at those waiting at the crossroads beyond the church.

Juste was pierced through the upper back and trying to get to his knees. The weight of the shaft caused the javelin to flop sideways and the pain drove him down.

Tannahuser drew his sword and laid it on the wagon and took the *spontone*.

A musket boomed. Too far away for smoke or pan flash. He heard screams.

Grégoire's screams.

Tannahuser saw him squirming, in Clementine's blood and his own.

Bone shards waved from beneath one leg of his new red breeches.

The spear in Juste was tipped with a long, thin, triangular head. It had skated up over his left shoulder blade and pierced the upper chest, maybe the lung; they'd see.

Tannhauser stooped and grabbed the shaft and put a foot on Juste's back and drew the javelin out. He hefted it and caught it at the sweet spot and spun and cast it overarm, picking his man on the turn from among the three too slow to scatter. The javelin broached the burliest through the chest and the others turned tail.

Tannhauser dragged Juste to his feet. The boy's eyes were glassy. Tannhauser grabbed him by the jaw and bent over into his face.

'Grégoire is dying. Go and cut a length of the traces and tie it round his leg.'

He put a dagger in his hand and slapped him on the back and Juste staggered towards his friend. As he reached him, he skidded in the blood and fell by Grégoire. He rolled to his knees in the mire and scrabbled for one of the severed traces with his left hand. He cried out at the pain in his wounds, but turned it into a scream of defiance. He dragged the strap between his teeth to anchor it, and began to saw through the leather.

Something uncorked in Tannhauser's chest.

His lads were down; and probably done.

He let the something flow through him, lest he burst.

Another musket shot. He turned sideways to offer the narrowest target. Two long guns. He saw the smoke plume at the crossroads. Dominic's guards? He welcomed the rage. It scoured his exhaustion and grief. Pilgrims emerged from the side street with the steadiness of frightened men who had determined to be brave. About a dozen. Three ranks. Four spears out front. He let them come on until they blocked the distant muskets.

Grégoire fell silent.

Tannhauser took a scythe grip on the *spontone*.

'*Allahu akabar.*'

CHAPTER THIRTY-SIX

The Hanged Man

C arla felt Grymonde's pain throb through the massive heart that hammered at her ribs through his shirt. She had seen many die with gut wounds. At the Hospital in Malta, they had set such unfortunates aside without spending any effort to save them, for such efforts would have been futile. The contents of his intestines were corroding him from within. His stomach was already as stiff as an oak board. He made no complaint. His determination to spare her the slightest discomfort was complete, as if at last he had a task he could take pride in. Compared to the wagon his arms were a feather bed and she was glad of them; yet whatever the two mad men might claim, she knew her weight exacerbated his agony and hastened his end, and she felt guilty.

She heard a gunshot somewhere in the darkness of the city behind them.

She looked back and saw nothing. They had turned north towards the river. She looked ahead. Hugon was bent under the weight of his baggage. Both lanterns clanked in one hand; he hefted her violl in the other. She would have left the violl, and so would Mattias, but her instinct knew why Hugon had chosen to bring it. He wasn't going to abandon a dream. The twins they called the Mice walked behind him. Pascale had disappeared.

'Grymonde, please, set me down. I can walk.'

'Carla, prithee. If I set you down I will kneel in the dirt and wait for your husband to kill me.' He took a breath. 'A shame I would rather forego.'

'He'll help you to the quay.'

'If he hadn't needed me to replace that old grey mare, he'd have cut my throat with no more thought than he'll waste on cutting hers.'

Carla did not dispute this. 'You shouldn't talk.'

'It's the last conversation I'll ever have. And more precious than all the conversation I had in my life. Though, since most was of a base nature, perhaps that's saying little.'

'I don't believe that from someone raised by Alice.'

'Didn't we have precious conversations, too?' asked Estelle.

'Is a dying man to be denied his morbid rhetoric?'

Carla couldn't help but study Grymonde's face; it was inches from hers. His strange yeasty smell came off him in waves. Sweat ran down his brow and funnelled into the ridges melted in his sockets, from whose roofs the drips fell to pool in the scarred floors. Runnels spilled over his cheeks as he took each step. She remembered the wild brown eyes that had spared her life on a whim. More than a whim. Her baby had been born into his murderous hands. The brown eyes were gone, and the murderous hands were carrying them both through as dark a night as anyone alive could have known. It was a story she didn't understand; for some other, untold, story lay underneath it; but one day she would. The stories were in her.

'What does he mean?' asked Estelle, from above Grymonde's head.

'He means he overstates his case, as a means to ignoring our advice.'

'Very well, I give in. You're both right. My mother's words I didn't listen to, though I heard them And your words, La Rossa, were the crown jewels of my kingdom.'

'Truly?' demanded Estelle.

Carla looked up at her fierce little face.

'I remember every word you ever spoke, for I played them in my mind like music on many a dark night, and on many a sunny day, and the day and the night both were made brighter.'

'I remember them, too,' said Estelle. 'But I bet you can't remember every one.'

Grymonde bared his teeth at Carla, in what she supposed was a grin.

'Just the same as the grandmother.'

Carla said, 'So you still won't say what you know.'

'I know what we have, now, she and I. We don't want our wings to become limbs. One day, perhaps, but I'll leave you to be the judge of that. If you'll do that for me.'

Carla swallowed on a sudden sob. She nodded. He couldn't see, but he felt her.

'Carla, why doesn't he say what he means?'

'He does say what he means. I'll explain when we get home. When you're older.'

Estelle considered this.

'Does that mean home is very, very far away?'

Grymonde laughed. Carla laughed, too. Pain cut them both short.

'It's far but not that far,' said Carla. 'I'm happy you're coming.'

'Tannzer said I could carry Amparo home.'

'You already have,' said Carla. 'And you'll carry her farther still.'

'It was the wren saved us, if you think about it,' said Grymonde.

Carla did. It was true; in many ways. She wondered if Grymonde would have killed her if she hadn't been pregnant. She wondered if that was what he meant. She didn't ask.

'Not the wren, the nightingale,' said Estelle.

'I've never seen a nightingale, and nor have you, but I can tell a wren when I see one.' He gave a short laugh. 'Can you?'

'No,' said Estelle, 'but you can't see Amparo and I can.'

'Exactly, my darling, which is why I see a wren in my brain. As long as the wren is alive, we're winning.'

Pascale emerged from the dark.

'Militia have come through the houses. We'll cut across the market.'

Carla looked across a broad patch of cobbled ground. They would be exposed.

'It's shorter,' said Pascale. 'That light by the stable, and we're almost there.'

She waved Hugon towards a glow and Hugon seemed to think it a fair idea. Estelle somehow turned Grymonde after him, and they moved out across the paled cobbles.

Pascale skipped beside them, looking back and forth through the dark like some feral cat: absolutely afraid, absolutely alive, absolutely determined to get through the night.

'The cards, you see,' said Grymonde. 'My mother said it was bad luck to look at another's draw, for you don't know what it is you're looking at, and you'll read only your own doom. How right she was. But I won't say the judgement has been harsh, for I deserved worse.' His teeth gaped into Carla's face. 'In fact, I'd say it's been generous.'

'How could it not be generous to the king of the Land of Plenty?'

'Too late the king, and too late the plenty, and yet –'

Grymonde's head turned this way and that, as if comparing a series of paintings in the gallery of his mind. Carla wondered if his knowledge of himself somehow ran in parallel with Alice's knowledge of the world, and thus they had never crossed. He had never listened to her. Because the only thing about which he knew more than Alice was him, and, from knowing that, he had tried to protect her. Grymonde shrugged what was left of his brows.

'It's not the death I wished for. I've killed no one and the prospects are grim.'

'You killed Rody,' said Estelle.

'But you shot him first, so he doesn't enter my reckoning.'

'I shot the bravo, too, remember? But Tannzer killed him, so who enters that reckoning?

'Tannzer wouldn't claim it.' He sniffed. 'But, then, he can afford not to.'

'Oh, but I killed Papin all by myself. And Irène.'

Pascale seemed as shocked as Carla, though not at all appalled. 'You killed Irène?' said Pascale.

'Who was Irène?' asked Grymonde.

'In the heart,' said Estelle. 'You can ask Tannzer. He said "Good".'

'I suppose that's all we need to know,' said Grymonde.

'There was the creature under the wagon, too,' conceded Pascale.

'Of course! I'd forgotten Petit Christian. He really deserved it.'

Pascale said, 'They all deserve it.'

Carla sensed the fear that Pascale must have endured for most of her life, and the cruelty that had taken its place. Mattias had hatched these children into killers. He must have had strong reason. He had steered Orlandu clear of violence. She hadn't dwelled on Orlandu or where he might be for hours. Before she could do so, Pascale lunged away and vanished.

'Stop in the name of the King!'

Carla looked back over Grymonde's shoulder. Two men carrying swords were advancing across the market ground from the west. One held a torch.

Neither Carla nor Grymonde could run. To try would invite attack. She had to induce them to take her, and themselves, into the path of Mattias.

'Grymonde, stop. Don't turn until I signal, just so.'

She clenched her leg on his arm. He nodded.

'If I signal again, give voice to your anguish.'

'And the wren?' asked Grymonde.

'Your anguish won't harm her.' She called out. 'Officers! Quickly, come here!'

The two militiamen broke into a trot. A good start. They slowed as they got close. She didn't recognise them but they wore red and white ribbons, and might have taken part in the attack on Cockaigne.

'I am the Comtesse de La Penautier. Take me to Bernard Garnier at once.'

She flexed her knee and Grymonde turned about. The men stopped short.

'Jesus Christ on the Cross.'

Their swords came up and wavered.

'That's him. That's the Infant. Or it's his ghost.'

'Is the beggar's brat a ghost, too?'

'Messieurs, we don't have much time. Ghost he may be, but while he carries me he seems docile. I fear his temper if he should be made to set me down.'

She clenched her leg again. Grymonde let out a howl so haunting she felt as if her heart would halt from pity. She looked down and saw Amparo open her eyes. They gazed up into the spangled sky as if searching for the source, as if so awful and beautiful a sound could only have its origin in those infinitely distant fires. She showed no distress, only wonder.

The swordsmen retreated. In the light of their torch, Pascale appeared behind them. The girl's rashness alarmed Carla. She couldn't stop her. She held their attention.

'Estelle, if she be the subject of your slanders, is my daughter, but your apologies can wait. If my good Captain Garnier is not close by, I suggest you take us to Notre-Dame.'

The gunshot startled Amparo into trembling. The torchbearer folded like damp cloth, a black fountain spouting from the smoke that engulfed the back of his skull. Even as he fell, Pascale sprang back and aside. The other soldier turned with a forehand swipe of his sword and missed her by a yard. Pascale darted in behind the arc, Grymonde's pistol extended in two hands, and shot him beneath the ribcage from such close range the muzzle blast ballooned his tunic and flames lanced out through its fabric. At once she sprang away again, like some juvenile harpy sent to practise her antics. Her victim reeled and toppled with a gasped blasphemy.

Carla scanned the edges of the square and saw no one. She saw Pascale doing the same. Their eyes met for a moment in the flicker of the torch flames on the ground.

Pascale drew on what was dark in Mattias; Carla drew on what was light.

Pascale's face broke into an eager, girlish smile. She wanted to be liked.

Amparo was crying. Carla turned away to comfort her.

Pascale ran over, breathless with elation, and offered the smoking pistol to Carla.

'Gramercy, madame. Your stratagem was better crafted than mine, and made my work easy. Now I need my hands free. Will you carry this?'

'I'll carry it,' said Estelle. 'It's a Peter Peck, and it's mine anyway, Tannzer said so.'

Pascale hid a stab of pique behind fluttered lashes and gave her the gun.

'Girls contend with fiends while I make faces like a clown,' said Grymonde. 'Was this in the cards?'

'Alice put great store in the Lunatic,' said Carla.

'I thank both of you for that,' he said, his bitterness no less sharp.

'Grymonde, go,' said Pascale. 'Hugon's waiting.'

'Pray give him no weapons, for if he too –'

'Go,' said Estelle.

She kicked Grymonde in the armpit with one heel and rested the weight of the pistol on his head. He chuckled at some inner fancy and set off. Amparo quieted in her animal skin and Carla looked back to watch Pascale as they stumped away.

The girl picked up a sword. The torchbearer had doubled back on his knees as he crumpled. His head still smoked from the rear, as if that substance had been all it had contained. Pascale jammed the sword into his chest and threw her weight into an extra shove to make sure it would stand upright. She walked past the fallen torch to the other man.

The girl was leaving them to be discovered with their own weapons stuck through them. She was doing what she thought Mattias would do.

Carla was disturbed. She could almost see Pascale thinking as she took the second sword in both hands and stood over its owner, who was struggling up onto his elbows. He craned his neck to look up at her. The two figures glimmered in the light reflected from the cobbles. They seemed like actors in some story from the Bible's oldest books. Pascale raised the sword in both hands and Carla thought she would try to decapitate him. Instead she took a step and chopped through both his Achilles tendons. His legs kicked up and fell as he screamed. She raised the sword again in a dagger grip and stepped astride him.

Carla turned away. Another scream followed, more outraged than the last. It jarred her, confused her. She had no feeling for the soldier. But his cry somehow told her that Pascale shared something with Mattias that she did not.

They passed the smell of a stable and the Mice led Hugon to an alley.

'Hugon, wait.' Pascale ran up with the torch. 'I'll go first.'

She slipped down the alley. Carla saw that she and Grymonde wouldn't fit.

'Grymonde, I must walk. We've reached an alley too narrow for us to pass. And I smell the river, we're at the quays. You've done it.'

Grymonde lowered her down. Her legs took her weight without shaking. She'd been so exhausted that the rest in Grymonde's arms had restored more strength than she could have hoped for. Grymonde clenched his teeth and raised his arms and plucked Estelle from his shoulders and her face shone with delight as she flew through the air. He stopped halfway as if, had he not, he would have dropped her. Then he lowered her gently to her feet and doubled over, his hands on his knees, and panted, though not for want of breath. His shoulders stiffened until they shook. He tossed his head. He growled.

'Go on.'

'We can't go on,' said Carla.

'You can't see,' explained Estelle. 'So we can't leave you.'

'Take my hand,' said Carla. 'We'll go down the alley sideways.'

Grymonde walked his palms up his thighs. He pushed himself upright.

Carla settled Amparo against her heart and slipped her right hand into Grymonde's left. His huge fingers closed. He squeezed her harder than he realised, but not as hard as he could. His battle wasn't with blindness or pain. His battle was to be the man he felt he had to be. Carla felt a deeper sadness for him than any she had felt before. He had fought that battle all his life and had won it a thousand times over. The squeeze gave her a vision not of that man, but of the man he might have been. Grymonde turned his face towards hers. The moist holes seemed to read her more clearly than any other gaze could have. He had glimpsed that other man, too, said the holes, but the vision had come too late.

'The Hanged Man smiles because he doesn't know he's hanged. Much less that he was the hangman. The Lunatic smiles because he does know.'

'Estelle, give the pistol to Grymonde and hold his little finger.'

Carla led them down the alley after the Mice and the lanterns. Grymonde's back and chest scraped either wall, as almost did his chin and the back of his head. Hugon's strength was so taxed by the weight he had carried, he bounced from one wall to the other; but he wrestled the violl case ahead of him with low grunts of determination, which, as Carla got closer, she discovered were inventive obscenities. She wondered where Mattias was. She had hoped he would be here by now, given their delay. If they were both to die, she wanted to die with him. She scolded herself.

'Grymonde, cheer me up. Let me hear some more morbid rhetoric.'

'We shall hear some from my bowels if I don't get out of this alley.'

Pascale's torch swished into the mouth of the slit, beyond Hugon and the Mice.

'Everyone turn back. They're coming across the river in boats.'

CHAPTER THIRTY-SEVEN

Horses and Boys

Tannhauser gestured to the left of the front rank and sent all four spearheads swinging that way. Had they read his body, not the gesture, they'd have seen he was headed to the right.

Halberd, partisan, *spontone*. The beauty and the danger of pole arms lay in the weight. The heavier a weapon, the harder it was to use well. Once committed, such force was the devil to ward; but by the same law it was as hard to alter its course; with the wrong grip or stance, it was impossible, at least within the instants that death left available to avoid him. Footwork, posture, ebb and flow; the natural geometry; the circle and the line. There was music to be played with a *spontone*. Most who drilled with pike or spear were like donkeys trying to sing.

In a stride he was inside their draught and their points were useless. With stoop and sweep, thrust and pull, he scythed the two outer Pilgrims across the shins, and felt three good bites. As a swing and twist brought the iron-shod shaft against his hip, he switched length and forward grip, underhand, and shouldered the nearest Pilgrim aside while he was hopping on his one good leg. The Pilgrim fell on his crippled comrade and Tannhauser jabbed the man behind him through the goitre in his throat – windpipe, gullet – not too deep, twist and out. The goitre burst like a bad fruit and the torch in his hand swung wide among his friends as he sucked the poison through his lungs.

Tannhauser avoided a panicked sword swipe from elsewhere in the pack and darted round the flank of the outer file. Scythe grip, high port, slice and shove; chest, arm, shoulder, hip; his run behind it, too. The rear-rank man was lifted from his feet, the blade so entrenched beneath the hinges of his jaw that Tannhauser felt it splinter the base of his skull. A gust of blood through the nose and teeth. Stop, backstep, turn and pull.

Tannhauser ran the next rear-ranker through the loin from where he stood and carved him to the backbone and swept out and up to bat away the sword of the last in the rank. He followed through on the push, the pull, the hip, the circle, chopping through the side of his face to the depth of yonder nostril. He rolled the shaft with both hands as if cranking water from a well and felt the crackle as the blade prised the upper jaw from the rest of his face like an obstinate clamshell. The *spontone* slid free as he stepped back and he rammed him up under the breastbone and hoisted, and pitched him into the legs of the congested.

Tannhauser took the first breath he had needed.

A body of men needed training to work as a unit; and then they needed command; and their function was to tackle other such bodies, or in this case the wholly defenceless. While the lamed caterwauled and floundered, and the throatless sprayed blood and terror, the rest yelled instructions at each other while trying not to injure the same with their brandished arms. They were young enough to boast a deal of belligerence; but they were not to know that in the space of that single breath the fight had been decided and they were done.

He reversed grips, a left-handed stance, to exploit the angle and the wall. He gored his way through the rest with contempt, like a man shovelling shit. Yet as always he marked his targets and what the blade told him, noting any deviation of the result from his intention; for in future such deviation might cost him a wound. Rising strokes under the ribcage. Upwards, piercing the Pilgrim nearest the wall above the left hip, clipping the front of the spine as it burst the aorta. And out. Upwards through the side of the gut of the next as he turned; a half-squat and turn on the pull, the muscle and skin parting like cloth, the entrails mobile, tenacious, clinging to the tip as it pulled them out through the slit. And upwards, beneath the floating ribs from behind, kidney, tripes, the point bursting from the belly, pull back, hip twist, shove, slice, and out as a scarlet mouth spewed from the loin.

Tannhauser took a second breath. The air was befouled with the evacuations of the slain and the disembowelled. Red and white ribbons added a gaudy note to the shambles. If the whole affair had taken half a minute, he would be embarrassed. There were two still standing. A third bent against the wall, braying as he inhaled his ruptured goitre.

The farther of the two yet unmolested ran, towards the lads. Tannhauser snapped his head towards the nearer, who held a torch and a sword, and screamed in his face.

'Drop the sword.'

The youth, for such he was, recoiled and obeyed. Tannhauser took a half-step back, arming the *spontone* like a javelin as he reckoned the fugitive's distance and pace. He made the cast, arcing the shaft into the spot beyond its prey. The *spontone* wasn't built for casting but the range wasn't far, and by the time it got there, so had the fugitive. It cut through his left shoulder blade as if it were parchment, and didn't stop until the wings dug deep. The Pilgrim plunged into the blood that oozed about the wagon from horse and boys.

Tannhauser drew the lapis lazuli dagger and slapped aside the torch the youth held and stabbed him through the base of the neck. He picked up the sword. Its quality was common. It was streaked with crusted blood, though likely shed in murder, not combat. He stepped over to the first of the lamed and cut his head off, or would have done so clean with a decent blade. He slashed the strings of flesh that remained. It was useful to have such a token to fling down the street if the moment came. The second cripple curled in the filth and covered his head with his arms. Tannhauser planted the sword through his armpit and let it stand.

Both the fallen torches were fresher than that on the wagon. He picked one up. He left the man by the wall to inhale his goitre and the gutted to pray for the end.

He recovered his own sword from the wagon and sheathed it. He swapped the torch in the bracket and stuck the dimmer one between the spokes. He knelt over Grégoire and collected the dagger Juste had used and sheathed it. Juste had wrapped the trace strap around Grégoire's thigh and was trying to tighten the knot with one hand and his teeth. Tannhauser took over. The blood came in pulses. The artery. He staunched the flow.

'Good work, Juste. Plug your own holes with that axle grease.'

Tannhauser examined Grégoire's leg. The ball had struck below the right knee, from the side, and shattered the larger bone like a stick of chalk. There was an exit hole in the fossa behind the knee, from whence the bleeding had been worst.

Tannhauser mastered a surge of nausea, as if his stomach knew before he did what was required of it. Strange, the different songs that butchery sang. He could do it, if he stopped the song from sounding in his heart. Don't look at his face. He stood up.

He took the shaft of the *spontone* and pulled. It was lodged fast in the Pilgrim. He used it to drag him out of the way, levered it free with the help of his heel. He propped the *spontone* on the wagon and dragged out the mattress and slung it away. He lifted the unconscious boy in his arms and laid him out on the wagon bed, the ruined leg closest to the edge. He looked at his face.

Grégoire breathed noisily. Tannhauser put a hand on his forehead.

Clammy, cool. He stroked the hair away. He saw the lad's ugly, gaping mouth.

He choked on a knot of emotion. His nerve failed him.

Loosen the strap. Let the lad slip away in peace.

'Juste, help me, brother. Should we let him die?'

'What? Grégoire? How can we let him die?'

'Well said. Come here. Hold this leg high and steady. Keep your back to me.'

He lifted Grégoire's left leg perpendicular and placed Juste to hold it thus. A musket ball splintered the wagon bench. Tannhauser stooped to the halberds and brushed a thumb across the axe edge of each and chose the sharper. As he took the shaft his nausea returned and he let it come and vomited into the blood pool. He spat and wiped his lips on the hairs of his forearm.

He straightened and stepped back and chose a grip and judged the angle.

He summoned all his strength, body and spirit.

Tannhauser chopped Grégoire's leg off.

Grégoire sat up and screamed over Juste's shoulder.

Tannhauser met the boy's eyes. The pain he saw there he expected. The utter bewilderment – the unspoken '*You?*' – laid waste to his heart.

He looked away.

He had aimed to split the boards beneath the leg and had done so. He levered the axe head free and propped the shaft. Grégoire clung onto Juste, oblivious to his friend's dire wounds, and Juste let the good leg fall, and clasped him to his chest with his one good arm, and cried with him. Another musket ball whirred by. Tannhauser dug out the half-stone of opium. He stooped for the wineskin and pulled the stopper with his teeth. He slipped the opium through Grégoire's deformed lips and pinched his nose and poured wine down his throat. Tannhauser dropped the skin and clamped a hand over his mouth.

'Swallow, lad, swallow. We're with you. We need you.'

Grégoire swallowed and he let him go and the boy coughed but the stone stayed down. Tannhauser corked the skin. He put a hand on Juste's head. He felt the sobs.

'We need you, too, Juste. Hold him fast.'

Tannhauser took the amputated leg by the foot and threw it out of sight. He took the torch from between the spokes. He saw his shirt behind the bench and grabbed it. He spun the shirt twice around his open left hand and turned his back to Grégoire and lifted the stump. The second bone had been severed clean, level with the fragments of the first. The stub of the calf muscle had contracted under the skin; so had the vessels he had to cauterise. Tannhauser held the knee joint tight and applied the torch to the stump.

He said an *Ave*, steadily, to time himself.

He couldn't hear it over the screams.

'*Hail Mary, full of grace, the Lord is with thee.*'

Grégoire kicked him frenziedly. He prayed for Grégoire to pass out.

*'Blessed art thou among women, and blessed is the fruit of thy womb,
Jesus.'*

He rolled the burning sponge of the torch over the raw surfaces.

'Holy Mary, mother of God, pray for us sinners . . .'

He pressed deep on the contracted tissues to seal the vessels.

'. . . now, and at the hour of our death.'

His own hand started to burn through the shirt.

'Amen.'

Grégoire fell limp in Juste's embrace.

Tannhauser withdrew the torch and the smell of burned flesh hit
him. Smoke rose from the stump. Pitch flared and died in the wound.
The scorched shirt smoked, too. Tannhauser dropped the torch and
slackened the strap. The slight ooze congealed as it appeared. A thin,
blackened bone poked forth from the seared skin and muscle. It was
ugly, but the job was done. He wrapped the shirt over the stump and
tied it around the thigh by the sleeves. He heard a pistol shot from
the north.

Another.

Pascale.

Amparo. Estelle.

Carla.

Whatever had happened would be over before he got there.

He heard hooves at the canter and looked up the street at a
horseman charging from the crossroads. He took the halberd and
advanced to meet him.

Unless seasoned by war, the horse would likely refuse at the
corpses choking the street, or even sooner, for though he couldn't
smell the marsh of blood, horses could, and it unnerved them. They
were wary of the sharp end of a pike, too, if they spotted it. He
reached the edge of the dead and wedged the butt into a rut beneath
the nearest, who was headless. He picked the head up by its saturated locks. He tilted the blade towards the horse and turned it in
the light of the fallen torch to catch some winks from the steel. At
worst he'd let the poor creature impale itself; with luck, he'd come
away with the mount he needed.

The rider wasn't Garnier. He wasn't big enough. A breastplate.

A helm. A brandished sword that flapped too much. He didn't sit like a man who had ever lived in the saddle, much less at the charge. Tannhauser let out his own reading of Grégoire's snarl and slung the severed head down the street as he might have slung an axe.

The shout and the stench of gore, and the sight of corpses, missile and blade, caught the horse all at once and it baulked and swerved to its right for the side street. Its hooves pranced and slid in search of a new gait, and the severed head slammed into the rider's breastplate, and Tannhauser dropped the halberd and ran.

The rider reeled back, and in lurching forward to right himself tilted steeply to the off side. He might have kept the saddle, but he wasn't used to the weight of his gear. As he tumbled to earth among the groans of the disembowelled, Tannhauser hurdled his legs, intent on the horse, but in its terror the horse was too quick. He watched its tail flutter down the side street. He turned and saw the first of the crowd who had advanced on foot behind their champion, and who now had to decide whether to die for him.

Tannhauser retrieved the crossbow he had left at the corner.

He shot said first in the belly to aid the rest in their cogitations.

The advance stopped. Tannhauser dropped the crossbow. He unslung the short bow from across his chest and grabbed a handful of bloodslaked broadheads and nocked and loosed. The shafts were a fair match for the pull. He nocked and thumbed and drew and loosed. He spared the torchbearers for their light was handy. He shot at the crotch of each target. The first two arrows flew high. He corrected for the third. A hero burst from the herd. His valour inspired a second to follow. Tannhauser shot the first in the chest and nocked while the man made three more strides and carved apart the insides of his thorax. The second slowed, as much from the realisation he was alone as from fear. He looked back to confirm his comrades' shame and was doing the same for them when Tannhauser ferried an inch of steel through his colon.

Time to show them how the janissaries advanced.

He grabbed his last fistful of arrows from the quiver.

He glanced back as he nocked a bodkin and saw the rider on

his knees, clambering up the wall of a house with his hands. Tannhauser shot him through the arse. At this range he heard the thud as the point hammered deep into the timbers beyond. He nocked and turned and strode towards the wavering torches.

He drew and loosed and killed and nocked. Those at the front started screaming at those behind them. The street before him roiled with terror run riot and he shot another in the back and nocked and kept walking. Torches dropped as the sharper of the thronged scum realised the virtue of the stratagem. The ribbons of the Pilgrims provided useful markers and he shot into the turmoil at chest height. The throng parted and began to spill away. The parting revealed a musket man jostled by the routed and struggling to level his barrel on a forked wooden rest. Tannhauser drew and aimed the last of his arrows beneath the muzzle and loosed. The fork and the gun tumbled without firing.

Tannhauser drew his sword and ran for the matchlock. He spotted the second musket man, stranded by the retreat and taking aim. Tannhauser kept running, his eye on the small red glow of the match. He slashed the bowstring and dropped the bow. He threw away the quiver. The glow snapped down and he feigned left but swerved right and the muzzle jerked left as it flamed. He felt its heat. Two strides. He ran the musketeer through the belly and cut him wide on the crank and pull.

He stood the musket on its stock and smashed the cock from the lock plate with the ricasso. He ran back to the unfired gun and collected it and stripped the match, and ran on through abandoned torches and the bodies of the squirming and the slain. He stopped by the rider nailed to the house. Blood leaked down the back of his thighs and pooled around his knees. He saw his face. It wasn't Dominic. He tapped the shaft of the arrow with the gun barrel and set it to vibrating. The rider whimpered and his fingers clawed the wall.

'Where are Bernard Garnier and Dominic Le Tellier?'

'Millers' Bridge. We heard you were there.'

'You must be Crucé.'

Crucé shifted around on the arrow, each movement exacerbating the pain it hoped to relieve. His eyes veered sidewise to plead with Tannhauser's. He was terrified. He watched Tannhauser tip the point of his sword in shit.

'Aye. I'm Crucé.'

Tannhauser put the point under the angle of Crucé's jaw.

'Crucified up the arse is how you'll be remembered.'

Tannhauser shoved the blade up through the root of Crucé's tongue, a gritty texture that eased as the tip burst into his mouth and pierced the palate. Crucé gargled on horror and gore. Tannhauser twisted the hilt through three-quarters of a rotation. He walked to the wagon and left him to strangle slowly on the swelling and the blood.

He propped the musket by the *spontone* and threw the match in the wagon. Grégoire was still unconscious. Tannhauser turned Juste towards him and explored his wounds by hand through the neck of his shirt. They were greased and not much bleeding; they could kill him later by a diversity of crueller methods, but not right now. For now they would only hurt and disable him. He folded Juste's arm across his stomach and buttoned the tail of his shirt up over it.

'We're not giving up, then,' said Juste.

The revelation seemed to daze him as much as blood loss and pain.

'Give up? You and I are more outlawed now than we were this morning.'

Tannhauser grinned and got a smile out of him. He squatted by Clementine's head and pulled her lip down. There was no blood or foam around the nostrils or teeth. The lungs were sound, her injuries not unlike Grymonde's. Movement was agony. Tannhauser looked her in the face. A large eye rolled towards him.

'I don't believe you, old girl. You can get up for us. Come on.'

He stuck his left hand under the angle of her enormous jaw and grabbed a fistful of her mane with the other. He lifted her head and twisted her neck along its axis and snarled in her ear and heaved as he straightened his legs. Clementine turned with him and drew her forelegs under her chest and a spasm spurred her on and she rose to all four feet so fast she almost lifted him off the ground. He thanked her and slapped her, and ran a hand under the girth strap. She was clenched tighter than an oyster. He lowered the stirrups.

'Juste, one arm round my neck. Foot in the stirrup.'

He hoisted Juste by the waist and Juste got a foot in the stirrup and his hand on the rim of the saddle. Tannhauser gave him a shove from below and the lad rose and landed. Clementine didn't move.

'Shuffle forward. More. Here.'

Tannhauser gave him the reins. He stacked the *spontone* blade-down against his leg.

'Grégoire will ride behind you. Pull his arms round your waist.'

'Will he scream again?'

'If he screams, we know he's alive.'

Tannhauser hung the wineskin from the saddle. He went to the wagon and donned Altan's quiver and strung the horn bow around his chest. He took the match and blew it yellow and cocked it to the arquebus and aimed it into the darkness that ruled the far crossroads. He couldn't see a target, but if any had stayed it would keep them on pins. Between here and there half a dozen abandoned flames spiralled skyward from the ground. Dark mounds heaped the dirt down fifty yards of street, like the droppings of some monstrous beast. It occurred to him that he'd got this far without firing a gun. He wasn't against the practice in principle, but the world would be nobler without them.

He pulled the match and threw it in the blood, and smashed the lock apart on the rim of the wagon wheel, and dumped the gun. He cut the string on Juste's bow. There were no more reasons to delay. He feared Grégoire's screams more than Juste did.

He took Grégoire by the shoulders and sat him on the edge of the wagon. The boy's head flopped forward and Tannhauser put a hand on his chest. The ribs poked through his shirt; his heart fluttered like a bird's. Tannhauser slipped his arm around him and the other under his thighs. He gauged the move and picked him up and carried him to Clementine and tossed him upwards and across, and managed to part his thighs and land him astride. The stump caught and Grégoire flailed and cried out. He hadn't the strength to do either with any vigour; and it was too soon for him to be feeling the virtue of the opium. Tannhauser crammed him against Juste's back, and Grégoire clung on.

Tannhauser mounted behind them and took the *spontone* and the reins in his left hand. He held the shaft across Juste's chest to stop him falling off. Grégoire was pressed firm between them. He grabbed the torch from the bracket.

'Lucifer!' said Juste. 'Look, Grégoire! He's back!'

The bald dog checked the street as if to confirm that all was quiet. He cast a dubious glance at the horse, as if assessing her frailty, then took up his station

'You see, Grégoire?' said Tannhauser. 'Despicable though he is, Lucifer holds true to his hardy, stout and resolute mates.'

'Lucifer isn't despicable,' said Juste.

Tannhauser gave Clementine a good kick with his heels. She didn't move.

'Clementine,' called Grégoire.

The mare stumbled forward in an ungainly walk. Tannhauser tapped her on the haunch with the torch and she broke into an agonised trot. Grégoire's punishment was hardly less arduous. The boy muffled a cry each time they landed. Each time Tannhauser felt the shorn limb flap against his leg. He kept them moving.

They passed two dead in the marketplace, staked out by their own swords. The printer's daughter, now his own, stamped her name once more on his heart. The lamp he'd left by the stable still burned but he kept a course straight north, to the west of the lamp. Beyond the market was the wharf where produce was unloaded. He reached the river and turned east and followed the curve of the bank. He saw lights and knots of men on the edge of the Place de Grève, where earlier he'd seen their dead carts unload. They were watching something on this side, but not him.

Tannhauser dropped the torch in a vegetable garden.

He rounded the shoulder of the bend and saw the barges. He saw no sign of Carla or her party on the quays. He saw lights on the water. Oars rose up to be shipped as a rowboat slid up to the bank on the far side of the coal barge. Five or six men on board.

A larger boat, a fishing skiff, wasn't far behind them. It was danger-
ously overmanned but they hadn't chanced more than fifty yards.

Tannhauser stopped Clementine and she blew her nostrils as if
glad to oblige. He swung down and walked her to the dark lee of
the houses and gave the reins to Juste. He could think of no intelligent advice. The lads wouldn't have known what to do with it.

He advanced through the narrow gardens in the shadows.

Pascale didn't need intelligent advice. She had taken Carla
and the others to hide at Irène's. And it would work. The militia
had nothing to accomplish on the quays. Let them go and find
the Devil's faeces heaped in yonder streets, and let them ponder
their futures. He liked the look of the skiff. If there was a mast
and a sail in the bottom – and from its cut there should be – he
could sail them all the way to Bordeaux.

He wanted it.

He slowed his stride. The first boat tied up and the militia
clambered out as the skiff slid past them to dock tight behind the
coal barge. They were thirty yards away, blinded by their lanterns
and idle talk, and unaware of any threat. He stopped. Let the skiff
tie up. Let them muster and leave. He saw hands thread the rope
of the skiff through an iron ring. He had to get the lads off the
quay and hide them. He turned around.

A hiss. A whisper. Very close.

'Tannzer!'

He turned back. An enormous head loomed from the dark,
almost in front of him.

Estelle wasn't on his shoulders.

Tannhauser felt her take his hand.

In Grymonde's hands, he saw knives.

'My Infant. You and Estelle should be indoors.'

'Perhaps, but, as you have noticed, I am not.'

'Wait here, stay stealthy.'

'If I find no role in your design, I have one in my own.'

'Estelle, tell me, what is the Infant's design?'

'I'll push him straight at the soldiers, then run away and hide
at Irène's.'

'Opium's designs are best enjoyed in peace,' said Tannhauser. 'Wait here.'

'You'll have to kill me.'

'My Infant, you don't have any eyes.'

'Did it take a man with eyes to crush the Philistines?'

Grymonde neglected to whisper and heads turned on the quay. Lanterns were brandished. Swords. A shouted challenge. The lights in the second boat bobbed.

Tannhauser wanted that skiff.

A flame lanced from a nearby house. The sound of his own rifle. A figure lurched from the cluster of disembarked militia and fell into the river.

'Estelle, run and hide now. I'll do the pushing.'

CHAPTER THIRTY-EIGHT

Something of the Lore

'I knew he would come.' Pascale stood watch at the open window of the kitchen. 'The militia are out of the first boat. He's found Grymonde'

Carla watched her heft Mattias's rifle and lay the barrel across the ledge. Carla had seen what a long gun could do to an unprepared shoulder; and to unintended targets. She didn't want her to shoot Mattias. But she wasn't going to infringe the girl's authority, not least because any such advice would be rebuffed as surely as that she had offered Grymonde. She had no right to argue with any of them. Her own decisions had been just as reckless. The folly they held in common was the power that had kept them alive. Folly and Mattias, who didn't consider himself reckless at all.

It was Carla's job to protect the stillness at the eye of the storm.

Grymonde was right: the eye was Amparo.

The kitchen was dark but for a faint glow that crept from the parlour, where they had left the torch and the lanterns, along with Hugon and the Mice. Carla groped about the cold stove behind her and found a hemp towel. She wadded it and took it over.

'Pascale? Cushion the butt with this. When you shoot, keep the shoulder tight.'

Pascale was terrified. So was Carla. Carla knew that terror was too exhausting to be borne for long, and she had learned how to let it rave alone in some locked and far-flung cellar of her mind. She had never seen anyone transmute terror into so focused a state of elation as Pascale. Nature had cast her eyes with a very slight prominence; along with the gap between her teeth, they held her short of prettiness; and their present clarity of purpose was itself frightening. Carla had noted it when they had arrived here via the street and Pascale, with an effort that should have been beyond her strength, had dragged a dead *sergent* to the cellar door and rolled him down the steps. She had shoved a dead woman down after him. Pascale took the wadded towel.

'Thank you, madame. Have you ever fired this gun?'

'No, but I know something of the lore. You're standing a little too straight, and your stance is a little too narrow. If you bring your right foot further back, and bend your front knee, you can turn with the recoil instead of resisting it, which may well cause you an injury.'

Pascale did as suggested and nodded.

'Let the line become the circle,' said Carla. 'Then it won't knock you backwards.'

Pascale enacted the motion. 'Let the line become the circle.'

'I quote Mattias. As also: "But you have to be quick."'

'I am quick.'

They both turned towards a shout from the quay.

'They've been spotted,' said Pascale. 'Go to the parlour.'

Carla had already begun that retreat to spare Amparo the smoke and noise, or the worst of it. Pascale bent to sight down the barrel.

'Aim low,' said Carla.

'I will, for their balls. When you return bring the lanterns, if you please.'

Carla placed her back against the parlour wall inside the doorway. She saw Hugon squatting over the open violl case as if it were piled with treasure. As of course it was. He glanced up, neither frightened nor guilty. The grotesque events in which he was swept up seemed not to make much impression on him. He lowered the lid and locked the brass hooks and reached for the straps.

'I can see how you stretch the strings,' he said, 'but how do you tighten them?'

'You mean tune them, so that they are in harmony with each other.'

The rifle shot shook the house. Powder smoke rolled into the room.

'Hugon, open the window. Bring that lantern to the kitchen, and that sack. Fill it with whatever provisions you can find.'

Carla took the other lantern. She saw the Mice. They sat at the table playing some game with their hands. They had the gift of excluding the outer world entirely from their own. No doubt they had needed it to survive. Carla had exchanged not a word with them, yet they had won her affection. She glanced into the kitchen. Pascale was still standing. She was swabbing the bore of the rifle with the rammer. She had set the table with a powder flask and a sack of ball, and three large pistols.

'Thank you, madame. The towel and the circle helped. I killed one, and sowed confusion in the others. Please, put the lantern on the table.'

'There's gunpowder on the table.'

Carla set the lantern on the stove and went to the window.

Two large shapes ran at a confused knot of militia, though running was not quite the notion. At another moment it might have been comical. Mattias held Grymonde by the back of his belt and hoisted him forward, while Grymonde lifted his knees unnaturally high and propelled himself in great, ungainly leaps. Each must have been more painful than taking another arrow. He howled at the militia, though this time she heard no anguish, only a rage so intense it sounded like joy.

Amparo let out a short cry. Carla looked down at her. Her eyelids were half-open and two tiny points of light gleamed out. Her tongue poked through her lips.

'My beauty can't be hungry yet.'

Whether Amparo needed feeding or not, the pull was overwhelming. They might never get another chance to share the pleasure, and it was as agreeable a delight as either of them had ever known. She heard Alice's coarse laugh. Carla took her left breast out and put Amparo to her nipple and the delight of all three was enjoined.

Estelle burst through the door from the quays and Carla heard Grymonde more distinctly. She doubted anyone else could have found either word or meaning in the sound. No sound like it had ever been made but there was no one else alive who knew him as she did. All his shame, all his pride, all his regret, in that sound. Grymonde screamed his mother's name as he plunged into the fire.

CHAPTER THIRTY-NINE

The Quays At Saint-Landry

A t least the quays were paved.

Tannhauser couched the *spontone* beneath his left arm, though no knight before had made such a charge nor reined so wild a beast. The blinded Infant dragged him along and it was all he could do to steer him away from the water. Tannhauser expected with every step to see Grymonde fall but the man roared on, less a raging bull than some Minotaur deranged and at last broken free from the gaol that had so long bewildered him.

The crew of the farther, smaller boat stood on the quay. The fishing skiff was still crammed with men. As they passed the skiff, the first Pilgrim to attempt to disembark leaned out and rested both hands on the stones. Tannhauser stuck out the *spontone* on the fly and the blade of the left wing caught him in the bridge of the nose. The blow was glancing but not one that many would have welcomed. It pitched him among his shipmates in a spray of snot and gore and set the skiff rolling on the swell.

Tannhauser and Grymonde charged on.

Five men waited for them. One had drifted out to the rim of the quay, drawn by the option of abandoning dry land. The other four were braced in an improvised phalanx, two swords raised, two levelled. Head-on was no good way to take them, but that die too had been cast. Tannhauser shouted in Grymonde's ear and unleashed him.

'For Cockaigne.'

With a primordial cry whose ecstasy compared to janissaries rising from the last ditch, Grymonde brandished his knives and fell on the swordsmen.

Tannhauser rushed the flanker, who dropped his weapon and

674

clapped both hands to his eyes, and turned and hunched forward, too raddled with fear even to try for the water. Tannhauser lanced him through kidney, gut and spleen, and caught the familiar and foetid whiff of involuntarily evacuated bowels. He forked him braying blood into the boat and spun towards the melee.

The outer two of the four sprawled some several paces distant from their stand. Both were trying to rise; both had been stabbed in the chest. The other two had been driven back almost as far but hadn't fallen. They couldn't. Grymonde had them wrapped in his arms and had buried a knife in the lower back of each. He churned the hilts, and the organs within, with the motion of an either-handed cook beating eggs. They were dead.

Tannhauser punched both the wounded through the skull with the spike on the butt of the *spontone*. He looked downriver and saw what he least hoped to see. The men in the skiff had decided not to fight for the quays at Saint-Landry. None had put ashore. One was fumbling to unhitch the line that tied their vessel to the dock cleat. If Tannhauser lost the skiff, it would be free to harass the barges.

As he ran back past Grymonde he glimpsed the tips of two sword blades protruding from his back above either hip but didn't stop. He wheeled the *spontone*, scythe grip, and skirted the rim of the quay, the blade angled down and out above the overmanned skiff.

The militia, nine, ten of them, hastened to squat and sway beyond its arc. The boat rocked violently. A sword swept for his ankles. He jumped it. An oar rose to block his spear. He stopped short and stabbed the one who had raised it under the cheekbone. As the texture of lettuce yielded to something like pine, he cranked the shaft, shoved and pulled, and left him to amuse his shipmates. He jumped the dropped oar and wheeled the *spontone* about his right hip, shortened his grip, and drove the counterspike at the head of he who struggled with the rope around the cleat. The head moved. The spike bored through his upper neck south of his ear and chiselled a wedge from his spine. Tannhauser twisted and pulled and struck backwards with the blade, and lanced another militiaman through the sternum as he flailed for balance. He cranked the broached ribcage wide and pulled the steel free in a black cascade and glanced back.

The dock line was still fast.

Tannhauser grabbed the socket of the spike with his right hand, clenching tight through the coating of blood, and struck long and down. He pierced a gawping Pilgrim through the throat notch. As the wounded bawled and flailed about in this barque of the suddenly doomed, the panic among those yet living was extreme. Tannhauser leaned forward and raised his voice above the din.

'Any man who stays in this boat will die.'

Three men jumped in the water. One vanished as if his feet were anvils. The others floundered in their gear. Of the three left in the boat without mortal wounds, one grovelled in the bilges snorting blood and two clung to the gunnels as they pitched up and down.

'You two. Look sharp. Throw these corpses overboard.'

He stooped over the quay and speared the groveller through the loin.

'Start with him. Don't swamp the boat.'

Tannhauser looked towards the curve in the bank where he had left his lads and beckoned. He glanced towards a splash. Today the Seine was a graveyard. The groveller had joined it. So, too, it seemed, had other would-be swimmers. He ran to Grymonde.

The Infant leaned on his thighs over the sword hilts protruding from his belly; one to either side, where Tannhauser might have inflicted a slow kill. Tannhauser grabbed one hilt and braced the staff of the *spontone* against the web of Grymonde's neck. In the cannon-ball muscle of Grymonde's shoulder, a deep cut welled waves of blood.

'Do you want me to piss or shit?'

Tannhauser dragged the sword out and dropped it.

'Did I get them all?'

'All four.'

'I'll have the next Immortal then.'

'I've none to waste.' Tannhauser grabbed the second hilt.

'Waste? Do I have to list my wounds? Do I even have the time?'

'What are a few more leaks to the mighty Infant?'

Tannhauser pulled the second sword. He stooped and cut the white armband from the nearest corpse. He dropped the sword and took the armband. He glanced at Irène's. Carla waved from the window. Pascale stood at the back door with his rifle. He gestured to them to wait. He stuffed the armband into the shoulder wound and hoped it would stay packed. Grymonde didn't notice.

'I allow you your jest,' he said. 'Forgive me if I don't laugh.'

'You'll be dead before the opium starts to work.'

'You've been promising death for hours.'

Tannhauser returned to the skiff. Clementine plodded towards him by the barges. The sparks had gone from her hoof strikes; they landed as if each one broke another string in her heart. Two small shapes, shrunken almost into one, sat on her back.

'This young rascal is still alive, sire. Blood coming out of his eyes.'

Tannhauser looked down at the speaker.

'It seems a bit harsh, sire. Some might even say unchristian.'

'Do you want to get out of that boat or not?'

'Indeed I do, sire. I already feel right queasy.'

The oarsman whose face was split in two screamed and struggled, but they got him over the side without falling in. Tannhauser saw the mast, yard and furled sail in the hull.

'Drop your knives in the boat. Get up here while I'm feeling kind.'

'Gramercy, sire, and your kindness is well known.'

They clambered up. Tannhauser motioned them a few steps downstream. The speaker tossed three small purses at his feet, much as a dog might offer a dead rat. From the sound they made when they hit the flags, they weren't worth very much more.

'Waste not, want not, sire.'

Tannhauser stabbed the quiet one in the stomach and the speaker sprang forward. Tannhauser pulled the *spontone* and stepped back to skewer him, but the speaker grabbed his dying associate and guided him backwards off the quay. A splash. The speaker turned and dusted his hands.

'That's that then, sire. Job done. Anything else I can do to oblige?'

The man wasn't bright enough for drollery, nor guile.

'Do you know where Captain Garnier is?'

'I'm afraid I don't, sire. Ensign Bonnett sent us.'

Tannhauser levelled the *spontone*. The man seemed amazed he was to die.

'That's Hervé the plasterer,' said Juste.

'Right you are, young master,' said Hervé.

Tannhauser had a fair memory for faces, but Hervé's had left no shadow on his brain. He put the *spontone* flat on the ground and added Altan's bow and quiver. He took Grégoire by the waist and lifted him from the saddle. The boy was floppy but conscious. His face contorted with agony, but he lacked the strength to cry out. His screams had gored Tannhauser to the bone; right now they would have reassured him.

'Hervé, hold him, gently, as if he were the child Jesus.'

Hervé took him in his arms. 'Poor lad. I did warn him about that dog.'

'Lucifer didn't bite his leg off,' said Juste.

'Perhaps not, young master, but he does have the evil eye.'

Tannhauser lifted Juste down.

'Lucifer took us to Cockaigne,' said Grégoire. 'He found the baby.'

'Raving, sire. I'd say it looks quite bad.'

'Silence,' said Tannhauser. 'The lad needs peace.'

Tannhauser bent to the girth strap. Clementine's belly was so distended he couldn't get a finger under. He unbuckled it and Clementine staggered with relief. He removed the saddle and blanket and spread them on the quay. He took Grégoire and laid him flat on the blanket and rested his mutilated leg over the saddle. Juste sat cross-legged beside him and held Grégoire's hand. Tannhauser gave him the wineskin.

'See if he'll take a mouthful. You, too.'

Tannhauser studied the charcoal barge. It was filled to the gunwales with gaping sacks of lump char, stacked to within four feet of the tiller. The sacks were footed with damp from the rain. What he had in mind might have been designed by Grymonde under opium. He took one of the lumps. It crumbled easily. Not smelting quality, but that meant it would ignite more readily. The problem was to get it to ignite at all.

'This lot must be worth a franc or two, sire.'

Tannhauser sized up Hervé.

'Hervé, I'm going to put you to work.'

'You'll not find a man more willing, sire.'

Tannhauser illustrated with his hands.

'Take those sacks from the rear row and empty them on top of the sacks at the front of the barge, midship. Spread a nice loose bed, two palms deep. Cover the tops of about six sacks, longwise with the barge. Understand?'

'Spread it and bed it, sire. You don't have to tell me twice.'

'Take more sacks from the back and make two rows, the sacks end on end, like so, on either side of the bed, again, longwise with the barge.'

'It might help if I knew what we're up to, sire.'

'I'm going to set fire to it.'

Tannhauser took the *spontone* and led Clementine to a nearby garden. The boys were too lost in pain and fatigue to see him go. He stopped her and stepped back and took a short grip, the shaft over his shoulder. The mare rolled one large eye to look at him.

'You deserved a better life, and a better death, but in that you're not alone.'

Clementine seemed satisfied with this valediction. She turned her head away. Tannhauser lanced her clean through the upper neck behind the jaws and felt the scrape of the spine along the upper edge. He whipped his arm over the shaft and threw down with his weight and pulled and severed her neck, outwards through the throat. The mare staggered sideways and her front legs folded and he stepped back as she fell towards him. An immense surge of blood swilled over his boots and he felt a twinge of nausea. He welcomed the scant evidence it offered of some remnant to his humanity. Clementine's eyes rolled white and her chest heaved for air and the blood whistled and bubbled from her windpipe. The sounds weren't loud enough to carry. Tannhauser blinked the grit from his eyes. For the spilling of human blood he could afford no such qualms. He wiped the *spontone* on the scarred and quivering hide, and turned away, and left the old grey mare to her passing.

He stepped down into the skiff. It smelled of fish and tar. They'd had their pick from the craft on the Right Bank and someone had known how to choose. Clinker-built, fifteen feet long and four and a half in the beam; full ends. The long yardarm and its pivot with the mast made it a lateen sail, with which he was well acquainted. The whole rig could be lowered and raised with ease for passing under bridges. Three oars. He recovered the fourth from the quay. A boathook. Two lanterns. He picked up three swords and threw them on the quay, and stowed the knives and a fourth sword safe beneath the helmsman's seat. A built-in chest that he didn't open. He checked the rudder. A sturdy boat, river or sea. He climbed out.

He went to the smaller boat and found two oars and a lantern. He snuffed the lantern and added his finds to the swords on the quay.

Grymonde hadn't moved since he'd left him. His hands still clenched his thighs. But for the blood that trickled from his shirt and overbrimmed the tops of his boots, he might have been the stony idol of some race from ancient myth.

Tannhauser walked past him to Irène's. Pascale met him at the door. His rifle was propped against the wall. His saddle wallets and two holstered pistols draped her either shoulder. The twin-barrelled pistol was stuck in her belt. Pure pride kept her standing. If he'd had a heart to spare, he would have broken it for her. He mustered a grin instead. It came easily enough. She grinned back and he saw the gap in her teeth that had given him his first faint intimation of her mettle. He pointed at the Peter Peck in her belt.

'Did the Devil's Apprentice reload?'

'It's easier than setting type.'

'I fear country life will disappoint you. Wait here.'

He took her by the waist and pulled her aside and went through the door.

Carla had Amparo in her arms, with Estelle and the Mice in front of her, ready to go. Hugon stood behind her with a satchel over either hip and a sack in each fist. Tannhauser beckoned them outside. He took the wallets and holsters from Pascale and loaded them onto Hugon, who swayed beneath the weight.

'Why can't she carry 'em?'

'Put this gear in the skiff. Keep the powder dry.'

'This gear? There is no more. I'm carrying the lot.'

'If the burden's too great I'll take that gold collar back.'

Hugon reeled towards the boat. Tannhauser went in the kitchen. He saw a wicker basket filled with faggots. He took the kitchen table, turned it on its side and dragged it outside and flipped it on its top. The legs were braced with panels fore and aft.

'Pascale, I need kindling. Faggots, candles, lamp oil. Stack it in here.'

He put an arm around Carla and walked her to the skiff. Estelle and the Mice followed them.

'There's a boom across the river at the Louvre,' said Tannhauser, 'boats chained end to end. Much the greater danger will come from the Right Bank, from Garnier. On the Left Bank there shouldn't be more than a token guard, and few or none to reinforce them. I'm going to hit the boom right of centre. I'll bring the barge in sideways, stern to port. The fire in the bow will stop them crossing on foot from the Right Bank. I'll board the boom and break it.'

'How?'

'A chain's not going to stop me. What do you think?'

Carla looked away to see the scheme in her mind. She looked back at him.

'A chain's not going to stop us.'

Tannhauser grinned.

'I want you to hold back until I signal to you to pick me up. They should be shooting at me, but if you can pull around the head of the island when we part, I'll feel better.'

'There are two small islands off the tip of the City. We can hold there.'

'There's a dock at the Hôtel-Dieu, I doubt Notre-Dame will be guarded. If I fail –'

'I'll hear no such talk.'

'Carla, I've been meaning to tell you. You've never looked more beautiful.'

She smiled. 'I'll hear no lies either.'

The world was in flames all around her, yet she still had a smile to strengthen his spirit. Her courage overwhelmed him. He swallowed.

'I never spoke truer in my life.'

Carla squeezed his hand, heedless of the blood that stained it. Tannhauser squeezed hers.

'Now,' he said, 'if I have my bearings right, we've three furlongs of water between the Millers' Bridge and the boom. The militia don't boast many archers or guns, but I can't say what help they've recruited. If we come under fire, it will be from the wharves on that stretch. When we clear the bridges, fall in on my larboard side until we reach the islands.'

'Beware the sandbanks,' she said. 'Especially the Right Bank.'

'The run-off from the rain should give us some leeway. Now, if you see the boom open but you don't see me –'

'Then stay in sight.'

They stopped at the skiff. He pulled her to him. He looked at Amparo. She seemed to gaze back at him. He sensed the wheel of eternity turn, its speed either too great to imagine or with so little haste he could not know if it had ever shifted at all. He felt Carla's eyes on him and he looked at her. Her face was so pale. His chest tightened. He didn't know what to say. Carla stood on tiptoe and kissed him.

'We'll meet you at the boom.'

Carla stepped back. He had covered her frock with blood.

'Don't worry,' he said. 'It isn't mine.'

She gave him one of her smiles. 'I love your oldest jokes.'

'Which reminds me, Orlandu loves his new sister and is strong in heart.'

'You mean he's hurt.'

'Orlandu's a Maltese yard boy. He's as tough as the Infant.'

He saw her bite on many questions. She held his hand tighter and climbed down into the skiff. With a sure step she settled at the tiller and studied the boat.

Tannhauser turned to the boys and saw Grégoire's stump. He picked him up. The lad murmured and flinched. The opium was working.

'Hugon, take the saddle and blanket, make a place for him, near Carla.'

Grégoire opened his eyes. They were dreamy.

'Is Clementine gone?'

'Clementine's soul is free, as her body never was.'

'Clementine helped save the baby, too, didn't she?'

'You saved the baby, brother. You saved me.'

'Master? Can I ask you a favour?'

'You never asked before, so ask away.'

'Don't kill Hervé.'

Grégoire's eyes were as clear as a silver mirror.

Tannhauser blinked at what he saw therein. He nodded.

Grégoire closed his eyes.

'Hugon, jump out and hold her steady.'

Tannhauser stepped into the skiff and settled Grégoire on the strakes as best he could. He reached up and beckoned the Mice and lifted them down one by one. He called Juste. Hugon pulled Juste up by his good arm and the boy gasped with pain but didn't protest. Tannhauser saw him into the boat and sat him with the others. No one complained about the blood. He had left the rowing benches unoccupied. He climbed out.

'Are you an oarsman, Hugon?'

'No.'

'Go and help Pascale fetch the kindling. Drag the whole table.'

'It would be nice if Pascale helped me.'

'You've got forty years' wages round your neck.'

Tannhauser picked up the oars and the swords and went to the charcoal barge. The fire pit had been built with such perfection that even Hervé, checking that the angles were true from the stern, appeared to find no flaw. He had left palm-width gaps between the upper sacks to improve the draught. Tannhauser detected a faint cross-breeze.

'Hervé, when I buy the Louvre and turn it into a brothel, I'll hire you to plaster it.'

'You'll find none more reasonable, sire, especially for a job that size, though there's them as would say that no such alteration would be needed.'

'Now, I want you to build a redoubt, there, to the right of the tiller.'

'You mean a kind of wall, sire?'

'Exactly.'

Hervé pointed to a collection on the quay. 'I found them on that other barge, sire. Not strictly honest, I'll allow, but they'll burn a treat. Caulking pitch in the bucket, the coil of rope is tarred, and so is that rain canvas. Spread that on top and whoosh.'

Tannhauser turned as Pascale and Hugon reeled over and dropped their improvised handbarrow, which they'd carried by its legs. They were stunned with fatigue. Had any but Tannhauser received them, Pascale would have sunk to the stones. Had she not been a girl, so would Hugon. The table was heaped with combustible materials. The char was hardly needed.

'Excellent,' said Tannhauser. 'I want you to build a fire in this pit. Pour the pitch over the bed, then the faggots, not too tight, leave me a trough at the back for the torch. Next –'

'We know how to build a fire,' said Hugon.

'We?' said Pascale. 'I thought you didn't like girls.'

'I don't.'

Tannhauser saw Grymonde talking with Estelle on the quay. He went over. The Infant still hadn't moved, his pain such that each word stole his breath.

'La Rossa, on these very quays, you once asked me –' Grymonde faltered. He set himself. He beamed at her with gapped teeth. 'If one day we could sail away.'

Estelle near danced on the spot. 'You do remember every word!'

'Now we will sail away. We'll be on different boats, and mine will go farther than yours. If I'm lucky, and luck runs in the family, it will go more swiftly, too. But now you must remember my words. Wherever you go, the dragon will be with you. Always.'

'Estelle,' said Tannhauser. 'Get in the skiff. Careful of the wounded.'

'Tannzer, Pascale's got my Peter Peck and won't give it back.'

'I'll see you get it. For now, go and help Carla and your sister.'

Estelle looked at Grymonde. He nodded. She skipped away. Tannhauser picked up the two swords he had pulled from Grymonde's gut.

'I'm not easily moved to pity,' he began.

Grymonde clenched his teeth on a short laugh. 'Prithee, peace.'

'Say the word and I'll kill you now.'

Grymonde shoved on his thighs and stood tall. The sightless holes turned.

'Spend that rarest of coins on him who needs it. Put me on your hell ship.'

Grymonde swayed. Tannhauser already knew he wasn't fit to pole the barge.

'The hell ship is full. Can you handle a pair of oars?'

'I was born by this river.'

'What I ask is do you have the strength?'

Grymonde groped for Tannhauser's forearm and squeezed.

'My Infant, my hand is turning black.'

'It will match your filthy soul.'

'Carla has the tiller. Mark her orders.'

'I've been marking your wife's orders since the moment I met her.'

'That, too, we have in common.'

'Too?'

Tannhauser guided him to the skiff, Grymonde forcing the pace.

'Pascale will man the second bench,' said Tannhauser.

'Must that girl best me at the rowlocks as well?'

'We're here. Stop. I want you on your arse, legs over the quay. I'll take you under the arms from behind and let you down.'

Tannhauser dropped the swords. He wrestled Grymonde's

immense weight to the flags and manoeuvred his legs into the boat, just astern of the for'ard row bench. He put Grymonde's right hand to the gunwale and held the boat steady with both his own.

'Your left leg is hard to the bench. Put your left hand on the bench and sit.'

Grymonde bent and took his weight on his hands and groaned and hoisted and twisted and landed square. The skiff swayed. Estelle clapped. The Mice joined in. Tannhauser ran the oars through the locks and across Grymonde's lap.

Grymonde doubled over in a spasm. He couldn't contain an awful groan.

'My Infant, if you're going to die, die backwards.'

'One dark day, my friend, you will hear grim laughter behind you, and you will turn. And you will see nothing. But be assured, it will be me.'

Tannhauser collected the five swords and chose the best of a poor lot, and stowed it by the tiller of the barge. Hervé had built a three-step redoubt which, at its top, was two sacks deep and nearly a yard taller than the gunwale. It would protect the pilot from all but a cannonball. He gestured with the rolled tarpaulin he carried under one arm.

'With your permission, sire, I thought I'd drape this over the fire. Light up the whole town, sire, when this goes up.'

Tannhauser decided to keep the tarred canvas in reserve until he reached the boom, where just such an effect would give the most advantage.

'No, leave it there. Fetch that table. Stack that on top instead.'

Tannhauser walked across the sacks to examine the fire.

Hugon and Pascale had latticed the pit with inflammables, end to end.

'Magnificent. Hugon, get in the skiff. Pascale –'

'The violl! I left the violl!' Hugon ran towards Irène's.

'Pascale, do you see that torch flame yonder?'

Tannhauser pointed up the quay to where he had dropped it.

'Yes, but I have another in Irène's fireplace, and your rifle's there.'

He nodded. He laid the swords in a gridiron across the sacks, above the kindling. He laid the oars lengthwise across the swords. He pulled three fresh sacks of char and piled them side by side on top of the grid. The lantern had cooled. He pulled the stopper and sprinkled whale oil over the sacks. On top of the sacks he coiled the heavy, tarred rope. Hervé gave him a hand to slot the legs of the table over the whole ensemble.

Tannhauser stepped back and nodded.

'If that lot doesn't get it burning, it isn't charcoal.'

'My word, sire, I believe that's Captain Garnier. Over on the square.'

Tannhauser vaulted to the quay and dashed to his bow and quiver as he looked across the river to the Place de Grève. The black beams of the gallows rose above a horseman who sat his saddle and watched him. A big man. Breastplate. Helm. Sixty yards. He had made plenty of better shots but the chances of killing an armoured man with a broadhead were slim. He was loath to waste an arrow. Get him on the turn? He recalled Garnier leaving Le Tellier's. Fluted back plates. A full cuirass.

He slung the quiver and walked to the edge of the quay behind Carla. Garnier reined his horse into a half-turn. Tannhauser waved Altan's bow above his head and Garnier paused. Tannhauser pulled an arrow and waggled it from his crotch. Laughter drifted from the militia on the Place de Grève. Garnier shook his fist and rode away through his men.

The Pilgrims would be waiting at the boom. Tannhauser wondered where Dominic was. He restored the arrow and slung Altan's bow across his chest. He unhitched his sheathed sword from his belt. Pascale ran over from the house. In one hand she carried his rifle and in the other a torch. Over one shoulder she had a bow and quiver.

'I took it from one of the *sergents*. Can I bring it home?'

Bodkins. He took the weapons and hung them over his shoulder.

'Where's Hugon?' he asked.

'Hugon's gone.'

'Gone?'

'The violl has gone, too.'

'Hugon won't be back.' Grymonde swung his head back and forth, trying to find Carla. 'I saw it right off, in the birthing room. Can't blame a thief for thieving. I'm surprised he waited this long. But then, Hugon was always a queer lad.'

'If he had asked for the violl,' said Carla, 'I would have given it to him.'

'He knows you love it. He heard you play.'

Tannhauser took the torch from Pascale and gave her his sword.

'Won't you need this?' she said.

'I need to be nimble.' He took her hand. 'Get in the skiff. You're second oar, if needed. Do as Carla tells you.'

She nodded. Her black eyes gleamed.

He squeezed. 'You're the only able body in the boat.'

'I'll look after them.'

'I know you will. I saw the bodies in the market.'

She beamed. He helped her aboard. He heard Estelle, somewhat wounded.

'I'm an able body, too. Aren't I, Carla?'

He untied and coiled the dock line and threw it behind Grymonde.

'Are we done, then, good sire?' Hervé hovered on the quay.

'Hervé, you are done. Know that you owe your life to Grégoire.'

'Then I'm very grateful to him, sire.'

'Stay away from the militias. Go home to your wife.'

'Wife, sire?'

Grégoire cried out.

Carla's voice, sharp. 'Agnès, Marie, sit back down at once.'

Tannhauser turned to a sudden turmoil in the skiff. The Mice stood holding hands and were leaning back so far against the river-ward gunwale they would have fallen in had they been much taller. They both stared at Hervé with closed expressions.

Tannhauser was sickened.

The Mice looked at him and he saw that they were afraid. Of him. The colour of their fear appalled him. They didn't fear pain or death; they feared betrayal. He supposed they hadn't known much else. He loved the Mice. They endured. If they didn't survive, none of them would. He looked at Hervé. The man was oblivious to his own depravity.

'Tannzer?' Estelle had reclaimed Amparo and was cradling her inside her frock. 'Do you know what I think?'

Hervé smiled at the Mice and waved. He opened his mouth to speak.

Tannhauser chopped him in the throat with the edge of his hand and kicked his legs from under him. The back of Hervé's skull cracked on the quay. Tannhauser looked at the Mice. Their faces were closed again, but the fear at least was gone. They sat down.

'You'll be safe with Carla,' he said. 'You will always be safe with Carla.'

Tannhauser looked at Grégoire.

'Grégoire, will you release me from my promise?'

The lad's agony was extreme; but he understood what had just passed.

He glanced at Hervé. He nodded.

Tannhauser pushed the skiff out into the river.

'Obey Carla. All you have to do is sail through the breach in the boom.'

He dragged Hervé by the scruff of his jerkin to the front of the barge, and laid down the torch and the *spontone*. He squatted and picked him up in both arms and stood and dropped him arse down into the space between the bow and the sacks, his feet in the air to either side of the stem. He unhitched the dock line and used it to bind Hervé's ankles to the prow. Hervé coughed and blinked. His head and shoulders were a yard forward of the fire pit above him.

Tannhauser pushed the bow out from the quay. He loaded his weapons and untied the stern and boarded. He checked the rudder, whose crest was decorated with a large-breasted and much-fondled mermaid carved in wood. The sternpost was sheathed in iron. He bent for the pole and his back stabbed him as he straightened. He propped the pole on the redoubt. He looked over the sacks of char at Carla, who held the rudder hard to port to stay the skiff. Grymonde called out from the oars.

'La Rossa! Do we still have my satchel?'

'Yes, it's here.'

'Open it, look inside.'

Tannhauser climbed on the sacks and walked forward with the torch. Down in the bilges beyond the fire pit, Hervé craned his head backwards.

'Begging your pardon, sire, but if I stay here I'll be roasted like a chestnut.'

'Try to stay alive until your comrades catch the spectacle.'

Tannhauser shoved the torch into the kindling and blew on it. Smoke spiralled upward. He stepped back and away. Flames erupted from either end of the pit. The oil on the sacks beneath the table caught and bright yellow rags fluttered skyward. Hervé lunged with his arms, his fingers straining towards the knots cutting into his ankles. The movement wedged him more deeply in his fiery tomb. He screamed for mercy above the pop and crackle of the faggots. Tannhauser walked back to the stern.

A thousand yards to the boom. Tannhauser reckoned the current at no more than three knots; with pole and rudder, under ten minutes. He rolled his neck. He butted the pole to the quay and pushed. The barge slid out into the current and passed the skiff.

Grymonde's eyeholes bored into him across the water. They were tunnels of absolute darkness. His smile was horrible. He waved a roll of brown paper.

'You may hear that laughter underwater, my friend. We have the caul.'

CHAPTER FORTY

Ghosts of the Unrepentant Damned

C arla steered towards the fire that floated down the black and
silver river ahead, towards the wild and bloodstained ferryman
whose figure quavered and warped against the flames he had kindled
from wood and human bone. He passed beneath the Pont Notre-
Dame and the flames filled the stone archway entire, and Carla
could see nothing beyond them, as if fire were all that lay before
him and all that he could promise those who followed in his wake.
In Malta, he had followed her into the fire, on the promise of a
piece of music. He had done the same here, in Paris.

Carla realised she was the fire. She was his fire.

Her love for him caught in her throat. She swallowed.

'Grymonde, blades in, let her run.'

Grymonde had claimed the role of sole rower and she hadn't
argued with him. His strokes were few but with each the water
plumed from either side of the bow. He pulled his oars across his
lap and bent over them and growled words she couldn't hear.

The boat freighted so much pain it was a wonder it didn't founder.
The two boys lay in the bilges side by side, as if through proximity
they might assuage each other's hurts. Pascale had lost her sister and
her father, and bore other unseen wounds that she didn't yet know
she had sustained. Carla knew little of the lives of Agnès and Marie,
but little was enough. Estelle sat at her feet with Amparo in her
shirt. Both seemed happy in the spell each cast upon the other, yet
Estelle, too, had witnessed and taken part in abominable cruelties.
And Amparo, her baby? She had done more than any to bring them
together, to bind them together. What had she felt and seen?

Carla's love for her baby caught in her throat.

Her love for all of the children.

The skiff handled well as she took it under the arch. Despite the run-off, the current was steady. Mattias and his flames sailed under the Pont au Change.

'Grymonde, three strokes, then blades in.'

As they ran the next bridge Carla saw a woman's body caught up in the pilings. She was naked, gashed, her mouth agape in an expression of unreckonable disillusion.

The paddle wheels of the watermills churned three boat lengths beyond, closer than she had expected. Mattias steered the barge between the two most southerly wheels. She followed and rode the spume and the river opened out before them. The shimmer of moonlight that divided it ran clear to the boom. Most of the barrier's length was hidden by the islands. From the Right Bank torches and lanterns crept out along the low black line of chained boats.

'Grymonde, pull.'

Carla steered to draw parallel with the barge. Mattias held the tiller between his knees and poled without hurry. He glanced over his shoulder and waved. The prow seemed a waterborne volcano, the flames roaring upwards from the banked rim of glowing char. She glimpsed a writhing figure on its farmost slope, blackened and hairless, his flailing arms smoking from the scorched tatters of his sleeves. The cruelty repelled her; Mattias's cruelty; but she had raised no objection when she might have and the cruelty was hers, too.

Carla turned away.

The beach of the City, below the Conciergerie, was strewn with the corpses of the massacred. Their murderers stood among them, legs caked to the knees in bloody mortar, and they bawled curses and brandished their knives like the ghosts of the unrepentant damned. By the clock tower above it was a half past midnight. In the shadow of the prison she saw a turmoil of Huguenots, a score or more, encircled about their collective waist by a rope held by a militiaman. As the skiff passed by, the desperate throng buckled and reeled and arms and cries reached out towards her.

Carla turned away.

'Carla, look.'

Pascale pointed at the shore. A young woman ducked the rope

and broke free and ran down the beach. She beckoned them with one arm and pointed to the water's edge further downstream. In her other arm she held a tiny child. There was a shout and two of the ghosts sprang after her. Carla pushed the tiller to starboard and the skiff swung landward.

'Grymonde, give me your best.'

Grymonde heaved and howled and the skiff leapt forward. Three more ghosts joined the pursuit, as if the murder of an unknown woman and her child were the greatest prize on earth. Waterlogged bodies congested the shallows. Carla had made an error. She carried that prize in the skiff and had put it at hazard. She had seconds to correct her course. Her hand clenched the tiller to steer away and her womb clenched harder in reply.

If you don't try, you will be damned, too.

Carla held steady.

'Grymonde, larboard blade in.'

The bow ploughed through the floating dead and slowed.

The woman splashed into the shallows. The ghost on her tail lunged with a sword and stabbed her in the back. She staggered and twisted and struck the blade away and the ghost stumbled and went down on one knee. Love and desperation gave her the strength to wade on, her mouth gaping for air. She saw Carla. She held out her baby at arm's length. Carla aimed the bow to skim past the dying woman.

'Pascale, take the child.'

Carla felt the scrape of sand on the hull. Pascale straddled her bench and leaned out and called to the woman. The woman faltered, thigh-deep, and pulled the baby back into her breast for balance. The ghost gained on her and raised his sword. An arrow hissed into his chest and he spun and fell.

The skiff was close enough now for Carla to see the woman's face. She saw her try to extend her child, saw something burst inside her. She saw her eyelids fall shut. She saw the wash from the skiff lap into her chest. She saw the woman fall backwards into the river, a foot short of Pascale's hands, her baby still cradled in her arms.

Pascale plunged over the gunwale, her legs wrapped under the bench, and her head and shoulders vanished under the surface. She stayed under so long, Carla almost reached out to pull her in. Pascale reared back up, her empty fists clenched above her head, and she screamed through the water running down her face, all her grief and all her rage unleashed, the sound of her soul being torn from its moorings in whatever she had ever known or believed about Life Her-own-self.

Carla couldn't afford to heed it.

A second arrow hissed to her right. A thud and a curse and a splash.

The ghosts were wading out behind her.

'Grymonde, pull.'

Carla turned the skiff for the fire barge.

Pascale glanced past her and bared her teeth and leapt from her bench, treading on Juste and Grégoire. The tiller jerked in Carla's hand. A ghost had seized the rudder.

Carla twisted, her belly cramping, half-rising to her feet and pushing with all the strength in her thighs to right it. The rudder shifted, then heaved back hard against her. Pascale landed on the seat to the other side of the tiller on her knees, and her arm came over and down with a flash of steel. Carla heard screams – Pascale's, the ghost's – and she glimpsed a pierced and spurting neck and face, the blade plunging down into the hole of the opened mouth. The tiller sprang free. She saw Mattias raise his bow and shoot. She heard another body hit the water in her wake. He raised up and drew again, then relaxed and lowered without loosing. Carla took it that they were clear.

She looked astern. There was no sign of the woman or her babe. The remaining ghosts vented their indignation on the roped and clamouring innocents. Spear and sword, boots and knives. Then the night enshrouded the just and the damned in the same impenetrable darkness, and Carla turned away.

Pascale wiped her dagger on her skirt and sheathed it. Blood was splashed across her cheeks, her lips, her throat. She didn't look at Carla. She returned to her bench and put her face in her hands and wept. Juste and Grégoire cried with her. Estelle looked up at

Carla, her lip trembling, too. They had put on a sterner front for Mattias, but that was no surprise. She felt obscurely accused and though none deserved it anger flared in her chest, as if the core of some hidden force had opened inside her.

'Pascale, that woman died in hope. She died on her feet. She died fighting for her child. She didn't live, but she won.'

Pascale kept her hands over her face. She stopped weeping.

Carla heard Alice's voice.

They're all your sons and daughters, now, love.

You are the mother.

You were always the mother.

Carla had never known the feeling before. She had never felt entitled to be Orlandu's mother, though he had grown inside her, just as Amparo had. She hadn't earned the role; she had betrayed it. Now it was there, the knowing. Alice had healed the wound that could not be healed. She was a mother. They were all her sons and daughters. The weight of the notion was fantastic; yet in its weight she felt its power and beauty.

'Pascale.'

Pascale dropped her hands and looked at her. Carla took a breath. She had become so accustomed to the girl's courage that the naked despair in her face appalled her. Pascale was hardly more than a child. Her failure to save the unknown child must have evoked other failures more awful still.

'Pascale, you are a braver girl than ever I was.'

Pascale didn't speak.

'So be more than brave. If we sailed the five rivers of Hades end to end we'd not find such desperation as crowds the shores of this one. Yet in the middle of all this – all this – you gave that woman hope – you – and she took it into her soul with her dying breath. Tonight there is no more precious a gift. Not even life.'

'Tonight life is worth nothing.'

'Listen to Carla, girl.'

Grymonde feathered and leaned and dipped and pulled. His agony must have been immense. The holes in his face were incandescent with moonbeams and a strange peace.

'Don't abandon your hope or you'll leave the lot of us short, and we'll not find any more on these dark waters. As to life, it's naught but a burst of flame, so let's burn bright.'

Pascale wiped her face and turned towards him. 'You mean like Hervé?'

Grymonde's laughter doubled him over the oars. Agnès and Marie giggled.

'I adore a woman with a sharp tongue.'

'I want to row,' said Pascale.

Grymonde drew his oars across his lap and Pascale looked at Carla and she nodded. Pascale slotted her oars into the rowlocks. Her arms were thin but all sinew. Her strokes were shorter and weaker than Grymonde's but they were faster. They gained on the barge.

The sand on the shore of the Right Bank was blackened with gore and carnage but there Carla saw no ghosts. Many boats had been beached there but none had dared put out to take on the fire barge. She saw laggards climbing the stairs to the wharves, and on the wharves milling bands of militia. A horseman. Shouts. Surges of movement.

All were being marshalled towards the boom.

The boom was no more than a furlong away. The closer they got, the more formidable it appeared. Lighters made up the greater part of its length. Their flat bottoms lent less resistance to the current and provided better footing. At least one spearman stood in every boat, in some, groups of three or four. Closer still. She saw that the men in groups weren't holding spears, but long poles. They intended to hold the fire barge at bay.

Mattias pushed onward. The firelight glimmered from his sweat. He drew the pole from the water and stowed it. He turned to Carla and pointed to the approaching break between the Île de la Cité and the tiny island off its tip. She nodded. Mattias put his fingertips to his lips and flung his arm out towards her. Carla was too moved to return the kiss. She swore she saw him grin. He turned back to the tiller and swung the burning prow towards the centre of the boom.

Carla steered for the break. The western end of the City was surrounded by a defensive wall. A watchtower overlooked the fork in the river and she saw a helmet move on top. The tiny island was low and flat, and too regularly flooded to be inhabited. Beyond it was a second, somewhat broader, with a short channel in between the two.

'Pascale, let her run.'

Pascale raised the oars.

'Carla, look,' said Estelle.

The girl was pointing at the fire barge, now dead ahead of them and set on an oblique course to plough into the boom, right of centre. Mattias loosed an arrow and Carla watched one of the pole men fly backwards from the left half of the boom. The men either side of him dived for the deck. Carla turned away and piloted the skiff into the break.

'No, look again, in the water.'

Estelle cupped her hands to her mouth.

'Tannzer!'

Carla ignored her and turned the skiff again, from the break into the channel. She pulled the tiller over and the skiff bobbed short of the channel mouth where the two arms of the Seine rejoined each other. The boom spread before them, a hundred yards distant and as many broad. It ran from the Tour de Nelle on the Left Bank to the Tour au Coin on the Right.

The volcano slid into view beyond the island.

The fire barge had abruptly changed course.

Carla saw Mattias.

He was bent double over the stern, reaching down to the rudder. It must have fouled. The burning prow was sheering to larboard. Unless he threw the rudder hard over, the fire would block the left side of the barrier, the reverse of his intention. He would have to break the boom while open to attack from the forces Garnier was massing on the Right Bank. At the speed the current was carrying him, Carla reckoned he had a minute before he hit the boom, and half that time to make the correction.

Plumes of powder smoke and gunfire exploded from the wharf.

Carla shut her eyes.

She opened them.

Wood splinters blown from the stern of the barge by the volley fluttered down in the wake. She couldn't see Mattias. The barge appeared unmanned and uncontrolled.

Juste had risen to his knees. Grégoire grabbed his good arm with both hands and hauled himself up to hook his elbows over the starboard gunwale.

Estelle took Carla's hand.

The children watched, all of them, in silence.

Carla couldn't. She looked at Amparo, tucked under Estelle's chin.

Amparo's eyes roved this way and that, and then settled on her face. Amparo was unperturbed. She was right. Carla ignored the crushing tightness in her chest. They could make it back to the cathedral. They would survive. And in time she would see both Bernard Garnier and Dominic Le Tellier die on their knees as they begged for her mercy. She swore it. She reached down and touched Amparo's lips.

'I swear it on your life.'

She had never imagined an oath so terrible.

Nor that her tongue might ever speak such words.

But she had spoken them.

She felt hands on her shoulders, yet there was nothing behind her but water.

Old hands, gentle, but strong.

The tightness vanished.

Carla nodded. 'Thank you, Alice.'

'We have a blind man aboard. Will someone tell him what's happening?'

'Pascale,' said Carla, her eyes still on her babe. 'Is Mattias alive?'

'Alive and printing in red.'

Carla looked up across the water.

The barge was floating broadside into the boom, its stern to the Right Bank and close enough to the shallows to permit assault, from either side, by men wading from the beach. Mattias loosed arrows at the wharf, the sinews of his back flexing and relaxing in the violent beauty of his art. Carla threw herself inside his mind.

Mattias will take the musket men first, while they reload.

He will drive the rabble from the boom, for they fear death and he does not.

He will attempt to breach the boom in the respite.

Then Garnier will come, and that unblooded bastard has not the guts to come alone.

If the boom isn't broken by then, even Mattias might be overwhelmed.

Pascale said, 'Carla, tell me what to do. Or I'm going to start rowing.'

The girl was game to the backbone, her oars already poised above the water.

The other children turned to look at Carla. They were all of them game.

Carla looked down again at Amparo.

'Your father won't approve.'

Amparo cooed.

Carla looked at Pascale and Pascale bared her teeth.

'Pascale. Take us to the boom.'

CHAPTER FORTY-ONE

The Devil's Causeway

Fortuna, so it was said, wore a blindfold, but Tannhauser didn't believe it. When the fancy took her she moved her pieces with far too exuberant an esprit. He saluted her for it, though he doubted she cared.

He had the barge running a few degrees to port. At fifty yards he'd alter course to strike the boom at forty-five degrees, where the two rightmost quarters of its shallow arc met. If the boom broke there and then, all the better. If it didn't, the stern would sheer larboard under the force of the current, towards the centre of the boom, and the barge would come to rest alongside. Once moored, the prow fire would render him invisible to the wharves on the Right Bank, as too, from this approach, did the redoubt, which left him free to harry the pole men on the boats ahead.

The char had ignited before the first bridge and by the shade of red at the rim was hot enough to smelt iron deeper down. Hot enough, too, to set light to other sacks well beyond the reach of the flames. The brightness denied him sight of the central third of the boom, but across the starboard gunwale he chose the vessel he intended to board and shot its sole occupant in the chest. He looked across the larboard side and saw a cluster of four on a lighter. He winged an arrow into the middle of them. By the time he'd dropped a third there was no one left to shoot at. Some had fled for the Left Bank across the pontoons; most were lying low and likely to stay there.

He had used the *sergent*'s bow Pascale had found at Irène's, and he left the tiller for at most five seconds, to lay the weapon on the step of the redoubt and return two arrows to the quiver. He felt the larboard sheer at once and turned.

The tiller had swung hard over behind him. He grabbed it and shoved. The rudder moved as if through mud and then stuck. He heard a thin yell. He saw a small white hand snatch the mermaid's tail. The hand held on.

Tannhauser let go of the tiller and it swung over as he lunged head and shoulders across the stern. A boy clung onto the starboard side of the rudder. He coughed up gouts of river water, fighting too hard for life to be merely panicked. The barge must have overtaken him and the lad had seized his chance. He was naked as far as Tannhauser could see, and kicking his legs with what strength he had left to push himself from the water. The only result was to swing the rudder even harder over and increase the sheer.

Tannhauser knelt on the thwart and reached down to haul him aboard.

In Tannhauser's experience, when facing a smoothbore musket ball at much over thirty yards the safest man to be was the target. The use of muskets – the infliction of fear aside – was in massed volley fire against a massed foe. Dominic's men had placed themselves well and shown patience. Their six muskets were massed in volley and the barge was massy enough. The sudden sheer had denied the stern the protection of the redoubt.

Tannhauser grabbed the boy by his left arm and right armpit. As he hauled him up and over he saw the sparks from a row of flashing pans and clasped the boy tight and dived sideways for the deck. He felt the ball poke him hard in the stomach and landed heavily, his wind robbed by either or both. He rolled onto his back. He felt blood spill down his flanks; but he knew it wasn't his. The boy was a dead weight. Tannhauser lifted the boy from his chest and raised his head and looked down across his gore-clogged body hair. The musket ball sat in the quag of blood on his belly. He set the boy aside and rose to one knee and the ball dropped and skittered away.

The tiller.

His eye stopped him in mid-turn before his mind knew what it had seen.

He knelt back down.

On his neck, below the angle of his jaw, the boy had a strawberry birthmark.

Tannhauser saw a mother's hand quicken to cover the mark, as if she feared he would read it as a sign of evil. This boy had given him a smile at the gates of Paris. And the gladdest sight it had been in many a day. He picked the boy up by the shoulders. The boy's head flopped and twisted, its weight an obscure obscenity to Tannhauser's sinews.

'You were gone. Why did you come back?'

Tannhauser didn't know why he felt so pierced. There were more dead boys in the river than fish. He had dragged the like from Grymonde's path without giving them so much as an Amen.

'I don't know you, boy. How did you know me?'

The cesspit of disgust, whose earliest contents were the stuff of his earliest memories, and which he rarely dared admit he carried inside him, overflowed into his throat. He knew the boy. He envied the boy. For the boy it was over and done.

He lowered the boy down. He let go of his shoulders.

He stood up and pulled the tiller.

It didn't move.

He shook it back and forth. It was stuck, solid. He bent over the stern and ran his fingers down between the sternpost and the rudder. A musket ball the bore of his thumb was wedged between the eye of the upmost gudgeon and the wood of the rudder, its upper rim shaved square by the arm of the pintle. The ball was still warm. He tried to pluck it free and broke a fingernail. The hot lead had squeezed into the gap and welded itself to the iron. The rudder was jammed to larboard. He grabbed the back of the rudder with both hands and heaved and shoved. Timber crunched; and resisted. He fingered the lead again. It was further deformed, but just as surely fixed. To whittle it out with a dagger would take more minutes than the current would give him.

The Right Bank wheeled across his vision. A mass of moored boats on the beach. The church of Saint-Germain-l'Auxerrois. The square where he had scolded Juste. The conical towers of the Louvre. He was set to drift broadside into the boom with the fire in the prow pointing in the wrong direction, towards the Left Bank, not the Right. He would have to break the boom within a half of its length from its anchorage by the palace, and without anything to deter an attack from the wharf. Anything except himself.

He gave Fortuna her due and abandoned the rudder.

He took a fistful of arrows from the quiver on the sacks. He glanced at the boom as he took up the *sergent*'s bow and nocked. The stern would run into the boom some four boats short of the beach; with luck, five. They were all lighters, twenty-five-footers or thereabouts, a foot or two of chain stretched between them. He marked the wharf jutting out into the water, the six musket men ranked along its edge. The same wharf from which other men had fired at other fugitives not twenty hours before. They were all ramming their scouring sticks with a fury.

Tannhauser drew and shot the rightmost musket man.

He nocked and drew and shot the leftmost.

Gut shots both, to the feathers.

When the second fell, the two in the middle realised that they'd never charge another pan. As they fled he shot one in the back. He nocked as the other vanished. A fifth added speed to his escape by dropping his gun. Tannhauser shot him, and nocked, and laid the pride of the last as he turned to follow. The bodkin skewered his thighs, one to the other, and, with a wail that must have tickled the fallen angels awaiting his soul, he tripped and splashed to his grave.

Tannhauser nocked. Between this wharf and the next a row of wide steps led down to the beach. At the top he saw torches and bands of militia, a gaudy flag aloft, red and white ribbons on their arms. A pilgrimage of woe, if he had any say in it. He flew an arrow into their midst to let them know he did. Their consternation was immediate and general.

The stern continued its implacable arc to starboard.

The second wharf was stage to a horde of gaping Pilgrims, the charred plasterer exciting their particular curiosity. Tannhauser shot one in the face to give them something else to talk about. Six shafts left in the quiver; he shouldered it; a dozen for Altan's bow. Not as many as he would have liked. He glanced over the redoubt.

The boom appeared deserted. Hundreds of corpses bobbed against the hulls. As if the barrier had been made for that purpose the massacred collected towards the centre in a morbid scum, black and undulant on the swell, as if still possessing motive and eager to be on their way. The landward flatboat was moored to the outer face of a timber jetty. The current seemed to have doubled its speed. The barge was thirty seconds from the collision.

Tannhauser bent for the *spontone* and saw the rolled tarpaulin and grabbed that instead. He took the barge pole and tossed it lengthwise on the sacks and climbed up onto the char and took three steps for'ard before the furnace stopped him. He unfurled the tarred canvas to fall across the top third of the pole and the rim of the red shimmer that extended from the blaze. He turned and waded back as the canvas erupted.

He jumped from the sacks and hoisted the pole aloft.

The burning tarpaulin howled above his head and a shower of molten tar droplets sprinkled him. For an instant his arms and chest lit up with dozens of tiny flames. They died on the caked gore before he felt their sting. He pitched the flaming canvas over the stern and into the third flatboat of the boom as he passed it by. He grabbed the *spontone* and the sword and shouldered the *sergent's* bow. A tremor ran through the timbers from the prow and he relaxed for the fall.

The barge collided broadside and threw him into the sacks of the redoubt.

Couplings moaned and timbers creaked. The prow ploughed forward a few yards more and wedged itself to a halt. The whole boom swayed. The chains held.

Tannhauser mounted the stern gunwale. The gunwale of the fourth lighter rode almost a foot higher. He stepped up and gave himself a shove with the *spontone* and jumped and landed halfway down the flatboat's length. A man squatted by a lantern four feet away, his back to the hull, his hands over his face. He dropped the hands and Tannhauser glimpsed his terror in the yellow light as he lanced him in the neck.

He was on the boom.

Beyond, the river rolled unhindered towards the sea.

Tannhauser scooped up the lantern and strode through the blood in the bilges to the stern. He was some seventy feet from the jetty, three boat lengths. In the next lighter two burning figures clambered over the side and plunged for the water. The flames of the tarpaulin were already shrinking from their height. A third figure rose to his feet in their midst, his face a confection of bubbles, the incinerating canvas draped around his shoulders like the vestments of some suicidal priesthood. He waved his arms and fire leapt into his mouth as he sucked for air. He toppled backwards to complete his role as burnt offerings.

Tannhauser studied the coupling between the two craft. A length of half-inch chain was looped around the larboard stern cleat, the horns wedged through two links. The arms of the chain then twisted into a single strand, two feet long, before they parted again to hook the horns of the bow cleat on the next boat. Behind that cleat, the links were secured by a padlock. Both cleats were cast from iron and secured by bolts fore and aft of the central pillar of the horns.

Tannhauser laid up the *sergent*'s bow and the sword. He hung the lantern and set himself and drove the chiselled spike of the *spontone*'s counterweight into the wood, two inches short of the forward bolt. He levered upwards and a wedge splintered away. Two minutes; if it took him three he'd deserve to drown. Smoke and sparks drifted back from the inferno in the charcoal barge. He chiselled and pried; short, fast strokes; thin wedges that came up easily with the grain. He excavated the shaft of the bolt until the spike broke through the bottom of the timber. He levered up the front edge of the cleat plate; the forward bolt was free. He shoved the spike deeper and levered again, hoping sheer force would unseat the second bolt. He felt some cracks give in the wood but the shaft of the *spontone* bowed too severely and he relaxed and pulled it out.

The second bolt was obscured by the twisted chain. He stepped up and across and into the bow of the third boat for a better angle. The fire around the smouldering acolyte had subsided to the last folds of the sheet. He chiselled under the aft edge of the cleat and pried up a good splinter and ripped the fragments clear. He felt the footsteps on the strakes before he heard them.

He turned as the spearhead of a halberd lunged from the tar smoke. He trapped the shaft in the winged jaw of the *spontone* and twisted it aside. The halberd point crunched into the bow and he dropped the *spontone* and moved in, drawing his dagger. He stabbed the halberdier up beneath the left ribs, and again through the neck and vented his throat. Warm gore sprayed Tannhauser's chest as the corpse fell and he squinted through the haze.

At least four more men advanced along the second lighter; more loomed behind them in the first and on the quay. Others waded out into the shallows, either side of the boom, though by the bow of the landward boat they were thigh-deep.

Tannhauser flicked and sheathed the dagger and left his chisel where he'd need it and claimed the halberd. He stepped on the burned acolyte and the body bucked and twisted under his tread. He steadied himself against the hull with the halberd and stomped on the melted face, and his heel slithered as bones crackled and the face sheared away from the skull. He stomped him through the chest and the ribcage stove inwards into the lungs. The draught pumped from under the corpse blew a final flaring from the canvas, and flame spiralled up around Tannhauser's hips. He saw the next Pilgrim stop, one foot on the stern, his face slack at the spectacle that confronted him.

Tannhauser charged and speared him under the sternum and followed him over the gunwales as he pitched him backward into his mates, which latter crowded each other and clucked the usual self-defeating advice. He tugged the spear free as he landed and rotated from the hips and twirled the shaft and cut sidewise with the axe at the foremost Pilgrim. The blade cleaved the side of his skull to the nose through the socket of the eye and the eyeball popped. Tannhauser cranked his head apart like a half-split log. The Pilgrim following caught the brained man round the waist, as if afraid the fall might harm him. Tannhauser split his skull to the nostrils with an overhead swing.

He was vexed by these poor imbeciles. Their very lack of skill offended him. Their lives weren't worth the seconds of his time required to slaughter them.

A pike lunged up from the water and he swayed back and let it pass his chest and chopped down over the gunwale and axed the oaf who wielded it above the ear. The stroke wasn't clean but the heavy blade peeled the side of his head like a turnip and unhinged one side of his jaw in a cascade of blood and bad teeth.

These dogs weren't foes, they were victims.

He straddled the dead and bore down on the fourth Pilgrim as he backed away. A fifth jumped into the stern, and a greater fool than the rest he must have been for his spear was encumbered with a flag. The fourth attempted a parade-ground lunge with a half-pike, and Tannhauser swayed aside and shortened his grip and stepped in and clove him square through the web of the neck. The axe trimmed the top three ribs from their jointing to the breastbone and sundered the mediastinum. He wrenched the blade from the carcass in a catastrophic fountain. The fifth was clambering onto the stern, his flag draped around his head and shoulders by the frenzy of his retreat. Tannhauser swung the axe and severed his right foot through the instep.

The Pilgrim dropped his flagstaff and fell to the thwart on his knees, his arms reaching astern to the landward lighter. He screamed to his comrades to pull him clear.

Tannhauser shook sweat from his brow and rolled the ache from his shoulders and chest. He looked at the advancing comrades and they saw him and stopped amidships. Six of them. He employed the gunwale as a chopping block and severed the flag-bearer's right arm above the elbow. The six watched it fall in the river. Tannhauser changed his angle and severed the left arm. The Pilgrim screamed himself breathless and slid downwards. Tannhauser rammed one boot into the flag that shrouded his shoulders and trapped his chest against the transom. He looked at the six again.

'This is the Devil's causeway. Take a kinder road.'

The front man turned and pushed his way back past his fellows.

Some sound made Tannhauser glance backwards.

The skiff floated alongside the third lighter, lit by the ochre pandemonium floating on the water beyond. Grymonde held fast to the lighter's gunwale with one hand. Carla was looking up from the tiller. Pascale had boarded the boom. The girl had assumed Tannhauser's job and was levering the *spontone* to pry out the cleat. She was using the long blade, not the chisel, and, though he couldn't see it, the imagined bend in the steel made him cringe. He had seen the damage a snapped blade could inflict.

'Pascale! Stop!'

She turned and looked at him through the smoke.

He waved his hand in a circle, over and down.

'Use the other end! The spike! The blade may snap like a sword!'

He made the inverting gesture again, in greater earnest. It didn't matter. With the axe of the halberd he'd have the cleat out in a minute and the carnage he'd left along forty feet of deck would buy them more than that. He flapped his hand down.

'Just stop! Leave it for me!'

Pascale stepped back from the cleat and raised and planted the *spontone*.

A voice rose behind him, above the caterwauls of the amputated flag-bearer.

'Let us take poor Jean away, for the love of Christ.'

Tannhauser turned.

Beyond the six, the jetty, the wharves, the square, were mobbed with Pilgrims, spear points gleaming by torch and moon. A dozen or so spilled down the steps onto the beach. At the top of the steps, eighty feet away, a hulking figure appeared in a cuirass. Garnier looked at Tannhauser.

They all looked at Tannhauser, scores of them.

Tannhauser took his boot from poor Jean and indicated his gaudy shroud.

'Is that not the sacred banner of Saint-Jacques?'

'Aye, we'll not leave it to you nor the Devil.'

'That's what we fight and die for.'

Tannhauser levered his cock out with one hand.

'Die for this.'

He pissed on poor Jean and the banner of Saint-Jacques.

Such a silence fell upon his audience, near and far, he wondered if Garnier could hear the splash. Tannhauser shook his cock and put it away.

'Good as an hour's sleep.'

He stooped for the half-pike and the six retreated a step towards the jetty.

'Poor Jean stays here, with me and the Devil. So does the banner.'

Tannhauser raised the half-pike at arm's length and nailed Jean and the flag on his back to the transom. He looked at the six. None met his eyes. He looked at Garnier, who apart from putting his fists on his hips had not moved, and looked disinclined to do so. The other soldiers of Christ were content to follow his example. If they would swallow an insult like that, they were no more of a threat than the bodies in the river.

Tannhauser turned to start for the cleat and frowned. He saw Juste clamber past Pascale and charge down the smoking hull towards him. She shouted after him and Juste half-turned to shout back, then kept on coming. What was the boy up to?

Tannhauser called out. 'Juste, stay there. I'm coming.'

He strode forward, his hand raised to forestall him, but the lad came on, pale with the blood he had lost, pale with bravery and fear, as if possessed by the need to fling himself like a bag of sand against the malice drowning the world. As if that way lay redemption. He was beautiful; and the world was not.

In his hand he clutched Tannhauser's sword.

Tannhauser ran towards him.

'Juste stop. Go back. Back.'

Juste climbed the stern thwart, to cross onto the bow of the second lighter. His good arm waved the sword for balance as he teetered on the swell. On this side of the chain the rim of the bow gleamed with fresh gore. The boy's shoes were slathered in the same, and his front foot skidded in more as it landed. The arm of his pierced shoulder flapped in its improvised sling. Uninjured, he might have regained his poise, but the pain twisted his body into an ungainly pirouette.

Juste fell into the river downstream of the boom and vanished.

Tannhauser reached the spot in two strides and dropped the halberd and bent double over the gunwale. Altan's bowstring cut into his neck. The hilt of his sword appeared above the waters and he lunged and grabbed it by the sheathed blade with his left hand and pulled. Juste's arm surfaced, his head and shoulders. He heaved for air. His hand slid six inches down the sheath as the current sucked him. With all the desperation of his own heart Tannhauser shouted in his face.

'Squeeze, boy. Hold tight.'

He felt a tremor run along the hull as the Pilgrims jumped in. Footfalls echoed as they charged. He grabbed the hilt and shouted again.

'I'm going to draw the sword. Hold tight to the sheath, like a rope.'

The soft leather, if anything, would give them both an easier grip. He drew and Juste held on and Tannhauser glanced back across his shoulder, his weapon concealed, his perceptions racing faster than his thoughts.

The first Pilgrim wielded a sword above his head as he stumbled over the bodies. Behind him, a pikeman, the spear point extended two feet ahead of the man in front and to the latter's right. A good formation; compared to his own, a masterpiece. To ward the pike sideways with strength alone, if it could be done, would knock the shaft against the body of the front man, and alter its aim but little.

He slashed backhand, over the spear point that lunged for his ribs; in the same instant he snapped his leg up, a fraction behind his arm, and kicked the pike shaft upwards with the side of his foot. The pike passed an inch above his head. His sword carved the front man upwards through the armpit and shattered the collarbone from below. With the muscles of his chest and back severed from his arm, the man reeled sideways, his sword falling to the hull from his nerveless hand. The stroke left Tannhauser canted sideways with both arms wide as the pikeman fell on him. The weight smashed him against the gunwale and the brute changed grip and rammed the pike shaft broadside at Tannhauser's throat.

Tannhauser ducked his head beneath the shaft and caught a

blow across the top of the skull. He tugged on the sheath to affirm Juste's weight and shoved his head up between the pikeman's arms and sank his teeth into his lower lip. He closed his eyes as the pikeman screamed and phlegm sprayed his cheek. He tasted blood and beard and foul breath. He pulled his sword in hard, underhand, and felt the edge bite a thigh and sawed in fast, short strokes. The muscles parted and he canted the angle and carved down and felt a thick fillet peel away from the bone. The screaming in his face became frenzied. He felt the shaft wedged across his shoulder blades fall and hands grabbed for his throat, and he bit harder and shook his head and the hands pulled away and so did the face as the lip tore away. He pulled the sword from the spurting flap of thigh and as the pikeman squirmed away along the gunwale, Tannhauser spat out the lip and stabbed him deep through the gut above the hip bone. All this in seconds and small pieces of seconds, Juste's weight still tugging on his left hand, then the third man was on him, sword raised.

As Tannhauser chose his stroke, the *spontone* embossed the swordsman through the belly to its wings and Pascale screamed at him to die as she sprang across the gap in the boom. She pulled as he fell and stood over him and lanced him again, twice, her shoulders heaving. She looked at Tannhauser. He saw no further foes in the boats. He met Pascale's eyes and gave her his blessing and nodded at the swordsman he had crippled. The swordsman saw the gesture and tried to stagger away. Pascale lanced him through the back below the right ribs and he bawled and fell and whimpered in the pooled gore and Pascale stabbed him again in the neck.

Tannhauser propped his sword and leaned over the gunwale.

Juste was all but spent, and with more than merely blood loss and exhaustion. His face was indistinct in the dark. He seemed to be staring at the Louvre, where his journey into the degeneracy of mankind had begun. His hand was two feet beyond Tannhauser's reach, his body bobbing at the length of his arm, as fragile a thread as any a life might hang from.

'Juste.'

Juste looked up at him. He spat water. His eyes were clear.

'I can see the cage,' he said. 'The place of dead monkeys.'

'I'm going to pull you closer and grab your wrist. Just hold on. I'll do the rest.'

'My brothers are over there, too. I saw them, with the pigs and the dogs.'

'Squeeze tight. Nice and steady, now.'

Tannhauser started to pull the sheath in, hand over hand. He didn't dare rush for fear of plucking the leather from the boy's grip.

Juste said, 'I feel like going home.'

'We'll get you home, lad. Don't worry.'

'I'm not worried. I'm tired.'

Juste drew his knees up close to the hull. He smiled a strange smile.

'I've seen Flore,' he said. 'She's waiting for me.'

Tannhauser lunged at full stretch.

Juste let go of the sheath and shoved his feet into the hull.

Tannhauser missed the hand as Juste snatched it away.

'Tell Grégoire I will miss him.'

Pascale let out a cry of absolute sorrow.

Tannhauser clenched his jaws.

Juste floated away downstream on his back, still facing them.

Pascale dropped the *spontone* and sat on the gunwale and swung her legs over the side. Tannhauser threw an arm around her waist and pulled her to his chest.

She sobbed. She screamed at him through her tears.

'If you won't go after him, let me go.'

Tannhauser had learned to swim since the time he had almost drowned in Malta, but he wasn't swimmer enough, in the gear that he was wearing, to save Juste. It wasn't a risk he had the expertise to take. Nor would he risk Pascale, whatever her skill.

'Juste's moment has come,' he said. 'He's taken it. Let him go home.'

Juste was still afloat, twenty feet distant and drifting at a yard a second.

'Why did he bring me my sword?' asked Tannhauser.

Pascale said, 'He said he'd heard you call for it.'

'I didn't.'

Pascale twisted her head to look at him.

'You said my spear might snap like the blade of a sword.'

Tannhauser nodded. So. He had killed all four brothers.

He might as well show some gratitude for Juste's valour.

He raised the sword high in salute.

Juste's arm rose in reply.

'Juste!' cried Pascale.

Juste slid beneath the Seine and was gone.

Tannhauser set the sword down and lifted Pascale in both arms.

'He loved us,' she said. 'He loved you.'

Her eyes were painted in infinite shades of pain.

Tannhauser let the pain penetrate him. Pascale blinked.

He leaned his face close to hers.

'You and I have crossed the bridge but not the boom. Be strong.'

Pascale turned away and looked at the water. She nodded.

Tannhauser carried her to the bow and leaned over the chain and set her down in the stern of the third lighter. He heard a groan. Grymonde had thrown a leg over the side and with an effort that should have been beyond him he hoisted himself up and fell in. He landed in the hull with a roar of pain and a billow of pitch smoke.

Tannhauser was glad to see him; they could do without a dying giant in the skiff. Grymonde had concluded the same. Tannhauser picked up the *spontone* and passed it to Pascale. He sheathed the sword and reattached it to his belt. He recovered the halberd and checked the jetty. The causeway was empty but for the dead. The Pilgrims voiced their outrage at a safe distance. Garnier stood paralysed by the burden of command.

Tannhauser suppressed the itch to shoot the windbag. To the others it might be a provocation too far, and he owed it to Carla to be gone. He climbed back into the third lighter. It wasn't ten minutes since he had left it. It seemed longer. By the length of a life no more to be lived. He put Juste from his mind.

He rolled Grymonde onto his belly amid charred flesh and canvas, and dragged him to his knees, and thence to his feet. The

Infant couldn't be bleeding fast enough to die, but his entrails were dissolving inside him. He clenched his jaws against a spasm.

'So you're not leaving Paris,' said Tannhauser.

The blinded holes glowered.

'I've never left Paris in my life. Why would I want to?'

Tannhauser took the *spontone* from Pascale. He put it in Grymonde's fist.

'Good. You can guard the Devil's causeway.'

Grymonde leaned on the shaft.

'May it please God they try to take it before I go.'

Tannhauser stepped past him and looked down into the skiff. It was held firm to the boom by a boathook anchored by Agnès and Marie. Grégoire lay unconscious. Estelle sat with Amparo in her shirt. Carla held the rudder hard to larboard. She knew Juste was gone. He could see that she felt responsible; but the claimants for that honour stretched all the way back to Krakow. He mustered a smile.

'We're on our way, love. Be ready for the boom to shift.'

He sized up the cleat again and set himself to swing the halberd. The chain had shifted an inch or two and the field was clearer. He sank the axe into the wood and felt the blade strike the bolt. He levered, slowly, and the splinter gave and the bolt shifted. He freed the axe and worked six inches of the spear point under the iron plate. He levered the shaft, slowly. Both bolts had been unseated. The whole cleat rose a quarter of an inch, held only by the great weight on the chain. He stopped and left the halberd jammed in place.

'Pascale, get in the skiff.'

As he helped Pascale mount the gunwale he saw Carla's face.

She was staring ashore. She was stricken.

Tannhauser followed her gaze.

A tall figure walked along the beach from the east, from behind the moored boats. There was purpose in his stride. He was headed for the wharf steps and Bernard Garnier.

'Mattias,' said Carla. 'That's Orlandu.'

Orlandu carried a bucket in his one good hand.

'Aye. It is.'

Tannhauser rolled his neck.

He pulled Pascale back down.

'Mattias,' said Carla. 'What's he doing?'

Tannhauser knew what Orlandu was doing. He might well have done the same himself. He might have left him to it, too, but the dread and confusion in Carla's voice spared him that decision. She turned to look at him. Her lips trembled.

In all the time he had known her, through every heartbreak and horror, he had never seen so much as the ghost of a chance that her spirit might be broken. Her spirit had only broken once, long before they had met, and she had tempered it anew, from metals unknown even to him. It was Orlandu who had broken her before, though he had not known it then, any more than he knew that he was about to do so now.

'Mattias?'

'Orlandu's buying time that we no longer need.'

It was only half the truth, but Tannhauser didn't reveal his other intuitions.

He added, 'But he's not to know that.'

Carla nodded. He reached down and she took his hand. It was cold and wet, and her touch choked him. He found another smile.

'You look after our daughter and I'll look after our son.'

Tannhauser showed Pascale the cleat and how to lever the halberd.

'Four or five cranks, a little at a time, and the river is open. Show Grymonde how to do it. If the militia come down the causeway, tell him to break the boom and get in the boat and go. I leave my wife and family in your hands, so do as I would, and do it cold. The decision to go is yours, not Carla's, do you understand?'

Pascale grabbed his arm.

'Don't. Stay here.'

'I can't let all the boys go down.' He grinned. 'I'd be the only one left.'

Pascale let go of his arm. She nodded.

Tannhauser put a hand on Grymonde's shoulder and squeezed.

'My Infant, I have business on shore, with a boy and a bucket.'

'You are a stubborn man.'

'It's a good day for being stubborn. Do as Pascale tells you.'

'I've become accustomed to taking orders from children and women,' said Grymonde. 'I recommend it.'

'If in doubt break the boom, for La Rossa and the nightingale.'

Tannhauser started down the causeway.

'So what's in this bucket?' called Grymonde.

Tannhauser didn't answer. No point upsetting Carla.

The last circle was waiting to be closed.

At the place of dead monkeys.

CHAPTER FORTY-TWO

The Place of Dead Monkeys

Tannhauser unslung Altan's bow and drew four arrows. The string was bloody but the Turks wove them with such conditions in mind. Pure silk spun straight from the cocoon, and stiffened with isinglass and resin. He nocked and stopped by the impaled and sodden corpse. The last flatboat was deserted, an open grave for any who dared try to cross it. Tannhauser looked at the Pilgrims on the jetty, thirty feet away. They sneered and scowled, and one displayed his arse, but their invitations to battle couldn't disguise their hope that he'd decline. Some were sincere in their truculence, but it was a rare man who had the nerve to be the one to start a war.

Taken as a whole, they just wanted him to leave.

A hundred feet east of the jetty, Garnier aped a general stunned by events passably well, but he lacked the experience that made a general a general, good or bad: that of sending an uncertain number of his men to their certain deaths, and watching them die for nothing.

Dominic might have done better. But if Tannhauser's intuitions were right, Dominic's severed head was in Orlandu's bucket.

He couldn't think of any other use for the bucket, unless Orlandu had decided to deliver milk to the troops. If there was a head in there, he could think of no other head it might be. Orlandu had gone from the bridge to the Hôtel Le Tellier. He had waited behind the door by the piled slain. When Dominic had returned in search of Petit Christian, he had found the chandelier embellished with his father's face.

It took iron in the gut to saw through a man's spine. Especially one-handed, with a knife. Every eye ashore was fixed on Tannhauser but they were watching the wrong man. Tannhauser looked up the beach.

Orlandu was passing through a scatter of Pilgrims. They paid him little mind. He was one of them, the disciple of Marcel Le Tellier, no less. He had tied red and white ribbons around his wounded arm. His face was in shadow but Tannhauser sensed the light in his eyes. He must have seen Tannhauser, and Grymonde, and the chidren and his mother in the skiff. He was too intelligent not to read the field, the situation too peculiar not to strike him for what it was. All combatants were inclined to go their ways without further bloodshed. Even Tannhauser, or he'd have been hard at them already.

Orlandu was the man who had the nerve.

He aimed to make amends for starting one war by starting yet another. A practice hallowed by a thousand kings.

He'd get Garnier to look at the head, then he'd stab him. A grand gesture on a grand stage; followed, in all likelihood, by heroic death, perhaps even immortality.

Tannhauser understood. Not only Orlundu's need to right the wrong he had done, but that excruciating tension whose allure transgressed and transcended all other experience. He understood why that feeling was worth dying for. It gave him no joy to steal another man's thunder; but the price Carla would pay was too high.

If Tannhauser summoned him to the boom, Orlandu could probably make the forty yards across the beach without anyone trying to stop him. If he refused, Tannhauser, at this range, could put a broadhead though Garnier's thighs for a certainty. That done, Orlandu's bucket might as well contain milk. With his grand stage in turmoil and his moment gone, he would heed the call of survival, though the odds would be thinner.

Orlandu reached the foot of the broad wooden stair. Garnier glanced down at him, and away, as if the youth were irrelevant to his troubles. Orlandu was just eight steps from the wharf and another reckless lunge for redemption. Tannhauser feared to endanger him with too particular a greeting; and he wanted a space around him to create a killing zone for any rash enough to enter it. He let him climb three steps and called out.

'We're ready to go.'

Orlandu stopped and looked at him.

Garnier, his bombast undiminished by shame, mistook Tannhauser's intention.

'Then for God's sake go!' he said. 'I have no power to pursue you!'

The moon shone full on Garnier's face. He was sweating in his steel plate. His flag had been pissed on, his private army decimated, his day of glory defiled. Beneath the rage and malice, he exuded self-pity and fear.

Tannhauser said, 'The Devil requires thy soul of thee tonight.'

Garnier put his fist to his heart, as if to lend himself a flavour of gallantry.

'I was never Le Tellier's man. I admired you. None of this was necessary.'

Orlandu hadn't moved, though his options must have been clear.

Tannhauser gestured to the vast and howling necropolis.

'Speak not to me of what was necessary.'

'Don't you hear me, chevalier? I yield. You've won.'

Orlandu turned away, as if the struggle with his conscience was done. He set the bucket down. He was going to submit to reason. If Tannhauser could spin out this farce for another minute, Orlandu would be on the boom before anyone noticed, much less cared. Garnier, disturbed by his silence, proved a fine fellow buffoon.

'You take all the honours, man. What more do you want?'

Tannhauser caught a glimpse of blue at Garnier's throat. He'd recognised Carla's scarf when Garnier left the Hôtel Le Tellier, and had guessed how she had used it.

'Is that my wife's scarf you're wearing?'

Someone guffawed. A gust of nervous laughter blew across the square.

Tannhauser grinned. Let them warm to him, if that was possible.

Garnier lifted the scarf from round his neck as if it were a noose.

Orlandu pulled a cloth from the mouth of the bucket.

Tannhauser's scalp clenched.

The fanatic's son was going to show Garnier the head. He wasn't vacating his stage, he was taking it back. Tannhauser understood that, too, but it was no longer a matter of conscience. The wrong had been righted well enough when he murdered Dominic.

'You. The man with one arm and a bucket. Fetch me Carla's scarf.'

Orlandu dropped the cloth but neither turned nor straightened up.

'Carla is tired and I am impatient. Do not test my goodwill.'

Orlandu hesitated.

He reached in the bucket.

He had to declare his manhood.

It was time to see at what cost.

As Orlandu hoisted Dominic's head by its hair, Tannhauser drew and shot.

The weight of the pull was enormous. The Turkish string sang like a harp.

Orlandu flung the head up the steps, but no one much noticed.

The broadhead ploughed through Garnier's crotch a thumb's width below his cuirass. It must have hit a heavy bone, for it spun him around like some gigantic marionette. He hit the timbers with a sound so dire his troops moaned with him. Dominic's head rolled to a stop inches in front of his face, but his agony was more compelling than the sight of it.

Tannhauser nocked. While the Pilgrims gaped at their captain's fall, and before the spectacle provoked them to revolt, Tannhauser gave them something else to watch.

'Fetch me the scarf, man. Now. Or I'll drop you on the spot and find some other to fill your shoes.'

Orlandu looked at him. He didn't expect to get shot, but the deeper interpretations did not elude him. He nodded. He turned and climbed the steps.

'Leave your trophy where it lies. Your mates can admire it later.'

The threat, along with the suggestion that the head was that of some poor Huguenot, should seal the masquerade. Tannhauser watched the watchers.

Orlandu stooped and pulled the scarf from under Garnier's body. If Garnier now knew that Orlandu was no Pilgrim, he conveyed the fact only with guttural grunts of pain. Orlandu walked along the edge of the square to the jetty. Several Pilgrims muttered encouragement. Orlandu stepped down into the flatboat. He looked at Tannhauser.

Tannhauser beckoned him, his eyes still on the mob.

Orlandu walked the length of the boat and Tannhauser stepped back. Orlandu climbed across the chain and into the stern. He proffered the scarf. He was scared; he was sick; he was weak; and he hid it all well. But not from Tannhauser.

'Give it to your mother.'

'She won't want to take it from me.'

'Carla would take it from you if it carried the plague. I told her you were buying time we didn't need. Since you bought that in plenty, you've no good reason to gainsay me.'

'The truth is a bad reason?'

'The truth serves only your vanity. She already has one baby to feed.'

Orlandu flinched.

'You proved what you needed to prove to me,' said Tannhauser. 'If you didn't prove it to yourself the venture was a failure and you're still a boy. That's for you to decide. All your mother needs to know is that you're alive. So I ask you, man to man, to spare her your guilt, your truth, your metaphysical doubts, and whatever other hogwash you've been dining on.'

Orlandu tucked the scarf in his sling.

'I bought time you didn't need.'

'We'd didn't need the time to get away. But I'm grateful for every minute.'

Orlandu didn't understand. He couldn't imagine what his return meant to Carla. Such ignorance was a son's birthright; and a certain sort of stupidity the privilege of youth.

'I'm grateful for Dominic, too,' said Tannhauser, 'if that head be his.'

Orlandu pulled a knife from the sling and cut the ribbons from his arm.

'It was the vilest thing I ever did.'

'I'm glad to hear that. Your mother need not.'

'She won't.'

Tannhauser slapped him on the back and stood aside.

'Tell Grymonde to break the boom.'

Orlandu walked by. Tannhauser almost told him not to fall in the water, but to a Maltese, even one sore wounded, the insult would have been too great. He watched him pick his way through the bloodbath and cross the gap to the third lighter. Tannhauser was exhausted down to bones he didn't know he had, and he was testy, but he reckoned that the privilege of age. He turned back to the jetty.

The conversation had taken place beyond earshot of the Pilgrims, though Tannhauser had kept one eye on their puzzlement. Now that they had their solution, and could add treachery, deception and the pleasure of being gulled to their humiliations, they were enraged. The tide of oaths and insults was more heartfelt than before, but he saw none who wanted to die so close to bedtime.

He asked himself why his life had made him so familiar with such swine, but before he had a chance to mount an answer, a scream echoed across the beach. The scream was of so harrowing a quality even Tannhauser might have been moved had it not been Bernard Garnier's. Gut, muscle and bone. The edges Altan had honed on the arrowhead were carving the captain's entrails with every breath and squirm. Garnier screamed again.

'By the blood of Saint-Jacques!'

Tannhauser heard a man praying for a miracle, but a figure knelt by the captain, and he heard it different. He stood up. It was Ensign Bonnett. Since Tannhauser had left Notre-Dame, the zealous little turd had inconvenienced him more than any other. His first instinct was to shoot him, but again the provocation seemed unwise. He hesitated and learned again why he mistrusted the practice.

'By the blood of Saint-Jacques!' shouted Bonnett. 'For God and the King!'

The mob roared, at first without form. The rallying cry was taken up.

Tannhauser shot Ensign Bonnett in the chest.

Bonnett dropped across his master and exacerbated his anguish.

Tannhauser turned away.

He saw Orlandu slide over the gunwale into the skiff.

Grymonde had both hands on the halberd but wasn't cranking it. Pascale was shouting in his face.

'Pascale,' called Tannhauser. 'All aboard.'

She stopped and looked at him. Tannhauser pointed at the skiff. He turned back to the mob.

A surge from the rear of the jetty pushed two Pilgrims to stumble into the flatboat. A third jumped in behind them of his own accord, and then a fourth. Tannhauser let an untidy file assemble, then drew and shot the Pilgrim in front. The fletchings vanished through his belly and he fell, and the man behind him sank to his knees with the bloody feathers protruding from his privates. Tannhauser nocked the last of the arrows in his fist and pinned the next two together like a pair of rutting dogs. His shoulders ached already from the weight of Altan's bow. He stretched them as he looked back.

Grymonde was cranking the halberd under the cleat. He paused after each movement as atrocious spasms waxed and waned within his body. Only Paris could have made him; only Paris could have brought him down. Everything he had left, and, had his heart not been so great, that would have been nothing, was thrown into his final task, of liberating the children who had liberated him.

Tannhauser would be sorry to leave the Infant behind. He was relieved not to see Pascale. Everyone who needed to be in the skiff was in it, except he.

He turned again.

The fervour on the jetty had cooled, the invasion of the flatboat abandoned.

On the beach, the wharf, the square, jeers and battle cries continued, though those who voiced them showed no inclination to move. God. King. Saint-Jacques. Saint-Jacques.

By his holy blood.

Blood, blood, blood.

They wouldn't have vexed him so much if they'd known what they were talking about. Tannhauser's skin was caked in a blackening slurry, in places half an inch thick. He was covered in the blood of men he despised. His body was as drained as he had ever known it to be. His belly was empty. He was thirsty. His loins ached. So did his feet.

And none of this was necessary.

He turned his back on them, but found himself unwilling to take the next step. He had no good reasons, very few bad ones, and many of the highest order, moral and practical, to the contrary. But it didn't sit well with him. These dogs had been snapping at his heels all night, and he had run from them. He had thinned the pack, but the rest would go home and tell a different tale, and before long they'd believe it themselves. Their tale was no concern of Tannhauser's; but his own was. He had chided Orlandu for impulses not dissimilar; but that was a privilege of age, too. The memory of cowards and child murderers spitting at his back as he walked away wasn't of the species he knew how to carry.

'My Infant.'

Grymonde stopped. At this range, his eyes seemed bored right through him.

Tannhauser unslung the quiver, and laid it down with Altan's bow.

'Will you give me a minute?' he said.

'If you'll let me come with you,' said Grymonde.

'You're already with me.'

'You are a stubborn man.'

Tannhauser stepped past the desecrated flag and into the last flatboat.

He picked up a spear. He looked at the jeerers, and curiosity quieted them.

Tannhauser said, 'Give me that cage.'

'What cage?'

Tannhauser pointed with the spear.

'Load it on this lighter and I'll let you kiss your wives goodnight.'

Several of those nearest the cage took a closer look.

'It's a cage of dead cats. Or rats.'

'Monkeys, I'd say, from Africa.'

'Christ. They're horrible.'

'They could be poxed.'

'Tell him to come and get 'em himself.'

'Come and get 'em yourself!'

Two of the men Tannhauser had shot were still alive. He stuck the first in the throat notch, and the foremost spokesman stepped back, and so did the rest. Tannhauser stabbed the second wretch in the spleen from behind and walked to the stern of the boat.

One step onto the thwart and another onto the jetty.

Pride obliged the spokesman to advance into the space he had vacated and lower his half-pike. Tannhauser evaded a thrust and as he rose from the thwart and mounted the jetty he lanced him between the bollocks and the anus and pitched him, shrieking, into the river. The spectacle of so vile a death drove his fellows backwards another step. They levelled half a dozen spears at Tannhauser. Those Pilgrims behind this rank were clustered too tight to point their weapons anywhere but skyward.

Tannhauser was aware that in this position Carla could clearly see him. Out of respect for her gaze and her feelings, he gave them another chance.

'I told you to fetch me the cage.'

'For Christ's sake, what do you want it for?'

'I want it so that you'll tell me to get it myself.'

No one did. Neither did any have the wit to bring the cage.

'He must be raving mad.'

Tannhauser raised the spear overarm in a throwing grip, aimed at the centre of the line, and the two there turned to flee, one into the other, and their spears crossed.

Tannhauser charged the right flank, and warded the two outer spear shafts towards the middle with a sweep, and closed, and grabbed the outermost by his belt and threw him off the edge into

725

the water, and lanced the man behind him in the gut and let him grab the spear. He drew the lapis dagger and stabbed the newly rightmost man in the armpit and drew his second dagger. With a double lunge to the guts, he stabbed the outermost two in the next rank while they wondered what to do. He slid into the gap between the first and second lines, both already buckling with panic, and stabbed the next man to either side at the same time. Ten-inch blades. The root of the neck; the heart. He ducked and wove, his senses and instincts working faster than his brain, the killing strokes plotted three, four men in advance of their execution. Their spears at this range were worse than useless; their senses and their instincts, slack at best, now stupefied by the gusts of blood venting from the bodies of their friends, by the urge to void their bowels, by the speed and fury of Death's plenipotentiary on the Seine.

Footwork and targets; right dagger left, left dagger right; straddle a pike shaft. A fist came at his head and he rolled with it and stabbed its owner in the liver. Trust the blades, get ahead of the dead as they fall; heart, neck, neck, gut; a knife: stab him in the forearm, stab him in the chest. He killed five; he killed seven in fewer than that many beats of his heart. The gore on his hide oiled his progress through the press. Dying fingers slithered over his skin. He turned his face away from a fountain of bloody vomit. Behind him an entanglement of woe; before him of unrectified panic. There were no more ranks, just a mass who hadn't yet realised they were fleeing, those who would have fought struggling past the throng of those who wouldn't, and both varieties lambs to his rage.

He killed eleven.

He glimpsed the mazement in their eyes as they died.

He killed fifteen and then lost the count as he killed more.

A wide space opened on this side of the tangled retreat, and he left both daggers in the chest of the last and plucked the fellow's halberd from his hands.

He gored a charging swordsman and pitched him into the legs of a second, and set himself, and dashed that second's brains from his skull with the axe. He axed a third through the thorax and judged the distance to the next man, and that man saw him and turned to run, and Tannhauser pursued him and spiked him between the shoulders at the full length of the shaft. He followed him down and spiked him again through the base of the skull.

Tannhauser felt better than he had felt all day. He felt as well as he had ever felt in his life. He felt the Quintessence of all that Destiny had meant him to be flow through his veins, the good and the evil, the crimson and the white, and it felt true. He felt true. He defied God to strike him down for his transgressions. And God did not.

Tannhauser took a breath and surveyed the field.

He'd cleared the jetty and was a good way onto the square. The random stacks of building materiel provided cover, but he saw no lurkers. The east wing of the Louvre was dark but for the lantern above the gatehouse, and another light burning in the tower. There were maybe twenty Pilgrims left, and a dozen more on the beach, but the closest was too far to be hounded. Half were headed elsewhere at a healthy pace and they weren't looking back. Among the rest, most were delayed by shock or the compulsion to find out what happened next. There were a few still sizing him up, war veterans perhaps, but what had most veterans done but stand in a line and take orders? The dullest knew he'd be butchered like a shoat, and the best had no idea how to tackle him.

Garnier lay ten paces away, moaning under Bonnett's weight like a badly butchered steer in his own abattoir. Tannhauser walked over and put a foot on Bonnett's chest, and pulled out the arrow there transfixing him, and stuck it in his belt. He kicked Bonnett aside to better see the arrow in Garnier's groin. A foot of shaft was visible beyond the fletchings. The other two feet had skated up from his pelvis and through his intestines. A slow and mortal wound, and no less than he deserved, but his death would give the laggards some sense of finality. Tannhauser looked the captain in the eyes, but the man was incapable of knowing aught but pain. Tannhauser raised the halberd in both hands, on the vertical. He drove the point through Garnier's mouth and impaled him to the timbers of the wharf through the nape of his neck.

He looked at the laggards and drew his sword, and they turned and hurried towards the warrens of the Ville. Those on the beach trudged east, past the moored boats.

Tannhauser strode through the shambles to the jetty. Four crawlers grovelled in the moon-blacked spillings of the slain like penitents at the altar of some Mexican temple. He beheaded them, one by one, and cleaned his blade, and reckoned his bloodlust slaked. He retrieved his daggers and flicked and sheathed them. He picked up a cap and towelled his brows and dropped the cap.

He walked to the cage of dead monkeys.

It lay on its side, the tiny, exquisite creatures still piled inside it. The heat and damp of the day had merged their carcasses into one grotesque mass, multi-headed and multi-limbed, as if it were the single pelt of some fairy-tale monster.

He dragged the cage to the downriver edge of the jetty. The door of the cage comprised one entire wall, and he cut through the leather hinges and opened it. He tipped the cage over and emptied its prisoners into the water.

If all had believed him mad he would have had no means to contradict them. But the square was deserted of all but the dead, and so was the jetty, and so the beach and the boom. There was no one left to ask the question but he, and he was indifferent to the answer.

He sheathed his sword.

On the upriver side, steps led down to the beach and he took them, and waded into the water up to the knees of his high boots. He bent from the waist and rinsed his hands, and scrubbed the gore-matted hair on his forearms, his shoulders, his chest. He scooped handfuls of river into his armpits and over his face. He spread his legs wide and doubled over and ducked his head beneath the water. He scraped handfuls of clots from his hair and let the current carry them away. He squeezed the nape of his neck in the palm of his hand. He stood up.

He felt fit to join the small collection of humanity in the skiff. If they'd have him.

He climbed back to the jetty and looked at them.

Carla stood up from the stern thwart and turned towards him.

Burning wood and charcoal threw a wall of flame behind her. The
river seemed of molten gold and silver. The full moon hung high
above her head and he couldn't see her face. She could have been
some ancient spirit risen from the deep.

Carla raised Amparo above her head in both hands.

Tannhauser breathed deep.

He was forgiven, then, which, if such he needed to be, was all
to the good.

He'd come to find his wife and was taking home a daughter,
too.

Five daughters. He grinned. Why not?

He crossed the jetty and stepped onto the bloody causeway. He
retrieved a serviceable broadhead from a body in the first lighter.
In the second, he stooped to return the recovered arrows to their
quiver. He reclaimed Altan's bow. Behind him he heard the perfect
cadence of soldiers who knew how to march.

Eleven Swiss Guard advanced from the Louvre to the jetty.

He couldn't decide if he was too tired to run or too tired to
fight.

He looked again. Ten guards.

A rotund figure stepped forward and bowed his head. It was
Arnauld de Torcy. Arnauld motioned to Stefano, who commanded
the section. Stefano gestured to the slain that littered the ground
thereabouts. His men stacked their halberds and separated in pairs,
and set to throwing the corpses into the Seine.

'Tannhauser,' said Arnauld. 'One day you'll walk across one
square too many.'

'Is the King abed?'

'His Majesty has had a trying day. There's no need to try him
further.'

Tannhauser glanced at the guards, slithering on the gore-slaked
planks as they grunted and heaved. He raised one brow at Arnauld.

'A traitors' grave,' said Arnauld. 'They did not act for His
Majesty.'

'Neither did I.'

'You were not sworn to.'

'Our young ward, Juste, is dead.'

'I saw it all,' said Arnauld. 'From the tower.'

'Does the King know that tomorrow will be worse than today?'

Arnauld didn't answer. He had made his choice and he would prosper.

'Good luck, my friend,' said Tannhauser. 'Adieu.'

His legs tensed as the hull rolled underneath him.

The boom was broken.

He turned and in the third boat saw Grymonde prop his haunches on the bow, and swing his legs across the gunwale. Beyond him the burning barge drifted away as the current unfurled the greater length of the boom towards the Left Bank.

Tannhauser ran.

'My Infant, wait.'

Grymonde's shoulders flexed as he shoved himself into the Seine.

CHAPTER FORTY-THREE

For Whom My Tears Have Made Me Blind

When Mattias almost started towards the skiff, but didn't, Carla knew he was going to turn back into a darkness blacker than the night. A complexity of painful feelings knotted inside her. She knew he didn't need to go back. And she knew that he did.

She took Amparo from Estelle, and cuddled her. The baby they had made gave her comfort while she watched Mattias bathe in blood.

His descent into violent madness shocked the children, even Pascale, who adored him. They thought they had known him; and they thought they had known him to be a bloody man, yet now they were appalled. They were terrified. For a moment, so was Carla. She cared nothing for the dying as they tumbled by threes and fours into bleeding piles. She trusted they were bound for Hell. But Mattias wasn't killing them for justice or creed; or even to defend the boom. He killed them because they were there and because he could and because this was his calling.

He had hurt her by turning back. She couldn't help but fear for him, and of fear she had had her fill. His spree was spent inside a minute or two, and the whole arena was cleared inside of five, but they were long ones. He prowled among the heaps of slain, his skin wet and black in the moonlight. He decapitated the wounded, as if their continued existence affronted his. She had no idea what thing he emptied from the cage, nor why it was so important he commit it to the river, and when Estelle voiced those very questions no one there could give her an answer.

Carla watched Mattias wash himself, and though she tried to

731

contain a surge of love so deep it felt more painful than giving birth, the sight overwhelmed her, and sobs racked her shoulders, and tears fell down her cheeks and onto her babe. The man she loved was a man wedded to bloodshed. No feeling she might know would change the fact. He had pledged that fidelity long before he had known what it was that he vowed, when men not unlike these now extirpated on the shore had scourged the life he might have had from the realm of possibility. Perhaps it was for that that Carla wept, for such possibilities would have kept him forever from her arms, and from Orlandu and Amparo, too, and those joys she would not have foregone for any price; not even peace for Mattias's turbulent spirit. And so, she had no right to censure his fury, for without it he would never have been hers, nor she his, and if she couldn't love all that he was, she deserved none of him.

The children wept, too, all except Grégoire, who moaned in a drugged sleep on his horse blanket. They had endured intolerable hazards and intolerable loss with extreme courage. They did not cry for their own troubles. They cried because they loved Mattias and because they feared the loss of his soul.

Orlandu did not cry, but he was a child no longer. He had kissed her and returned her blue scarf, and she had thanked him, and he had sat down on the middle thwart, next to Pascale, and had said no more.

Amparo did not cry either. She was wide awake and seemed not in the least perplexed or upset by the surrounding woe. Her face was turned to Carla's.

Carla smiled. The song and dance of Life Her-own-self went on.

'Will Tannzer come back?' asked Estelle.

'Of course he will,' said Pascale.

'Yes,' said Carla. 'Of course he will. And he will need us to take care of him, so let's dry our tears and show him he can count on us.'

'I didn't think Tannzer needed to be taken care of,' said Estelle.

'Yes, he does,' said Carla. 'He needs us more than we need him.'

'He'd never admit to that,' said Pascale.

'I think you'd be surprised.'

Carla watched Mattias wade dripping from the river and climb back to the jetty. He looked at her, and though she couldn't see his face, in his posture she saw a certain, insincere, remorse. For her sake.

For his sake, Carla stood up and raised Amparo towards him.

Above the river of the dead.

Beneath the stars and the full of the moon.

The burden of insincerity flew from his shoulders.

He stepped down onto the boom.

Carla lowered the baby. A late cramp clenched her and she sat down and waited for it to pass. The pang dried what was left of her weeping. She could feel absolute exhaustion lurking, waiting to consume her. She saw the Swiss Guard, and Mattias facing them, and her fear was refreshed. Ten Swiss were more dangerous than three score Pilgrims, and she didn't put it past Mattias to go back again.

The guards started hoisting the dead into the water.

She heard Mattias wish their spokesman Adieu.

She heard a grinding of iron on wood.

The current was tearing the boom in two.

Grymonde tossed the halberd behind him and lunged across the bow as the cleat he had half-unseated popped from its mooring. It seemed he hoped to grab the drifting stern and hold the entire boom together by sheer force of will. His hands grasped only the air. Carla was about to call to him when the release of tension and the unopposed current caused the skiff to shift away from the hull of the lighter.

The boathook twisted free of the gunwale. The pole slipped from the hands of Agnès and Marie, who had been as racked by tears as any. Their dismay at their failure was immense and their hands snatched out together. Pascale reached for the boathook, too, and so did Orlandu. But all were too late and it fell into the water and slipped away.

The skiff was adrift and the children panicked.

Carla realised they were afraid of losing Mattias.

'Pascale, get the dock line.'

Carla pointed to the coiled rope beyond the forward bench.

Pascale leapt across her bench and scrambled for the line.

'Throw it to Grymonde. Grymonde!'

Grymonde was sitting on the bow, his legs above the water. He had wrapped the chain still attached to the lighter around his left wrist. He pushed himself in. For a moment she didn't understand what he was doing, then the jaws of the broken boom gaped and the skiff was carried into the gap.

'Pascale, Orlandu, ready the oars.'

Grymonde was ready before them. With a roar that conveyed his rage at the pain inside him, he hauled himself up by the chain and reached out, and grabbed hold of the skiff by the stern, his eyeholes brimming with water, and held onto it in defiance of the current.

Carla could do nothing to help him. She could have told him to let go, that his agony wasn't necessary, but that would be to steal the only precious thing he had left.

Orlandu slotted an oar in the larboard lock with one hand, and Pascale took her place beside him, and picked up the other. They weren't going to leave Mattias behind. But they would be leaving Grymonde.

Grymonde would have stayed behind anyway. Of course. But she hadn't had the thought until now. The knowledge filled her with a confusion of feelings, sadness foremost. No. Foremost was love. His enormous hand was inches from hers, the fingers as thick as pike shafts gripping the gunwale as if they would splinter it. She put her hand on his and turned to look at him. The weight of the loaded skiff had stretched him like a man crucified. He spat water as the current wafted them slowly shoreward. The holes in his scorched and deformed face were indifferent to his agony. They simply saw everything.

'Grymonde.' Carla didn't know how to go on.

'It wasn't tears made this man blind, so he'll have none shed for him.'

'Grymonde!' Estelle stood up.

Carla put an arm around her to hold her steady.

'La Rossa, my darling. Be true to your sister and her mother.'

'I will.'

'I will be watching you.'

'Like an angel?'

Grymonde heaved for breath as membranes burst inside him.

'A black angel?' Estelle looked up. 'Like Tannzer's?'

Mattias leaned over the bow above Grymonde, and extended a halberd and secured the skiff with its hook and pulled it in. Grymonde held on, but sank in the water.

'My Infant, you are in my way.'

'Then step around me, for to such am I accustomed.'

Mattias changed the hook's purchase, to the other side of Carla, and she shifted over. Mattias swung a leg over the side, then the other, and stepped onto the thwart, and threw the halberd in the river while keeping hold of the lighter with his free hand.

A sound heard by no others before them exploded through the night.

Carla turned towards it, as did they all.

Freed from the widening arms of the broken boom, the fire barge rotated slowly as the current made off with it. It seemed to float on a carpet of bodies. A fountain of steam erupted skyward abaft of the prow. The sound was that of a thousand coals surrendering their fire to the river.

'My Infant, we're all aboard, and we've paid our coin.'

'Then be gone. And wait for the sound of my laughter.'

Mattias released his grip and the skiff drifted away to the outer limit of Grymonde's arms. Estelle cried out and clutched Amparo and pushed deeper into Carla's breast.

Grymonde held on, teeth bared, his eyeholes staring at the stars.

Mattias made his way to the forward rowing bench and unloaded his gear. He beckoned Pascale and Orlandu to pass the oars, and he took his seat and fitted the oars to the locks. He leaned forward and laid the blades flat on the water, and paused. He smiled at Carla from behind the sad, young faces. He awaited her command.

Carla took the tiller and nodded.

Mattias dipped the oars and pulled.

As Grymonde felt the stroke he opened his hand and reversed it, and his fingers caressed Carla's. The skiff pulled away and the hand fell into the water. Carla glanced down at Amparo. The babe was still awake, still enraptured by the world.

Carla turned as Grymonde's chin fell to his chest.

His great, mutilated head sank below the water.

All that remained above the surface was his arm, his huge hand splayed and blue, his wrist bound to the broken boom by the chain.

Mattias rowed and the skiff pulled away. They passed the dying barge as it wheeled towards the shore and threw rolls of smoke across the floating dead. The towers of the Louvre were black against the midnight sky and getting smaller. She saw the torches on the wall that surrounded the city. They had left Paris.

Carla turned away.

Estelle did not. She stared across the water at the drifting boom.

'He moved. Look, Carla! The dragon's not dead.'

Carla looked back at the chained arm. It might have been some trick of moonlight, smoke and water, but she believed Grymonde's hand had clenched into a fist.

'Estelle?' said Mattias.

Estelle wiped her face and turned to look at him.

'It wouldn't sit right with the Infant to be an angel.'

'Why not?'

'An angel's wings aren't strong enough to carry such as he.'

Estelle brightened. 'But a dragon has wings.'

'Aye. And a dragon shares something else in common with the angels.'

'What's that?'

'A dragon never dies.'

CHAPTER FORTY-FOUR

Nameless Ways

Hugon waited in the alley by the stable until all he could hear were distant screams. When the screams hadn't moved in five minutes, and were getting weaker, he made his way through the darkest shadows he could find to the Pont Notre-Dame.

He looked down as the bald dog trotted up alongside him.

'I told you not to go with 'em last night, but you wouldn't listen, would you? Had to follow the pack. Look where it got you.'

The dog seemed pleased enough with his adventures. So was Hugon. He'd done all right. He'd taken some chances. The bodies in the river had almost pulled him down with them. But you had to take chances if you wanted what you wanted, especially when everyone else wanted what they wanted and reckoned you weren't worth much more than a bald dog.

None of them really knew who he was. That was the way Hugon liked it. Keep them guessing. Not even Alice knew him, though he thought she thought she did. He was sad Alice was gone, but she hadn't been long for this world; he'd known that for a while. Grymonde, too. Tannzer had surprised him – he hadn't been kidding about the forty years' wages; what was that about? – but that just went to show how stupid it was to think you could see into a person, without waiting to see what they did. Mind you, he wouldn't want to get on the wrong side of the man; that didn't take any guessing at all.

As for Carla, well, Christ, she would have him guessing for the rest of his days. If it wasn't for the fact that he was carrying her violl, he would have thought he had dreamed her. He was sorry she'd gone off with the others. She had secrets he wanted to know. He couldn't say that of anyone else he had ever met. But he had the violl. He knew it didn't make much sense, but the violl felt a lot more precious than the forty years' wages hanging round his neck.

He would have to think of a name for the dog when he had the time, if the dog stuck around. He was a tough little thing, and he had the Devil's luck, so Hugon hoped he would. Tannzer's boys had called him Lucifer, but what kind of name was that for a bald dog?

When he got there the bridge was deserted, except for the little girl.

The girl was of no great interest to him. He didn't even know her name. But she looked lost, not because she didn't know where she was, but because she was alone.

It didn't do to care too much. He'd always known that, and today had proved it, and so would tomorrow. Yet it was funny. Carla would never know, and she probably thought him a right bastard for stealing her violl, but he felt he owed it to her.

He walked over to the girl and she turned, and he saw she knew him.

'What's your name, then? I'm Hugon.'

'I'm Antoinette. Where's Carla?'

'She's gone, down the river, to wherever she's going. Though I wouldn't bet much on her getting there.'

'Why did Carla leave me in the cathedral?'

He almost said: *Maybe they didn't want you*, which seemed the likeliest reason.

'I don't know. Maybe she just forgot.'

'You saw me in the cathedral.'

'Yes, but it wasn't up to me, was it?'

She could see that this was true enough, and it was. But she was still puzzled. Maybe she was even a bit hurt. He shrugged and felt the weight of the collar.

'Tannzer said the cathedral was the safest place in the city. Said you were better off in there than they were out here, and if you'd seen the state they left in, you'd not disagree. You could have lost a leg, easy.'

This explanation seemed to give her some comfort.

'Who's Tannzer?' she said.

Hugon didn't know where to begin. He thought Tannzer should probably be chained to a muck cart and given a shovel, for he was lunatic enough, but he didn't say so.

'Just a man.'

'Will you take me home?'

'I don't know where you live.'

'Aren't you going back to the Yards?'

'Where else? At least, for the time being. I got what I wanted. And more.'

'Take me home to the Yards – that's what I meant. Can I come with you?'

'I suppose so. But I'm not looking after you.'

He didn't know whether she wanted him to or not.

She took hold of his hand and he let her hang onto it.

He started across the bridge, in the shadows, where he felt good.

Antoinette looked at the violl case.

'Did Carla give you that?'

'She said I should learn to play it. I attack the strings with spirit, she said.'

'Carla was always telling us to attack with spirit. But it's not so easy on a recorder.'

'What do you mean?' asked Hugon.

'Blowing doesn't feel like attacking.'

'No, I mean when did she tell you?'

'When we played music.'

'What, you and Carla played music?'

'Yes, every day. With Lucien and Charité and Martin. And Mama.'

Hugon took another look at the girl.

'Are you saying you know music, then?'

'I can read music.'

'How can I believe that? You're just a kid.'

'Mama taught me. It's easier than reading books.'

Hugon grunted. 'Never seen anyone dance or cry from reading a book. Can you teach me? I mean, how to read music?'

'I can try. If you've got some.'

'What do you mean?'

'What do *you* mean?'

Hugon decided that this matter was best tackled some other time.

They walked on and the girl got puzzled again.

'Hugon? Why didn't they leave you in the cathedral?'

'They needed me to lug their gear.'

'But why didn't you go with them?'

Hugon frowned. The idea of going with them had never occurred to him. He'd been well aware that going with them had been a possibility: they had expected it of him; taken it for granted in fact, though none had taken the trouble to ask him if he wanted to. But that had only served to sharpen his sense of the right time to escape, with the violl. He had had no doubt, for a start, that the older girl, Pascale, would have shot him down for the pleasure of seeing him fall.

'I done my bit, didn't I?' he said. 'And more. So did you.'

'I don't know.' She thought about it. 'I didn't do anything.'

'Kept Carla company, didn't you? And she needed it, believe me. I followed you from Cockaigne, see, on the roofs. I saw you. You held her hand all the way.'

'I suppose so. Yes, I did hold her hand.'

'And if I remember right, you were holding it when she arrived in Cockaigne. Just like you're holding mine, now. You're good at it.'

'Am I?'

'I'm starving. Let's find something to eat.'

They stopped at the chain on the ground at the end of the bridge and he spied up and down the streets along the river. They were dark and empty. He heard gunfire in the distance. A volley, as they called it. He saw the lanterns outside the Châtelet, but no movement. Bastards. He was glad there was no one left around to tell how Rody had caught him; especially Rody. He'd enjoyed watching the Infant give him a seeing to.

Hugon dragged Antoinette as he ran across the road and ducked into the Savonnerie, and on into the nameless ways and alleys east of Saint-Denis.

He felt safer. They could take the alleys all the way to the Yards. 'We've done all right, you and me. We'll be fine.'

'I think so, too.' She didn't sound sure.

'As long as we don't take anyone at their word.'

He sensed he had contradicted himself, but she didn't seem to notice.

'Things'll be different now, anyway. No more "Hugon, bring the wine and fetch the water." It'll be "Hugon, you were there, with the Infant and Tannzer. What happened? What did they do? How did they do it?"'

'What did happen?' asked Antoinette.

Hugon didn't think that question deserved an answer.

But the other one she'd asked him, on the bridge, still itched him.

'Anyway. Why would I want to leave Paris?'

The night trembled with the thunder and the clamour of a thousand doomed beasts being driven to the abattoirs. Hugon could no longer see Antoinette's face. He held her hand tight.

'Like the Infant says, it's the greatest city in the world.'

ENVIRONED WITH A WILDERNESS

The massacre in Paris grew in reach and vindictiveness through the rest of that second day, Monday 25th August 1572.

On Tuesday the crusade against the Huguenots reached the peak of its frenzy.

Though the weak of stomach and faint of heart had by then had their fill, and the ranks of the killers were thereby somewhat reduced, those that woke with the dawn and took up arms for Christ were of the most ambitious and committed sort. Thus unencumbered by the feeble, they managed to exceed in pitilessness and depravity all that had gone before. Militia captains seeking prestige, and winning it, led the gangs with flag and drum, and priests blessed the blood on their swords in the names of their patron saints. Rape was anointed a sacred instrument. Women were beaten to death with their own babies. Children were baptised in the blood of the parents whose slaughter they were forced to witness. Men were buried alive in dunghills.

The apathy of the supposed forces of order – royal, military and civic – emboldened confraternities and criminals alike. The King dared not unleash his guards on his own most fervent supporters, for beyond them he had few left. The envoys who conveyed his disapproval of his capital's ruin were mocked and ignored. Those despatched by the Bureau de Ville found themselves in danger of their lives. The Military Governor did his duty and defended the walls, though no structure in the city was in smaller danger of assault.

Catholics, too, continued to fall under the tide of vengeance and crime, but the powers at the Châtelet minded their own affairs. These latter were more Byzantine than usual, for the struggle for

Marcel Le Tellier's throne was fierce. In the absence of witnesses to rack, reliable or otherwise, the responsibility for Le Tellier's murder was pinned on the Cockaigne Infant – the notorious Grymonde – who was captured and killed on Monday morning, by the commissioner who later inherited Le Tellier's mantle.

Grymonde's body – curiously bloated with water, as some pointed out, for one said to have died in a desperate sword fight – was cut into quarters and the segments displayed at the principal city gates, though, in the circumstance, the audiences were smaller than usual. His enormous head was impaled on a pike outside the Châtelet, and while some wondered how a man with no eyes could have accomplished a crime so daring, or have fought to the last with such defiance, this very riddle nurtured and sustained the legend of the King of Cockaigne.

Later, his conqueror had the skull boiled clean and the brain sucked out of the spine hole. The skull made a fine conversation piece for the rest of his long career, and he willed it to the School of Law at the University of Padua, a bizarre whim blamed on advanced old age. For all that anyone knows, the Infant's skull resides in the vaults of that august institution to this day.

On Wednesday, his authority having proved too puny to tame the anarchy, the King assembled Parlement, and claimed that all that had occurred to date had been by his own express commandment, 'to prevent the execution of an unfortunate and detestable conspiracy'.

The results of this stratagem were most agreeable. His people discovered, briefly, that they loved him after all. Poems were written to his courage and wisdom, and to the angel that had guided him. Sacred processions, displaying the Blessed Sacrament and the relics of Sainte-Geneviève, rendered thanks to Almighty God for the defeat of the Huguenots. The King had a gold medal struck, depicting himself as Hercules slaying the Hydra of heresy. The distant elites, *Les Messieurs*, made money. In Rome and Madrid and elsewhere, the news was received with rejoicing, and Giorgio Vasari was hired to paint frescoes in the Vatican to commemorate the affair.

On the whole, then, the outcome was considered a good one.

And in its way the counsel provided to the King proved sound.

While the massacre did not destroy the Huguenot movement, the blow crippled them, almost fatally, and they never recovered. Its principal leaders were gone, and with them the means to finance further conflict. Thousands of Huguenots renounced their faith, appalled that God could allow his children to be butchered with such impunity. They sought baptism and went on with their lives. Many more fled to other countries, where the bonfires were reserved for unbelievers of other stripes.

The destruction of Protestant power in France did nothing to prevent another twenty years and more of civil war, for in such matters the elites are endlessly inventive. They found other ways to persuade the people to slaughter each other and continued until the Valois were no more and the first of the Bourbon kings could hardly afford a pot to piss in. This new king starved Paris by siege to bring it to heel, and though he failed, for Paris is ever stubborn, he killed more than thirty thousand of its citizens. When peace within the kingdom was finally secured, he led the nation into a new war with Spain.

He ended his reign, as had his predecessor, at the point of an assassin's knife.

In the aftermath of Saint Bartholomew's Day, the murder spree in Paris lingered on for a month more, its wane due more to a lack of plausible victims than for want of enthusiasm. And the massacres spread, like the waves from a pebble cast into a pool, across the whole of France. Such pebbles were cast often enough in the affairs of men; in the end the pool always settled to await the next. But Tannhauser could not avoid the inner knowledge that the pebble that had splashed into Paris he had helped to throw.

He and Carla, and the children, encountered its bloody ripples on their journey home. They survived them unscathed, at least in body. Though he knew no qualms of conscience for any he had killed by his own hand, not even the unlucky minstrel nor the

Huguenot knelt and bound on the Parvis, Tannhauser felt tarnished, forever, by his conversation with Retz.

He did not imagine that his counsel had tipped the scales in the direction they had dropped. He could not thus flatter himself. Such counsel was available from anyone versed in the nature of power and war; and that was what so diminished him in front of himself. He had been gulled by his own vanity. For the privilege of riding half a mile on lavender-scented cushions, and in return for feeling important enough to be asked he had regurgitated a pail of swill that could be heard in any tavern, or read in any cheap pamphlet written by the likes of Petit Christian. And though no one such pail could pollute much more than a few more minds, enough of them made a stream, a torrent, a sea; a world awash and drowning in shit. In that shit he wallowed deeper than most.

No wonder his need to bathe himself in blood had been so dire.

A truth smouldered at the core of his being.

Tannhauser knew that he should lay down the sword.

At any cost, even be it that of the lives of Carla and his children.

He believed he had the will to do it, for to do it was within his power.

But he did not want to.

As Petrus Grubenius had said, Truth was the burden impossible to bear. Which was why men devised lesser truths, lighter truths; and made of them their gods.

Because Tannhauser had the will, but did not want to exercise it, he told none of this to Carla, and this diminished him further. He did not tell her for he feared she would tell him he was right, and if she did, the Truth, and his will, would have had no hole to hide in.

It was not that she disapproved of his crimes; she didn't. Great as they were, they had never broken the boundary of her love and her compassion. Such crimes as would do so, he had no fear of committing. Yet such sophistry was too inelegant to fool him. If he told her he had to lay down the sword, he did not believe she would love him any the less, even if she would neither love him more; for he was so bewildered by her love that he believed she loved him that completely.

Something had changed in Carla in Paris. Something that intensified her mystery, her strength. A woman called Alice, the Infant's mother, had changed her. So had the children who sailed with them down the Seine. Amparo had transformed her. The change threw the nature of his own love into question, for his love became so deep that its abyss gaped at his feet, and the drop terrified him. He had changed, too; or perhaps he merely felt that he ought to have.

At times his melancholy was so great he didn't dare trust his own thoughts.

Outside Castets, not a day's ride from La Penautier, they encountered a band of deserters bent on easy plunder. Tannhauser slew them and his melancholy vanished, and he put the truth of what he ought to do aside, for some other time, and some other place, in a world unlikely to be this one.

In this one he resolved to stop giving his opinions instead.

On the night of their escape from Paris, Tannhauser rowed the skiff until the break of dawn. Orlandu and Pascale took turns to man the tiller. Carla slept exhausted on the strakes with Amparo on her breast. Estelle and Grégoire and the Mice clustered around her, and they kept each other warm.

Tannhauser watched the sun come up. He saw no other craft on the river and the banks to either side were uninhabited. Birdsong. Wild flowers. Trees. Long light. An eerie tranquillity so sweet they might have passed through some elvish veil into the realms of legend. He looked at the children, sleeping in bare feet and bloody rags.

Outside of the Hell whose flames had welded his destiny to theirs, and theirs to his, their faces, for a moment, were innocent of all cares. He felt as though he was seeing them, each of them, for the very first time. They were so small and so young and so fragile, and as he watched them sleep his chest filled to bursting with the ache of their inexpressible beauty.

He had reached the end of his own rope. He motioned to Orlandu and they pulled in to the shore. He tied up and none of the sleepers were roused and he left them in peace. He unloaded his wallets and the sacks, and he and Orlandu collected wood and built a fire without speaking. They two had shared many fires together. This one felt particular and it felt good. They smiled. Tannhauser explored the sacks and laid out the fare and found they had more than enough for a decent breakfast.

It looked right welcoming.

He looked at Orlandu, who nodded in agreement.

He woke Carla and helped her onshore. He kissed her and won a pale smile. He took her to the camp and the look on her face was enough to fend off his weariness. Carla sat cross-legged and took out one breast and fed Amparo, who was keen and altogether brimful with life. Still no one spoke, for it seemed that they were walking through a dream and none dared break its spell.

It was broken soon enough, as was the tranquillity, though the morning was by no means the worse on that account. Estelle had never seen a forest before, nor a campfire beneath a tree, nor a greensward spread with cheese and bread and sausage. Neither had the Mice. Neither had Pascale. They fell on the food as children will, like starving lions. They chattered and the Mice laughed. Pascale made tart remarks at Orlandu's expense, and was delighted to be paid back in kind.

It was a sight to remember. Yet the truest among them, if such there could be, was missing. Without him there would have been no feast. Without him, it would be no right feast at all.

'Leave something for Grégoire, even if you leave naught for me.'

They jeered him roundly but promised to preserve a full share for their shipmate.

Tannhauser returned to the boat.

He wasn't alarmed to see that the boy hadn't moved. Opium entitled him to sleep even sounder than the rest. Tannhauser wondered if he shouldn't leave him be while it lasted. He'd witnessed the agonies of those who'd lost a leg. They got worse for a long time before they got better. On the other hand, the feast would do the lad's heart a power of good, and he'd need that as much as the food.

Grégoire liked his food.

Tannhauser climbed into the skiff and saw that Grégoire had moved since they had docked. The boy clutched something in his hand, some crumpled rag. Tannhauser stooped and saw the once-white ribbon in the boy's fingers. The package from the market in the Grand Hall. The cloth-of-silver christening robe. What a lad. Tannhauser worked his arms beneath him. The body was limp but not cold. He lifted him to his chest.

It wasn't until he stepped ashore that he realised Grégoire was dead.

He wasn't breathing. His lips, and the wide strip of exposed gum, were blue.

More than that, he could feel in his heart that the boy's ghost had flown.

Something in Tannhauser flew after him.

He knew that neither the something nor the ghost would ever come back.

Why had he died? There was no blood in the boat. Was his blood poisoned by the wound? The opium would have killed him much sooner if it was going to. He would never have woken up, yet he had roused himself to take the gown from the satchel. How could so small an effort have killed him?

It made no sense to die now, here, when it was over.

Tannhauser wanted to shake him.

He remembered the boy with the strawberry birthmark.

He remembered Juste.

Grégoire's last act had been an act of loyalty.

Of love.

Tannhauser carried Grégoire into the forest.

He circled around the camp and its revellers. None of them had really known Grégoire. He had been too busy ferrying them about the bloody streets of his city. They didn't need to see another dead child. He would tell Estelle he'd seen the dragon fly him away. The Mice might believe it, too. The others would understand. He stopped beyond the edge of the sounds of joy they made. He was in a small glade and the morning light was gentle and green. He laid Grégoire on the grass. He knelt on one knee beside him.

'You were the only one who didn't have to die. The only one with no good reason to come with me. The only one I chose when I didn't have to choose.'

Tannhauser stopped. His voice broke and he didn't care.

'You loved horses. And I'd say they loved you, and I'd not blame them. You found my daughter in the darkest night. You put Carla in my arms. You were with me, you stayed with me, you guided me, through blood and death and thunder, and you never flinched. If we two never had met, you'd still be loving horses. But though my heart be breaking I'll not lie. I wouldn't wish it otherwise. I've nothing that suits the purpose to dig with, so I'm going to leave you here, in the wilderness, to be eaten by wild beasts and birds. I'd expect the same. A warrior's grave, we call it. And never more bravely earned.'

Tannhauser took in Grégoire's face, for he wouldn't get the chance again.

The boy was as ugly in death as he'd been in life.

'Call him the most beautiful.'

Tannhauser lowered his head and let grief consume him.

He didn't know for how long.

He heard the laughter of girls and raised his head from his chest.

He found Carla kneeling beside him. She took his hand.

Amparo slept in the cradle of her arm.

'Carla. You have never looked more lovely.'

'I hope that's another tender falsehood.'

'It is not.'

'We miss you. The children miss you.'

'It doesn't sound like they do.'

'I think they're laughing about you.'

Tannhauser grinned.

'Let me hold my daughter. Amparo.'

Tannhauser took the babe. She rode well on his arm. He felt like she belonged there. And so did Amparo. After all, she did. So tiny. So extreme. So there.

Amparo was.

'What's Grégoire holding?' asked Carla.

Tannhauser had forgotten about the package.

He took it from Grégoire's hand.

'We bought it for you and the nightingale, he and I. Grégoire never let go of it.'

He gave the package to Carla.

She pulled the ribbon and opened it and held up the robe.

It was striped with dark stains.

'It's a little big,' said Tannhauser, 'but she'll grow into it.'

'It's charming. I love it.'

She kissed him. He looked at her.

'I'm sorry I wasn't with you,' he said. 'I should have been.'

Her eyes filled and he knew that she agreed.

She smiled and, despite that she agreed, he believed what she said.

'You were always with me.'

He stood up and took her hand and pulled her to him. He put his arm around her waist. They walked back to the camp through the green morning.

There were a thousand bodies in the river more deserving of the privilege than he, and another in the glade for whom he would have died, but Tannhauser was alive to watch his daughter suck the milk from her mother's breast. He sat down by the fire with Amparo in his arm and she stared at him while he ate, and he took pains to make a fool of himself, and the children laughed at him.

The Mice.

Estelle.

Pascale.

Orlandu.

Carla, the woman of his life.

Amparo cooed and he looked down.

Tannhauser laughed, too.

He had come a long way to spend but a day in the greatest city in the world. Now it was a long road home. But he gave thanks to Death and the Devil, and to Fortuna, blindfold or not, for the treasures he had discovered and the wonders he had been shown, for the dance he had been led upon and the songs he had sung in his soul, for the wagers won and the wagers lost, for the sight of his woman's bliss, for the love chiselled deep in the stone of his heart by the Twelve Children of Paris.